9 Stories of Finding Shelter and
Love in a Wintry Frontier

A PIONEER
Christmas
COLLECTION

Lauraine Snelling, Margaret Brownley
Kathleen Fuller, Marcia Gruver, Cynthia Hickey,
Vickie McDonough, Shannon McNear, Michelle Ule, Anna Urquhart

BARBOUR BOOKS
An Imprint of Barbour Publishing, Inc.

Print ISBN 978-1-63409-031-5

eBook Editions:
Adobe Digital Edition (.epub) 978-1-63409-629-4
Kindle and MobiPocket Edition (.prc) 978-1-63409-630-0

Published by Barbour Books, an imprint of Barbour Publishing, Inc., P.O. Box 719, Uhrichsville, Ohio 44683, www.barbourbooks.com

Our mission is to publish and distribute inspirational products offering exceptional value and biblical encouragement to the masses.

 Member of the
Evangelical Christian
Publishers Association

Printed in the United States of America.

Contents

Defending Truth

Shannon McNear

Historical Note

Truth and her papa and siblings are fictional, but I've anchored them within an actual historical family. Anthony Bledsoe was indeed captain of the home guard while the others rode away to hunt Ferguson, and genealogical records reveal a much younger half brother by the whimsical name of Loving Bledsoe—by some accounts, Lovin or Loven. Where I could, I matched family members as well as events with historical records. Although I kept their location deliberately vague, they probably lived in or around the Watauga Valley in what is now eastern Tennessee, but was then western North Carolina.

In reality, Truth's younger brother would have been considered old enough to run the hills and go hunting for the family, so that was a bit of dramatic license on my part. I did not, however, exaggerate the tales told after the terrible battle at Kings Mountain, which was a major turning point in the war for independence.

My apologies to the descendents of Joseph Greer, for painting that bold and daring young man in a less than flattering light.

Dedication

For all of you who believed, even when I dared not.

Chapter 1

Late October 1780

Papa would tan her hide if he knew she was out here again. Too many Indians to worry about. Not to mention Tories. But Papa was still gone, fighting the British, and the young'uns needed fed.

Truth Bledsoe took a better grip on her grandfather's long rifle and peered through the cold fog of the western North Carolina morning. The narrow path up the mountain lay beneath a carpet of reds and golds, slick with rain. All but a few yards ahead faded into the mist. The forest was still except for the occasional drip of moisture and creak of branch.

With a deep breath, she trudged on, until out of the mist loomed a great boulder tucked into a fold of the mountainside.

Her favorite hunting perch. She slid the rifle up over the edge then, with fingers and toes in various cracks, hoisted herself onto the top. There she settled herself to wait for whatever game might wander past.

She'd taken her share of deer, turkey, and squirrel from this rock. Seen the occasional panther. Even glimpsed a few Indians. Today she was just hoping for something to fill the stew pot.

Her ears strained for shreds of sound. Everything would be muffled in the fog, whether the whoosh of a deer's snort or the rustle of a squirrel in the leaves.

The snap of a twig, when it came, drew her almost straight up, gun to her shoulder.

"Don't shoot!" came a sharp cry.

Sighted there at the end of her rifle was a man—young, unkempt, hollow cheeked. Not one she recognized from the near settlements.

"Please. For the love of God, don't shoot."

She did not move or lower the rifle. She'd take no chances. "Who are you?"

"I—" He swallowed, dark gaze flicking over her.

No hat, no rifle, no gear to speak of, not even a haversack. Filthy from head to toe. Hunting frock and breeches tattered, and were those—bloodstains?

"Answer," she said. "Now."

His already pale face went a shade lighter. His mouth flattened, and his brows came down. "No one of consequence."

"So, there's no one to miss you if I shoot."

"I didn't say that!"

A wry smile tugged at the corner of her mouth. "Tell me, then, why I should not shoot you. Besides the love of God, of course." Not a small reason, that.

He swayed a little on his feet. "Because. . ." His voice dropped. "Because the battle is over."

Her heart hitched. The love of God, indeed.

She kept the rifle aimed—a girl must be prudent, after all—but lifted her head. Those were most certainly bloodstains then. "Are you wounded?"

He shook his head.

"How long since you last ate?"

Behind the curtain of stringy brown hair, his dark eyes remained wary. One shoulder lifted and fell.

Nothing for it then. Venting a sigh, she propped the rifle against her hip, keeping it leveled toward him, and reached her other hand into her haversack. The man's gaze shifted, curious, hungry.

When she found the double-fist-sized chunk of johnnycake wrapped in a napkin, she pulled it out and tossed it to him. He caught it midair with only the slightest fumble.

"There," she said. "Eat up."

He didn't need to be told twice.

"Slowly. You'll choke otherwise." She reached this time for her canteen and swung it toward him. He easily snagged the strap as it sailed through the air.

Still eyeing her with caution and expectation, he unstopped the wooden vessel and took a drink before making short work of the last handful of her flat corn bread.

"Nearly out of sugar, so 'tain't as sweet as I'd like," she said.

He wiped one sleeve across his mouth. "Tastes mighty fine. My thanks to you."

The rifle was getting heavy, but she ignored the burn in her arms and shoulders. "What battle, now?"

He stilled. His gaze darted to hers and away. "King's Mountain."

The chill those words gave her went all the way from toes to scalp. *Lord, have mercy! He must be a Tory.*

❧

He'd thought nothing could ever unsettle him again, not after the battle and the horrors he'd witnessed in the days following. Not even being held at gunpoint by a fierce over-the-mountain girl.

He'd thought wrong.

After the initial scare they'd given each other, Micah Elliot tried to keep his movements slow and steady. No telling how twitchy she might get with that rifle—and a fine one it was, too, a Pennsylvania model, as long as she was tall.

The girl, now, he couldn't tell, wrapped as she was in a man's hunting frock, her head covered in a felt hat, one edge cocked and decorated with a turkey feather. Eyes as pale as the mist and almost as cold peered at him from beneath the brim, and her mouth was a thin line above a pointed chin.

He hadn't reckoned on her taking pity on him and giving him food, either, but he was right grateful for that. And he wasn't lying about the corn cake being tasty.

"Now." Her eyes narrowed. "I know you're not from around here. Who are you, and why are you here?"

How much could he trust her? Colonels Shelby and Sevier had at least tried to be fair after the battle, but he'd had a taste of the legendary savagery of the over-the-mountain men. Worse than Indians, it was said. Whether that was so, he could not say, but his body still carried the aches and bruises of their smoldering fury.

And his head was still a little swimmy, making it hard to pull his tattered thoughts together and come up with a defense. "Who are you, and why are *you* here?"

She hefted the rifle, and her faded blue skirt swayed a little beneath the coat. "I asked first."

He fished and came up with a short form of his middle name. "Will." That was common enough.

"Will. . . ?"

"Williams."

Did he imagine it, or did the corner of her mouth lift? Her gaze lost none of its fire. "Well then, Will Williams, and from where do you hail?"

"East." The word was out before he could stop it.

"Oh, so amusing, you are." She tilted her head, and the misty light outlined a strong cheekbone and jaw. "Get a little johnnycake down your gullet, and you have all kinds of sass."

He wasn't going to tell her that the bread barely eased the ache in his gut. "Well, you did feed me. You're less likely to spend a rifle ball on someone you've just given your own provisions to."

But he stepped back a couple of paces, just to show his goodwill. No sense in tempting the pretty hand of Fortune.

"King's Mountain, you say." Her face resumed its grimness. "We heard tell of Ferguson's men meeting a bloody end there. You were on the Tory side, then?"

Right smart she was. He held his tongue. Nothing to say there.

"Well," she muttered. "At least you didn't lie about that."

"The truth means much to you?"

She gave him what approached a real smile. "My *name* is Truth. Truth Bledsoe. My uncle is captain of the home guard for our settlements."

Would it help his case or hurt it to tell her he was a coward? An escaped loyalist prisoner who could no longer face how neighbor fought neighbor and brother fought brother back home?

"Then I expect you're mighty handy with that rifle."

Her chin came up. "I'm near to fair."

Likely a crack shot, the way she handled it. He didn't want to test that.

"You going to tell me why you're here?" she asked, her voice low.

She stood, balanced in a small hollow in the side of the boulder, skirts swaying just a little, but she held that long rifle as steady as could be.

She had to be as scared of him as he was of her, maybe more.

"How long's it been since you ate?" she pressed.

"A week, maybe longer." And not much, even then. They weren't exactly generous with rations for prisoners.

Her mouth thinned a little more.

His gut growled, the hunger sharper than ever. It was becoming more difficult to keep the tremors out of his limbs, standing here under her eye. Better to take the chance of trusting her and die here quickly than dissemble and die of slow starvation. "I was part of the North Carolina militia from above Charlotte Town. Those of us what didn't die at King's Mountain were taken by the rebels—I. . .I mean—"

She nodded slowly. "See? I knew you were Tory."

"Loyalist."

Her fingers lifted on the gun barrel. "Makes no never mind. Go ahead."

His heart pounded inside his chest so hard he was sure she heard it. "They carried us to Gilbert Town. Nine of us were hanged. And the rest—"

He couldn't say the words. Couldn't inflict the horror of it on her, a mere girl—

But she'd fed him. She deserved an explanation.

"There was unspeakable abuse," he said. "You don't know." He shook his head again.

"Ferguson threatened our settlements with unspeakable things," she said.

He swallowed. "I know what you must think of me, but I promise I mean you no harm. You or the settlements. Regardless of what Ferguson said."

And how could he? He didn't even know where his loyalties lay anymore.

Chapter 2

What was I thinking?

Truth huffed. She'd stomp back down the trail if she weren't so particular about stepping downhill on wet leaves. She'd not just spared a Tory—one who'd doubtless faced her father across a battlefield—but fed him. And then bid him go back into hiding.

And she still didn't have anything to fill the pot at home.

Telling him, "Shoo, go away, I need to finish hunting," didn't sit well with her, but what could she do? He was noisy enough to scare away game for a mile in any direction. And he should know better.

She thought of the way he'd swayed, stumbled a little, and caught himself. Bone weary, he'd looked. . .maybe soul weary as well. That was the reason she'd had pity on him and not only warned him back into hiding but promised to bring him more food.

What *was* she thinking?

His plea still wrung at her. *For the love of God.* Likely he'd meant it as a common oath. Maybe. But maybe not.

Now, after wasting so much time, she had to see to her sisters and younger brother. Get off the mountain, back to the cabin, and while she was at it, see if Uncle Anthony had any word on Papa. It had been a good two weeks. If he was helping guard prisoners from the battle, then it could be a bit longer, and she'd learned not to fret overmuch when he was out riding with Colonel Sevier and the others.

There was unspeakable abuse. You don't know.

A chill swept her as the young man's words came back to mind. From Papa? Never. Oh, he could be stern. 'Specially after losing Mama three years back, there were times Truth wasn't sure he was still the papa she'd always known. But maybe that was just on account of growing older herself and seeing life a bit more clearly.

But abuse? No. Maybe he'd lost his temper a time or two, but he was more likely to leave the cabin than take it out on her or the young'uns.

So if Papa was there, that meant he either couldn't stop it, or—

She rounded a bend of the trail and skidded to a halt. Outlined in the thinning mist stood a perfect six-point buck.

Ah Lord! Could it be? And in the unlikeliest of places as well.

Without another thought, she swung the rifle to her shoulder, took aim, and squeezed the trigger. There was no turning down provision when it appeared for the taking.

The familiar recoil of the weapon slammed into her shoulder. Smoke puffed into the air and was lost in the fog. She peered again into the gloom—and there lay the buck, dropped with the single shot.

That surely was a miracle.

By long habit, she first reloaded the rifle. Afterward she made quick work of field dressing the animal, saving the organ meats, and tying the cord she always kept in her haversack to the buck's hind legs for dragging the carcass home. Now her main concern was leaving before a hungry bear caught wind of her kill.

Back at the cabin, her next youngest sister Patience had milked the cow and set the cream to rise, and Thomas had brought in wood. A bright, cheery fire warmed the inside of the cabin, and her two youngest sisters, Thankful and Mercy, were at their morning chore of brushing and braiding each other's hair.

Thomas's head came up at her entrance. "Fresh meat?"

Setting her rifle in the corner, she flashed him a grin. "A deer. Six-point buck."

His blue eyes rounded. With a whoop, he went to gather the knives and bowls they used for cutting up the meat.

She tugged off her hat and hung it on its peg. And how would she get food to—what was his name, Will?—without a dozen questions from the young'uns?

Will. . .Williams. With a snort, she slid out of the worn, fringed hunting frock and hung it up as well.

Together, she knew they'd make short work of it—skinning, cutting the meat into strips for smoking, and saving aside a haunch for roasting. And she set little Mercy to the side on a chair, with the Bible open before her.

"Behold," Mercy read, her clear, high voice steady, "the heaven and the heaven of heavens is the Lord thy God's, the earth also, with all that therein is."

Truth thought of the wildness of the mountains. How great God must be for shaping them.

"For the Lord your God is God of gods, and Lord of lords, a great God, a mighty, and a terrible, which regardeth not persons, nor taketh reward: He doth execute the judgment of the fatherless and widow, and loveth the stranger, in giving him food and raiment. Love ye therefore the stranger: for ye were strangers in the land of Egypt."

Her hands slowed at her task. *Giving him food and raiment.* Well, that settled it. She had to do something about that half-starved, soon-to-be-naked man up the mountain whether or not she liked it. She'd just have to figure out a way to do so without the others finding out.

Or Papa, once he returned.

&

There was only the pop and thunder of rifle and musket fire, the tang of smoke, the screams of the wounded, and the chilling war whoops from the rebel forces surrounding the mountain. Micah crouched, gripping the musket, his bayonet at the ready. Why was the colonel taking so long on the order to charge?

And over everything, Ferguson's whistle, with which he signaled above the din of battle. Would Micah even be able to hear the under-officer's order? He strained for the shout, but only the rebel screams and shriek of the whistle ripped at his eardrums. Still, none of his company moved, even when the fire pouring from below tore bloody holes in their hunting coats.

Inexplicably, Ferguson's whistle now sounded like a whip-poor-will, each beat of the three-beat call punctuated by a rifle wound hitting the breast of the man on Micah's right. . . .

He wrested himself awake with a gasp. Oh Lord, would he never stop dreaming about it?

As his eyes adjusted to the faint daylight outside the cave where he'd sheltered the last few nights, he heard again the call: *Whip-poor-will! Whip-poor-will!*

But it was deep autumn, long past the season the woodland bird would customarily take up the mournful, rhythmic melody that gave it its name. And the time of day was all wrong.

He sat up, crept to the mouth of the cave, and listened. Silence, then more slowly, *Whip-poor-will?*

Heart pounding, he put two fingers to his lips then hesitated. Indians sometimes used such calls, but something told him it wasn't an Indian. That over-the-mountain girl Truth—aye, a severe name for an equally severe female—had promised to bring him more food.

Not for the first time, he cursed his own need. How he'd managed to leave behind even his knife—

He answered with a two-note whistle. *Bobwhite!*

Would she recognize it?

Whip-poor-will?

He spotted her then, a skirted form with a hunting frock over, as before, pressed against a massive, gnarled oak. Stiffly, he crawled from the cave and stood.

Rifle in one hand, she reached for something behind the tree and stepped out as well. For a long moment, they merely stared at each other.

He hadn't told her where he was hiding.

"You said to meet at the rock," he ventured at last.

"I couldn't wait," she said, her voice soft in the predawn gloom. "And I know most of the caves hereabouts. Didn't figure it could be so hard to narrow it down." Was it his imagination, or did her lips curve a little? "I hoped the whip-poor-will call would help."

He tried a smile in return. "Was that a play on my name?"

She snorted, but the curl of amusement held. "If it is your true name."

Better not to answer that yet.

He looked at the bundle she held. Despite her suspicions, she had come. His eyes burned, and he hoped he didn't appear too desperate. Those few bites yesterday had reawakened not just his hunger but all his hope of life, it seemed.

She stepped forward and gave the bundle a gentle toss toward his feet then backed away. Still not trusting him either. "I found a few things that might be helpful."

Micah knelt and tugged at the knot of what he could see now was a wool blanket, worn and much mended. Inside lay a knife, also much used if the nicks of grip and blade were anything to judge by, but the relief of having steel to hand again after losing his own was almost as great as that of the prospect of another meal.

And a meal she'd brought—more johnnycake, with cold roasted venison and an apple, all wrapped in half a handkerchief. His mouth watered, and he took a great bite of the apple. The sweet flavor burst across his tongue.

At the moment, he nearly didn't mind the shame of having admitted to her yesterday that he'd lost everything in his escape from the rebels. Or of having her stand over him as he set the apple aside and tore into the venison.

He glanced up, forcing himself to chew more slowly then swallow. "My thanks."

She nodded, and apparently convinced he wouldn't turn savage, crouched opposite him, the rifle cradled in her arms. Her eyes were but a glint beneath the brim of her hat. "Have you family?"

Another bite. Chew, swallow. "Two sisters, both married." *A brother, turned rebel. My father, dead of the heartbreak.* "A brother who is a captain of the local militia."

She was very still. "Tories, all?"

He nodded, bit off another mouthful.

"That's all? Sisters and a brother?"

Another nod. "And you? Besides the uncle who's captain of the home guard."

"My father and another uncle rode with Colonel Sevier to hunt Ferguson."

He considered her clothing and the rifle. "And left you to fend for yourself?"

No reply there. He must have hit too close to the truth.

"The settlement is near enough by," she said at last. "And both of my uncles have families."

He finished the venison and started in on the johnnycakes. She stirred and, with the gun stock set against the ground, rose. "I must get back. Wish there was more, but it's all I could spare for now."

"It's—plenty," he said, and meant it. It was more than he'd had at one time since before the battle. "I thank you, again."

Hesitating, she gave a single nod then took off her hat and held it out to him. "This was an extra. I expect you'll need it."

This one was flat brimmed and plain, he realized, while the one she wore yesterday was cocked.

"Wearing it myself was the easiest way to avoid untoward questions," she added.

Stepping close enough to reach for the hat, he took hold of the brim—and stopped. The morning light caught her eyes and made them a pale blue, soft as a twilight sky. Dark hair, now uncovered, lay caught in a braid that disappeared inside the wide, fringed collar of her coat, but stray wisps curled about her face and framed the angular cheekbones with unexpected softness.

Last thing he'd looked for was her to be so completely fetching.

Eyes widening, she let go of the hat and stepped back. "Well then. Don't get yourself into too much trouble now, with that knife."

In a flash, she was gone, darting away between the trees.

Chapter 3

Why didn't you go back?"

It had been a week since she'd been surprised by the Tory hiding on the mountain, and with each visit, Truth coaxed a bit more of his story out of him—traded food and gear for it, more like. But he didn't seem unhappy about the exchange, though he still hadn't told her his true name.

And today he'd surprised her by cleaning up. The figure that met her—this time at the hunting rock and not his cave just over the mountain spur—was not the starved, bedraggled one of the first day. He'd put her offerings of well-mended castoff shirt and stockings to use, brushed out his waistcoat, and washed his breeches and hunting frock. His moccasins, though worn and missing laces, were no longer muddy. Most startling of all, however, was finding him clean shaven with hair combed and tied back, dark eyes watching the forest intently for her approach as she walked up the path.

Only that particular intensity let her know this truly was Will—as well as her father's old hat dangling from his hand and the spare knife stuck in his belt.

And when his eyes lit on her, that strange flutter went through her insides, like she'd felt when he stopped and stared at her the morning she'd given him the hat. He'd gone all still, and his eyes had widened, as if—

Ah, that thought was folly. Hadn't she had her fill of the settlement boys chasing after her? She'd no time for such foolishness, especially not with Papa gone, which ate more at her as the days passed. No more word had come of the battle, except what little she'd gleaned from Will, so she knew not what to expect.

They sat for the moment almost side by side. A fine, clear morning it was, almost warm, though a light snow had fallen two days before and melted off. Will chewed at the bone of the turkey leg she'd brought and stared off into the forest, as if he hadn't heard her question. But she knew he had. His quiet was too studied.

He peeled back a piece of the bone and brought it to his mouth to suck the marrow out. "I can't keep taking your charity."

Now, that she hadn't expected either. He was brighter of eye than even a day or two ago. Surer of hand and step, of a certain.

"It's not my intent to sound ungrateful," he went on. "But you hardly need another mouth to feed."

Fear jagged through her chest. What did he know?

He turned his head and met her gaze. "Why did you take pity on me, Truth Bledsoe?"

She swallowed and looked away. "Can't just shoot a hurt, starving critter."

He gave a low laugh. "You can if it deserves shooting."

"Did you?" She couldn't help but stare again.

"I—I ran away." He blinked, but a bitter smile still twisted his mouth. "Hoped to find death over the mountains rather than face another night hearing the groans of the wounded. Or the thought of facing my brother with this loss on our hands." His chest rose and fell with a breath. "But I'm there again, every night in my dreams."

She could find no reply to that.

"I'm weary of the fighting. Not a week went by, back home, that someone wasn't getting lynched, or tarred and feathered, or. . ."

He fell silent, dragging a hand across his face.

"Well, you've come to the wrong place if you don't like fighting," she said. His dark gaze returned to her, questioning. "Indians," she continued. "Three years ago it was so bad they called it 'the Bloody Seventy-seven.'" The reason she was so set on learning to shoot and carry a rifle. "They say the British set the Cherokee against us because the Crown doesn't recognize our right to settle here."

"And why did you settle here?"

Truth shrugged. "Same as anyone, I reckon. The chance to make a life for ourselves, to work the land and raise a family." They were words Papa had spoken often, but they came alive for her now. "Papa and the others bought the land fairly from the Cherokee. Trouble is, some of their people don't recognize that either, but we came here by God's grace, and by His grace we'll remain."

Will sat back, frowning. "God's grace," he said, softly. "The loyalist side speaks of that as well. 'Obey the king; he is God's instrument of judgment.' But in the end, whose side is God on?"

How to answer a question like that? "His own, I expect."

The question haunted her still, once she was home. Scrubbing linens in the washtub in the side yard, boiling them, hanging them out to dry. All she could hear was Will's quiet but impassioned voice, later in the conversation. *Where is the grace in neighbor rising up against neighbor? Men who not five years ago worked alongside each other, helped each other build houses and barns. I cannot go home until I know which side I am willing to lay down my life to defend.*

What was it about him that tugged at her heart? Compelled her to think of how to get him enough food to bring his strength up, to mend the odd castoff item so he could use—

"Hullo the house!" a deep male voice called.

She looked up to see her uncle Anthony crossing the yard. She straightened the shirt across the rail fence beside the barn then stepped back, wiping her hands down her blue linen skirt. "Any news of Papa?"

He shook his head.

❧

Who was that man?

In his hiding place on the slope above what he presumed was the Bledsoe farm, Micah shifted for a better look. Three days ago the malaise of starvation had faded enough that he'd crept down the mountain after Truth, for no good reason but curiosity. He hadn't been overly sure as to her identity the first time she'd walked outside without the hat and hunting frock—especially since a proper cap covered her hair—but the springy, determined stride from house to barn left little doubt. Two other girls were obviously younger, by height, and another girl had flaxen rather than dark hair. He'd also counted only one boy, tallish, but likely too young to be hunting far from the house.

If his guess was right that Truth was the eldest and her father was off fighting, Micah didn't blame her for being so protective of herself and her family.

Now he watched Truth straighten from her task of washing laundry and greet the rawboned over-the-mountain man approaching with such familiarity. He looked much as the other men at King's Mountain, and his garb not so different from Micah's and that of other men from the backcountry, but rougher and hard edged. He wasn't her father, judging by the restraint of her response. More likely her captain-of-the-home-guard uncle.

The man stayed but a short time, conversing with Truth, casting constant glances toward the trees above the house. Micah knew how to remain still and thus unseen.

Even after the man departed, Micah stayed where he was. Truth's soft words echoed in his mind. *Hospitality is not for repaying.*

And yet he couldn't not at least try. Especially when, to all appearances, she and her sisters and brother were alone.

Chapter 4

Meeting day. Truth beat eggs into a bowl, measured in handfuls of cornmeal, added milk, and stirred. She'd already warned Will not to expect her today, as they'd be walking to church this morning. It'd be the first time in a while, and she was feeling a longing to be there.

She had traded with a neighbor some of her stitching for a ham, and slices of it sizzled in an iron skillet on the coals. Their own hog was ready for butchering, but it wandered the woods until Papa returned. While she stirred the johnnycake batter, she drew a deep breath of the fragrant meat. If there were some left after—not likely with Thomas's appetite of late—she might could slip away up the mountain—

The front door flew open and bounced against the wall behind. Patience stood there, cheeks flushed and chest heaving as if she'd just run half a mile.

A small jolt went through Truth. Was it Indians?

"Who is that man out in the barn milking our cow?" Patience asked.

Suspicion trickled through her. *He wouldn't!* Truth dropped the wooden spoon against the side of the bowl and pushed it away. "Fry the batter when the ham is done, will you?" she told Patience then brushed past.

He would, she knew. That obstinate Tory!

Her strides gained fervor until she reached the barn. Mindful of the livestock, she forced herself not to storm inside. Sure enough, a lean male figure in shirtsleeves, with dark hair pulled smoothly back, sat at the cow's flank, milking away as if he belonged there.

In an effort not to fly at him, she leaned back against the sturdy log wall. "I see you know how to milk, at least."

He glanced over his shoulder and grinned, flashing dimples and an impressive set of teeth. Gracious, that wasn't fair. His gaze lingered on her, though his hands never broke rhythm. "There's little difference between a Carolina backcountry cow and an over-the-mountain one, except that the latter's a bit more feisty."

She knotted her hands in her skirts. Idiot man, in *her* barn, and he dared make a joke? "Where did you find the pail?"

He tipped his head toward the corner. "I washed it first, if you're wondering."

"Good thing. I'd hate to waste the milk."

Another grin. Then he turned back to the cow.

"Why are you here?"

Senseless question, since she knew already, but she had to ask.

"You need the help."

"We're getting along just fine, thank you."

He tossed another half smile over his shoulder. "That you are. You and—is it three younger sisters and a brother? Or are there more?"

She clenched her teeth on at least a dozen heated replies, most of which were an insult to his politics, parentage, and character. She must not allow him the upper hand by losing her temper.

"How long have you been watching us?" she said, when she could trust herself to speak civilly.

His milking slowed, as he stripped the last rich drops from the cow. "Three days." Another glance. "Did you expect me to stay in the cave?"

Another deep, long breath. How on earth was she to suffer this insolence? "I'm glad you're better," she said, stammering a little. "But truly—"

He rose, milk pail in one hand, stool in the other, and faced her. His eyes, black in the shadows of the barn, bored into hers. "You're alone. You need help. You've fed and clothed me for a week. At least allow me to ease some of the burden while your father is gone."

Though soft, his voice left no room for argument.

"And what am I to tell others about your being here?" She fought to keep her own voice from trembling.

"What others? You're not overclose to the main settlement here. I'd stay well enough out of the way."

"My uncle and aunts. And other folks of the settlement do drop by of an occasion." He didn't move, and she grew desperate. "What of my father when he returns?"

"I can be gone by then."

She shook her head, but he stepped closer. "Please. Put me to work. At least for a few days. I can't bear staying up on the mountain, letting you provide for me while I do naught."

Just as on that first day, something about him caught her. *I know next to nothing about him!* her reason argued. *What is it they were always called—filthy Tories?* But this one hadn't proven himself anything like what she'd been led to believe Tories were. Perhaps his loyalties were misguided and he could be persuaded to see the right of it. Hadn't he admitted to doubts?

She swallowed but drew herself straighter. "What is your true name, *Will Williams?* Trust me with that, and I'll let you stay."

The dazzling smile appeared again. "Will is good enough for now."

Hissing, she stepped back. Unfortunately, she understood his reluctance to tell her, and she couldn't deny the appeal of a strong back and arms around the farm. Perhaps, since he'd trusted her enough to let her bring him provisions and then followed her home and watched without taking advantage—

She shivered. "Lord help us all. For a few days only, and you'll sleep in the barn."

Was it her imagination, or did relief glint in his eyes? "Fair enough."

A scuff behind her drew her attention, and she turned to find Patience and Thomas standing in the doorway.

"I brought your rifle," Patience said, scooting the weapon into view, "but it don't look like you need it at the moment."

Thomas scratched his nose. "Is he the one you been sneaking away to meet every morning?"

A groan escaped through gritted teeth as she took the rifle and pushed past them. "Come to the house, and now. We'll be having meeting at home again."

There was no way she'd leave the place under Will's care, however pretty he was all cleaned up.

Halfway across the yard, she snarled back over her shoulder, "You might as well come, too."

At least feeding him would be simpler this way.

❧

Did she know how magnificent she was when angry?

Micah handed the milk pail off to the girl who, now that he had a good look, was almost certainly the second eldest, but he couldn't help gazing after Truth. A slender thing she was, without the bulk of her hunting coat, but with more than enough fire to make any man want to step down.

And he nearly had, except that he knew her need must be as great as his in its own way.

The boy lingered by the barn door. His eyes were pale, reminding Micah of Truth's, and a scattering of freckles dusted the boy's nose. "Waiting on me?" Micah asked.

The boy gave a single, grave nod. Micah stowed the milking stool and pointed to the cow. "Do I leave her, or. . ."

"Turn 'er out in the pen for now."

Micah nodded, led the beast from her stall, and returned her to the split-rail pen adjoining the barn. Without a word, he followed the boy to the house.

Was that ham he smelled? He was like to drool if he wasn't careful.

Truth was dishing food to the plank table with the help of the two youngest girls, both of whom peered at him with doubtful blue eyes. Truth herself refused to look directly at him, but after a moment of turning this way and that, she pointed at a bench near the head of the table. "You. Sit there."

He settled, back to the wall. He'd barely time to glance about the snug interior of the place before she was there again, a stoneware mug in hand. "It's a poor excuse for coffee, but it'll have to do. Drink and be welcome, since you're here."

He cradled the vessel in his hands, savoring its warmth, and inhaled. His eyes slid closed. Weak, perhaps, but it was real coffee. He sipped and glanced across to find Truth watching him.

Would he ever be able to repay his debt of gratitude to her?

She nodded toward the boy, standing nearly at his elbow. "This is Thomas. These are my sisters Thankful and Mercy"—she indicated the younger girls—"and my sister Patience." A nod toward the girl now bending over the hearth, from whence he caught the definite aroma of corn cake. "And this," she went on, "is Will." She hesitated as if to give him time to correct her. "He was, ah, in the battle with Papa earlier this month."

The younger children, but Thomas especially, came alive at that. "A battle! Will you tell us about it?"

He sent a questioning glance toward Truth, and she nodded slightly.

What could he share that wouldn't betray his part in it?

Thomas scooted into the spot beside Micah. "Did they get that rascal Ferguson?"

"Thomas, eat," Truth said. Her gaze flicked to Micah's, guarded.

The girls piled in around the table as well, and Truth slid a wooden plate of food in front of Micah before gracefully seating herself opposite him.

A plate—a real table—how long had it been? Somehow he'd never appreciated it before.

"Did you know Papa?" one of the younger girls asked shyly. Mercy, he remembered.

Micah shook his head. "I'm from Burke County, North Carolina. Different units." Very different.

"So why are you here, and Papa ain't?" Thomas this time. That boy was as sharp as his eldest sister.

He chewed a bite of his ham. The flavor filled his mouth, and for a moment, all he could think of was his sheer unworthiness to be here.

"Your papa," he said, when his mouth was cleared, "was with the men guarding the prisoners after the battle." He didn't know for sure—he seemed to remember the name Bledsoe but couldn't put a face with it. God willing he wasn't of those beating or slashing at the prisoners in their fury and frustration on the march northward. "I was—I was released from duty."

Thomas frowned. "But if your home is eastward—"

Truth cleared her throat and leaned forward. "God sent him."

Chapter 5

Micah met Truth's eyes across the table. "You believe that." It was more a statement than a question.

"I do." Deliberately, as if daring him to argue, she went back to her food.

"Well then." Micah took up a paring knife and sketched an elongated oval on top of his johnnycake. "This is the top of a place called King's Mountain, a long, isolated hilltop on the eastern edge of the mountains, roughly west of Charlotte Town."

Thomas and the girls leaned in to watch.

"Here," he pointed to a place near one end of the oval, "is where Ferguson and his men made camp and took their stand. Loyalists all, no British regulars among them but Ferguson himself."

He hesitated. Had he betrayed himself by use of that term, and not "Tory," as the rebel side called them? But no one moved or behaved as though he'd acted amiss.

"Here," and he pointed around the west and south perimeters of the johnnycake map, "your over-the-mountain men climbed, while militia from the backcountry of North and South Carolina and Virginia surrounded from the other. They whooped and hollered, fit to strike terror into the hearts of the Tories, officers and ordinary soldiers alike."

Micah glanced up into the faces surrounding him. Children of one of those men, furious at the threat Ferguson had made to lay waste with fire and sword to their homes.

The chill of those war cries still lodged in his chest, but sitting here among the children provided an odd comfort. They deserved to hear the tale of how bravely their father had fought.

"When the loyalists found that their musket fire couldn't match the long rifles, they resorted to bayonets. Three times they pushed their attackers down the mountain, and three times the over-the-mountain men drove them back up, until the loyalists were surrounded and caught in crossfire from both sides."

Food was forgotten as everyone, Truth included, sat round-eyed. Micah fought to keep his voice level as he recounted what had been the stuff of nightmares every night since. "Some tied handkerchiefs to their musket barrels and tried to surrender, but Ferguson rode the field, swinging his sword and cutting down anyone who raised a white flag."

One of Micah's cousins had fallen at his side for this very reason.

"At last, as more men surrendered, Ferguson himself tried to leave the field, but he was shot from his saddle and dragged."

"Did he die?" Thomas asked, barely breathing.

Col. Patrick Ferguson, the Scotsman who'd rallied the backcountry loyalists as no one else, who'd made the militia into real troops with endless drills and that hated whistle, who'd thought to threaten the over-the-mountain rebels into submission.

Who'd obviously underestimated the fury that threat would stir.

"He did, indeed," Micah said.

❧

He was quick witted, she'd give him that.

Truth had desperately wanted to stay angry with Will. To not admire the way he'd spun the tale for her family's benefit and not given away his own loyalties. But the slight tremor in his voice reminded her of that first day, when he'd begged her not to shoot. . . .

Please. For the love of God. The battle is over.

She could see him now, surrounded by men trying to surrender. A commander who wouldn't let them. And then—

"Why did you lie for me?"

Will's low voice startled her from her musing. She'd stepped outside after breakfast, and apparently he had followed her out.

She rounded on him but kept her own voice down. "I did not lie."

His eyes narrowed, and a muscle in his lean cheek flexed. "Helped hide me then. Why?"

A sigh escaped her. "Does it never cross your mind that what I said was, indeed, true? That God directed your path here?"

He stared at her so long she had to turn away.

"Very well then," he said. "Put me to work."

❧

And work he did, from sunup to sundown, without complaint, without hesitation. Mending the cow pen fence, patching the cabin roof. Cutting wood, during which chore Truth made a point of busying herself elsewhere so she'd not be tempted to watch his strong shoulders and arms swinging the ax. More folly—there were fine, manly forms aplenty in the settlements for her to have gone featherheaded over, if she were interested in such. Will would only be here until Papa returned.

But with each passing day, he seemed more at ease. Bantered with Thomas and the girls. Volunteered to fetch the hog from the woods, aided Truth in setting up the smokehouse and doing the butchering.

She couldn't remember that task ever being so enjoyable.

Yet with each passing day, an unrest gnawed inside her over Papa's whereabouts. Despite Will's assurance that Sevier, Shelby, and the other over-the-mountain men had, best he'd heard, committed to escorting the Tory prisoners to a parole camp north of Charlotte Town, as October trickled into November and the weather grew colder and stormier, so did her own worries grow.

She rose from her bed one night when a nearly full moon shone on the frost and, bundled in a woolen blanket, padded over to peer out the window. She pushed open the shutter just a crack. Icy cold air poured in and swirled around her feet. Across the yard, the roof of the barn glinted in the moonlight.

So far, Will had escaped notice from others in the settlement, but that couldn't continue forever. And then what would she do? Papa was sure to be angry when he returned and found she'd harbored an escaped Tory.

For this past week and more, however, he'd been a Tory no longer. He was simply Will, who had come and somehow made himself needed and necessary.

She didn't know how to deal with him being here—but now, she wasn't so sure she wanted him to leave.

The threat of rain the next morning sent Truth scurrying to make sure enough wood was brought in—although Will had been good about keeping the pile stocked—and to bring in anything that shouldn't be out in the wet. After breakfast, when Will returned to the barn, Truth left Patience in charge of overseeing the younger children's lessons and slipped out after him.

When she entered, he looked up from where he sat on a bench, carving at a piece of wood. "What are you working on?" she asked.

One shoulder lifted. "Something small for Mercy or Thankful. Haven't decided which." He opened his hand to reveal a rough but recognizable cow, emerging from a palm-sized burl of wood. Truth smiled, but he laid aside the carving and the knife. "Did you need aught?"

"Only to bring you this." She pulled a small rolled bundle from beneath her coat and handed it to him.

Bemused, he untied the rawhide thongs binding it then unfurled two lengths of gray wool.

"Gaiters," she said.

"As if you haven't already done enough." He took one length and wrapped it about his leg, from foot to above the knee.

"Yes, well, you've done more than your share, too." Truth's fingers itched to help with smoothing the gaiter and tying it down, but she could not fathom why. Will was plenty capable of tying his own.

He finished the second in short order and stood, stretching first one leg then the other. That grin made an appearance. "Very snug. My thanks, as always."

An answering smile tugged at her own lips. "You'll need them. I think I smell snow coming."

He nodded but absently. "It's about time for your father and the other settlement men to be returning, I'd think."

She clasped her hands behind her back. This was the conversation she wasn't keen on having. But what else was there but for Will to go? "Will you be returning home?"

A tiny shake of his head. "Not yet." His eyes did not leave hers. "I'm indebted to you, Truth Bledsoe."

Unaccountably, her heart gave an unsteady leap. She swallowed. "You've repaid that debt by now, Will Williams."

A softer smile lighted his lean features, tilted the corners of his dark eyes upward. Had he stepped closer just then? "Micah," he said.

Her heart was fairly pounding. "What?"

"Micah Elliot. That's my true name. Micah William Elliot."

She mouthed, *Will*, then aloud, "Micah."

Closer this time, without a doubt.

"Micah Elliot," she breathed. "It's a good, strong name."

The smile held, as did his gaze. "Would that I were strong enough to be worthy of it."

"I think. . .I think you're worthy enough."

Sadness flickered across his face. He touched her cheek. "If you think so. . ." Leaving the thought unfinished, he went suddenly still. "How old are you, Truth?"

And why. . . ? "Eighteen, come the first of the year."

His hand lingering, he gave another little nod then leaned in. His lips touched hers, held for a heartbeat, then brushed across and were gone.

Will—no, *Micah*—drew back with a look that was at once triumphant and full of wonder. Of their own volition, her hands stole upward to his face and neck, and this time she rose on tiptoe to meet his kiss. Micah gathered her into his arms—

From outside the barn came a male voice. "Halloo the house!"

Chapter 6

Uncle Loven!" Ignoring her own breathlessness, Truth dashed out of the barn and into the yard, where two horses stood, and a rider dismounted.

The youngest of her three uncles, just a few years older than herself, and the one who'd always seemed more like a big brother. He turned and caught her in a quick hug, which Truth returned despite the grime of his leggings and hunting frock. "My, you're a mess," she said. If only her heart would stop fluttering—perhaps Loven would think it was merely excitement over Papa returning, and not—something else.

He gave her a thin smile. "Fighting Tories will do that to a body."

Another pang of guilt hit her, and she glanced around. "Where's Papa? In the house already?"

Loven took off his worn felt hat, scrubbed his forehead with one sleeve, and then shook his head.

Truth shot him a look, but he only gazed back, the pale blue eyes grave.

Two horses, one rider. She turned. Papa's rifle and gear—things he'd normally wear strapped to himself—tied instead to the saddle of his horse.

She opened her mouth, but no sound would come out. A crushing weight caught her chest and would not ease.

"Loven?" she croaked.

He shook his head again. "I'm sorry, girl. There's no easy way to break the news. Your papa took a ball to the side at King's Mountain. The doc said if he didn't move, he had a chance at recovering, but—you know my brother. He insisted on riding with us and took a turn for the worse a week or so ago. We buried him on the way home."

Everything around her blurred, and Truth put out a hand to steady herself against Papa's horse. Loven's hands settled on her shoulders and tugged her toward him. "So sorry, Truth. His last words were for you and the young'uns."

Her sisters and brother. She had to tell them. Had to be strong for them.

And then there was Will—Micah—

Oh Micah.

Oh Lord, how could I?

She pushed away from Loven and stumbled back toward the barn.

❧

Micah saw her coming and held his ground. He'd been listening through the open window, out of sight.

This couldn't end well.

She threw back the barn door and stood, shoulders heaving. Where a few moments ago she'd been all softness, now her grief gave her the fire of an avenging angel.

Not that he blamed her. He'd seen it before.

"Tell me again, please." She took a few steps toward him and stopped. Her voice shook. "Which side of the mountain did you fight on? That south and east end, or—"

He didn't dare touch her, though his arms ached to catch her close. "The Burke County militia from both sides were fighting each other. We could hear the over-the-mountain men, but we didn't face them."

At least until later, and he couldn't remember whether he'd gotten off any shots at that point. They were too busy figuring out how to face that wicked crossfire.

Two strides, and she was nearly nose to nose with him. "But how do you know? Do you know of a certain?"

He couldn't help it—he reached for her, his hands cupping above her elbows. But she turned to fury at his touch, shrieking and flinging both fists repeatedly against his chest. "How do you *know*?" she sobbed, nearly incoherent.

Micah closed his eyes for a moment and let her pound on him. "I don't," he said at last.

She gave a wail that lifted the hairs on his neck and collapsed against him.

To apologize at this moment felt so inadequate. He slid his arms around her, laid his cheek against the linen cap covering her hair, and searched for the words anyway.

With a gasp, she pulled herself upright, eyes red-rimmed, lips trembling. "And I fed you. Gave you clothing and shelter. Oh Lord—*kissed* you—"

One hand over her mouth, she stared at him as if he'd become something awful, and then fled the barn.

Past the tall, rawboned man she'd called uncle, framed in the doorway.

The uncle, who appeared not much older than Micah himself, glanced after Truth then stepped inside the barn. "How did you think to take advantage of Truth?"

Would to God that Micah's life would not end here, spilled into the floor of Truth's barn. "I was not taking advantage."

"Of a certain you were." The other man strode forward and peered at him more closely. "And I believe I know you."

Micah remembered him as well—oh yes.

Truth's uncle bared his teeth, brows lowering. "You're a filthy ___ those from King's Mountain. Escaped, did you? What business have you ___ the mountains?"

No time for dissembling. And if this man had half as much heart as Truth. . . "I had. . .doubts after King's Mountain. Many of us did. Unlike others, I couldn't return home. One of my brothers had gone rebel, and my oldest brother nearly killed him for it. So I kept running. Next I knew, I was deep in the mountains." He drew a breath. "Truth found me one morning while out hunting. She's the one who offered food. The only shred of grace I asked of her was to spare my life. I asked nothing beyond that, I swear."

The hard-eyed man neither moved nor spoke.

"I'm well aware I deserve none of it," Micah went on. "And as for being here—well, I only sought to repay her kindness. It was my intent to leave as soon as her father returned."

"Then do so," Truth's uncle said.

❧

Truth sat before the fire, her arms around her younger sisters. Mercy still wept into Truth's skirt, but Thankful had quieted. Beside her, Thomas stared, stony faced, into the fire. Patience was sweeping the floor for what seemed the third time.

Papa would not be returning. She and Patience and the young'uns were well and truly alone.

And Micah. . .it hurt to breathe at just the thought of him. How could she have been so foolish?

Behind her, the door opened and shut. "Your Tory is packed up and gone." Loven's rumble carried the words to her.

"He's not my Tory," Truth said.

Thomas sat up, eyes wide. "What Tory?"

Patience had stilled, broom in her hands. "You mean Will?"

"His name is Micah." The words fell from Truth's lips of their own accord. She tightened her embrace around the younger girls.

Thankful squirmed out from under Truth's arm. "How could Will be a Tory?" Thomas's gaze reflected the fire. "He is not."

Truth's eyes burned. She hadn't wept since returning to the house, and here she was, nearly in tears, over a—a— "He was, yes. What he is now, only the Lord knows."

Thomas's face was very pale. "If he was a Tory and he was at King's Mountain, then. . ."

Shaking her head, she released Mercy and fled to the tiny lean-to her parents had shared as a bedroom. With the door shut, she flung herself on the bed, buried her face in the coverlet, and let the weeping come.

29

Chapter 7

The cold lay bitter over the mountains, and the red-gold carpet of leaves was fast turning brown. Truth led Thomas and the girls down the well-known path toward the settlement and toward church, but she glanced upward at the mountain slopes. She had no need to hunt the last few weeks, not with a smokehouse stocked with ham and bacon. And for the better, given the rumor of Indians on the warpath.

She missed her hunting frock and felt hat, but for Sunday meeting, proper won out over practical. A wide-brimmed straw hat covered her cap and a wool cape her gown and petticoats. All was in place, right down to her stays.

Downhill, it wasn't a strenuous walk, and the young'uns chatter should have kept her thoughts busy. But she couldn't help but wonder where Micah was: Had he returned home? How long did it take him to get there, or had he stubbornly remained in the mountains? Was he again cold and hungry?

And either way, why did she care?

They arrived at church with time to spare, and inside the log building, Truth herded the family onto their customary bench. Others were arriving as well, but she kept her head down to avoid meeting anyone's eyes. Afterward was the soonest she could face the pitying looks and sad smiles.

The service itself passed in a haze. She usually had little trouble paying attention, but today the words of the hymns and the minister's sermon seemed to slide over her and trickle away like snow melting across the rocky mountainside. She stood when necessary, sat at the appropriate times, kept her hands folded in her lap. Oddly, Thomas and the younger girls managed to hold still as well.

Afterward they filed out of the building. Outside, where quiet conversation was more acceptable, a trio of women, one older and two younger, stood waiting. Her aunts—Anthony's and Loven's wives—and a cousin.

"Aunt Mary. Sarah. Aunt Milly." Truth greeted them and accepted an embrace from each, in turn.

"Good to see you, dear," Aunt Mary said. "How are you faring?"

The concern in their eyes, as she feared, made her own burn. "Well enough, thank you."

She glanced about to see where the young'uns had gone. Thomas and one of the other boys had run for the edge of the churchyard, kicking leaves in their wake. Thankful and Mercy had a pair of small cousins by the hands and were likewise skipping in the crisp air. Mama would have chided them for it, but Papa would have laughed and told her to let them be children while they could.

Milly cleared her throat. "We're a little concerned about you being up there all alone."

"We're just fine, thank you," Truth said.

Aunt Mary pressed in. "You can't honestly be thinking of staying there? Think, Truth—you and the young'uns through the winter? With threat of—"

She broke off, but Truth could hear the unspoken words. *With threat of Indian attack.* She straightened, pulling her shoulders back. "The smokehouse is stocked. I need some things from the fort, but otherwise, truly, we're fine."

We even have an extra rifle. A tiny sigh escaped her at the thought of Papa's standing in its corner next to hers.

"How did you get your hog slaughtered?" Aunt Mary asked.

Truth suppressed a wince at the thought of Micah. The image of him, knife in hand, strong and laughing at some sardonic quip she'd made, flashed through her mind. "We had—help."

Aunt Mary's gaze narrowed. "Still. It wouldn't be fitting."

"And why ever not?"

Milly turned. "Loven!" Her youngest uncle was nearly at his wife's elbow already. She looped her arm through his and tugged him closer. "Please tell Truth she and the young'uns can't possibly stay there alone this winter. We could take them in—or Anthony and Mary would be glad to as well."

Loven's eyes went cool and speculating, his mouth flat—but he held his tongue.

Milly shook his arm. "Tell her!"

"She knows," he said at last and tugged his wife away.

And he knew entirely too much himself. Had he told Milly and Mary about her fugitive Tory?

He isn't my Tory, her mind insisted, but her heart broke afresh.

Papa had lost his life, possibly at Micah's hand—and she'd spared his.

She stirred to find herself standing alone, or nearly so. Aunt Mary had followed in Milly's wake, and Sarah lingered, but only to talk in low tones to her beau. Truth edged away and headed across the churchyard.

"We gave them just what Reverend Doak said, the sword of the Lord and of Gideon!"

The ringing voice carried from a cluster of men several paces away. Truth halted, her eyes snapping shut. Another ribbon of pain laced across her breast.

"No more than what they deserved," another said.

Oh Papa.

Oh Micah.

How could she feel so torn? She'd heard the threats Ferguson had made, to hang their leaders and lay waste to the settlements with fire and sword if they did not stay out of the conflict between the colonies and Crown.

But Micah was not of that ilk. She knew this.

And yet—if there was the slightest breath of possibility that his hand held the gun that took Papa—

She made herself think of Papa, his last embrace, smelling of leather and bear grease, and his gruff admonition to be strong. The way he'd tucked each of the young'uns in close and whispered to them as well. Perhaps her aunts were right and she should consider moving to one of their farms, at least for the winter. After all, how could she be enough for them all, with him gone?

Almighty Lord, I cannot do this alone. . . .

"Truth girl."

She started, but it was only Loven sidling up to her, and by himself, more's the wonder.

"Of a certain, how are you faring?"

The admission of his concern nearly broke her. She tucked her head, swallowed, and only answered when she thought she could contain herself. "Well enough."

He tipped his head, considering her. "You're not pining over that Tory, are you?"

She'd been right—his pale eyes saw far too much.

"No." It was not a lie. If anything, she pined over her own loss of strength and good sense.

"Good." He chewed the side of his mouth, glanced over to the other men, still loudly reminiscing over the battle, then refocused on her. "Was he courting you?"

Her cheeks heated at the memory of what he must have overheard—her admission that she'd gone soft and let Micah kiss her—no, further, had kissed him back. She shook her head. "I think not. It didn't get so far."

He sniffed. "I wonder. 'Tain't like you let anyone try before. Sooner shoot them as let them talk pretty to you." The corner of his mouth twitched. "You deserve better'n him. And if you're finally of a mind, Joe Greer will be returning soon—"

"I don't want Joe Greer." *Preening peacock.*

"He's at least a real man, not a yellow-hearted Tory."

She waved a hand then covered her eyes for a moment. "He didn't run from you, did he?"

Silence then, "No. He didn't."

Truth waited. He'd have more to say, doubtless.

When it came, his voice was oddly gentle. "I just expected you to have more sense than that, Truth girl."

She released a long breath. "So did I, Loven. So did I."

With the blade of his knife against stone, Micah struck sparks into the tinder he'd made from shredded bark then blew them to flame until the twigs he'd collected ignited.

He customarily used coals from the previous fire to start the new, but in his ranging, the fire had been out too long. But his tinder was good and dry from being stored off to the side in the cave, and the kindling caught quickly enough. He added a few smaller pieces of wood then sat back, tipping his head to scan the sparkling, rippled surface of the cave ceiling. The rear part of the cave was damp, with a passage leading downward to a stream, but here the floor remained dry and sandy.

Inside the low opening, the cave was wide enough for a man to stand up comfortably and deep enough for several to find shelter. And unlike during the early days here, he was one blanket richer, along with one knife, one hat, and assorted proper gear.

All thanks to Truth.

Why he could not simply cross back over the mountains and head for home was a mystery. She'd made it clear enough that he was no longer welcome—and he blamed her not a whit. But something compelled him to stay. Whether it was because he'd left his heart down at that farm at the mountain's foot or something else, he couldn't say.

Did staying still make him a coward?

He let his mind play back over the past few years since the war's outbreak. It hadn't seemed to touch them much in North Carolina. A few skirmishes here and there, neighbors snarling at each other over fences—until the British firmly took Savannah and Charles Town and started their push into the backcountry. Then men's blood truly began to boil.

He was weary of it, truth be told.

When the fire was warm enough, he lit a torch he'd made from mosses and took himself down the rear passage to the stream. Being careful not to slide on the rocky bottom, he bathed and then washed out his shirt and breeches.

Afterward, shivering—though the temperature of the cave was constant and far warmer than outdoors, it was still cool to his bare, wet skin—he made his way back to the fire to dry himself and his clothing.

The welts and deep bruises of two months past were faded now, except for the occasional ache in his ribs. He stretched, pulling on the shirt, then held the breeches out toward the flames. He'd swam the creek many a time, even in the cold, and tramped the countryside with wet clothing, but taking the edge off the damp would certainly make them more comfortable.

The thought of home pricked at him. Christmas was near. Did his sisters wonder what had befallen him and mourn? Did John care a whit that his absence might cause them pain, or did he merely curse and rave at Micah's disappearance, certain that another brother had gone rebel?

And then the image of Truth, with her wry smile and light blue eyes, flashed before him. The younger children, shy but laughing. Christmas couldn't be aught but a gloomy affair for them. And what if that was indeed his fault? Truth's wild grief at that possibility chilled him even now.

And even now, he could feel the softness of her lips and of her slight form as for that moment she'd yielded to his embrace.

Just for a moment, but it was enough. He'd never be the same after kissing Truth.

A kiss was not sufficient, however, to erase the horror of where he'd been, that her father could have met his end at Micah's hand.

All the more reason my life should be spent making up for that loss.

The strength of that thought stole his breath. His eyes snapped shut. A lifetime at Truth's side—providing for her, protecting her—nothing until now had seemed as worthy a cause to spend himself upon.

But could she be persuaded to see it thus? And would she ever forgive him for being in the wrong place at the wrong time?

Chapter 8

Micah went steadily but as silently as he could through the twilight, across the slopes that would take him back to the cave. After being here for more than a month, he could find his way in the near dark with little trouble. He'd ranged far today, and the last glow from the sunset had faded as the first stars glittered above, leaving the mountains in crisp, bitter cold. His snares had netted him a pair of rabbits—lean as far as meat went, but at least he'd not starve again, yet.

As he picked his way through the laurel and around a fall of boulders, an owl's hoot broke the stillness, then another. At the third one, from a different direction, he stopped. A chill brushed his skin, lifting the hairs on the back of his neck.

He slid into a man-sized crack between the boulders. The owl hoot came again, closer. Forcing his breathing to shallowness, he waited. Muscles cramped and skin prickled.

Voices, low at first, then rising in agitation. Micah caught a few words—Cherokee, if he didn't mistake what his brother had taught him, with English mixed in.

Settlements. . . Warpath.

Micah's blood turned to ice in his veins.

Was he understanding them aright? What if his memory served him wrong and they were merely talking of a hunt?

On the other hand, what Indians hunted ordinary prey at night, well after sunset?

The voices fell silent, and he held himself still, barely breathing. There was a rush, as of a wind sweeping through the winter-bare trees. Micah peeked out, and the dark shapes of two or three dozen bodies, perhaps more, streamed past the boulders. Downhill, and definitely toward the settlement.

Between here and there lay Truth's farm.

Micah waited until the last echo of the war party—if it was such—had faded. Then he slid out of his hiding place, considered his direction, and took off down the mountain as well.

❧

Young'uns tucked in bed, at last. Truth listened to the last shuffling sounds of Thomas and the girls in the loft above as, shawl-wrapped, she made her rounds, padding from door to windows, making sure all was shut and barred.

Of late, this was the moment she looked forward to most all day. The house quiet, the young'uns settled, and the first breath of rest since she'd lifted her head from the pillow that morning. She couldn't remember it ever being this hard before, but then she'd always had Papa's return to look forward to.

No longer.

She paused at one window, fingertips on the barred shutter. If not for the cold, she'd open it and just stand there, soaking in the evening's peace. Tonight a shiver ran through her, and she turned away.

Sighing, she rubbed a hand across her face. It would be Christmas in just a few days. Memories assailed her of Mama and Papa gathering them all by the fire for a reading of scripture, the house fragrant with roast bird and pie and sweets that Mama had labored over for what seemed like days. There'd be no more of that for the young'uns unless she made the effort. She had enough sugar for a small cake, but she'd have to borrow cream and eggs from Aunt Milly. Her own cow had gone dry a couple of weeks ago and would not come fresh again until early spring after her calf was born.

They could have a very decent day of it if none of them dissolved into tears as had been their habit of late. . . .

A thumping on the front door drew a gasp from her lips and spun her around. Who might—

"Truth! Open up. It's Micah."

Heart pounding, she flew to the door then reached for her rifle before she lifted the bar. Fumbling, she pulled it open. The wild man who stood there, hat in hand, illuminated in candle- and firelight—bearded, hair mussed, eyes wide—reminded her again of that first day. And once again, she could hardly move. "Micah?"

His name escaped her throat in a squeak.

"There's no time—may I come in?"

She stepped back, and he did so, shutting the door behind him. His gaze fastened on hers, every bit as intent as she remembered.

"Indian attack," he said, breathless. "I came to warn you."

She put out a hand, and he gripped her arm, steadying her.

"The settlement," she gasped.

"Aye. I'll go." He tipped his head, gesturing with his free arm, and for a moment his mouth flattened in what looked like a rueful half smile. "I know the way. Been scouting about this past month."

Heat flashed through her. He hadn't left. He'd stayed—but why?

The cold took her again, and she found herself trembling.

His gaze swept the room before coming back to her. "I'll be back as soon as I can. Just—stand ready." A definite smile this time, sweet and tender and heart-piercing. "I know how well you can use that rifle. Give 'em fire if they're here before I return."

Then he was gone, the door shutting behind him with a solid thud. Truth shook herself and set the bar back in place.

Whirling, she stared about her. So much to be done. But first—

She went to the table and blew out the candle. Then at the fireplace, she set aside the rifle and dropped to her knees. With the poker, she spread the logs apart so the flames would die more quickly to embers.

And there she lingered, in prayer for the young man she'd sent away but who'd somehow returned to warn them all of danger.

To her amazement, the house stayed quiet.

&

Micah's lungs burned from the cold, but still he ran, across the fields undoubtedly cleared and worked by Truth's father, through a stand of thick timber, down a ravine. He dodged mossy boulders and leaped a narrow, swift stream, still gurgling despite the recent freeze. In the dark his foot slipped, went down in a pool so cold his foot was instantly numb, but he scrambled up and kept going.

The lingering fear for Truth and her sisters and brother nipped hard at his heels, making the short distance to the farm of Truth's uncle seem miles longer than he knew it to be.

If there had been anyone else closer, Micah would go there, but it made more sense to warn her uncle first—even if it was the youngest uncle, Loven, rather than the hard-faced oldest.

Micah only hoped the man wouldn't shoot him on sight.

He'd barely reached the next harvest-bare field before a hound bayed somewhere ahead of him. He set his teeth and put on a last burst of speed. The baying became more urgent.

Halfway across the field, he slowed. "Ho the house!"

A door opened, silhouetting a man in shirtsleeves holding a rifle. He gave a low command, and the baying subsided to a growl and whine. "Who is it?" the man called.

"A friend." Heaving for breath, Micah walked to the edge of the porch where the light touched him and leaned his hands on his knees for a moment.

"You," the man grunted.

Micah lifted his head then straightened. "Aye, it's me. Shoot me if you wish, but I came to warn you there's what looks like a war party of Indians headed this way."

Loven Bledsoe's head came up, apparently searching the darkness behind Micah. He beckoned Micah inside.

The man's wife stood near the fire, still poised in shock. Micah dipped her a quick bow then turned back to Truth's uncle. "Thirty or forty braves met together then passed me up on the mountain. I overheard them talking—fairly certain they mean to attack, although my Cherokee's a bit rusty."

"Well." The iron set of Loven's jaw did not ease, but he put down the rifle and reached for his hunting frock, hanging behind the door. "We're too far from the fort to take refuge there, but I'll need to spread the word. Did you warn Truth?"

Micah sucked in another deep breath, grateful for the warmth of the snug cabin. "Went there first."

Loven gave a quick nod and buckled his belt around the coat. His gaze flicked over Micah. "And you're going back, I expect?"

"I am. She and the children shouldn't be alone."

"Somethin' we agree on," Loven muttered, reaching for his hat. He held one arm out to the woman, who stepped close for a quick kiss and embrace. "Bundle yourselves and the young'uns, follow him over to Truth's." Another glance at Micah. "You'll not mind?"

"I'd be honored," Micah said.

Chapter 9

Truth heard the voices before the soft scratching came at the door. She opened to find Milly and her two young'uns standing outside. Behind them, Micah was tying a huge dog to the corner of the porch.

Her heart did a strange flutter. "Loven let Micah bring Brutus?"

Milly flashed a smile. "The hound is useful for sounding alarm." She stepped past Truth to the lean-to bedroom, leading the bundled little boys.

Finished with the dog, Micah stood back, hat in hand, his expression lost in shadow. "Get inside," Truth whispered and barred the door after him.

She took his hat and hung it on a peg beside hers. She'd not think about how Papa's hung there day after day.

Loven trusted Micah with his hound. . .and his wife and young'uns.

Micah stood entirely too close. She twitched away, reached for Papa's rifle, and thrust it into Micah's hands. "Here." She kept her voice low, but it sounded harsh in the stillness. "Make yourself useful. Can you reload, or should I set Milly to do it for you?"

She knew without looking that his bearded mouth would be curling in a grin. "My older brother has a fine Pennsylvania longrifle. I've handled it a time or two."

"That'll do then." She handed him a shot bag—she'd counted more than twenty balls—and a powder horn.

Both Papa's. Again, she'd not think about it.

He huffed the breath of a laugh. "Where do you want me?"

She pointed at the window to the left of the door. "There. Reckon we'll have to unbar the windows to properly keep watch."

With a nod, Micah moved into position. After opening the window, he slung the pouch and powder horn straps over his body and, between glances outside, counted the balls. "Is this all you have?" he said, hushed.

"I've an equal amount saved back." She swallowed. "Will the Indians head straight for the settlement, do you think, or burn houses and farms as they go?"

He gave a little shake of his head. "Hard to say. They'd have been here by now if they intended to hit as they go. Doesn't mean the danger's over."

Milly came, rustling softly, from the lean-to. "I've put the boys to bed. What do you need me to do?"

Truth considered. "There's a small window near the bed. You could keep watch there, whistle if you hear anything amiss."

Milly hesitated, glanced toward Micah. The curiosity must be burning inside her, but they must not make idle conversation. "We have water?"

"Enough till morning, at least."

And if they did not survive until then—it wouldn't matter.

Milly whisked away to the back room.

Truth carried a stool to her chosen post, placed it carefully, and eased open the shutter where not an hour ago she'd stood. Peering out now was a different matter entirely, but with a gust of cold, only the deep quiet of evening greeted her. A sullen quiet, it seemed.

She exchanged her shawl for hunting frock and slipped her own shot pouch and powder horn into place, slung across her body. She'd already removed her cap and stowed it in her pocket, so as not to make more of a target than they already were. With rifle leaning upright against her shoulder, she settled onto the stool, a little back from the window.

Were they out there even now, waiting? She suppressed a shudder. Her own grandfather had disappeared in the wilderness, presumably at the hand of some Indian brave. She couldn't visit the merchants at the fort without hearing talk of Indian attacks, with the horrors of being scalped or captured described in detail.

Papa had often said that he and his brothers had moved farther out on the frontier to escape government interference and political squabbling, but which was worse? The Cherokee remained as divided as any over the white men's land purchases this side of the mountains.

Yet this was the life she knew. She wanted naught else, unless it was to have Papa back, and Mama. And God willing, someday a family of her own.

Her eyes strayed across to Micah. She could just see the outline of his form beside the open window. Feet set apart, shoulders wide under the fringed double collar of the hunting frock. Dark hair loose over that, the hint of a strong brow and straight nose as he gazed out into the night.

Her throat tightened. Why did he agitate her so? Was it merely the knowledge that Micah was there—where Papa took the musket ball that later took his life—and could have been the one to deliver it? Or was there more?

God sent you.

Her own words haunted her.

As if she'd spoken aloud, Micah turned his head, meeting her gaze in the dark. Neither of them moved.

❧

Even in the dark, he could see the hint of curls around her face. His memory filled in the tilt of her cheekbones and chin.

Did she despise the necessity of him being here? Or was that spark he'd seen in her eyes when she'd first opened the door to him one of relief and gladness? It would be easy enough to imagine it as such. Too soon to tell whether she tolerated his presence simply because she needed him to fire a rifle if the Indians attacked.

Which he should be watching for, instead of letting her distract him.

He turned back to the window. All was quiet, including that great hound Loven had insisted he bring along. Not that he was ungrateful—as Loven's wife had said, the dog would be useful to raise an alarm should anything happen.

And Truth's expression of surprise had warmed him clear through.

He stole another glance at her, but she'd returned to looking outward as well, perfectly still and straight, one hand curled around the barrel of that rifle.

Brave, fetching girl. He had so much to say to her if they lived through this night.

Please, Almighty God. I'm not in the habit of praying anymore, but. . .protect and spare her. Protect these people.

And—if I did shoot the ball that took her father, I ask that You pardon my soul. Did we not all only do what we felt was right?

Only the silence echoed back to him, but a small measure of ease filled his heart.

The night wore on. A distant wolf howled, then an owl hooted. The hairs on Micah's neck lifted again. He raised the rifle, held it half at ready, but nothing stirred nearby. The hound growled but only the once.

A creaking came from the ladder to the loft. Truth's next youngest sister, Patience, descended and tiptoed over to her. They whispered briefly; then Patience went to the pail on the table, dipped a tin cup of water, and brought it to Micah. He nodded his thanks and drank it down.

After he handed her back the cup, Patience stood there like she also wanted to ask him something. Micah glanced at her, but after a moment she returned to Truth's side.

The next hour or two passed without event. Micah reckoned it to be close to midnight, and he scrubbed at his face in the attempt to stay awake.

Truth sidled up to him, her presence more felt than heard. "Think we dare sleep? If Brutus will bark or growl. . ."

He shrugged. The temptation to sleep was strong, but the later the hour, the more likely the Indians would double back from their planned target. And if the two of them weren't both awake, ready to respond the moment of attack, could they hold them off?

"Been thinking," he murmured. "If they come, we should do all we can to make it seem there's more than two of us."

"We could take turns firing and loading, moving from one window to the other."

"Should work." He forced himself to sound calm, but just having her standing there, elbow nearly touching his, set all his senses at the ready. It wasn't sleep he wished to dare, suddenly, but to tuck her into his arms again, and—"Do you have more than the two rifles? An old musket as well, perhaps?"

"No. But I have Papa's tomahawk and hunting knife, if need be."

A smile tugged at his mouth. "You'd be right fierce with either of those, I expect."

She huffed softly—was that a laugh for his benefit or merely derision? He let himself look at her. Between the pert nose and chin, her mouth was firm, all outlined in shadow.

"I'm going to feel mighty foolish if this turns out to be for naught," he said.

At that, she turned, her gaze catching his. "Don't."

Her eyes widened, as if she'd just admitted something she didn't want him to know. Her lips parted and shut, and she glanced away. He imagined if there were enough light he would have seen her flush.

"I—I was overharsh with you, weeks ago, that day when Loven came home," she said. "You couldn't have known—"

She broke off, half turned away. He reached out and caught her arm, but gently.

"The news of your papa was a terrible shock," he said.

Her eyes glimmering, she looked up again. He let his fingers slide down her sleeve until they closed over her hand.

"If I could bring him back to you," he said, "I would. If somehow I could go back there and exchange myself for him. . ."

Her grip tightened on his. "Don't—not that either. 'Tain't fitting to question what God has decreed."

For a long moment, they stood almost nose to nose, unmoving. "It isn't questioning God to admit you grieve," he said. "I remember what it's like to lose a mother and father. And if it pains you that I'm here and your papa isn't, well, no one can blame you for that."

She drew a soft, uneven breath. Then, tough over-the-mountain girl that she was, she sagged against him, forehead to his shoulder.

Outside, the hound shot to his feet, baying.

Chapter 10

Truth sped back to her window. Her eyes strained through the darkness—was that movement at the far corner of the barn? If Brutus's continued baying was any indication, yes. She raised the rifle and sighted.

Micah was at her shoulder. "The hound's pointed toward the cow pen. Could be there, and maybe beyond the house a little. Don't fire just yet, until you're sure what it is."

An unearthly shriek split the night, chilling Truth to the marrow. She remembered that cry from the night in the fort, three years past. "I'm sure," she said, and pointing the rifle at the nearest flicker, just beyond the rail fence, pulled the trigger.

The boom of the gun shook the house as the rifle stock kicked against her shoulder. The acrid smell of burnt powder filled her nostrils. She stepped back to let Micah take position and upended the rifle for reloading while thumbing open the powder horn. A measure of powder, tipped down the barrel, then a patch and ball from inside the pouch on her other side. Ramrod out, then—

A flash and a blast heralded Micah's shot. She had the ball and patch tamped nearly down the barrel. Micah slid to the wall opposite her and began reloading as well.

Ramrod back in place. Truth lifted the rifle, primed the pan with a slight dusting of powder, dropped the horn, and swung the rifle to her shoulder again. More shrieks, overlaid with Brutus's frantic yips and howls.

"Wait," came Micah's voice, steady and low. "Wait. . .and. . .there."

Movement accompanied the nearest-sounding war cry. She pointed and fired again. Stepped back. Tipped up rifle, powder horn in hand.

Lord in heaven, preserve us! She had twenty or so balls and plenty of powder. Could they hold off a full-scale attack?

And how many times had Papa and her uncles and the other men faced battle? Had Papa felt this white-hot determination to fight until last breath?

Ramrod down. . . Next to her, Micah fired again and moved aside. She slid the rod into place, primed the pan, stepped up.

She mustn't waste balls. *Oh God, let me shoot true. For my sisters and brother. For Milly and the boys—*

A flash from past the barn betrayed return fire, and Truth heard the ball hit somewhere beside the open window.

Squeeze the trigger. Flame and smoke, and the kick against her shoulder. Move back and reload again.

A thin cry—one of the girls—came from above then was drowned by the roar of Micah's next shot.

Ramrod down—down—this ball was stubborn—

The cry was muffled now.

Micah reloaded, glancing out the window. Truth slid the ramrod home and stepped up.

Milly came scurrying out of the back room. "There's more," she panted, "behind the house."

Micah darted away before Truth could move. She gritted her teeth, torn between the desire to just shoot and the knowledge that she mustn't just blaze away into the night. Every shot counted. But now—

The thunder of Micah's rifle echoed from the tiny lean-to. One of the boys yelped—likely Isaac, the younger.

How long before the Indians figured out that it was just the two of them shooting and made their attack in that precious half-minute while they were reloading?

She searched for movement. Brutus's baying changed in pitch—was he pointed another direction? She leaned to one side to see back past the porch—there, a flash and boom, and a shutter at the other window exploded in splinters.

Without thought, Truth raced across the room, lifted the gun, and sighted. She fired then ducked back to reload.

A flurry of shouts echoed from the field beyond the barn; the crackle of gunfire echoed after. The settlement men in pursuit of the war party?

Or reinforcements for the attack?

Her breath came in gasps. The next moments would tell. As a second boom rolled across the cabin from the lean-to, she made her hands continue the task—ball, patch, ramrod. Slide the ramrod back into place—sidestep to the window, rifle to her shoulder.

Oh Lord. . .merciful Lord. . .

A few more shots rang out. The war cries seemed to scatter and fade. Truth waited, still at the ready. Behind her, someone scuttled up the loft ladder—most likely Milly. Patience had gone back to bed hours ago.

"Halloo the house!" came a call as Brutus's baying quieted to a yelp and a growl.

Truth sagged against the wall and closed her eyes.

❧

Micah made sure their attackers were on the run. Then with the barest glance toward the two boys huddled on the bed, he left the back room and crossed to where Truth leaned, rifle cradled in her arms. He set a hand on her shoulder, and her eyes fluttered open.

"It wasn't for naught," she said, and he shook his head slowly.

"Truth, be you there?" The deep voice of one of her uncles carried through the open window.

She pushed upright and glided past Micah to the door. The rawboned man outside wasn't Loven but the older one he'd seen speaking to her weeks before. She threw herself into his embrace. "Uncle Anthony!"

"Is everyone safe?" His gaze swept the room and came back to Micah with a sternness that made Micah think he might be better off facing the Cherokee.

Loven's wife and Patience descended the ladder, followed by the younger children. "We're all well," Loven's wife said.

The two boys spilled out of the back room. Half the children aimed for Truth and her uncle, but Thomas, Thankful, and Mercy all surrounded Micah. "Will!" Mercy exclaimed and launched herself at him.

He caught the girl in a quick hug. The other two hung back a little, eyeing him uncertainly. Thomas lifted his chin. "It's Micah now, Truth said."

He let out a rueful laugh. "Will is part of my middle name."

Thankful still glared. "Why did you leave without sayin' farewell?"

"Are you back to stay?" Mercy chimed.

He shook his head. "I only came to warn the settlement about the Indian attack."

Amid the girl's expression of disappointment, Truth's uncle, who'd apparently been listening to the exchange, looked pointedly at Micah and cleared his throat. "I'm following the chase up the mountain. You coming? We could use another rifle."

Micah checked his gear and reached for his hat. Truth made to come as well, but Anthony Bledsoe shook his head. "You stay here with the young'uns. Just in case."

Her shoulders dropped like a chastened child's, but Micah thought she didn't look as disappointed as she might.

The night had been harder on her than she wished to let on, he guessed.

As her uncle slipped outside, Micah stopped and caught Truth by the elbow. "I'll be back later."

Her lips thinned, but she gave a quick nod then glanced away. Throwing herself into his embrace as she had her uncle's would have been more encouraging, but—there was no helping it for the moment.

Out into the clear cold, he followed, running after the war cries echoing down from the mountainside timber above.

They gave chase, some on horseback and some on foot, until dawn began to lighten the skies. At last the other men agreed that the Cherokee were long gone and it was safe to return to their homes. Some stayed out to keep watch, and Micah accompanied the rest down to the valley's edge.

Not far from Truth's farm, they stopped, gathering in a rough circle. Loven had already told the others of Micah's part in sounding the alarm. Thanks and handshakes were offered from all around, while Loven smirked knowingly from a short distance. Some of them, like Loven, Micah recalled by face from those long days as a prisoner after the battle. Being back in their company, greeted as an equal at the edge of deep forest where his arms couldn't but half span the biggest trees and where just hours earlier the war whoops of Indian and white man had echoed—it was eerily like King's Mountain, yet unlike.

When the other men had said their farewells and gone, Loven Bledsoe lingered behind. Anthony had gone with those riding patrol for the day. "Since I need to go collect Milly and the boys," Loven said, "I'll walk with you down to Jacob's place."

Truth's father's name. Micah hesitated for a moment, but Loven beckoned to him and set off. The man's long, braided hair swung on his back as he walked.

Micah trotted to catch up.

"No use pretending that ain't where you're headed next." Loven glanced over. The look in his pale eyes was so reminiscent of Truth, it made Micah's throat ache. "Wonder how many of those young bucks will be after your hide when they find out you aim to marry her."

Micah wondered that himself, but he wouldn't say so to her uncle. "If she'll have me."

Loven snorted. "She's gone terrible soft where you're concerned, make no mistake about it." He stopped and swung toward Micah, studying him with a frown. "Why did the young'uns call you Will?"

"It's what I went by when Truth first found me. My middle name. Didn't want anyone to know who I was, where I'd come from."

"And you are. . . ?"

"Micah Elliot. Lieutenant in the militia, Burke County, North Carolina."

Loven's expression remained still. "And you think you can make a life here over the mountains?"

Micah lifted one hand, palm upward, then let it fall. "There's a girl down there what makes me want to try."

Another long look. Loven blew out a breath. "If you ever hurt Truth—"

He straightened and met Loven's eyes with a stern gaze of his own. "I'd never intentionally hurt her. Never."

The ghost of a smile crossed the other man's mouth. "Well. See to it then."

And he set off walking once more.

Chapter 11

Truth ignored the quivering in her limbs as she and Milly led the young'uns, after daylight, in all the ordinary things that needed doing after such a night—fetching water and wood, tending spooked livestock, mending the broken shutter, emptying chamber pots. The attack had been over hours ago, and now all that was left was the weariness and the need to keep moving lest she fall asleep on the spot.

One of the young'uns gave a cry, and she turned to see Loven striding across the yard. Milly ran to meet him, she and their boys, and not until they closed about him did Truth notice who followed after.

Micah.

He tipped his head, watching her from beneath the brim of his hat, not smiling but walking with purpose. Toward her.

For some odd reason, she could not move. Last night, she'd found herself weakening toward him again, but today, in daylight, things seemed more difficult. He slowed as he neared her, as if he felt it as well.

"We saved you some breakfast," Milly said, addressing Loven but turning to include Micah.

"You're welcome to stay and eat," Truth murmured, her gaze never leaving Micah's.

He half smiled and dipped his head toward Milly then removed his hat. "If it'd be no trouble."

But when Loven and Milly and the young'uns all continued toward the house, he didn't follow.

Truth's chest felt strangely tight as Micah studied her, long-lashed dark eyes narrowing, one hand raking back his hair. All at once, she remembered her manners. "I thank you for what you did last night."

The lashes fell, and he shook his head, mouth curving slightly. "It's I what should thank you, for giving me back my life."

Sensible thought fled. She'd only done what she felt compelled to by Christian charity.

She'd not admit it had become far more than that.

Head tilted, he looked at her again. "Truth Bledsoe, I have something I need to say to you, so hear me out. Recall when I told you I wouldn't decide about returning home until I found something worth laying my life down for?"

The intentness of his gaze begged a reply, and she gave a quick nod.

"Well, I've found it. It's you, sweet Truth. I'd gladly spend the rest of my life as I did last night—standing beside you, defending you. That is, if"—he went shy and shifted from one foot to another, cradling Papa's rifle in his arms—"if you'd be willing."

His gaze became direct again. "You need the help, you and the girls and Thomas. But I'll not make a pest of myself or demand an answer before you're ready to give it. You take your time, and when you've decided, you know where to find me."

The fine morning blurred before her eyes, and she could not speak for the thickness of her throat. Blast him, what was this he did to her?

If it pains you that I'm here and your papa isn't . . .

She blinked, swallowed, tried to speak.

He smiled a little then held out the rifle. "It's a fine piece," he said softly, and once her hands closed about it, he took off the shot pouch and powder horn and handed those to her as well. "My thanks for the use of them."

She fumbled with the straps, but he curled her fingers around them. He hesitated then leaned in, lips pressing to hers and lingering for but a moment.

He smelled like the wild forest.

In the next moment, he backed away. "It was a long night. Rest soon."

And then he was gone.

Could she walk back into the cabin and pretend nothing was amiss? Her feet carried her there, regardless. Inside, she sank onto a stool as Milly and Loven stared at her.

"Well," Loven said. "That didn't end as I expected."

"Isn't he staying for breakfast?" Milly asked.

"No," Truth said.

"What happened?"

Truth blinked. Her sister-in-law's gentle but probing tone brooked nothing short of a reply. "He asked me—" What exactly had he asked, anyway? Of a certain, something far more than *Let me sleep in your barn and fix your fences.* He'd said the words "for the rest of my life."

"He asked me to marry him," she said and buried her face in her hands.

It felt like the whole cabin stopped to hear what she'd said.

"Oh, Truth," Milly said.

"And—do you want to?" Loven asked.

She made herself breathe—in and out—then pressed her hands to her knees and looked at them. Patience stood on the other side of the table as well, poised to listen.

"How can I marry him and not be untrue to Papa?"

The silence was broken only by the laughter outside of the young'uns at play.

Loven's gaze was steady. "Your papa would want you to do whatever is best for you and the young'uns."

"And that would be—?"

He let out a long breath. "It's my thought that what took place at King's Mountain is best left there."

Something Micah had said pricked in her memory. "And what of—what took place after."

Was it her imagination, or did Loven flinch just a little? He swallowed. "That, too. Our rage was slow to die, Truth girl. But Ferguson threatened our homes and families, and the threat of the Cherokee has been hard enough without the Crown trying to bully us directly. Micah understands that now. Think of what he risked to come down here last night to warn us."

What he had risked—to defend her. The words wrapped her about.

But Papa. . . Papa would have tanned her hide if he'd thought she'd gone soft over a Tory.

"I just don't know." She rose and turned toward the back room. "I'm tired. Patience, wake me up long about noon, will you?"

❧

Days later, she still didn't know.

It was Christmas Eve. A sudden snow kept them from going anywhere, so Truth had sat the young'uns down for the traditional reading from Scripture. As she turned to the familiar passage about a cold night and a passel of frightened shepherds visited by angels, the pages kept falling open to other places, and the odd sentence would leap to her attention. *"But love ye your enemies, and do good, hoping for nothing again. . . . Be ye therefore merciful, as your Father also is merciful."*

"If your enemy hungers."

Her hands stilled on the pages. She'd given of what she had, not expecting a reward—and God had been merciful in sparing their lives.

God sent you. . . .

What if He truly had sent Micah to be more to her?

She pressed ahead to the Christmas passage. *"Fear not: for behold, I bring you good tidings of great joy. . . . On earth peace, good will to men."*

And farther down, *"Mine eyes have seen thy salvation."*

Hours after, she could not sleep. The cabin was quiet, but as her habit in the nights since the attack, she couldn't seem to settle. She lay in her bed and listened to the howling wind and wondered for the hundredth time where Micah was. Closing her eyes, she let herself think about his mouth on hers, the warmth of his breath on her cheek, those dark eyes, and his dimpled grin. The kiss in the barn—again. The feel of his arms around her for that moment, lean and strong, and his shoulder beneath her cheek.

She rose from her bed, wrapped a blanket around herself, and pushed her feet into worn fur-lined moccasins, then paced the main room as soundlessly as she could.

Salvation through the hand of a Tory. Was that so difficult to believe? For some, perhaps. She knew, and others as well—she'd heard Loven and Milly speaking of it—that it was salvation from the hand of God. Not only on that night so recently passed, but—for the span of their lives—through that Child born so long ago.

"Forgive us our trespasses, as we forgive those who trespass against us."

She dropped onto a chair, weeping.

Lord in heaven, can I forgive? And if I do not, how can I, in turn, merit Your great grace?

She did not merit it, then or now. Else it was not grace.

Chapter 12

Truth peeked out through the shutter as the sky held the colors of a newborn day. The overnight snowstorm left everything covered in glittering white. Each tree branch and twig bore its own delicate coating, reminding her of lace or sugar glaze.

She'd finally returned to bed and, lulled at last by the relative safety of snow and wind, slept until just about dawn, when she awoke with a fresh sense of purpose and a strange, sharp joy.

Patience tiptoed up to peer out as well. Truth opened her blanket, offering to share the warmth. The younger girl nestled against her side, and Truth tugged the blanket around them both.

"It's beautiful," Patience breathed.

"It is that. Merry Christmas, little sister."

Patience giggled. "Merry Christmas."

Thomas popped up on their other side. "Shall I fetch the ham now?"

He was getting near as tall as her, she noted. "Hmm, in a bit. First, I want you to run over and let Uncle Loven know that we won't be coming to church or dinner today."

Both Patience and Thomas stared at her, but she only smiled. "Shoo now. I have other plans brewing, but don't tell them that."

Thomas dashed off to finish dressing. With a regretful sigh, Truth closed the shutter and set Patience to build a fire. They'd not be here long, but the front room was ice cold.

In the lean-to, which she'd been making her own after the news of Papa's death, she lingered over the decision of what to wear. The odd desire to look her best warred with the need for practicality—but she'd be climbing the mountain today after all. Over her shift, she tied on a set of jumps rather than the boned stays. Over that, her pocket and two layers of petticoats, a quilted calico first, then the faded indigo she usually wore. Her red-and-blue-flowered short gown went next—it had been one of Mama's—and the knitted elbow-length mitts she was never without during the colder months. And under, of course, went stockings and leggings and moccasins.

Her cap, however—she tucked that into her pocket, after brushing and braiding her hair. She would not be tramping up the mountain in a mere hood and cape if she could help it.

Out in the main room, she gathered what they'd need—the frame for the iron spit, half a dozen small pumpkins for roasting, sugar and spices folded carefully into a clean cloth, the dried berry pie she'd baked the day before similarly wrapped. Their great Bible in its own carrying pouch. All of it, settled carefully into haversacks and blanket bundles for carrying.

Thomas returned, and she sent him to the smokehouse for the ham she'd selected the day before. Milly and Loven would be missing it, but they had meat put up as well—and this was too important.

Making sure everyone else was dressed for the trek up the mountain, Truth put on her hunting coat and strapped both hers and Papa's shot pouches and powder horns across her body. Lastly, she returned to the back room for the bundle she'd prepared the night before. Once that was slung in place, she put on her hat, took both her rifle and Papa's in hand, and led off into the snowy morning.

"Where are we going?" Mercy asked.

"I bet it has something to do with Micah," Thomas said.

"Silly, we're taking Christmas to him," Patience said.

Truth smiled a little. Her sister was as sharp as any.

"Are you going to marry him, Truth?" Thankful asked.

"We saw him kiss you," Thomas said.

"How could you not?" Truth muttered, but she smiled wider.

Micah, unashamed, kissing her in the front yard for God and everyone to see. "*Are* you going to marry him?" Patience asked.

She laughed. "I just might."

Thomas and the younger girls broke out into whoops and huzzahs.

"Wait," Mercy said. "Is he still a Tory?"

Truth laughed until she was breathless—which wasn't long, considering they'd hit a steep portion of the trail.

❧

Micah had always loved snow. On this morning, he stepped out of the cave and was struck breathless by the clear glory surrounding him.

As pure as the first Christmas morning, he was sure.

Filling his lungs with the crisp, clean-washed mountain air, he scanned the forest. Did he risk leaving tracks for a quick run to the lookout at the summit?

Aye, how could he not?

The chill air burned his nostrils and invigorated him as he raced up the now-familiar track. Glimpses of the snow-covered distance flashed between the trees, white and shadow stark in the dawn, but he pressed on until he came to the familiar tumble of boulders.

At the top, he feasted his eyes. First toward the east, and away southward in the misty distance, past the rippled mountaintops, the land that had birthed and bred him. He thought of his parents, gone these many years, and of the bitter struggle between John and Zacharias during the early part of the war, before Zach had gone to join the Continentals. His sisters, busying themselves in their growing families and only speaking of Zach in whispers afterward.

His own idealistic fervor until the awfulness that was King's Mountain.

The world did not hold enough treasure to tempt him to trade places with the rebels, not with the way their officers had left the fallen prisoners to be trampled to death on the march by day and then vented their fury upon them by night. But after watching the settlements scratching for survival here on the frontier, and furthermore, living it as he'd sought to help Truth, his heart had changed. He was no stranger to hardship, being backcountry folk himself, but their raw determination amazed him.

He turned slowly, his gaze marking where hillside fell away into river valley. Could he indeed find his place here if Truth made the decision to accept him?

And if she did not, where would he go? Possibly home, to see his sisters one last time, at least. But then what?

Heart aching, he searched the edge of the valley where he knew Truth's farm lay past the folds of the mountainsides. *Oh God, can she forgive who I am. . .who I was?*

Then there was the matter of how long she might wait to let him know what she'd decided. Would she make him stay here the whole winter long, hoping he'd simply leave?

He blew out a long breath, watching the plume of steam disappear on the breeze. Enough already. Christmas Day or no, he had snares to check. At the least, he'd have a bundle of furs to carry down to the fort and trade in a few weeks. The keeper of the post had promised whatever provisions he wished in exchange. It was just rabbit and squirrel now, but if he could barter or work for a decent rifle, there was more to be made in deer or bear pelts.

The longing hit him like a blow to the chest, and he shut his eyes. *Oh Truth. . .*

A shot echoed across the mountainside, and he looked up again, scanning the forest. An odd morning for someone to be out hunting, and this community didn't seem to be given to the customary *feu de joie* of the lower country. But no more shots followed, and after a few minutes of listening, Micah climbed down off the rocks and went to check his snares.

They'd passed Truth's favorite hunting rock, and as they neared the cave where she'd found Micah taking shelter all those weeks ago, she found her heart beating unaccountably fast.

You know where to find me. Would he even be there?

Ah Lord, let him be there!

They rounded the last bend, and she made everyone stop at the big oak where she'd stood signaling for him that first time. She handed the rifles off to Patience, and then facing the half-hidden cave entrance, she pursed her lips and sent out the call again. *Whip-poor-will! Whip-poor-will!*

Silence, and the wind in the bare treetops above, rattling the few browned leaves remaining.

Her heart plummeted. What if he'd gone away already?

Then her eye caught on the fresh prints laid in the snow, leading from the cave entrance. Her pulse leaped anew.

"Here—hold my rifle and stay here until I tell you otherwise," she said, taking Papa's rifle from Patience.

She wouldn't go far—surely he'd be back, and they had plenty of preparations to make before their feast would be ready. But she couldn't resist tracking him a short distance, at least.

Cradling the rifle, she set off up the trail. She recognized the winding path— so he'd gone to the lookout? It had been a while since she'd been there herself—

And then—there he was, climbing toward her from a slightly different path, winding upward through the laurel. He stopped, eyes widening, then hurried on toward her. A pair of rabbits dangled from his hand.

Suddenly, she could hardly breathe.

He stopped a few paces from her, head angled, eyes searching her face. His chest rose and fell—the climb, or her sudden appearance? Warmth shivered through her at the thought that she might affect him at least as much as he did her. She certainly couldn't seem to find her tongue.

"Truth," he breathed.

Of habit, she glanced over his gear—haversack, knife, hat, gaiters, mittens. "You're missing a few things there," she blurted.

The corner of his mouth tipped. "I've been doing all right."

"Well—" She forced her feet to move forward a step. "You need—this."

And she held out Papa's rifle.

A flush crossed his pale cheek. He searched her eyes then hesitantly reached for it. "You're—certain?"

She nodded, sure her own cheeks must be red as holly berries. They felt hot enough to catch on fire.

He gently, reverently took the piece from her hands. Her throat closed, and she unstrapped Papa's powder horn and shot bag. "These too," she whispered.

He took them, looped them one-handed across his shoulders and over his body. "Figured you'd be saving these for Thomas," he murmured.

She shook her head, swallowing. "It's my thought—they won't be leaving the family."

He went still, and she could not tear herself away from the hope in his dark eyes.

"If what you said to me last time means what I think it does," she went on.

A smile dawned, flashed into a grin. "Sweet Truth. This is your answer?"

Oh, he made her both soft and weak. She could only manage another nod.

What if she'd mistaken his intent?

He eased closer, knuckles brushing her cheek. His brows knitted for a moment. "You'd forgive me enough to marry me?"

Another nod. She was drowning in those eyes.

He took off his hat, swept an arm around her, and kissed her with such suddenness that her own hat fell off. But she only kissed him back, reveling in the contrast of warm lips and cold cheekbone, and in the strength of him in her arms.

After a very long moment—or several—he pulled back, breathless. "Surely you didn't come alone?"

She giggled. "No. I left the young'uns at the cave. We brought Christmas dinner."

❧

Micah could hardly believe the happy blur of the next hours. Tramping hand in hand back to the cave, he'd seen Thomas and all three girls jump for joy and cheer then fly toward him with open arms. They'd brought not only a ham but a turkey—that was the shot he'd heard from the lookout—and half of them set to dressing the bird while the other half stoked the fire inside the cave and set up the spit. The pumpkins were tucked around the edges of the fire for roasting, and when all was set for the long wait of cooking, Truth sat them all down and laid the Bible in his lap. "Would you do us the honor of reading?"

He met her pleading half smile with a grin of his own then opened to where she'd already marked the passage with a scrap of ribbon. The print read, "The Gospel According to Luke," and she pointed to chapter 2.

This task had always been taken by his father and then by his eldest brother. It wasn't that he disbelieved, but Micah had felt detached from the words they'd read—pronouncements and decrees from an ancient, distant God. But today, touching the pages and seeing the expectant faces surrounding him as the firelight flickered on the cave walls, Micah thought he sensed the nearness of God as never before.

Had God truly heard and answered his prayers?

Truth leaned toward him, her fingers covering his on the page. "We had our reading last night, for Christmas Eve. But this—this is why we came today." Her eyes, pale as mist, begged him to understand. "Just—read it, and I'll explain."

With a nod, he found his place and began. " 'And it came to pass in those days, that a decree went out from Caesar Augustus, that all the world should be taxed. . . .

" 'For mine eyes have seen thy salvation, which thou hast prepared before the face of all people; a light to lighten the Gentiles, and the glory of thy people Israel.'"

Truth's hand covered his again, and he looked up.

"This is why," she said, her voice soft, her gaze earnest. "On Christmas we celebrate the birth of the Christ, yes? The One that God sent to later die for our sins. Mine, Micah, as well as yours."

"And what sins might you have, sweet Truth?" He knew well his own.

"Pride," she answered without hesitation. "But—His grace covers it all. And I cannot expect Him to forgive me if I'm not willing to forgive you.

"Whether or not you were directly responsible for Papa's death. . ." She faltered and blinked. "You did not know, and it's past. You are here now. And I'd be wrong to refuse this gift of grace that God is offering me, in you."

He turned his hand to clasp hers, and she gripped it tightly. Those misty eyes shimmered in the firelight.

For a moment, he nearly forgot they were not alone.

"And I confess I've become"—he was sure she blushed—"accustomed to having you about."

A chorus of giggles greeted that pronouncement. With a grin, he took them all in. "And what are your thoughts about this?"

Patience only smiled shyly, but Thomas snorted and said, "You'd better marry her while you can. She's never let anyone else get close enough to kiss her."

While they all laughed—Micah and Truth included—Micah set aside the Bible, rose to his feet, and drew Truth into his arms. She nestled into his embrace then tipped her head so her mouth was close to his ear. "Of a certain, you're the only one I'd want defending me," she whispered.

Warmed through, and not by the fire, he tucked her closer. "For the rest of my life," he murmured back.

The Calling

Kathleen Fuller

Chapter 1

Unionville, Ohio
1820

Milly Kent! When's a fair lass like you gonna settle down?"

Milly laughed along with Mr. O'Reardon, a man old enough to be her father. "I suppose when the good Lord tells me to." She put a plate of sliced cold beef, chunks of white cheese, and a thick piece of rye bread slathered with fresh butter in front of him. The tin plate thudded against the wooden table.

Mr. O'Reardon smiled. The balding Irishman was missing nearly all his bottom teeth, but with his twinkling eyes and natural Irish charm, she barely noticed. "The man the good Lord brings ye will be a lucky one, indeed."

"Thank you." Milly curtsied, which made him grin all the more. She went back behind the tavern counter, wiped her hands on a towel, and looked out the large window facing the road. Flakes of snow floated down, landing on the grassy yard in front of the tavern like powdered sugar over an apple fritter.

"Milly, quit your daydreaming." Cornelius Kent burst out of the kitchen, his wide forehead slick with sweat despite the December chill outside. "The dishes need washing, Daughter."

"All four of them?" Milly winked. It was two days before Christmas, and the tavern was nearly empty. The last stagecoach was scheduled to arrive about an hour from now, and she doubted there would be many passengers. Winter traveling was dangerous, especially with the unpredictable snowfall between here and Buffalo, New York.

"Yes, all four of them." Cornelius wiped his brow with the back of his hand and looked at the front door. A shadow passed in front of it. He groaned. "Lands, doesn't that woman take a day off?"

The door opened, and Milly's aunt Louise bustled inside, dusting the snow off her thick woolen shawl. She lifted her heavy chin and waddled to the counter.

"Mrs. Crosby." Mr. O'Reardon stood and took off his cap. He lifted the corners of his mouth in a jaunty smile.

"Mr. O'Reardon." She passed by, giving him the barest of polite glances.

O'Reardon's jovial expression faded as he shrugged and sat back down. He pulled a folded newspaper out of the breast pocket of his wool coat, unfolded it, and chewed on a piece of cheese as he started reading.

"Louise." Milly's father took a couple of steps back. "I was just heading to the kitchen—"

"Then my timing is impeccable, as always. I'll take a roast beef sandwich. With plenty of gravy. And if you have any of those little potatoes, add a decent portion to the plate. Don't skimp."

"Anything else?" Cornelius spoke through gritted teeth.

"Make sure the roast beef slices are tender, Cornelius." Aunt Louise fiddled with her shawl. "Yesterday they were filled with gristle."

"Yes *ma'am*." Cornelius disappeared into the kitchen, muttering something about marrying into the wrong family.

Milly turned to her aunt and smiled. Unlike her father, who could barely stand her aunt Louise's company, Milly thought she was amusing. Except when she was matchmaking. Her aunt didn't understand that Milly wasn't interested in anyone in town. Only one man had captured her attention, but he wasn't aware of her feelings. Milly intended to keep it that way, for both their sakes.

Aunt Louise leaned over the counter. "Don't make any plans for Sunday eve."

"Why?" Milly asked.

"I invited that nice young man Carl Weatherspoon to sup with us."

"And why would you do that?"

Aunt Louise sighed. "Don't be coy, Millicent Kent. You won't find a suitable man in this"—she looked around the tavern and sniffed—"establishment. I shudder to think of the kind of men that frequent this place."

"*You* frequent this place."

"That's different." She peered at Milly over her upturned nose, the same shape as Milly's. The same shape her mother's had been. "You spend all of your time here, except when you attend church service."

"I live here. Plus I enjoy my work. Interesting people stop by." Milly thought of one person in particular. She tried to hide her smile but failed.

"I see nothing humorous about this conversation, Millicent. Now, Sunday supper. My house. Six sharp. Don't be late."

Cornelius came out with Louise's food. He walked across the dining room to the table farthest from the kitchen and set the plate down with a clatter. A piece of potato fell off the edge and onto the table. "Your dinner," he said before storming back into the kitchen.

Aunt Louise wrinkled her nose. "Humph. Your father could learn some manners."

"My mother found his manners just fine, Aunt Louise."

"Your mother, God rest her soul, had the patience of a saint." Louise looked at her food then back at Milly. "Now if you'll excuse me, I don't want my lunch to get cold."

Milly nodded. As her aunt walked away, Milly added, "You do know I supped with you and Mr. Weatherspoon three weeks ago."

Louise turned around, her thick eyebrows narrowing. "You did?"

"Yes. We didn't hit it off very well."

"But Mr. Weatherspoon accepted my invitation right away. Why would he do that if he didn't like you?"

Milly sighed. "I think he likes me too much. Auntie"—she lowered her voice—"he was a bit. . .pushy."

"Ah." Aunt Louise's plump cheeks turned red. "I apologize then. I will cancel the invitation posthaste."

"Thank you."

"Not to worry." She tapped her thick finger against her chin. "Have you met my friend Kate's nephew Franklin?"

"Your dinner is getting cold, Auntie."

"Oh yes it is." She bustled to the table. "We'll discuss Franklin at a further date."

Milly heard Mr. O'Reardon chuckle. When she looked at him, he moved the paper in front of his face.

The sound of horses' hooves penetrated the walls of the tavern. Her heart pounded in time with the cadence. She knew it was improbable, but she couldn't help but hope the man who held her heart would be on the stage. His image filtered through her mind—his black hair that curled at the ends, his slender frame, and the crispness of his suits, which were always precisely tailored. But more importantly she thought about his kindness, his unending politeness, and the brilliant smiles he gave her, smiles seemingly meant just for her.

But they weren't. A wonderful man like Elijah Montgomery would want little to do with a tavern girl. And that's all she would ever be.

❧

"You cannot ignore the Lord's calling any longer!" Percival Montgomery slammed his fist against his mahogany desk. "Remember what happened to Jonah? He was punished for his disobedience and spent three days in the belly of a great fish."

Elijah Montgomery fisted his hand at his sides. He was more than familiar with the biblical tale. He looked at the florid face of his father then to the disappointed one of his mother as she stood by her husband's side. It wasn't the first time his parents had accused him of avoiding his destiny. But today would be the last.

The stagecoach lurched forward, jerking Elijah out of his slumber. He blinked, looking around the dimly lit coach and trying to gain his bearings. He'd been in a deep sleep, which was unusual for him. He'd gotten little rest in the past year, since his parents had told him he was destined to preach in the western territories. "My son will be a great voice in the wilderness," his father had said to almost anyone who would listen.

Elijah didn't think he'd be a great voice anywhere. But his parents were insistent that he was called to preach, like his father and his grandfather. Unlike them, Elijah had the opportunity to go west, to follow other preachers and deliver the Word of God—just like the prophets of old.

The thought made his stomach turn. Not that he didn't love the Lord. He did with all his heart. But the few times he'd preached in his father's stead had been disastrous. One time he lost his place during his sermon, and it took him several minutes to find it again and continue. The next time he broke out in a cold sweat on a freezing winter day before he even started speaking. When he delivered his last message, he had quoted so many wrong verses and chapters his father had cut Elijah's preaching short.

How could Elijah be called to preach when he had no gift for it?

He looked out the window, watching the familiar scenery, and pushed the uneasy thoughts from his mind. Despite his inner turmoil, a heady feeling rushed through him at the thought of seeing Milly Kent again. The lovely tavern maid, always quick with a sweet smile and encouraging word, warmed his heart whenever he saw her.

The stage pulled up to the front of the tavern. Elijah grabbed his case from the floor and waited for the driver to open the door.

"Thank you." Elijah stepped down, the only passenger on the afternoon stage. He placed a few coins in the driver's hand. "When will we depart for Cleveland?"

"Tomorrow morning, bright and early." The driver gripped the coins in his gloved hand. "Thank you, sir."

Elijah nodded, blowing out a puff of frosty air as he headed for the tavern door. The snow that had started to fall an hour ago now lay in an inch-thick carpet on the grass and roads. Light glowed from the tavern window, a warm beacon in the fading daylight.

He opened the door and stepped inside. As he expected, it was nearly empty. Unionville wasn't a large town, just a small village with a tavern serving as a stagecoach stop. He hadn't spent much time in the area, but he knew that several families lived nearby and that they had built a small schoolhouse that doubled as a church on Sundays.

He glanced around and saw the Irishman O'Reardon at his usual table, reading the paper. In the back corner of the tavern sat a plump woman Elijah recognized as Milly's aunt. He continued to search the room. Where was Milly?

Finally, she appeared from the kitchen, tying a white apron around her narrow waist. Elijah removed his hat, flakes of snow falling from the brim. He looked at her and couldn't help but smile. His heart flipped as she smiled in return.

"Welcome, Mr. Montgomery." She walked from behind the counter. "I'm glad you're visiting us again. I'm surprised, considering the holiday. We may not have many guests tonight."

That was fine by him. He wouldn't mind a bit if only he and Milly were there, although her father might have something to say about that.

They held each other's gazes for a moment, and his pulse began to thrum. Sometimes he thought she might have feelings for him, especially when she looked at him with such sweetness. Then again, it was possibly an empty wish on his part.

She clasped her hands in front of her, her eyes never leaving his. "I hope you enjoy your stay at our tavern."

It was her standard greeting to all their guests. He'd heard it several times during his previous visits. And as he usually did, he responded, "I will, Miss Kent. I always do."

Milly lowered her eyes before looking at him again, this time with enough sparkle to make his smile widen. All the thoughts and doubts of his trip west vanished.

Chapter 2

"Can I take your coat and hat?" Milly asked, willing her hands not to tremble. He was here. She couldn't believe it. And as he handed her his top hat and thick, black wool coat, she gazed up at him—tall, lanky, and with shock of black hair that curled over his forehead and brushed against his collar. She hadn't seen him for months, but he hadn't changed. Except for being even more handsome than she remembered.

She pulled her gaze away, lest he realize she was staring. She'd been smitten with Elijah Montgomery since he first walked into the tavern almost two years ago, on his first trip west of Cleveland. She'd kept her feelings for him a secret, something she dared not change. She wouldn't make a fool of herself or open her heart to rejection, because nothing would ever come of her attraction to him. This fine man, whose father was a prominent preacher in Buffalo, wouldn't settle for a simple tavern girl.

Yet he would settle for a meal. Despite his gangly frame, he enjoyed eating. "I suppose you're ready for supper, Mr. Montgomery?"

He nodded. "Yes, Miss Kent. I am famished."

She draped his coat over her arm. "I'll let Father know. In the meantime, I'll prepare your room."

"Don't go to too much trouble, Miss Kent."

She smiled. He was so kind. "It's no trouble at all." Milly left the dining room and walked into the kitchen. Her father was shoving wood into the stove. He shut the small iron door, stood, and wiped his damp forehead.

"Mr. Montgomery is here," she said. "Along with the stage driver. I believe it's Mr. Menough this eve."

Her father lifted a bushy eyebrow. "I wasn't expecting anyone to arrive until after Christmas." He shrugged. "I suppose Montgomery is ready to eat?"

"Isn't he always?" Before she could catch herself, Milly's cheeks heated like the burning embers in the fireplace. She quickly turned her face away from her father. "I should get the gentlemen's rooms ready." She rushed out of the kitchen and hurried upstairs. A chill hit her as soon as she reached the top step.

Milly opened the first door on the right, which opened to what would be Elijah's room. She placed his hat and coat on the stand in the corner of the room, letting her fingers linger over the rough wool, still damp from the falling snow outside. Then she quickly built a fire, pulled an extra quilt out of the cedar chest at the end of the bed, and turned down one corner of the bedding. One last fluff of the pillow and she moved on to Mr. Menough's room.

When she finished, she went downstairs. "Milly!" her father called out from the kitchen.

Her father was piling a plate high with slices of tender roast beef and small boiled potatoes. He placed a thick slice of bread on the side and handed the dish to Milly. "For Montgomery."

She grabbed a knife, fork, and cloth napkin and took them to the dining room. Elijah was sitting at a wooden table nearest to the kitchen. She put his meal in front of him. He inhaled. "Smells wonderful."

Milly glanced around the dining room. Her aunt was still there, along with Mr. O'Reardon, but they were ignoring each other. "Where is Mr. Menough?"

"He said something about taking a look at the stagecoach after he settled the horses."

"Is there something wrong?"

Elijah snapped the napkin open and laid it in his lap. "I don't know. The ride wasn't any different than it normally is. Bumpy, as usual." He started to fold his hands but stopped to look at her. "Have you eaten?"

The question took her off guard for a moment. "No I haven't."

"Well then, would you—" He glanced away for a moment. Then his gaze met hers. "Would you mind joining me?"

Her heart flipped. He'd never asked her to eat with him before. Surely it was only out of kindness. It was suppertime, and she did have to eat. Although she normally ate with her father in the kitchen or sometimes behind the long counter where they kept the glasses and beverages—

"Miss Kent?"

She gave her head a quick shake and looked at him. Then she realized that Mr. Menough hadn't returned. Her father would never let her eat without the guests being tended to first. "Thank you for the offer, Mr. Montgomery. But I'm afraid I can't, as I'm working right now."

"But surely you can break for a meal."

Was that disappointment she saw on his face? How odd and thrilling at the same time.

"Milly."

She turned at the sound of her father's voice. He approached the table and stretched out his hand to Elijah. "Nice to see you, Mr. Montgomery. I hope your trip from Buffalo was uneventful."

Elijah accepted her father's beefy hand. "Very much so, fortunately. Albeit a little chilly."

"Milly, bring Mr. Montgomery a cup of coffee, will you?" Her father turned to her.

"Yes sir." She glanced at Elijah again before getting the coffee. When she returned, he had his head bowed in silent prayer. She waited until she heard him whisper, "Amen," before giving him his coffee. "Do you need anything else?" she asked.

He took a sip of the coffee. "No thank you."

She smiled. "Let me know if you need anything, Mr. Montgomery." Milly moved to walk away. Suddenly, he put his hand on her forearm, stopping her. Then he jerked back. When she looked at him, his cheeks were slightly flushed.

"Elijah," he said. "Please, call me Elijah."

She gazed at him for a moment. He'd never been so informal with her before, and she didn't mind it one bit. "Elijah."

His mouth tilted upward as he picked up his fork and started eating.

Milly practically floated to the kitchen, her thoughts so filled with Elijah's smile that she bumped into her father.

"Milly!" Water sloshed from the bucket in his hand. "Watch where you're going, girl."

"Sorry." She walked to the counter and put a linen towel over the sliced bread in the basket.

"Have all our guests been taken care of?" he asked.

"Yes," Milly said. "Except for Mr. Menough. He's still outside." Her stomach rumbled. How she wished she could have joined Elijah for supper. But their guests came first.

"Make sure he's taken care of when he comes inside." He set the bucket down. "Is Mr. Montgomery satisfied with his meal?"

Milly walked to the swinging kitchen door and peeked outside. As he usually did when he was a guest at the tavern, he was eating his food with relish.

"He seems to be."

"Good." Her father bent over and rinsed his hands in the bucket. "He's one of our frequent customers. I don't want to disappoint him."

She took one last look at Elijah before shutting the door. *Me either.*

Elijah bit into the tender roast beef. The meal, as always when he stayed here, was delicious and satisfying. But he couldn't concentrate on the food, not when he kept glancing at the kitchen door, wishing Milly would come out.

She seemed to grow more beautiful each time he came to Unionville Tavern. Her soft, kind voice only enhanced her loveliness. Inviting her to dine with him had been a rash decision, but he'd hoped she would have agreed. Her refusal, while not surprising, was disappointing nevertheless.

"Ye have to try harder than that, son." Mr. O'Reardon sat down in the chair next to him uninvited, but Elijah didn't mind. O'Reardon always seemed to be here, even though he had a small house a few yards down the road. "I've noticed ye been eyeing the lass for a while now."

Elijah looked down at his plate. He thought to deny O'Reardon's words, but it would be a lie. "I didn't intend to be so obvious."

"Nay, you're not." O'Reardon gave him a sly smile. "At least not to her. But this old lad's been around a time or two. I know a smitten look when I see one."

Elijah stabbed at a piece of potato with his fork. "Not that it makes a difference."

"Why would ye say that?"

He looked at O'Reardon, the Irishman's hat perched at a jaunty angle. "After today, I won't be returning to Unionville."

O'Reardon frowned, stretching the craggy lines of his face. "And why not?"

"Because." He put down his fork. "It's time I quit running from my responsibilities." Elijah sighed. "My *calling*."

"I see." O'Reardon leaned back in the chair. "Well, ye must do what ye must. But a word o' advice, son."

"Yes?"

"The heart, it has a mind of its own. Sometimes ye have to listen to what it's tellin' ye, instead of what yer noggin's sayin'."

Elijah frowned. "What?"

"Ye'll know what I mean when the time comes." He stood then clapped Elijah on the back.

Milly appeared beside O'Reardon. She looked at Elijah's plate. "Can I get you anything else?"

Elijah stared at her, his heart pulsing. *You*, he wanted to say, but dragged the thought back into the recesses of his mind where it belonged. O'Reardon's friendly advice changed nothing. Elijah was on a path chosen by God, one that didn't include Milly. He could only imagine his parents' reaction if he admitted that he'd rather stay in Unionville and court Milly—if she would allow him to—instead of preaching. They had made it perfectly clear that his focus was on God's work and nothing else.

"We have a few slices of apple pie left," she said, clasping her hands in front of her, the insides of her wrists brushing against her white apron. The sturdy cloth was covered with food stains, some fresh, some faded from time and repeated washings. Milly worked hard. He'd always respected that about her.

"Go on, lad." O'Reardon gave him a little shove on the shoulder. "The pie is delicious." He winked again and walked back to the table.

"What was that about?" Milly asked, glancing at the man as he crossed the room. O'Reardon sat down and resumed reading his newspaper.

"Nothing. He was just making conversation."

"I see. So, about the pie?"

The tension released in his shoulders. At least he had the night before he was back on the road again. He might as well enjoy it. "Yes, Miss Kent. Some pie would be agreeable to me."

"I'll be right back." But she didn't move. "As long as you promise me one thing."

"What's that?"

"If you want me to call you Elijah, then you must call me Milly. It's only fair."

Milly. He liked how her name rolled off his tongue. She'd been his Milly for a while now—only she never knew it. "Milly it is."

Chapter 3

A few hours later, Elijah rose from bed. He stoked the fire a bit, poking at the warm coals. Other than the soft pop and hiss from the fading fire, silence surrounded him. Sleep had been elusive, as it had been for the past week. Every time he closed his eyes, he'd hear his father's coercive voice prodding, pushing.

Where is your obedience? Why do you disappoint the Lord with excuses, Elijah? He always equips us for His will. This fear you have is not of God, Son. It is from the evil one.

He closed his eyes against the words, against the memory of disapproval in his mother's eyes as his father lectured him yet again, reminding him not only of his duty but of his legacy.

You are our only child. Our miracle that we prayed for, like Hannah prayed for Samuel. And like her, we dedicated you for God's purpose. And you continually turn your back on Him—and on us!

He was failing them. He knew, they knew. And by failing them, he was also failing God.

He opened his eyes, threaded his trembling fingers through his hair, and rested his elbows on his crouched knees. They were right. He felt that failure deep inside. It pulled at his conscience, draining him. He tried to keep up the facade, at least on the outside. But he couldn't manage it for much longer.

Failure and cowardice. Yet innumerable prayers beseeching God to give him confidence and peace about being a circuit preacher in the western territories had gone unanswered. Instead, more turmoil churned inside him.

Elijah stood. Paced the room until his foot hit a creaky board. He froze. Everyone else was asleep; he didn't want to wake them, especially Mr. Menough, who was so exhausted he had barely made it up the stairs to his room.

Elijah put on his robe and slippers and crept downstairs.

When he reached the bottom, he saw the warm glow of firelight in the large fireplace on the opposite side of the tavern entrance. A wooden mantel protruded from the sand-colored stone surrounding the hearth. Two high-backed chairs braced the fireplace. If he couldn't find peace, perhaps he could at least find physical warmth from the glowing coals.

But when he rounded the staircase, he halted his steps. Someone was sitting in one of the chairs. He thought to go back upstairs again, but when he turned, another board creaked.

Milly jumped up from the chair. She peered in the darkness. "Hello?"

"I'm sorry. I didn't mean to disturb you."

She moved toward him, a shadowy figure outlined by flickering light from the fireplace. "Elijah?"

Sheepish, he pressed his lips together. "Yes."

She hugged her slender body, her hands rubbing the arms of her night wrapper.

"Are you cold?" He moved toward her and saw the fire was starting to die down.

"A bit." She didn't return to her chair. "I was just about to add another log."

"Allow me." He picked up one of the short pieces of split wood from the pile on the stone hearth and put it in the fireplace. He grabbed the poker nearby and settled the log until it had caught fire. Heat surrounded them.

"Ah," she said, her palms facing the fireplace. "That's better. Thank you."

He nodded. "I'll leave you to it then." He moved to head upstairs when her sweet voice stopped him.

"Elijah?"

He turned and looked at her.

"Please. Stay."

"Are you sure? I don't want to intrude."

"You're not." She gestured to the opposite chair. When he sat down, she added, "I couldn't sleep."

"Me either."

She sat down. Fingered the ribbons on her night wrap. "I hoped some time to myself by the fire might still my thoughts."

Elijah frowned. He hated the idea that she was troubled. "Do you want to talk about it?"

She sighed. "You'll think me silly."

"I doubt I could ever do that, Milly."

She smiled as she gazed at the fire. "I'm trying to figure out how to avoid my aunt. Actually, not avoid her per se but her incessant matchmaking."

Jealousy stabbed at him. He cleared his throat. "I can see how that would be a problem."

Milly glanced at him. "Are you mocking me, Elijah?"

He shook his head. "Of course not." He leaned forward, his forearms on his thighs. "It's obvious you're not happy with her attempts." He did find that a little gratifying.

"Definitely not. She means well. . .and she's right."

"About what?"

"About getting married." Milly tilted her head as she gazed at the flickering flames. "I had just hoped. . . ." She glanced down at her lap. "I mean I wished things could be different."

"In what way?"

"That someday I could run this tavern. Take the business over from my father."

"It is your dream then?"

She nodded. "Yes. Foolish, isn't it?"

He gazed at her. "Not at all. We all have dreams, Milly."

"And sometimes they come true. But not this one." She smiled, but her lips were tight at the corners. "I have two choices. Work here for my father and hope he sells the tavern to someone who would want to keep me on. Or get married."

"Do you not want to marry?"

She looked up at him but didn't answer right away. Finally, she said, "I do."

Milly stared at the fire, unable to look at Elijah. She'd spoken more about her thoughts and dreams tonight than she had to anyone. She finally glanced at him. He, too, looked at the fire, the flames casting flickering shadows on his profile. Perhaps she shouldn't have said anything so personal. Yet speaking to him about this was so natural. And cathartic.

He turned his face to her. An unfamiliar but comforting warmth filled her as she met his caring, dark eyes. They held no judgment. Instead, they seemed to be full of understanding.

"Why haven't you married yet, Milly?"

His question took her off guard. After a moment, she said, "I haven't found the right man." But she wanted to tell him so much more. How she couldn't settle for what her aunt or father wanted. Her aunt especially didn't seem to care who she wed, as long as Milly had a husband. But Milly wanted more. She wanted the love her parents had shared. She wanted to marry for love.

And the only man she could imagine herself with—was him.

Her cheeks heated, and not from the warmth of the fire. Then suddenly she remembered he was a guest. She should be seeing to his comfort, not indulging in her own imaginings. "Would you like something to drink? I could prepare a quick cup of tea or coffee." She looked at him. "Or would you rather have a snack?"

Elijah shook his head. "I'm fine. And even if I wasn't, I wouldn't want you to go to the trouble."

She popped up from the chair. "It's no trouble—"

He gestured for her to sit down. "Please. I don't need anything to eat or drink." He paused, looking up at her. "What I need. . .is a friend."

As Milly sat down, she willed her pulse to slow. *A friend.* She ran the words through her mind a couple of times. He needed a friend, not a silly girl with a crush.

They both stared at the fire for a few moments. Finally, she spoke. "Do you mind if I ask you a question?"

He nodded. "Considering I asked you something quite personal, please do. I hope you weren't offended by my inquiry, by the way."

"Of course not." She smiled. "I was the one who brought up the subject of matchmaking."

He angled himself toward her. "Good. I would never want to offend you, Milly."

The pull of attraction intensified inside her. She reminded herself that he'd asked for her friendship and folded her hands in her lap.

"What is your question?" he asked.

"Why are you not in Buffalo?" She glanced at her lap. "If I'm not being too nosy."

"You're not."

"It's just that I assumed you would be spending the holiday with your family."

He leaned back in the chair and let out a long sigh. "They made other plans."

"Without you?"

"Yes."

There was no doubting his sour tone. "I didn't realize your business in Cleveland was so important."

"I don't have business in Cleveland."

Her brow lifted. "But—"

"Why do I travel back and forth from Buffalo to Cleveland several times a year?" His chin dipped. "Because I'm a coward."

Milly scoffed. "You are not."

"I am." He looked directly at her, his eyes haunted. "I'm Jonah, Milly. I'm ignoring God's instructions. His direction." He shook his head. "I'm just as cowardly as he was."

She frowned. Why would he make such a negative, and surely untrue, statement? "I don't understand."

He rubbed the back of his neck and turned to the fire again. "Ever since I can remember, my parents told me I was going to be a preacher. When I turned sixteen, my father said I was called to go to the western territories and preach the Gospel. 'You will be on a great commission,' he would say. 'Like the prophets of old.' My mother believed it, too."

Milly leaned forward in her chair. "Do you?"

He rubbed the palms of his hands on his thighs. "I want to. My father is a preacher. My grandfather, too. My great-great grandfather left England for the chance to practice his faith here. It's not just a calling; it's my legacy."

"Yet you're not sure."

Elijah let out a brittle laugh. "I'm an awful preacher, Milly. I'm not like my father. He always says the right thing in the pulpit. He's strong in his convictions. Strong in his faith."

Milly's heart went out to him. She could see he had wrestled with this for a long while. "Have you ever thought your father could be wrong?"

"My father is never wrong."

"He can't be perfect. None of us are."

"He's close. And what he says makes sense—we cannot have a spirit of fear. That's scriptural. He says I'm afraid and that's what's holding me back." His gaze held hers. "I'm terrified. That's why I always come back. But this time, I have to go."

"Even if you have doubts?"

"It doesn't matter what I think. Or what I feel. They told me this time not to come back." He stared at his upturned palms. "I don't have a choice anymore."

"Elijah." She looked at him. "There's always a choice." She shook her head. "Your father sounds like Aunt Louise. They are so sure about what's right for *our* futures. Don't we have a say in what we do?" *And whom we'll marry?*

He didn't answer. Then he stood. "Mr. Menough said we're leaving early in the morning."

It didn't escape her that he had evaded her question. "Elijah—"

"I imagine he's eager to see his family in Cleveland for Christmas." He glanced at her. "I should get some sleep."

Milly paused then nodded. She would respect his wish not to discuss the issue further. "I should retire as well." She rose. "Father and I will have breakfast ready for you both in the morning."

He started toward the stairs. Then he stopped, hesitated, and touched her shoulder for a brief moment before pulling back. "Thank you for listening, Milly. I hope what I told you won't lower your estimation of me. I. . .I couldn't bear that." Before she could answer, he hurried upstairs.

She heard the door to his room click shut. Knowing he was in turmoil pained her. Nothing could lower her estimation of Elijah Montgomery. He'd been honest and vulnerable. If anything, she was drawn to him more than ever.

And now she knew that not only was he setting out on a journey he feared, but he had to do it alone, and on Christmas of all days. *No, not alone.* She bowed her head and prayed for him.

Chapter 4

Milly rose early the next morning after only a few hours of sleep. She was bleary eyed, and her heart still carried Elijah's burden. But it was more than that. Each time he left the tavern, she always knew he was coming back. Now she knew for certain he wasn't.

She put aside her despair, determined to make Elijah's last breakfast at Unionville Tavern the best one he'd ever had. She had the biscuits cut and ready, the sausage sliced, and the eggs scrambled in a bowl by the time her father entered the kitchen. His eyes widened. "You've been busy."

"I had trouble sleeping, so I thought I'd get to work."

Her father yawned and nodded. "Good thing. Thought I heard our guests stirring about upstairs."

A short while later, Milly pulled the fluffy biscuits out of the oven. The eggs were cooked to perfection; the sausage still sizzled in the cast-iron skillet on top of the stove. She prepared two heaping plates and took them to the dining room.

Elijah was crouched by the fireplace, stoking the fire in the hearth. "Needed more wood," he said, tossing in another log. He stood. "Breakfast smells delicious."

His smile didn't reach his eyes. Perhaps he was fighting the same thoughts as she, that this would be their last time together. More likely, he was worried about his trip west. He had more things to concern himself with than her. She internally chastised herself as she placed the plates on the table. "Where is Mr. Menough?"

"Taking care of the horses. He will be here in a moment." Elijah sat down at the table. "Thank you, Milly."

"You're welcome."

He bowed his head in silent prayer. She joined him, praying for his safety not just on the trip to Cleveland but also as he headed to a new world. She'd never been farther west than Unionville. She never had occasion to be and didn't have a yearning for travel. Yet she'd heard from travelers passing through that the west was untamed country, filled with dangers from Indians, harsh weather, and more often than not, solitude. People had surrounded Milly all of her life. She couldn't imagine leaving behind everything she knew and going out on her own.

From his words last night, Elijah didn't want to either. But he was being obedient to his parents and to God. At least she hoped he was right about his journey west being about God's calling and not his parents pushing him to fulfill their own dreams.

Just as they finished praying, Mr. Menough entered, his bulbous nose red from the chilled air outside. "Gonna be a cold trip, Mr. Montgomery."

Elijah nodded, glancing at Milly. "I believe it is," he said, his voice filled with sadness.

Mr. Menough sat down across from Elijah. Milly excused herself and went to the kitchen. She stood in front of the sink and tried to shove the sadness away.

"Milly?" Her father came up beside her. "Something wrong?"

"No." She took a deep breath and turned to him, forcing a smile. "Everything is fine."

"Good." He stepped away and scraped the sausage grease off the skillet. "Snow's coming down pretty heavy. Once Montgomery leaves, I don't think we'll have any more guests. At least not for a while."

She swallowed the hard lump in her throat and nodded.

An hour later, Milly approached Elijah, who stood near the front door of the tavern. Mr. Menough was already outside, seated at the top of the stagecoach and ready to go. Elijah tipped his hat at Milly, giving her a long gaze. Finally, he said, "I guess this is good-bye, then."

"Wait." She gave him a square package wrapped in brown paper and tied with one of her light green hair ribbons. "I prepared a couple of sandwiches for you. In case you get hungry before you reach Cleveland."

Elijah smiled, accepting the package. "That is kind of you, Milly." He stared at her one more time. "Good-bye, Milly," he said before walking out the door.

She touched the glass window as the stagecoach pulled away. The glass was as cold as her heart. "Good-bye, Elijah."

❧

The stagecoach lurched as Elijah fingered Milly's hair ribbon. A lump caught in his throat as he remembered the sadness in her eyes when he left the tavern. Had she been mourning their last few moments together? He shook his head. More likely she pitied him.

He wished he hadn't told her his secret. He'd asked her not to think less of him, but how could she not?

He forced the thoughts out of his mind as the stagecoach slogged through the thick snow. He gripped the edge of his seat, partly from the bumpy ride, mostly from nerves. There was no looking back now. He had to put Milly out of his mind and heart forever and focus on the task ahead of him.

The stagecoach lurched forward, along with his stomach. He'd expected a bumpy, slog of a ride through the snow. But not something that would make him nauseous—

The stagecoach suddenly tipped on its side. Milly's package flew out of his hands as he searched for purchase in the coach.

"Whoa!" Menough shouted at the horses.

Elijah reached for the door, his stomach dropping as the coach continued to fall on its side.

"I said, 'Whoa!' "

Just as Elijah thought they would land sideways, the coach righted itself and dragged to a halt. He froze for a moment, catching his breath. What in the world had happened?

He exited right away, landing in almost knee-deep snow. Visibility had worsened since they'd left the tavern. He looked up at the driver. "Mr. Menough? Sir, are you all right?"

Menough's chest heaved as he sat in the driver's seat, his hands, encased in thick leather gloves, still gripping the reins. Large puffs of air mingled with thick wet snowflakes falling to the ground. "Yes sir," he gasped. "I'm fine." Then he let out a groan. "Can't say the same for the coach."

Elijah turned and looked. Immediately he saw the problem—a broken axle. It was a miracle and a test of Menough's strength that he had kept the horses under control. "Well done, Mr. Menough."

Menough wrapped the reins around the seat and jumped to the ground. He removed his hat and scratched his thick red hair. Snowfall surrounded them like a white curtain. "Thank you, Mr. Montgomery. I thought for certain we'd be lying in the snow by now. I'm thankful we're all safe, including my horses." He patted one of their flanks. He looked at the stagecoach and grimaced. "I'm not sure we can fix it right now. I have a few tools, but I don't have the supplies to fix the axle. There's a livery a few miles up the road. I can walk there—"

"With the snow coming down the way it is, I wouldn't want you to." Elijah pulled out his pocket watch. "How far did we go?"

"From the tavern? Not too far, I'm afraid."

"We should go back there then."

Menough put his hat back on. "I agree. I'm sorry for the inconvenience."

"Don't worry about that." Elijah hid his relief from the driver. Although he wouldn't have wished a broken axle or any other kind of accident for Menough and his horses, it did give Elijah another night's reprieve. He said a hasty prayer of thanks for that and their safety before saying to Menough, "This wasn't your fault. Can I help you with the horses?"

Menough nodded, and together they unhitched the two horses from their harness. Elijah brushed a bit of snow off one of the horse's chestnut-colored noses. A pointless gesture, as fresh snow immediately replaced it.

They guided the horses back toward Unionville, each man leading a horse and carrying a satchel. Elijah walked a few steps, only to stop. How could he have forgotten? "Mr. Menough? Wait one moment, please." He handed the reins to Menough and hurried back to the stagecoach. He dashed inside, searched around, and spotted what he was looking for. He pocketed the sandwich packet Milly had given him. But it wasn't the sandwich that was on his mind. It was her ribbon. He couldn't leave that token behind.

Chapter 5

Milly laid out two pine boughs on the mantel over the fireplace in the dining room. She breathed in the pine scent. Her mother immediately came to mind. She remembered how Mother used to decorate the tavern with the fragrant boughs for Christmas each year. Milly couldn't wait for the day she was old enough to help. She remembered the first time her mother had allowed her to arrange the pine boughs.

Milly stood on a short ladder, placing a thick branch on the mantel.

"Now Milly, make sure we can see the pine cones. They're an important part of the branch, too."

"Yes, Mother." Milly reached up and made sure the fattest pinecone balanced on the edge of the polished wood. "How's that?"

"Lovely, dear one. Be careful as you climb down the ladder."

Milly stepped down and stood beside her mother. She felt Mother's gentle arm wrap around her shoulder. Milly leaned against her, her cheek touching the soft fabric of her mother's red apron, the one she wore only on Christmas.

Milly's mind came back to the present. She touched a sharp point on one of the pinecones. Now Christmas decorating always had a tinge of sadness, even amid the happiness of celebration.

Her father came out of the kitchen, wiping his hands on a stained linen towel. He stood next to Milly. "Smells like Christmas in here."

Milly nodded, her throat thick with bittersweet memories. She placed a small candle in the middle of the mantel. It was a fancy white one her mother had bought when Milly was a little girl. Like the red apron, it was used only at Christmas.

Father took the candle, running his thumb over the dried wax drippings. "It's nearly gone."

Milly caught the catch in his voice. She cleared her throat. "Perhaps I shouldn't light it this year."

He shook his head. "Your mother wouldn't want that." He placed the candle back on the mantel and sighed. "I miss her most this time of year," he whispered. He turned to Milly, giving her a half smile. She could see a trace of warmth in his eyes. "Thank you."

"For what?"

"For this." He gestured to the decorations. "For being here."

She replied, "I'll always be here for you, Father."

"As much as I would like that, it wouldn't be fair to you. You deserve more than spending your life with your old father."

"Forty-five is hardly old." Sure his brown hair had started graying at the temples over the past couple of years, but he still moved with the same energy he'd always had.

He put his hand on her shoulder and patted it awkwardly. "That's nice of you to say. But as much as I hate to agree with Louise about anything, she's right about your future."

"My future is here."

"But not forever." He sighed. "We've talked about this before. I don't want you running the tavern by yourself. I'd sell it before I'd let that happen."

She crossed her arms. "I'm perfectly capable of taking care of this business. I've done it all my life."

"I'm not saying you're incapable. But you know as well as I do—owning a business is not a woman's place."

"Maybe I should buck the trend."

Her father chuckled. "If anyone could, it would be you." His mirth faded. "You have to think about yourself—"

"I am—"

"Let me finish. I want you to be happy. And I know you enjoy working here. But we're isolated at times." He glanced away. "I've been lonely since your mother's death."

She reached out to her father. Sadness filled his eyes. He often became melancholy during the holidays, but for some reason this seemed different. "I'm sorry."

He looked at her. "It's okay. And I've realized it's my lot in life, at least right now. But I don't want you to live with that emptiness. This building"—he gestured at the dining room—"it isn't a substitute for true companionship. People come and go, yet you rarely get to know them beyond polite conversation."

Milly thought about her talk with Elijah last night, and she had to admit her father was right. She and Elijah had moved past being polite and had revealed parts of their inner struggles to each other. And that brief conversation had meant more to her than all the small talk she'd engaged in with their guests over the years.

"I don't want you to be alone, Milly," her father continued. "So don't dismiss Louise's determination in finding you a beau. She knows everyone in town, plus who they're related to, what they do for a living, and most of all, who is suitable and who you should stay away from. For once her nosiness is useful."

He chuckled, but it came out strained. "Milly, you and I, we don't venture past these walls very much. Mostly just to church and back, and to the general store and post office when we need to. And I'm to blame for that, relying on you being here so much."

"I don't mind."

"I know, but that doesn't make it right or fair. Louise, in her own way, is trying to secure a stable future for you. Believe it or not, it's the one thing we both want."

"But. . ." She turned her back on her father, unsure if she could admit her fear out loud.

"What is it, Daughter?"

She spun around. "What if I don't find love?" She stopped at the point of admitting that the man she loved had just left her forever.

"As long as your heart is closed, you won't."

She thought about his words. Could she open her heart to someone else? Right now, with Elijah so fresh in her mind, she couldn't fathom it.

Her father fiddled with the candle on the mantel. "Enough talk of such things. Instead, we should be celebrating."

Milly swallowed the knot in her throat, grateful her father changed the subject. "Right. Celebrating."

His lips formed a tight, wooden smile. He was trying to move on like she was. Yet this time of the year was harder than most. "Will you help me make the Christmas cake? Your aunt will be expecting it."

Milly glanced outside. The snow was so thick she could barely see the grove of trees across the road. "Do you think she'll come in this weather?"

"Have you ever known Louise to miss a Christmas here? Even if she has to strap on snowshoes, she'll walk through that door."

She smiled. "True. I'll be there in a minute."

Her father disappeared into the kitchen. Milly adjusted the boughs and centered the candle again. She knelt down to put another log on the fire, but she couldn't keep her thoughts free of what her father said. Would he really sell the tavern? But what were the chances of her finding a husband who would be willing to run it? Or even more, let her be in charge? She had to figure out a way for them to keep the tavern.

She looked around the dining room, taking in the empty tables and chairs, the long wooden counter where she prepared drinks for weary travelers. She was happy here.

Yet her father was right. Up until Elijah's departure this morning, she hadn't felt lonely. But now, knowing she would never see him again, an ache appeared in her heart. One she couldn't easily dismiss, even by focusing on Christmas preparations.

She sat down in a chair, leaning her forehead against her hands and closing her eyes. *Dear Lord, give me the wisdom to know what to do about my future. Take from me my worry about my father and the tavern, and help me leave them in Your hands. Most of all, please help me forget about Elijah Montgomery.*

A knock sounded at the front door. Her eyes flew open. Through the heavy snow whirling outside, she could make out the shape of a man standing in front of the tavern window, waving at her. She hurried to the window. . .and despite her sincere prayer to forget about Elijah, she couldn't help but smile when she opened the door.

❧

Elijah held out his shivering hands in front of the fire. Milly put a quilt over his shoulders. He closed his eyes, letting his body soak in the warmth. Then he opened his eyes and looked at her. "Mr. Menough and I parted ways when we reached the tavern. I gave him the other horse. Has he come inside?"

"Not yet. Father is helping him in the barn. He took out some hot coffee to help him warm up while they took care of the horses."

He shrugged the quilt from his shoulders. "I should be out there with them—"

"Mr. Menough is dressed more warmly than you." She put the quilt back on his shoulders. "He will be fine, Mr. Montgomery."

Were they back to formalities again? Perhaps that was best. Even though he'd been given a small respite from his trip west, he still had to leave once the storm was over and Menough fixed the stagecoach.

She disappeared, only to reappear again with a steaming mug in her hand. "You're still shaking. This will help relieve the chill."

He sat down in the chair and took the coffee from her. "Thank you."

"Are you getting warmer?"

He nodded and took a sip of the coffee. "Yes. Much better."

"Good. You were practically frozen." She perched on the chair opposite him. "How long did you walk in the storm?"

He shrugged. "More than an hour. Maybe two. I didn't realize we'd gone so far before the axle broke. I don't think Mr. Menough realized it either." He gazed at her again. "I'm glad to be here."

She looked away then stood and busied herself with the fire, even though it didn't need tending. She took an iron poker and jabbed it into a log. "Do you need anything else?"

"Not right now." He leaned back in the chair. Warm and cozy now, he found it easy to let the brutal walk through the thickening snow and dipping temperatures slip from his memory. He had dressed warm enough to travel in a stagecoach but not to walk in a near blizzard.

Cornelius and Menough came into the dining room. "Horses are settled in," Menough said, his large nose red from the cold.

"When the snow let's up, I'll go with you to the livery," Cornelius said. "The owner, Jonathan Cooper, is a friend of mine. Between the three of us, we can get that axle fixed quickly."

"That's kind of you, sir," Menough said. He glanced at Elijah. "Mr.

Montgomery has been delayed long enough."

Elijah gripped the mug of coffee. If only Menough knew how fortuitous Elijah considered this delay. Not only would he have more time before he'd have to go on his quest, but he'd also have more time with Milly. Both prospects brought a smile to his lips.

Cornelius gestured to Menough. "Now have a seat in front of the fire. Milly, bring the man some coffee."

"Yes, Father."

She turned toward the kitchen, but the front door of the tavern opened. A frozen wind cloaked the dining area. Louise Crosby bustled in, pushing against the door to get it shut.

"Lands, it's not fit for man or beast out there." She brushed the dense snow off the shoulders of her woolen shawl.

Cornelius put his hands on his hips. "Louise, you should have waited until the snow storm stopped."

Louise tilted her lips in a smile. "Worried about me, Cornelius?"

"More worried about having to find you in this mess."

"Humph. I suppose it would be too much to ask for a cup of coffee or tea to warm me?"

Milly looked at her father and smiled. "No trouble at all, Aunt Louise."

The door opened again. This time O'Reardon stepped inside. "Aye, what a storm. We don't get these back in me fair Ireland." He stomped his snow-covered boots on the mat in front of the door. "Almost got lost crossing the street," he said, removing his cap and shaking off the snow. He looked at the widow. "Louise."

"O'Reardon."

Their greeting was colder than the air outside. Elijah suppressed a chuckle. O'Reardon should follow his own advice when it came to the heart. Anyone could see he had designs on Louise—everyone but Louise, apparently.

Cornelius turned to Milly. "Milly—"

"Three cups of coffee. Got it."

Elijah watched as she left the room. Ever since he'd known her, she'd always seemed eager to serve the tavern guests.

"Looks like everyone will be spending the night tonight," Cornelius said.

O'Reardon shook his head. "I just came for a bit to eat. Then I'll be on me way."

"No you won't." Milly's father crossed the room and clapped O'Reardon on the shoulder. "I won't have anyone going out in this storm tonight. No exceptions."

The Irishman nodded and sat down at a table, making sure he was as far from Louise as possible. But Elijah didn't miss the quick glance O'Reardon gave her.

He smiled and looked at the fire again. For the first time in a long time he was content. And he couldn't think of a better way to spend Christmas Eve tomorrow than with the people right here in Unionville Tavern.

Chapter 6

The next morning, Milly scraped at the frost on her bedroom window and peered outside. The snowfall that had thickened overnight showed no signs of slowing. Drifts as high as the middle of the huge oak tree on the back property of the tavern made Milly's eyes widen. She couldn't remember the last time it had snowed this hard and for this long.

She dressed and quickly went downstairs. Her father and Menough walked into the dining room. Elijah was kneeling by the fire, laying a few logs on top of the glowing embers. His back was to her, and he wore the same tailored suit coat he'd had on the past couple of days, with his dark, curly hair just past the back of his collar.

"Everyone is up rather early," she said.

"I'd hoped the weather had improved enough for us to fix the stagecoach." Menough plopped into the chair.

"No one's going anywhere in this." Her father's nose and cheeks were as red as holly berries. "I'm sure the coach is halfway buried by now."

Menough tapped his fingers on the arm of the chair. "At least the horses are happy in the barn," he said. "It's nice and toasty for them in there. Please accept my apologies, Mr. Montgomery. Again."

Milly glanced at Elijah. He looked over his shoulder at the driver, his expression serene. "Don't worry about it, Mr. Menough. My business in Cleveland can wait." He turned his gaze to Milly and winked. She gave him a quick grin. He returned it, causing her cheeks to heat.

"Milly?" Her father interrupted her thoughts. "Help in the kitchen, please."

But she couldn't pull away from Elijah's gaze. Not yet.

"We don't have all morning, Milly."

At Father's words, she yanked away her gaze and hurried to the kitchen. When she entered, her father was leaning against the counter. His thick brows formed a V over his puzzled eyes.

"What's wrong?" she asked.

He paused. "Do you. . ."

When he didn't finish his thought, she moved toward him. "Do I what?"

He shook his head. "Nothing. It's. . .nothing." He turned to the stove and began cracking eggs into the cast-iron skillet.

She shrugged and started helping with breakfast. But her thoughts never strayed far from Elijah. Even as she worked in the kitchen, first cooking then cleaning after breakfast was done, she thought about him in the dining room, sitting with Mr. O'Reardon and talking. She hadn't seen him this relaxed before, and she was glad for it.

Later that morning, Milly finished decorating for Christmas Eve. Their guests had retired for a few hours to their respective rooms, except for Aunt Louise, who had disappeared in the kitchen.

Milly hummed as she tied scarlet-colored bows on the backs of the chairs. Polished the counter until it gleamed. Pulled out the pine garland she'd made two days earlier by tying the boughs together end to end. It had dried a bit but was still fresh. She had just gotten out the short ladder, the same one she used as a child, to put the garland around the door frame when Elijah entered the room.

He glanced around, his eyes shining with approval. "Looks nice." He slipped his hands into his pockets. "You always work so hard, Milly."

"I don't mind." She smiled and started to climb the ladder. Outside the snow continued to come down. It seemed like it would never stop.

"Can I help?" Elijah asked.

"You can hand me the garland on the counter." She paused in the middle of the ladder.

"I have a better idea." He held his hand out to her. "How about I put the garland up for you?"

"I do this every year. So it's no bother—"

"I know, Milly. Nothing is a bother for you." He smiled. "But allow me the privilege of doing something for you for a change."

Milly hesitated, touched by the gesture. She looked at his hand then slipped hers into it. His long fingers folded over hers as he helped her down the ladder. When he let go, she could still feel the tingle of his touch on her skin.

When he ascended the top step, Milly reached for the garland. Her aunt's loud voice carried through the swinging kitchen door.

"Cornelius, I will not abide you destroying my sister's stuffing recipe."

Milly glanced over her shoulder as her father and aunt came out of the kitchen.

"I'm not destroying anything." Her father's bushy eyebrows straightened into a line across his sunken blue eyes. "You tasted it. It's perfect."

"Perfectly dreadful." Louise wiped her mouth with a dainty handkerchief. "You used too much sage."

"I used the exact amount my wife always used."

Milly shook her head and grabbed the garland. She couldn't believe they were arguing over the stuffing. Again. Every year they had the same disagreement. Over sage, of all things. The stuffing always tasted delicious. For some reason, her father and aunt couldn't go a day without bickering.

"Milly?"

She turned to look at Elijah. "I'm sorry. Here." She started to hand him the garland when a large cracking sound made her jump.

Suddenly, the ladder gave way under his feet.

"Elijah!" she shouted.

He flailed in the air for a moment before hitting the ground. She knelt beside him. "Are you all right?"

He moaned and slowly sat up. "Yes, I think so."

She breathed out a sigh of relief. "Good thing it's a short ladder. You could have been injured."

He rubbed his arm. "I think my shoulder disagrees with you."

Her father came up behind them. "Mr. Montgomery, are you—"

"All right?" Elijah smiled ruefully. "Only thing truly wounded is my pride."

Aunt Louise looked at the broken ladder and wrinkled her nose. "If you ask me, Cornelius, you should have gotten rid of that ladder a long time ago. It's only useful for kindling now."

Milly looked at the ladder then at her father. Even broken, she didn't want to part with it. But she couldn't admit it out loud, not without sounding silly and overly sentimental over a few old pieces of wood that had nearly caused Elijah serious harm. Her father nodded slightly, picked up the ladder, and looked at Aunt Louise.

"No one asked you, Louise." He took the broken ladder and disappeared into the kitchen.

Louise crossed her chubby arms across her chest. "Well, I never!"

"For the love o' peace and quiet," O'Reardon said, descending the staircase. "Don't tell me ye and Cornelius are at it again."

"Yes," Milly and Elijah said at the same time. They both laughed, and she noticed he moved closer to her.

"I don't see anything funny, young lady." Aunt Louise gave Milly a stern look.

"Relax, Mrs. Crosby. We're all just havin' a bit o' fun."

"You were not invited to take part in this conversation, Mr. O'Reardon."

"Louise," her father said, coming out of the kitchen. "You do realize you're free to leave anytime if you find the company here at the tavern not to your liking."

"You're the one who didn't want anyone going out in this horrid weather." Aunt Louise sniffed. "It's as if you want me to get lost in the blizzard."

Her father sighed. "If only."

O'Reardon shook his head. "The two of you are acting like children, ye are."

Aunt Louise turned, narrowing her gaze. "Excuse me?"

O'Reardon straightened to his full, yet still diminutive, height. "You and Cornelius. Always fightin'. Yer family, not boxing mates."

Breathing in a gasp, Aunt Louise said, "You have a lot of nerve, nosing into our business."

"Yer always loud enough to make it everyone's business."

Milly curled her bottom lip inward. Elijah stood stock still, as did her father, while O'Reardon and Aunt Louise eyed each other like the adversaries they seemed to be.

"If you think for one minute I'm about to take advice from a man who has nothing better to do than hang out at a tavern—"

"The same tavern ye be hangin' out in, I must remind ye."

"Then you are sorely mistaken." She leaned forward. "Your words are of little consequence, Mr. O'Reardon. Wait, my mistake. They are of *no* consequence."

"Aunt Louise," Milly whispered, shocked that her aunt could be so mean, especially to a man who was trying to bring peace between her and Father. Her father placed his hand on Milly's arm, silencing her.

O'Reardon didn't back down. "Mrs. Crosby, did ye ever stop to think I come here for the same reason ye do?"

"I can't imagine our reasons are the same. I come to spend time with my niece. The fact that her father is intolerable most of the time is a burden I must bear."

"Oh brother," Elijah whispered. He leaned over to speak in Milly's ear. "I mean no offense, but is your aunt always this. . ."

"Insufferable?" Milly shook her head as she whispered, "But today she seems especially cranky."

O'Reardon moved closer to Aunt Louise. "Ye can make up all the excuses ye want, but I know the truth. Ye come here because yer lonely." He rubbed his finger back and forth underneath the reddish-gray stubble on his upper lip. "Same as me."

"Mr. O'Reardon! I demand you take that back."

"I will not, because it's the truth. Ye know it plain as I do." He adjusted his cap, turned, and without another word walked upstairs.

The room remained completely silent. Milly looked at her aunt. The defiance so evident in her eyes a moment ago had disappeared.

"I–I'm not lonely," she said. She lifted her chin, which quivered slightly. "I'm perfectly. . .happy." She burst into tears and fled upstairs.

Cornelius leaned against the stair banister. Weariness edged his expression. "Well. That was unexpected." He looked at Elijah. "My apologies, Mr. Montgomery. I'm sorry you had to see that."

"It's all right." He glanced at Milly, his eyes filled with concern. Then he looked back at her father. "That was tame compared to some of our family spats."

Her father shook his head. "I guess I didn't realize she felt that way. And that O'Reardon did, too. And here I thought Louise was the cross I was forced to bear. Seems we all have more in common than we thought." He sighed and left the room.

Milly felt Elijah's gaze on her. She looked up at him.

"It seems we do," he said, lightly touching his fingers to hers. Then he snatched his hand away, as if the gesture had been out of his control. He moved past her. "We should finish hanging the garland," he said.

She thought his voice sounded thicker than usual. Did he experience the same thrill she did at his touch? She didn't dare hope so. "Yes," she said, glad she sounded somewhat normal. "We should."

❧

Early that afternoon, Milly started setting the table for Christmas Eve supper. Her father had been busy preparing the meal in the kitchen, while Aunt Louise and Mr. O'Reardon had stayed in their rooms upstairs. She wondered if they would come down for supper. She hoped so, as she added two more plates to the table.

Footsteps sounded on the stairs. She looked up, smiling when she saw Elijah. He looked especially handsome, dressed in a black suit and white cravat. His attire was fancier than she'd seen him wear before, and far more elegant than the men in her village wore. However, as he neared, she could see the suit was fraying at the shoulders, and the cravat was limp. He had used this suit often, probably when he had given his sermons. But she didn't care about the condition of his suit. Not when she knew the condition of his heart.

"Can I help with anything?" he asked as he approached the table.

"No, I'm just about finished."

He looked at the counter where a stack of red napkins waited to be folded. He walked over and started the task.

"You don't have to do that."

"I don't mind." He finished folding a napkin in a small square. Simple, and a little lopsided.

She hid a grin.

He looked at the napkin. "It's a little crooked."

"It's fine." She smiled. "No one will notice anyway."

Elijah picked up another napkin. "Oh, my mother would. So would Father." He half smiled. "If he knew I was doing something as domestic as folding napkins, he'd have more than a few words for me." His smile disappeared. "He always has more than a few words."

Milly heard the disappointment in his voice, the same tone he'd had when they had talked about the reason for his trip west the other night. "Does your father ever have anything nice to say?"

Elijah froze in the middle of folding the napkin. "I. . .I suppose he does." He looked down and resumed folding. "But it seems I only remember the negative things." He faced Milly. "That's the power of words. They can build. . .or destroy. And it's why I worry that I won't say the right ones when I start preaching."

She opened her mouth to respond, but the door to the tavern flew open. She spun around. A young couple, covered with so much snow they were both nearly white, staggered into the tavern.

Milly rushed to the door in time to see the man's lips were blue. He embraced his wife, whose arms were folded over her chest, as if she was cradling something under her coat.

"Are you all right?" Elijah joined her.

"C–c–cold," the man said. "My w–w–wife. . ."

Milly brushed snow from the woman's shoulders as she led her toward the fire. Then she heard a quiet mewling. A baby's cry.

Chapter 7

M y baby." The woman looked at Milly. "P–p–please. . .take her."

"Let's get in front of the fire, first." Panic filled her. The couple was nearly frozen. It was a miracle they could move. She hadn't heard anything else from the baby the woman held underneath her coat. Dread filled her. What was she supposed to do?

She looked at Elijah. "Get Aunt Louise." She raised her voice. "Hurry."

Elijah ran up the stairs. Milly turned to the woman. "Where is the child?"

She opened her woolen shawl with shaking hands, cradling a swaddled bundle.

"Will she be o–o–kay?" The man approached the fire, melting snow dripping from his face.

Milly couldn't answer. She looked at the seemingly lifeless bundle, afraid for the worst. Aunt Louise and Elijah came down the stairs.

"What happened?" Aunt Louise asked as she bustled toward them. Her gaze landed on the baby. "Milly, take these two to your room. Elijah, you go with them. Start a fire in the hearth."

"What can I do?"

Milly's father had appeared in the room. Louise nodded at him. "Gather blankets and warm them by the fire. Then bring them back to the bedroom." She looked at the young father. "Are you all right?"

He nodded. "Cold. Worried." He trembled as he spoke, his eyes wild and fretful.

"Get yourself warmed up, too." She turned to the stairs. "Mr. O'Reardon?"

The man was already half down the stairs. "Aye?"

"Coffee for everyone."

He nodded and went to the kitchen.

Milly led the woman and babe back to her bedroom, Elijah and her aunt trailing them. She said a prayer for the baby. . .for all of them.

After he'd built the fire in Milly's room, Elijah left Milly and her aunt to take care of the baby and mother. When he walked into the main room of the tavern, he saw the man pacing in front of the fire. He stopped when Elijah came near.

"Are they all right?" His face was nearly as white as the snow outside.

"They're warming up." Feeling the words were inadequate, he added, "They're in good hands. Milly and Louise will take care of them."

The man whipped off his hat, revealing a thick shock of sandy brown hair. "I was so foolish. We should have never left the house."

"How long were you out there? Elijah asked.

The man faced the fire. "I don't know. Time slipped away when we got lost. We just moved here a few weeks ago from Pittsburgh. Ethel has a large family, and she's been homesick. When we got an invitation for Christmas Eve supper from the neighbors, she was desperate to go. I wasn't sure." He sighed. "Ethel had Anne a month ago. She said it would be okay. We weren't going far." He turned to Elijah. "But once we stepped outside, we couldn't see anything. . .not even the house."

Elijah put his hand on the man's back. "What's your name?"

"William Tomlinson. But everyone calls me Billy," he added.

Cornelius came downstairs with a pile of quilts in his arms. He laid them as close to the fire as he dared. O'Reardon appeared from the kitchen, trying to steady coffee cups on a tray.

"Let me help you with that," Cornelius said. He took two mugs and handed them to Billy and Elijah. Billy took his but didn't drink.

Louise hurried into the room. She looked at Cornelius, her face a picture of calm. "Are those blankets ready?" Her voice didn't hold nearly the sharpness it usually did when she spoke to him.

Elijah was impressed with her poise.

Her father crouched and put his hand on one of them. "This one is a little warm."

"I'll take it."

Cornelius handed her the blanket. Billy moved toward her. "My wife and baby. . .are they okay?"

Louise nodded, but Elijah saw the worry in her eyes. Apparently Billy did too, because he turned away, his shoulders drooping.

"Just keep the warm blankets and hot coffee coming," Louise said. She glanced at O'Reardon then disappeared back to Milly's room.

"I used the last of the hot coffee," O'Reardon told Cornelius.

"We'll go make more. Won't take but a few minutes."

O'Reardon followed Cornelius to the kitchen, leaving Elijah alone with Billy. He stood next to him. "Why don't you sit down? Drink some of that coffee?"

Billy shook his head. "I don't know what I'll do if something happens to them." He turned to Elijah. "They're my life. . . . I won't be able to go on without them—"

Elijah put his hand on Billy's shoulder. He looked him square in the eyes. "Then we will pray you won't have to."

Billy hung his head. "I'm not much of a praying man."

"That's all right." Elijah suddenly felt a confidence he'd never experienced before. "If you'll allow me, I'd like to pray for you and your family."

Billy nodded. "I'd like that."

Elijah closed his eyes, keeping his hand on Billy's shoulder. He prayed aloud, his voice growing stronger as he asked the Lord to keep Ethel and Anne safe, to give Billy peace, to bring them all together to celebrate the miracle of Jesus' birth. When he finished praying, he squeezed Billy's shoulder and said, "Amen."

Billy turned to Elijah, tears in his eyes. "Thank you, Preacher."

Stunned, Elijah dropped his hand from Billy's shoulder. "I'm not a preacher."

"The way you prayed, you could have fooled me."

Chapter 8

Hᴏw are you doing, Ethel?" Milly asked. She stood away from the bed but close enough to follow her aunt's instructions.

From beneath a pile of quilts, Ethel smiled. Baby Anne's little face, now pink with health and warmth, peeked out from beneath her blankets. "Much better, thank you. I never thought I'd get warm." She glanced down at her daughter. "And if I was so cold, I could only imagine Anne being chilled through."

"You kept her warm enough under your shawl," Aunt Louise said. "Are you ready to drink a bit of the coffee?" Anne started to fuss. Aunt Louise chuckled. "Seems the babe might be hungry."

"I'll feed her first."

Milly stood back, noticing the care with which Aunt Louise spoke to Ethel. She hadn't seen this side of her aunt since her mother had died. She thought about what Mr. O'Reardon had said about her aunt being lonely. Milly had never considered it. Her uncle had died years ago, before Milly was born, and they had never had any children. But Aunt Louise had several friends, mostly those she went to church with. She thought her aunt came to the tavern so she didn't have to cook and because she liked needling Milly's father.

But as she watched her aunt look at baby Anne so tenderly, with a wistfulness in her eyes, she knew Mr. O'Reardon was right. Her aunt was lonely. Milly should have seen it before now.

"We'll give you your privacy," Aunt Louise said. "But don't hesitate to let us know if you need anything."

Ethel nodded. As Milly put her hand on the doorknob, Ethel said, "Wait."

"Yes?" Milly asked.

"Could you send Billy back here? I know he's so worried and blames himself for this. He shouldn't. I'm the one who wanted to leave the house and visit the neighbors. He tried to talk me out of it." Her smile was bittersweet. "He's a kind man. I can't let him think this is his fault."

Aunt Louise walked over to Ethel and patted her hand. "Neither one of you need to blame yourselves. The three of you are all right—that's what matters."

As Milly and Louise left the room, Milly stopped her aunt in the hallway. "You were wonderful with them, Aunt Louise."

Her aunt huffed. "It was a simple thing to get them warmed up."

"But you kept them calm. You kept all of us calm." Milly leaned over and kissed her aunt's cheek.

Aunt Louise touched her face. "What was that for?"

"To let you know I love you." A lump caught in Milly's throat. "I don't tell you that often enough." Milly headed for the main room, but her aunt didn't follow.

"I'll be there in a moment." Aunt Louise's voice sounded thick. Milly nodded and left her aunt alone, respecting her privacy.

When she entered the main room, Elijah and Billy were sitting in the chairs near the fire. Both men popped up from their seats when they saw her.

"How is Ethel?" Billy asked, walking toward her. "Anne?"

Milly smiled. "They're both fine. Ethel is asking for you."

Billy nodded and started to leave. He paused and looked at Elijah over his shoulder. "Thank you," he said, giving Elijah a nod. Then he disappeared.

Milly joined Elijah by the fire. "What was that about?"

Elijah shrugged and stared at the fire. "I don't know. I just prayed with him."

"Obviously that meant a lot to him."

"I suppose so."

Milly frowned. Elijah seemed distant, lost in thought. "Is something wrong?"

He paused then shook his head. He looked at Milly and smiled. "Everything's fine."

But his smile didn't quite reach his eyes. She was about to press him further when Mr. Menough came downstairs. She and Elijah watched as he yawned and stretched his arms when he reached the bottom.

"Haven't slept that well in ages," he said, moving to stand by the fire. "I don't think a stampede of horses could have woken me up."

Elijah chuckled. "Apparently."

Menough lifted a questioning eyebrow. "Did I miss something?"

❧

The rest of the afternoon and early evening, Milly helped her father prepare the Christmas Eve meal. Aunt Louise sauntered in at one point, only to get a glare from Milly's father. "If you're going to badger me about the sage again, you're too late. I've already prepared the stuffing."

Aunt Louise straightened her shoulders. "I wasn't going to say anything about the sage."

Her father's harsh expression softened. "Louise—"

"But I will take that as my cue to leave. You seem eager to have me gone as soon as possible anyway."

"Louise, I didn't mean—"

But her aunt had already left. Father wiped the beads of perspiration off his forehead with the back of his hand. "I will never understand that woman."

Milly thought her father probably understood her aunt more than he realized.

A few moments later, O'Reardon came in. "Can I help with anythin'? I'm feelin' a little at loose ends while ye two are workin' so hard."

"I'm sure Milly wouldn't mind if you washed the dishes." Her father grinned.

"Not at all," Milly said, handing O'Reardon the dishcloth. "If you don't mind, that is."

"Washed plenty o'dishes in me time, lass. Have no choice, seein' as I'm a lifelong bachelor." He smiled, but Milly knew better. They all did since hearing O'Reardon's confession. She marveled that she had known her aunt her entire life and Mr. O'Reardon for several years but never really understood their personal struggles, which mirrored not only her father's but also a bit of her own.

As she walked away from the sink, she thought about Elijah. His calling was filled with loneliness, too. Heading to almost uncharted territory alone. Again she both admired and feared for him. But she knew that fear didn't come from the Lord. Still, it reminded her to pray not only for his safety but also for his emotional state.

By the time they finished preparing supper, darkness had descended outside. Mr. Menough had gone out earlier to check on the horses again. "Snow's drifted past two feet," he said. "Worst blizzard I've seen in years. And living in Buffalo, I've seen plenty of blizzards."

Milly surveyed the tables. Earlier she had pushed three of them together to make one long table and covered it with one of her grandmother's white tablecloths. In the center, several candles flickered, illuminating the room with a soft glow as the fire crackled in the hearth. Other than waiting for the guests to arrive, there was nothing else for her to do. She untied her apron and folded it, placing it behind the dining counter.

Billy, Ethel, and baby Anne entered the dining room. They had been together in the back the entire afternoon. Ethel cradled their daughter and stopped at the edge of the room. "Perhaps we should go back in the bedroom," she murmured to her husband. "We don't want to intrude."

"Absolutely not." Milly led the family to the center of the long group of tables. "The more the merrier."

"Are you sure?"

"We're sure." Cornelius entered the room carrying a platter of sliced turkey, O'Reardon following him. "The good Lord knew what He was doing when He provided us an abundance of food this Christmas."

Soon Elijah and Mr. Menough came down the staircase. At last Aunt Louise appeared, not looking at either Milly's father or Mr. O'Reardon. Instead, she took her traditional place at the opposite end of the table from Milly's father.

Then Milly noticed that while everyone sat in a chair, Elijah held back. He'd been quiet that afternoon, sitting by the fire. She moved to stand next to him.

"Aren't you going to sit down?"

"I thought I'd wait until everyone found a seat."

"It looks like they have." Milly saw there were two empty chairs left, right next to each other.

"Then, after you." Elijah held his hand out and gestured for her to walk in front of him. When they reached the table, he pulled the chair out for her. She sat down, and he joined her, his elbow touching hers as they sat.

This was turning out to be one of the best Christmas Eves she'd ever had.

"Just a moment," her father said, standing up. "Before we pray, I want to say a word of thanks to our guests tonight." He smiled, his broad grin warming Milly's heart. Her father wasn't normally sentimental. She knew what it took for him to stand up and say those words.

"Usually for Christmas Eve it's just me and Milly. . .and Louise." He glanced at Aunt Louise, her face pinched as if she were ready for a verbal blow. "And as much as I love my family, it's nice to have a few extra friends to join our celebration." He held up a glass filled with eggnog. "Thank you, Mr. Montgomery, Mr. Menough, and the Tomlinson family for joining us. O'Reardon, you know you're always welcome, and from now on you have an open invitation to join us anytime."

"Thank ye," O'Reardon said. He stared at his plate.

"And Louise."

Aunt Louise folded her arms. "Yes, Cornelius?"

"I promise"—he took a deep breath—"I promise to make a better effort not to argue with you this coming year. At least not as much."

"Amen," O'Reardon said.

Everyone laughed, and even Aunt Louise mustered a chuckle. Elijah looked at Milly and grinned.

Her father sipped his eggnog and sat down. "Mr. Montgomery, would you do us the honor of praying over our meal?"

Milly sensed Elijah tensing. He looked up at her father. "Mr. Kent, are you sure?"

"Yes, son." His gaze was serious. "I'm sure." He held out his hands, and everyone joined together.

Milly slipped her hand into Elijah's. His fingers were cold, and she felt the dampness of his palms. She gently squeezed his hand and smiled before bowing her head.

Elijah started to pray, his voice shaky at first. But as he gave thanks for the Lord's provision and blessings, the timbre grew in strength and confidence. By the time he finished the prayer, Milly could feel God's presence with them at the table. She also realized that any doubts Elijah had about his calling or his effectiveness with words weren't from the Lord.

"Nice prayer, Preacher." Billy grinned at Elijah.

"I told you I'm not—"

"A preacher. I know." He put his arm around Ethel's shoulder. Anne was sound asleep in her mother's arms. "But you've just about got me convinced to try out that church down the road in Unionville."

"That's God's prodding, not mine," Elijah said.

"God works through his people," O'Reardon said, taking a long swig of his eggnog. "'Tis what me sainted mother used to say."

Aunt Louise reached for the platter of turkey. "I didn't realize you were a man of faith, Mr. O'Reardon."

He looked directly at her. "You never asked, Mrs. Crosby."

Milly looked around the table as everyone started talking and laughing as they filled their plates. Tears suddenly came to her eyes. Not just because of what her father had said or because her aunt and Mr. O'Reardon kept looking at each other when they didn't think the other one was paying attention. Instead, she thought about Elijah. The real love he had for God. How his heart was revealed in a simple act of prayer. How his words had an effect on Billy Tomlinson, a man he barely knew.

"Excuse me," she said, scooting back from the table before the tears spilled over her cheeks.

"Milly?" Her father held his fork in midair.

"We need more butter. I'll be right back." She flew out of the room, wiping her cheeks as she left.

Chapter 9

Concerned, Elijah looked at Cornelius. Everyone else seemed to accept Milly's excuse to leave, but Elijah knew differently, and not because there were three full butter dishes already on the table.

Cornelius nodded, and Elijah excused himself. He went into the kitchen. "Milly?"

She stood by the sink, her back was to him, but he could see her wiping her cheeks. She turned and faced him, her lips forming a watery smile. "What are you doing here?"

"I came to check on you."

"I don't know why. Nothing's wrong." Her voice sounded higher pitched than normal. She glanced wildly around the kitchen. "Now where did I put that butter?"

"Milly." He softened his tone as he approached her. "We don't need any more butter."

"Oh. My mistake then." Her smiled widened, as if it would threaten to permanently wrinkle her smooth skin. "No reason we should be standing in the kitchen then." She started to move past him.

He put his hand on her arm. "Please. Tell me what's wrong. You were crying."

She looked up at him, her eyes glazing again. "I always miss my mother the most this time of year."

He took a deep breath. "Of course. I wasn't thinking. . . . I should have allowed you a moment of privacy."

Her gaze didn't flinch from his. "That's all right, Elijah. It. . .it means a lot to me that you care."

He did care, more at this moment than he ever had before. How could he leave her? How could he be apart from her forever? He leaned forward, taking in the beauty of her blue eyes, drowning in the depths of them. Without thinking, he touched her cheek, where a stream of tears had started to fall. He wiped them away with his fingertip.

"I'm sorry," he murmured.

She didn't move from his touch. "For what?"

Leaving you. "That Christmas is so difficult for you. I wish things were different."

Milly took his hand in hers. "I wish they were, too." She squeezed his fingers before letting go. "We should get back before we're missed."

He nodded, but he didn't want to go back. He wanted to capture this moment in his memory forever. Because soon, memories would be all he had.

&

After everyone had finished eating, Milly started removing the empty dishes. Clearing the table was easier than clearing her head, which replayed Elijah's tender words and expression over and over. He had offered her comfort in her grief, but she suspected there were more to his words. She wanted to believe it to be true.

She took the last of the silverware to the kitchen and put it in the sink.

"I see why my matchmaking has utterly failed with you, Millicent."

Milly whirled around to face her aunt Louise. "I don't know what you're talking about."

"I believe you do." Her aunt's normally stern expression softened. "Elijah is a good man, Milly. I can see why you're taken with him."

"That's nice of you to say, but you're mistaken." She poured water from the large pail on the floor into the sink basin.

"That you have feelings for him? I don't believe I'm mistaken at all."

Milly paused. To deny her aunt's words would be a lie. "It doesn't matter how I feel, Aunt Louise. Elijah and I can never be."

"Well, why on earth not? Surely he realizes what a prize you are."

She put the pail back on the floor and looked at her aunt again. "I'm not so sure. And even if he did, it wouldn't matter. He's leaving tomorrow." She explained to her about Elijah's calling west, in as little detail as possible. "He has no choice but to do God's will."

"Humph." Her aunt uncrossed her arms. Then she sighed. "You're right. No wonder that young man has been so quiet today. Pensive even. I don't believe for a minute he wants to leave you any more than you want him to go."

"His hesitation has little to do with me," Milly said.

"You're far too modest, young lady. You are a big part of why he's in no hurry to leave."

If only that were true. But she had to be realistic. He had only shown her kindness. And friendship. "I would never stand in his way, Aunt Louise." Her voice caught.

Her aunt drew her into her soft embrace. "Of course you wouldn't. Yet it doesn't make things any easier, does it?"

Milly leaned her cheek against her aunt's shoulder. "No. It doesn't." She pulled away and wiped her eyes. "I'd better finish cleaning up. I'm sure Father is getting out his Bible as we speak."

"I'll help," Aunt Louise said. She reached for one of Milly's aprons hanging on a peg on the back of the door. She tied it around her wide waist, the strings barely knotting together. Then she turned and started washing the dishes in the sink.

Despite Milly's sorrow over Elijah's approaching departure, she couldn't help but smile as her aunt started washing dishes with enthusiasm. She'd never offered to help in the kitchen before. This truly was a time for miracles.

After she and Aunt Louise made quick work of the kitchen, they went into the dining room. A fire blazed in the hearth. The Tomlinsons sat next to each other in the high-backed chairs, Ethel cradling a sleeping Anne. O'Reardon was seated a little farther away in one of the wooden chairs. Father and Mr. Menough were seated on the other side of the hearth, a little closer to the fire. As Milly had thought, her father had his Bible in his lap.

But where was Elijah?

"Where are we supposed to sit?" Aunt Louise peered down her nose. "Milly and I worked tirelessly in the kitchen—"

"An' I saved a seat for ya." O'Reardon patted the empty chair next to him. "If yer done talkin' and are ready to sit down."

Aunt Louise froze. She looked at the seat. Milly gave her a nudge, and she cleared her throat. "Thank you, Mr. O'Reardon. That was very. . .thoughtful."

"That's me. Thoughtful."

Milly thought she detected a small smile as Aunt Louise sat next to O'Reardon. Although she did move the chair a few inches away from him.

"Milly, come sit down by the fire," her father said. "It's time to read the Christmas story."

"We should wait for Mr. Montgomery."

Once again her father gave her a strange look, similar to the one he'd given in the kitchen earlier that day. "We'll wait for him. He just ran upstairs for a moment."

"Oh." Milly felt as if they were all looking at her as she took her place on the floor at her father's feet. He had already put one of her mother's old quilts in front of the fireplace for her to sit on. Every year he read from the book of Luke. But this evening was the first time in years when they'd had more than Aunt Louise for company. Milly had just settled in when Elijah came downstairs.

"Sorry to keep you all waiting." He stood near the fire, and Milly noticed he had something tucked underneath his arm.

"Mr. Montgomery, there's a place right here for you." Father pointed to the empty place beside Milly.

She held in her breath as Elijah looked at the quilt. What was her father doing, asking a guest to sit on the floor? But Elijah didn't hesitate and sat next to Milly.

"There." Father sat back and opened his Bible. He started reading from the second chapter of Luke.

Milly gazed at the fire while her father read, soaking in every word. She'd heard this story every year ever since she could remember, yet it never failed to amaze her. She thought about how blessed she was, surrounded by family and friends, listening to her Savior's inauspicious beginnings. She glanced up and saw Billy staring at his daughter, his eyes filled with love.

When her father finished, he closed his Bible.

"Never get tired o' that story." O'Reardon leaned back in his chair. " 'Tis a beautiful tale."

"Yes it is," Mr. Menough agreed.

Milly looked at Elijah. He hadn't moved since he sat down. Suddenly, he turned to her father. "If you don't mind, Mr. Kent, I'd like to share something."

"Of course."

Elijah rose and turned his back to the fire. He opened the weathered black book he'd held in hands during the Bible reading. "We've always had a tradition in our family, too. One that goes back to before I was born, when my family first came to America from England." He pulled out a delicate, worn letter. "My parents gave this to me right before I left Buffalo." He glanced down at Milly and smiled. "They thought it would provide encouragement during my. . .travels." He gazed at everyone else. "I think it's appropriate for tonight."

Chapter 10

Then by all means, Mr. Montgomery," Cornelius said. "Share with the rest of us."

He looked at Billy Tomlinson, who nodded. At O'Reardon, who gave him a nod before sneaking a look at Louise, who was sharing a glance with Milly. Elijah held the letter in his hand. Usually his father read these words on Christmas Eve, in a strong, clear voice honed by years in the pulpit guiding his flock. Elijah hoped he could do them justice.

"This is a letter from my great-great-grandfather." Elijah cleared his throat. "He was too weak from consumption to make the voyage across the ocean with the rest of his family. He gave this letter to his oldest son, Elijah, my great-grandfather and namesake.

> *My dearest family,*
>
> *It is with utmost regret that I must say good-bye to you, that I will not be able to join you in freely worshipping our Savior. Know that I will miss all of you terribly but that you are following the highest calling possible— God's will.*
>
> *Never forget the purpose of your journey—not to escape persecution for our faith here in England, but to be steadfast in your devotion to the Lord. Remember that Jesus, our King, was born in a foreign land, rejected even before His birth. Remember the sacrifice His earthly parents made, traveling across the desert, the threat of death looming over them, forced to spend the night in the humblest of places—a manger.*
>
> *In the New World, you will endure hardship. You will have moments of doubt. Of worry. Of fear. Do not allow these to take root in your soul. Rather, look to the Lord, our most sovereign God, for strength and guidance. Keep your eyes and heart on Him, and you will not fail.*
>
> *Do not mourn for me, my loved ones. Know that I am in the safety*

of God's steady hand, and that I will pray for you hourly for the rest of my days.

Your loving husband and father,
Elijah E. Montgomery

Elijah folded the letter. For years he'd heard these words but had never truly listened to them. As a youth, he had pretended to listen, more interested in thinking about the presents he would receive the next morning. When he was called to go west, each year he felt the sting of those words and indictment of his own cowardice.

But tonight. . .tonight the words pierced his heart. He put the paper back in his grandfather's Bible and sat down. He avoided looking at everyone, keeping his gaze on the fire. But he could feel Milly looking at him.

Finally, Cornelius spoke. "Thank you for reading that," he said. His voice sounded a little heavy.

"Yes," Louise chimed in. "What a wonderful man your great-great-grandfather must have been."

"He was," Elijah said, not looking at her. "I never appreciated it until now."

Cornelius yawned. "Well, I don't know about you all, but it's been a long day. Billy, you and Ethel and the baby are welcome to stay in Milly's room. And I'll brook no argument about that."

"Thank you, sir," Billy said.

The flames crackled and burned as they all took their leave and went to their respective rooms for the night. Everyone but Milly.

She remained by Elijah's side, not saying anything. The silence between them, instead of being awkward, felt comfortable. He wished it could last forever.

"He was a brave man," Milly finally said.

"Yes he was. He not only was facing his own death, but he had to tell his family good-bye." He clasped his hands over his bent knees. "This was the first time I really understood what he was saying." He looked at Milly. "I'm not afraid anymore." It was the truth. He finally had let go of the fear. It happened sometime when he was reading the letter. He could feel the paralyzing doubt melt away.

"I'm happy for you, Elijah." She smiled.

"Thank you."

Her smile quickly faded. "I should be getting to bed. The snow started to lighten up earlier."

"I overheard Menough and O'Reardon talking about it. O'Reardon said he would help with the repairs. Did you know he used to make stages back in Ireland?"

"Apparently there are a lot of things we don't know about Mr. O'Reardon." She stood. Smoothed the skirt of her dress. "I'm glad you're at peace, Elijah. Good night."

"Good night." He watched her go upstairs to one of the guest rooms. But he didn't follow. Not yet.

He was at peace about his calling. But he wasn't at peace with leaving Milly. He wondered if he ever would be.

❧

The next morning when Milly woke up, there wasn't a flake in the sky. It was Christmas Day, but a heaviness still settled over her. She was truthful when she told Elijah she was glad he was at peace with his mission. But she didn't want to say good-bye. And there wouldn't be another storm or broken axle to bring him back to her.

She got up and quickly dressed then went downstairs. She checked the kitchen, then the barn, but didn't see anyone. She heard the sound of a baby's cry coming from her bedroom. The baby quickly quieted.

Milly went into the kitchen and started breakfast, trying to ignore the pain in her heart. Having Elijah here for the extra time had only reinforced how much she cared about him. But she had to let him go. And it was even harder this time than it had been the last.

She had finished cooking breakfast and was keeping it warm on the stove while she waited for the men to return. The Tomlinsons came out of the room, dressed and ready to go.

"Thank you, Milly," Billy said as Ethel stood beside him. "We appreciate the hospitality. We'll recommend this place to our friends for sure."

"Don't be strangers." Milly smiled. "Perhaps we'll see you at church this Sunday."

Ethel looked at her husband. After a pause, he nodded. "Perhaps."

"You sure you don't want breakfast before you go?"

Ethel shook her head. "We're eager to get back home." The family headed for the door.

"Merry Christmas," she called out to them.

"Merry Christmas," Billy and Ethel said and waved at her before disappearing out the door.

Milly walked over to the window. The sun shone brightly, making the thick drifts of snow sparkle in the sunlight. It was hard to believe only yesterday the sky had been cloaked in gray, the air filled with a curtain of snow.

She heard the familiar creak of her aunt bustling down the stairs. She turned. Aunt Louise was already dressed, her woolen shawl draped around her shoulders.

"You're not staying for breakfast either?" Milly asked.

"I don't want to wear out my welcome." Aunt Louise gave her a sheepish smile. "I suppose if Cornelius is willing to make an effort, so can I." She kissed Milly's cheek. "Merry Christmas, darling. I'll see you at church on Sunday. And I promise, you do not have to keep your appointment with Frederick."

Milly frowned. "Who?"

"Exactly." Aunt Louise chuckled. "I'll be back later this evening for supper."

"I'll make sure to tell Mr. O'Reardon." Milly winked.

Aunt Louise huffed but didn't say anything.

An hour after her aunt left, the men returned, cherry-cheeked and red-nosed. Milly brought out a tray of hot coffee. Each man took a mug in his glove-covered hands.

"You're right quick with the repairs," Menough said to O'Reardon. "We'd still be there fixing the stage if it wasn't for you."

Milly couldn't tell for sure, but she thought she saw O'Reardon blush. "Nay, you blokes could have done just as well. Many hands make less work, me sainted mother used to say."

"Your sainted mother had a lot of sayings," Milly's father said with a laugh.

"Aye, her favorite being 'I'll take a switch to ye, Patrick O'Reardon.' She never did though. Which is why she was such a saint."

"Mr. Montgomery," Menough said after taking a sip of his coffee. "We'll be ready to go as soon as you are. You've been delayed long enough."

Elijah glanced at Milly. He gave her a grim smile. "I'll run upstairs and fetch my case."

"But what about breakfast?" She thought she would at least have a little more time with him.

"Pack them a basket of food, Milly." Her father took Elijah's mug. "Enough to fill their bellies until they get to Cleveland."

"Yes, Father." She turned to Elijah, but he had already started up the stairs. Now that he felt at peace with his calling, he seemed eager to get started.

A short time later, she brought a wicker basket laden with turkey sandwiches, thick cheese slices, two flasks of mulled cider, and large squares of apple cake. Menough took the basket from her. "Much obliged, Miss Kent. I'll give you the basket back when I pass through next week."

"No hurry," her father said. He clapped Menough on the shoulder. "Godspeed."

Menough nodded, tipped his hat to O'Reardon, who was seated at his usual table near the counter, and left. Moments later Elijah came downstairs, his satchel in hand, his top hat perched on his head.

"O'Reardon, would you mind helping me out in the barn?" Father's lips curved into a quick smile as he looked at Milly.

O'Reardon jumped out of his seat. "Wouldn't mind a'tall." He shook Elijah's hand. "Good luck to ye, Montgomery. Hopefully we'll see you back 'ere in Unionville someday."

Elijah nodded but didn't reply. When O'Reardon and Milly's father disappeared, he picked up his case and headed toward Milly.

She couldn't stop her chin from trembling. Then she noticed his cravat was crooked. "May I?" she asked, pointing at the white cloth around his neck.

"Please."

As Milly straightened Elijah's cravat, she searched for something to say. They had said their good-byes before. She didn't want to go through that again, because this time she knew in her heart that when he walked out that door, he would never walk through it again.

"I wish some things could be different, Milly."

His voice, low and soft, sent a tingling sensation through her. "Things are as they should be," she said, releasing his cravat and taking a step back. Finally, she was able to look him in the face. "I'm just glad this is God's call on your life and not just what your family wanted you to do."

He nodded. "I did have my doubts about that. But now I know I have to head west. I have to discover the truth for myself." He reached out and touched her face. "I must admit I'm not eager to set out on this journey alone."

Sadness entered his eyes. But not the fear and doubt she'd seen there before. An impulse came over her, one she couldn't control.

"Good-bye, Mil—"

She reached up and kissed him. With tears spilling over her cheeks, she fled upstairs.

Chapter 11

One year later

Christmas Eve again. As Milly laid out fresh pine boughs on the mantel, she thought about the past year. The Tomlinsons had become good friends, especially Billy and her father. They were also regular attendees at Sunday service. And now that little Anna was walking, they could barely keep up with her when the Tomlinsons visited the tavern, which they did almost once a week. Milly had just finished making Anna's doll last week. It lay on Milly's bed upstairs, ready to be wrapped in brown paper and tied with one of Milly's hair ribbons. She couldn't wait to give it to her honorary niece tonight at supper.

"You were singing the words wrong, Patrick."

Milly turned around as Aunt Louise and Mr. O'Reardon walked into the tavern. Both gave Milly a nod then sat down at their usual table—where they had been sitting together since New Year's Day.

"Ye need to get yer hearin' checked, woman." Mr. O'Reardon's scowl was coupled with a smirk. "I was singin' that hymn perfectly."

"It was perfectly dreadful." Aunt Louise looked down at her wool shawl then gave a pointed but kind look to Mr. O'Reardon. He jumped up from the chair and removed her shawl, hanging it on the wooden coat tree near the front door.

"Thank you, Patrick."

"Anything for you, me dear." O'Reardon sat down, and they both looked at each other for a long moment before they started bickering about song lyrics again.

"I don't see how O'Reardon puts up with that cantankerous woman." Milly's father appeared at her side.

"He enjoys the challenge." Milly crossed her arms. "Look at them. They're so well suited for each other."

"Good thing, too. The more time she spends with him, the less time she has to criticize me. You know she hasn't said a word about the amount of sage I put in the dressing this year."

Milly chuckled. "She must be in love."

Her father laughed, but the sound quickly faded as Milly turned around and put the Christmas candle in the middle of the mantel. "Have you heard from him, Milly?"

She shook her head. "Not since September." She swallowed, forced a smile, and faced her father. "Which is fine. It truly is. I hadn't expected to hear from him at all."

When she'd first received a letter from Elijah a week after he left last Christmas, she'd been delighted to hear from him. Over the past nine months, he had written fairly frequently, regaling her with tales of the wilderness, of the Indian tribes he'd encountered and the rugged pioneers he'd met in the Dakota territories.

While his missionary opportunities sounded exciting, the letters were bittersweet. She could sense him withdrawing from her and knew his correspondence would stop eventually. Perhaps he found someone who shared his passion for his calling. The idea pained her, but she hoped he was happy.

As for her, she was content working at the tavern. But she couldn't deny her loneliness, even more acute knowing that Elijah was so far away. Yet in the past month she had come to accept reality and had even had Sunday supper last week with a young man who had just moved to Unionville with his family over the summer. He was pleasant enough, but he wasn't Elijah.

"I should get back to the kitchen," her father said, interrupting her thoughts. "I could use your help, Milly."

"I'll be there in a moment." She adjusted the candle one more time as her father left. She touched the hardened drips of wax as she ran her finger around the candle's rim. More than ever she wished her mother was here to offer her advice. Her heart was so confused.

She heard the door open again but didn't turn around, assuming her aunt and Mr. O'Reardon had left, since the tavern had suddenly grown quiet. And unlike last Christmas, not a flake of snow disturbed the ground. The Tomlinsons weren't expected to arrive for a few hours, so she had some time to get things prepared—

"Milly?"

Milly froze at the familiar voice. She slowly turned, willing herself to believe her ears. Sure enough, standing in the middle of the tavern dining room was Elijah Montgomery. He looked different. Older. Confident. His curly hair shorter, a black, neatly trimmed mustache on his upper lip.

Then he smiled, and she hurried toward him, stopping only a few inches away. "Elijah? What are you doing here?"

He glanced around the empty room. "Where is everyone?"

"I don't know." At that moment she didn't care. "I never thought I'd see you again. Are you here for a visit?"

"No, Milly. I'm here for good."

"But what about your ministry? I thought you enjoyed living out west."

"I did, for a time." He set down his satchel and removed his hat, placing it on a nearby table. "And I'm sorry I haven't written recently. But I had a few things to sort out between me and God."

"I don't understand."

"I didn't either at first. But I realized something, Milly. I don't have to travel great distances to minister to others. I just have to be open to the opportunities God brings my way."

"Like Billy Tomlinson."

He nodded. "I was pleased to hear he and his family are attending services."

"They never miss." She smiled.

"A wise Irishman once told me the heart has a mind of its own. Now I know he was right." He took her hands in his. "You have my heart, Milly. You always have. I have to go where God leads. And He led me here. . .back to you."

"Are you sure?"

"I've never been so sure of anything in my entire life."

The front door opened. Milly peered over Elijah's shoulder as he turned around.

"Kiss her already, lad!" O'Reardon laughed. A chubby hand appeared behind him and grabbed him by the collar of his coat. When he didn't budge, Aunt Louise wedged herself in between him and the door.

"Mind your own business, Patrick!" Aunt Louise tugged.

"Keep yer hands off me, woman. At least in public."

"Patrick!" Aunt Louise gasped.

O'Reardon winked at Elijah and Milly and disappeared out the door with Aunt Louise.

Elijah turned to Milly, "Are they. . . ?"

"They're something. We just haven't figured out what yet."

He chuckled then drew her close. "I hope you don't mind me visiting the tavern again, Miss Kent."

"You're always welcome here, Mr. Montgomery."

Elijah leaned his head toward hers. "Would I be too forward in asking for a kiss?"

Milly grinned and shook her head. "Considering the last time we kissed, I didn't even bother asking, I would say you're being most polite."

He bent down and kissed her tenderly. "Merry Christmas, Milly."

She looked into his dark eyes and thanked God for the best gift she'd ever received. "Merry Christmas."

A Silent Night

Anna C. Urquhart

Chapter 1

Edinburgh, Scotland
March 29, 1824

Y ou'll sign the papers today?" Lorna asked as she looked across the table at Iain.

Iain looked up from his plate of boiled eggs on toast and nodded. "I told Angus McCracken I'd come at lunch and sign. The ship leaves in four weeks for Boston."

Lorna lifted the china teapot with lilac sprigs abloom around its base and poured a stream of steaming amber liquid into a matching sprigged teacup. She could feel Iain watching her but didn't raise her eyes. She didn't need to see him to know he was anxious. Anxious to have things settled. Anxious to be under way. Anxious for her, his new wife, to embrace this venture, this new life they were about to begin.

"Two lumps?" Lorna asked. She spooned a small piece of sugar from the bowl. Iain tilted his head, as if chastising her for asking a question to which she knew the answer. She grinned and clucked her tongue as she dropped a second lump into his tea.

"What are we to do with such extravagance, dear Iain?"

As she handed him the teacup, his hand brushed hers. She met his eyes— dark brown eyes with honey-gold flecks. Eyes that made the backs of her knees tingle. A smile came over his face. Lorna waited for the dimple in his right cheek to appear. It did. He couldn't hide his enthusiasm for this new adventure.

For several minutes, only the clink of Lorna's spoon against the rim of her teacup interrupted the silence. Iain's smile, Lorna observed, waned as he stared into his tea.

"It's a new start," he said finally. She rubbed her fingers over a small scratch in the tabletop. She placed her palm flat against the solid, gold-hued surface. Iain had made this table out of sturdy oak. Dove-tailed joints. Beveled edges. Sturdy, scrolled legs. Tongue-in-groove surface perfectly aligned. At this table, Iain had promised, their children would surround them. Each Christmas they would lay a feast and sing and laugh and gorge themselves on Lorna's Christmas pudding. The place her palm rested grew damp from her own heat, yet she did not withdraw her hand. Instead, she pressed harder, resisting the change that had already begun.

"It's such a long time." Her voice neared a whisper.

"It's five years." Iain made five years sound like five days. "Five years I'll be indentured to the McCrackens in Boston. After that we'll be free."

"We're free now." She brought her gaze to his. She wanted—no, needed—him to understand her fear.

"You know what I mean." Iain leaned forward, placed his hand atop Lorna's that still pressed on the table. "I want more for us. For our family."

Lorna may have married Iain only four months ago, but she had known him most of her life. She knew he was a man for open spaces—a man who loved to work with his hands, longed to be his own master, and dreamed of breathing and digging deeply in land that was all his own. He couldn't do that in Edinburgh. At one time his idealism had been intoxicating. Now it prompted fear.

Lorna lifted the teacup to her lips and glanced out the window into Mrs. Ross's garden where lilacs and bougainvillea bloomed. She listened to Iain explain—again—that, with the Erie Canal's completion, it was as perfect an opportunity as they would ever have. Five years' indenture in Boston. Then onto a boat—a canal boat—through the Erie Canal into Michigan Territory. To Wayne County. A town near Detroit—Spring Wells, was it? A place, Iain assured her, where they would build a home. A place where their children would run freely. A place where they would sing Gaelic Christmas carols beneath a million sparkling stars without the fog of the city to cloud the sky, nor the noise to drown the birdsong.

Lorna placed a hand against her abdomen. Never, in all her dreaming, did she think she would carry their first child into the yawning dark of the unknown. Away from the familiar. From family and friends. From safety. The weight of that decision, that responsibility, hung on her like a yoke. But she loved Iain; she trusted him. And she had made a vow.

Iain stood, swallowed the dregs of his tea, and smacked his lips. The cup clacked against the saucer as he set it down. He gave Lorna a look that brought a warm flush she could feel creeping up her neck.

"I have one condition," she said.

Iain raised an eyebrow.

Lorna, her hand still atop the table, sighed. "This table comes with us."

Iain chuckled. "That's your condition?"

"You promised." Lorna rose to her feet and looked at her husband. "You promised our family, for the next eighty years, would gather around this table. It comes with us."

Iain laughed a loud, throaty laugh that came from down deep within him.

Lorna finally laughed, too.

"Lorna!" Iain wrapped his arms around her waist, lifting her in the air, exultant. He set her back on her feet and kissed her fully on the mouth. Lorna brought her hands up to his chest, pressed her palms against him, feeling his heart pulse. She wanted to soak up every ounce of him—of his enthusiasm, his confidence—in this one kiss. Iain pulled back, his eyes bright, and he began to hum. He hummed the strains of a ballad, grasped her around the waist, and spun her through the steps of a highland reel. The same reel they had danced together at their first ceilidh in Collin McGregor's barn when they were twelve, the night she knew she would one day marry Iain Findlay.

" 'O my Luve's like a red, red rose that's newly sprung in June,' " Iain crooned in Lorna's ear. " 'O my Luve's like the melodie that's sweetly play'd in tune. As fair art thou, my bonnie lass, so deep in luve am I. And I will luve thee still, my dear, till a' the seas gang dry.' " Even now she could hear the strains of the fiddles, the smell of hay and barley. She imagined a ceilidh in Michigan, in the barn Iain assured her they would have. Maybe they could make Michigan home, Lorna mused, as the tenor of Iain's voice smoothed the edges of her fear.

Iain's singing stopped. He dropped to one knee before Lorna and placed his hand—his long, strong fingers that carved and sculpted the flesh of wood—upon her stomach.

"And this wee one," he whispered, "will be born in a new world."

Lorna placed her hand atop Iain's. "This wee one I fear for the most."

Iain lifted her hand, kissed the tips of her fingers. "Trust in the Lord, my sweet," he said. He stood, clapped his hat on his head, and whistling, strode out the door to his work. Where he would shape willing, vulnerable pieces of oak and cedar. Until midday, when he would sign a paper and shape the rest of their lives. A red-breasted robin tugged at a worm in the garden then flitted off into the morning sunbeams as Lorna sat at the table and finished her tea.

Chapter 2

Michigan Territory
November 26, 1830

Iain is dead. Lorna repeated the phrase over in her head, as though looking at a vaguely familiar face whose name she was unable to remember. She rolled over in bed, moving into the empty space Iain had filled. For three weeks her eyes had opened expecting to find him next to her. Yet each morning she found only cold emptiness. *Iain is dead.* She was conscious of this new, horrible reality but could do no more than hold that truth in her mind for mere seconds before laying it down and moving to calmer, safer thoughts. Thoughts of kneading bread and setting it to rise. Thoughts of the ache in her back while bending over the fire—an ache she never previously had, but one that arrived with the cold of Michigan. Lorna exhaled into the rough ticking of the mattress.

"Mama?"

Lorna lift her head to look at her daughter Afton, who stood next to the bed.

"What is it, kitten?" Lorna slowly sat up to face her six-year-old.

"Harry wants out." Afton pointed to where Harry, their mutt with scruffy russet fur jutting out in all directions, sniffed and pawed at the door to be released into morning sunlight.

Lorna sighed, scooted to the edge of the bed, wrapped her black woolen shawl around her, and winced as she placed her bare feet on the icy floorboards—boards Iain had felled and split and planed with his own capable hands. Lorna pressed a fist to her chest where the ache was so fierce she thought her heart would stop. She was almost surprised to feel it thrum, hard and sure, beneath her hand.

"Have you used the privy yet?" Lorna asked.

"Yes."

The metal latch of the door was stiff, and Lorna gave it a firm, two-handed tug. The door groaned open. Harry sprinted into the world outside where the sunrise pinked the tops of the spruce trees. *That dog is sure to return muddy,* Lorna thought. But what was a little more muck added to the disorder the cabin had become? She shut the door. Her eyes roved up to the back corner of the cabin, the corner opposite the stone fireplace and the bedroom Lorna and Afton shared. Thatching of pine and spruce boughs covered a hole that looked to be about the length and width of a buckboard. Leaves and twigs, small birds seeking shelter, and icy fingers of wind all penetrated this makeshift covering, leaving a continual mess in their small home.

This portion of roof was all that was left to be finished. Three weeks ago, Iain had planned a final trip into the forest to fell a tree for lumber. "I'll be home soon, my love," he had said to Lorna. He gave her cheek a quick kiss. "Then our home will be complete." She had watched Iain ride off on Goldie—their horse's name so chosen by Afton for the golden tone of the mare's coat—down by the stream and out of the clearing. The red of his wool shirt disappearing among the trees. Hours later, as the sun began to hide itself behind the trees, Goldie sauntered into the clearing alone.

Lorna again pressed her fist to her chest. She handed Afton her coat and lifted the water bucket from its place by the door, the layer of water left in the bottom overnight now a sheath of milky ice.

"It's cold out there," Afton whined.

"The sooner we get water, the sooner we get breakfast," Lorna answered.

With an exaggerated moan, Afton shrugged into her coat, the bright red one of which she was so proud, and took the pail from her mother's hand. Lorna remembered when Afton had gotten lost in the vastness of that coat last winter in Boston. Now it fit perfectly. Lorna studied her daughter, the long length of her stride, her squared shoulders, and the uplifted tilt of her chin. Afton was every inch the image of Iain. With what seemed all the energy she possessed, Lorna followed Afton to the edge of the clearing where the stream burbled and spun down a narrow bed of its own making.

A mockingbird chirruped in a tree nearby. Lorna squinted but could not see the songbird. *That wee bird should be heading south,* Lorna thought, *before winter arrives. No one survives winter here alone.* Lorna's breath seemed to snag then freeze in the back of her throat. The mockingbird's song disappeared as though it had never begun.

Lorna looked at the hill rising behind their cabin. On that hill Lorna and Iain had first set eyes on this land upon which they would build their home. On that hill they had walked as a family in the evenings, Iain and Afton at times bursting into song. And on that hill Lorna had, with the help of Mr. Edgar, placed a marker for her husband. There was no casket. No grave. No body was ever found. On a quiet night she thought she could still hear him on the hill, singing old hymns they had learned as children. Lorna swallowed. Afton dipped the pail into the water. Harry, next to her, licked her face, her hand, the pail as water trickled down the side. Afton giggled. Lorna wanted to reach out, touch the sunlit, silky hair of her daughter. Run the backs of her fingers along Afton's soft cheek. Remind herself of what she still had.

"This is where our roots will go down," Iain had told Lorna as he held her in bed the night before the forest claimed him. "I feel, at last, we've come home."

Lorna breathed in the earthiness of the air, the scent of pine. *We've come home.* It was not a home of her choosing; it was the home Iain had chosen. He cleared the trees. Constructed their cabin and the barn. He even bought a goat they named Nanny! If Lorna left now, then it was all for nothing. Those five years toiling in Boston. Those three babies she had carried such a short time and lost. The typhoid fever they all endured—the fever that seemed to close her womb forever. She had survived it all. She—and Afton—would survive this, too.

"We've come home," Lorna said aloud. Afton looked at her, smiled with a dimple appearing in one cheek. Her brown eyes the same shade as Iain's.

"Of course we're home, Mama," Afton said, her voice musical. The handle of the bucket cut into Lorna's fingers as she lifted the burden from her daughter.

"Let's make breakfast, kitten," she said and smiled at her daughter. The first smile she'd been able to offer in weeks. They walked toward the cabin. Lorna tilted her shoulders to counterbalance the weight of the pail. The first thing to do, she determined, was to finish the roof. Lorna lifted her chin, hearing again the song of the mockingbird burst from the trees.

&

"Hallo, Mrs. Findlay!"

Startled, Lorna stopped the ax midswing. The ax head landed with a whump on the hard earth. Their neighbor Mr. Edgar, aloft on his pinto, lifted his hat and called out again as was expected when approaching a homestead. With the continual threat of Indians and wild animals, folks here were skittish.

Lorna raised her hand in greeting then let it drop. It felt as weighted as the ax. She dragged the ax to the sparse woodpile and propped its handle against the stacked logs. Her palms felt gritty, raw. She wiped them against the apron she had tied around the outside of her gray woolen coat and forced a wooden smile onto her face. Her cheeks felt stiff, maybe from the cold. Edgar rode toward her, dismounted, walked the remaining distance. His horse plodded behind.

"Good morning, Mr. Edgar."

"As I said before, please call me Joseph," Mr. Edgar said with a pleasant smile. Lorna fidgeted with her apron. "Can I help you with some of this?" He pointed at the ax and the empty chopping block. The small log Lorna had been hacking at had fallen forlornly off the block. It lay on the ground like an old boot tossed to the dog for gnawing.

Without awaiting an answer, Edgar handed Lorna his horse's reins, set his hat and heavy coat atop the woodpile, and grasped the ax. He set the log back onto the block, heaved the ax over his head, and in a single stroke, split the log cleanly through. Lorna felt her shoulders sag. Edgar set up another log then split it. The pieces separated like an egg cracking open. He grinned at her, hoping, she supposed, for her admiration. She turned away, walked the horse to the post outside the barn, and tied him up.

"Where's that girl of yours?" Edgar asked. Another drop of the ax, another log split. Afton should be fetching Nanny, Lorna thought. That goat needed set out to graze before it gnawed a hole through the pen. Lorna looked around. She reached behind her back to untie her apron strings that had stubbornly knotted themselves.

"She and Harry were just here," she mumbled more to herself. She squinted through the trees for a glimpse of a red coat, strained to hear Afton's laughter or Harry's bark. Nothing. Lorna's hands began to shake and her breaths shortened. Edgar lowered the ax.

"I'm sure they haven't gone far," he said. His tone was soothing, almost patronizing, Lorna thought. She glanced at him. Had she so quickly betrayed her panic? She again forced forward her smile, hating that he thought he knew what she was thinking. She took a step away from Edgar, her fingers still fighting the knot of her apron. She had heard only last week of a man killed in his fields by two passing Indians.

Her chest tightened. With quick strides she moved toward the stream. In a frenzy of fear, she felt a scream trying to push its way out from her lungs. She opened her mouth, her daughter's name on her tongue.

A crashing of brush sounded. Harry broke through the tree line with a bark and ran for the stream. Afton trailed behind with a fistful of ferns raised above her head. Lorna exhaled, her shoulders hunched forward. She managed to stay on her feet despite the tremble of her legs. Afton waved the clump of ferns at Lorna, who waved back. Lorna's other hand rose to her chest.

Afton and Harry tramped to the stream where Lorna knew Harry would get terribly muddy, and Afton would spend the next hour floating fern leaves, like a tiny armada, down the water's spinning current. Frosty signs of approaching winter licked the water's edge. Nanny could wait a little longer, Lorna decided. She reached back to attempt again to untie her apron.

"May I help?" Mr. Edgar asked, his voice close behind her. She turned and, finding Edgar only inches from her, moved back several steps.

"Mr. Edgar, I—"

Edgar held up a hand as if to assure her of his innocent intentions.

"I'm sorry," he said, his hand still raised. "Your apron. I just want to help."

"Indeed, Mr. Edgar," Lorna nodded, reminded that she needed this man's help. There would be no finishing her roof without him. "There was something I wished to speak to you about." She began to explain her decision to stay in Michigan with Afton and her need to complete her roof. As she spoke, she watched a look of mild humor spread across Edgar's face. Irritated, Lorna continued until Edgar finally held up his hand again, this time to stop her.

"I admire your sentimentality, Mrs. Findlay," he said, seemingly unable to hide his amusement. "Clearly you are attached to this homestead you—and your husband— began. But," he paused to hide his laughter behind a cough, "you can barely chop wood. Your mare is fat and restless because she's not been ridden in weeks. Your land's overrun with brush, and you haven't a decent roof on your cabin. Your beasts are kept warmer than you are." He stepped toward her, his grin replaced by a somber, pointed look at Lorna. "No woman can survive out here alone."

Lorna stiffened, angry at Edgar's laughter, resentful that he saw her determination as mere sentimentality. "Sissy has managed," Lorna retorted. The image of Sissy Cousins, a hardened neighbor woman in her sixties, loomed in Lorna's mind. Sissy had buried her husband and five of her six children. Sissy was a survivor.

"Sissy's tougher than the devil," Edgar said. He crossed his arms. "Death took one bite of her and threw her back. You seem to lack her. . .tenacity."

A gust of wind swiped a piece of hair across Lorna's forehead, and she brushed it away. The giggles of her daughter brought her attention to the stream, where Afton pulled a small leaf from the fern, held it up for Harry to sniff, then released it into the swirl of the current. Lorna bit down on her lower lip. Mr. Edgar was a seasoned frontiersman. A man who had survived many winters here. Lorna stared at the coarse green fabric of Edgar's shirt, the sleeves rolled past his wrists, a splinter of wood caught in one sleeve. He was easily ten—if not twenty—years older than she, though the weathered condition of his face made his age difficult to gauge. His hands, wrinkled and calloused, ought to be cold in the November wind, but it didn't seem to bother him. He didn't seem to feel anything. Was this what she must become—someone weathered, calloused? Someone without feeling?

"I suppose an arrangement could be made," Mr. Edgar said, his voice hesitant. "A marriage arrangement. That is, if you are determined to stay."

Lorna blinked several times before she understood what Edgar, with his pleasant smile and rough hands, offered to her.

"You—" She paused to clear her throat, her mind. "You know that my husband has been. . .been gone only three weeks."

"I do," Edgar replied, his voice not unkind. "I offer out of consideration. No woman can survive out here alone."

Lorna stared at him. Her mind howled like the wind that swept around their cabin at night. She glanced at Afton, who had paused in the launching of her leafy ships and, as though sensing the magnitude of the conversation, had turned to watch Lorna. Something hard knotted in Lorna's stomach. Edgar seemed to translate her silence as possible assent. "The winter is coming," he continued. "You have this place to manage, a daughter to care for. And Michigan is not kind in winter."

Michigan is not kind in any season, Lorna thought. Her blood pulsed in her ears. She gritted her back teeth to keep away the tears. Joseph Edgar would not see her cry. Edgar smiled, the creases in his forehead and around his eyes deepened like folds of worn leather.

"We could marry immediately. You and Afton would have a home," he lifted his eyes to the latticed patching on the roof, "and no reason to fear the coming snows."

Lorna closed her eyes and saw their table spread with food, Afton singing Christmas carols, and Iain's seat empty. She didn't fear winter for the snow. How was she to survive Christmas without Iain? Lorna opened her eyes, blinking hard to keep them dry. Edgar walked away, setting the ax by the woodpile and retrieving his coat and hat. He released the reins of his horse from the post with the snap of leather against wood. The pinto snorted as Edgar mounted.

"I'll let you think on my offer," he said and dipped the brim of his hat at Lorna.

Lorna waited until he rode down the lane out of sight then hurried into the barn and heaved the door closed behind her. A sob burst from her throat. She clapped both hands over her mouth. Afton didn't need to hear her mother crying. Tears streaked down Lorna's face. Goldie lifted her head over her stall and stared at Lorna with gentle gray eyes, while Nanny, mildly curious, gnawed on the post of her pen.

With the sleeve of her coat, Lorna scrubbed away the tears that continued to fall, lifted her chin, refused to dissolve into this grief that threatened to consume her. She walked to Goldie, touched the horse's velvet muzzle with the back of her fingers. "What do I do?" Lorna whispered into the stillness. How could she replace her own husband? Replace her child's father? Lorna knew that in the wilderness these marriages of convenience happened daily. It was expected when a spouse was lost that a replacement be quickly found in order to survive.

"What do I do?" Another tear driveled alongside her nose. She knew what Iain's answer would be even before her whispered question, like a prayer, rose into the eaves of the barn. Iain would kiss the tips of her fingers and say, "Trust in the Lord, my sweet." A swallow—or was it a sparrow?—flapped around the barn roof, trapped.

The barn door creaked open, admitting a shaft of sunlight to carve away some of the shadows. Afton's face appeared, and Lorna again swiped away her tears.

"Mama?"

"Yes, kitten?"

Afton sauntered farther into the barn. She stopped at Nanny's pen.

"What are you doing?"

Lorna drew a deep breath, exhaled heavily. "Fetching Nanny."

Afton peered into her mother's face, a crease of concern lining her forehead, the corners of her little mouth turned down. "I'm sorry I forgot, Mama," Afton's face strained as though she might cry. "I promise I'll remember to take Nanny out tomorrow." Lorna pulled Afton, in her red coat, against her. Afton wrapped her small arms around Lorna's waist and squeezed.

"Thank you, little one." Lorna held tightly to her daughter, kissing the top of her small head and inhaling the soft scent of soap that lingered there.

Chapter 3

November 30, 1830

The wooden handle of the small saw chafed Lorna's palm. Iain had used this tool to craft exquisite furniture—Windsor chairs, highboys, dining tables. Now she used it to hack at brush and thin young trees that crowded the west side of their cabin outside the bedroom window. She stamped down onto a lithe, bending stalk—the beginnings of what looked like a Hemlock—and two-handed she sawed at the base of the plant. Sissy had told her that these small trees often sheltered critters that tended to come visiting indoors once the snows arrived. "Best clear them shoots out afore they get sturdy roots," Sissy had advised.

These roots are already sturdy, Lorna grumbled. Roots that refused to relinquish their hold on the earth. So, instead of battling the roots, Lorna found Iain's saw. Her upper body rocked as she sawed until the green flesh of the infant tree was exposed then severed. Lorna wiped the back of her hand across her forehead, clearing away the beading sweat. One baby hemlock gone, a dozen more to go. She grabbed ahold of the next shoot, pleased that it seemed thinner than the last.

"Your sun must have been stolen," she said to the gangly plant. She bent it the whole way to the ground, trapped the rangy trunk with her foot, and sawed at its base. The roots, she knew, would survive beneath the ground through the winter, only to bud again. Lorna shook her head. She would deal with the roots in the spring.

Afton whooshed around the corner of the cabin along with a gust of wind. Lorna looked up, her blade halfway through the small trunk.

"He's gone!" Afton cried. Her brown eyes spilled giant tears, her face scrunched with worry.

"Harry?" Lorna asked. "Is he locked in the barn again?" She straightened, let go of the saw's handle, its blade wedged in the wood. Her foot stayed securely on the trunk.

Afton shook her head. "I looked there. And down the lane."

"Did you try the hill?" Lorna asked. She glanced at the hill rising above the cabin. Harry wandered daily up that hill expecting, Lorna believed, to find Iain there. Instead, he found a wooden marker and a biting wind. Afton, too, looked at the hill, her eyes hopeful. Lorna nearly offered to climb the hill in search of Harry, but the ache in her chest choked away the words.

"I'm sure he'll come home," Lorna said. "He always does." But from Afton's expression, Lorna knew there would be no more clearing trees till Harry was found. Lorna sighed. That dog got into more scrapes—with bobcats and porcupines and hostile badgers—that at some point Lorna knew his luck would end. She watched as fear creased her daughter's face. She wanted to smooth away those creases with whispered words and gentle kisses, but kisses and words would not assuage Afton's fear.

"Give me a minute, kitten, all right?"

Afton nodded and gave a hint of a smile. Two hands again on the saw, Lorna hewed through the rest of the tree. Its severed body dropped lifeless onto the stiff, browning grass. She placed the saw on the ground, gripped the two small saplings she had felled by the ends of their narrow trunks, and dragged them around back of the cabin, well away from the cabin wall so no critters would welcome themselves inside. Lorna returned to Afton, retrieved the saw, and held out her hand. Afton wiped a grimy hand across her wet cheek, leaving a streak of dirt. She took Lorna's hand, and they walked along the front of the cabin, across the yard, past the chopping block and the paltry woodpile, to the barn. Past Nanny tied to a post where she nibbled back the dying grass.

Lorna lifted the wooden latch, shoved it open. The damp dung smell pushed out from the barn's depths. Another job—mucking out Goldie's stall—which would have to wait. The shadows of the barn faded as Lorna's eyes adjusted to the dim light. Goldie whinnied. Lorna walked to Iain's workbench opposite Goldie's stall and replaced the saw. She turned to Afton, who looked at her expectantly. Lorna swallowed. What should she do? Saddle up Goldie and roam thousands of acres of swampy woodland to find a dog that didn't know he was lost?

"We'll walk up the hill and look." She cleared her throat. "If he's not there, we can go along the north road toward Spring Wells."

"What about the woods," Afton asked, "on the other side of the stream?"

Lorna stared at her daughter but didn't actually see her. Instead, she saw Goldie, riderless, wandering from the woods beyond the stream. The sound of barking brought a squeal from Afton, and she spun and sprinted out of the barn. Lorna heaved out a breath, relieved—though not at the safety of Harry. Lorna touched Goldie's soft muzzle then walked out into sunlight. Up the lane Harry walked—limped—alongside a man. A trapper Lorna had never seen, though she had seen plenty of these grizzled men trading fur in Spring Wells. A thick beard covered most of the man's face, and animal pelts coated the rest of his body. A donkey, burdened with animal furs and skins, ambled behind him. Lorna's stomach knotted. She wished Iain's musket was close at hand and not ferreted away beneath her bed.

Harry continued to bark and hobble, his left forepaw lifted and held close to his body. His tail wagged frantically at the sight of Afton.

"Harry!" Afton called, undaunted by the burly man towering beside the dog. She ran to Harry before Lorna could call out to stop her. Lorna hurried forward. Afton dropped to her knees and allowed Harry to lick her face.

"Mama said you would come home, you naughty dog," Afton prattled. "But what did you do to your foot? Have you fought with a porcupine again? Better than a skunk. Mama wouldn't have let you into the house smelling of skunk."

Afton inspected Harry's paw, which he seemed reluctant to let her touch. Coming near, Lorna felt the man's eyes on her before she was able to see them amid the low-slung hat and overgrown beard. The hair on her arm prickled, and she reached for Afton instinctively.

"Mama," Afton protested to Lorna's grip on her arm. "Harry needs help."

"Take Harry into the house," she instructed without looking down at her daughter. "We'll tend him inside."

She trained her eyes on the trapper as Afton escorted the hobbling Harry to the house, her stream of chatter unabated. The intensity of the trapper's eyes—vibrant blue eyes the color of cornflowers—startled Lorna once she found them. Yet he had a distant, almost distracted look. Too much solitude, Iain had once told her. These trappers spend months alone in the wilderness. Solitude makes them crazy, Iain said. Was this man crazy? Lorna wondered. Again she thought of Iain's musket.

"Thank you, sir, for bringing Harry home," she said hesitantly.

The man nodded and passed his donkey's lead rope from one hand to the other. He seemed to be waiting for something, but Lorna wasn't sure what. His expression was hidden, impossible to read. With his hand—nails black, skin brown and leathered—he pushed his hat back on his head, revealing a shock of curly, matted blond hair. It seemed as if he intended to tip his cap then thought better of it. Instead, he rubbed the back of his knuckles across his forehead then pulled his hat back down.

"You're welcome." His voice was gravelly and low, as if unaccustomed to use. A small feather of sadness settled on Lorna for this man alone in the wilderness. She looked back at the cabin and saw Afton had gone inside. Lorna turned again to the trapper but didn't know what else to say. From behind the trapper came the whinny of a horse. Lorna looked past the large, fur-clad man to see Mr. Edgar riding up the lane. He slowed his pinto as he neared Lorna and her visitor. The donkey snorted and sidestepped at the arrival of a new, larger beast.

"Mrs. Findlay," Mr. Edgar said, though he did not dismount. Lorna cocked her head, surprised at the cold edge of Edgar's voice.

"Everything all right, Mrs. Findlay?" Edgar asked without looking at her. He trained hard, dark eyes on the trapper. Lorna could see the trapper would be easily a head taller than Edgar. Was Edgar intimidated? She couldn't tell. It seemed Edgar stayed on his horse as if wanting to keep the upper hand, the higher ground. The trapper showed no signs of fear.

Lorna nodded. "This man just returned our Harry to us. Afton and I are quite relieved."

"Charles Grayson." Edgar edged his horse closer to the trapper. The trapper lifted cold blue eyes to Edgar. He gave a nod to acknowledge the curt greeting then turned again to Lorna.

"Good day, ma'am," came the voice again from deep in the folds of fur. He gave the lead rope a yank, which brought an ornery *haw* from his donkey, then turned and walked down the lane to the road. He didn't shuffle or amble as Lorna would have expected, as even his beast did. He walked as though solitude hadn't yet broken his pride.

"I came to help chop some of that wood," Edgar said, dismounting. Lorna knew Mr. Edgar had come to see about something besides firewood. She studied the trapper's retreating form.

"Thank you, Mr. Edgar," she said. "The ax is in the barn. Excuse me. I should check on Afton." She left Mr. Edgar standing in the cold with his horse.

❧

For nearly an hour, Lorna listened to the steady whump of the ax. The wind whistled through the thatched corner of the cabin. In waning daylight, Lorna shrugged on her coat and went outside. A potato-and-carrot soup made mostly of broth bubbled in the pot over the fire. Afton had wrapped Harry's wounded paw—a wound that appeared superficial—in a scrap of muslin Lorna had torn from an old petticoat. Lorna walked toward the woodpile, stopped, and watched Mr. Edgar. His back was to her, and his hands gripped the ax handle, poised directly above his head. He heaved down. The wood, with a splintering sound, divided and toppled off both sides of the block. The ax blade lodged, rigid, in the chopping block. Mr. Edgar raised his fist to his mouth and blew hot breath into it.

Guilt nudged Lorna. Edgar had been good to them—when Iain was alive and after. It was Edgar who had helped Iain clear the land for the cabin. It was Edgar who had gone with Lorna into the forest to look for Iain. It was Edgar who had tried to comfort her when they found the blood smeared across the fallen tree and trailed into the forest. So much blood. Lorna's chest tightened and stomach churned at the memory of blood. For three weeks she had kept that memory, that gruesome image, from her mind. Again she heaved it away and stepped forward.

"Mr. Edgar?"

He spun, the ax still lodged, its handle stiffly pointing to the sky. "Mrs. Findlay, I'm sorry, I—" He appeared flustered, which unnerved her, and she wasn't sure why.

"You've been out here awhile," she said.

"I said I'd chop your wood," he replied. He retrieved the split pieces of log, walked to the woodpile, and stacked them. He turned to look at her, and she tried to smile but couldn't.

"Would you like dinner?" she offered.

He watched her for a second, as though trying to interpret the intent of her invitation, then looked at the sky. "I should get along. Don't want to be caught out after dark."

She nodded, knowing the darkness in this land was palpable, had a density that swallowed a person left alone without a lantern.

"You didn't come here just to chop wood." Lorna had to force the words out, not knowing their result, not wanting any more change.

He sniffed. "You certainly need it."

"I do." A small corner of her mind reminded her it could be wise to accept him. Everything else within her resisted, as though a voice down in the deeps of her spirit whispered, *Wait*. She knew if she waited, she and Afton would be alone. A heavy, empty solitude. The tall form of the trapper came to her mind. The resolve in each of his steps. She drew in a breath of cold Michigan air.

"I'm sorry," she whispered.

Edgar leaned in. "What?"

"You have been kind," Lorna said, louder now, "but I cannot accept. . .your offer." She exhaled. "I'm sorry."

Edgar stared at the ground and cleared his throat several times. Lorna frowned. Was he crying? she wondered. Yet when he lifted his head, she saw no sadness. His features had hardened, his jaw flexed as it would if he was grinding his teeth. Lorna stepped back. This hardness, this anger, surprised her. For a moment, the ambivalence of fearing the consequences of the wrong decision and fearing the consequences of the right one nearly sent her fleeing back inside to Afton and the warmth of the fire. Edgar yanked the ax out of the chopping block, stalked to the barn, and disappeared inside. Seconds later he returned, his horse in tow. He mounted, the cold leather of the saddle creaking. Lorna felt the burn of his glare.

"You know what this means?" His voice was gruff. Lorna stuck out her chin and brought her eyes to his. A shiver of fear ran through her, but she refused to shift her gaze. "Enjoy your first winter in Michigan." Edgar gave his horse's flanks a kick and galloped down the lane. The yowling wind—or was it a coyote?—devoured the sounds of his retreat.

Chapter 4

December 1, 1830

Host much farther?" Afton asked, her voice muffled against Lorna's back, her arms around Lorna's waist. "My bum hurts." Giant breath-clouds puffed from Goldie as she plodded along the uphill trail that led to Sissy's farm.

Lorna patted Afton's arms. "Soon."

The crest of the hill flattened into a grassy plateau that overlooked a basin of land. At the front edge of the shallow valley stood a solitary cabin and barn, a narrow creek snaking behind. A row of hemlocks stood as sentinels just beyond the barn. Acres and acres of fallow fields spread beyond the hemlocks till land blurred into sky. Sissy, despite her rigor, once admitted to Lorna of her inability to manage the planting and plowing alone. Lorna tried to imagine Sissy in young wifehood, motherhood. The budding fields in spring, green with new life.

Pale smoke ribboned from the cabin's chimney, blended with the ashen sky. The brown, brittle grasses around Lorna and Afton rustled as though surprised by their presence. Lorna nudged Goldie to hurry along.

༄

Lorna saw the barrel of the musket before she saw Sissy peering through the half-opened cabin door. Goldie snorted as Lorna jerked on the reins.

"Should to call out when coming 'pon a homestead," Sissy said. She lowered her musket and left the shadows of her doorway. Lorna nodded, dismounted, relieved at the feel of solid ground. She reached for Afton, who dropped from the mare into her mother's arms. As Lorna tied Goldie to a rail nearby, she offered an apology for not announcing their arrival. Then she and Afton followed Sissy inside.

"Tea?" Sissy asked. She set her musket on a high shelf by the door. Lorna stared at the weapon. Soon she would need to hunt, she thought. The stores of meat Iain had smoked and the root vegetables and herbs she had dried in summer were dwindling. Iain had taught her to fire his flintlock. Yet she had hidden the musket, rendered it useless, beneath her bed. She knew Iain would be cross Lorna hadn't brought the musket with her on the four-mile journey to Sissy's. Not that she could load it quickly enough to fight off an attacking animal or Indian or any of the other dangers of this wild region. She might do better to club an attacker with the musket rather than shoot. She looked at Afton, who played by the hearth with Sissy's tabby cat. Lorna resolved to retrieve the musket once they returned home. The fire snapped and spit as Sissy stoked it with a poker. Lorna nodded when tea was offered for the second time, thankful Sissy didn't serve the bitter coffee Americans—particularly those in the territory—seemed to fancy.

"So why've you come?" Sissy asked once tea had been poured. Lorna and Sissy sat at a small, round table. Not a table pounded together quickly, perfunctorily while building a homestead. Someone had taken care to curve its edges, to round its shape to a perfect circle. The table sat next to the cabin's only window that looked out across the desolate fields. The warbled panes of glass melted and skewed the landscape like a batch of swirling, churning butter.

"You's didn't come four miles for tea," Sissy said. Lorna stopped tracing the rim of her china cup and took a small sip.

"Indeed," Lorna set her cup in its saucer. "We need a buckboard. My roof needs to be finished, and I haven't the lumber to do it."

Sissy nodded, seeming thoughtful. Such a stark contrast from the woman who greeted Lorna with a rifle to the woman who served from a china tea service. Deep creases around Sissy's eyes and mouth pulled her face down into what seemed a perpetual scowl. Yet the older woman's hair, silver with hints of the black it once had been, was pulled loosely back and woven at the nape of her neck in a braided chignon, softening the rough lines of Sissy's face. Lorna had met women—hardened from homesteading—when she, Iain, and Afton had stayed in Detroit before buying their land. The women's faces were weathered like Mr. Edgar's hands. Their eyes hollowed. Their hair twisted into tight, unforgiving buns or hidden under dark, shabby fabrics. Lorna shook her head. Edgar was wrong about Sissy.

"Thought Edgar would've tended to that roof afore now," Sissy said. Her empty cup rattled hollowly against its saucer. Lorna pursed her lips and glanced at Afton.

"I see," Sissy said with a nod. "He wanted payment for his help."

"I refused his marriage proposal." Lorna kept her voice low. The words in her mouth tasted foreign, brackish—like stale, unsugared coffee.

Sissy poured herself more tea. "Man's a weasel for asking."

Lorna smiled and for an instant felt lightened, thankful for Sissy's words. Then the familiar weight settled back on her shoulders. "He thinks we won't survive," she said. Sissy smacked the teapot down on the table. The lid rattled so hard Lorna thought it might break.

"You'll survive." Sissy sounded sure, absolute. She stared at Lorna, who felt the world, for a moment, suspend, all creation holding its breath. Lorna wanted—needed—to believe Sissy. Then a low vibration—not quite a laugh, not quite a moan—came from the older woman, intoning an old sadness. "I buried my husband and five young'uns. When Ronald, my last, rode off ta Detroit for work, I refused ta leave. Tol' him this ere's my home. He said I'd not survive." Sissy looked out the window. "'Twas nine years ago."

Lorna leaned in. "How did you do it?"

Sissy's sadness was consumed by something burning just behind her eyes.

"You fight." Sissy pointed a gnarled finger at Lorna. "Fight ta keep hold a' hope. Ta keep trust in the Almighty when it 'pears He's forgot you. He clothes the field lilies. He sees the sparrow. You hold ta that."

Lorna bit her lower lip. She could almost feel Iain's finger lifting her chin, pointing her to the heavens. Lorna looked out at the sky. Sunbeams shifted—appearing and disappearing—with the movement of steely clouds.

"Miz Findlay," Sissy's voice returned Lorna to the small table, to Afton stroking the tabby that had curled into her lap. "No woman I know woulda refused Edgar, not with winter comin'. You did." Sissy dropped her hands into her lap, leaned back, studied Lorna. "Goin' a town next Tuesday. I'll come early." Sissy nodded at Afton. "Bring your girl; we'll get your lumber." Lorna watched Afton's small hand stroke the silky fur of the sleeping cat and felt in her gut a slight undoing of the knot of fear.

"Thank you, Sissy."

Sissy shook her head. "Thank me next spring."

❧

Lorna kissed Afton's cheek just next to her ear and whispered, "Sleep well, love." Afton shifted on her small bed that pulled from beneath Lorna's. Lorna stood, reached for the candle that danced, its light an orb chasing off some of the night's shadows. Afton's hand appeared from beneath the heavy quilt, caught Lorna's hand, and tugged her back down. The candle Lorna held wobbled, and the flame shimmied then settled.

"Will you pray with me?" Afton asked. Lorna brushed a strand of hair back from Afton's forehead.

"Pray with you?" Lorna had lost the habit of praying. Afton nodded, the candlelight reflected in her dark eyes. "What should we pray?"

What looked like relief crossed Afton's face. "Pray for Papa."

Lorna blinked and shifted her weight, the bed creaking beneath her. Harry pattered into the room, climbed onto the foot of Afton's bed, and laid down.

"Pray for Papa?"

Afton nodded. "Ask God to send him home for Christmas."

Lorna could not find her voice. The candle grew heavy in her hand. Careful not to spill wax, she set the candle on the small table by her bed.

"We talked about this, kitten, remember?" She brushed a tear from her lashes.

Again Afton nodded. "You said Papa died." The words fell easily, simply, from Afton's lips into the space between them. Hearing them, helpless to make them not true, Lorna wanted to weep. She stroked Afton's hand. "But Sissy told me," Afton continued, "God can do miracles. 'Specially at Christmas. Couldn't God bring Papa back? That'd be a miracle."

Another tear trickled alongside Lorna's nose. On the table, the flame of the candle flickered, startled by a draft of air. Harry's tail began to thump against the bed. Lorna had neither the breath nor the will to destroy the hope living on Afton's face. Suddenly, violently, Lorna yearned to protect—to preserve—that hope. She raised Afton's hand to her lips.

"Of course we can pray, love."

Chapter 5

December 8, 1830

Lorna's back ached from the jolts of the buckboard. Afton, wedged between Lorna and Sissy, didn't seem to mind the incessant jouncing. Spring Wells offered only basic necessities—musket powder, flour, whiskey, tobacco, sugar. Lumber could only be found in Detroit, a city that seemed far away this morning as Lorna and Afton rose before the sun. Now the city surrounded them like a clapboard forest, but without birdsong. Lorna shifted, careful not to kick Iain's musket on the floor, proud she had not forgotten to bring it. The noise of the city jarred her—clangor created by civilization. Strange, thin rivers, their water an oily gray, ran through the rutted street. Faces that turned toward her carried a wan, weathered look.

At the mill, Sissy told Lorna and Afton, "Stay put," though Lorna stood in the buckboard and stretched. An itch of guilt troubled Lorna as she watched Sissy haggle with the mill hand over the lumber. Lorna felt useless. Once they reached the mercantile, Afton's hand gripped in hers, Lorna marched to the counter and informed a small, bespectacled man reading the *Gazette Française* that she needed nails. Slowly he laid down his newspaper and tilted his head. Sissy appeared beside Lorna and plunked a cut nail onto the countertop.

"*Nous avons besoin de plus des clous.*"

Lorna stared at Sissy and felt her jaw go slack. The man nodded, stood from his stool, and walked through a door to what Lorna assumed was a storeroom.

"Wh–what did you say?"

Sissy shrugged while pointing to the *Gazette Française*. "He speaks French." She lifted the nail. "I said we need more nails." Lorna looked at the nail, her laugh incredulous.

"Why don't you go where they speak English?"

"Jacques is honest," Sissy said.

"And you speak French?"

Sissy set the nail back down. "M'late husband was French Canadian."

Lorna, again, could only laugh. Any guilt she had felt at Sissy taking charge evaporated.

"Can you teach me to say French?" Afton asked Sissy.

"*Speak* French," Lorna corrected.

"*Oui. Un jour,*" Sissy nodded.

❧

The next morning, when the sky was pinked in expectation of the sun's arrival but before the sun sent its first rays through the trees, Lorna gently woke Afton. Today they would finish the roof. The planks were stacked knee high against the side of the cabin. Lorna ran her hands across their length, feeling the prick of the splintery surface. She had seen Iain touch his hands to wood in much the same way. He always said, "Every piece of wood has potential for something." Lorna pulled her coat tighter, pushing back the wind that fingered through her collar and scratched at her throat. She pulled Iain's thick work gloves from her pocket and slid her hands into them, her fingers too small to fill the space where Iain's hands had stretched the leather. She had found these in Goldie's saddlebag. Afton, her red coat open and flapping like a cardinal taking flight, ran from the barn.

"I need your help," Lorna said. She reached down and buttoned Afton's coat. "Can you hold the ladder steady?"

Afton ran to the ladder propped against the cornice of the roof and clutched the sides in her small, eager hands. Lorna climbed onto the first rung, then the second and third. She paused as the ladder shuddered. Once Lorna's head was above the roof, she peered back down at Afton, at the hard packed earth and the pile of lumber beneath her, the chopping block and ax several paces back. *Hoisting the boards will be difficult,* Lorna thought, feeling on her cheeks the first warm rays of morning sun. Above the roof's edge, first her head, then her shoulders rose.

Before her the boughs that enclosed the roof were cluttered with leaves, wispy feathers, and abandoned bird nests. Lorna swung her leg over the ladder's top rung and set her foot squarely on the roof. Hands on her hips, her toes pushing up into the tops of her shoes, she stood, a momentary conqueror. Afton, standing on the bottom rung of the ladder, stared up from below. Lorna knelt, steadied herself, and gripped the end of a pine branch. The knots of the wood jabbed her palm through the gloves. Hand over hand, she pulled the branch toward her. The branch resisted, its splayed fingers intertwined and held by other branches. A small portholelike opening appeared as Lorna wrenched the bough free. She dropped the branch to the ground, where it landed in a whorl of dry, spinning needles.

Lorna looked at Afton. "I'm going to keep throwing down branches. I need you to drag them back beside the barn. Make a pile."

Afton grinned. "Come on, Harry!"

For only a second, Lorna watched Afton wrestle with the branch then she gripped the next. The hole widened, more of their home laid bare. But the wound must be opened to be properly mended.

After an hour, Lorna had cleared away all the branches. A pile had amassed on the ground as Lorna's productivity outpaced Afton's. Lorna pitched the last branch over the roof's edge. Afton, with Harry at her heels, came sauntering back from the barn. She grabbed ahold of another branch then yelped in pain. Lorna carefully climbed down and went to her daughter. Afton held up her hand for her mother's inspection. A small spot of blood appeared in the center of her dirt-flecked palm where a branch had pierced the skin. With the hem of her skirt Lorna wiped the blood away and kissed the scratch.

"Must be careful," Lorna said, knowing her words were too late. Afton tearfully nodded. Lorna took off one of her gloves and handed it to her daughter. A one-dimpled smile appeared on Afton's face.

"This is Papa's glove."

Lorna drew in a breath, held it, then released it. "It'll keep your hand a wee bit safer." She slid the glove over Afton's hand, her child-sized fingers lost in the man-sized glove. Again Afton grasped the end of the pine bough and pulled it from the pile, then dragged it behind her as she plodded toward the barn. Lorna went in search of rope. The grass, thick with frost, crunched beneath her feet.

๛

The chimney was her ally. Lorna had backed Goldie around so that the horse faced away from the cabin. She tied the end of a length of rope to the saddle horn, slung the rope around the chimney, and attached the other end to a plank. She called to Afton, who stood atop the chopping block watching. Afton hopped to Lorna, who had ahold of Goldie's bridle. The two of them led Goldie toward the barn, away from the cabin. The rope tensed. The leather of the saddle creaked. The *whish* of the rope against the stone of the chimney budded new hope in Lorna. Goldie pressed forward. The board lifted, wobbled, tilted, and began to stagger in the air.

"Whoa!" Lorna said. Goldie halted, and Lorna handed the reins to Afton. "Keep her still." Then she ran to the board and steadied it against the ladder. She nodded at Afton, who gave Goldie's reins a tug. Lorna watched the plank lift higher and higher; with each step of the mare, the roots of Lorna's budding hope burrowed deeper, grew stronger.

"That'll do!" she called to Afton.

"Whoa, Goldie!" Afton said, her voice singsongy. She turned to see the plank's progress. "We did it!"

Lorna raised her hands in the air, a celebration of this small victory.

"Keep her still," she reminded, pointing at Goldie. Then she climbed toward the piece of lumber hanging above her. Spreading her feet as wide as she could on the rung, Lorna lifted the board up over the uprights of the ladder. It clattered onto the rooftop.

"Forward one more step!" She called down. Goldie moved. The board shifted higher on the roof. The roof felt steeper than when Lorna had torn away the thatching. She knelt and slid the board over the freshly opened hole. Untying the end of the rope, she threw it off the roof to be secured onto the next board and reached into her pocket for a nail. From her other pocket she retrieved the hammer, its handle protruding like a ladle in a pot. Then she began to pound. One nail. Then another. She struck her fingers several times and bent two nails, but still she hammered on. Occasionally Lorna glanced at Afton, who never moved. Goldie, next to her, flicked her tail. But Afton's gaze was fixed to her mother. Lorna felt a surprising flourish of pride.

Despite the cold, sweat beaded on Lorna's forehead and dampened the back of her neck. She and Afton stopped only a short time for lunch then resumed their work. On her knees, Lorna pounded a final nail into the board. The breach in the roof was half covered, the lumber half consumed, the sun past its zenith. She stood, arched her back, and looked down. The pile of branches that Afton hadn't hauled yet to the barn was spread below like the green ticking of a mattress. They should be moved once the roof was finished, hopefully by nightfall, Lorna thought. She exhaled in relief.

"Back Goldie up!"

She could hear Afton speaking to the mare. Keeping hold of the rope, Lorna climbed down the ladder. She knotted the rope around another plank. "Okay!" she called over her shoulder. Afton, with a funny clack of her tongue, led Goldie forward. The plank began its ascent. Once the plank lurched over the top of the ladder, Lorna stepped onto the roof and released the rope.

"How does the inside of our cabin look from up there?" Afton called.

Lorna again looked down through the chasm that was only about the span of her arms outspread. As she leaned forward, Lorna thought of what to say, how to describe what she saw as she looked through this peephole into a room so familiar yet unfamiliar from this vantage. A strong arm of wind swung from the hill. Lorna widened her stance to brace against its push. Her foot landed atop the head of the hammer. The hammer shifted. Her foot rolled, slid. Balance lost, Lorna flailed her arms but met only air. She stumbled against the top of the ladder, which, like a felled tree, tipped and calmly fell away from the roof. Just as Lorna, with a cry, fell back into the emptiness where the roof ended and the sky began.

❧

Lorna could hear Afton crying but could not find her through the darkness. Were her eyes open? Lorna couldn't tell. Each breath brought a choking pain through her chest. Something warm touched her cheek, huffed air into her ear. Harry. No sooner did the thought appear than it vanished in the pain of her next breath. Afton's cries were so close and sounded so desperate.

Lorna found a shred of daylight, followed it, and pushed open heavy eyes. She tried to turn her head and couldn't. The overwhelming urge to vomit held her still. She moved only her eyes toward the cries. Afton knelt, lifting Lorna's hand, kissing it, shaking it. Tears streaked Afton's face, dripped from her chin, and left damp dark patches on her red coat. Lorna breathed in to speak and moaned in agony. Afton's face—nose running, cheeks wet and chapped—came so close Lorna felt her daughter's breath on her face. Blinking, Lorna tried to clear her vision. She moved her head slightly, squinted. Her head throbbed. The earth rustled and crunched beneath her like brittle, autumn leaves. The branches, Lorna realized. She lay on the branches discarded from the roof. The sun was still in the sky but lower now. She had not been unconscious long. She heard Goldie whinny nearby.

"The stick, Mama," Afton whimpered.

Lorna grimaced and tried to follow Afton's gaze. The front of Lorna's coat was thrown open. A sturdy branch, about the thickness of her thumb, pointed stiffly, defiantly at the sky, its tip red the color of Afton's coat. Lorna's hand trembled as she reached down and touched her side just below her ribs. The flesh puckered open through the torn fabric of her dress. A spreading stain of scarlet seeped through the faded green of her dress. Her pulse hammered in her ears. The world began to tilt as Lorna laid her head back down.

"I'm going to get Mr. Edgar," Afton said.

Lorna raised her hand. "No," she rasped. Afton grasped her hand.

"Or Sissy?"

"Don't leave."

"Mama, we need help!" Afton's grip on Lorna's hand tightened. Lorna's eyes closed, and she wasn't sure she could open them again. She squeezed Afton's hand.

"No," Lorna repeated. She swallowed. "Stay—with me."

She could hear Afton whispering, "Help, get help." Was she praying? Or sending Harry on a mission that would end in chasing squirrels? Again Lorna pushed open her eyes to ward off the deep dark that lured her. The sky carried the amber of late afternoon. The cold, already biting, would come ravaging once the sun disappeared. Time was slipping.

"My apron," Lorna whispered. Afton disappeared, the sound of her running feet faded then returned.

"Your apron," Afton said, her breathing heavy.

Lorna swallowed. "Put it on the—the—blood."

Afton wadded the apron, pressed it against Lorna's side. Lorna drew in a shallow breath, her head screaming in pain and fear. *God, what do I do?*

Keep hold a' hope, Lorna heard Sissy say.

"What next, Mama?" Dirty and tear-streaked, Afton's face was stern, focused on her work. She stared hard at her own little hands. Blood stained her fingers. The composure of her daughter shocked Lorna—her child no longer a child. Lorna's eyes burned.

"We must—get inside." Lorna's hands shook at the thought of trying to move. She panted with the effort of speaking. "Can you help. . .me to stand?" Afton released the pressure from Lorna's wound, which brought a ripping pain. Bile rose into Lorna's throat. She swallowed it down. "Lift my—shoulders. Just a little."

Small hands slid beneath Lorna's shoulder and arm. "Stop!" Lorna screamed in pain. Afton froze. The fragile sound of a stifled sob sounded near Lorna's ear. Wheezing, Lorna pulled in as much breath as she could manage and braced herself. "Again," she commanded. Afton pressed up against Lorna's shoulder then against her back, lifting her. After what seemed an eternity of fractional movement and screams of pain, Lorna was halfway sitting. The sun was halfway hidden behind the hill. *Keep breathing,* Lorna told herself. *Don't let darkness take hold. Not yet.*

Goldie, still by the chopping block, stamped her hooves. Afton froze. Lorna held her breath. "Harry's back." Afton's voice was near Lorna's ear. Lorna heard both hope and alarm in her daughter's voice. Weary, the darkness too unwavering, Lorna closed her eyes.

"Someone's coming," Afton said. Lorna, through heavy fog, tried to listen. The world sounded submerged in water. Or maybe it was Lorna submerged.

"Sissy?" Lorna's head drooped against Afton's shoulder.

"No." Afton brought her mouth next to Lorna's ear. "The trapper."

Footsteps crunched over brittle grasses. Lorna felt the man's presence. He said nothing—nothing she could hear—but she felt Afton move away as though following unspoken instructions. Lorna slumped against the branches. Pain, like rivulets of heat waves, volleyed through her, even into her fingertips. Her heart raced, pulsed behind her eyes. Then she felt a hand—no, an arm—around her shoulder. Another beneath her thighs. More bile burning the back of her throat as she was lifted, freed from the branches.

"Be still," came a voice above her. Her breath came in gasps. Noises echoed, hollow and far off. Heavy boots treading on the wooden floor rumbled, distant thunder in Lorna's head. They were inside the cabin. The image of Afton's bloodied hands and her whispered words, "We need help," brought a weak sob from Lorna. Then a feeling of falling, sinking into the earth slowed her heart. Her throbbing head cradled in softness. The familiar scent of her pillow. The trapper pulled her arm free of her coat sleeve. Then he rolled Lorna onto her side, leaving her other, wounded side exposed. Lorna heard Afton's scuffling steps draw near the bed.

"I'll need a needle. Some thread," the trapper said. Lorna ignored the words. The cabin, Afton's cries, the crackle of distant fire ebbed away. Her hand reached across, rested on the empty pillow beside her. The pain of her side—the ache in her heart—dissolved to nothing. The dark no longer fearsome.

Chapter 6

December 11, 1830

Daylight blazed, even behind closed eyelids. Lorna resisted waking until her eyes, working without consent, lifted. White light blinded her then receded.

"Wondered if you'd join us." The voice sounded distant, muddled. Lorna worked to place it. The musk of tobacco hung in the air. The room eased into focus. She was in her bed. Sissy sat nearby, a cob pipe in her mouth.

"Mama?" Afton stood at the foot of the bed, watching with worried brown eyes.

"Afton," Lorna whispered. She tried to smile, but her lips and tongue were thick and clumsy. She extended her hand, and Afton—quivering like an excited pup—crawled onto the bed next to her. Lorna shifted and sucked in her breath at the pain beneath her ribs. She fingered the place where, last she remembered, had been seeping blood.

"When—did you come?" Lorna whispered.

"Grayson fetched me. Said you'd been hurt," Sissy said. "Didn't know how bad till I arrived. You've been out two days."

Lorna closed her eyes. She heard what Sissy said, but the words seemed to jumble in her head. "Water?" she croaked. Afton scrambled off the bed, jostling Lorna, igniting fresh sparks of pain. A second later Afton returned with a full cup. Lorna slurped at the cool water and cleared her throat several times. The weight of her tongue and the tightness of her throat began to lessen. She drank more. Handing Afton the empty cup, she again touched her side.

"He sewed it up," Afton said, her look serious. She reached her hand toward Lorna's wound but didn't touch it. "He used your red thread. I wanted to give him. . .another color." Lorna patted Afton's hand and smiled.

"He made some foul-smelling paste we've slathered on the last few days." Sissy puffed out a curl of smoke. "Seems ta work."

"Where is Mr. Grayson now?"

"Left yesterday"—Sissy jabbed her pipe up toward the cabin's main room—"after he fixed the roof."

❦

Sissy stayed two more days. Lorna watched first from her bed then from a chair by the fire as Sissy and Afton made meals, churned butter, fed the animals, kneaded dough, and filled chinks in the walls with a putty made from mud and straw. Snow fell and coated the world in white, and Lorna thanked God the roof was finished. As the moon rose, after kissing Afton good night and listening again to her daughter pray for her papa to come home, Lorna slowly got up from her bed and limped back to the fireplace to sit with Sissy, who darned one of Afton's stockings. They sat in silence. The snap of the fire kept its own conversation.

"I nearly orphaned my daughter," Lorna said, voicing the guilt she had carried since waking. Sissy pushed her needle through the stocking, lifted, pulled, began again. Lorna watched the rhythmical movement then looked back into the fire. "She wanted to fetch you. I wouldn't let her." Still Sissy pushed the needle, lifted, pulled. Lorna sighed. "I suppose I'm lucky."

Sissy grunted. The needle stopped. The fire spit out a flaming cinder onto the hearth. Lorna watched it glow bright ochre then slowly die to a lifeless gray. "No luck about it," Sissy said then resumed her darning.

"Do you know Mr. Grayson well?" Lorna reached into her sewing basket for a piece of darning to work on, to occupy her hands. She pulled out what she thought was one of her socks. It was Iain's. She dropped it back into the basket and stared back into the fire, her hand on her chest.

"The hurt fades," Sissy said, her fingers continually active. Lorna's hand dropped to her lap. "No, I don't know Grayson well," Sissy answered, as though sensing Lorna's need for conversation, something to talk of other than her own loss. "I knew his wife."

Lorna lifted her eyebrows. "His wife?"

Sissy nodded. "They homesteaded out here 'bout ten year ago. He, Amelia, and their son. Son was four or five, I s'ppose. Luke. Spitting image of Grayson. Few years back, Grayson made a run into Detroit, came home to his house burned to the ground. Wife and son inside."

Lorna blinked. Grayson, stride strong, shoulders squared, alone in the wilderness. Like Job, left with nothing. Lorna stared out the window into the dark. The pale forms of snow-laden trees gazed calmly back at her.

"Since his wife died, Mr. Grayson's been living as a trapper?" Lorna asked. "Keeping to himself?"

Sissy nodded.

"Then why would Mr. Edgar dislike him?" Lorna asked, remembering that first encounter.

"Amelia was Edgar's sister," Sissy said. "Most folks blamed some Chippewa that were passing through. But Edgar blamed Grayson for not attending his family." Sissy knotted her thread and snipped the needle free with a pair of Lorna's small shears. "Just Edgar's hurt talking. No one coulda done a thing."

She dropped the shears into the basket. "Should be getting on tomorrow. Fixing to go into town afore more snows come. Need anything?"

Lorna thought for a moment. "Sugar."

Chapter 7

December 16, 1830

That's the beautifulest thing I've ever seen," Afton breathed. Lorna lifted the delaine dress from the cedar chest. From the first time she had seen the fabric on Princes Street in Edinburgh, its sapphire sheen had charmed her. Still it charmed. She laid the dress on the bed, where Afton with timid fingers touched the smooth pearl buttons trailing down the bodice like stepping stones. Lorna smiled. She returned the other belongings she had removed back into the chest, her hand brushing the emerald tartan of Iain's kilt.

"Your *wedding* dress," Afton whispered. Lorna lifted the dress, raised it high, and gave it a shake to clear away some creases. She winced at the twinge in her side. Her wound seemed slow to heal, though only a week had passed since her fall. Lorna walked from the bedroom, Afton at her heels, into the kitchen, where a fire roared. She spread the dress across the oak table. Her hands practiced, she smoothed down the folds of the fabric. Each seam, each stitch, familiar. Tears threatened, but Lorna ignored them, cleared her throat, and turned to Afton.

"Can you bring my sewing basket?" she asked. Afton returned, the basket hoisted in both hands. Last night Lorna had dismantled one of Afton's dresses, seam by seam, for a pattern, though she would cut the new pieces a bit larger to give Afton room to grow. She might be inept at mending roofs, but sewing was as natural to her as breathing. As Iain's hands took to wood, so Lorna's to fabric. Lorna placed the pieces of Afton's old, faded-yellow dress atop the sea of blue. She felt Afton's eyes on her hands without looking at her daughter. This dress would have life again on Afton's growing frame, far more than if it stayed entombed in a chest. Lorna lifted the cutting shears from her basket. The weight of them seemed to drag her hand back down as though they resisted the task ahead. Lorna's side began to throb. She swallowed, brought the shears to the fabric, and spread the blades to cut.

Your eyes are aglow, Iain had said as they danced after the ceremony that had joined them as man and wife. Lorna had smiled, rested her cheek against his shoulder. The rough fabric of the bridal sash brushed across her throat, the sash made of the deep greens and blues of the Findlay tartan. The same tartan of Iain's kilt. She belonged to a new family now, the sash representing the transference of the family name, the traditions to uphold, the honor to bear. She pressed her forehead against the warm skin of Iain's neck, felt the rise and fall of his chest.

A knock tore Lorna away from her memories. The shears clattered to the floor. Harry barked. Lorna exhaled, put her hand to her throbbing side. Afton ran to the door and opened it before Lorna could tell her to wait.

"Mr. Grayson," Lorna said, surprised. She walked forward, gestured to him to come in. He looked at her a moment, then, still on the doorstep, raised two dead rabbits up by their hind legs.

"Brought these," he said.

Lorna reached out, took the rabbits. "Um, thank you." She felt she should say more, but with two dead animals in her hands and a towering man in her doorway, words abandoned her.

Grayson removed his fur cap, his blond hair wild and wiry. He knelt in front of Afton, who had half hidden herself behind Lorna's skirt. He gave Afton a smile, the first smile Lorna had seen on him. A gentle smile, warm. From beneath his coat, he produced another hat—a miniature version of his own. Made of gray and white fur and a leather tie for beneath the chin. Afton stepped forward, and he placed the hat on her head. She giggled. Mr. Grayson replaced his own hat. His smile faded as he stood.

"Will you stay for dinner?" Lorna offered.

Grayson shook his head. "Headed to town. Few days I'll be back."

Lorna smiled. "Thank you," she said, lifting the limp rabbits. "For everything."

Grayson nodded then pointed at the rabbits, "Save the pelts. Make fine mittens." Lorna and Afton, her furry hat swallowing her head, waved from the doorway as Mr. Grayson walked with his burro down the lane. Lorna shut the door then looked at the two rabbits in her hand. She would make some stew with these—some highland rabbit stew with wild onions and mushrooms Sissy and Afton had found. Iain had loved rabbit stew. Lorna laid the rabbits on the hearth, where Harry began sniffing at them. Dinner would not need tending for a few more hours. Lorna wiped her hands on her apron and retrieved the shears from the floor where they had fallen. With her left hand she kept the fabric flat and still and, with her right, Lorna cut into the sapphire sea.

Several days later, Mr. Grayson appeared with a dead turkey, feathers still on. Lorna again invited him in, but he shook his head and hung the turkey on the peg by the door. He took the rabbit pelts Lorna had saved, and in two days returned with mittens for Afton. He seemed pleased that Afton wore the hat he had made, though his face was so bearded and shadowed that Lorna struggled to read his expression. Each time Grayson arrived, Lorna felt a thawing of the icy fear within her. She was indebted to him. He had saved her life and now saved her the indignity of having to hunt—another task at which she knew she would miserably fail. Yet she felt a shadow of shame pass over her that she could do nothing for him in return. Just as she so often felt helpless to repay Sissy. Lorna had become familiar with such shadows.

Grayson knelt before Afton, her rabbit mittens on her hands. From a pouch that hung on his back, he pulled an animal skin and unrolled it to reveal a luminous mahogany fur.

"Beaver," Grayson said.

Lorna shook her head. "Mr. Grayson, it is too much. You should not be giving away these things you work so hard for."

Grayson's blue eyes blinked at her, and again she struggled to read his expression.

"Who says I work hard for these?" he asked.

Lorna detected a small smile beneath the scraggle of beard. She looked at Afton, who rubbed her mittened hand across the silky pelt.

"Well," Lorna said, "if it's not such hard work, perhaps you can provide a bear skin next. I hear they are wonderfully warm."

A sound, more like a cough than a laugh, came from Grayson and caught Lorna by surprise. The blue of his eyes hinted of a cloudless highland sky.

"Bear skins," he said. "They are. . .more difficult."

"Well, regardless, you must stay for dinner," Lorna replied.

Grayson shook his head, as was his habit.

"You can't keep standing on my doorstep handing me dead animals." Lorna put her hands on her hips. "What will people think?" She caught another hint of a smile, though Grayson held firm, shaking his head again.

"Be back in two days," he said, looking at the steely sky. "Before the snow comes."

Lorna glanced at the decaying snow that littered the ground, looked at Afton still petting the beaver fur with Harry sniffing its edges. "Two days will be Christmas Eve," Lorna said, her voice near a whisper. She looked at Grayson, whose eyes now held the same gray of the sky holding back its snow.

"You will stay for dinner on Christmas Eve," she said with a lift of her chin. He started to shake his head. She held up her hand, insistent. "There will be a place at our table for you."

Chapter 8

December 24, 1830

The rumble of a wagon drew Lorna's eyes from her sweeping and the broom's hypnotic *tssh, tssh, tssh* across the floorboards. Harry barked and sniffed at the cabin door. Afton, who had been staring at the sock in her hand, looked up from her seat at the table. Lorna had spent the morning teaching Afton to darn and had offered Iain's sock that she had found in her sewing basket as a sacrifice to her daughter's untrained fingers. Through the pocked glass of the window, Lorna saw Sissy pull back the reins, her team jostling to a stop. The horses' breath puffed from their nostrils like smoke. Lorna set her broom with its fraying broomcorn bristles in the corner behind the door. The wind stung her cheeks and neck as she opened the door.

"Tea?" Lorna offered as Sissy clomped inside and began to shrug from her coat.

"Surely," Sissy replied. She hung her coat on one of the pegs by the door, next to Afton's red coat. The same peg Grayson had used to hang the dead turkey. Then she walked to the table and sat next to Afton, who greeted her with a yowl of pain. The sock and needle dropped to the table as Afton stuck her pricked finger into her mouth. Lorna bent over the hearth and set the kettle close to the glowing coals.

"Returning from town?" Lorna asked, pleased to have company.

Sissy nodded and pulled a small sack from her coat pocket. "Price a sugar's gone up."

Lorna took the sugar from Sissy. "Thank you." She smiled, enjoying the small weight of this luxury.

What are we going to do with such extravagance, dear Iain? Iain and Edinburgh and memories of a time when hope came easily circled round Lorna. She could almost hear Iain singing softly in her ear. And for just a moment, she allowed it all in—allowed herself to see Iain's face, the lilac china, Mrs. Ross's bougainvillea. Then, with a gust of breath exhaled, she expelled it all. She placed the sugar in a small, empty flour canister and set it on the shelf next to the dishes.

"Saw Edgar in town," Sissy offered, nodding at the stitch Afton placed into the sock without injury. "He asked after you. I told 'im you took a fall but Grayson patched you up." Sissy grinned without looking up from Afton's darning. "Tol' him Grayson mended the roof, too."

Lorna poured the tea and handed Sissy a steaming cup. "Can't imagine Mr. Edgar took that well."

Sissy sipped the scalding liquid without a flinch. "Nope."

❧

Lorna waved good-bye to Sissy as she drove her team down the lane. She had hoped Sissy might join them for Christmas Eve tonight, too. *No one should be alone on Christmas Eve,* Lorna thought as she closed the door. Sissy had insisted she couldn't be caught out in the snow. Though, when Lorna mentioned mincemeat pies, Sissy's resolve wavered. Lorna touched the top of the table, where she had begun to roll out the dough for the pies. She was almost sure Grayson wouldn't come either, but she would make him a pie all the same. She studied Afton's furrowed brows as she concentrated on the sock. Lorna smiled, savoring the unfamiliar sense of satisfaction. Afton's dress was complete. Many nights while Afton slept, Lorna had sat sewing by the fire. Last night she had added the finishing touch—the pearl buttons.

Lorna pressed her fists deep into the dough. She would roll the dough flat and cut it into small circles, which she would fill with gravy and minced turkey from the wild tom she and Afton had watched Harry miraculously capture up on the hill and drag home victorious. The first piece of usefulness she had seen from that dog, Lorna had thought but not spoken aloud. She would bake the pies near the coals of the fire until the crusts turned golden brown. With the leftover dough, she would form small, coin-sized pockets filled with wild raspberry jam she had made in early summer and stored for a special occasion. Lorna kneaded harder, the dough forming around the heel of her hand.

"How's this?" Afton asked, holding up Iain's sock. Lorna inspected the haphazard stitching along the toe that she knew would rip free the first time it was worn. But this sock would never again be worn.

"Not bad," she lied. She patted Afton on the head. "Do you want to try again?"

Afton groaned.

"Or you can go fetch more firewood," Lorna offered. Afton dropped the darning on the table, flew to the door, and flung it open. "Your coat!" Lorna called. Afton jerked her coat from its peg and, as she ran, shoved her arms into the sleeves.

Lorna turned to the fire to stir the mixture of turkey, onions, and gravy that bubbled in the pot. She wrapped her hand in her apron, pulled the pot away from the fire. A knock came at the door. She tucked a stray strand of hair behind her ear. The latch on the door snapped up, and the hinges whined as it opened. Had Lorna not recognized his fur coat, she never would have known Charles

Grayson stood at her door. His beard was trimmed close to his cheek and jaw. His wild hair was combed, smoothed down, as she remembered Iain doing each Sunday when preparing for church. Grayson clutched his hat in both hands. Afton, a skinny log under each arm, sauntered up behind Grayson.

"Hello, Mr. Gray—" Afton stared, just as Lorna stared, at the familiar yet foreign face. Only his blue eyes were the same. He looked at Afton. A thin smile appeared, and he took the logs from her.

"Do please come in," Lorna said, finding her voice. "So glad you've come."

Grayson looked down. Lorna did the same, seeing even his worn boots had been polished. He stared at the threshold as if deciding whether to cross it.

"Com'on in, Mr. Grayson." Afton broke the silence. She tugged at his coat sleeve and led him inside. He had to duck slightly to get through the door. His presence, the sheer size of him, seemed to fill the room. The bulk of his coat made him seem bearlike. Outside in the wide expanse of the world, he hadn't seemed so large. Inside, he seemed enormous. Even Afton stood for a moment looking up at him. Then, quick to recover, she began to pull on the sleeve of Grayson's coat. Lorna took his coat and hung it up. Wearing a tan flannel shirt, brown breeches, and black suspenders, Charles Grayson looked. . .ordinary. Well, not quite ordinary with his intense blue eyes that seemed to catch and weigh everything. Yet he looked like a man who belonged in a cabin eating dinner and speaking of the weather.

"Dinner's nearly ready," Lorna said. "Would you care to sit?"

"Actually," Afton jumped in, "Mr. Grayson and I have something. . .to take care of."

"But he's just arrived," Lorna replied, surprised. "He doesn't want to go back ou—" Before her objection could fully form, the two disappeared outside. Lorna watched from the window, the gloaming light throwing strange shadows and making it difficult to see properly. Grayson's donkey brayed as it was released from the hitching post, the inelegant sound making Lorna chuckle. She lit the lantern on the table then the one in the window. Three thin mouths pulled open on the surface of each pie as Lorna made three small slits to release steam as they baked. She set the pies atop hot stones at the side of the fireplace and set several stones around them to keep off the ash.

Kettle in hand, Lorna walked outside. The wind nipped at her nose and ears. Dense clouds hid the stars that should be appearing now, making the gathering night feel darker than usual. The air smelled of pine and snow. She dumped the dregs of tea from the kettle. Afton's giggle signaled the approach of her daughter and Grayson before the crunch of their footsteps. Lorna's breath fogged before her, and she hurried inside to get warm.

At dinner little was said. The sound of clinking utensils and the crackle of the fire seemed all that was needed. Harry's tail whumped against the floor as Afton donated to him pieces of her dinner. After the pies were finished and plates cleared, Lorna set out the jelly pasties. She placed the plate before Afton then caught Afton's hand as she lurched for the dessert.

"Wait for tea," Lorna instructed. In a flurry of tossing braids and flapping arms, Afton jumped from her chair, darted to her coat by the door, and pulled something from the pocket. She returned to Lorna with a small, burlap-wrapped parcel. The parcel she placed on the table as gently as though tending a newly hatched sparrow. Her eyes danced with firelight.

"Happy Christmas!" Afton said, looking proudly at Lorna.

Steam rose from the spout of the kettle Lorna held as she looked from Afton to the parcel and back to Afton. Swallowing down a lump that grew in her throat, Lorna set the kettle on an iron trivet atop the table. She peeled away the burlap. A china tea cup and saucer the color of pearls nestled inside the rough cloth. Lorna bit her lower lip to still its quiver.

Afton watched, wide-eyed. "Do you like it, Mama?"

Lorna traced her finger along perfect pink roses and leafy green vines that trailed along a surface as smooth as Afton's cheek. " 'O my Luve's like a red, red rose that's newly sprung in June,' " Lorna recited. She pulled Afton toward her. " 'O my Luve's like the melodie that's sweetly play'd in tune.' "

"That's Papa's favorite!"

Lorna kissed Afton's dimpled cheek. "Thank you, dear one." The logs in the fire shifted, sending sparks onto the hearth. "Wait here." Lorna walked to the bedroom. The trunk lid creaked as Lorna lifted it and retrieved Afton's dress. She dropped the chest lid without allowing herself a glance at Iain's kilt. She held the dress against her and walked from the bedroom.

"I had planned to give you this tomorrow," she said, "but right now seems. . .fitting."

Afton squealed and clapped her hands, her smile brighter, fuller, than Lorna had seen since Iain—

She handed the folded dress to Afton, who shook it open, pressed it against herself, and bent over, trying to see how it might look.

"Would you like to try it on?" Lorna asked. In answer, Afton rushed to the bedroom. A feeling of buoyant delight near to giddiness swelled in Lorna. She sat down, blinked at Grayson, just remembering his presence.

"I had planned to give her the dress tomorrow," Lorna repeated almost in apology. "I have only tea to offer you, I'm afraid. Though I also have sugar." A familiar ache frayed the edges of the moment's pleasure.

" 'Tis enough," he said and cleared his throat.

She retrieved the forgotten kettle and poured the tea. She placed the bowl of sugar before Grayson, though he did not take any. As she resumed her seat, she tried to remember him with the wild, shaggy beard and couldn't. It seemed as though he'd always looked this way. Lorna studied the smooth, white handle of her tea cup, the gracefulness of it. *Where would Grayson have gone had he not come tonight?* she wondered. *Does he feel the same deep ache I feel?*

"What do you—" She cleared her throat. "Where do you stay once the snow comes?"

The blue of Grayson's eyes faded slightly. Silence spooled between them. Lorna worried that she had misspoken.

"I rent a room in Detroit," he said. He lifted his cup to his lips then returned it to the table. "Though Sissy's offered a room if I help tend her animals. Maybe tend her fields next spring."

Lorna tilted her head. "You would work for Sissy?" The idea seemed so foreign. Sissy admitted to needing someone to plow and to plant, but it surprised Lorna that Sissy would ask Grayson for help. Though the more she thought about it, the more fitting it seemed.

" 'Tis a difficult life we lead." Grayson's words were measured, as though training serious thought on each one before allowing it to be spoken. "Alone is more alone here than elsewhere. Sissy knows to ask for help when it's needed." Lorna could hear Afton shuffling and talking to Harry behind the bedroom door. Lorna envisioned Afton touching each button, just as Lorna had touched her teacup.

"Do you ever think of leaving?" Lorna asked. From the window she could see the first snow begin to fall lightly on the dirty, pitted patches of old snow. The blanket of white created a smooth, seamless surface.

Grayson shook his head. "I'm where I'm s'posed to be."

"But you could start fresh. Have a family again." Lorna wanted to seize back her words, feeling she had stepped across an unseen, unmarked boundary. But Grayson didn't appear troubled. He set down his cup, circled his ruddy hands around it as though collecting warmth.

"If I was s'posed to have a family, I'd still have one."

Afton swept out from the shadows of the bedroom. Firelight seemed to set her aglow. She twirled. Her skirt flumed outward then settled against her legs. Giggles shook her as she ran to Lorna and wrapped her arms around her neck.

"It's perfect!" Afton said.

Lorna remembered that familiar blue beneath the tartan sash she had worn and smiled knowing her dress had new life. Harry barked, scampered to the door, and started to sniff. Lorna stood. Who would be out in this dark and snow? On Christmas Eve? Afton climbed into Lorna's chair and studied the teacup. Grayson rose, seeming to sense Lorna's uncertainty. Then a knock sounded. Lorna walked to the door, lifted the latch, and peered into the dark.

"Mrs. Findlay."

Lorna's hand tightened on the door as the beauty of the evening slipped away into the night.

Chapter 9

Do come in, Mr. Edgar." Lorna nudged Harry back with her foot so she could open the door wider. She looked at Grayson, who stood by the window, lips pursed, eyes half closed, as if trying to blend into the logged wall. Edgar, from where he stood outside the door, could not see Grayson. He held his hat in his hand, offering apologies. Though she hoped he would refuse, Lorna again asked him inside. A few brave snowflakes wisped in onto the floor and instantly melted. Edgar stepped forward.

"I thought being Christmas Eve you might like company," he said, as Lorna closed the door. He turned to hang his hat and froze, the peg he sought occupied by Grayson's coat. Edgar turned his stare from the fur coat to Grayson, who stood with his head tilted, watching.

"I see you don't lack for visitors," said Edgar. He clenched the brim of his hat in both fists. Lorna, feeling tense and awkward, offered Mr. Edgar tea. He declined with a shake of his head, but Lorna poured some anyway for something to do. Edgar fidgeted, shifting from side to side. He opened his mouth twice as if to speak then closed it again. Afton, a crease across her forehead, looked from Grayson to Edgar, Lorna's teacup in her hands.

"So you've come to stake your claim," Edgar said. His tone sounded playful, yet a sharp edge belied his civility.

Grayson, silent, moved to Afton and sat in the chair next to her—the table a barrier between himself and Edgar. Afton studied Grayson. He lifted the corner of his mouth in a half smile and winked. Afton returned his smile and tried to wink by squeezing both eyes closed. Lorna handed Edgar the cup of tea, which he took from her without taking his eyes from Grayson. Lorna searched for something—anything—to say.

"Mr. Grayson has been quite helpful to us, hasn't he, Afton?"

Afton nodded and made another attempt at winking. Grayson again gave her a small grin.

"I'm sure he has," Edgar said. He set his cup of tea on the table, untouched.

His eyes rose to the far corner of the ceiling. "Roof's finished, I see. You always were good with your hands."

Lorna stood by the fireplace, speechless, desperate for Edgar to leave yet reminded that he was still a friend. His argument—though it appeared one-sided—was with Grayson. Grayson tilted his head and caught Lorna's glance. His eyes seemed to convey something she couldn't quite read—something close to sadness.

"Are you friends?" Afton asked Grayson. She pointed to Edgar.

Edgar stepped toward Afton, his laugh loud and raspy. "Long ago, child," he answered. "But this man is no friend of mine. Not after he murdered my sister and her child."

Grayson leaped up, his chair crashing to the floor behind him. He lunged around the table at Edgar. Lorna sprang forward and, arms extended, set herself between the two men. Her heart hammered in her ears. The men glared at each other above the top of Lorna's head. Lorna touched the fist Grayson had formed. Slowly Grayson took a step back, though his breath came in quick gasps, his body rigid. Afton, wide eyed, started to cry. She stood by the table, fat tears falling down her cheeks. She ran to Lorna, who lifted her as she had when her daughter was small and would run to her with arms upheld. Lorna gasped at the ripping pain in her side. She nearly dropped Afton, but Afton clung to her, buried her face in Lorna's neck. Lorna could feel the teacup and saucer Afton still held pressing against her collarbone. She tried to breathe deeply, tried to ignore the pain radiating up into her chest and down her arm. She was afraid the red thread that closed her skin had broken. Yet she held tightly to Afton.

"Mr. Edgar, you really should leave." Lorna spoke through little gasps of painful breath. A new burning anger heated her words. Silence held sway for several seconds. Afton's cries faded. She grew heavy in Lorna's arms. Lorna's side throbbed, but she still held on.

"Aye," Edgar finally said, a cold stare aimed at Grayson, "Seems so."

Grayson's shoulders shifted as though shrugging off a weight. Lorna set Afton down, exhaling in quiet relief, and retrieved the lantern from the window.

"I'll see you out," she said. Edgar moved toward the door. With a moan, the door opened. Edgar took the lantern from Lorna and leaned toward her, his breath hot and rank with the sour scent of whiskey.

"Best beware, Mrs. Findlay"—Edgar's voice was a gruff whisper, yet clearly intended for everyone to hear—"or your bed is the next hole he'll be filling."

Lorna jerked away from the foulness as Grayson stormed from behind. One hand then another seized Edgar's coat. Harry began to bark. Edgar fought the grip, his fists flailing, but Grayson did not flinch. He shook Edgar like a child's rattle. Afton again started to cry. Wind and tufts of snow swirled in through the open doorway.

"She said leave," Grayson growled, his face inches from Edgar, whose face purpled, eyes bulged. The captive man grunted, cursed, and struggled to free himself. He swung a fist, hitting Grayson's shoulder. With his other hand he swung the lantern—his only weapon—at Grayson's head. Grayson ducked. The lantern, a bird in flight, soared over the table. Lorna gasped as it shattered against the wall, exploding into flames.

Lorna ran straight to Afton, who stood frozen. The sudden roar of the flames mottled and muffled all sound. Grayson threw the stammering Edgar out into the snow. Then Grayson seized his own coat and began beating at the spreading fire. Lorna grabbed hold of Afton's wrist and dashed to the door, where she snatched Afton's coat and hat. Harry ran alongside them, nearly tripping Lorna in the doorway. Once outside Harry bolted into the night. Lorna led Afton well back from the cabin, near the stream, and handed her daughter her coat and hat.

"Put them on!" she ordered then ran back inside. The flames ate at the roof, spreading across like an ink spill toward the newly mended corner. Grayson, face and arms streaked black, thrashed at the devouring flame. Dense smoke rolled over Lorna. Her eyes burned. Each breath seared her lungs. She snatched her coat and began to beat the fingers of fire along the wall. The roof creaked and groaned till a section splintered and gave way.

"Grayson!"

Grayson leaped aside as chunks of flame and wood collapsed, the debris catching his shoulder. He staggered, kicked through the rubble, ran to Lorna.

"Get out!" he yelled, grabbed her arm. More wreckage crashed onto the chair Lorna had occupied at dinner. Lorna coughed, gagged, feared another breath would never come. Grayson pulled her outside, her coat dragging behind. Its hem smoldered. Afton stood by the stream, her red coat aglow. Lorna stumbled to her, picked the hat up from the snow, and pulled it down over Afton's ears. Afton still pressed the teacup to her chest as though to shield it from the blaze. Lorna pulled Afton against her and looked again at their cabin through stinging tears. More splintering of wood. Through the doorway, Lorna saw it land on the table. She leaped to her feet, a wail tearing through her lungs, her throat. She sprinted toward the door. Grayson caught her arm.

"Iain's table!" Lorna shrieked. "I can't let it burn!"

As though far off, Lorna heard Afton screaming for her. Weeping, Lorna pleaded with Grayson to free her. Grayson clenched both her arms, his face a hair's breadth from hers.

"Wait."

The sound of the fire dimmed, and Lorna grew still, watching fragile flakes of snow collect in Grayson's hair. Grayson released her and sprinted with his coat to the stream. Then, his dripping coat over his head, he raced back into the inferno. Lorna dropped to her knees. She thought to pray, but words had lost meaning. Smoke and flame spurted through the front door, the front window, the roof. She was scantly aware of Afton coming beside her, clutching her arm. Snow—creamy like the china of her teacup—mingled with ash in the air. Lorna trembled. A roar grew in the bowels of the cabin. Then Grayson appeared in the doorway, his coat afire. He dove into the snow, threw off his coat, then ran back to the door. Inch by inch, he pulled Iain's table free.

The table was black and mangled, one of the legs gone, two still afire. Clear of the cabin, Grayson tipped the table on its side. The flames *hissed* and died in the snow. Lorna wrapped her arms around Afton, both of them shaking, Afton's tears warm on Lorna's neck. Lorna stared, almost mesmerized, at the relentless blaze. Grayson dropped to his knees beside her, his shirt torn at both shoulders. His face, neck, and hands were black. A final thundering—the death rattle—and the entire roof caved in. Lorna noticed blood staining the front of her dress, the red thread broken, her wound reopened. But she felt nothing. No pain—or perhaps pain of such intensity her mind refused it recognition.

Lorna turned away from the cabin, from the flames, to the barn to see Edgar mount his horse and skulk away. Night swallowed him; snow expunged his trail. The world seemed to hush. And Lorna waited. For the fire to end. For Afton's cries to subside. For God, who sees the sparrow, to appear. She waited as snow continued to fall, and the night was silent.

Chapter 10

Christmas Day 1830

Sensing morning, Lorna buried deeper into sleep. The surrounding warmth soothed her and brought forgetfulness till a soft whinny reminded her of where she was. She lay in the barn, hay beneath her. Several furs Grayson had pulled from his donkey blanketed her. Afton in her arms, Lorna had drifted to sleep. Now her arms were empty. Lorna sat up.

"She's gone looking for Harry."

The voice brought Lorna to her feet. Her coat smelled of ash. She shivered, wrapped a fur round her shoulders, and peered above Goldie's stall. Grayson stood saddling the mare. He looked across the animal at Lorna. "I dozed off near sunrise," he said. "She must've slipped out."

All breath left her. Lorna covered her face with her hands.

"Oh God," she whispered. "No more."

A single tear dripped free but none followed. Her eyes dried quickly with the cold. She looked up. Grayson stood before her, the wall of the stall between them. He was so near she could feel a tingle of his breath on her face. He closed his eyes. A calm settled on him, suffused the space between them. After several moments of watching in wonder, Lorna realized he was praying. His mouth didn't move. But strangely, he seemed to rise. A lifting of his being, though his feet stood firmly aground.

Lorna let go of the fur around her, grasped the top of the stall, and lowered her forehead to the wood between her hands. She closed her eyes, breathed in the calm. Words too had gone dry; prayer was beyond her. Yet it felt as though, by his nearness, Grayson's words would speak for them both.

"The storm is over." Grayson's voice was so close, Lorna drew sudden breath. "She's left clear tracks. I'll find her." Lorna didn't lift her head, only heard Grayson move off. Heard Goldie's hooves upon hay as she was led from the stall. Heard, though muffled by snow, horse and rider gallop away.

"Oh God." Lorna breathed again. She lifted her head. The teacup on Iain's workbench caught her eye. She turned away and shuffled to the barn door. Her numb fingers made buttoning her coat difficult. A button was missing, the hem of her coat singed and black. She hefted open the barn door to blinding white. The storm had ended, the world made new. Tree branches bent low with the weight of snow. Blue jays chattered back and forth. Sunbeams ignited the white banks of the stream. Lorna stepped out of the musty shadows of the barn into a patch of sun. The snow rose above her boots, nearly to her knees. Her breath clouded before her.

The smoldering remains of the cabin stood wraithlike against the bright world. Tall and whole, the stone chimney pointed skyward, its stones black but unmoved. The wood round the chimney looked like a charred ribcage. Tendrils of smoke rose in places. Several paces from where the front door had been, Iain's table lay on its side, snow mounded atop it. Lorna trudged toward it, forging a path through the snow. Her hands clenched and unclenched. Then she remembered Iain's gloves in her pockets. She felt somehow braver once she had them on.

At the table, its leg jutting out like a stiff carcass, Lorna brushed away the thick coat of snow. She walked around, hunkered down, and found the table's edge. She tried to hoist the table upright, then gasped, dropping it back into the snow. Gingerly she touched her side. Though she had resisted examining the injury, the bleeding seemed to have stopped. The stain on her dress, now hidden beneath her coat, felt stiff with blood long dried. She blew out a gust of air. Slowly, favoring her tender side, she stood the table on its three legs. The fire had gorged itself on the top, though it had not eaten completely through. Lorna raked her fingers across the crumbling wood, remembering Iain's voice soft in her ear, feeling a horrible relief that Iain would never know what had happened here. Her relief was replaced by anger—anger she could not explain. And then fear.

Lorna shoved her hands into her pockets. She walked to the front of the cabin, the threshold disintegrating underfoot. A tingling warmth emanated from the smoldering ruins. A few stones of the fireplace had broken free, but it appeared mostly intact. Lorna kicked some rubble aside and stooped to pull the iron cooking pot from the ash. It was empty. The remains of their dinner burnt to nothing. With scrubbing, the pot could still be used. Lorna shook her head to clear it. The eddying smoke brought a strange dizziness, a surreal headiness.

Pot in hand, she walked from the cabin toward the stream, dragging her feet through the snow as she went. Movement was labored, but she needed a path. Her return would be easier for it. At the stream she pounded at the thin, newly formed layer of ice with the pot, smashing a hole to reach the water that rushed—as it always did—beneath the surface. Lorna filled the bottom of the pot, swished the water around, then dumped it. Rivulets spread and quickly froze, black flecks of charred debris marring the opaque ice. Even with Iain's gloves, Lorna's hands ached from cold. Her shoulders shook. The tears were upon her cheeks before she realized she shook from her cries.

A stifling weight fell on Lorna. A weight she was helpless to throw off. Her eyes lifted to the hill, the same hill Harry would loll about on, where the tips of giant firs seemed to reach into the clouds. The hill where an empty grave sat and a placard memorialized the man she loved. The rising sun climbed behind her, the snow of the hill reflecting it with such intensity Lorna was forced to look away. *Trust in the Lord, my sweet,* Iain had said. She had trusted, but heartbreak had come. Three babies dead. Iain disappeared. Their home destroyed. Now Afton. . . *Keep hold a hope,* said Sissy. Lorna dropped the pot into the snow. She knelt, rocking back and forth, her tears unattended, unnoticed. *He sees the sparrow.* Lorna squinted at the sky. The unfettered sun shone on everything alike. She closed her eyes and understood her fear. Fear of finding that, in the end, God was not good. Was indifferent to her pain. Did not see the sparrow. Her fear suffocated more than the smoke that had choked her. Fear, a boulder, compressed her chest, her hope.

The warble of birdsong trilled from the trees. Lorna stopped rocking. She opened her eyes, lifted her chin. *Keep hold of hope.*

"I trust You."

The prickling wind and the burbling water beneath the ice smothered her words. She said it again, this time louder. Her chin rose higher. Breath came—in and out, in and out—more easily. And she understood for the first time freedom. The freedom born in trust. She grasped the handle of the pot, leaned forward, and again filled it. Two cardinals flapped from a nearby spruce and chased each other over the water, their crimson feathers creating red ribbons across the ice. Lorna paused to watch.

A shadow passed across the sun. Then the sun burst free, seeming to shine all the brighter. Lorna stood. Two figures appeared on the hilltop. The beat of her heart quickened. Had Grayson found Afton? No, it was two men. She studied them as they began to descend the hill. They wore tanned buckskin, furs.

Indians.

They were halfway down the hill. Lorna's hand tightened around the handle of the pot. She had no weapon—Iain's musket lost to the fire. The snow made movement difficult, running impossible. One Indian with long black hair—she could see him now—lifted an arm. She knew she was spotted. Her stomach churned, heart hammered. She began to backtrack along the path she had plowed, back toward the table. Wincing, she tipped the table back on its side, leaned her weight on the black, grizzled leg until, with a crunching sound, it broke off into the snow. She could still fight.

They would be here soon. The wind had died. The birds in the trees were silent. All Lorna could hear was the racketing of her own heart. Her side throbbed. Then she heard the *shwa, shwa* of footsteps through snow. The two Indians appeared round the woodpile between the house and barn. Lorna lifted her weapon—the table leg—above her head. Her eyes wide, focused.

"Lorna?"

Her heart pounded up near her throat. The second Indian with a thick black beard and fur cap raised a white hand. She blinked, lifted the table leg higher.

"Lorna."

She shook her head, could feel her breath come in quick gasps. The man removed his hat, his dark hair thick and curling. He stepped toward her, and she instinctively pointed the leg of wood directly at him as if a loaded musket. He stopped. His brown eyes moist, watching her.

"It cannot be," she whispered through an erupting sob. "Iain?"

Her legs refused to support her. She dropped to her knees, her weapon falling useless into the snow. Iain ran toward her, the snow parting like the waters of the Jordan. She felt his arms surround her. His breath in her hair. She pressed her face to his neck and breathed the scent of him. Lorna lifted her head. Her hands gripped the front of his coat in refusal to let go.

"You're alive."

"Ay," Iain smiled. "Barely, but alive."

Lorna shook her head. "I saw the blood. So much"—her voice caught—"so much blood."

Again Iain nodded. "I felled the tree and did nae move away fast enough," he said, pointing to the side of his head. The red line of a freshly healing wound ran from his forehead, along his temple, and down behind his ear. "I would have died, surely, but Lalawethika here"—he nodded at the Indian behind him— "found me. Carried me to his Shawnee village, tended to me. When it was time for them to move on, move south, they took me along. I wasn't conscious of time or place for weeks." Iain leaned forward, brushed his lips against Lorna's. Lorna traced her fingers over her husband's familiar face. Along his woolly jaw. His dimple hidden in the underbrush of beard. "When finally I woke, I tried to send word, but there was only wilderness. No settlements, trading posts. The only word I could send was to bring myself home."

Lorna's hands, nose, and ears were numb. Her knees soaked through. But she could not bring herself to move for fear of Iain disappearing.

"How far have you traveled?" she finally asked.

"Eight days," Iain replied. "We would have arrived sooner, but we lost our way in the storm."

Lorna turned toward the blackened skeleton of their home. "And now there is no home left." She sniffed, wiped a sleeve beneath her nose. "The fire. It took it all. And now Afton—"

Iain's laugh startled her. "The fire saved us!" Iain's smile was as bright as sun on snow. "Had we not seen the blaze, we would have frozen to death wandering in the forest. That fire led us through the storm." Iain leaned forward, slowly, as though afraid Lorna might dissolve, and kissed her.

"Papa!"

Lorna leaped to her feet, wincing, pressing a hand to her side. Afton, holding tight to Grayson on the back of Goldie, wriggled and waved wildly. Harry, alongside, pounced through the snow. Iain and Lorna both pushed past the blackened table toward Afton. As Iain reached Goldie, Afton flung herself into his upheld arms.

"That's my wee lass!" he said, his voice muffled in Afton's hair. Lorna wrapped her arms around the pair, emotion stealing her voice. Goldie shifted her weight, and Lorna looked up at Grayson. His eyes were closed, his face lifted to the sun.

"Where have you been, my girl?" Iain asked.

"Looking for Harry," Afton replied as though it were nothing of consequence. "I found him. Then Mr. Grayson found me."

Iain, as though for the first time, noticed the man astride his own horse and extended his hand. "I thank you, sir."

"We have much to thank Mr. Grayson for," Lorna said.

A brusque "Halloo!" brought everyone looking down the lane as Sissy, astride one horse and leading another, rode into the clearing.

"Sissy!" Afton squealed. "God brought Papa home! A Christmas miracle!"

"Suppose it's to my house for tea then," Sissy called back.

The journey to Sissy's was slow. Iain had asked Lalawethika, whom Iain called simply Thika, to come with them, share a meal before his journey home. Thika shook his head. Iain said Lalawethika in Shawnee meant "he makes noise." He seemed to understand what Iain was saying, but Thika never uttered a word. *He must make noise elsewhere,* Lorna thought. Thika shifted his shoulders, signaled with his head toward the hill. Iain extended his hand, and the Indian grasped it.

"Thank you," Iain said. With bobbing head, Thika turned and treaded back the way he came till he disappeared behind the hemlock on the hill where rested the memorial for Iain—now buried beneath the snow.

Once the barn was battened tight, they rode—Lorna with Iain, Afton with Sissy. Grayson tied Nanny and his own donkey to his saddle horn, neither beast cooperative. They stopped once because Nanny had eaten through her rope, but the snow was too deep for her to run off. Harry waggled and bounded through the snow to keep up. Sissy's cabin came in sight. The sun had lasted long enough for their arrival. Then it stowed its rays and slipped away to the sound of Iain and Afton singing Christmas carols. Grayson, Iain—and Afton, too, who wouldn't leave her Papa's side—walked to the barn to put up all the animals, while Sissy and Lorna tromped in to make an impromptu Christmas meal. Sissy hunkered in front of the fireplace, stoking the dormant coals. The fire leaped to life.

"We've work to do," Sissy said, dusting off her hands. They walked to where several jars of preserves sat on the table alongside a portion of smoked ham and a globe of dough for biscuits. Lorna attacked the dough while Sissy cut the ham into thick slices.

"You'll be needin' a place to roost till spring," Sissy said. She didn't look up or stop the movement of her knife through the meat.

Lorna paused, her fingers pressing holes—like rabbit burrows—into the dough.

"I suppose we will," she said.

"If that husband of yours don't mind bunkin' with Grayson," Sissy nodded, still studying the ham, "you's are welcome here."

"Are you sure, Sissy?" Lorna knew they could find a room in Spring Wells—or even Detroit—if needed. She would feel like an imposition if they stayed here.

Sissy snorted. "Wouldn't offer if I wasn't." She raised her eyes. "Be nice to have the rafters full again. Grayson said he might try his hand at farming, and my fields have been fallow long 'nough. Seems we're all tired of lonely."

Lorna reached across the table and squeezed Sissy's hand. "Sissy, I don't recall ever hearing you talk this way. I do believe you're fond of us." Sissy snorted again and stabbed her knife into the ham.

Soon they all sat round the table, fed and thankful. Lorna reached over to Iain sitting next to her and claimed his hand. He gave her a wink. Sissy retrieved her Bible from the mantel and handed it to Grayson, instructing him to read from the second chapter of the book of Luke, the story of the first Christmas. Grayson's voice was quiet and expressive as he read of the journey of Joseph and Mary. Afton, next to Iain, squirmed in her seat. Iain lifted her from her chair and set her on his lap. Her head against Iain's shoulder, Afton fingered the pearly buttons on her blue Christmas dress—now the only dress she possessed. Grayson read of the angels and the shepherds. The candles on the table flickered as though excited by the appearance of heavenly hosts.

" 'And the shepherds returned,' " Grayson read, " 'glorifying and praising God for all the things that they had heard and seen, as it was told unto them.' " He closed the Bible, placed it on the table. No one spoke. Softly Iain started to sing a song from the Scottish psalter, an old song Lorna remembered singing while standing amid the pews of the stone parish church of her childhood:

"Praise ye the Lord for it is good,
Praise to our God to sing,
For it is pleasant and to praise,
It is a comely thing."

Iain's sonorous tenor expanded, filling the room. He gave Lorna's hand a squeeze. Lorna, warmth spreading through her, began to hum:

"Those that are broken in their heart
and grieved in their minds
He healeth, and their painful wounds
He tenderly up-binds.
He counts the number of the stars;
He names them every one.
Great is our Lord, and of great pow'r;
His wisdom search can none."

Sissy began to serve the tea. Lorna sipped from her rosebud teacup that

Afton had carried through the snow to Sissy's. Iain shifted Afton on his lap and spooned into his cup two lumps of sugar. *Such extravagance*, Lorna thought and smiled. She turned to the window—to the clear night, silent and spread with stars. The snow returned the starlight and set the world aglow.

A Pony Express Christmas

Margaret Brownley

Dedication

This story was written in memory of the brave young horsemen who risked life and limb to deliver the mail for the Pony Express.

The LORD is my rock, and my fortress, and my deliverer;
my God, my strength, in whom I will trust.
PSALM 18:2

Pony Express Rider Oath

I, _____, do hereby swear, before the Great and Living God, that during my engagement, and while I am an employee of Russell, Majors, and Waddell, I will, under no circumstances, use profane language, that I will drink no intoxicating liquors, that I will not quarrel or fight with any other employee of the firm, and that in every respect I will conduct myself honestly, be faithful to my duties, and so direct all my acts as to win the confidence of my employers, so help me God.

WANTED

Young, skinny, wiry fellows. Not over 18. Must be expert riders. Willing to risk death daily. Orphans preferred.

—California newspaper, 1860

Chapter 1

Nebraska Territory, 1862

Are we there, yet?
—Carved into Chimney Rock in 1861 by Jimmy Watts, age eight

Oh no you don't!" Hands at her waist, Ellie-May Newman glared at the back of her fast-retreating trail guide. She'd paid the man good money to take her to Chimney Rock, but at the least sign of trouble, he'd taken off like a horse with his tail afire.

Chasing after him, she stumbled over a rock. "Come back, you hear? Come back or I'll—"

By the time she scrambled to her feet, it was too late to follow through with her threats. Already the scrawny lad had leaped into his saddle and raced away.

Sputtering, she marched back to her covered wagon and gave the broken wheel a good kick. It did nothing for the wagon and didn't do much for her foot either, except make her want to scream.

A fine pickle! Now she was stranded in the wilds of Nebraska Territory with two stubborn mules, a disabled wagon, and 190 miles still to go. All because her guide thought he saw a couple of. . .

Indians!

With a quick glance around, she choked back a cry and rushed to the wagon for her double-barrel shotgun. Weapon in hand, she turned slowly and scanned the nearby woods. A slight breeze rustled the trees and tugged at the hem of her knee-high skirt and bloomers.

Betsy the mule perked her ears forward—not a good sign. Next to her, Josie flipped her skinny tail and turned her short thick head toward the thick growth of trees at the side of the rutted trail.

Ellie-May followed the mule's gaze, and her nerves tensed. After seeing nothing for days but brown prairie grass and prickly pear cactus, the tall cedars had been a welcome sight. But since her guide ran out of those very same woods looking like he'd seen a ghost, danger now seemed to lurk behind every moving shadow.

Holding her shotgun as steady as trembling hands allowed, Ellie-May ducked under a low piney branch. Ever so softly, she stepped over a fallen tree trunk and crossed a dry gully. A twig snapped beneath her foot, and she jumped. She stopped and listened. Tom-toms! She was just about to turn and run when she realized that the thumps came from her fast-beating heart.

Moistening her lips, she moved forward on what seemed like wooden limbs. The trees closed in overhead, blocking out the hazy sun. No bird call joined the chorus of whispering wind and pounding heart.

She stepped into a small clearing. *Voices.* Something moved, and she ducked behind a tree. Holding her breath, she peered ever so cautiously around the trunk. Two saddled horses were tied to a bush. Her fool guide was wrong; those weren't Indian horses.

Head low, she followed the sound of voices to where three men stood. Two had their backs turned. Only the top of the third man's head was visible.

She hesitated, but only because she didn't want to interrupt what sounded like an argument. *God, please don't let them be robbers or murderers or. . .or worse.*

Gathering as much courage as she could muster, she called out, "H–hello there."

Two men swung around, and one reached to his side for his gun. After looking her up and down, he withdrew his hand with a smirk.

She was used to people laughing at her bloomers, but this man had the nerve to leer. She kept her shotgun pointed straight at him. A woman alone couldn't afford to take chances.

"Well, what have we here?" He raked her up and down with bloodshot eyes; a toothless grin parted a scraggly beard.

"I wonder if you would be kind enough to help—" She realized with a start that the middle man's hands were tied and he had a rope around his neck. The other end of the rope was slung over a tree branch and tied to the saddle of one of the horses. Dumbstruck, she could only stare.

The man pointing a gun at the prisoner's chest didn't fare much better than his partner, appearance-wise, though he was a tad thinner. A nasty red scar cut a path from his brow to his chin whiskers, making his face appear lopsided.

Scarface looked her up and down, while next to him, Toothless lifted a brown jug to his mouth and took a swig. The two hangmen weren't exactly drunk, but they weren't exactly sober either.

Of the three strangers, the one with the rope around his neck, looked the most promising. Or at least the most clearheaded.

Swallowing, she found her voice. "Surely you don't intend to hang that man." They didn't look like lawmen, at least no lawmen she'd had occasion to meet.

"Found him snoopin' around," Toothless said. "Cain't have no thievery."

Doubting that Toothless and his partner had anything worth stealing, she studied the prisoner. The whiskers shadowing his square-cut jaw didn't seem to belong with his neatly trimmed hair. Cut shorter than the current style, his brown hair fell to the side of his head from a single part. Intense cobalt eyes appeared to be conveying a private message.

Scarface spat, and a stream of chewing tobacco hit the ground with a plop. "As you can see, ma'am, we're kind of occupied at the moment. So 'less you have bus'ness here, I suggest you mosey along."

She pulled her gaze away from the captive. "I'll leave. Soon as you tell me where I might find a nearby farm or ranch."

Toothless scratched his chest. "Used to be about ten miles north, but you won't find nothin' there now. Indians burned it to the ground."

Her heart sank. Since leaving St. Jo, good news had been scarce as hen's teeth.

"How far to Plum Creek?"

"I'd say about fifteen miles. What do you say, Big Red?"

His partner nodded. "Sounds 'bout right to me."

She would never make it that far on foot before nightfall. That would mean spending the night alone on the trail without so much as a guide.

"Is there nothing closer?" she asked.

Toothless hung his thumbs from his suspenders. "You look like one a them—whatcha callums—a modern miss." The gummy smile grew bigger. "So you probably won't take no offense if me and my pardner here invite you back to our cabin. It's only a half mile downstream." He took another gulp, tossed the empty brown jug to the ground, and wiped his mouth with his shirt sleeve. "You're welcome to stay long as you want. We'll show you a good time."

Scarface concurred. "A *real* good time." He licked his lips and scratched his belly with his weapon-free hand.

She glanced at the jug on the ground and then swung her gaze to the prisoner. "I can offer you both a better time."

Big Red's eyes grew round as wagon wheels. "Can you now?"

"I'll give you twenty-five dollars to let the prisoner go." It was money she could ill-afford to part with. The proceeds from the sale of the family farm would have to last until she found another source of income, and who knew how long that would take? Already the trip had cost more than she'd planned. Still, she wasn't about to let a man be hanged at the whim of a couple of hard-drinking scoundrels.

"You can buy a lot of moonshine for twenty-five bucks," she added.

Toothless considered this a moment before advancing toward her. "I like our plan better."

"Don't. . .don't come any closer, or I'll shoot." She pointed her shotgun and thumbed back the hammer. The *shh-click-click* of metal did what her threats failed to do; stopped him in his tracks.

"Now what'sha want to go and do that fer?" he slurred.

She stepped back. The heel of her boot snagged on a tree branch, and her feet flew out from under her. Just as her backside hit the ground, her shotgun fired. The blast blew the hat clear off his head. He turned white and slapped his hands on top of his shiny bald pate.

Her mouth dropped open. If she was in any way responsible for the lack of fur on his head, she'd proven herself a better shot by accident than she ever was on purpose.

Fortunately, she managed to regain her composure before Toothless found his. She staggered to her feet, and moving her finger to the second trigger, swung the barrel of her gun from man to man.

The captive's gaze followed her shotgun from side to side. He looked more worried about her weapon than the rope around his neck.

She cleared her voice. "Twenty-five dollars for your friend there. Do we have a deal or don't we?"

Toothless looked at Scarface, who shrugged. He then turned back to Ellie-May. "Deal."

She nodded. Whew! That was close. Confidence restored, she lifted her chin and rose to her full five-foot-five height. "Now tell your friend to put away his gun and cut the prisoner loose."

Toothless reached for his crownless hat. He slapped the felt brim on his head, and his shiny bald cranium stuck out like an egg in a nest. "You heard the lady," he slurred.

Scarface pulled an Arkansas toothpick out of his waist and cut the rope. He then replaced his knife.

"Now step away from him," she ordered, indicating with her weapon where she wanted them to go. She reached into her skirt pocket, drew out two gold coins—one a double eagle— and tossed them onto the ground. "Not git, both of you!"

Scarface scooped up the money and ran, spurs jingling, toward the horses, his partner at his heels. Soon the pounding of hooves signaled their fast departures.

The prisoner picked his wide-brim hat off the ground, slapped it against his thigh, and pressed it on his head. He stood straight and tall, shoulders wide, giving his dusty trousers, rumpled shirt, and wrinkled vest more dignity than they deserved.

"Thank you, ma'am. Sure appreciate it. The name's Corbett. Michael Corbett. And you are. . . ?"

"Ellie-May Newman."

"Much obliged, Miss Newman." He then turned and casually walked away, the second man to do so that day.

"Wait!" she yelled. "Where do you think you're going?" He kept walking, so she lifted the shotgun skyward and fired.

That stopped him. He held his back toward her for a full moment before making a slow turn. "Gonna get the horse those hombres stole from me."

She frowned. "That sounds like a bad idea."

"I paid ten dollars for that sorry mare not two days ago."

"And I paid twenty-five dollars for you."

He hung his thumbs from his vest pockets. "That was your mistake, ma'am. I'm not worth more than fifteen."

"Maybe so, but I intend to get what I paid for."

He considered this a moment before asking, "And what might that be, Miss Newman?"

"You, Mr. Corbett, are going to help me find my brother."

Chapter 2

Traveled 1,000 miles and aged 10 years.
At this rate I'll be an old man by Christmas.
—Carved into Chimney Rock in 1862 by Edgar Dobbs

Mike Corbett circled Miss Newman's covered wagon. It was a simple farm conveyance, homemade by the looks of it, and fitted with a canvas bonnet. The wagon had seen better days, but he doubted the mules had. The woman said she was heading for Chimney Rock. She had to be kidding. She'd be lucky to make it to the next farm.

"Where'd you get them mules?" he asked.

"They belonged to my pa, and I kept them when I sold the farm," she said. "Bought the wagon from a neighbor." After a pause, she added, "Cost less than you did."

"I believe it."

The iron rim on the back left wheel had slipped and the wood cracked, but at least Miss Newman had the good sense to carry a spare.

"Tools?" he asked.

"In the wagon."

He walked to the back and peered inside the wagon bed. Two polished wooden trunks sat side by side. He opened the nearest one, and a faint smell of lavender wafted from its depths. A white lacey garment lay on top of a pile of neatly folded clothes. His gaze traveled through the inside of the wagon.

He could see Miss Newman tending the mules through the canvas opening in front. She'd removed her floppy straw hat, and tendrils of blond hair had slipped out of her bun and blew around her face.

She was pretty, he realized with a start. Mighty pretty. Couldn't imagine why it took so long to notice, unless it was that confounded outfit. *Is that what women wore these days? Knee-high skirts over ankle-bound trousers? A man is locked away for two years, and look what happens.*

His gaze settled on the satiny underriggings in the trunk. It was hard to believe that the strong-willed, gun-wielding woman would favor such feminine frippery. Especially one who obviously preferred comfort and practicality over fashion. He closed the lid of the first trunk and opened the second.

This one was filled with bolts, linchpins, skeins, and nails. It also held a homemade jack.

She left him alone as he worked, and in no time at all, he'd changed the wheel and checked the other three.

He hung the broken wheel on the outside of the wagon and returned the tools to their proper place, but he couldn't help taking another look at the wooden trunk carrying the lady's apparel. The sweet smell of lavender still lingered in the air. Deprived of anything pleasant for longer than he cared to remember, he allowed himself the luxury of inhaling the delicate fragrance for a moment before turning away.

At the nearby stream, he washed his hands and face, the cold water stinging his skin. Still, it felt good. Just being alive and free felt good.

He still couldn't believe he'd let those ruffians sneak up on him. Nothing like that would have happened in the past. The last two years hadn't just knocked the stuffing out of him but had evidently dulled his senses.

Returning to camp, he accepted a cup of coffee from the lady. It was hot and strong, just as he liked it. The smell of bacon sizzling over a campfire made his stomach growl, and he tried to recall the last time he ate anything that smelled that good.

Miss Newman sat by the fire and tended the bacon, allowing him to study her unnoticed. In the light of the fast-fading sun, her hair looked like spun gold.

"Soon as you reach civilization, you better have a blacksmith repair that wheel to use as a spare."

"I'll do that, Mr. Corbett."

He leaned against the wagon and sipped his coffee. The crisp air promised a cold night ahead. The blanket spread out on the ground was set with two tin plates and silverware.

"Why are you looking for your brother?" he asked.

She glanced up at him. "He's missing."

"I figured that."

She stabbed at the bacon with a fork and placed the strips one by one on a tin plate. "He was a Pony Express rider. After the company shut down last fall, I expected him to come back home to the farm. He didn't."

"No surprise there. Once a man sees the world, he's not likely to want to go back to his old ways."

"Speaking from experience, Mr. Corbett?"

"Experience is all I have, ma'am."

She studied him a moment before rising to her feet. She set the plate in the center of the blanket, along with a loaf of bread. "Sorry I can't offer you more."

He sat on a rock next to the blanket. "Looks mighty appetizin'." He filled his plate and gobbled his food. He'd almost forgotten how good a meal could taste.

Aware that she was staring at him, he frowned.

"What?"

"Would you care to join me in grace, Mr. Corbett?"

"Anything you say, ma'am." He dropped his fork and lowered his head and tried to remember the last time he'd talked to the Lord. Giving thanks for the slop fed him over the last two years would have been an insult to God.

The moment she said *amen*, he dove back into his food, giving no mind to manners. That would come later. Now he had to fill the hunger gnawing at his insides.

"So when's the last time you heard from your brother?" he asked between bites.

"It's been awhile, and there's been nothing from him since the Pony Express stopped running. However, I did receive a package from the Russell, Majors, and Waddell Company."

"The express firm."

She nodded. "The package contained a small calfskin Bible with his name inside. I tried contacting them for more information, but the company was bought out, and no one knows what happened to the records."

"Every express rider was given a Bible and a gun," he said. The riders had been told to use the Bible at all times and the gun only when necessary. Seemed to him they got that backwards.

"The package contained nothing else. Not even a sketch."

He looked up from his plate. "A sketch?"

"My brother was an artist." She reached into a pocket and drew out a sheet of paper, which she carefully unfolded. It was a drawing. "It's called Chimney Rock," she explained, "but my brother named it the Hand of God." She pointed to the tall, funnel-shaped rock surrounded by clouds. "He said this was God's finger pointing the way."

Corbett was no expert in art, but even he could see the boy had talent. "It's a fine drawing." His compliment brought a smile to her face, and he suddenly realized how young she was—probably no more than nineteen or twenty.

She carefully refolded the paper. "His dream is that one day his work will be displayed in art galleries around the world and maybe even kings' palaces."

He wiped his mouth with the back of his hand and reached for the remainder of the bread. Her brother's aspirations struck him as odd. Who cared what hung on obscure walls viewed only by the rich or elite? Nonetheless, he envied the boy his dreams. Been a long time since he had dreams of his own.

"You said the company mailed the Bible to you," he said.

She nodded. "That's what makes me believe my brother's in trouble. He would never willingly give up his Bible."

He helped himself to more bacon and slapped it on the bread. "How do you propose finding him?"

"I think Chimney Rock might have been his home station. I hope to find a ledger or records of some kind with his current address—maybe even someone who knows him. If not, I'll visit every last Pony Express station between there and Sacramento. I've already checked the ones between here and St. Jo."

He did some quick calculations and thought out loud. "The stations are placed approximately ten to twenty miles apart, depending on terrain and water supplies. That means there has to be something like—"

"A hundred and ninety. Many are deserted, and a few are in ruins." After a short pause, she added, "I hope I don't have to travel as far as Sacramento."

He glanced at the rickety wagon and two homely mules. "Me, too, ma'am. Me, too."

She took a dainty bite of bacon before continuing. "That's why I need your help, Mr. Corbett. I need someone to keep the wagon in good repair."

He gazed at the wagon again, but when a vision of white lace came to mind, he quickly looked away. "And who is going to fight off Indians and robbers?"

She slanted her head. "I was hoping you could help me in that regard. I have a spare gun you can use and—"

"You gonna trust me with a gun?" He stuffed another piece of bacon in his mouth. "You know nothing about me."

"I know you have an honest face. I doubt you're a thief like those men said." She tossed a nod at the empty plates and raised her eyebrows. "I also know you have a voracious appetite."

He leaned forward "And here's what you *don't* know. I'm not crazy." He tossed away the grounds from his coffee cup. "It's almost December. Do you know what that means? Has it occurred to you why one of the busiest western-bound trails is now deserted? Anyone with half a brain knows not to start a journey this late in the year."

"My trail guide assured me we would reach Castle Rock before the winter snows!"

"And you believed him?" He glanced around. "And where is your trail guide now?"

Two spots of red flared on her cheeks "He. . .he ran off."

"Smart man." Corbett reached for the coffeepot and filled his cup. If he had a lick of sense, he'd follow in the trail guide's tracks. He set the pot down. "You haven't the chance of a bug in an anthill of making it to Chimney Rock before it snows. Not with that wagon."

"Oh ye of little faith," she said.

He narrowed his eyes. Did she think this was some sort of joke? "Indians and thieves are the least of it. Have you ever been in a blizzard?"

"We have blizzards in Iowa."

"Then you know it's cold and miserable and you can't see a blasted thing."

She rose from the blanket. "I guess we won't have to worry about being attacked, then, will we, Mr. Corbett? If we can't see a thing, neither can anyone else."

Chapter 3

What war?
—Carved into Chimney Rock in 1862 by Deadwood Dave Hugo

Ellie May couldn't sleep. The night was filled with sounds. Identifying them gave her little peace of mind. With every coyote howl and owl's hoot, she imagined Indians creeping through the dark, tomahawks raised.

Fearing she would wake and find Mr. Corbett gone, she kept peering out of the wagon to the dark shape on the ground. Odd as it seemed, she found comfort in the surly man's presence even as he slept.

She felt in the dark for her brother's Bible and clutched it to her chest. *Where are you, Andy?*

The day her brother left home seemed like only yesterday. He had no interest in taking over the family farm and spent every spare moment with his sketch pads.

Their father was a simple man with no appreciation for art. Manual labor is what he knew, so he and her brother argued. But the day Andy left home was the worst, for that was the day her father tossed her brother's drawings into the fire. She'd tried to save them, burning her hands in the process, but it was too late. It was also too late to stop her brother from leaving, never to return.

Her papa wept after Andy left. Realizing what he had done, he shoveled the ashes out of the fireplace as if to make amends. He buried them in the family plot next to Mama, who would have loved Andy's work.

Papa was never the same after that day. He had been fighting a cough for months, and after Andy left, it seemed to take over his entire body. On his deathbed, he made her promise to find Andy. "Ask him to forgive me," he pleaded.

It was the first time he'd mentioned Andy's name in more than two years. Now the memory brought tears to her eyes, and she whispered in the darkness. "I'll find him, Papa. I promise."

It was almost dawn by the time she fell asleep. She woke a short while later to the scent of freshly brewed coffee.

She dressed, ran a brush through her long tresses, and pinned her hair into a bun before stepping out of the wagon.

Mr. Corbett sat on a fallen log, drinking coffee from a tin cup. Her map was spread on the ground in front of him. She'd taken great pains to mark each Pony Express station with an X, and he traced the line she'd drawn with his finger.

"I see you decided to stay," she said. She'd honestly feared he would desert her in the middle of the night.

He looked up. "Wouldn't get very far without a horse."

"I reckon not," she said.

She grabbed a flour-sack towel and a bar of soap and walked to the stream to wash. When she returned, Mr. Corbett handed her a cup of coffee.

"Thank you." She moved closer to the fire for warmth.

"We need to talk." His tone was as brusque as his manner.

"Save your breath. I'm not turning back." She took a sip of the hot brew.

"So you said." He hesitated. "You should know that I spent two years in prison."

She choked and spilled her coffee.

He waited for her to recover before adding, "Don't look so worried. I didn't escape. I served my full term."

She stared at him. Was that why he acted like he hadn't had a decent meal in a month of Sundays? And why he looked as lean as a desert grasshopper?

"I'm relieved to hear that, Mr. Corbett." An ex-prisoner was better than an escaped one, or at least she hoped so.

"I was on the way to Omaha when I spotted a cabin. Thought I could get a meal there. Instead, I got attacked by those two scoundrels."

"Do you mind telling me why you were in prison?" she asked. "You didn't. . .kill anyone, did you?"

"Only in the line of duty," he drawled. "I was a U.S. deputy marshal, but when I refused to do what they asked of me, I got hauled off to prison."

"Most people simply get fired for refusing to do a job."

He scoffed. "Most people aren't expected to track down runaway slaves like animals."

"Is that why you went to prison?" She studied him. "Because you refused to chase down slaves?"

"There's a thousand-dollar fine for not obeyin' the Fugitive Slave law." He shrugged. "When I refused to pay it, they locked me up." After a beat, he added, "Sometimes a man has to stand for what he believes in."

"So does a woman, Mr. Corbett. Which is why I refuse to turn back until I find my brother."

He eyed her over the rim of his cup as he sipped his coffee. "What makes you think you'll find him? It's a big country. A man can get lost out there."

"My brother and I are twins."

"What's that supposed to mean? You got some sort of special bond or something?" His voice held a note of mockery, which she ignored.

"Not only do my brother and I look similar, we think alike. When we were children, he had the habit of wandering off. I was the only one who could find him. I intend to do so again."

He lowered his cup and stared at the map. "I'll stay with you as far as Chimney Rock, but that's all." He cast a glance at the mules. "Twenty miles a day should get us there in little more than two weeks. I doubt the weather will hold that long, but we can hope. If you don't find your brother, my advice is to get you a place to stay till spring."

She bit her lip. Her chances of finding a place to stay in the wilderness ahead looked mighty slim.

"Twenty miles a day, huh?" Out of those mules? That she had to see. "Why have you decided to help me?"

"I didn't decide anything. You paid twenty-five dollars for me. I aim to give you your money's worth."

॰ॐ

Later, after he'd hitched the mules to the wagon, the lady offered him a gun in a holster.

He couldn't believe it. "You gonna trust me with that?" he asked. "Even after I told you I was in prison?"

"It's because of what you told me that I trust you," she said.

He shrugged. No accounting for the way a woman's mind worked. He took the holster and checked out the gun. It was a Smith and Wesson. He'd prefer a Colt Dragoon, but beggars couldn't be choosers. The firearm was loaded.

He buckled the holster around his waist. The heavy gun drooped to his side, but it felt good to be armed. If he had a horse, he'd feel almost normal.

The lady watched him like a hawk. If the dubious look on her face gave any indication, she already had second thoughts about trusting him with a weapon.

"We better get started," he said gruffly. "Got a long day ahead."

Chapter 4

Been lost for three weeks straight.
That's the last time I'll let a woman read a map!
—Painted on Chimney Rock in 1860 by Walter "Buckeye" Sands

Mr. Corbett insisted on driving the wagon, and Ellie-May was happy to let him. For the most part, the mules behaved, but the rutted trail made progress slow. Twenty miles, indeed. At this rate they'd be lucky to make five.

She held her brother's Bible as they rode. That and his drawing were the only tangible links she had to him, and they comforted her.

Every hour or so, Josie the mule stopped walking and refused to budge. With surprising patience, Mr. Corbett climbed out of the wagon on each occasion to pet and talk to her. Just as surprising, Josie would then lumber along for another hour or so without stopping.

"I do believe Josie is sweet on you, Mr. Corbett," she said after one such occasion.

He released the brake and tugged on the reins, and the wagon rolled forward.

"I seem to have that effect on ladies," he said.

"Do you now?" She studied him through the fringe of her lashes. Even with several days' growth of whiskers, he was a nice-looking man—some might even say handsome. If only he would smile.

"Do you have family?" she asked.

"Yep." Keeping his hands on the reins, he met her gaze. "In Texas. My pa's a preacher. He doesn't have much use for a son who gets himself thrown in prison."

"Even if it was for a noble cause?" she asked.

He shrugged. "Prison's prison."

"I guess he doesn't have much use for the apostle Paul either," she said.

"Guess not."

"It sounds like you and my brother have something in common."

His eyebrows shot up. "Your brother spent time in prison, too?"

"No." Though Andy might have thought the farm a prison. "You both were at odds with your fathers."

"Is that why he left home? 'Cause he didn't get along with his pa?"

She nodded, and a heavy feeling filled her heart. She dreaded having to tell Andy that Pa was dead, but he had the right to know. He was also entitled to half the money from the sale of the farm, though he'd probably turn it down.

"So where were you heading?" she asked. "Back to Texas?"

He shook his head. "Omaha. Heard work was plentiful." He clicked his tongue, and the mules picked up speed. "It's either land a job up north or join the Union army."

"Considering how you feel about slaves, I'm surprised you don't want to fight for them." Secretly, she worried that her brother had done that very thing. Papa accused Andy of being less than a man. Getting hired with the Pony Express was Andy's way of proving otherwise. It wasn't hard to imagine Andy joining the army for the same reason.

"I've been fighting for two years just to stay alive." The steely edge of Corbett's voice faded away. "I don't have any more fight left in me."

She fervently hoped that wasn't true; especially since they were traveling through Indian country. His closed expression forbid further comment, and they rode the rest of the morning in silence.

❧

They traveled all day without seeing a single Indian, or anyone else for that matter. Nor had they found a single Pony Express station. Ellie-May studied the map and scanned the landscape.

Finally, something caught her eye. Shading her eyes against the late afternoon sun, she spotted a man behind a horse-drawn plow.

"Over there," she said, pointing.

Corbett pulled the wagon alongside a wooden fence.

She rose from the seat and cupped her hands around her mouth. "We're looking for a ranch that once served as a Pony Express station," she called.

The man brought his dappled horse to a stop. "You found her." He tossed a nod in the direction of a small building made of logs.

Calling the little farm a ranch was like calling a spoon a shovel, but the farmer seemed friendly enough.

"Do you mind if I ask you some questions?" she asked. "About the Pony Express?"

The man whipped off his hat and brushed an arm across his forehead. His face was as wrinkled as a burnt leather boot. "Wait at the house. I'll finish up here and join you."

Ellie-May waved, and Mr. Corbett guided the wagon toward the little farmhouse with a click of his tongue. "We can't stay long," he said, impatience written all over his face. "We barely put on five miles today."

"I'm not leaving till I talk to the rancher. He might know something."

"We only have two, three hours of light left."

She tossed her head. "I don't care."

"You better care," he snapped. "I'm not driving this wagon in the dark."

They were so busy arguing that it was several moments before she noticed a round-figured woman watching them from a short distance away.

Ellie-May jumped to the ground. "I'm Ellie-May Newman. Your husband told us to come here."

The woman smiled. "I'm Mrs. Wender." She spoke with an Irish brogue. A frilly cap rode upon her white hair. A spotless, starched apron covered the front of her gingham dress. The woman's eyes widened as she took in Ellie-May's bloomers, but no disapproval showed in her manner.

"Pleased to meet you. You, too, Mr. Newman."

"Oh, we're not—" Ellie-May's cheek flared. "This is Mr. Corbett. He's my. . .trail guide."

Mrs. Wender's gaze swung between them. "Bless my soul. The way you two were carrying on, I'd have sworn you were husband and wife."

Ellie-May ventured a glance at Mr. Corbett, who seemed to suddenly take a great interest in Josie and Molly.

"So what brings you two here?" Mrs. Wender asked.

"I have some questions about the Pony Express."

Mrs. Wender rolled her eyes and waved her arms up and down as if shaking out a blanket. "You get Harold yammering about the Pony Express, and you won't be able to shut him up. You better plan on staying for supper. We're having lamb stew."

Ellie-May expected Mr. Corbett to decline, but at the mention of food, he quickly followed the rancher's wife up the porch steps. In his eagerness, he failed to duck, and the low threshold knocked off his hat.

Ellie-May picked it up and handed it to him. Their gazes met for an instant before he turned and stomped into the house. Shaking her head, she trailed behind him. Mention food and the man would follow you like a tick on a lamb's tail.

Built from hewn logs and mortar, the house was small but comfortable. Sheets of canvas divided the main room into two parts. One half served as both a kitchen and small parlor. A wood block table with four chairs vied for space with a cast-iron cookstove. Two upholstered chairs with matching footstools were arranged in front of a stone fireplace. Orange flames licked lazily at a log.

The other half of the room served as a small general store. Rough wooden shelves lined an entire wall and were piled high with canned goods and tins of coffee. Bags of flour and rice were stacked on the floor.

"Make yourselves comfortable," Mrs. Wender said. "You're the first travelers we've seen for weeks. Most are in California and Oregon by now. Last thing you want is to get caught traveling in snow."

Ellie-May tried to ignore Corbett's "I told you so" look.

"We do a booming business in the early summer," Mrs. Wender continued in her lilting brogue. "Two years ago I remember counting more than eighteen hundred wagons passing by in a single day, and we sold out of supplies by noon.

Of course, things have slowed down this past year because of the war."

As she spoke, she arranged two additional place settings on the table, along with a plate of freshly baked biscuits. "You're lucky it hasn't snowed yet. You think the road is bad now? Just wait."

Ellie-May couldn't imagine the road much worse than it already was. "It was very kind of you to invite us to supper," she said, "but we don't want to be a bother."

"Yes we do," Mr. Corbett whispered in her ear. His breath sent warm ripples along her neck. Surprised by her quickening pulse, she glanced back at him and was horrified to find that he'd already helped himself to a bread roll. Such poor manners!

Fortunately, Mrs. Wender didn't seem to notice. "No bother." She walked to the stove, lifted a lid off a cast-iron pot, and stirred. The savory smell of stew wafted across the room, and Ellie-May's mouth watered.

Mrs. Wender set the stirring spoon down and wiped her hands on her apron. "You wanted to ask about the Pony Express."

"My brother was a rider. His name is Andrew Newman; Andy for short. He's an artist, and one day his work will hang in art galleries and kings' palaces."

"My word," Mrs. Wender exclaimed, clearly impressed.

Ellie-May continued. "He worked out of Chimney Rock. I'm hoping to find someone who might know his whereabouts."

"Sorry, I can't help you, but then riders seldom rode farther than a hundred and twenty miles from a home station. If his run included Chimney Rock, he wouldn't have traveled this far east."

It was disappointing news but not altogether unexpected. Basically it's what she'd been told at previous stations.

Close to an hour after they had arrived, Mr. Wender stomped into the house and pecked his wife on the cheek before peering into the stew pot. "Ah, my favorite." He reached for a spoon to dip it into the pot, but his wife gave his hand a playful tap.

"Sit down and entertain our guests while I serve our meal."

He took his seat at the head of the table with Ellie-May and Mr. Corbett on either side of him. Corbett grabbed another biscuit. She tried to catch his eye, but he was too busy reaching for the butter.

"So what did you want to ask me?" the rancher asked.

Ellie-May explained her reason for following the trail.

"Newman, you say. Hmm." He thought for a moment. "Don't remember anyone by the name, but that don't mean nothing. There was somethin' like eighty or more riders, and I got to know only a couple."

"It's a shame that the Pony Express went out of business so quickly," she said.

"No surprise there. It was a successful enterprise for eighteen months in all ways but one: it never made a dime."

Mrs. Wender set a bowl of stew in front of Ellie-May. "Now we have the telegram. Soon as they complete the lines, we'll be able to send messages all around the country. Can you imagine? If we can just get the buffalo and Indians to cooperate, that is."

"Cooperate how?" Ellie-May asked.

While Mrs. Wender finished serving the meal, her husband explained. "The buffalo rub against the poles and sometimes knock them clear out of the ground. Somebody got the idea to put spikes at the bottom of the poles, but that made the problem worse."

Mrs. Wender took her seat. "The buffalo used the spikes to comb their hides."

"What about the Indians?" Ellie-May asked. Buffalo didn't worry her; Indians did.

Mr. Wender tucked his napkin into his shirt. "It didn't take 'em long to figure out that the movement of troops follow the telegraph, so they simply burn the poles down. 'Course, you won't find many troops around now. Most were sent to fight in the war."

Ellie-May glanced at Corbett, who was making fast work of his stew. Hoping their hosts didn't notice that he'd begun eating, she gave Corbett's leg a nudge with her foot.

He looked up, and she mouthed, "Your manners." To his credit, he set down his fork and waited for his host to give the blessing.

As they ate, Mr. Wender continued to talk about the Pony Express. He had many fond memories of the riders stopping at his station.

"Most of them were just kids," he said, dabbing his mustache with his napkin. "But it was a man's job. Once the mochila left St. Joe, the rider didn't stop for anything."

"What's a mochila?" she asked.

"That's what we called the locked saddlebag that held the mail." He pointed to the wall where a four-pocket, sheep-leather satchel hung from two hooks.

Mrs. Wender nodded. "At first the riders were given a horn to blow to tell us when they were coming. But we could hear the pounding of horses' hooves, so the horns were soon abandoned."

Mr. Wender's fork stilled. "The rider was allowed two minutes to change horses, but we got it down to fifteen seconds if the weather was good. Longer during a snowstorm. Once it snowed so hard that one poor fellow got turned around. Instead of reaching the next station, he ended up back here where he started."

Ellie-May shuddered to think of her gentle-natured brother working under such harsh conditions. Certainly working on the farm wouldn't have been any harder. If only he hadn't inherited Pa's stubborn streak.

"Is there anyone at the Chimney Rock station?" she asked.

Wender and his wife exchanged a glance. "That I can't say."

Mrs. Wender jumped to her feet. "I hope you all saved room for berry pie."

Just as abruptly, her husband began a lively discourse on the raging war. Puzzled by the sudden change of topic, she glanced at Corbett, busy slathering butter on the last biscuit. He didn't seem to notice anything odd, so perhaps she'd only imagined it.

Chapter 5

Left my infant on the trale, along with a peace of my hart.
—Carved into Chimney Rock in 1859 by Mrs. Hannah Snow

Early the following morning, Corbett fed and watered the mules and hitched them to the wagon.

He hadn't expected to spend the night at the Wender ranch, but by the time they finished supper, it had been too dark to travel. Miss Newman slept in the house, and he had bedded down in the hayloft.

The breakfast alone had been worth the stay—that and the bucket-and-rope shower behind the barn. The water had been icy cold, but no more so than prison showers. Mrs. Wender insisted he help himself to clothing left by former express riders.

The trousers were too short but fit okay around the waist. The fringed tops fit better and were a whole lot warmer than the thin shirt allotted by the prison upon his release. He wiped his clean-shaven chin. The Wenders told him to help himself to a razor, toothbrush, and comb in the general store, and he felt human again. Almost.

He headed for the little shed next to the stables and barn where Wender was repairing Miss Newman's wagon wheel.

The gray sky reminded him of dingy prison walls and looked almost as ominous. Last night's rain left puddles on the muddied ground. The damp air chilled him to the bone, and he put his hands beneath his armpits to keep warm. Snow couldn't be that far away.

He stepped into the shed, and Mr. Wender greeted him with a nod of his grizzled head. The shed was furnished with blacksmith tools ranging from a sharp-pointed anvil to a redbrick forge.

"That should do it," Mr. Wender said. He checked the steel rim before handing the wheel to Corbett.

"Much obliged." He hesitated. He hated letting a woman pay his way, but right now it was the only choice he had. He'd spent the last of his prison allotment on that flea-ridden horse stolen from him. "How much do we owe you?"

Wender shook his head. "It's on the house."

"You've done enough already. Letting us stay overnight, feeding us. I'm much obliged." He had every intention of repaying Wender after finding employment. He wasn't completely without manners, no matter what Miss Newman might think.

"No need to thank me. It's our Christian duty to help one another." He gave Corbett a sly look. "I reckon you got your hands full helping Miss Newman."

Corbett cracked a smile, his first in he didn't know how long. It was amazing what some fresh-cooked cackleberries and ham in the morning will do to a man's disposition. The tough, leathery fare that passed as prison meat had never oinked or mooed, that's for sure.

"I reckon so."

Wender wiped his hands on a rag. "You take care of your lady friend, and I'll consider us even."

"She's not my. . .lady friend. I'm just her trail guide."

"Right. Trail guide." Wender walked out of the blacksmith shed, grabbed a bucket of slop, and headed for the pigpen.

Corbett hung the newly repaired wheel on the outside of the wagon before joining him. Josie protested his walking away with a show of her teeth and a loud bray that practically scared the feathers off a nearby hen.

"I'll be back," Corbett called over his shoulder.

Upon reaching the pigpen, Corbett hung his folded hands over the top rail of the fence. "When Miss Newman asked about Chimney Rock, I got the feeling you were holding something back."

Wender dumped the contents of the bucket into a trough, and a hefty sow rolled out of a mud hole, sauntered over, and poked her snout into the slop.

"I didn't want to worry her needlessly."

Corbett grimaced. That's what he was afraid of. "Feel free to worry *me*."

Wender set the empty pail down and turned to face him. "There was some Indian trouble out that way just before the express went bankrupt. Couple of people killed."

Corbett's breath came out in a white misty plume. "Miss Newman's brother?"

"Don't know. Could be."

The news was as welcome as a rattler in a bedroll. If something happened to her twin, Miss Newman would be heartbroken. A surge of protectiveness rushed through him, catching him off guard. He couldn't imagine where it came from. Certainly not from his overworked mother. Not from his preacher father either, who used the pulpit like a judge's bench and the Bible like a mallet.

He wasn't even sure Miss Newman needed his protection. He could still picture her pointing her shotgun at his two would-be hangmen. Her serious demeanor didn't seem to belong to those ridiculous bloomers she favored.

Sucking in his breath, he touched a finger to his hat. "Thank you again for your hospitality."

Mr. Wender picked up his pail. "My pleasure." He frowned. "If you don't mind my saying so, you couldn't have picked a worse time of year to travel."

"Believe me, it wasn't my choice." Corbett headed for the wagon, and Josie lifted up a thick lip in greeting. If he didn't know better, he would swear the mule smiled at him.

Miss Newman emerged from the house looking mighty pretty. After hugging Mrs. Wender, she hurried toward him, a basket slung over her arm.

Today she wore a blue plaid skirt over white pantaloons and stockings. A short white cape was wrapped around her shoulders and tied in front with a blue ribbon. As always, she wore her floppy straw hat.

He felt an unexpected jolt, not unlike the earlier surge of protectiveness, and quickly looked away.

She placed the basket in the wagon and took her place on the seat next to him. "Mrs. Wender insisted upon packing us a picnic basket."

Nodding approval, he tipped his hat to the rancher's wife, and she waved back. He snapped the reins, and the wagon rolled forward.

Miss Newman was in a chatty mood, but his mind kept wandering back to the conversation with Mr. Wender. He didn't know what worried him more: the Indian attack at Chimney Rock or the ominous dark skies ahead.

⊱

With each passing hour, it got colder. The wind flattened the prairie grass and threatened to blow the canvas cover clear off the wagon. Nothing but a stone foundation was left of the next Pony Express station, and it was a good twenty miles to another.

Finally, he'd had enough. The trail widened, allowing him free rein to turn the wagon around and head in the direction they'd come.

Miss Newman's entire body stiffened, and she sat forward. "What do you think you're doing?"

"What does it look like I'm doing?" The wind forced him to yell. "I'm going back to the Wender farm. With luck we'll get there before dark."

Her eyes flashed. "Stop at once," she shouted. "You hear? I said stop!"

He kept turning the wagon. "There's a storm coming."

"I don't care." She reached for the shotgun and pointed it straight at him. "I said stop."

No doubt she was all bluster. But after seeing her shoot a hat clear off a man's head, he wasn't about to take chances. He tugged on the reins, and the wagon rolled to a standstill.

"Now turn the wagon back the other way."

"Turn it around yourself." He jumped to the ground. Soon as she realized she was on her own, she'd give up her foolhardy plan.

To his surprise, she moved to the driver's seat, grabbed the reins, and circled the wagon around till it faced west again.

He crossed his arms and watched. She was bluffing. Had to be.

Only she wasn't. The wagon took off like the first rattler out of a box, slinging mud everywhere. Josie gave a loud harsh bray, but for once Miss Newman's fierce determination prevailed over mule-headed stubbornness.

When the wagon was but a mere dot on the horizon, he pulled off his hat and tossed it to the ground. The wind picked it up and carried it away, forcing him to give chase.

In the wrong direction.

Chapter 6

Oregon or bust.
—Carved into Chimney Rock in 1861 by the James family

Come on, Josie. Pull!"

Ellie-May dropped the mule's harness and brushed her forehead with the back of her hand. It was no good. Ever since she'd left Corbett behind, Josie had kept trying to turn back. It was exhausting to keep the mules heading west while one stubborn mule kept trying to turn in the opposite direction.

To top it off, the wagon was now hopelessly stuck in mud. Slipping and sliding in the tarlike slush, she gave the harness one more yank and glared at Josie. "We're in a fine mess, thanks to you!"

Molly strained forward but without success. Josie stood like a statue and wouldn't budge. Doleful brown eyes gazed straight ahead from beneath a heavy brow.

At wit's end, Ellie-May blinked back tears. *What am I supposed to do now, God? Will You tell me that?*

She'd been so certain God had wanted her to make this trip. At first, everything seemed to fall into place, including the quick sale of the farm. It was as if God had smiled on her decision to find her brother. Then everything went wrong, postponing her journey for nearly three months. That's how long it took her to straighten out the mess at the bank before they would release her funds. Now this. . . .

She gave herself a good shake. "Ellie-May Newman, it's no time to feel sorry for yourself." At least the wind had died down, and that was a blessing.

Who needed Corbett anyway? She didn't miss him one iota. How could she? He had the manners of a hog and the disposition to match. He also had the bluest eyes she'd ever seen. Come to think of it, the rest of him wasn't that bad to look at either. Though she'd only known him a short while, his face seemed to have filled out, or at least look less gaunt. A little more meat on his bones and he would be mighty pleasing to the eye.

With an irritated shrug, she clamped down on her wayward thoughts and scanned the landscape, hoping to see a structure, wagon—anything other than the stark prairie land and mucky river stretching ahead as far as the eye could see.

The Platte was at least a mile wide but appeared to be only a few inches deep. A hand-written sign warned against drinking the water. The word *cholera* was etched onto wooden gravestones dotting both sides of the muddied trail.

Fortunately, the mules had gotten their fill from a freshwater spring earlier, and now Molly contently nibbled at the tall grass while Josie continued to pout.

Ellie-May slapped Josie on the rump. Blasted mule! She was worse than a spoiled child. Josie switched her tail, lifted a back leg, and stomped it down onto the ground, splashing mud all over Ellie-May's skirt.

Hearty male laughter rang out, and Ellie-May spun around. Mr. Corbett stood a short distance away, and Ellie-May's pulse quickened.

Not wanting to admit how glad she was to see him—or how good it was to hear him laugh—she scowled. "What's so funny?"

"You." He looked at the sunken wheel, glanced at her mud-splattered skirt, and burst out laughing again.

She folded her arms. "If you came to gloat, you can leave now," she said, though secretly she hoped he'd stay. The thought of spending the night alone in the wilderness filled her with dread.

He arched a dark eyebrow. "If I had the brains God gave a grasshopper, I would. And wouldn't you be in a fine mess?"

She was already in a fine mess, but she didn't want to give him the satisfaction of admitting it. She was also having a hard time staying annoyed.

His clean-shaven chin and amused expression did wonders for his appearance. So did the way the fringed shirt molded his form. Still it was no reason for her heart to do flip-flops at the mere sight of him.

He ran his hand along Josie's rough neck. The mule twitched her ears and lifted her tail. "Hee-haaaw."

The short, thick head rested on Corbett's shoulder, and Ellie-May rolled her eyes.

It was disgusting the way Josie fawned over Corbett.

"You two deserve each other."

Corbett held her gaze. "It's nice to know someone appreciates me."

Her cheeks flared beneath his studied gaze, but fortunately a few large drops of rain drew his attention away.

Freeing himself from Josie's affections, he rushed to the back of the wagon. "Give me a hand," he called, hauling out a wooden chest.

It took only a few minutes to lighten the load. Following his instructions, she climbed into the driver's seat while Corbett planted his shoulder next to the stuck wheel.

"Go!" he yelled.

She grabbed hold of the reins and snapped the whip through the air. "Git up!"

The mules strained forward. With a loud sucking sound, the wheel pulled out of the mud, and the wagon sprang free with a jolt.

She steered to solid ground and climbed down. "We did it!"

Corbett stood in the middle of the trail, covered from head to toe in mud, his arms straight out like a scarecrow.

Both hands on her mouth, she stared at him over her fingertips and laughed.

Corbett had barely finished putting the trunks back into the wagon when it began to pour. Miss Newman scrambled inside, but he waited until the rain had washed away the mud from his clothes before joining her.

"You're soaking wet," she said, as if he couldn't figure that out for himself.

He was also cold and hungry. The canvas provided protection from the downpour, but not from the chilled air.

She knelt by the trunks, a shawl wrapped around her shoulders. While he was cleaning off outside, she'd changed into fresh clothes but missed an intriguing speck of dirt on the tip of her upturned nose.

She tossed him a black woolen shawl. "It's not much, but at least it's dry."

After unbuckling his holster, he pulled off his fringed shirt. Miss Newman quickly turned her back and busied herself with Mrs. Wender's picnic basket.

He couldn't help but smile. Two drunken thugs hadn't fazed her, but a man pulling off his shirt definitely did.

He quickly changed into dry clothes, and a pleasant whiff of lavender greeted him as he wrapped the wool shawl around his shoulders.

"You can look now."

She shyly met his gaze before turning her attention back to the basket. "Supper's ready."

Cheese, dry meat, and bread were spread on a wooden trunk, alongside a lit lantern. He didn't have to guess which trunk it was, as a tiny piece of lace hung out over the side. He swallowed hard and looked away.

She handed him a tin plate, and he helped himself to a wedge of cheese.

"Mrs. Wender saved the day," she said. "At least we don't have to worry about dying of starvation."

"No," he grumbled. "We just have to worry about pneumonia."

"Your *optimism* never fails to amaze me, Mr. Corbett."

"I deal with facts, Miss Newman, and right now, you and I are in danger of being washed away."

"Then I suggest we pray," she said.

He studied her, surprised to find himself wishing he had her kind of faith. "You think God answers prayers?"

"He already did. When my wagon got stuck, I prayed for help, and there you were."

He laughed. He couldn't help himself. "Never thought I'd be the answer to anyone's prayer."

"Why *did* you come back, Mr. Corbett?"

Biting off a piece of dry meat, he tried to think of an answer. He worried about her safety, of course, a woman alone in the wilderness. And Chimney Rock. That worried him, too. But he was at a loss to explain his utter dismay when she'd driven away.

"I figured Josie needed me."

Her face darkened with disappointment—or was that just wishful thinking on his part? Had she hoped for another answer? A more personal one? Or was his mind playing tricks on him?

"What if you don't find what you're looking for?" he asked.

"Then I'll find what God wants me to find," she said.

He reached over and rubbed the speck of mud away from her nose. She stared at him for a moment before lowering dark lashes.

After hotfooting after her most of the day, he should be madder than blazes. If only she didn't look so appealing. Unable to make up his mind whether to wring her pretty neck or kiss her, he drew his hand away.

"I'll go outside soon as it stops raining," he said.

Her lashes flew upward. "Y–you can stay here tonight, Mr. Corbett. In the wagon."

"I'm no expert, but I'm pretty sure God is against an unmarried man and woman"—he cleared his throat—"spending the night together."

Her cheeks turned pink, but her gaze never left his face. "God will understand. He makes exceptions for such occasions," she said.

He frowned. The God Miss Newman worshipped bore little resemblance to the angry, punishing one his father preached about. "You sure about that?"

"Quite sure, Mr. Corbett."

He was equally certain she was wrong, but he was too cold to argue.

"I. . ." She cleared her voice. "I don't have anything to worry about, do I, Mr. Corbett? From you, I mean."

He hesitated. "Nope, nothing to worry about." If only her dewy lips didn't look so downright. . .kissable.

Avoiding her eyes, he arranged the bedroll the best he could before sliding into the cotton flannel depths. "You keep watch while I get some shut-eye," he said in a gruff voice. Earlier he had heard tom-toms and didn't want to take chances. "I'll take the midnight shift."

"Do you think anyone will bother us in the rain?" she asked. "Bandits or. . .or Indians?"

"You just never know, Miss Newman." Now that kissing was on his mind, he couldn't trust himself with the lady. "If I were you, I'd keep that shotgun handy."

Real handy.

❧

Something woke her. Annoyed at herself for falling asleep, she sat up. The lantern had burned out, and she couldn't see a thing. She strained her ears. The rain had stopped, but the squishy sound of footsteps outside made her heart thump.

"Mr. Corbett," she whispered, but no movement came from his side of the wagon.

She reached in the dark for her shotgun. Forcing her voice low to sound like a man's, she asked, "Who's there?"

The high-pitched voice that answered was obviously a man trying to sound like a woman. "It's just me."

"Mr. Corbett!" She took a deep breath. "You nearly scared the life out of me."

He stuck his head through the canvas opening. "It stopped raining, and I was just checking on the mules."

"What time is it?"

"Almost dawn. We need to get an early start."

She groaned. Miraculously, neither had succumbed to pneumonia, but every bone in her body ached from sleeping in cramped quarters. With the two of them sleeping inside, there was hardly room to turn over, let alone stretch out.

She was still yawning moments later when she climbed out of the wagon. The eastern sky was gunmetal gray; the western sky still dark. Noticing his steady gaze, she blushed and regretted letting her hair cascade down her back.

Abruptly, he looked away. "No coffee," he said. "Too wet to make a fire." He chomped down on a piece of dried meat left over from last night's supper.

"Maybe someone is still living at the next Pony Express station." According to the map, it was five or six miles away. "If so, we can get coffee there."

"Don't count on it," he growled.

She quickly pinned up her hair, plopped on her hat, and started for the driver's seat.

His hand clamped her shoulder. "Before we start, we need to get a few things straight."

She pulled away from his grip. "Like what, Mr. Corbett?"

"From now on, I do the driving."

She pulled on her gloves. "I'm perfectly capable of driving my own wagon."

"Which explains how you broke a wagon wheel and got stuck in the mud."

"I suppose you can do better."

"A coyote could do better."

"I see. Will that be all?" she asked in a cool voice.

His gaze bored into her. "Just one more thing. Be nice to Josie."

Chapter 7

Can't stay here. Can't go back. Gotta keep going.
—Carved into Chimney Rock in 1861 by Paul Shoemaker

They traveled in silence for most of the morning.

Ellie-May pulled off a glove and fingered her brother's leather-bound Bible and prayed for strength to continue her journey. *Oh Andy. . . Why didn't you come home or at least let us know where you are?*

The question was very much on her mind as they plodded along the wet trail. More than once Corbett was forced to make a detour around a pond-sized mud hole. As a result, it was late afternoon before they arrived at the next relay station, a low-slung hut built from what was commonly called dobie brick. Grass grew on the thatched roof, and a hole cut in the wall two feet from the door served as the only window.

Inside, it smelled moldy and dank. The hut had a fireplace but no furnishings. Cobwebs clung to grease-spattered walls, and the glass pane of the single window was cracked. Empty tin cans and other trash littered the dirt floor. Two mice scampered by, and Ellie-May jumped back.

Her brother had written about the horrible conditions of some of the stations. If this one was any indication, his complaints were valid.

She held herself still, but Andy and even God seemed far away.

Corbett stepped into the house behind her, the thump of his boots causing yet another mouse to scurry across the floor and into a pile of dry leaves.

"Find anything?" he asked.

She shook her head. It was disappointing not to find anyone living there, but not all that surprising. "This wasn't part of Andy's run."

He laid a hand on her shoulder. Unlike the firm hold he had on her earlier, his touch was gentle, seeming to reach inside her. Since her father's death, she had been very much alone. Until that moment, she hadn't realized how much.

"Do you mind if I call you Michael?"

He removed his hand. "If we get too personal, I might be inclined to kiss you," he said, his voice husky.

She spun around, but he was already walking out the door. It took several moments to control her pounding heart enough to follow.

Not ready to face him—and torn by conflicting emotions—she walked around the hut toward the stables in back, hoping to find feed for the mules. *I might be inclined to. . .*

The idea was intriguing—no, alarming. Intriguing *and* alarming. She gnawed on a fingernail. She didn't want him to kiss her. Of course she didn't. Absolutely not! Never crossed her mind until he put it there.

She was so lost in her thoughts she failed to notice that she was no longer alone until a movement caught her eye.

An Indian stood not twenty feet away. Heart leaping to her throat, she shrank back. Every horror story she'd ever heard about Indians raced through her mind. His beaded buckskins didn't look menacing, but the dark eyes glittering from beneath a heavy brow certainly did. His head was shaved at the sides with only a turf of black on top, falling to a single braid in back.

He said something that could have been a greeting or a threat. She didn't know, didn't care to know, and didn't stay around long enough to find out.

Running for dear life, she screamed, "Mr. Corbett. . .Mr. Corbett. . .Michael!"

In her panic she ran straight into him, and he toppled backward, taking her with him. They landed in a pile of damp leaves. Startled eyes met hers but only for the instant it took for him to wrap his arms around her waist and kiss her gently, firmly, crazily on the lips.

His moist, warm lips demanded a response, and without a moment's hesitation, she kissed him back. Her senses reeled and shot to dizzying heights. His hands explored the hollows of her back, and her flesh tingled with pleasure.

He moaned aloud, shocking her into reality. She pulled back and pushed against his chest.

Questioning eyes met her. "Ellie?"

Her mouth flapped like a loose cellar door before she could get the words out. "Mr. Corbett!"

His eyebrows knitted. "You called me Michael. I told you what would happen if we got too personal."

"I—" A nearby movement reminded her that Corbett's nearness was the least of her worries. She quickly rolled off him and scrambled to her feet. "There's a—"

She gasped. Not just one but three Indians stood a short distance away, and each looked equally menacing.

Corbett's gaze followed hers, and the blood drained from his face. He jumped to his feet, leaves clinging to his back. "Let me handle this."

One brave pointed to her and laughed, and his companions laughed with him.

She placed her hands on her hips. The nerve. They were laughing at her bloomers! "How dare they?"

"Hush, we don't want to upset them," Corbett cautioned. In a louder voice, he asked, "What can we do for you?"

One Indian stepped forward. "Swap."

"What. . .what did he say?" she whispered.

"I think he wants to make a trade."

"Well, he can't have my bloomers," she said with a huff.

Corbett lifted his voice. "No swap."

The brave held up two fish and pointed to the wagon. "Two fish. One mule."

Ellie-May stiffened. "No deal."

The Indian's eyebrows met. "Two fish. One mule," he thundered, and this time it sounded more like a declaration of war than a trade negotiation.

"I don't think they'll take no for an answer," Corbett said, his voice hushed. He reached for his gun, and just as quickly all three Indians lifted their spears.

Corbett held his hands forward, palm sides out. "We swap."

"You're giving up?" she stormed. "Just like that? What kind of marshal were you?"

"The kind who knows when he's outnumbered." He arched a dark eyebrow. "I'm trying to look on the bright side."

"There is no bright side to losing a mule," she snapped

"Sure there is. Tonight we'll enjoy a nice fish dinner." Corbett signaled the Indians to follow him with a toss of his head.

"Wait!" She ran after them.

One brave swung around to face her, spear raised head-high. Without her shotgun, she wasn't about to challenge him, except to return his glare with one of her own.

Corbett unhitched Josie and led the mule to the brave who handed him the fish.

Talking among themselves and giving Ellie-May's bloomers one last laugh, the braves took off with Josie in tow.

"Oooh." Hands on her hips, she clenched her teeth. "You had no right to give away my mule!"

"I didn't give her away. I swapped." Grinning, he held up two catfish.

The twinkle in his eyes only incensed her more, and she practically spit fire. "There's no way Molly can pull this wagon by herself. Now I'll never get to Chimney Rock!"

He shook his head. "And you accuse me of having little faith."

She frowned. "And what is that supposed to mean?"

"You'll see."

A loud scream, followed by gut-wrenching shouts, made her spin around. In the distance, Josie kicked and bucked and made a terrible racket. The three braves did their best to contain her, but they proved no match for the flying hooves and snapping teeth.

Josie butted one Indian head-on, sending him flying back like a rag doll. Ellie-May covered her mouth in horror. The mule then turned on the others. Ears pinned back, tail whipping around in a circle, she charged. The two braves turned and ran for their lives, the third Indian not far behind.

Corbett laughed, his loud guffaws filling the air.

"It's not funny," she said. "Someone could have been seriously hurt."

"It would have served them right." He put out his hand. "Ah, here she comes."

Josie didn't even glance at Ellie-May. Instead, she strutted right up to Corbett and pressed her nose into the palm of his hand.

Corbett gave the mule an affectionate pat on the head. "That's my girl. I knew you could do it."

Josie bobbed her head up and down as if to agree.

Ellie-May's mouth dropped open. "You knew she would get away, didn't you?"

" 'Course I knew," he said with a silly grin. "I told you to be nice to Josie."

Chapter 8

Excitement was plentiful during my two years' service as a Pony Express rider.
—Carved into Chimney Rock in 1861 by Bill Cody

The days that followed were long and dreary. Sometimes it rained, on occasion it snowed, but always it was cold. The trail grew increasingly worse, and some days they barely covered more than a few miles.

November turned to December, and with it the air turned frigid. The wagon rocked back and forth on the rutted trail like a ship on a stormy sea. More than once, Corbett had to pound away ice before they could reach springwater.

They stopped at every former Pony Express relay station along the way. Some were deserted, one had burned down, another was nowhere to be found. But some, like the Starr Ranch, still served as trading posts, offering a place to rest and purchase supplies.

None of the ranches had much in the way of livestock. Supplying traveler needs was far more profitable than raising horses or cattle.

The fort established to protect the trail was all but deserted; federal troops had been sent south to fight rebel forces. Since no private enterprises were placed on government land, the fort was never home to the Pony Express, but riders often stopped for supplies or simply to share news. No one had heard of Andy.

Talk around the fort was of a possible Indian uprising now that the troops were gone, but the few braves they met were more of a help than a hindrance. For a handsome fee, two Lakotas even ferried them across the Platte River at Cottonwood Canyon.

They encountered herds of antelope, but it was the buffalo that fascinated Ellie-May most. Never had she seen more odd-looking animals. It hardly seemed possible that such skinny legs could hold up the thick, bulky bodies.

If the long, torturous journey wasn't bad enough, the tension between her and Mr. Corbett was taut as a fiddle string. He didn't mention the kiss, nor did she. But the memory seemed to take on a life of its own, making it imperative to watch every word and gesture.

Even the slightest touch of hands, no matter how accidental, made her heart skip a beat. So she carefully called him Mr. Corbett, and he was equally scrupulous in formality.

"Did you see the size of that buffalo, Mr. Corbett?"

"Indeed I did, Miss Newman."

The farther west they traveled, the more graves they passed. Late one afternoon, they reached an area where hardly a foot separated one grave from the next. Ellie-May's spirits plummeted as she read the hastily scrawled epitaphs. Several siblings in one family succumbed within a twenty-four-hour period.

Overcome with emotion, she directed her gaze straight ahead and willed herself not to look left or right.

"Have any brothers or sisters?" she asked.

"Five living," Corbett replied. "All older than me. One brother drowned."

She studied his profile, and the urge to smooth away his tight expression was almost unbearable. If it wasn't for the memory of his lips on hers, she might have done just that, friend to friend.

"I saved Andy from drowning once," she said. "It was a long time ago, and I doubt he even remembers."

"He remembers," he said.

The certainty in his voice surprised her. "How do you know?"

"You always remember the one who saved you."

Somehow she knew they were no longer talking about drownings or even brothers. Something more personal had crept into the conversation. Something that had hovered like a shadow since the day they kissed now threatened to take shape.

He held her gaze for a moment before they both turned away: he to coax the mules into picking up speed and she to read the name on yet another grave.

❧

At long last they reached Mud Springs. The sod station had lost its battle with mud, and sludge oozed from its stone foundation.

Corbett didn't even bother to stop. Instead, he drove the wagon around a muddy buffalo wallow, and a flock of brown-speckled birds took to the sky.

He pointed ahead. "Look."

Ellie-May craned her neck. "What is it?" She was shivering so much she could hardly get the words out.

"Courthouse Rock," he said. "The smaller one is Jail Rock."

The larger rock was well named, its huge ragged shape giving an impression of judicial protection.

"Chimney Rock is about twelve miles west of them," he added.

"Praise the Lord," she whispered. "We're almost there."

"Not quite. We're still a good twenty-five miles away."

She closed her eyes and envisioned her brother with sketchbook in hand and tongue between his teeth. He was probably drawing even now.

Drawings of the war had started to appear in newspapers. Was that what Andy was doing? Drawing war pictures? It would certainly explain why she hadn't heard from him; he didn't want to worry her. The thought depressed her. She couldn't imagine her gentle brother sketching battle scenes. He much preferred God's world to man's, and that's why he held such high regard for Chimney Rock. Nothing like it existed in Iowa.

She opened her eyes, and her brother's vision faded away. She ran her hands along her arms for warmth.

Corbett reached behind and pulled a blanket out of the wagon. "Wrap yourself in this."

She pulled the blanket around her shoulders. "We're getting close to finding Andy," she said. "I can feel it in my bones."

"Are you sure that's not just the cold?'

"What I'm sure about, Mr. Corbett, is that God wouldn't bring me all this way for nothing."

His eyebrows knitted. "How do you know that?"

"He sent you along when I most needed help. Not just once, but twice. I don't think that was an accident, do you?"

"Seems to me you got that backwards. I was the one with the rope around my neck."

"We were both in desperate straits. It's a miracle that we found each other when we did."

He narrowed his eyes but kept his gaze focused on the trail ahead. "Don't put much stock in miracles," he said. "I'm what you call a realist."

"So am I, Mr. Corbett. So am I."

∂⌐

Corbett tightened his hold on the reins and shifted his cramped legs. Realistic? Miss Newman? What a laugh. She was about as realistic as a mirage.

Her upturned nose was red from the cold, and her glazed eyes worried him, but as usual she sat straight as a schoolmarm, her dainty hands gripping her brother's Bible. The gaze glued to the shadowy rocks ahead held no room for doubt, and he envied her faith, however misplaced he feared it might be.

It was hard to look at her rigid exterior without thinking about the warm, soft, and passionate woman he'd held in his arms and kissed. Would he ever see that side of her again? He doubted it. If she found out he kept the Chimney Rock Indian attack from her, she might not want anything more to do with him.

Not that he could blame her. He should have told her. Wanted to, had even started to, but the words wouldn't come. And the longer he hesitated, the easier it was to justify his silence. The express company would have notified Andy's family had he been killed. They wouldn't send a package without explanation, would they?

Coward. Corbett clenched his jaw. Like it or not, she had the right to know about the Indian attack. That way she could prepare herself for the worst.

Tonight he would tell her as soon as they set up camp. No more excuses. He glanced at her and frowned. Telling her would break her heart; but not telling her was breaking his.

Chapter 9

Here he comes! And there he goes. The fleeting ghost of a Pony Express rider.
—Carved into Chimney Rock in 1861 by Samuel Clemens

For the next few hours, Ellie-May hardly took her gaze off the clay and sandstone formations ahead. They could now pick out Chimney Rock. They'd driven several miles since first spotting the distant landmark, but it didn't appear one whit closer.

She pulled the blanket tight around her shoulders and yawned. She tried to stay awake, but her lids felt heavy as cast iron. Talking to Corbett was no use. He'd grown increasingly silent in the last few hours. A broom would offer more in the way of companionship.

She tried praying, but she couldn't concentrate. Never had she felt such bone-wrenching exhaustion.

It was still light when Corbett drove the wagon beneath a grove of trees, but it would soon be dark.

He hopped to the ground and stood by the side of the wagon, looking up at her. "We should reach Chimney Rock by tomorrow afternoon."

"A whole week before Christmas." She forced a smile. "I'd say that was a miracle, wouldn't you?"

"I'll withhold judgment until we get there."

Her gaze drifted to the distant landmark her brother called the hand of God. "Sometimes you can best appreciate miracles from a distance," she said. It took years before the miracle of Jesus' birth was fully realized.

"Guess you could say the same about trouble." He started to add something more but stopped abruptly and walked away, muttering something about tending the mules.

She watched him for a moment before climbing out of her seat. Feeling breathless, she stopped to rest before ambling to the back of the wagon on rubbery legs.

After sitting all day, a walk wouldn't hurt. She reached into the wagon bed for the empty basket and walked slowly through the tall prairie grass, looking for firewood. It was too cold for snakes—a blessing, indeed.

The few twigs scattered about would make good kindling but little else. Her throat parched, she felt lightheaded, and a wave of nausea washed over her.

Leaning against a tree, she waited for the dizziness to pass. If only it wasn't so hot. What was wrong with her? *Please, God, don't let me be ill. Not now. Not when I'm so close to finding Andy.*

She pulled off her hat and fanned herself. Never could she remember feeling so tired. Her body ached, and her head hurt. It took awhile before she was able to gather enough strength to drag herself back to camp.

Vision blurring, the basket slipped from her hand. "Mr. Cor—"

Everything went black. The ground gave way beneath her feet, taking her with it. Suddenly, she felt herself rise, and her head fell against a soft warm cloud. At first she thought she was in heaven, but a quick flutter of eyelids told her she was in Mr. Corbett's arms.

&

Corbett hated traveling at night, but he didn't dare wait till morning. Not with Miss Newman so ill. After she had collapsed in his arms, he'd carried her to the wagon and laid her down. He took off her boots and sponged her fevered brow. He did everything he could to make her comfortable, but her breathing grew more labored with each passing hour. Fearing she wouldn't survive the night, he hitched the mules to the wagon and set out, hoping against hope he would find a farm, a ranch—something that would shelter them against the bitter cold.

Surprisingly, neither Josie nor Molly balked at having to travel all night. It was as if they somehow sensed the urgency that drove him, smelled the metallic fear coating his mouth.

Never had he known such unforgiving darkness. Not even in his prison cell during the year spent in the black hole of solitary confinement. The air was dank with the threat of rain if not snow.

One rut or badger hole could break a mule's leg, and that would be disastrous. To prevent such a misfortune, he walked ahead of the animals, swinging a lantern back and forth. The light barely penetrated the black shroud of night, but it was better than nothing.

No one in their right mind would travel under such conditions. He wasn't even sure if he was still heading west. Without so much as a single star to lead the way, he could just as easily be traveling south or east or in circles.

Not only the road worried him; so many stations they'd passed had been deserted. It was entirely possible that Chimney Rock Station would be, too.

Miss Newman accused him of having little or no faith. So what was he supposed to do? Trust God to lead him to a ranch house? Or better yet, a doctor?

Now *that* would be a miracle.

He grimaced. Weeks ago he had walked out of prison with his life in tatters and faith in God shattered. Inside, he'd felt as hollow as an empty barrel. He never thought to smile again, let alone feel. But this intriguing woman in her ridiculous bloomers and floppy straw hat changed all that. Not only did she make him laugh, but she'd somehow managed to break down the protective wall meant to keep people out.

That wasn't all that crazy woman had done; now she got him thinking about miracles. Got him thinking about God. Not his father's unrelenting and punishing God—no comfort there. Instead, he found himself hoping—more than that believing as Ellie-May did—that a kind, loving, and merciful God was guiding him through that long, lonely night.

The thunder of horse's hooves filled the air. Ellie-May ran outside and stared at the spot in the distance until it grew large enough that she could make out the rider. It was a man on a sorrel; actually it was a boy. Though they were the same age, everyone always thought Andy younger, and she had come to think of him that way, too.

He was dressed in black trousers and red shirt, a slouch hat perched upon his golden hair. He handed her something as he flew by—a picture—but when she looked down, the canvas was blank.

Her eyes flew open. "Andy?"

Only it wasn't Andy looking back at her, washcloth in hand. It was an older face. Rugged. A kind face. Concerned. Her mind scrambled until she remembered his name.

"Mr. Corbett."

"Hello. . ." He cleared his throat and turned to toss a washcloth into a basin. "I'm sure glad to see you."

She placed a hand on her forehead and stared at the wood-beam ceiling. She moistened her parched lips. "Where am I?"

"We're at the Madison farm. Harvey Madison and his wife took us in." He filled a glass with water from a pitcher and slipped a hand beneath her head. "Madison was the Chimney Rock Pony Express station keeper." He held the glass while she drank.

The water soothed her dry throat. He lowered her head to the pillow and set the glass on the bed stand.

Trying to make sense of her muddled thoughts, she waited for the fog to clear before asking, "How. . .how did we get here?"

He explained how he walked all night to find help. "You were burning up with fever."

She studied his face. "You did that for me?" She thought about the times he'd adamantly refused to travel at night.

He gave her a crooked smile. "I can't take all the credit. I'd have walked right by the house had it not been for Josie. She stopped and refused to budge. That's when I smelled smoke from a chimney fire."

"Josie did that?" She rubbed her forehead. "How long have I been sick?"

"Seven days."

"Seven!" It didn't seem possible.

"Christmas is tomorrow. You pretty near slept right through it."

She grimaced with disappointment. She wanted so much to spend Christmas Day with Andy. "Did. . .did you talk to the station keeper about my brother?"

"Yes." He set the glass on the bed table. "He remembers him well."

Even in her weakened condition, her heart leaped with joy. She tried sitting up, and the room turned topsy-turvy.

He sprang to her side. "Whoa. Take it easy."

"I have to talk to him. Maybe he knows where Andy is now."

Hands on her shoulders, he gently pushed her back until her head landed on the pillow. "There'll be time later for that. Right now, you need to get your strength back."

His serious expression gave her pause. Was it her health he worried about or something else? "What is it? Tell me."

He straightened. "You've been very sick. Didn't think you'd make it." His voice broke. Dark shadows skirted his eyes, and fine lines creased his normally smooth forehead. Had he lost sleep over her?

"I'm sorry." She took hold of his hand. Sometimes she could be so single-minded. "I don't know what I'd have done without you."

His eyes darkened with emotion. "Wanted to make sure you got your twenty-five dollars' worth."

Recalling the crazy way they met, she forced a wan smile. "I got more than my money's worth." His debt fully paid, he had no reason to stay, but the thought of him leaving was like a knife turning inside.

He laid her hand on the bed. "I'll get your breakfast." He turned.

"Thank you," she whispered.

His back to her, he stood motionless for several moments before leaving the room.

Chapter 10

I fought Indians, rattlers and thieves for this? To deliver a bag of advertisements?
—Carved into Chimney Rock in 1861 by Wild Bill Hickok

How is she doing?" Harvey Madison asked from his chair in front of the fire. One foot on a stool, the former station keeper leaned over to rub his leg. The flames cast a copper glow on his rugged face and turned his white beard orange.

Corbett sat opposite him. "She's awake."

Mrs. Madison stood at the kitchen door, wiping her hands on her apron. She was a tall, thin woman with white hair and a well-lined face. "I'll heat up some soup for her."

Corbett nodded. "Much obliged."

Harvey sat back. "I still can't get over how you found us in the dark."

"Lucky for me you had a fire going."

Madison had explained that by some stroke of luck, he'd risen before dawn and started a fire, hoping the warmth would help ease the pain in his leg.

"Never thought this bum leg would be good for anything, but if it helped you find us. I guess that's something. The good Lord works in mysterious ways."

"That's for sure." Corbett rubbed his whiskered chin. He needed to shave. Hadn't done much of anything these past few days except tend the mules. Mostly he sat by Ellie-May's side and forced liquids down her throat. Sleep, if it came at all, was spent on the floor by her bed. At times he read aloud from Andy's Bible, hoping the sound of his voice would coax her back to consciousness.

"I don't think we should tell her about her brother," he said. "At least not until she's stronger."

Madison stroked his beard. "Such a waste. Nice kid. Had the same blond hair as his sister. Always drawing. Said he wanted to be an artist like that Audubon fellow." He shook his head. "The rider from the fort was late arriving. Had he been on time, Andy would have already left and might have escaped the Indian attack." He paused. "Soon as I heard gunfire, I grabbed my rifle, but it was already too late. The Indians had taken off with all our horses."

Four had died that day, including two riders and two stock tenders. All were buried a short distance from the now-deserted relay station seen from the stables.

Elbows on his lap, Corbett rubbed his hands together. For once the smell of bacon and freshly ground coffee held no interest for him. How could he best tell Ellie-May about her brother?

He wasn't good with words. Never had been. Even his teachers had complained. Hadn't bothered him before. Being a man of few words had actually been an asset when he was a U.S. Deputy Marshal. Talk was cheap, and one thing outlaws knew was value. If his height didn't impress them, his gun certainly did. Nothing worse than a silent man holding a weapon.

The rules were different when dealing with a woman. You couldn't just look at a woman and expect her to know what you were thinking. Otherwise, Ellie-May would know he loved her. She would know how much he longed to hold and kiss her. Know how much he wanted to comfort and protect her. He couldn't come right out and say that, of course. Without a job or any kind of a future, he had nothing to offer except a criminal record. She deserved so much more.

"I should have told her what Wender said about the Indian attack. That would have prepared her for her brother's death—"

A gargled cry stabbed at his heart, and his gaze shot across the room.

Ellie-May stood by the doorway, clad in a white flannel gown, her eyes wide with horror.

Anguish seared through him as he jumped to his feet. "Ellie—"He almost fell over a chair trying to reach her. He held out his arms, but she slapped his hands away.

Accusatory eyes bored into him. "You knew?"

"I didn't know, not really. I knew there was a possibility, but—"

She shook her head and lashed out at him. "You let me come all this way and never said a word!"

"I wanted to." He rubbed his forehead and tried to think. "Please—"

"Don't touch me!" With a moan of distress, she spun around and slammed the door in his face.

಄

The next day—Christmas—Ellie almost missed the grave markers. Four of them stuck barely six inches out of the snow and twenty feet from the deserted relay station. A wooden sign hanging over the front door of the rectangular sod building read: PONY EXPRESS.

She fell on her knees and frantically raked through the white powder with gloved hands.

The first two headstones belonged to Joseph Wells and Eric Beller. Jimmy Dorring was the name on the third one, which meant the fourth and last marker had to be Andy's.

Gasping for air, she frantically brushed away the snow, blinded by tears. Blinking, she sat back on her heels. Andrew Newman's name was burned into the wood in big, bold letters. She didn't want to believe what her eyes told her was true; her dear brother was gone.

"No, no, no!" she cried. His name didn't belong here. It belonged in art galleries and on palace walls. That was his dream. Not this!

Her body wracked with sobs, she rocked back and forth, crying his name and shouting at God. "You brought me all the way here for this?" Finally, she collapsed in the snow.

She might have frozen to death had Corbett not found her. By then she was too distressed to fight him off. He wrapped her in a warm coat and lifted her ever so gently into his arms and carried her into the deserted Pony Express building.

Unlike most other relay stations, this one was neat and clean and furnished with a table, four chairs, and a cookstove. Gingham curtains and a quilt-covered sofa provided a homey feel.

Corbett set her on the bear rug in front of the stone fireplace. He quickly arranged a stack of logs in the firebox and struck a match to a clump of dry leaves. Hot flames climbed up the chimney, and warmth began radiating outward.

He pulled off her gloves and rubbed her frozen fingers with his own until the red flesh faded to a healthier pink.

He then pulled her sobbing into his arms. He ran a hand down her back with soothing strokes until her sobs subsided.

"I was wrong," he said in a hoarse whisper. "I should have told you about the Indian attack." He lifted her chin and gazed into her eyes. "You had such hope and faith, and I hadn't seen much of that. Not for two years. Maybe longer. I couldn't bear to take that away from you. From. . .from us." His voice grew husky. "Can you ever forgive me?"

His words stabbed at her. He wanted her forgiveness, just as her father wanted Andy's. Only it was too late for Pa.

Fresh tears stung her eyes as she lifted her hand to his cheek, his rough whiskers poking through her numbness. How could she not forgive this man? He'd stayed by her side for days and weeks and truly saved her life.

"I don't blame you for not telling me," she choked out. "I would probably have done the same."

He pulled her into his arms and held her close. She clung to him, and somehow his nearness made the terrible pain inside more bearable. When at last he pulled away and stood, she feared the black hole of grief would consume her.

"Are you ready to go back to the house?" he asked. "You haven't fully recovered from your illness."

Glancing around the room, she shook her head. Her brother had been here, had probably warmed himself in front of this very fire. Perhaps even sketched at that very table. "I want to stay here." Near Andy.

"Will you be all right if I leave?"

She gazed up at him. "Don't go."

He looked down at the hand clutching his arm. "I'll only be gone a short while. I want to tell Mrs. Madison to go ahead and start Christmas dinner without us."

"You should eat," she said.

"Not without you." He hesitated, his face suffused with unreadable emotions. "I'll be back."

అ

After Corbett left, she spotted a mochila on the floor, and her breath caught. Was it Andy's? She scrambled to her feet and quickly checked each pocket— nothing. She wanted so much to find something of Andy's—his sketchbook— and it sickened her to think it had probably fallen into the hands of his killers.

She then noticed a door ajar, and this led to a second room furnished with four bunks. Anguish seared through her as she touched each tick mattress in turn, but nothing indicated which, if any, had been Andy's.

Overcome with grief, she left the room and threw herself on the rug in front of the fire. She must have fallen asleep, because the next thing she knew, Corbett walked through the doorway brandishing a basket covered with red gingham and tied with a big red bow.

"Mrs. Madison insisted on packing us Christmas dinner complete with roast beef, squash, potatoes, and mincemeat pie."

She had no desire to eat, but she forced a smile for his sake.

He set the basket on the table and added another log to the fire. "Josie's missing. I should go and look for her."

Alarm shot through her. Oddly enough she'd grown quite fond of that fool mule. "Oh no."

"Mrs. Madison thinks she escaped while looking for me."

"Knowing how Josie feels about you, I'm not surprised." She rose. "We must find her."

"It's getting ready to snow."

"Then we'd better hurry."

He looked about to argue but instead picked the coat off the floor and wrapped it around her, his hands lingering on her shoulders. "Are you sure you don't want to stay here?" he whispered, his breath warm against her ear.

"I'm sure."

Outside, the sky was gunmetal gray. A slight north wind blew, and a few white flakes drifted through the air like tiny feathers.

Corbett cupped his hands around his mouth. "Josie."

Ellie-May's breath caught at sight of the four headstones, and she quickly looked away. "Maybe she went to the river."

He shook his head and pointed to indentations in the snow. "She went that way."

Hand in hand, they walked. The white powder swallowed their legs as they followed the mule's hoofprints toward Chimney Rock.

The looming landmark was quite impressive from a distance, but even more so close up. The tall spire was about fifty feet square and rose from a conical base to more than two hundred feet in the air. The top sloped like a pointed finger and looked identical to the drawing Andy had sent. The thought made her gasp for air. Seen through her brother's eyes, it really did look like the hand of God.

"Hee-haaaw."

"Over there!" she said, pointing. "By the side of the rock." In her anxiety to reach the animal, she nearly tripped. Had it not been for Corbett's steady hold, she would have fallen into a snowdrift.

Josie let out another loud bray. Ears pinned back, the mule scampered toward Corbett, practically knocking him over. "Whoa, girl," Corbett said, laughing.

While the two greeted each other, Ellie-May moved closer to the rock. Travelers had left names, dates, and comments on the sandstone base all the way up to the funnel. Some messages were written in paint; a few had been penned with wagon tar or gunpowder mixed with grease. Others were carefully etched into the sandstone with knives. Loved ones sadly left on the trail were memorialized, but most travelers expressed desire for a better future.

Her gaze jumped from one inscription to the next, and she felt a kinship with the strangers who had passed this way before her.

The remains of hundreds of burnt candles on the ground puzzled her. Was this some sort of altar? She lifted her gaze and gasped. For above the makeshift altar was a magnificent drawing of a weary traveler on his knees praying. A hand reached out of the heavens and touched his shoulder. Written in big bold print were these words: *Put your trust in God. He is the Rock.*

She pressed her hand to her mouth. She recognized Andy's work even before she saw his initials. Carved deep into the sandstone, the art stood out just as she'd imagined his work standing out among masters. The empty canvas of her dreams now had a vision.

Her brother had died far too young. His work would never be seen in fancy art galleries; nor would it ever grace a palace's ivory walls. Instead, his art was displayed on God's masterpiece in all its glory, greeting thousands of weary travelers with its message of faith, hope, and love.

Turning away with tear-filled eyes, she rushed into Corbett's waiting arms.

It started snowing hard, and Corbett led her back to the relay station with Josie close behind. The mule followed them inside the small building with the look Ellie-May had come to dread. Nothing or no one was going to convince that mule to go back outside.

Corbett laughed. "All we need is a babe in a manger."

"And maybe a wise man or two," Ellie-May said.

He reached for the picnic basket and began arranging silverware and plates on the table. He raised a quizzical brow. "You okay?"

She nodded and took a seat. "If it wasn't for Josie, I might never have found my brother's artwork."

"See? I told you to be nice to her." He finished emptying the basket and quickly filled two plates.

At first she didn't think she could eat, but when Corbett set a plate in front of her, her stomach growled. She tasted the potatoes first and then started on the roast beef.

Corbett cleared his throat, and she looked up. "What?"

"Would you care to join me in grace?" he asked.

Blushing, she put down her fork. "I do believe I've been hanging around you too long."

He chuckled and tossed a handful of cooked carrots on the floor for Josie. "Not long enough," he said, lowering his head in prayer.

Later they sat on the bear-skin rug, and Corbett threw another log on the fire.

"Now that your journey has ended, what are your plans?" he asked.

She hugged her knees to her chest. "I. . .I don't know." She didn't want to think about a future without her beloved brother. "What are yours?"

He scooted to her side. "While Mrs. Madison packed our Christmas dinner, her husband mentioned that Shorter County is looking for lawmen. He knows the sheriff and agreed to put in a good word for me."

"That's wonderful," she exclaimed. "Does. . .he know you were incarcerated?"

"He knows." He grimaced as if pained to say it, even now.

Her heart ached, and she covered his hand with her own. "You didn't deserve to be in prison. Not for what you did."

A shadow hovered at his brow as he stared at the fire. "Nebraska will grow by leaps and bounds once the railroad is built."

"Why, Mr. Corbett, is that optimism I hear?"

He slanted a glance at her. "There's got to be a reason God brought me all the way out here."

The thought took her breath away. Or maybe it was the way he said it with none of his usual skepticism. "Next you'll be telling me you believe in miracles."

"When I think about how we met, it's hard not to."

Heart pounding, she gazed at him and realized, suddenly, how much he meant to her.

They both started speaking at once. "What do you—"

"Do you think we can—"

They laughed. "You go," she said.

He shook his head. "Ladies first." His brows rose. "Don't look so surprised. I do have *some* manners."

She smiled, and her heart swelled with tenderness as she gazed at him. Today was one of the worst days of her life. It made no sense to think that it was also one of the best, but there it was. For today she found something she didn't even know she was looking for, and it was something that would last a whole lot longer than the terrible grief she felt. For today she found love.

"You go first," she said. "I insist."

He shook his head. "It's not the right time. You just learned about your brother. What I want to say can wait."

He was wrong about that. Nothing that needed saying should ever wait. That was the one thing she had learned on this trip as she passed the many graves along the way. Life was short and often unpredictable. Had she had it to do over, she would have told her brother how much she loved him. No doubt her father would have done the same. Sadly, she couldn't change the past, only the future.

"What I want to say *can't* wait," she said. It had to be said now, and it had to be said in language this handsome, wonderful man of few words would understand.

"Merry Christmas, *Michael*."

He stared at her as if to make sure he'd heard right. "I told you what would happen if things got too personal between us."

She nodded. "I know, and I intend to hold you to your word."

A smile inched across his face. Then with a whoop of joy, he pulled her in his arms and kissed her like she'd never before been kissed. "Merry Christmas, Ellie-May."

Just as he moved to kiss her again, Josie stuck her nose between them with an approving nod and an ear-splitting *hee-haaaw*!

Epilogue

*We're here with our adorable twins, Ellie and Andy,
and our youngest daughter, Josie. God is our Rock.*

—Carved into Chimney Rock in 1866 by
Sheriff and Mrs. Michael Corbett

Author's Note

The quotations from Chimney Rock are fictional, however, they are based on writings in old diaries and on tombstones. Those attributed to Mark Twain and Wild Bill Hickok come from their writings.

A Christmas Castle

Cynthia Hickey

Chapter 1

Prescott, Arizona
December 1867

Annie Morgan looped her horse's reins over the hitching post, slung her rifle over her shoulder, and marched into one of the many saloons in Prescott, Arizona. Every head turned in her direction. Every conversation ceased. Every glance increased her heart rate.

"I'm looking for Bill Morgan." She lifted her chin, causing her floppy hat to slide to one side. She righted it and glared at the bearded faces turned toward her. "Well, is he here or not?" Her insides quaked. *Please, somebody answer before my last nerve flies out the window.* Her new husband should have been at the livery to meet her. Instead, the grizzled old man who worked there had sent her here.

"He ain't here." The bartender swiped the inside of a glass with a towel. "Maybe you ought to check his land. Heard tell he ain't left it in a couple of days." He grinned at a group of men playing cards. "If you're his new bride, I'm betting he's got a surprise for you."

Well, Annie had one for him, too. The man didn't make a good impression by not meeting her. So far, he wasn't anything like his letters. "Can you direct me to his land?"

The man snickered. "Head straight west about half-a-day's ride. There's a big pile of junk with a sign that says, 'Morgan's Ranch.' If you veer to the northeast a bit, you'll find your nearest neighbor, a man named Carter. He has another surprise for you." He winked at the card players.

This town seemed full of surprises, and Annie had a feeling they weren't pleasant ones. "Thank you kindly." She straightened her hat and shoved through the swinging doors. Something strange was going on, and she aimed to find out what.

Sure enough, four hours later she stopped in front of a sagging fence with a weathered sign stating MORGAN'S RANCH. In the distance, brown cattle grazed, walking over and around a mound of dirt covered on one side by more weathered boards. A few mustangs stood, heads down, in a nearby corral. Chickens squawked, running free.

Annie dismounted and led her horse through a gate ready to fall off its hinges. Already her head spun with a list of things that needed improvement. She'd mention them to Bill at the first opportunity.

She lifted her face to the sun. Although a chill filled the air, the day's moderate weather amazed her. Back home, snow covered the ground and cold bit at your cheeks. She'd heard tell, though, that the area could have snow after the first of the year, if not sooner. It'd be nice not to have to worry about freezing when a body rolled out of bed in the mornings.

Had her new husband lost cattle because of a shoddy fence? Could he possibly be out looking for them? What had she gotten herself into? The letters she'd received from Bill proclaimed him an ambitious man. Annie's first impression showed otherwise.

Certain that God had led her to wed Bill Morgan, sight unseen, she'd had no qualms about leaving Missouri and traveling to Arizona. Now she hovered beside her gelding, filled with indecision. Where was the man?

Seeing no house, Annie let her horse graze on dried grass and wandered the strange land. A small stand of trees—oak, pine, and another she thought might be the Arizona ash she'd heard about—bordered what she hoped was a creek. Bill had written her about one. She headed in that direction, letting her hat hang down her back by its drawstring.

Sure enough, a clear stream ran over rocks. Annie dropped to her knees and splashed her face with the frigid water before cupping her hand for a drink.

Crashing sounds in the nearby brush had her spinning and grabbing for her gun. A wiry-haired mongrel appeared, tail wagging. She grinned. "Well, hello there, boy. Do you live here?" She scratched behind his ears. "Could you possibly be Scout?"

The dog answered with a slobbery kiss.

"Where's your master, boy?" Annie straightened and glanced around. The land showed promise. Not as fertile as Missouri, perhaps, but promising all the same.

The sun sat low in the sky, and the temperature dropped. Forgetting her irritation at Bill's nonappearance, now she was worried. She snapped her fingers for the dog to follow and headed for the mound of junk.

Wait. A board cross next to the creek caught her attention. She rushed over and read the crude letters burned into the wood. BILL MORGAN. REST IN PEACE.

She fell to her knees. This must be the surprise the townsmen thought so humorous.

A widow before ever meeting her husband. Tears pricked her eyes. What would she do now? There was nothing left for her in Missouri. No parents, no family. Why would God bring her this far only to leave her alone again?

Planting her hands on her thighs, she pushed to her feet. First order of business: she needed to find the house, then the neighbor who supposedly had another surprise for her.

Slapping her hat back over her braids, she headed for the pile of wood around the mound, leaving Scout to continue investigating whatever he felt the desire to stick his nose in.

If she had to sleep outside, it wouldn't be the first time, but she needed to start a fire. Once the sun slipped below the horizon, the temperature would drop fast.

She stopped by the mound. Her heart sank. Why was there a door propped against the dirt?

෴

"Hold it right there, mister." Drake held his shotgun on the trespasser and tried to ignore the tight hold of the child sitting on the horse behind him. He prayed there wouldn't be gunfire, not with the little one so close. *She's already seen enough violence in her life.*

The stranger put his hands up and turned to face Drake. When he tilted his head, his hat fell, releasing mahogany braids that reached to his—no—her waist.

"You're a woman." Sparks flew from hazel eyes. He couldn't recall ever seeing a prettier woman, leather pants or not. She must be Bill's bride. He'd told him she was scheduled to arrive that day.

"Last time I looked in the mirror, I was."

"But you're wearing britches." Drake shook his head and lowered his gun. "Who are you?"

"Annie Templeton. No, it's Morgan now, and you're on my land."

She sure wasn't what Drake expected. Bill had filled him with tales of a lady. A woman excited about helping him run his ranch. Drake needed to get to town more, or at least make the rounds of neighbors. "When did you get in?"

"I arrived a little bit ago, expecting to meet my new husband, but instead. . ." She waved a hand toward the creek bed. "We were married by proxy not more than a week ago. Who are you?"

"Drake Carter. I'm your closest neighbor. My place is an hour's ride from here, right across the boundary line." He reached behind him and lowered May to the ground then tossed her pack next to her. "Since you're Bill's widow, seems like this is your new daughter, May."

Annie's eyes widened, and her skin paled, making her freckles look like drops of watered-down coffee. "Daughter? Bill didn't say anything about a child."

"Well, he had one." Drake dismounted. "Guess you found the grave."

"Did you bury him?"

"Yep, two days ago." He nudged May forward. "Found the little one and the dog sitting all alone in the house." The child shrank back against him and stuck her thumb in her mouth.

"I'm obliged." Annie took her lower lip between her teeth. "How'd he die?"

"Scoundrels after his land." Drake shrugged. "I was checking the boundary fence and heard gunfire. By the time I got here, it was too late." Seemed like most folks died that way out here, or by disease. He studied the pretty woman in front of him. How would she manage several hundred acres of land and cattle all on her own? What if Hayward returned with his hired hands? The poor thing wouldn't stand a chance.

"Where's the house?"

"You're looking at it."

She frowned. "Where?"

"That door leads to a dugout. A good-sized one, too. I reckon Bill dug out a good ten-by-fifteen foot of space."

"A hole in the ground?"

Drake didn't think it possible, but she paled further. He took a step forward in case she fainted. Instead, she whipped her rifle around and had it pointed at him before he took the second step. "Whoa." He held up his hands. "I mean you no harm. I thought you might faint."

"I've never fainted in my life." She narrowed her eyes. "Child, come over here behind me."

May shook her head and ducked behind Drake.

"Go on, sweetheart. This is your new mama." He lifted her and set her down by Annie. "She ain't never had a mom. Hers died in childbirth. It's always been her and Bill."

"How old is she?"

"Four." Drake didn't feel right leaving the two alone, but there wasn't much help for it. The sun was setting fast, and he needed to get home. "I'll show you around the place, then I've get to git." He pulled on the flimsy dugout door. "Come see your place. Bill installed a new cookstove a short while ago, most likely in preparation for your coming. He hadn't gotten around to putting in a stovepipe yet. I'll light a lantern, but take care on the steps leading down. A couple of them need repairing." He rushed down the stairs and lit a lamp on the table before watching Annie, who now clutched May's hand like a lifeline, enter.

"It isn't much, but it'll do until you get a proper cabin built. There's two bunks, a dry sink, a table, two chairs, and that's pretty much it." He'd lived in a dugout while building his own cabin and hadn't thought much of what a woman would think until now. The place sure looked sparse. And dirty. "That crack over there is big enough to point a rifle barrel through if the need arises. It's also all you've got in the way of a window."

"Oh my." She released May's hand and turned slowly in a circle. "It's. . .different." She speared him with a glance. "Without a husband, how can I be expected to build a cabin?"

Right. Looks like Drake had another job added to his list. "Bill already cut the lumber."

She pressed her lips together. "I'll make do. Thank you for taking care of. . .May." She plopped on one of the bunks, releasing a cloud of dust.

"I reckon you could sell out and head back to where you came from." Drake crossed his arms. He refused to allow himself to feel guilty. Annie should've made sure things were more to her liking before hitching herself to a man like Bill.

"You'd like that, wouldn't you?" She tossed her hat on the rickety table. "After all, didn't you say Bill died because of his land? Are you offering to buy, or should I wait for the next no-good scalawag to make an offer?"

"Now, wait one minute." Did she just compare him to the men who killed Bill? He ought to leave her to her own devices. He turned for the door. "I'm an hour's ride due east. You can't miss the house. After I buried, Bill, I've been coming every day to tend to the stock. Now that you're here, I've plenty work of my own."

"Wait. My apologies. It's. . . I've got a lot to take in right now. I'd offer you a cup of coffee, but. . ." She waved a hand.

"The shelves are fairly well stocked. There's what's left of Bill's cash in May's bag, and he's got a running credit at the Grayson's. You let me know if I can help you in any other way." He took the steps two at a time until he darted back into sunshine. Closed in spaces always made him feel as if he were in a cage. The six months he'd lived in a dugout were the longest of his life.

He called to his horse and then mounted in one motion. From this higher vantage point, he could see all the improvements that needed to be made. He shook his head. If he offered, it'd take up most of his day, and he still had a ride home. But the good Lord wouldn't look kindly on a man who didn't offer. He'd be back tomorrow with May's clothes and a hammer and nails.

With a click of his tongue, he steered toward home, his mind listing the things he could accomplish in a day and the things that would take longer. Between his place and Annie's, he'd be busier than a three-legged dog after a jackrabbit.

He laughed, envisioning the first time Annie would try to give May a bath. He still had the teeth imprints in his hand from his one attempt.

Oh to be a fly on the wall in that dugout tonight.

Chapter 2

Annie rolled off the cot, keeping the quilt wrapped around her shoulders. Seemed yesterday's mild weather had given in to winter's cold. She padded to the cookstove and added more kindling to the low embers.

What had she gotten into? She cast a glance to where May still slept. She hadn't liked letting the child go to bed filthy, but exhaustion won out. Today a bath would definitely be in order.

With the fire building in the stove, she perused the contents of the shelves and decided on flapjacks for breakfast. Later she'd make their hole in the ground habitable. She had a trunk arriving on tomorrow's stagecoach with a few of her mother's things. She hoped they'd help make the place a home.

She faced the table. May sat staring up at her with big eyes the color of blue bonnets.

"You can go play while I fix breakfast." Annie picked up a cast-iron skillet. "Do you have any toys?"

May shook her head and stuck her dirty thumb in her mouth.

No toys? "Not even a doll?"

Another shake of the head.

Well, Christmas was on the horizon. Annie was a fair seamstress. She'd sew May a doll, and the little girl a dress to match. Just because Annie found wearing pants more convenient didn't mean that the child shouldn't have the option to choose for herself.

What if May didn't like her, even after Annie took care of her? Annie had no younger siblings and had rarely had neighbor children to play with. She glanced at May. She'd treat the girl like a small adult; she didn't know any other way to respond to a person. Hopefully it would be sufficient. With her own melancholy and mentally absent mother, Annie definitely knew what not to do in regard to raising a child.

She dropped a blob of lard onto the hot skillet and listened to the pleasing sizzle. She had a bit of red flannel in her trunk. Maybe May would enjoy making ribbons to decorate greenery around the dugout. As a child, Annie had loved decorating for Christmas. Since it appeared she now had a young'un of her own, she'd introduce the little girl to some of the things she'd loved and give them some time to get to know each other.

After mixing the batter, she poured some into the hot skillet. Soon the smell of frying flapjacks filled the room. "Okay, May, I'm going to tell you everything I need to do today. You help me remember." What did one talk about to a little girl with eyes as big as saucers?

"First thing is to get as much of the dust out of here as possible. That most likely means washing the linens. Then we need to find the hole in the chicken coop and round up them feathered rascals." She glanced out of the corner of her eye. May's gaze never left her. Annie smiled. "Then, I think we'll give you a bath."

"I hate baths!" May dashed up the stairs and out the door.

Annie removed the pan from the fire and raced after her. Outside, she barreled into the little girl and wrapped her arms around her to prevent taking them both to the ground. May pointed toward the gate. Scout dashed from the woods and barked, running to May's side.

Squinting, Annie made out the form of four men on horseback. She whirled and dragged May into the dugout. "Stay here." She grabbed her rifle and headed back outside.

Annie aimed her gun at the biggest target: a man dressed in black sitting tall on his horse. "State your business." She narrowed her eyes.

"My name's Ben Hayward." He removed his hat. "I'm here only to welcome you to Prescott, Mrs. Morgan. It isn't every day that a comely widow moves to these parts. I've come to offer my services."

She snapped at the still barking dog. "Hush, Scout." The noise set her nerves on edge.

"In what capacity? If you've come to make an offer on my land, you can turn around and leave. I have no intention of selling."

"Mrs. Morgan." Hayward swung a leg over the horse to begin his dismount.

"Don't bother getting down." Annie's arm was starting to shake from holding the gun steady for several minutes. "You can talk just as well from the saddle."

Hayward sighed. "I haven't come to make an offer on your land but rather to offer you my hand in marriage."

"Whatever for?"

"Women are scarce out here, and one as beautiful as yourself shouldn't be left to tend to a ranch alone. I'm willing to care for you and the child while joining our acreage together. It's a winning situation for both of us."

"Are you the skunk who murdered my husband?"

"Now, Mrs. Morgan, that was an unfortunate accident. I made the man a fair offer, and he pulled a gun on me and my men." Hayward held up his hands. "We mean you no harm."

"Turn around and leave, Mr. Hayward, before I put a bullet through your scheming heart."

❧

Drake slowed his horse at the sight of Annie struggling to lift her gate into place. Why didn't the stubborn woman wait for him? He grunted. Had he even mentioned he'd be back today? He stopped and dismounted. "Let me do that. It's too heavy for you."

She rubbed the back of her gloved hand across her already dirty face.

Instead of making her unattractive, the fruits of her hard labor appealed to Drake, and he pulled away to focus on the task at hand. It wouldn't do to pay too much attention to Annie. He was here to do a job, nothing more.

"Thank you. The sorry thing was already falling, but then one of Hayward's men knocked it completely down when I refused to marry him. The whole fence looks like it would fall with a brisk wind."

"Marry who? The hired hand?" This couldn't be good. In town less than twenty-four hours and already Annie had a target on her back. There had to be more to Hayward's attention than water rights.

"No. Mr. Hayward."

Drake lifted the gate into place. "I take it he didn't care for your answer."

"Nope." Annie leaned against the fence and helped hold the gate while Drake hammered. "I don't understand the man's intentions." She stared toward town.

"I'm wondering whether the man's thirsting for more here than water." Drake motioned her to step back while he swung the gate back and forth. "That ought to hold. What else would you like me to do?"

She tilted her head. "Don't you have work of your own?"

"Yep, but I can't rest easy knowing what a mess Bill left you." Nor, could he, in good conscience, leave her be while a snake like Hayward hung around.

"I need to give May a bath. Could you round up the chickens and fix the coop? Oh, and there are a couple of pigs rooting in the woods. Can you build an enclosure for them?"

"Sure." Easy enough jobs.

"And tomorrow, I've a trunk coming in on the stage. I don't feel comfortable going into town with Hayward sniffing around. Could you fetch it for me?"

Drake sighed. He knew offering his help would result in a lot of nonsense. Why didn't the woman hire someone to deliver the dratted thing? No help for it now. He guessed if it all came down to most desirable job, he'd rather muck out a pigpen, fix a chicken coop, and waste a day riding to town than try giving May a bath.

Annie marched to the dugout and disappeared inside its dark depths. Within a few minutes, she returned with a plate of flapjacks.

"Eat," she said. "I'll call when lunch is ready."

Drake watched her retreat back into her hole. A beautiful but strange woman. He wondered what caused her to let go of the familiar and travel west to marry a man she'd never met. He shrugged.

He needed to get things fixed as soon as possible and avoid Annie Templeton Morgan as much as possible. He had no desire, or time, to get tangled up with a woman no matter how pretty, and it was none of his concern as to why she married Bill. It was his Christian duty to make sure she didn't harm herself or the child, and that was best done by making repairs around her property.

The flapjacks melted in his mouth. Maybe he could work out a way of having Annie cook for him in return for repairs. He hated his own cooking. When he'd finished, he set the plate on a stump and got back to work.

A shriek rose over the sound of Drake's hammer. He whirled, hand on the butt of his gun. He relaxed and chuckled.

Annie had a kicking May slung over her shoulder as she marched toward the creek. This, Drake had to see. He propped his tools against the fence and jogged after them.

"The water's cold!" May squirmed until Annie dropped her into the creek.

"If you hadn't knocked over the tub, you would have a warm bath."

"You're mean." May threw a handful of mud at Annie. It hit with a splat and slid down the front of her faded yellow shirt.

Drake crossed his arms and leaned against a pine tree. The scene before him beat working for sure.

Annie pulled a bar of soap from her pocket, toed off her boots, and waded into the creek after May. She wrapped an arm around the flailing child and started scrubbing.

"Your lips are turning blue." Drake didn't know what he'd expected, but it sure wasn't for Annie to join the child in the cold water.

"No doubt." Annie grunted and took both her and May under the water. They came up sputtering, and Annie struggled to drag May back to the bank.

Drake stepped forward and offered her a hand. He froze at the sight of her wet blouse clinging to curves better left disguised. He averted his gaze and pulled.

"Thank you." Annie slung May back over her shoulder and headed home. "Next time I tell you to take a bath, I'm guessing you'll listen, and don't think you're going to get out of helping me mop up the mud in the house."

Maybe Annie would be all right out here after all. Drake shook his head and followed. He'd never met a more strong-willed person, male or female. Poor little May didn't stand a chance.

By the time he entered the dugout after fetching his tools, Annie and May huddled together by the stove. May sat on Annie's lap, her head tucked under the woman's chin. Well, what do you know? Maybe Drake had been too easy on the little tyke. Her father, too. All the child needed was a firm hand and then a consoling shoulder when it was all over.

"I'll get you something to eat in a bit," Annie said over her shoulder. "Gotta take the chill off first."

"No hurry." Drake backed out of the small space. "I'll work on the coop." He'd have to take his meal outside. Just stepping into the dugout caused his heart to race. There didn't seem to be enough air to breathe, not to mention the lack of space for a man well over six feet tall.

The coop sat behind the dugout, out of sight of the road. Drake found the hole. Looked chewed through by an animal. He nailed a couple of boards over the hole. Once he found the chickens, Annie would have fresh eggs every morning.

He didn't know how many fowl Bill had, but he found a rooster and three hens among the forest's foliage. He tossed them into the repaired coop and then stretched the kinks from his back.

"Now it all makes sense." Hayward stepped from the trees, a cigar dangling from his lips. "The lovely widow doesn't want me because she already has you. Well played, Carter. A beautiful woman, desirable acreage—why, you've got it all."

"What is it you want, Hayward?" Drake's fingers itched for his gun.

"Don't play stupid." Hayward blew a smoke ring in the air. "I want the mineral rights to this land. Bill flashed gold all over town. The fool even tossed several nuggets on the bar. It's simple, really, what I'm after. His having a beautiful widow only sweetened the pot."

"You can't have her if she's already married to me."

Chapter 3

Drake wanted to bite his tongue. What would Annie do if Hayward confronted her with the fact she was marrying him? He struggled to keep his composure. What a blasted fool. How was he going to tell Annie they were getting married?

"We have ourselves a predicament, Mr. Carter." Hayward tossed his cigar butt at Drake's feet. "I want this land we stand on and the creek that runs through it. Somewhere on this land is gold, unless Morgan lied, which I doubt."

"Did he actually say he found the gold here?" Drake kept his fingers close to his gun and crushed the burning ember of the cigar under his boot. Drake knew Bill had found gold, but it wasn't on this land. Most likely it was found somewhere else and brought to Arizona in a saddlebag. Either way, that type of rumor could only spell danger to Annie—and to him.

"Not in so many words." Hayward frowned. "But his meaning was clear. When a man buys horses with gold, people take notice. I want this land, and I intend to have it."

"Over my dead body."

"I don't kill, Mr. Carter." Hayward melted back into the shadows. "Until next time."

No, he just let his hired hands kill for him. Drake's blood ran cold. The man was as heartless as a rabid wolf and every bit as dangerous. Drake couldn't waste any time in coming up with a plan to protect Annie and May. He hadn't thought to marry, but he would if it kept them safe.

After a few minutes without seeing any more signs of Hayward or his men, Drake gathered his tools and meandered back to the dugout. He'd decline the offer of lunch and head back to his place. His mind whirled like a dust devil, and he wasn't any closer to coming up with an answer to his loco remark to shut up Hayward. He needed to find a different solution than getting hitched.

As he rode home, he expected to feel a bullet rip between his shoulder blades. Tension knotted his shoulders.

He, a grown man, had raced away from a woman like she was a porcupine

215

ready to stab him with her quills. He shook his head. If being around a good-looking woman left him this addled, he definitely needed to get to town more.

Tomorrow. He sighed. He'd promised her he'd fetch her trunk tomorrow.

Smoke rose on the horizon. Drake's mouth dried up. He spurred his horse to a gallop and raced for home.

∾

Annie pulled a small drawstring bag out of May's things and peeked inside. Gold? Was there gold on her land? Was that why Hayward was determined to claim it?

She glanced around the dugout. Where could she hide it? Why hadn't Mr. Carter mentioned it, or had he not even bothered to go through May's few items of clothing? From the looks of the child yesterday, Annie would guess not.

The spittoon. She'd clean it out and stuff the bag in there. With no one around who chewed tobacco, the gold should be safe and left undetected from marauders.

She didn't deserve the money. Having never met Bill, much less loved him as a wife should, she didn't feel she was due the inheritance. But she knew from his letters that he had no one else, and she had nowhere else to go. Her gaze fell on May. She'd take care of the land and the money for the sake of Bill's daughter.

Leaving the child wrapped in blankets, Annie donned her clothes and slipped out into the morning cold to take care of the stock and gather eggs. The peace of the morning surrounded her with a gentle embrace. She might feel guilty at enjoying land she felt she had no claim to, but for the first time in her life, she had something that actually belonged to her.

Scout bounded to her side and sent the chickens into a panic. Annie laughed and glanced at the repairs Mr. Carter had managed to make the day before. The next thing on the list would be to fix the fence. She could do that herself. None of the chores were too difficult if she set her mind to doing them.

She studied the dugout. Surely there was a way to make the place look less like a junk heap. She pulled her coat tight. But the dugout served its purpose of keeping out the cold. Most likely, it would stay cool in the summer as well. Maybe she could live with its ugliness for a while.

Would Mr. Carter bring the trunk today? If so, he wouldn't show up until at least the noon hour. She finished collecting eggs and headed back to the dugout to fix breakfast.

A cloud of dust rose on the horizon. She set the basket on a stump and grabbed her rifle. Surely Hayward wouldn't bother her so early in the morning.

Cattle and horses thundered toward her. Annie whistled for Scout and dashed inside the dugout. Underground was the safest place she could think of to be in a stampede. She gathered May in her arms and waited for the pounding of hooves overhead. None came. Instead, a whistle pierced the day. She slowly emerged into the sunlight.

Drake marched toward her, his face set in grim lines. Soot marked his skin and clothing. Strange cattle mingled with hers.

"What's happening?" Annie peered into his face.

"You're coming with me to collect your trunk." He slapped his hat against his thigh, sending puffs of dust and ashes into the air.

"Are these your cattle?"

"Yes."

"I don't understand." Whatever it was, she didn't want to hear it.

"My place is gone. Burned to the ground. House, barn, everything."

"Hayward?"

"That's my guess." Drake slapped his hat back on his head. "So we're going into town and getting hitched."

Annie froze. "Excuse me?"

"We're getting married. I told Hayward we were."

Fire burned through her limbs. If she didn't know better, she'd think smoke came out her ears. "And why, pray tell, would you do something so stupid?" She stuck her hands in her pockets to prevent herself from punching him.

"It's the only way to keep you and May safe. If you're married, Hayward can't pester you to marry him. Any deals he wants to try to make would go through your husband." Drake waved an arm at the mingling cattle. "I've combined our stock, removed the boundary fence, and come to stay until I have time to build another house. I can't do that unless we're married. It wouldn't be proper."

"Neither is doing all that without consulting me!" Annie stepped close enough that her nose practically touched his chin. "I haven't been married a month yet, nor widowed for much less time than that. Perhaps I don't wish to wed again."

"Do you have a better idea?" Drake planted his hands on his hips and stared into her eyes.

My, a woman could forget herself. His eyes were so blue. No, there were other things to contend with. "We were doing just fine as we were."

"I can't ride back and forth every day. I can't watch both places at the same time."

"Then I'll care for myself." Annie whirled, grabbed her basket of eggs with enough force to send several crashing to the ground, and stomped down the stairs of the dugout.

The man was plumb loco. She slammed the door and cringed as dirt rained on her head. She set the basket on the table and plopped on the edge of her cot. May watched her, silent as usual unless the subject of a bath came up.

Was there reason in Mr. Carter's proposition? True, having a man around full-time would be convenient and safer, but Annie had always dreamed of a proper proposal. Her first marriage occurred on paper. Why did she expect another one to be better? She took a deep breath and filled a kettle with water.

If today was going to be her wedding day, she might as well wash up. She ran her hands down her buckskin pants. Since she'd grown old enough to know her own mind, her insistence on wearing britches had been a point of consternation with her ma. Now the idea of wearing a dress seemed foreign. What would Mr. Carter think if she started dressing like a woman? What should she care? Pants were more practical.

Would God ever send her a man to love, or would her marriages always be ones of convenience? And what about Christmas? The dugout had no room for a tree. Annie doubted May had ever experienced Christmas, and it had been years since she had. What a silly woman, worried over something as trivial as holiday decorations.

She stood and cracked eggs into the skillet. "Go tell Mr. Carter that breakfast is almost ready."

May dashed outside. She returned by the time Annie set plates of scrambled eggs and bacon on the table. "He says he'll eat outside."

"I don't think so." She exited the dugout and approached Mr. Carter by the well. "If I'm to marry you without a proper proposal, then the least you can do is eat with your soon-to-be family." She crossed her arms.

"I don't like closed-in spaces."

"Then how in tarnation do you expect to have a place to sleep?" Annie glanced around her land. "I don't even have a barn."

"Reckon I didn't think that far ahead."

She narrowed her eyes. "There's no time like the present to get over your fears. Come on." She marched away, knowing without looking that he would follow. She grinned. No man liked to be outwitted by a woman.

Ignoring the fact that Mr. Carter paused at the dugout's entrance, Annie took her seat at the table, raised the wick on the lantern to cast more light around the room, and waited. Drake joined her with all the enthusiasm of a man going to his own hanging.

"So, you'll marry me?" He sat across from her.

"I reckon, although I've heard of better proposals." She flushed at the sight of her cot behind him. "May will sleep with me, and you can have the other cot."

"Fair enough." Mr. Carter spooned a healthy serving of eggs onto his plate. "We'll head into town after breakfast and hunt down the preacher."

"And fetch my things." Annie set her hand over his and gave it a squeeze.

He raised a startled glance.

She glared at him. "Here's a warning for you. If you try to take my gold, I'll shoot you, husband or not."

Chapter 4

Annie followed her husband-to-be into town with May perched on the horse behind her. At least this wedding would have a physical groom in attendance.

By the time they reached town, snow flurries drifted from a gray sky. Annie shivered and pulled her wool coat closer around her. She could feel May's shudders and wondered how much credit Bill had at the mercantile. Clearly, they both needed warmer coats.

She peered in the window of Grayson's as they rode past. A scarlet dress adorned a headless dress form. What would it feel like to dress like a girl for once? A woman? She shrugged. A dress around a rundown ranch. Britches were more practical. She ran a hand over her thigh. Besides, she was the one who killed the doe whose skin she'd used.

Mr. Carter stopped in front of a clapboard building with a small steeple. He dismounted and helped May down from the back of Annie's horse. With her heart in her throat, Annie followed him inside. Marriage was forever, "till death do you part." And she knew less about this man than she'd known about Bill. At least with Bill, she'd corresponded over the course of several months.

"Are you okay?" Mr. Carter removed his hat. "It's not too late to back out, although I still think marriage is the safest recourse."

"No, I'm not changing my mind. There's strength in numbers, and we can't fight together unless we're wed." She wiped sweaty palms down the legs of her pants and wondered again about purchasing a dress. How would Mr. Carter look at her if she looked like a woman?

Would she see admiration in his eyes or the same weary resignation he exhibited now?

He crooked his arm and gave her a small smile. She slid her hand in the crook of his elbow and allowed him to lead her to the pastor's residence. Before she knew it, Annie Templeton Morgan added Carter to her name.

"Your trunk is most likely at the livery. Is there somewhere else you'd like to go while we're in town?" Mr. Carter escorted her outside.

"The mercantile, please." Annie had a list in her mind and knew that a full day back and forth would make trips to town few and far between.

He nodded. "Why don't you do that while I rent a buckboard for your trunk? You should probably buy necessities for the winter, too. Mine burned with the house."

Annie took May's hand and rushed across the street. Pa rarely wanted to wait while Ma shopped. Perhaps her latest husband was the same.

A bell tinkled over the door when she pushed it open, and a round woman behind the counter greeted them with a smile. Annie sent May to sit by the woodstove radiating heat in the center of the store while she browsed.

"I'm Mrs. Grayson," the shopkeeper told her. "Is there something I can help you with?"

"I'm Mrs. Morgan—no, now Mrs. Carter." Would she ever be able to keep her names straight? Annie leaned closer to the woman. "I'm looking for a doll."

"For the little one?" Mrs. Grayson grinned. "Oh, hello, little May. I remember you from when you visited with your pa in the spring." She lowered her voice. "I have just the thing. A pretty, curly haired doll with a blue dress." She pulled a box from under the counter. "I've yet to set them on the shelf."

"Do you have a child's dress to match?" Annie peered under the lid. Her breath caught at the doll's beauty. She'd always wanted one.

"We do." Mrs. Grayson came around the counter and led Annie to a rack of readymade clothing. "This looks about the child's size." She removed a dress the same shade as May's eyes. The garment had white ruffles around the neck and hem. It was perfect. "What about for yourself?"

Could she? Annie looked down at her calico blouse and stained britches. "The dress in the window." She exhaled. She was buying a dress. Had she lost her mind? Pa would say she was growing silly in her adult years. She didn't care. A red dress for Christmas!

"Lovely. Do you need flour, sugar. . .?"

"Yes, and heavy coats. I'll be back in the spring to settle my account." On a whim, she grabbed a forest-green man's shirt from the rack and added it to the pile, along with wool and cotton to sew clothing. If Mr. Carter's food had burned, then so had his clothes, and he needed something under the tree on Christmas morning, too.

For as long as Annie could remember, she'd wanted something of her own. Now she had land, a child, and a husband. One more thing than her poor ma and pa had had. Poor sharecroppers, they'd rarely had anything to call their own, much less land. She'd work hard to keep all three, whether her marriage had love or not. Over time, God willing, they could at least have mutual respect.

"Which account should I put these on? Mr. Morgan's or Mr. Carter's?" Mrs. Grayson opened a thick leather-bound book. "Or should I combine the two?"

"Yes, please." She supposed she'd have to let her husband know.

May tugged on Annie's sleeve. "That man is staring." She pointed.

Annie turned to the window. Mr. Hayward stood on the sidewalk. He tipped his hat and continued on his way. "Add some ammunition to that pile of supplies, would you, Mrs. Grayson?"

So much for flights of fancy. Life would be spent keeping May safe and holding on to her land. There wasn't time for foolishness or daydreaming or wondering *what ifs* about love.

❧

Drake hitched the horses to the buckboard and glared at Hayward as the man paced the sidewalk in front of the mercantile. He was sure it was all around town that the Widow Morgan and he were hitched. Word spread fast in those parts. Why couldn't the man leave well enough alone?

If there was gold on Bill's land, he would have said something. Even a fool who bothered to ask questions would know Bill recently came from California. That's how he'd had the funds to purchase his land in the first place. He'd earned the gold working in a gaming hall.

Drake had told his neighbor plenty of times not to flash the nuggets around, but he'd wanted to buy the supplies to build a cabin for his new bride. Drake shook his head. All for nothing. Now he was dead over a squabble. Drake hooked the tugs to the evener. And now he was married with a child.

Life could take a huge turn in a short amount of time. It was all a man could do to keep up.

Horses hitched, he led them across the street in order to load the supplies. Hayward nodded and moved toward the saloon. Good riddance.

Annie came out of the mercantile. "Why doesn't he shoot us and get it over with?" She boosted May into the wagon. "If that's his intention."

"I don't think he intends to kill anyone." Drake watched the man push through the saloon's swinging doors. "Bill was an accident, Hayward said. He said Bill fired first."

"You believe him?"

"I do. If Hayward was a murdering a man, we'd be dead for sure. No, he intends to run us off or force us to sell, and he'll burn us out if he has to."

"Like he did you." Annie marched back into the mercantile and returned with her arms loaded.

"I'll get those. You watch May." He took the bundles from her.

"I can carry things." Her eyes flashed.

Drake didn't think she could get any prettier than when riled. "Let me do the heavy work. A woman has enough to do. Hasn't a man ever taken care of you?"

She tilted her chin. "No. I don't want a man to take care of me. I want a man to let me work alongside him as God intended."

"How so?" Drake leaned against the wagon. This ought to be interesting.

"Do you believe in the Bible, Mr. Carter?"

"Drake."

"Excuse me?"

"It's Drake. We're married, and yes, I believe in the truth of God's Word."

"Then you know Eve was created as a helpmate for Adam." She crossed her arms and fixed her eyes on his.

"Point taken. Suit yourself. We'll load the wagon together." He marched inside and slung a bag of flour over his shoulder, chuckling as Annie struggled to do the same. He wanted to tell her to take the smaller things just to get her riled again but thought better of it. The ride home was long, and could be even longer with an angry woman.

By the time they got the wagon loaded, snow fell heavier. It'd most likely turn to rain by morning. Drake looked at the pile of supplies and shook his head, knowing he'd have to go back to the livery to get a canvas covering. Seemed like women required a lot of things. He would start on a shed first thing in the morning in which to store it all, and then he'd start a cabin, weather permitting.

He hoisted himself on the wagon seat and flicked the reins. Annie's thigh brushed against his, sending a wave of heat through the layers of both their pants. Separate cots or not, he doubted he'd get much sleep that night. Not with her breathing a few feet away and him having to sleep inside such a closed-in space like the dugout.

"Here." Annie draped a thick wool coat over him. "I bought us all new coats."

"Really?" Knowing she'd thought of him warmed him more than any coat. He took another look at her and May. Sure enough, they both wore new coats. Good thing, because with the way the snow was coming down, the horses would be knee deep in the stuff by the time they got home.

"I'm much obliged." He didn't begrudge her the pile in the back of the wagon. As sweet as she was proving to be, he'd be hard pressed not to shower her with gifts himself. Maybe he should have gotten hitched a long time ago.

Late afternoon looked like nightfall when they reached home. Drake sent the females inside while he unhitched the animals and sent them to their corral and lean-to. He stomped his feet to warm them. The supplies could stay where they were. Covered with the tarp, they'd be all right until he found a place to put them. Bill would have piled them in a corner of the dugout, but Drake wanted to make the place less crowded. Maybe he could find a lock that hadn't burned in the fire at his place.

He gazed at the door. It'd be dim in there. Airless. He shuddered, whether from cold or nerves, he didn't know.

Annie opened the door. "You coming?"

"Yeah."

She stepped out, wrapping a blanket around her shoulders. "You're afraid. Why?"

The time had to come sooner or later. "When I was twelve, I went camping with my older cousins and followed them into a cave and got lost. I had no lantern and headed farther away from the opening. It took until the next day until I found my way out. Can't stomach small places to this day."

She tilted her head and peered up under the brim of his hat. "I can't make the dugout larger, but I can light a second lantern, and you can have the cot by the window so you can see the sky."

He wanted to kiss her. Grab her close and claim her lips. No one had ever been so thoughtful of him. Yet now he was married to a woman who didn't love him but wanted to make sure he was comfortable. He had nothing to give her in return but protection. He prayed it would be enough.

Chapter 5

Annie woke to darkness. Sometime during the night, Drake must have extinguished the lanterns. She smiled at his bravery. She wouldn't say a word. If he could sleep without a lit lantern, they'd save on fuel.

Glancing at his cot, she noted it was empty. The lack of laziness on Drake's part, even before their marriage, warmed her despite the chill in the room. It wasn't as freezing as the cabin back home, but even in a home underground, winter made itself felt.

She glanced out the slit of a window. The sun was just beginning its peek over the mountains, painting the sky with coral and pumpkin. A light dusting of snow covered the ground. Oh she hoped they'd have a white Christmas.

After lighting a lantern, she set to starting a fire in the stove. Breakfast would be ready by the time Drake returned from morning chores. She glanced at May and decided to let the little one sleep. Annie had lost sleep during the night because of the child's thrashing. May likely needed more rest.

Half an hour later, Drake returned with a pail of milk and a few eggs.

"We have a milk cow?" Pleasure rippled through Annie. There was so much she needed to discover about her new home.

"Two, now that I've combined our stock." He grinned. "Breakfast smells good."

"Flapjacks and bacon." His presence made the dugout that much smaller. How would they make it through the winter with three people in such a tight space? "Sit. It's about ready."

Maybe she could make cheese to sell at the mercantile. No, the long trek into town wouldn't make that practical. She smiled. For once, she'd have more food than three people could eat. The West truly was a land of milk and honey.

"I'll wake May." Drake gently shook her shoulder. "Time to rise and shine, sweetheart. After breakfast, I'll work on a shed for the supplies," he said, turning to Annie. "I'll have to use some of the wood intended for the cabin, but with Bill's gold, we can replace the wood easily enough."

Annie's hand stilled, spatula suspended over the flapjacks. Had Drake married her for the gold? Her heart sank. Too late to back out now. He'd known Bill better than she had anyway. He had as much of a right to it as she did, if you didn't factor in that she had been Bill's wife. She'd never laid eyes on the man. She sure would like to be loved for herself though. Someday, God willing.

She sighed and slid the flapjack onto a plate. "That's fine. I'm going to unpack my trunk and work on making this hole in the ground look more like a home." Annie smiled at May. "And we'll go looking for greenery to decorate with."

"Why?" Drake set his fork on his plate and glanced around the room. "Isn't it small enough in here without adding unnecessary things?"

"I've been looking forward to a real Christmas for years." What if Drake thought celebrating was a waste of time? She slumped in her seat. Pa hadn't liked holidays, but Bill's letters said he had. Annie should have known better than to get her hopes up.

"Are you wanting a tree, too?"

"Yes, even if only a small one." She tipped her head toward May. "I doubt she's ever had a Christmas. Look how excited she is." The little girl's eyes were as large as owl eyes, and she transferred her attention from Annie to Drake and back so fast that Annie thought her head might fall off.

"You can't be excited about something you've never had."

"Just a small tree in the center of the table." Annie wasn't going to budge on decorating. No matter how small the space, there was always something that could be done. She forked a bite of flapjack and lifted it to her mouth, her gaze not leaving Drake's face.

He ate like a man who hadn't eaten in weeks, shoveling the food into his mouth as fast as possible, glancing out the window every few seconds.

❧

Despite the rumbling of his stomach, Drake dreaded mealtimes in the dugout. Now that he was hitched, he wouldn't ask to eat outside anymore, for risk of hurting Annie's feelings. But now the crazy woman wanted to take up more valuable space with frilly decorations. His leg jerked up and down, bumping the table.

"What is that noise?" Annie bent to peer over the table.

Drake put his hand on his leg to still it. "I didn't hear anything."

"Are you feeling closed in right now? The sun is streaming through the window."

A slit of a window barely big enough for a rifle barrel. "I'm fine. Tell me why decorating for the holidays is so important to you." Anything to take his mind off the walls closing in.

"When I was real little, we celebrated, but then life got tough. Pa took to drink, and anything happy or frivolous flew out the window." Annie reached over and refilled Drake's coffee with a white speckled pot. "During my correspondence with Bill, he said he liked the holidays. I got my hopes up is all. We don't have to."

A tremor in her words belied the bravado. There was no way Drake could let the holidays go uncelebrated now. Not if it meant he'd hurt her feelings. He reached across the table and placed his hand over hers. "Do what you want."

Tears filled her eyes. Drake stood and fled outside. Nothing scared him more than a woman's tears.

Having a woman around to cook and serve him with a smile was nice, but Drake missed his own homestead. It hadn't escaped him that with his land and Annie's, they were quite wealthy. Not to mention Bill's pouch of gold. Yep, they were sitting pretty.

He selected the lumber he would need for the shed and located Bill's saw between the pig shelter and the fence. Sometimes the man stuck things in the oddest places or left them where he'd used them last. It might take Drake months to get the place operating correctly. Maybe he should consider hiring an extra hand, if they had a place for the man to sleep. Someone to help him make improvements, care for the stock, and build a cabin.

He grinned. The place was turning into a regular ranch. Between the two of them, they had approximately fifty head of cattle, three pigs, five chickens, a dog, and a family. Something Drake didn't think he'd have for a while yet, if ever.

After measuring the space for a shed a bit smaller than the dugout they called home, he hammered a simple frame together and then cut a hole for a door. If the shed was as warm as the dugout usually was in the winter, he'd suggest they move into it and get above ground. Dugouts felt too much like a grave. But, the wind would tear at the shed.

Scout sniffed around him as he worked. Then the dog stiffened and barked.

Drake studied the horizon. A lone figure of a horseman stood silhouetted against the sun. Drake still didn't know for sure why Hayward didn't shoot to kill. After all, with him and Annie gone, the land and stock would go up for sale. Most likely, a man could get them for next to nothing. He switched his attention as Annie and May came out of the dugout.

More than likely, she would make good on her promise to find some greenery. With Christmas only two weeks away, he figured she'd want to get it done before too much snow fell.

His heart stopped. Winter meant long days indoors. A lot of time spent in the dugout. He was doubly grateful for his new coat, knowing he'd use every available moment to step outside to work, no matter what the temperature.

By the time he started nailing boards to form the shed's doors, Annie and May had returned from the woods with their arms full of evergreen boughs. Drake glanced back at the horizon. Another silhouette joined the first.

Annie glanced that way then at him, before ushering May back into the dugout. She returned within minutes with her rifle cradled in her arms, instead of the evergreens, and marched in the direction of the unwanted visitors.

"What are you doing?" Drake stood.

"I'm going to send them on their way."

"No you're not." He took the gun from her. "They're likely to shoot you."

"Not if I shoot them first." She crossed her arms. "We shouldn't have to worry about folks watching every move we make."

Sweet one minute and like a caged boar the next. Drake had no idea living with a woman could be so interesting. "You can't go getting yourself killed. You have May to think of."

"I do." She nodded. "If something should happen to me, like it did to Bill, I want you to take her." She reached for the rifle.

Drake held it over his head. "Stop it. You're acting loco."

"I could just take it from you." Her eyes flashed. She was prettier than a snow-filled winter night.

His mouth crooked. "How do you reckon?"

She opened her mouth to say something, snapped it shut instead, and kicked his shin. The toe of her boots sent a shard of pain rippling through him. He loosened his grip. She jumped, grabbed the rifle, and continued her march toward the men.

The little wildcat. Drake rubbed his shin and then followed, grabbing his gun from where he had leaned it against the pigpen. "Have you always been this stubborn?" he asked, catching up with her.

"Most likely." She strode right up to the men and took aim. "What are you doing on my land?"

"We're outside the boundary fence," one of them replied.

"You're too close. What do you want?" Annie cocked the hammer. "Answer carefully if you don't want to meet your maker today."

She was going to get them killed. Drake stepped next to her, holding his gun loose at his side. "I'd do what she says, men. She isn't one to listen to reason."

"Hush," Annie hissed out the corner of her mouth. "You're not helping."

"And you're plumb crazy. My leg hurts."

"You shouldn't have taken my gun." She glared at him, lowering her guard.

He whipped the rifle from her hands. "Go on, men. Git. Tell Hayward we're not selling."

"There are ways to make you."

Drake shrugged, not taking his eyes off Annie's red face. "Yep, I'm sure there are."

Annie planted her fists on her hips. "You tell Hayward that if he shows his face around here, I'll shoot him." She lowered her voice and stepped closer to Drake. "But I won't really. I just want to scare him." She whirled and stormed back to the dugout.

Drake burst out laughing as the men rode away. A little bitty thing like her, scare a man like Hayward? He doubted it, but he'd like to see her in a face-off with the man. If guns weren't involved, that is. He had a feeling he'd miss the feisty Annie if something happened to her.

Of course, with her spirit, and if he were a betting man, Drake might just have to put his money on Annie winning.

Chapter 6

Drake stopped at the door to the dugout and peered inside. The place had been transformed. Green swags covered every surface they could lie on. Pinecones and red ribbons were scattered among the greenery.

The room didn't look as crowded as he'd feared. Instead, Annie had managed to bring the great outdoors inside.

Colorful quilts lay across both bunks. A crocheted runner ran down the center of the table. A two-foot pine tree took center stage, stuck in an empty coffee can. The place looked like Christmas. Like a home. Drake didn't have a clue how to react. He turned and dashed back outside.

His growling stomach could wait. He dropped to a stump and placed his head in his hands. What was the matter with him? First, he'd blamed his caginess on the dugout, but that wasn't the truth. Annie made him nervous, plain and simple. The way she looked up at him with those sparkling hazel eyes, the curve to her lips, the dusting of freckles—it was enough to make a man crazy. Not to mention the little snuffling sounds she made in her sleep.

Annie's heart sank. Drake hated the decorations. If not for the smile on May's face, she'd take everything down this minute. She sliced the fresh loaf of bread for sandwiches. Eventually he'd come back for lunch. After all, he did the work of two men and needed sustenance.

Sighing, she placed slabs of ham between the bread and handed it to May. "I'm going to take your new pa's lunch out to him. You stay here and eat. I'll be right back."

"Yes, Mama." May dutifully took a bite.

Annie's heart swelled. *Mama*. What a wonderful word. Maybe someday she'd hear the word *wife* fall from Drake's lips.

She found him slumped on a log. "Here's your lunch."

"Thank you." He exhaled loudly, sending her heart to the ground, and accepted the plate with two sandwiches.

"I apologize if I overdid the holidays. Would you like me to remove some decorations?" She twisted her hands together. "May is thrilled, but if it bothers you. . ."

He held up a hand. "It isn't the decorations."

"Then it's me." She forced the words past her frozen lips. Her husband disliked her, couldn't stand to be around her. "I'll let you be as much as possible. I know you felt you had to marry me, but. . ." She turned to leave.

He reached out a hand and grasped her elbow. "It isn't you. Please, sit and have one of the sandwiches."

She faced him, studying the grave intensity in his blue eyes. His brown hair curled over his collar. What would it feel like to run her fingers through those silky strands? Would he push her away or close his eyes and lean closer?

"Are you sure?"

"Positive." He handed her one of the sandwiches. "I see you unpacked your trunk. The dugout looks wonderful. A woman's touch makes all the difference. Please don't change anything on my account."

Confusion filled her mind. She took a bite of her food and stared at the almost finished shed. The wood gleamed new against the weathered boards of the chicken coop and pigpen. "Where will you build the cabin?"

"At first, I thought about building on the boundary line, but I like the idea of being closer to the creek. How about moving the corral fencing and putting the house where the horses are now?" He fixed his gaze on her.

Did he really want to know her opinion? No one had ever cared before. She looked at her land with new eyes. "I love that stand of birch. In the springtime, the green leaves will be so pretty against the white trunks. Can we build it there? That isn't far from where you'd planned."

Drake looked in the direction she mentioned. "I think that's a wonderful idea. We could call our ranch Birchwood. I'll make a branding iron to fit the name."

"Birchwood." She liked it. She cast a shy glance at Drake. "It sounds fancy."

He set his plate on the ground then leaned back on his arms. "This will be one of the finest ranches in northern Arizona in a few years. Why shouldn't it have a fancy name? I'll build us the finest two-story cabin you've ever laid eyes on. May will be the spoiled princess of our kingdom. When she grows up, no man will be good enough for her, and I'll meet them all at the door with my shotgun." He chuckled then stood. "Enough daydreaming, I've lots of work before the day is done, and I want to check the fence line."

She watched him go, his back strong and straight. Sure, May would be spoiled, and already the little girl owned a piece of Annie's heart, but Annie had always thought God would bless her with many children.

Was it wanton to crave Drake's arms around her? To wonder about the true physical side of marriage? She sighed and picked up the empty plate. She ought to be grateful she'd married a kind man, even if she did have suspicions regarding his interest in the gold. Things could have been worse. She could have been stuck with a fat man who hit her. But it sure would be nice if Drake didn't try to avoid her so often.

She'd liked their conversation about the ranch and wanted more enjoyable times together. Maybe she could draw him out at supper. Ask him more about his plans for their future. And maybe, if she had a moment of bravery, she'd tell him about hers.

❧

What a fool he was! Annie sat there next to him, willing to share his lunch, and he'd babbled on about a romantic name for the ranch. What was wrong with him? Ranches didn't need romantic names. This was the wilds of Arizona.

He needed to get away and do some thinking. He headed to the corral, saddled his horse, and decided to ride the split-rail fence, checking for spots that needed fixing. A cold wind picked up, and he pulled his coat tight, thankful for Annie's thoughtfulness.

Until he'd gotten himself hitched, he hadn't realized how lonely he'd been. Seeing Bill occasionally and the rare visits to town didn't satisfy like the company of a woman. God sure knew what He was doing when He'd made women.

At one section of fence, Drake dismounted and studied the broken rail. To his trained eye, it was clear it had been sawed through. Had it been springtime and the cattle grazing a larger area of the ranch, most of Annie's stock would have disappeared in a very short time. He tried to remember whether Bill had ever told him how many head of cattle he'd owned. The last time he'd checked, Drake had counted only fifty.

Was that how Hayward planned on running them out? By rustling the cattle? Drake almost expected to see Hayward and his men gallop over the nearest hill. Instead, the horizon contained nothing but trees and heavy gray clouds.

Looked like rain. Drake shivered and tugged up the collar of his coat. He'd best head home before the sky unleashed its burden.

He straightened. A blow to the back of his head drove him back to his knees. Darkness overtook him.

❧

With the thickest of the two quilts wrapped around her, Annie stood in the doorway of the dugout and watched for Drake. A slow rain fell, chilling the air and increasing her worry.

Night had fallen an hour ago. Suppertime had come and gone.

Drake had said the decorations didn't bother him. Had he lied? Had he left to do a chore and decided to keep riding? No, that wasn't possible. Not for an honorable man like Drake. But really, how well did Annie know him?

He'd combined the ranches without consulting her—not that it was a bad thing—made plans to wed her without a proper proposal, and mentioned the gold at regular intervals. She shook her head. Drake Carter was not out to harm her and take what belonged to her. Something else was wrong.

She hurried back into the dugout and grabbed her coat. "May, we've got to go look for your pa. Put your coat and mittens on, please." Annie grabbed her rifle and filled her pockets with ammunition before rushing May out of the house.

Please, God, let him be safe. Once she'd saddled her horse, she hefted May into the saddle and climbed on behind her. She'd follow the fence line, like Drake had said he would earlier.

The rain fell harder, soaking through her coat. Annie hunched over May, trying to keep the little girl as dry as possible. Why hadn't they found him yet? They'd long since passed the halfway mark on the property line, and night had erased day, leaving them riding through inky darkness. How would they ever find him?

Despair threatened to choke her, and Annie pressed against May, taking comfort from her presence. Surely God hadn't made her a widow twice in less than a month.

Wait. Drake's horse stood, head hanging, under a tree. On the ground next to the fence was a bump on the ground that was quickly covering with snow.

Annie guided her horse to his and slid to the ground. The bump wasn't a mar in the landscape but Drake, who didn't move when she approached him. "Drake?"

How would she get him home? She knelt in the mud by his side and checked for signs of life. A faint breath from his lips brushed her face. He was alive! Praise God. Her throat clogged with unshed tears.

She shook him. "Drake, please get up."

He groaned and rolled from his stomach to his back.

"If you can get on the horse, I can get you home." Annie tugged on his arm until he sat up. "What happened?"

"Someone surprised me and hit me on the back of the head." Drake put a hand to the back of his head. "I'm bleeding. You look blurry."

"I'll care for you when we get home." She scooted closer until he leaned on her shoulders. "Climb up, and I'll ride behind you." She prayed May was able to sit on the other horse alone.

With much effort, Annie helped Drake onto the horse then mounted behind him. Seemly or not, she pressed closer, giving him as much of her body heat as she could. With the reins of May's horse clutched in her hand, she set off.

Her arms ached from keeping Drake from tumbling to the ground, taking her with him. By the time they reached home, the dugout had never looked better. Annie helped May down and sent her into the house to change into dry clothes before she turned her attention to Drake.

"I'm fine." He slid down, and his knees buckled. He leaned heavily on her for a moment then straightened. "I'll put the horses away."

"You'll go to bed." Annie propped her shoulder under his arm. "The horses will have to wait."

"You're a bossy little thing."

"Yes I am." She struggled to stay upright under his weight and steered him inside and toward the cot. He sprawled on it with a moan. Her face heated as she stared down at him. She was the only one available to strip him of his wet clothes. Well, they were married, after all. "May, hide under the covers. Don't peek out until I say so."

Removing the soggy coat was no big deal, but by the time Annie's fingers worked on the buttons of Drake's shirt, she was shaking. The fact that he stared at her, eyes stormy, not moving, his chest rising and falling under her hands. . .made her want to turn tail and run. If doing so wouldn't put him at the risk of catching pneumonia and dying, she would have without a second thought.

When she moved to the buttons of his long underwear, Drake's eyes darkened. "Get the fire going and tend to May. I can finish this." He cleared his throat, his hand resting for a moment longer than necessary on hers.

She slid free. Her breath hitched as she turned away. What had she been thinking undressing him? What must he think of her? She busied herself tending to May. Anything to stay busy and not dwell on how she'd felt tending to him.

Annie Templeton Morgan Carter had fallen in love with her husband and had no idea what to do.

Chapter 7

Yesterday Drake had still had a fever and drifted in and out of consciousness. Today he seemed much cooler but still slept later than usual. Annie sponged his forehead and prayed. Lying on the wet ground for hours had left him struggling to breathe, and other than fighting his fever, she had no idea what to do. She'd tried tea but could only get Drake to take a few sips. What if his fever came back while she wasn't paying attention?

The dugout was easy to keep warm, but snow fell steadily outside, lazy flakes covering the ground with a light powder. She didn't know much about caring for stock. The pigs and chickens were easy—she'd had them back home—but cattle were another story. At least she knew how to milk a cow. "Please, get up quickly," she whispered. "We need you."

Would God hear her prayers in an underground home? Silly woman, of course He would. Her ma always said He was with her no matter where she abided, but right now, Annie felt alone and helpless.

"Mama?" May leaned against her.

Annie pulled the little girl into her lap. "Are you hungry? I can fix you some oatmeal if you'll keep putting cold water on your pa."

May nodded and took the rag from the bowl of water. "I'll make him better. He won't die like my other pa."

Annie prayed not. Each day, May's affection for her new ma and pa grew. Now one of them lay at death's door. What would that do to a small child? Annie was almost grown when her parents died of influenza, not a young'un still in need of raising.

One of the cows set up a bellow, reminding Annie she hadn't done the milking yet or gathered the eggs. "I need to do the chores. Keep wiping his face with cool water until I get back. Then I'll fix breakfast. Come get me immediately if he gets worse." She grabbed her coat and hurried outside. She'd need to hurry. What if Drake got worse and May didn't recognize the signs? What if she came looking for Annie and got lost in the snow?

She glanced over her shoulder, barely able to recognize the dugout in the snowy dawn. Surely once the sun fully rose anyone could find their way around, even a child. Annie worried too much.

Or maybe she didn't worry enough. Her steps faltered. Her hand shook as she reached for the milk bucket next to the cows' lean-to. Would Drake be out of harm's way if she'd gone looking for him sooner? How did he get a bump on both the front and back of his head? It seemed to her as if someone had hit him, and he fell forward, striking his head against a rock.

She slumped on the milk stool, her fingers already growing numb from the cold. With Drake gone, she'd have no choice but to sell out. She couldn't run the ranch on her own, not with the repairs it needed and a cabin and barn to build. She'd put on a brave face when Hayward approached her, but it was all an act. Fear took root in her stomach and grew, spreading its branches through her heart and mind.

For the first time in her life, someone wanted what she had and would do anything to get it. She shook the bad thoughts from her mind and let the splat of milk hitting the tin pail soothe her. Scout whined and sat next to her.

"Where do you stay out of the weather, boy?" Annie feared for him out in the winter cold. If not for Drake already feeling overcrowded, she'd invite the dog inside.

When she finished milking, she forked hay into the manger and moved to the chicken coop. By the time she finished hunting eggs and feeding the stock, the sun sat a few inches over the nearest eastern rise. She didn't know why, but she expected to see Hayward or one of his men up there, on horseback, watching everything that went on at Birchwood. She smiled. Even if Drake changed the name, the ranch would stay Birchwood to her.

With a basket of eggs in one hand and a bucket of milk in the other, Annie headed back to the dugout. In her hurry, milk sloshed over the rim of the bucket, soaking the hem of her pants.

She shoved open the dugout door and stepped sideways down the steps. After setting the eggs and milk on the table, she turned to the bed. Drake sat up, blanket pulled to his chin, gaze on her.

"You're up." Her heart fluttered. He was awake and looking very fine.

࿊

"Thanks for your ministrations." The blanket covering his bare chest slipped.

Annie's cheeks darkened, and she turned away. He wanted to tell her not to worry, that they were married and her looking upon him wasn't unseemly, but embarrassment over his vulnerability had him yanking the blanket up to his chin. He glanced at the sheet Annie had hung the first night in order to allow him to strip to the waist in privacy.

She nodded and pulled it partway closed. "Do you feel like some oatmeal?"

"That would be wonderful." His stomach rumbled. "And coffee, please." He moved his legs over the side of the cot and tried to stand. He wobbled like a newborn calf. Maybe he wasn't ready to get up.

"You'd better not be trying to stand," Annie called from the other side of his privacy curtain.

He grinned. She sure was a bossy little thing. "No ma'am."

She screamed.

Shoving the curtain aside, he lunged for the table. His hand came inches from a scorpion ready to strike. He jerked upright and fell back, tangling himself in the quilt curtain and falling to the bed.

"What is that?" Annie's shriek rang against his ears.

Drake fought against his fabric prison. "Don't touch it."

"It's a scorpion." May glanced up from her bowl of oatmeal.

"A what?" Annie's eyes were huge in her pale face. "Is that a type of insect?"

Managing to free himself, Drake stood. "Yep. Very poisonous, too. Most dangerous part is a person doesn't know how badly they'll react until they git stung. Guess he's been hiding in here because of the cold."

May grabbed her boot and squashed it. "Gone now. My other pa got bit once. Said it felt like his hand was on fire."

"Are there more of them?" Annie glanced around the floor, her words trembling.

"Most likely. We do live in a dugout. It's full of bugs." Drake leaned against the table, struggling to breathe through lungs full of sludge.

"I haven't seen any before." Annie slowly climbed onto the chair.

So, she was afraid of something. Drake had wondered. "Bill built the dugout sound with a good roof. Otherwise, bugs would be dropping on you while you sleep." He grinned.

"You're enjoying this!" She crossed her arms. "I want a proper cabin built immediately."

She sure was pretty when riled. Sometimes he felt tempted to start a fire between them just to see her eyes spark and her cheeks brighten.

He figured he'd work on a bigger bed before building a cabin and concentrate his efforts on making Annie his wife in every sense of the word. But first, he'd court her. With Christmas looming, he needed to come up with a gift. He'd go back to his burned cabin and see whether he could find his ma's ring. Maybe, with some polishing, he could make it lovely again. The sapphire stone would suit Annie just fine. He'd kept it in a metal lockbox. Surely, the fire spared that.

Clearing her throat, Annie nodded at him.

"What?" He turned in a circle. "Is there a bug on me? Oh." His long johns had slipped low on his hips, leaving more bared than not. He grabbed the fallen quilt and wrapped it around him. Face burning, he met her gaze.

Laughter bubbled from deep inside him. Clearly, his new wife wasn't overly shy. He'd never had time for false, coquettish women. His lips twitched. Within seconds, they both laughed like a couple of loons.

"Isn't anyone going to clean the smashed scorpion off the table?" May asked, looking from one of them to the other.

This made Drake and Annie laugh harder. Annie finally climbed down from the chair and handed Drake his clothes. "Not that I don't admire the scenery, but it isn't proper."

Her glittering eyes made Drake hotter than his fever had. He hurriedly donned his clothes and scooped up the scorpion with a piece of bark before tossing the thing into the stove. The simple act of dressing left him exhausted. A fine sheen of perspiration covered his forehead.

"You've overdone things." Annie set his breakfast in front of him. "It takes time to recover from a chill." She placed a cool hand against his forehead. "No fever. That's good."

"I'm just weak. It'll pass." It had to. He didn't cotton to Annie having to do the chores that belonged to him as the man of the house.

He took her hand in his. "Sit with me."

"Okay." She did, her gaze not leaving his face. "Is there something on your mind?"

A whole lot of things he wasn't quite ready to voice. "I don't like to eat alone."

"All right." She folded her hands on the table and continued to watch him.

He squirmed under her stare and struggled to find something to talk about. Something more serious than romantic notions about a ranch. "How long have you been afraid of bugs?"

"How long have you been afraid of the dark and small spaces?" She smiled.

"Point taken." He spooned oatmeal and honey into his mouth. Why did he feel tongue-tied all of a sudden? It couldn't be because she had caught him stumbling around the dugout in his under drawers. No, it had to be the fact that there was no one on earth in whose company he'd rather spend his time. The feeling was foreign.

Strength seemed to return with food. "I'm going to ride to my burned cabin and see if I can salvage anything."

"Should you? I mean. . . ." She took a deep breath. "It isn't my place to stop you, but you've been ill."

"I'll be fine. I'll keep my wits about me. No one is going to catch me unaware this time." He scooted back his bowl.

"If you aren't home by the noon hour, I'll come looking."

He patted her hand. "I'll be home."

Something bumped under the table. He looked under to see May crawling on the dirt floor. "What are you doing, sweetie?"

"Looking for bugs so Ma isn't scared."

"You're doing a fine job." He looked into Annie's teary eyes and clasped her hand. "We've a fine little family, don't we?" Nice, the way it was, but he wanted more. Much more. A big cabin, a passel of young'uns, and Annie by his side until the day he died. Now if he could work up the courage to say so. . .

She nodded. "The best." She fussed with her hair and stood. "I'd best clean up from breakfast. Be careful, Drake. I don't relish being a widow again so soon."

He chuckled. "I'll do my best to see that doesn't happen." He yanked on his boots and grabbed his coat and hat. With a final glance at Annie's lovely face, he headed out the door, praying he wouldn't collapse from exhaustion, and cursing his stubborn male pride.

Something about having a family made him want to be a hero in their eyes. A man had no time to be sick.

Chapter 8

Annie watched Drake ride away then closed the dugout door on the cold winter day. How could she have said the thing she'd said? Heavens, she was as wanton as a saloon girl. If she wasn't careful, she'd drive her husband away.

Sighing, she stacked the breakfast dishes on the drain board then reached for her yarn. She wanted to knit Drake a muffler for Christmas, along with a scarf and mittens for May. If she didn't work fast, the holiday would be upon them and she wouldn't be ready. She checked her seat for bugs then sat down.

It hadn't occurred to her that a house underground would contain pesky insects. Not that she hadn't seen plenty of bugs in Missouri, but most didn't run across the kitchen table with intent to harm. She'd be sure to check her bed covers before sliding in each night. She shuddered. Drake must think her a silly woman.

While May continued to search for bugs, Annie knitted, the click-clacking of the needles soothing her. With each stitch of the blue yarn, she envisioned how it would look with Drake's eyes. Heavenly, that's how. It should be a sin to look as fine as her husband. Surely the angels in heaven had nothing on his looks.

Scout barked outside. Annie set aside her work and peered out the window. Hayward sat on his horse, just feet from the house. Why hadn't the dog barked an earlier warning? What would the man do if Annie pretended not to be home?

"I see the smoke from the stovepipe, Mrs. Carter. I know you're home."

Bother. Annie shrugged into her coat and grabbed her rifle. "Stay in the house, May."

"Yes, Mama. I'm finding all kinds of bugs to toss in the stove."

Annie shuddered and went out to meet a two-legged pest. "You aren't welcome here, Mr. Hayward."

"Now, ma'am, is that anyway to greet a neighbor?" He dismounted and approached her, hands held loosely at his sides. "I've come to make another offer on your land."

"My husband and I have no intentions of selling." Maybe a bullet in his backside would convince the man. Words didn't seem to have any effect. "There is no gold on my property, if that's the illusion you're under. We've told you time and again."

"It's still prime land. With what I'm offering, you could afford to build a grand house, worthy of a fine lady such as yourself." His gaze ran over her pants and scuffed boots. "Maybe purchase yourself a wardrobe of fine fashions."

"I have no need of such things."

"That dugout must be mighty crowded now that you've hitched yourself to Mr. Carter." He grinned. "Had you taken me up on my first offer, you would be dining on china this evening."

"Fine food with swine is still slop."

The man's eyes narrowed. "You're a stubborn, foolish woman."

She shrugged and lifted her gun. "I've been called worse." *Please, don't let him see my knees shaking.* She struggled to hold her aim steady. "Get back on your horse and ride, Mr. Hayward."

"What of the child? Doesn't she deserve better than. . .this?" He waved his arm.

"She's the princess of her castle and is happy."

"I found another scorpion, Mama." At the doorway, May held out a jar with another of the evil creatures inside.

Mr. Hayward laughed. "Some princess." He turned and marched back to his horse. "There are other ways of convincing folks to sell out. I'll be back to show you one." He mounted and galloped away, leaving the gate open behind him.

Annie sagged and eyed the jar with disgust. "Throw that away. Jar and all." She leaned against the corral fence and closed her eyes. Why did the man insist on visiting when Drake was gone? Did he sit away somewhere and watch to see him leave? She had half a mind to ride to Drake's property and fetch him home right away. She lifted her gun to fire a warning shot but set it down before doing so.

No, he had his reasons for checking his land. She'd leave him to them. Casting her eyes on the sky, she sent up a prayer for her husband's safety.

Contentment spread through her as she looked around at all God had blessed her with. A field of cattle and other stock. A warm home for the winter. A husband willing to work hard in order to better their lives. Yes, she was indeed blessed and didn't need some high-handed cattle baron telling her otherwise.

She looked down at her pants. She had a half-finished dress in her trunk, nestled under the new scarlet gown. Maybe she should finish it. If she did, maybe folks would look at her differently. Even go so far as to give her more respect. She shook her head. If Drake came home to the sight of her in a dress for the first time for no apparent reason, he might think she'd lost her mind. Besides, a dress wouldn't make people like Mr. Hayward any kinder. She rubbed her face, her mind a muddle.

Wearing a dress was a new concept, one she'd toyed with for the last year since receiving letters from Bill. She straightened her shoulders. She'd do it. All she needed was to attach the bodice to the skirt, and she'd be decked out in a sunshine yellow calico when her husband came home. Then she'd save her britches for chores.

❧

Drake hefted a heavy beam out of the way and stopped to catch his breath after a fit of coughing. He prayed he'd caught nothing but a cold. It wouldn't be good to have pneumonia. There wasn't a doctor closer than town. The fact that his fever seemed to stay away gave him hope, but his head pounded something fierce.

Under the last scorched piece of wood, he found the lockbox, intact. Inside was his ma's ring, and his deed to his land. He tucked the box into his saddlebag and continued searching through the rubble for anything spared by the fire.

There wasn't much. A few tin dishes and some tools. No matter. The lockbox was the important thing. He glanced to where the barn had once stood and laughed at the sight of his laundry frozen stiff on the line. He'd forgotten he'd washed a couple of shirts and a pair of pants. Thank the good Lord, he had a change of clothes now. The ones he wore would most likely stand on their own if he let them. He grinned, remembering the sight of Annie's own stained buckskins.

If she were that pretty in men's clothes, what would she look like dressed in women's? He doubted his heart would be able to take the sight without exploding.

Having salvaged all that he could, and with saddlebags bulging, he turned his horse toward home. Never in his wildest dreams would he have thought he would ever call a dugout home. Went to show it wasn't the walls a man built but the people who lived within those walls that made the place special—that and the God who put them together.

Once home, he brushed down his horse, gave it some feed, then turned to the house. There were other chores that needing doing, but a nap would have to come first. Exhaustion dragged at him. He hefted his shoulder bags and headed to the dugout, stopping when he noticed unfamiliar hoof tracks in the snow. He sprinted for the house.

"Annie!" He barged inside and stopped.

She turned, wearing a bright dress, her hair piled high on her head, and a shy smile on her face. "You're back."

"You look like spring." He swallowed past the lump in his throat, all thoughts of a nap having flown out the slit of a window.

She brushed her hands down her skirt. "Do you like it? I just finished it today. Made May a skirt, too."

Sure enough, May wore a yellow skirt with her nut brown blouse, her hair tied into neat braids adorned with leather strips.

Drake set his bag on the table. "I think you two must be the prettiest gals in Arizona."

He thought his grin might split his face in half. For Annie to don a dress meant she might harbor feelings for him. At least he hoped. It had to be a sign of good times ahead. "What's the occasion?"

"I started sewing it when Bill proposed. I thought it was time to wear it."

Oh. She'd made the dress for Bill. Stupid of Drake to think it was for him. Why would she go to extra trouble for a man she barely knew? He noted the curtain rehung and headed for his cot. "I'm in need of a nap. Call me when lunch is ready." He ignored the hurt look on her face and ducked out of sight.

He dropped his boots to the floor with a thud and fell back on his thin pillow. Idiot, harboring dreams that Annie could grow to care for him. Him! Drake Carter, a full-grown man afraid of the dark. Most likely she laughed herself to sleep at night long after she blew out the light.

He heard her shush May and rolled to his side, his gaze landing on the tiny window. Barely any light managed to squeeze inside, but it was enough when he laid eyes on Annie's face. Now the winter sun barely broke through the gloom in his heart. Hitched to a woman in love with another man. What had he expected? She hadn't had time to grieve before he'd practically forced her to marry him.

What did she say to make him angry? Annie glanced down at her dress. He didn't like it. What was she going to do with the red one now? She'd feel foolish wearing it. Didn't Drake understand she wanted to look pretty for him?

She plopped into the nearest chair. Marriage was confusing. Crossing her arms, she rested her head on them and stared at the fire in the stove. Tears burned her cheeks, leaving paths as hot as the fire's flames.

"Why are you crying, Mama?" May burrowed her way into Annie's lap.

"No reason. Sometimes women cry." She wrapped her arms around her daughter, breathing in her clean scent. She'd managed to give her a sponge bath before Drake returned. The sweet thing hadn't fussed much at all, other than completely soaking Annie by the time they were finished.

"You're crying?" Drake stepped from around the curtain. "Do you miss Bill that much?"

Annie shook her head. "I didn't know Bill, so how could I miss him?" She swiped her hands across her eyes, wanting him to disappear back to his cot. She must look a fright with her eyes red and watery.

Instead, he knelt beside her. She turned her face away, only to have him turn it back to face him. "What did I do?"

"I put on this dress for you! Oh, you're such a. . .a. . . Oh." She pulled away and stormed outside.

The wind cut through the thin fabric of her dress. Why couldn't she have left things the way they were? She didn't know any other way of letting him know she loved him other than cooking, cleaning, and donning a silly dress.

"Annie?" Drake followed in his stocking feet.

She hid a grin. They'd both freeze to death from their foolishness. "Go back inside before you take ill again."

"You wore a dress for me?" He stood so close behind her, she could feel his body heat.

She nodded. "I'm sorry if you don't like it."

His arms wrapped around her waist, turning her in toward him. "Of course I like it. I thought you did it for Bill."

"You silly fool." She cupped his cheek. "Can't you see that I—"

A shot rang out.

Chapter 9

Drake shoved Annie behind him and down the dugout steps. He followed, making a beeline for his cot. More shots rang outside. He shoved his feet into his boots. If he should die that day, it wouldn't be in his stocking feet.

"Of all the days I choose to wear a dress." Annie shoved aside the curtain and pushed his rifle into his hands. "I'm hampered by yards of fabric, and we've a gunfight to tend to."

She made it sound as simple as gardening. "By the way, I should've mentioned that Hayward came by while you were gone. He threatened this very thing when I ran him off at gunpoint."

"Why didn't you tell me?"

"I didn't have the opportunity." She planted her fists on her hips. "I'm telling you now."

"Of all the. . ." He shook his head and upended the cot to get it out of the way so he could have better access to the window. The last thing he wanted right now was an argument. As soon as Hayward was dealt with, Drake had every intention of getting back to his previous conversation with his wife.

Hayward and six men circled the dugout on horseback, hooting and hollering, firing shots in the air like a bunch of drunken Indians. Drunk was probably true. Why else would the man leap from threats to lawlessness?

"May, get under the table." Drake pointed and watched as she scampered to do his bidding. "Annie, you, too."

"I will not." She grabbed her gun. "I intend to fight with you. There's power in numbers."

True enough, and they were definitely outnumbered. If something were to happen to her, though, he'd never be able to live with himself. "Then stay away from the window."

"Right." She gave a nod. "I'll shoot from the door."

"No." He yanked her back. "Fine, shoot with me from the window. But don't fire unless they actually aim for the house. I think they're only trying to scare us."

"Then I'm going out to show them we aren't afraid." She whirled and headed for the door. "They won't shoot a woman. This way, I'll distract them, and you can protect me from in here."

"Absolutely not." The thought made his stomach churn.

"Trust me." She cast him a smile and sailed out the door.

෴

Rifle aimed, Annie marched toward the galloping men. The winter wind whipped at her skirt and sent shivers through her. Her boots crunched on the thin layer of ice over the snow. Scout's barking promised to annoy everyone within earshot.

It wasn't that she meant to act foolhardy. Far from it. But sitting back and waiting for Hayward to make a move didn't sit well with her. He needed to know they wouldn't bow to his demands. "Stop this instant."

The men reined to a halt in front of her, eyes wide, most likely because of her stupid bravery. Hiding shaking legs was one thing a skirt was good for, and hers were as shaky as leaves on a windy fall day.

"So your husband sends you to fight his battles." Hayward leaned forward, arm resting on his saddle horn.

"His rifle is aimed at your heart, Mr. Hayward, while mine is aimed at your head. I guarantee we won't both miss."

"Should I shoot her?" One of his men glared at her. "She looks like she can handle a gun and might be a threat."

"Of course she can handle a gun, you fool." Hayward shook his head. "We don't want to shoot anyone, Mrs. Carter. Hand over your weapon and the deed to your land."

"Hard to do when I don't know where it is." She grinned. "I'm guessing it's safe in a bank deposit box in Prescott." If it needed a key, she'd be in trouble. The only proof she had that she had been married to Bill was a slip of paper in the bottom of her trunk, right under the newer sheet with Drake's name.

"Bank is open. We could take a ride." Hayward motioned for two of his men to skirt around her.

"Not a wise move, Hayward!" Drake's gun barrel showed through the open window. "You put one finger on my wife, and I'll put a bullet through your gut."

Annie knew the situation could spiral out of control faster than a twister across the prairie. Somehow she needed to calm the rising tempers. "Gentlemen, there's no need. . . ." She took a step forward.

One of the men's horses jerked, yanking hard on its bridle. A shot rang out. Something tugged at Annie's skirt.

She glanced down to see a rip through the fabric. "You shot my new dress." She leveled her gun at Hayward. "You've come on my land, given orders to me and my husband, threatened the welfare of my child, and ruined a perfectly good dress. I'm starting to get riled."

Hayward climbed from his saddle and strolled, hands up, to within a couple of feet of her. By the time the rancher reached Annie, Drake had rushed to her side.

"Not one more step." Drake's shoulder brushed Annie's. Immediately she felt as safe as if she were wrapped in his arms. "The land isn't for sale. Last time we were in town, I informed the sheriff of your actions and filed a complaint. He's sure to be suspicious if we don't show up alive within a couple of weeks." He narrowed his eyes. "Who do you think they'll look for first?"

Annie didn't know anything about a complaint. Maybe Drake was bluffing. If so, he had a great poker face. She could believe what he said with very little convincing.

By the way Hayward glared, she wasn't sure how much he believed. "Sheriff Olson is a friend of mine. I don't see him taking anyone's side but mine."

"Does that mean he can shoot us?" Annie leaned into Drake, her voice barely louder than the horse's breathing.

"Nobody is shooting anybody."

One of Hayward's men fired a shot in the air. "I got a whiskey waiting at the saloon. Either we get this gunfight started or I'm leaving."

As one, Drake and Annie transferred the aim of their guns to the whiskey-loving man. Annie shivered again. If she'd known it would take so long to run Hayward and his men off, she would've grabbed her coat. Her fingers tingled, threatening to grow numb. If it did come down to shooting, she wasn't sure she could hit the side of a barn.

"Go in the house, Annie, before you freeze." Drake stepped in front of her and took steps back, forcing her to move behind him.

"Only if you go." She felt his sigh rather than heard it. She hated to disobey him. After all, she'd vowed to honor her husband, but she wouldn't be able to live with herself if she hid in safety and left him to the devices of a man such as Hayward.

They shouldn't be doing this. Meeting violence with violence would not be the way God would have them handle the situation. Sure, Annie tried to reason with Hayward, but on the other end of a gun. She lowered her rifle and put a hand on Drake's shoulder. "Put the gun down, Drake."

"What?"

"We aren't handling this right. This isn't the way God would want us to act." She was sure of it, even more so as peace flooded her.

Drake nodded and propped his rifle on his shoulder. "Hayward, we aren't going to fight you over this. If you want our land, take it. By force, by law, however you want, but we will not start a gun battle with you."

"You're going to let God fight for you?" Hayward laughed, his steps halting two feet from Drake.

❧

"Yes, I reckon that's exactly what I'm doing." Drake shrugged. "If you take Annie's land, we still have mine. We'll be fine, unless you plan on killing us outright." He backed closer to the dugout, raising the barrel of his gun a bit to discourage any eager trigger fingers. Not that he didn't trust God but rather that he didn't trust man. If Annie didn't want a gunfight—and Drake agreed it was the least desirable option—then they'd wait Hayward out in the safety of their home. That Drake didn't already have a bullet between his eyes attested to the fact that Hayward possibly didn't want gunfire any more than he did.

"I didn't come out here to flap my jaws." One of Hayward's men aimed his pistol at Drake. "Somebody's taking a bullet."

"No." Annie pushed forward.

Drake tried to shove her out of the way at the same time Hayward stepped up. The bullet took the man in the back, toppling him into Annie. They both fell. Drake whipped his rifle into position and shot the other man off his horse. The five men who had remained silent observers turned their horses and galloped away, leaving Drake and the others in a state of shock.

"Help me." Annie rolled Hayward off her and pressed her hands to the hole in his shoulder.

"Are you hurt?" Drake pulled her to her feet and ran his hands down her arms, eyeing the blood across her stomach.

"No, but he is." She kept the pressure on Hayward's wound, this time using the hem of her skirt. "How's the other man?"

So much for no violence. Drake knelt beside the man he'd shot and felt for a heartbeat. Nothing. His shot had taken the man in the heart. He leaned back on his haunches, sick at knowing he'd killed a man but comforted in the fact the other man drew first. Drake was only defending the woman he loved. "This man is dead. Let's get Hayward inside."

Together they dragged Hayward inside and laid him on the table. "Annie, get the fire stoked. We've got to warm ourselves as well as Mr. Hayward. May, can you find me some clean rags?"

The little girl scampered off to do his bidding. Using his Bowie knife, Drake cut the man's shirt from his body and rolled him over so he could assess the damage. The bullet seemed to have gone through his shoulder and out the upper flesh of his arm. Good. He would survive, and it didn't look as if there was the need to dig a bullet out of his flesh.

After building the fire, Annie lit another lantern and placed both beside Drake, making it easier for him to see. The way she seemed to know his needs without his expressing them amazed him. It was as if the two truly were one.

"I think if we clean this good and keep him warm, he'll be fine and on his way home by Christmas." Another body added to an already crowded dugout. Drake shuddered as the walls closed in.

Annie's once sunny dress was stained with blood, her carefully upswept hairstyle falling around her face in disarray, yet the warm look in her eyes closed out the winter and bloodshed, leaving summer with them instead. With her here, Drake could survive the close quarters.

He could survive anything.

"I'm going to change, if you can care for Mr. Hayward." Annie plucked at the bodice of her dress.

"I can handle this." What he wasn't sure about was the idea of her changing behind a simple blanket while he was wide awake and standing only a couple of feet from her.

Hayward groaned, drawing Drake's attention back to him. "Don't move. I've got to get a bandage on you."

May handed Drake a handful of clean bandages. "Is he going to die?" Her eyes were wide and caught the flicker of the fire's flames.

"No, sweetheart. He won't die." Not if Drake could help it. "Why don't you sit on your bed and say a prayer?"

May nodded and scampered off.

Drake grinned, thinking on how the soft words of his wife had kept him from shooting Hayward himself and possibly having Annie killed in the process. One less thing on his conscience when God called him home.

When he'd heard the shot and seen her fall, he thought his world would stop spinning. Thank the Lord, they were both unharmed. Now he'd do his best to save the life of the man who started it all.

"I'm sorry." Hayward opened his eyes. "I'm a fool."

"You saved my wife's life, Mr. Hayward. There isn't enough gold in the world for that." Drake wrapped the fresh linen around his shoulder and tied it tight. "We've a few nuggets if you want it. I count it a small price to pay."

"Keep your money. I'm thinking on heading to Montana. Heard the cows almost raise themselves up there."

The man was a dreamer. Not a bad thing unless it consumed you. Drake glanced at the curtain. He had all he'd dreamed and more.

Chapter 10

Christmas morning! Annie leaped from bed, eager for breakfast—flapjacks with the last of their honey. Drake had shot some quail the day before, and she would prepare them for their Christmas dinner.

Hayward had left for his own place the day before, and Drake no longer slept curled on the floor beside his cot. Annie glanced at the kitchen table where she'd stuck wrapped packages around the tiny tree. She'd stayed up late many nights working on the scarves and mittens.

Oh! A small square she didn't recognize sat among the others. Her heart leaped. Had Drake gotten her a gift? Would today finally be the day when she found the opportunity to tell him how much she loved him? With the cramped space and their unwanted guest, the opportunity hadn't presented itself again after Hayward showed up with his men.

Annie grabbed a mixing bowl from the shelf and measured out the ingredients for breakfast. May would be so excited to find hair ribbons in her stockings when she went to pull them on, not to mention the wooden horse Drake had carved for her. The little girl was in for a day she wouldn't forget, probably her first real Christmas. And definitely the most enjoyable one for Annie in a good long while.

She hummed a new carol she'd heard right before moving to Arizona—"What Child Is This?"—and thought about Drake's response when she put on the red gown. If the way his eyes lit up when she donned the yellow one was any indication, he'd be speechless.

She couldn't count the number of blessings God had bestowed on her in the last few months. A husband, a home, and a child, food on the table, and money in the bank in the form of cattle. She knew other blessings would come to mind later, but these were the most important ones. She was a blessed woman indeed.

Hot water boiled for coffee, and flapjacks sizzled. She moved to wake May while glancing to where Drake slept. Why hadn't he awoken yet? Most mornings he rose and slid aside the curtain before she got out of bed, completing morning chores then coming in to breakfast.

"Merry Christmas, honey." Annie pulled the quilt off May. "Breakfast then presents. How does that sound?"

"Wonderful, Mama." May bounded to the table. She reached for the presents then withdrew her hands and sat on them.

Annie grinned. That was as good a way of not grabbing things as anything she could think of. She skirted the table and stood in front of Drake's quilt. "Drake?"

When he didn't answer, she moved aside the curtain. His cot was empty, the blankets pulled up. He must have forgotten to slide the quilt aside in his hurry to get outside. Well, she'd finish making breakfast and have things ready when he returned.

She rubbed her hands together, as excited as a child. She'd never given anyone gifts before and only received them when the church back home took pity on her and her parents. She couldn't wait to see May and Drake in their new clothes or see May hug her doll. Breakfast ready, she locked the door and hurried to dress in her Christmas finery.

&

Drake pounded the last nail in the bed frame. It might not be as big a piece of furniture as he hoped to have some day, but it would do for now. Tonight, God willing, Annie would become his wife in every way. Once he got a proper cabin built, then May could have this bed and he'd make a much larger one for himself and Annie. For now, the mattress would have to be filled with straw, but soon he'd start collecting feathers and give Annie something as soft as a cloud to sleep on.

The bed would also have to serve as seating. He grinned. It would take up a lot of space, but with the table shoved against it, the bed would make a fine bench.

Snowflakes danced like angels as he straightened from under the tarp and grabbed one end of the bed. If he hefted and dragged slowly, he ought to make it to the dugout with the frame in one piece.

Perspiration dotted his forehead. The cold air cut into his lungs. He leaned against the dugout door to catch his breath, slipped, and then rolled down the steps, landing in a heap at the feet of a queen in red.

"I'm sorry." Tears welled in Annie's eyes. "I opened the door to call you to breakfast. I had no idea you were leaning against it." She held out a hand to help him up.

He lay like a stranded fish, mouth opening and closing in an attempt to breathe. Finally, he pulled forth words. "You are the most beautiful thing I've ever seen."

Her cheeks pinked. "You hit your head when you fell." She turned. "Come eat. May is waiting for her presents."

Once they'd eaten and the dishes were cleared, Drake folded his hands. "There's something I've always wanted to do once I got a family, and that's read from the book of Luke at Christmastime. But my Bible burned in the fire, so I'll have to recite it the best I can."

"I've my ma's Bible." Annie jumped up and dragged her trunk from under the bed. "I think that's a wonderful tradition to start."

His face flushed. Whatever made Annie happy, he'd do to the best of his ability. He especially loved it when she was pleased with one of his ideas. Nothing built up a man more or made him feel stronger than the encouragement of a good woman.

She handed him a Bible with a worn leather cover and opened it to the Christmas story. "Ma didn't read out loud from it much, but I found this story once when I was hoping for presents. No gifts came that year, but the story filled an empty spot in my heart."

Drake would make sure she had gifts every year of their lives. Never again would sweet Annie want for anything, not if it was in his power to give it. He started to read, " 'And it came to pass in those days, that a decree went out from Caesar Augustus that all the world should be taxed. . . . And she brought forth her firstborn son, and wrapped him in swaddling clothes, and laid him in a manger; because there was no room for them in the inn.' "

Like their dugout, Bethlehem had been bursting at the seams, and the same as in that town of long ago, God provided the room needed for the celebration of Christ's birth. Drake finished reading of the angel's visit and closed the Bible.

"Now, presents?" May asked.

"Yes, now the presents." Drake ruffled her hair, noting the shiny blue ribbon. "You got new ribbons?"

"They were in my stocking." She wrinkled her brow. "Isn't that a strange place for them?"

"Very." He laughed then sobered as Annie handed him his gifts. He opened them, more than pleased with the shirt and muffler. "You are a fine seamstress, Annie." He stood. "I've something to show you that will test your skills if you don't mind a little snow."

"I love snow."

☙

What could he possibly have for her that he couldn't bring in? Annie headed for the stairs, anticipation adding a skip to her steps.

"Wait. There's something else I want to give you first." Drake reached for the box on the table.

With trembling fingers, Annie peeled off the thin slices of bark he'd tied on in place of paper. Inside was a small wood box with a gold clasp. The type of box that one might keep small treasures in. Holding her breath, she opened the box. Tears sprang to her eyes at the sight of the ring. "It's beautiful."

"No more so than the woman on whose finger I hope to place it." Drake took the box from her. "Will you wear it?"

She put her hand over her mouth and nodded, tears falling in steady rivulets down her cheeks.

"No longer are you the woman I married to save our land, but the woman of my heart. The other half of me." He slid the ring on her left ring finger.

Sobs shook her shoulders. He loved her as a husband loved his wife. She could hardly see through her tears. "I don't know what to say."

His eyes glistened. "Your response to the next gift will tell me all I need to know." Taking her hand, he led her up the steps and outside.

Waiting for them was a pine bed, big enough for two. When the implications of the bed occurred to her, Annie didn't need a coat to warm her. Her face burned. "How will we fit it in the house?"

"I've thought of that." Still holding her hand, Drake turned her to face him. "Will you share this gift with me?" His Adam's apple bobbed, showing his nervousness.

Knowing his emotions mirrored hers made Annie's decision that much easier to make. "Yes, I'd be most pleased to share my gift with you."

"I wish I had a finer place to share this day with you." He took her other hand in his and pulled her close.

"Anywhere that you are is a castle to me, my husband." She peered into his face. "I love you. I tried to tell you the other—"

He put a finger over her lips. "Merry Christmas. I love you." He bent and claimed her lips.

Annie felt like the most important woman in the world. She didn't care that she stood with snow covering her head and catching on her lashes or that the wind bit through the fabric of her dress. Drake's kiss warmed her to her toes and made her feel like the richest woman in Arizona.

The Cowboy's Angel

Lauraine Snelling

Prologue

B ut Pa, don't want you to go."

Anson Stedman picked up his four-year-old son and hugged him close. "I will be home soon. You must take good care of your ma."

"I will, but don't want you to go."

Belle smiled up at her husband, the firelight glinting off the blond strands in her hair. "Pa will be home soon, Abel. We need to take care of the cow and chickens, or they might freeze."

"I keep the fire going." He slid to the floor and hugged Rusty, his best friend in all the world. "You take care of Pa now, you hear me?"

Rusty, named for his color, cocked his head, one ear standing up, one flopping forward. He kissed Abel's cheek and wagged his feathered tail so hard he created a breeze.

Belle stood in the circle of her husband's arm, as they both smiled at the antics of boy and dog. She didn't want Anson to leave either, but he needed to make a trip for the much-needed supplies. He had planned to go earlier but various trials kept him home until they were desperate, and even now a storm could hit any day.

"I don't want to go, but if I don't, we and our animals won't make it through the winter." He hugged Belle one more time and, heaving a sigh, settled his knitted wool cap on his head and his flat-brimmed felt hat over it. With the scarf she last knitted for him tucked around his neck and under his wool coat, he waved good-bye. "Now don't you go standing on the stoop. You keep that baby inside where it's warm." His smile brought a return one from his wife, who with one hand on her mountainous belly and the other on her son's shoulder, smiled bravely. "And keep that rifle handy. You know how to use it if you have to." Together mother and son moved to the window to watch him drive the wagon hitched to their remaining mule toward the sun showing half a disk above the horizon.

The thought of using the rifle against a two-footed intruder had not entered her mind until they had one sometime before.

"Hurry home," she whispered. "Dear God, please keep him safe."

Chapter 1

Three weeks later
Two days before Christmas

W hen is Pa coming home?"

"Anytime now." Belle sucked in a deep breath. She looked at the calendar nailed to the bottom shelf on the wall of their sod house. She had marked off the days, every terrible, slow day, even though she kept busy enough for two people. That was the only way she could handle the terror.

Anson was more than two weeks overdue. He should have been gone ten or eleven days at the most. But when the big storm hit, she prayed he would stay in Fargo where he was safe. When it lasted for three of the longest days of her life, she reminded herself that God could see through a storm and protect her Anson. "Thou art my rock and firm foundation. I will not be afraid." She repeated the verse over and over and had finally set it to a tune to hum and sing. Singing it seemed the only way she knew to keep from going crazy. The weather never had really let up after that, but for one sunny day that seemed to be a promise that the storms wouldn't last forever.

But that depended on one's definition of forever.

In one lull, she and Abel had brought the cow and the ten chickens from the sod barn to the lean-to she and Anson had added the summer before. That way she could manage to care for them. Bringing in hay on the sled had taken much of an afternoon. At least Anson had prepared for winter storms by stringing a rope from the house to the barn. Like her, the cow was expecting any day.

"I should never have let him go," she reminded herself for the fiftieth time. As if she had had any choice in the matter. On the Dakota Territory plains in 1875, one did what had to be done, no matter what, if one wanted to stay alive. Winters were especially unforgiving. She'd heard tell that the wind drove some of the homesteaders outside to their deaths. After those three days of constant howling, screeching wind with no other adults around, she understood their desperation. But for her son and the baby she carried, she might have been tempted to do the same.

She added wood to the stove Anson had purchased in spite of her remonstrances that they couldn't afford it. While she kept the fireplace going for extra heat, she now cooked on the top of the woodstove. The stove was another thing to be thankful for since Abel could feed the woodstove more easily than the fireplace. In case he needed to.

"Lord, please bring Anson home soon." Digging her fists into her aching back, she tried to stretch and relieve the pain that came intermittently. So far she'd not given a name to the fear. Surely the pains were too soon.

"Ma?"

"Ja, Son."

"I'm hungry."

"Is it that time already?"

Abel nodded, the blond lock of hair falling over his forehead. He needed a haircut again. At least something around here besides her belly was growing.

"Did you look for eggs?"

He nodded and shrugged at the same time. Hens did not like to be moved, and not laying was their best revenge.

"When Tulip has her calf, we will have milk again."

"Ja, that is so." Belle brought the kettle of soup in from the box in the lean-to where she kept things cold. The skim of ice on top of the kettle was mute testimony to the cold even inside sod walls.

When she lifted the kettle to set it on the stove, a sharp pain started in her back and circled around the front, making her catch her breath. The baby was coming, no doubt about it now. When the soup was hot, she was not surprised that she no longer felt like eating.

At least she was as prepared as she could be. A folded cloth for a diaper, a knit wool soaker, a tiny gown and a strip of cloth to wrap around the baby's belly. Scissors to cut the cord and tiny ties for tying it off. Anson was prepared to serve as her midwife. Abel was too young. The packet was all wrapped and waiting.

The baby inside of her was not waiting. Over the next hours as the pains grew worse, she walked and gave Abel instructions to keep the fire burning. To melt water for the animals if the buckets of snow she'd brought in ran out. She only filled the line of buckets behind the stove half full so Abel could carry them. Good thing he took after his father in size and strength.

Almost Christmas and she was having a baby. Had Mary felt as she did right now? Was she afraid? At least she wasn't dealing with a Dakota snowstorm at the same time, and she'd not been alone. She'd had Joseph there.

Belle and Abel sat in the rocking chair together, and as she read to him the Christmas story, somehow the words found their way around her heart, too.

When the pains grew too strong, she told him, "You sit here, and Ma will walk and be right back." She paced the room from end to end, and when the spasm passed, they finished the story with the shepherds going back to tell everyone they met what they had seen. "Be not afraid," the angels commanded.

When Abel's eyes fluttered, she tucked him into the pallet on the floor by the stove where he would be warmest.

"Ma, I love you."

"And I love you. If you wake up and it's cold, you get up and put wood in the stove, all right?"

"Where will you be?"

"Right here. But you might wake up before I do."

He nodded and snuggled down.

She unrolled her pallet from the bed that was too far from the heat on a night like this and laid it beside his. And walked. Terror tore at her mind while the birthing pains ripped at her body. Surely it had not been this bad when Abel had been born. She muffled a scream with her hand. *Oh God, I can't do this. Walk. I can't walk.* She staggered back across the room, stopping to lean against the bedpost, using her breathing to help control the onslaught. Pain, waves of pain. Her mind tried to drift off.

"Put wood in the stove. Put wood in the fireplace." If she did both, they would run out of wood more quickly. The stove would have to do. *Lord, what do I do? Anson, where are you? Why did you leave me? Just when I finally learned to care for you, is God taking you away?* Rage fueled one trip across the room. But it was not his fault he had to leave. She gritted her teeth, and when that wasn't sufficient, she clamped down on a piece of cloth.

You cannot fall down! You cannot fall down. Through the blur of pain, she filled the stove again, set the damper to make the wood last longer, and collapsed on the pallet. The coals in the fireplace blinked like eyes, evil eyes waiting to pounce. *God help me!*

Chapter 2

Halloo the camp. Can I come in?"

Jeremiah Jensen waited for a reply. He'd known too many people who got blasted entering a stranger's camp. The fire was burning low, but he could see a form lying near it.

A dog barked. But he didn't come far from the campfire.

"I just want to use your fire to get some warmth back in these bones." The dog barked again.

Jeremiah listened closely. No, that was not a warning bark. He dismounted and, rifle at the ready, walked closer, his horse following him.

"Are you all right?"

Surely the blanket-wrapped form moved. Beyond the fire he could see a wagon. As he drew nearer, he realized the wagon was now only a frame. It appeared someone had been using the bed for firewood. The dog barked again, this time moving between Jeremiah and the man on the ground.

"Easy boy, not planning on hurting you or him." Jeremiah kept up the singsong he used for animals of all kinds and sometimes humans, too. The dog whined. Jeremiah moved slowly toward the man that he could now see was wrapped in a quilt and moving.

"I come to help you."

"Thank God." The answer was so weak as to be almost blown away on the slight breeze.

"Call off your dog, so's I can come to you."

"Rusty—no. Down."

The dog dropped to his belly, keeping his gaze on the stranger. Had Jeremiah not been watching, he'd have missed the tip of the tail that moved side to side. "Rusty, good boy. That's it now, easy." He reached the man's side. "Name's Jeremiah Jennings, and I'm heading north to work on a ranch. Mean no harm to you." While he spoke gently, he reached out a hand and laid it on the man's shoulder. "Can I roll you over here so I can see you or sit you up or. . . ?"

258

"Anson S–Stedman. I. . .I. . .too weak."

"Are you wounded?"

"No. Sick."

Jeremiah kept one eye on the dog, who was bellying closer. "Is your dog the bitin' kind?"

"N–no. Just doing his best to help."

"I'm going to put some wood on that fire, see if we can get you warmed up some. How long you been down?" He reached a hand out to the dog and got a sniff and a wag. He stood and pushed two boards farther into the fire, where they flared immediately. "I see you been burnin' the wagon. Do you have any food?"

"Someone stole it. Figured I was dead."

Jeremiah found a sack of beans under a bag of oats. A cook pot lay overturned the other side of the fire. He went to his saddlebags and pulled out some jerky and hard tack, his traveling food. So far he'd found farms that allowed him to bed down in the barn and even provided a meal or two. He'd left Texas four weeks earlier to go work for the same rancher who also had a spread on the western edge of Dakota Territory. The northern ranch needed a new general manager and horse breaker. The storms up here in the north country had slowed him down. He should have been there by now.

He filled the kettle with snow to melt and set it on the edge of the fire then returned to the man. "Can you sit up?"

"Don't know."

"I see. I'll be right back." He pulled the saddle off his horse and tied him to a wheel on what used to be the rear axle. Then he dumped the saddle on the ground and untied his bedroll. "I'm goin' to pull you up against that if you can sit." When the man slid to the side, Jeremiah tucked the quilt and the bedroll around him. "Be right back." He returned with the sack of oats and laid that so Anson could use it more as a pillow. Had to get him warmed up. "Good. Now I'm melting some snow, and I found beans, but in the meantime I got some hardtack here that I can soak soft enough that maybe you can eat it."

Anson coughed, but his effort was so weak it hardly raised the quilt. Mucus slithered from the side of his mouth.

"Where you headed?"

"Home."

"And you took sick?"

A nod. The dog crawled in next to the man on the ground, licked his cheek, and laid his head on Anson's shoulder.

"Good boy. Come on, snow, let's get to melting here." Shame he didn't have real firewood. Spread the warm around some. He returned to the wagon and pulled another board off, shoving the end in the fire like the others.

He poured the melted snow water into his own tin cup and set it by the fire to warm. Why did everything take so blasted long? Keep talkin' to him. "You sure got a good dog there. How'd you keep the fire goin'?" He didn't wait for an answer but broke off a piece of bread and dropped it in the water, stabbing it with his knife to soak faster. When it was warm, he took it to his patient. "Here we go. I'm goin' to spoon this into your mouth." He held the spoon of what was now gruel to Anson's mouth, but when nothing happened, he paused. "Anson, you got to eat this. Nice and soft, warm. Come on, open your mouth."

Anson's eyes fluttered. Slowly he complied. But the liquid leaked out the side.

"Come on, man, you got to swallow."

Eyes of such sadness as to make his throat catch stared at him. "Save Belle."

"Where is Belle?"

Anson gathered himself. "W–west. Near river." He collapsed, as if those words took all his strength. "Rusty."

"You mean the dog could show me where you live?"

The faintest of nods.

"We'll get you strong enough, and we'll set out."

A faint movement of his head was all Anson could muster. "Baby." His eyes opened again, and Jeremiah watched the life fade away. He closed the man's eyes, shaking his head. "Sorry I didn't get here sooner. Lord God, what am I to do now? Can't bury the body, no animal here to carry him. How far away is home? You got to be lis'nin'. You said You do."

He melted more snow and watered his horse. Shared some of his jerky with the dog, likewise a piece of hard tack. But his gaze kept returning to the body on the other side of the fire.

Rusty sat by his master as if he knew there was no way to warm him and stared off to the west.

"Rusty dog, I promise you, we'll start out first light." What a way to spend the night before the night before Christmas.

Chapter 3

Christmas Day

Belle floated awake on the most amazing dream. At least she figured it must be a dream. She laid there, eyes closed. No pain. Something moved next to her side. Eyes wide, she moved her head just enough to see a baby all wrapped and snuggled up to her side. Moving her head slightly, she realized she could see the fireplace at the end of her feet. No mountainous mound. Hadn't she decided not to add more wood to the fireplace, instead saving wood?

A clatter of the stove lids, and she saw Abel settling the lids back in place. He had replenished the stove. And the fireplace? Had she birthed and wrapped her baby and cared for herself without knowing? How could that be? She shut her eyes again, allowing herself to float back into her dream. A man had come. Who? Anson came home? She mentally shook her head. Abel would not be tending the stove were his pa here. But who and where was the man now?

His hands—he laid his hands on her belly, and with a wrench, the baby moved. The pain of it only teased the edges of her mind. No matter how she tried, she couldn't remember taking care of the baby or herself. She had fainted, that's why. But his voice. She heard his voice. But what had he said?

"Do not be afraid." That's what he said. Who was he?

"Thank you, Son." Her voice scratched. The baby nuzzled her side.

"Ma, you're awake. The man said you were, but you didn't wake up."

"What man?"

"The man who was here. He fixed the fire and said to take care of you. He said Pa was in heaven. He won't come back?"

Belle nodded. Somehow she heard the man's voice again. He had said that. "Did you see him leave?"

Abel knelt beside her. "No." He touched the baby's face. "I have a sister."

"How do you know that?"

"He said so."

"Oh." Such a little word with such a wealth of meaning.

"Merry Christmas, Ma, and Angel, too."

"Angel?"

Abel nodded in his definite four-year-old way. "I named her."

Belle heaved a sigh of relief, of joy, of. . . She wasn't sure what all, but their Angel was surely a gift of peace. The gift beside her squirmed again and whimpered, going to a full-throated wail on the next breath.

"She's hungry."

"Ja, she is." *Can I get up to sit in the rocker Anson made for me?* Without another thought, she rolled to her knees, babe in her arm, stood, and walked the three feet to the chair and sat. No pain, no weakness. "Please bring me your quilt, Abel."

Setting the baby to nursing was easy, too. Angel latched onto the nipple like she'd done this many times and nursed, her gaze on her mother's face. Belle sucked in a deep breath and let herself relax. *Thank You, dear Father, for the miracles I see all around me: Angel in my arms, and I am sure an angel came to visit us. Thank You for keeping my Anson safe and now home with You.* That the room was warm was miracle enough for right now. The others she would think about later. Now she understood the verse, "And Mary pondered all these things in her heart."

She put her daughter to her shoulder and rubbed her back to hear a loud burp that made Abel giggle.

Abel cocked his head and looked toward the door. "Did you hear him?"

"Who?"

"Rusty, that was Rusty's bark. Ma, Rusty's home."

Belle shook her head. "I'm sorry, Son, but—" She heard it, too. At the same time she realized the quiet. The wind had died.

"Pa!" But Abel shook his head. He said to himself, "Pa is in heaven with Jesus." The bark came again, closer, more insistent.

Abel leaped to his feet and headed for the door.

At that moment, a pounding on the door made him look around at his mother, his eyes rounder than the plates on the shelf.

"Bring me the rifle." She spoke softly and nodded to the gun in the corner. Abel did as she said, and when she had a firm grip on it and had it pointed at the door, she told him. "Go ahead, answer it." *Lord, how can this be? Rusty would not leave Anson. Right, but Anson was gone, the man said so.*

Abel lifted the bar and pulled the door open. A two-foot drift blocked the entry, but a brown-and-white bundle of fur leaped over and through it and threw himself at Abel, whining, whimpering, and yipping. The boy rolled on the floor, giggling and clutching at his best friend.

Belle had one eye on the dog and the other on the man with a flat-brimmed hat who filled the doorway.

"If you can give me a broom, I can sweep this out and close the door. That is if I can come in."

"Are you an angel?"

"Not that I know of. In fact, never been called an angel in all my life."

Belle started to rise, but he waved her back. "Let me get the door closed again, and then we can do the proper introductions." Abel had untangled himself from the dog and fetched the twig broom. He handed it to him.

"I think you are an angel, no matter what you say. My pa went to heaven."

"I know." He shut the door.

"How do you know?" Belle shook her head. Nothing more would ever surprise her. If someday she could ever sort all this out. "Come over and warm up at the fire. And Merry Christmas."

He nodded and removed his hat then unbuttoned his heavy wool coat. Standing in front of the fireplace, he rubbed his hands together in the heat. "This feels mighty fine, ma'am. Thank you."

Abel, one fist locked in Rusty's neck ruff, came over to look up in his face. "How come you talk funny?"

"Abel, that wasn't polite."

"Never mind, Miz Stedman. I got me a story to tell you. Wish it could have a happy endin'."

Belle nodded, one foot setting the rocker in motion. "Anson is gone."

"Yes ma'am. He is. He died when I was tryin' to get him to eat and drink something warm. I came upon his camp. Don't know how he kept that fire goin', sick as he was. Dog was watching over him, probably kept him from freezing to death. He said someone took all his supplies, left him for dead. He burned the boards on the wagon."

"I see." A tear rolled down her cheek and dropped on the blanketed infant. "And the mule?"

"Weren't no mule there. Maybe the robbers took that, too."

"How far away from here?"

"Fifteen miles or so. Guess he got too sick to continue. We'll most likely never know what all happened." He paused to remove his coat. "I wrapped his body in my ground sheet and put him under the wagon frame, blocked as well as I could. To keep the wild animals from him. Didn't find another farm between here and there. Didn't mean any disrespect."

Belle nodded. "I understand. Thank you for doing the best you could. And for being there with him." She closed her eyes for a moment, and when she opened them, she sucked in a deep breath at the same time. "Thank you. We don't have much for dinner, but you are welcome to join us."

"Ma'am, I reckon you don't need to be a-fixin' for me. Let me take care of that. You just tell me where to find things."

"We keep our food in a box in the lean-to." Abel looked up from his talk with Rusty. "I will show you."

"Did I hear a hen cacklin'?"

"We brought the chickens and our cow up to the lean-to 'cause Ma couldn't make it to the barn, and she said I was too little to take care of them."

The disgust in his voice made Belle roll her lips together.

"My pa said I was to take care of Ma and our baby. He didn't know if it was a boy or girl. But we got a girl, and her name is Angel."

"How about I go put my horse in the barn? I brought a sack of oats and one of beans. All the other supplies were gone."

"Anson was bringing our winter supplies back."

"So the wagon was full?"

She nodded. "Most likely."

He huffed a sigh. "Shame, ma'am. That surely is a shame. What will you do?"

"Pa always said God would provide." Abel spoke in all seriousness. "He sent us an angel."

"He sure did." Jeremiah smiled at Belle and indicated the baby.

"No, He sent us a real angel. You tell him, Ma."

"We will save that for another time." She watched the man in front of the fireplace. Perhaps God had sent them three angels. The baby in her arms, the visitor of the night, and the man standing right before her.

Chapter 4

S eems to me God got us in a real pickle here, Sanchez." Talking to his horse had become habit since Jeremiah rode alone so many miles. Otherwise he might have gone stark raving crazy. He'd heard that happened to homesteaders on these northern plains. The wind here was indeed something to respect. Opening the barn door required a shovel to move away the drifted snow.

That was one prepared woman, he told himself. Now, where would she or that poor husband of hers have kept the shovel?

"Mr. Jennings! Mr. Jennings!" Abel called as he came dragging the shovel. He was so light, he could walk on the snow, far easier than a man or a horse. Jeremiah scolded himself. The boy shouldn't have come out. He should have done something different. What?

Abel handed him the shovel.

"Thanks for the shovel. Now you'd better get back to the house before you freeze."

Abel gave him a disgusted look. "I shoveled snow before."

Backpedaling, Jeremiah figured he'd better be more observant and less opinionated. "I am sure you did. Are there two shovels?"

"One in the barn."

"Okay, we'll get that out, and you can help me."

The boy's eyes lit up. "Can I pet your horse?"

"His name is Sanchez, and he would like that right well." Jeremiah dug out the door enough to swing it open to let his horse in. He didn't need to clear it all. From the looks of the lowering sky, more snow was on its way. "Why don't you run back to the house and ask your ma. . ." What did he need? "Uh, if we need more hay up there."

"It's about gone. I fed the cow this morning."

"You want to lead Sanchez inside for me?"

"Ja, sure. You betcha. My pa used to say that." He took the reins and eased the horse around the half-open door.

He could hear Abel talking to his horse in the far stall of the three. A pile of hay filled the remainder of the barn. The other shovel hung on pegs Anson had driven into the sod wall.

Abel was struggling with the cinch strap when Jeremiah reached the stall.

"Here, let me help you." He loosened it, and Abel finished the job. Sanchez turned his head and nuzzled the boy's shoulder.

"He likes me."

Thank you, Sanchez. "He does. You petted him, and he sure does love to be petted." He threw the saddle over the half wall between stalls and stripped off the bridle.

"We melt snow on the stove for the animals to drink."

"You have a bin we can pour the oats in? Hate for the mice to eat it."

"We could take that to the house."

Talking to this child was about as good as talkin' to a man. Did his ma and pa realize how smart he was?

"Do the chickens and cow stay up there all winter?"

"No, first winter we had the lean-to. Pa and Ma built it during the summer."

"I see. You want to fork some hay in here?"

"Ja, I will."

When they finished taking care of the horse, Jeremiah asked if they had a sled to pull hay up to the house.

"I'll get it." The boy scampered out the door and returned, dragging the sled behind him. By the time they had it loaded and pulled to the house, dusk was already falling. Jeremiah parked the sled at the door to the lean-to, and together they forked it in. The chickens clucked as they settled on their roost across the far corner, and the cow rumbled deep in her throat—the comfortable sounds of contented animals. The baby whimpered in the other room, and the mother comforted her. More sounds that spelled home.

Jeremiah sucked in a deep breath. Sounds he had not heard for years immediately brought back a landslide of memories. He could picture his mother rocking the cradle of the newest addition to the family. Ten children had taken up her life. Jeremiah was the eldest and helped when he could. He and his pa and the others, as they grew old enough, planted the cotton, hoed it, and finally—when, thanks to God, there were no natural catastrophes—picked it. After hauling it to the gin, they had some money to buy more seed and even put food on the table. They grew most of their food themselves, with the smaller children helping the most there. He had left home when the others were old enough to take his place. Sharecropping was not the way he wanted to spend his life, so he headed west.

I hope they had a real Christmas this year. Not sure if he meant that as a prayer or. . .or what? *You decide, Lord, and thanks.*

And you haven't even written to them for how long? He tried to ignore the voice, but this was Christmas. He should have, he should have, he should have. . . .

In the main room, Mrs. Stedman was nursing her baby. He figured he should give her some privacy, hard to do in such small spaces. Yet whole families—even two families—lived in spaces like this for years. It made the house he grew up in look huge in his memory.

Today his memory was more enemy than friend.

"Mr. Jennings?" Abel opened the door and stuck his head out. "We can eat now."

Abel and his mother were already at the table with an empty chair waiting. The chair that would always be empty. How was she managing so serenely? After all, this was Christmas. He'd expect she would be dissolving into tears whenever the thoughts of her husband returned.

"Would you please say grace, Mr. Jennings?"

He bowed his head. How long it had been since he had said grace at a table with a woman and child present. "Dear Lord, we thank Thee for food and shelter and new life, and for Thy Son who saved us. Amen."

They joined in his *amen*. He looked up to see a smile so beautiful it made him catch his breath. She might as well be wearing a halo and be dressed in pure white. He swallowed and blinked and was able to breathe again. What had he seen?

"Are you all right, Mr. Jennings?"

"Yes, I am much more than all right. Thank you. And thank you for sharing your meal with me."

"A blessed Christmas, Mr. Jennings." The baby in the cradle beside her chair squeaked, for certain not a cry but—

"Please pass the corn cakes, but help yourself first."

He did as she asked and felt his ears get red. What was the matter with him, daydreaming—if that's what he could call it—like this? Even all those nights just him and Sanchez, his mind had not turned on him like this.

"Is everything all right, Mr. Jennings?"

"Thank you, ma'am. It will be." *What will you live on with no supplies this winter? Do you have enough wood or peat for the stoves?* He'd not seen an overly large wood pile anywhere outside. But then, surely the mister had left them with wood. But out here on the prairie, there was most certainly a lack of trees. What did the farmers burn?

"Would you care for more?"

"No thank you. I had plenty." He thought a moment. "I have some jerky and hard tack in my saddlebags. Would that help?"

"We can't use up your supplies. Thankfully, you already brought us that bag of beans. That will be a big help."

"Did your husband hunt? Surely there is game around here."

"He planned on that, but the weather has been so miserable even the animals went into hiding."

"We saw some. . ." Abel screwed up his face. "Four or two deer down by the river. They drink there, but now the river is solid frozen."

"Are there rabbits?"

"In the spring."

"Pa said they turn white in the winter so we can't see them."

"I see. Perhaps I could get you a deer?"

"That would be wonderful, but I hate to keep you from your destination. You already helped Anson."

"Not enough, I'm afraid."

Rusty yipped at the door, and Abel went to let him out. "Ma, come see." Belle rose. "Excuse me."

Jeremiah pushed back his chair. "Wait. There might be. . . ." But no one listened to him. Strange, she had met him with a gun and now went outside without even checking for strangers. Another strange thing to ponder about this place and situation. She drew her shawl around her shoulders and stepped outside with her son. Jeremiah got to the door as she sighed an ooh of pure delight. He stepped out and looked up where they pointed. The aurora borealis danced in every color of the rainbow against the cobalt sky, arcing and spearing to music no one heard but everyone always felt.

"I've never seen it so bright." She turned to Jeremiah, her hand on her son's shoulder. "Only the Lord could create such glory that it stops your breath."

The cold is what is stopping your breath. "Please go back in the house before you freeze out here."

They all rushed to the fireplace and warmed themselves.

"I'll be saying good night then," Jeremiah said when Abel started to yawn. "Do you mind if I sleep in the barn?"

"That would be fine, but perhaps you would like to sleep in the lean-to tonight? Up against the chimney would be warmer than the barn."

"Thank you. I will do that."

"Do you have enough bedding?"

"I have my bedroll." He rose and reached for his coat. "I'll go on out to the barn and get it." Hat in place, he tipped his head. "Thank you for welcoming me into your home." As he stepped into the night, he heard her say, "Lord bless your sleep, Mr. Jennings."

He stared up at the sky so deep blue as to be almost black with pinpoint stars tacking it in place. "You coulda done better by her, Lord. How on earth is she going to make it through the winter?"

Chapter 5

Good morning, Mr. Jennings. I'm sorry we have no real coffee, but I have some oats roasting, and that makes an adequate morning drink." She motioned to a pan over the fireplace fire.

"That smells good enough to eat."

"I know." She checked the sleeping baby under the blanket against her shoulder and lowered her gently into the cradle.

"Your rooster sure likes getting up early. Near to lifted me right out of bed."

"Yes, he figures getting the sun going is all up to him." Her smile made it real easy to return one.

He caught a yawn behind his hand and stretched his neck. "That cow looks like she'll be calving today,"

"Oh, I hope Abel can watch. The last calf was born out in the barn, and he was sad he missed it."

Jeremiah warmed his hands over the stove where snow was melting in the pot. "Did you never sleep?"

"Oh yes, but when a baby wants to eat every two hours or so. . . I've been up for a while. I don't mind—she is such a miracle." She stretched and crossed to the fire to use her apron to remove the dutch oven from the fire.

"Now I can use some of that water to make the coffee. In a couple of days, we'll have cream for the coffee again." As she talked, she poured water over the oats and put them back over the fire.

"Breakfast will be ready soon. Cornmeal mush, but at least it will be hot and filling."

He laid a once-white bag on the table. "Put some of that jerky in with the beans for flavor. I'm going to see if I can find rabbit or deer trails out there."

"Eat first."

"Ma, is Pa coming today?"

She watched her son's face collapse upon itself as awareness hit him.

269

"I want Pa to come back." Tears leaked down his cheeks, but he dashed them away.

She held out her arms, and he ran to them. Hugging him close, she smoothed his hair down and laid her cheek on his head, crooning softly all the while. She guided him over to the rocker and sat, lifting him to her lap. They rocked, and when she glanced up, Mr. Jennings was closing the door behind him. At her knee, Rusty looked toward the door and snuggled up as close to his boy as he was able, his quivering body doing everything he could to comfort.

Abel laid his hand on the dog's head. He sniffed and knuckle-rubbed his eyes. "He is with Jesus." His matter-of-fact tone said the tears were done for now. He slid to the floor and reached up to pat his mother's cheek. "I will feed the chickens."

"Mr. Jennings said Tulip might have her calf today."

"Good." He returned to the rope-strung bed he shared with his mother and pulled on his clothes. "Need more snow?"

Belle watched her son. Not yet five and so grown up. When his pa said he was to take care of her, Abel seemed to have left childhood behind and stepped into the role of a small man. How sad. How necessary. If she allowed her mind to go screaming forward, she would start to shake again. Instead, she did what her mother had taught her: thank God for what she had, for all His blessings, and rest in His mighty arms so He could take care of her. And He would. That baby sleeping in the cradle was proof of His mercy.

Abel finished tying his boots, stood, and stamped his feet. With a sniff he shrugged into his coat and stepped out into the lean-to.

Anson always did that. The thought sent an arrow straight through her heart. Sniffing back tears, she raised her chin. Abel did not need to see his mother dissolve into a puddle of tears. She'd cried plenty of them in the middle of the night when Angel let her know it was time to eat. That was when she'd comforted herself with the same words she gave her son. *Someday, Anson, I will see you again.*

But in the meantime. . . Angel started fussing in earnest. Saved by a baby's needs. Putting the light blanket over her shoulder, she set the round-faced baby to her breast and the rocker to creaking. In the quiet of the night, the rocker song had spoken to her of Anson's care for her and his family. He'd crafted this chair as a gift, a tangible proof of his caring that would stay with her. But he never had said he loved her.

She made the coffee, and she and Abel ate the mush. They poured the hot water over more snow to water the chickens and offered some to the cow, but she turned her head. It looked like their guest had shoveled the manure out the door. With the packed-dirt floor, it was relatively easy to clean up after the cow and the chickens.

After setting beans to cooking, adding small pieces of jerky, and moving the pot back to simmer, she swept the floor and brought in more snow to melt.

"A rifle shot!" Abel leaped up from playing with bits of wood on the floor in front of the fireplace. Together they ran to the frond-frosted window and blew on the glass enough to peek out, only to see snow and more snow. Footprints led toward the river. She motioned to Abel, and they stuck their heads out the door. Rusty pushed past them and headed out across the snow, his feet throwing up miniature snow clouds. She started to turn away when she saw a brown, flat-brimmed hat rising from the riverbank. As the man appeared, she realized he was dragging something. Something brown and, from the looks of it, very heavy.

"A deer. He shot a deer." Visions of chops frying and a haunch roasting over the fire floated through her mind. She could smell the fragrance and hear it sizzling. *Thank You, Lord.* Food to make it through at least the worst of the winter, especially if she hoarded it like a miser did gold.

Rusty darted back and forth, barking at the carcass, then danced around Mr. Jennings, yipping delight and throwing snow everywhere. True, even the dog would enjoy the spoils. "Oh Lord, thank You for providing again." Although she knew how to shoot a gun—Anson had made sure of that—she'd never shot at anything. Or killed something other than chickens. But she knew that if she had to learn to hunt, she would do that. With their nearest neighbor several miles away, the visits were few and far between. The homestead between this one and the other had been abandoned when the summer sun burned out the wheat crop. The oat harvest had been meager.

But she had hauled water from the river to water their garden enough to get at least some food that lasted through early December. After Anson left for supplies. She should have hoarded the vegetables more wisely.

"Come on, Ma, come see." Abel beckoned her from the door. He had gone outside shortly after he heard the shot.

Belle wrapped her shawl over her head and pulled on her winter coat. Stepping outside, she wished for a hat brim. Amazing how it could be storming one day or even one hour, and the next the sun blinded your eyes, reflecting off the sparkling snow.

"He was too heavy to carry," Mr. Jennings called. "I'll take the carcass to the barn. Did your husband set up a pulley system there for hanging game?"

"He did. You'll find the rope tied to a stall post. He carved the pulley himself."

"This should feed you for much of the winter." He stopped, his breath blowing clouds of steam around his face. His smile caught at her heart. What a shame he didn't use it more often. Anson had a smile, too, that had not had enough exercise. She wasn't surprised. This land stole smiles from lots of faces.

"You can fry the liver for dinner. And the heart could bake real well in that dutch oven in the fireplace. Come on, Abel, you can help me." He tipped his hat to Belle. "He can bring the liver up while I skin the rest."

"What a gift. Thank you, Mr. Jennings."

Some minutes later, Abel brought a bucket up with the heart and liver and grunted as he lifted the bucket up on the table. "Mr. Jennings said I am a good helper."

"He's right. You most certainly are. I think I heard a hen cackle when I was feeding Angel. You want to check for eggs, too?"

"Ma, come quick!" He motioned for her to hurry.

"Now what?"

"Tulip—she's falling apart."

Belle dipped her hands in a bucket of water heating on the stove and, drying them on her apron, joined him in the lean-to. Tulip lay on her side with two small hooves showing. She moaned, and the ankles appeared as the contraction did its job.

"That's the calf. Stay back. Now the legs, and see the nose is coming on top of the legs." *Oh you poor girl, I know just what you feel like.* "Come on, Tulip, push some more."

Abel looked up at his mother, eyes round as his mouth. "The calf is inside her."

"Yes." She steeled herself for his next question. Sure as that calf would soon be here, her son stared from her to the cow and back at her middle.

"Was Angel inside you?"

"Yes."

The cow moaned again and gave a mighty push, and the calf slithered out onto the hay scattered on the floor.

"Ooh, look." He started forward, but she stopped him with her hands on his shoulders. "You stay back in case she starts to move around." Belle bent over by the calf and, using a wisp of hay, cleared the mucus from the baby's nose. The cow lurched to her feet and started cleaning her now-alert baby up.

"Good girl," murmured Belle, looking around to see if there was anything to help dry the calf. "Go get one of those rags behind the stove."

Abel returned quickly and handed it to his mother. "Can I pet it? Is it a boy or a girl?"

He stepped forward, and the cow raised her head, glaring at him. "How come she doesn't like me anymore?"

"Because she has a calf and knows it is her job to protect her baby. And I don't know yet if it's a boy or girl."

The calf shook its head. The cow made noises deep in her throat and kept licking her baby. Within a few minutes, the calf tried straightening its legs. Rump in the air, it tried to do the same with the front legs but toppled back to the ground. On the third try, it stood.

"We have a male calf, a little bull."

"Like me."

Belle rolled her lips together and nodded, standing back to watch the little guy find his mother's udder and latch on to a teat.

"He's eating." Abel looked up to his mother, a grin splitting his face. "Tulip is a good mother."

"Ja, she is."

"Well, look at that." Jeremiah stopped in the doorway from the kitchen. "Looks to be a right smart calf there. What will you name it?"

Belle smiled down at her son. "You choose."

"I have to think about it. Can we eat now? I'm hungry."

"As soon as I fry the liver. Sorry, Mr. Jennings, we got a bit sidetracked here."

"The deer is hanging. I do hope it doesn't freeze tonight. We might want to hang it in here. Plenty cold but not freezing."

"Whatever you think best. I'm just thankful we have meat." Meat and beans and cornmeal, with milk soon. What a Christmas season this was turning into.

Chapter 6

I'm sorry, Reverend Swenson," Belle said to her pastor, who had arrived just as she was getting ready to cook up the liver. "I just cannot put someone out like that. Not unless it is absolutely necessary. I know my neighbors. They don't have any more than we have. And besides, Anson and I agreed if something happened to one of us, the other would stay right here."

Of course she didn't tell him that they never figured the mule would not be here and that one of them really would die. So soon at least. Although the fear of dying in childbirth had not really left until the angel came. Somehow, ever since that, she'd not been afraid of anything, not the wind and the wolves that howled, not being alone.

Had she really heard him say, "Do not be afraid"? Or? Or what? She most certainly had more questions than answers.

"Good of you to come check on us like this. I appreciate it."

"You are indeed welcome."

But what if Jeremiah leaves?

When had she started to think of him as Jeremiah? It wasn't like he had been here long, but somehow it seemed like half a lifetime.

"Well, the way that wind is picking up, I'd better be on my way. You know my wife will nail my hide to the cabin wall when I come back and tell her all this and you are not with me?"

"I'm sorry to hear that. You'll definitely do better with your hide in place."

He had the grace to smile at her attempt at humor. He stood and set his cup on the table.

"I'll get the heart for you." She headed out to the lean-to and the box they stored food in where she had set the heart and liver for protection. Tulip watched her, the calf peeking around his mother's dewlap. "I'm not going to bother you now, but tonight I will be milking you, so you better be prepared."

She wrapped the meat in a cloth with its ends tied together to make a sack of sorts and took it back to the reverend. "Tell the missus it weren't your fault. You gave it your best, but as Anson always said, 'Claribelle Stedman was just another name for stubborn.'"

She showed him to the door with a smile. The wind tried to grab the door, but she held tight. "You sure you should go out in this?"

"Not snowing yet, but that old horse of mine would find his way back to the feed box in a blizzard in the middle of the night." He tucked his scarf in around his neck and over the lower part of his face. "Fact is, he has. The good Lord makes sure I get where I need to go."

He mounted and rode off the way he came.

Belle shut the door and dropped the bar in place. The storm wasn't really on them yet—if it did indeed attack like the others had. Sometimes they just blew on by. Weather could be downright capricious.

She looked up to see Jeremiah shaking his head. "I can take you somewhere else soon as the weather lets up. You know that."

"I know, but I will tell you the same. I am staying here."

"What's so all-fired important about this piece of land that you won't leave even for a time?" He tried to keep the impatience out of his voice. After all, this was none of his business really, but the look she gave him let him know she got the point.

"I know you can't see it through the snow, but all our blood, sweat, and tears for four years watered this land. Anson has died for this land."

"Well, not exactly." He started to say something else and thought the better of it. "Think I'll go milk Tulip."

"Don't throw the colostrum away. The calf can drink it later, and the chickens will like it."

"My ma used to say colostrum was good for whatever ailed you."

"I'll make a pudding, and we even have sugar to put in it, thanks to Reverend Swenson. Oh such a treat this will be." She almost sang. She spun around. "We could even put a dollop of jam on top. Something lovely." She glanced at Jeremiah, to see him staring at her, a half smile in place, slightly shaking his head. "What?"

"Who were you before you married Anson and moved to the frontier?"

"This isn't exactly a frontier, you know. Why Dakota Territory might become a state sometime soon."

"Be that as it may. . ." He raised an eyebrow, along with a bucket, used and scrubbed so much it almost shone inside. "Use this for milking?"

"Yes. If it is big enough. I can make cheese, too. Ma used to make good cheese from the early milk." A cloud tried to darken the sunshine. "Before." She sucked in a breath and smiled down at her son. "Pretty soon you will have to learn to milk, too. If your hands are strong enough."

"Pa said I am strong."

"Ma said it, too."

He nodded. "Will the calf mind?"

"He might mind, but it will do no good. He will have to learn to drink from a bucket or Tulip won't keep producing enough milk for all of us."

"Why not?"

"Because the calf can't drink as much milk as Tulip can make."

"Oh." His brow wrinkled as he nodded. Then he looked up at his mother with a sun-kissed grin. "But we can."

"We can. We will have butter and cheese and cream in our coffee and buttermilk for us and the chickens and—"

Angel announced her displeasure at being ignored.

Belle blew up a breath from her lower lip that lifted the wisps of hair framing her face. And Anson wasn't there to enjoy this with them. The cloud tried to descend again. But Jeremiah was. He would like the pudding. And the cheese. If he stayed. He said he had to leave.

But I don't want him to leave. Where had that thought come from? Of course she didn't want him to leave in the middle of the storm, danger, all the things that were sure to assail him on his way north and west. She would be concerned for anyone going out in this.

So why did you not protest when Reverend Swenson left? Now that was a silly question. He had a home not more than three or four miles away, while Jeremiah was not exactly sure even where he was going. Well, he had a map, but he'd not been there before. Like when she and Anson came to the stakes he had set out when he filed his homestead papers.

She picked up Angel, and they nestled into the chair. Feeding her baby was one of the most pleasurable things she had ever done, even though it got a bit uncomfortable at times. But she remembered from nursing Abel that the discomfort went away—a small price to pay for the joy of a baby. With her toe, she pushed just enough to rock gently. Angel nursed like she'd not been fed for two days. Already she waved her tiny fist. Belle didn't remember Abel doing that until he was weeks or more old. Angel did not act like a three-day-old baby, that was for sure.

She could hear Abel talking to Jeremiah out in the lean-to. Peace filled the room and her heart. What if Jeremiah would stay? He couldn't stay here; that wasn't proper. What few neighbors she had would be terribly offended, first that someone beside Anson was living here, and second that she'd not honored the year-long decree of mourning behavior for a widow. *Lord God, I don't even own a black dress.* A dark blue one but not black. Anson used to make remarks about the strictures of society. He'd wanted no part of that.

But he was gone. That was the final line. Had she loved him? He had never said he loved her. Being a man of few words meant not wasting any. Was telling your wife that you loved her a waste of words?

Lord, why am I thinking all these outrageous thoughts now? I've never thought them before. Where did they come from?

"Ma!" Abel burst through the door. "The calf sucked on my fingers!" He held up his hand. "He liked them."

"Why?"

"'Cause I put my fingers into the milk like Mr. Jennings said." He wiggled his fingers and giggled.

Little boy laughter was entirely contagious, so she smiled back and then laughed, too. Laughter was a much-needed commodity in this household. Life was too serious. And death even more so. But today they could laugh. Was that a gift from the angel, too?

Chapter 7

That was really good," Jeremiah said as he leaned back in his chair after their delayed meal of fried liver.

"Thank you. I'm glad you liked it." Belle glanced over to the cradle where her daughter was making noises.

"Angel's crying," Abel said as if his mother should answer immediately.

"Thank you, but she's just waking up."

Angel took that moment to break into a wail.

Abel looked at his mother and shook his head, just the tiniest amount.

Belle stared at her son. "She wasn't really crying, you know."

His eyebrows twitched.

Belle rose and picked up her infant from the cradle, snuggling the baby against her shoulder. Angel calmed long enough to be laid down, but when Belle removed her diaper, she started in again. "Sh, sh, little one. I'm hurrying." Bundling her back up, she sat down in the rocker and, blanket over her shoulder, positioned the baby for nursing.

Jeremiah almost laughed at the byplay between mother and son. What made the boy so conscious of the baby? Was it because he'd never had a baby around before? He rose and gathered the dishes together, setting them in the pan of soapy water steaming on the stove.

"You don't have to do that," she said.

"I know. Abel and I are goin' to the barn this afternoon to check on that deer. Maybe bringing it up to the lean-to so it won't freeze, but the smell of blood might upset the new mother out there."

"Would it be terrible if the deer froze?"

"Need to cut it up first, and it should hang at least a day before we do that."

"I see."

She looked so peaceful he wanted to just sit and watch, but that wouldn't be polite, least ways the way he understood proper behavior. Not that handling cattle and living with other cowboys reminded one of polite behavior. But his mother had done her best to instill some sense of propriety in her family in spite of the sparseness of their lives.

So he pushed himself to his feet and, retrieving his coat while Abel did the same, stepped out into the lean-to. "We need to build some kind of a pen for that little varmint there so he can be shut away as his mother's real milk comes in."

"The white kind?"

"Right."

"But why can't he nurse anyway?"

"Cows, like other animals, have a way of making enough milk for their own baby, and we want her to make enough milk for your family. So if we pen the calf, she will keep producing more."

Abel stared at the cow, then up at the man. "How does she know all that? Who told her?"

"That's one of God's secrets, I guess."

"He can talk cow, too?"

The desire to laugh out loud felt so good, but instead Jeremiah nodded and smiled. "God can talk any kind of language He wants."

"Dog, too?"

"Dog, too." Jeremiah handed him the carved wooden pitchfork. "You want to clean out the manure? We'll put it by the house for now—helps keep the house warmer—but later it goes out in the garden. You do have a garden, right?"

Abel nodded and almost jabbed Jeremiah with the end of the pitchfork since the space was so crowded. "We got to fill the buckets with snow, too."

So many things he'd not had to do in Texas. While it snowed there a few times, it never stayed around long enough for more than a passing acquaintance. Not like this, where the snow took up residence for months on end. What would this country look like, all greened up for spring? Was the ranch he was heading for like this, or would it be more like Texas?

The urge to get on the trail again caught him by surprise. He'd given his word, and as far as Mr. Stubb knew, he was already there. He'd thought he heard the lonesome whistle of a train weeping out across the snowdrifted prairie. If he had any money, he'd have taken the train, but they'd been told it didn't go north and south yet, so what good would it do? The map he'd studied before leaving didn't begin to show him how far the ranch really was.

"You know if there are any boards out in the barn?"

"Some poles Pa brought back from the river one day."

"That'll work. Come on, you can show me."

By the time they had cut and pounded two rails into the sod wall across the corner and attached them to a movable post, dusk had blued the snowbanks. They watered the cow and horse and refilled all the buckets to melt again.

A small tub steamed on the stove.

"What you making, Ma?"

"Your baby sister needs clean diapers."

"You cook them?" He stared at her, making both adults chuckle.

"Don't worry, I made real food for us. We can eat as soon as you are ready."

Abel shook his head and glanced down at the cradle. "Babies are a lot of work."

Jeremiah laid a hand on the boy's shoulder. "Come on, let's get Tulip milked, and you can feed the calf. What are you goin' to name him?" They stepped back out into the nearly dark lean-to.

Abel shook his head. "I don't know." He stopped. "What about Nosey? He's always nosing for more to eat."

"Nosey it is."

The jerky-flavored beans made for a good meal. But that night in his bedroll, Jeremiah's mind would not shut down no matter how tired his body was. The realization was heavy with no easy answers. How would he ever be able to leave this woman and her children alone out here on the prairie with no near neighbors and not even a mule to go for help if needed? Yet he had given his word to take over the northern spread. *Dear Lord, what am I to do?*

Chapter 8

The next morning, Jeremiah couldn't decide whether the snow was still coming down or only blowing up from the earlier snowfall. Today was the day he absolutely should leave. But first he had to cut up that deer. If he quartered it, Belle could at least handle the sections, but even that would not be easy. Did she have a smokehouse? A box to let it freeze in? What should he do with the hide? Did she know how to tan a hide? So many questions and no easy answers.

He folded up his bedroll once he heard her in the kitchen. Now he could get a bucket to milk the cow again. After making pudding, Belle had set a pot of the colostrum to heating by the fire to make cheese. Once it turned to curd, she'd hang it to drain, and she said she'd start another pot. She was so thrilled to have the colostrum, he'd begun to realize she was happy to have anything. Instead of asking for more, she rejoiced over what she had just been given. He knew for certain there was a lesson there for him, too.

How can I leave her?

He kept coming back to that terrible, horrible question. He had to convince her to either get someone else to stay with them out here or go stay with someone else. Someone would make room at their house; that was the way things were done in the West.

"Good morning, Mr. Jennings. I'm sorry if I woke you."

"I was already awake."

"The coffee will be hot soon."

"Thank you." Such a stilted conversation. "How is Angel this morning?"

"She was hungry. That baby eats like none else I have known."

"She seems older than four days."

"Seems that way to me, too." She reached for one of the cups on the shelf and, cup in hand, turned to look at him. "I have to confess something."

"You do?" *Seems upside down to me. I'm the one who needs to confess—not just something, but a whole lot.*

"Yes." She looked down at the cup in her hand. "I feel so guilty that you are missing out on your job because you feel the need to stay here and take care of us. We will be all right. You have to believe that."

Jeremiah tipped his head back to stare at the rafters above. No wonder this house was cold—all the heat went up to the roof. The thought made him shake his head. As if that had anything to do with the fix they were in.

"The only way I can leave you here is if someone else comes to stay or you move into another house until spring comes."

"If I had a horse or mule, then I would be able to ride for help. Surely that would suffice."

"But what if you were the one who was sick? How would Abel, small as he is, go for help?"

"True." She stared into the empty cup.

He watched her face grow stern. When she looked at him, he saw a whole different person staring back at him.

"You are not responsible for me, for us, Jeremiah Jennings. Since Anson has gone to his reward, God and I are responsible for us. You keep your word, and I will keep mine."

He gritted his teeth, the urge to yell at her almost more than he could handle. "I am going to milk the cow. She at least will listen to reason. This can be used to water her, right?"

"Right!"

But he couldn't do it. He lost the inner battle. "You have to have help! You can—not—live—here—by—your—self!" He knew he was shouting, or at least raising his voice. He knew he cut each word with a sword. A sharp sword.

The baby started to cry. Abel woke up, crying and rubbing his eyes. Even the cow mooed and the rooster crowed.

"Why are you yelling at me? You have no—"

"Because I love you!"

You could have heard a feather float.

She paused in the act of lifting the baby and stared at him.

He stared at her.

A pint-sized warrior planted himself in front of Jeremiah. "Why are you yelling at my ma?" How could one small person, too little to mount a horse, pack so much venom into a simple sentence?

His mind screamed, *Run!* His body screamed, *Run!*

But Jeremiah Jennings could not run or turn or—

He took two steps forward, around the warrior with tears streaming down his cheeks and his fists planted firmly on his skinny hips, and three more steps to do a military halt in front of the woman who could never be his enemy and right now didn't believe he was a friend.

"Marry me!"

Tears erupted. "No one has ever said those words to me—'I love you.'"

"Well, I never said them before either, so that makes us even. But I have never meant anything more in my life. I love you. I love Abel and Angel. And I want to marry all of you. Right now, today."

She closed her eyes, but the tears refused to stop. "I—I can't."

"You can't what? Love me? Marry me? Pour the coffee? You can't what?" He didn't dare touch her, or he knew he would kiss her until they couldn't breathe. So he carefully set the bucket on the floor and glued his hands to his sides. *Lord, I need some real help here, right now!* He sniffed. "Please stop cryin'. I can't bear to see you cry. What can I do?"

"I—I c–can't."

He waited. Leaned forward. "You can't what?" Love me? I'll wait. Marry me? I'll wait. Quit crying? He dug in his pocket and brought out a handkerchief that had surely seen better days. He started to offer that to her but changed his mind. His handkerchief might make her throw up. He leaned over by the stove and snatched a cloth then mopped her cheeks, his touch like that of angel wings.

"Sh-sh-sh. Don't cry. All will be well. Don't cry." His mother always said that—*"All will be well."* He had come to believe every word of it through the years.

He repeated it, more strongly. He looked down to see Abel, fist wrapped in his mother's apron, staring up at him, question marks all over his face.

"It's all right, son. All will be well."

He guided Belle so her legs backed against the chair, and he lowered her into it. He mopped her tears again and smiled when she finally opened her eyes. "All right now?"

She nodded, swallowed, and swallowed again.

Angel whimpered.

Jeremiah sucked in a deep breath and squatted down to eye level with Abel. "Come on. Let's get you dressed before your feet freeze off."

The boy glanced down at his feet and nodded. He stuck his hand into Jeremiah's. "Can I help you milk Tulip?"

Jeremiah tried not to laugh, but the effort rocked him back, butt square on the floor. He didn't just laugh, he guffawed, pulling the boy into his lap, and gathered his little feet into one hand while he circled the child with his other arm. "Yep, you can help me milk Tulip. She'll be telling us to hurry on out there anytime now." He gave Belle a wink. "We'll be talking about this again. You can count on it." He surged to his feet, child in his arms. "You cannot milk a cow in your nightshirt. It just ain't proper."

He turned to smile at Belle. "I'll be back."

After brushing off Tulip's udder, he sat down, put the bucket between his knees, and planted his forehead in her flank. "This is the way you sit when you milk. Then, using two hands, you squeeze and release, pulling down gently at the same time. Like this, see?" The milk began squirting into the bucket. Once he'd milked so the bottom of the bucket was covered, he motioned Abel to come beside him. "Now you lean in here and put your hand on one teat, and I'll put my hand over yours." When the milk again squirted into the bucket, now foaming, Abel giggled.

"Feels warm and funny."

"That it does. Okay, tomorrow you can sit on the stool and try it. You pretend with me now. Right hand, left hand." The milk music picked up again. Nosey bawled from the pen where she now lived. "Right hand, left hand."

"Milking is hard work."

"Not so much after your arms and hands get used to it." When he'd finished, he stood and hung the stool back up on the peg on the wall. "Now you feed Nosey." He poured milk into another bucket.

Abel held the bucket in place and stuck his fingers down in the milk, and when Nosey remembered what she was supposed to do, she found his fingers and sucked away.

"Tonight you take your fingers away and see if she will do it alone."

Abel nodded and, when the bucket was empty, carried it into the house. "I did it. I sorta milked, and I fed Nosey. She likes my fingers." He looked down his arm and frowned. "I got my sleeve wet."

"Milk will wash out. I'm proud of you."

"When I can milk, you won't have to."

"That's right."

Jeremiah poured the milk through a towel into a kettle. "You want this by the fire, too?"

"Yes, please. The mush is ready."

Abel went to the window. "The sun is shining."

"I know. You need to bring in some wood."

While he did that, Jeremiah looked at Belle. "We need to talk."

She nodded. "That we do."

At least she looked more agreeable, he thought, puffing a sigh. "I'll sharpen the knives to cut the meat, and then we can let it freeze outside tonight. Tonight we'll talk."

She didn't smile when she nodded.

Maybe he didn't really want to talk, he thought. He might not like her answers.

Chapter 9

We have to talk. Jeremiah had talked too much already, way too much. Love her? He respected her, was proud of her, liked her and her fiery stubbornness. But love? He didn't even know what love was, not really. His mother bore his father ten kids, but did she love him? She called him *that hateful man* on more than one occasion. She got angry at him.

And Jeremiah was angry with this Belle Stedman right now. Her stubbornness endangered herself and her children. Endangered her man-cub Abel and her helpless baby. Maybe she didn't have any love. But no, that was foolish thinking. He thought about her gentle touch, the way she spoke to Abel, the way she cuddled her tiny girl. No, she was full of love. Just not for him.

He tossed Sanchez some hay and rubbed the nose of his easygoing old roan. But the horse was more interested in the hay than in his master just now. He dropped his grizzled head to the ground and began munching and crunching supper.

The last traces of sun were entirely gone, inside the barn and out. Jeremiah groped his way through the darkness down the rough-hewn stanchions to the door and stepped outside, closing the door behind him. There they were back again, the auroras, the mysterious, shimmering curtains moving among the stars.

Did anyone have any idea how or why those things appeared? They did not occur in Texas. That was for sure. Did the snow and the piercing cold play a part?

Who cared, really? There they were. *Ignore 'em, admire 'em, but just don't pick 'em apart.*

The path along the rope strung from the barn to the house had been packed down solid. It was part level track, part ice. He stomped the snow off his boots, rapped on the door, and entered.

Abel stirred on his pallet, but he was asleep. Belle was nearly asleep. Wrapped in a heavy woolen shawl, she rocked slowly, dreamily beside the woodstove with her baby on her lap.

She opened her eyes. She smiled then, and his whole world lit up.

He grabbed a stool from the table and plunked it down beside her rocker so he could sit on it facing her, his shoulder by her knee. The stove and its welcome heat was right in front of him. "I been thinking a good bit about what popped out of me earlier. Loving you." He didn't know how to say what he really thought. He'd never had to before, especially not to a woman. "Been thinking—maybe it isn't love. But if not, it's awful close."

She studied him. She didn't stare, didn't look surprised or angry or anything else. Thoughtful, if anything. He wasn't good at reading women's faces, but hers was about as easy to read as anyone's. She took a long, deep breath. "Are you married?"

"No. Never have been." He smiled. "Left home as soon as I could and grew up on a Texas ranch. You know how you have neighbors you can walk to? You don't walk to the neighbors in Texas; the spreads are scattered too far apart. And no women."

"You seem comfortable with Abel. The baby, too."

"Nine little brothers and sisters. I've changed a diaper before." The smile faded. "That's part of why I said that today, I think, about loving and marrying. I like kids. I like yours, a lot."

"You understand about homestead law?"

"Not really."

She licked her lips. "We laid a homestead claim on this property and marked it off. We developed it—that is, built a house and barns and fences and planted fields and gardens. Ran livestock of some sort. The cow counts as livestock, and the chickens. We used to have a pig, but we ate it. In short, we met the law by settling onto our claim like we're going to stay. If we stay on the land for five years and farm it, we prove it up. That means we gain title to it. If we leave the land, we have to start over somewhere else. That's the Homestead Act."

"How long have you been here?"

"This is starting into the fifth year. This land is nearly ours." Her voice broke. "Mine." She took another deep breath. Her voice went solid again. "You feel a need to go to your boss's other ranch."

"More than need. A responsibility."

She nodded. "If I were to go with you, I would be abandoning this land before it's proved up. Therefore I would lose it. This land is my children's future. Their legacy. Their father worked hard to provide this for them, and so did I. I can't leave it."

"So it's not just stubbornness." He nodded. He dropped forward to prop his elbows on his knees and stare at the floor awhile. Not floor. Rug. The floor was beaten earth, but she'd made some sort of braided rug to cover most of it. And that rug—how long had it taken to braid a rug this big out of wool scraps? The rug sort of said what she was saying—an untold lot of work had gone into this place to make it a home. A home forever. And he understood.

"Why is it such a responsibility? I thought a boss was someone you worked for, got your pay, and if you decided to work somewhere else, you quit and took the other job."

He smiled again. "That's how it usually works, yeah. But not this time. You see, I was sort of flounderin'. Seventeen years old, never worked at anything except sharecroppin'. Helpin' Pa in the fields. And helpin' Ma with the little brothers and sisters. Soon as Ellie Mae and Annie Mae were old enough to take care of the kids, I left. Pa was hoppin' mad. With sharecroppin', the more kids you have, the more money you can make. I promised to send money home, but I almost never did; I didn't make enough money to send anywhere. Then Mr. Stubb sort of took me under his wing."

"Mr. Stubb was your boss?"

The baby gurgled and stretched then began to fuss. Belle lifted her to her shoulder and rubbed her back.

Jeremiah nodded. "I came to his ranch looking for a job. No money, not a penny. Just a hungry, scrawny, grumpy kid. He fed me and hired me; took me in, really. He and the missus taught me manners, taught me ciphering, taught me about our Savior. Workin' in the fields back home, I never would've learnt any of that."

"So you owe him everything, even your eternal life."

She did understand. What a woman! He bobbed his head. "Exactly."

"Your father was a hard man."

"Still is. I guess. Haven't wrote home for a long time; don't know if he's livin' or dead." He looked at her. "What about you? What's your story?"

She didn't answer right away, as if she was thinking about it. Then she said, "It is incredibly difficult, maybe even impossible, for one person, man or woman, to prove up on a homestead. There's just too much to do. Too much work. But it's a way to own land, a farm, when you don't have any money. My father worked for the railroad, but only three days a week. Anson's father lost his job as a telegraph operator. Heavy drinking. So neither Anson nor I had any money. We knew each other from going to the same school. When we graduated from eighth grade."

"Where?"

"Missouri. Independence. Anson said, 'We can be farmers and landowners with this Homestead Act. Let's do it. Let's marry and do it.' So we married, claimed here near the railroad, and. . .well, that was the dream."

"Didn't you love him at all?"

"Oh, I liked him all right. He was a masterful craftsman. Look at this rocker. Graceful looking, but solid as a rock. And the house. He built the whole house; I only helped a little because I was busy with the garden and chickens, and then with Abel." She studied the rug, too. "And he was very good at accepting responsibility. He chose to be a family man, so he took care of his family. That has to be something to love."

"Love? Or respect?"

She smiled and sniffed and nodded. "*Respect* is a much better word. Yes, I respected him and all his hard work. It must not be lost."

His mind whirled as did his heart. He didn't like any of this. "So the best I can see, we're doomed."

"Doomed?"

"I gotta go to Mr. Stubb's ranch; you gotta stay here. I can't let you stay here alone, but I can't do anything else." He shrugged. "We're doomed." And then he asked what he was terribly afraid to ask but had to ask anyway. "Do you love me?"

She thought a moment. He admired that in her: not just saying whatever jumped into her head, like he did so often. "I don't know for sure. I don't know if I ever really felt love. I think I do." She smiled sadly. "But like you say, we're doomed."

Chapter 10

Jeremiah liked that Reverend Swenson fellow; he was a man of his word. Here he came up the track, driving a sleigh with two men on horseback at his side. Jeremiah laid aside the rail with which he was repairing the barn-side corral and walked out to meet them.

The reverend drove into the yard. "Mr. Jennings. Good morning."

Rusty came bounding over, tail flailing, and barked a greeting to his friends.

"Mornin', Reverend. Not quite sure about all this. Are you a pastor or a minister or a rector or a vicar?"

Reverend Swenson laughed. "A pastor. May I introduce Marcus Smith and Sam Barhold? They're members of our church in town. We've come out to retrieve the body of poor Anson Stedman."

"Ah, of course."

Belle stepped out onto the porch. "Good morning, Reverend! Marcus, Sam. Coffee's made."

The reverend tipped his hat. "We'd like Mr. Jennings here to take us out and show us where, uh, the mortal remains are."

She froze. And then—and this was very curious—Jeremiah could just about read her thoughts. Her heart moved from warm cheer and hospitality to sudden ice and sadness. And that was to be expected. "Of course, Reverend Swenson. Perhaps you all will stop by later."

"We shall indeed."

Jeremiah nodded. "I'll saddle up."

He hurried into the dark barn to his roan and saddled as quickly as possible. About the time his eyes were well adjusted to the gloom, he rode out into the brilliance of sun on snow. "Abel? Will you close the barn door, please?" He joined the party as the little boy darted toward the barn, and they all rode out to the east.

Now was a fine time to think of this, but he should have brought Rusty. The dog knew the way; he was not so certain, and he knew Sanchez didn't give a fig. There were precious few landmarks to guide his way on this vast prairie.

The reverend opened conversation. "Several people in our congregation this year have suffered pneumonia. Two died. Is that what struck down Mr. Stedman?"

"S'pose so, but I'm no doctor. He rattled when he breathed. That's usually pneumonia. But the cold had much to do with it."

The reverend nodded. "I understand that Russia refers to this season as 'General Winter.' The Russian army was no match for Napoleon's legions, but the winter cold was. It decimated the French. They were on the verge of taking Moscow—entered the city in fact—but they had to retreat because of the extreme cold. Most died on the way back to France."

Jeremiah nodded grimly. "I see your point. Same cold as this."

"Pretty much. Ah, Mr. Jennings, but wait until you experience spring and summer here. As close to heaven as earth ever gets. And autumn—crisp, clear, flowing gold. So to get to the beautiful seasons, if you will, we put up with the winter."

"Unless it kills you."

Silence.

Nice move, Jennings. You just cast a pall over the whole conversation.

Then the reverend asked, "You sound like you've come up from the South. The accent."

"I have. Texas. There's a man to whom I owe a great deal, a Mr. Stubb. He owns a ranch to the north and west of here. He asked me to take it over because of some problems there. So I'm on my way to do that."

"I see. And you stumbled upon Anson."

"Exactly so. Saw his campfire away up ahead, thought to warm myself, maybe share a meal."

The reverend nodded. "He was a fine man, a good Christian. And his wife no less."

"I figured that out, yes sir. Somebody did a fine job raisin' the both of 'em."

"Indeed." The reverend seemed thoughtful. "Sometimes, though, there's not much the parents can do if a child is wayward. Sparing the rod, applying the rod, doesn't seem to make much difference."

Jeremiah nodded. "That's so. I have two brothers like that." Where were they, anyway? This party, he meant, not his brothers. He knew where his brothers were: one was in jail and the other in Little Rock. "Can't imagine you with a wayward boy, Reverend."

The man smiled. "Not a boy. A niece. Always in trouble, it seems. Not trouble such as lying or stealing. Pranks. Roughhousing. She's twelve now, and old enough to know better. To at least act like a lady."

"I have a sister like that. You want to find her, start lookin' up in trees. Or in the creek catching crawdads. Not where you usually see a girl, like with a doll. And go, go, go."

"Yes! That is Cordellia, exactly. A sweet child but hardly proper."

He was pretty sure they were still on track, because there was a low rise off to the north that he seemed to remember; had a couple scrawny little trees on it like those. But this broad, broad prairie, barely undulating, looked too much the same. Funny how he could make his way across Texas plains just as flat as this and know exactly where he was, but this land? No.

Wait. Up ahead there. What they call a copse, a little rise with some mesquites on it. No, not mesquites this far north, but trees. Or bushes. Something. He pointed. "Let's head over there."

The reverend turned his sleigh aside.

An odd mound of new-fallen snow sat near the bushes. And the bushes were all cut off, as with a knife. Only the thickest branches, too stout to chop with a knife, stuck out, just as he remembered. He swung down, dropped a rein to ground-tie Sanchez, and started beating aside the mound with his hat. Yep. Here it was. Had to be God guidin' him, because he sure wouldn't have picked this out as the spot otherwise. There was the wagon, what was left that Stedman hadn't burned. Three wheels, the frame, the seat boards still attached. Was there anything left of Anson Stedman?

Under the wagon frame, the snow mounded a bit, and that is where he'd left Stedman. He brushed the snow off the mound at one end. A wool scarf. Jeremiah had wrapped the head in the scarf when he laid him out.

Grimly the reverend moved in beside him. Sam and Marcus pressed in close.

Jeremiah knelt at the mound and used his hand to brush away most of the snow from the scarf, tug it up over the head to reveal the corpse's face. Ghastly. That was the word. A strange bluish-white cast to the skin and frozen pure rock solid. His stomach flipped.

The reverend knelt and held a hand over the frozen face, muttering something. Then he said aloud, "I'm glad animals didn't get to him. I suppose that once the remains are frozen, they don't have much scent to attract varmints."

Sam nodded. "'Bout how it is with cattle. I've looked down on many a frozen cow and calf, but it was never like this."

"Amen," said Marcus, and he turned away and threw up.

Jeremiah stood up and tried to move the wagon frame, give them more working room, but it was frozen fast in the old snow. Wouldn't budge. So the four of them tugged and yanked and managed to get the body rolled out into the open.

Sam wrapped the scarf back around Mr. Stedman's face. Each on a corner, they toted him over to the sleigh and slid him in back, stiff as lumber. Reverend Swenson had had the foresight to bring rope, so they tied him down real good.

Sam looked at the reverend. "Take him by the missus first, so she can say good-bye?"

"Not with the boy there. Let her do it privately, in town."

Yep, Jeremiah liked this minister more and more. The man cared. To Jeremiah, that was the most important thing a man could do. Mr. Stubb had cared enough to invest in a worthless kid. That kid's own pa hadn't.

One of the things Jeremiah did for Mr. Stubb was to look around where cattle might have been rustled and try to get an idea of what happened. They'd caught three or four rustlers that way. The three men were waiting on him, he knew, but he started looking the area over good. He wanted to know. No tracks, of course. Any tracks were snowed under, not to be found. But the wagon frame told him some things.

The reverend asked, "Why did the robbers that fell upon him and stole his supplies not just take the wagon?"

"'Zactly what I was wonderin' myself." Jeremiah pointed to the near rear hub and axle. "Look close here. You expect it to be black from axle grease like the other hubs. But this black is different. It's charred." He gripped the wheel rim and strained mightily. Wouldn't budge.

Sam nodded. "His wheel wasn't greased enough, and it locked up. Quit turning. Probably smoking, so he had to stop. Pretty smart, Jennings."

Jeremiah pointed. "The off rear wheel is gone. He likely took it off. If I was out here and a wheel locked up, I'd pull the other wheels to steal some grease from each of them and get the bad wheel working again. Reckon that's what he was doing as well."

The reverend nodded. "Good surmise, Mr. Jennings. And if the pneumonia was upon him, he might have been too sick and weak to do much more than clear a spot and build a fire."

Sam said, "Cray Sheets at the hotel says Stedman stayed in town a week. Said he wanted to get back, but he was feeling poorly. Didn't think it was pneumonia though. Just blowing his nose and such. 'Sides, there was that bad storm to delay him, too."

The picture was coming clear. "He delayed in town, trying to feel better, and finally decided he had to get home. Maybe ran out of money; it's expensive staying in town. So he started out, got this far—too far to turn back—and his wheel locked up. And then the pneumonia came on him. And then the robbers. They couldn't move the wagon either, what with that wheel, so they left it and just took his supplies." Jeremiah shook his head. "Everything in the world went bad on him all at once."

Marcus sighed. "And he was such a good man, too."

" 'He sends His rain on the just and the unjust.' Matthew 5 something," Sam quoted.

"Matthew 5:45, I believe. Near the end of that chapter." The reverend took one last look at the forlorn wagon frame and climbed up into his sleigh. "Mr. Jennings, you may come into town with us if you wish, or return to tell the missus what we're doing here. I will take the remains in and then come visit her."

He pondered a moment. "Can the church give the missus a loan? I could get her some supplies."

Sam smiled. "I can spare a dollar or two."

"Me, too," said Marcus.

The reverend bobbed his head and twisted his horse aside to break his runners loose. "Excellent plan." He clucked his horse forward. "Mr. Jennings, you know pretty much what they need most. If you come with us, we'll load up this sleigh for the drive back to the Stedman place. We're not a wealthy church; in fact, most of us are poor as church mice, so to speak, so we cannot replace the stolen supplies. But we can ease her burden."

"Reverend Swenson, I'm much obliged to you."

Sam said, "And send some more out later, maybe."

Marcus added, "And axle grease. Lots of axle grease."

Chapter 11

Reverend said he would be out to visit you today." Jeremiah set the milk bucket on the table.

Belle nodded. "Thank you."

"Said he had a niece who was a bit of a handful. Twelve years old, and her parents are at the end of their patience with her."

"That's sad. Is she in trouble? With others, I mean."

"Not that he said—more high-spirited, it sounds like."

"Breakfast is ready. Give Abel a shake, please."

At the prompting, Abel climbed out of bed and shoved his feet into his boots then sat down at the table, still rubbing his eyes. Blue eyes widened when his mother set scrambled eggs with meat in them on the table. "Eggs!"

"I wish there were more, but at least we can enjoy a treat."

Jeremiah inhaled. "Smells like a corner of heaven."

She set a plate of cornmeal patties on the table, too. "One of these days I will make biscuits, but these will do for now." She sat down and smiled at her son. "How would you like to say grace, Abel?"

He nodded. "Thank You, Jesus, for food and milk and Nosey and eggs and that that mean old rooster missed me yesterday. Amen." His words had run into one long one, except for the *amen*, making his mother smile.

When they finished eating, Belle poured more oat coffee into their cups, filling Abel's with cream and then passing the pitcher to Jeremiah. "Cream makes even this kind of coffee palatable."

"It's hot and tastes fine to me."

Rusty scrambled up, his tail wagging on his way to the door where, nose to the edge, he announced they had company coming.

Abel jumped up and retrieved the rifle from the corner, handing it to his mother. When the knock came, he went to open it.

Belle caught Jeremiah's quizzical expression. "Anson insisted after we had an unwelcome visitor one time."

"Ma, it's Reverend Swenson."

"Well, invite him in."

Before the man stepped through the door, Belle put the rifle behind her skirts. "Welcome, Reverend. You're out early."

"Good morning. And a fine morning it is." He nodded to the young girl beside him. "I brought Cordellia along with me, my niece."

"Welcome, Cordellia, I'm Mrs. Stedman. My son, Abel. Our guest, Mr. Jennings. We have some roasted oats coffee if you would like a cup."

"Thank you. We have a few supplies along. Families donated some." He looked to Jeremiah. "And Sam decided he could loan you his old mule. He's getting kind of old for plowing and such, but he was hoping you might find a use for him in case you needed to go for help." He unwound his muffler from around his neck.

"I'll bring the things in." Jeremiah rose and grabbed his coat.

Belle smiled at the gangly girl. "Come sit over here."

Cordellia shook her head. "I'll go help Mr. Jennings if you don't mind."

When the two had left, the reverend took Jeremiah's chair. "I have a big favor to ask. Might you be willing to help us out by keeping Cordellia out here with you for a while? I know she can be a big help, and perhaps you can be a good influence on her. Her ma says she is a real good worker but tends to daydream a lot and has no interest in ladylike pursuits."

Thoughts darted through her mind like spring swallows on a bug hunt. The girl's blue eyes already haunted her. With freckles dusting a turned-up nose, Cordellia could not be called beautiful by any means, but since when did that matter? "We don't have a lot of room, as you know."

"She could sleep in the lean-to or on a pallet on the floor. Her ma said she could send out some flour and such in return for keeping her. Cordellia and your Abel here ought to get along right well."

"What about school? Shouldn't she be in school?"

"Well, I thought as how you can read and write and do sums, mayhap you would teach her." He dropped his voice. "She was the instigator behind several pranks at the schoolhouse, and she and the teacher don't get along too well."

Belle hid a grin. This girl sounded just like her younger sister. Leaving Amy behind was one of the hardest things she had ever done when she and Anson came west. Taking a deep breath, she nodded. "Of course she can stay with us. And while I think there might be a bit of conniving between you and Mr. Jennings, I do believe this will work out for all of us. Far better that she comes here than we get hauled off to stay with someone else."

"God does indeed provide."

The door opened, and Cordellia and Mr. Jennings entered, arms full of supplies, with Rusty dancing at their feet.

"Oh Reverend, how can I ever thank you?"

"It weren't me but the folks of our congregation. When they heard your supplies were stolen, they dug deep."

"How can I repay them?"

"By being a saving grace for Cordellia. With the mule, you'll be able to come to town for church one Sunday in the near future. Soon's we can bust your wagon out of the ice lock, we'll get it fixed and bring it back for you."

Belle sniffed then had to dab at her eyes.

"You got enough hay for both the cow and the mule?"

"I hope so."

He leaned forward. "Now I hate to get too personal, but do you have any cash on hand?"

She shook her head. "Anson took it all to buy supplies."

"Figured as much. Don't you go getting worried. God will provide, but you got to be honest with me and be willing to ask for help. Now I know that comes hard, but our Father gives us each other to make the road easier. Some people have a need to help, and if you don't ask, you cheat them out of doing what God is telling them to do."

Belle set the cradle to rocking with one foot. "All I can say is thank you."

"Thank Him, not just us."

Cordellia and Jeremiah set the last of the supplies on the floor. "That does it," Jeremiah said.

"Did you bring your things in?" Reverend Swenson asked the girl.

"No, but I will." She looked to Belle. "Are you sure, ma'am?" She glanced down, and her eye caught the cradle. "You have a baby?" Her voice wore awe like a coating of cream.

"Angel was born on Christmas Eve."

"Oh, I love babies. Can I touch her?"

"Of course."

Cordellia knelt by the cradle. "She is so beautiful. And you called her Angel."

"The man told me that was her name." Abel glanced at his mother as if asking if all was well.

"Really, what man?"

"We'll tell you the story later." Belle watched the girl. "Have you been around babies before?"

"Not for a long time." She rose. "I'll go get my things."

"Well, if that is all settled, I'd best be on my way. Jeremiah, you want to take that mule out to the barn? By the way, his name is Samson. Cordellia already made friends with him. The bridle stays with him."

"I cannot say thank you enough," Belle said. "And thank all those generous people for me, too."

"We'll get that wagon back for you as soon as we can. Don't want to leave it there too long, or it will walk off, too." He settled his hat on his head and stepped into the sleigh. "Lord bless and keep you." He clucked at the horse then stopped. "You tell Jeremiah that when he comes back through this way, he's already got family and friends here."

"I will." Belle waved him off and returned to the house, Cordellia right beside her.

"I'll help you put those supplies away."

"Thank you, I just have to figure where to put them all. Soon's the winter weather lets up, we can move the cow and chickens back out to the barn." She turned to the girl. "Do you know how to milk a cow?"

"Yes. I don't care much for chickens. They seem so flighty." She turned at the first whimper from the cradle. "Can I pick her up?"

Belle almost said no, but the look of pleading on the girl's face made her change her mind. "I take it you've been with babies before, then?"

"Like I said, not for a long time. I'll be careful. I promise."

Angel whimpered. Cordellia leaned over the cradle and gently, as if touching thistle down, slid her hands under the wrapped bundle of baby and held her in one arm against her chest. "Angel is such a perfect name for you." She rocked as if it were the most natural thing in the world. "You think it's time to eat?" Cordellia looked up to Belle, her eyes shining. "Thank you."

"I'll show you where to put some of those things while I change her and feed her." Belle did as she said and made herself and the baby comfortable in the rocker. "Abel went out to the barn?"

"I guess so." Cordellia opened each of the packets and filled the tins. "Mrs. March sent you some of her hundred-year sourdough starter. And some flour so you can keep it going. Someone else sent flour, too. Look here." She sniffed a can with a lid. "Someone sent bacon drippings. Now that's strange."

"No, that is wonderful. I can put it in so many things. Soon we'll have butter, too. Such riches." Belle blew out a breath. Now if only Jeremiah didn't have to leave, but she knew he would probably head out tomorrow.

That night Cordellia laid her pallet at the foot of the rope-strung bed, and both she and Abel were asleep within minutes. Jeremiah and Belle, she with the baby sleeping in her arms, sat in front of the fire. Jeremiah had a piece of wood he was carving on, brushing the chips into a pile.

"I meant what I said, you know."

"What—that you're leaving first thing in the morning?"

"Well, that too, but I have given this plenty of thought, and I do believe that I love you. The big question is, do you think you could come to love me?"

The words wanted to leap out of her mouth, but she bade her tongue and lips behave. "It is too soon yet."

"That wasn't the question."

"Oh." She rocked a couple of times, heaving a sigh. "But there are problems, you see."

"Such as?"

"I want to live here, and you will be living on a ranch way northwest of here."

"If you believe you can come to love me, then somehow that will work out." He scraped some chips unto the growing stack. "If I write to you, will you write to me?"

"Yes." There was no hesitation there.

"Good."

"When will you come back?"

"Not until after calving and branding and clearing whatever messes await me. So probably not before June. I will write to you." He dusted off his carving and handed her a wooden horse. "This is the first horse I will give Abel, but not the last." He brushed the shavings pile into a bag he kept handy for tinder.

"I have a feeling Cordellia is going to like it here." He nodded, thinking as he stared into the fire. "I think God sent her."

"Like He sent you?" She had a hard time believing she'd said that, but so truly God had been guiding Jeremiah.

"Maybe you can trade butter and cheese for hay or grain when you need it. Your wagon will take some fixin'."

"Are you sure you meant. . .ah, meant what you said?" Her heart felt like it might leap out of her mouth.

"That I love you?"

"Yes." She let the words nestle around her heart.

"Guess it gets easier with the saying."

"I guess."

He rose and leaned over, tipping her chin up with one finger. "And this is what love feels like."

His kiss not only warmed her lips but her heart and traveled deep into her soul. When he lifted his mouth, she let her head rest on the back of the rocker, staring up at him with seeking eyes.

"I will see you in June."

The next morning, his words echoed in her heart as she and Abel, along with Cordellia, waved him good-bye. They stood in front of the sod house, sun glinting on the snow, and waved until they couldn't see him. "The Lord keep thee safe," she whispered. Jeremiah's words, *All will be well*, echoed again in her heart. "Please Lord, let that be so."

Epilogue

You sure he will be here?" Cordellia asked with a skeptical look from under her brows.

"He said he would be." And he's never lied yet. Belle breathed a silent prayer. The last time someone didn't come home when he said was when Anson didn't return, and it wasn't his fault. *Dear Lord, not again, please.*

Abel burst into the room. "He's here! He's here!"

Belle felt her knees near to buckle. Relief could cause that, same as fear. *Thank You, Lord. You got me through before; thank You for now.* Every morning she woke with *thank You* on her mind. Thank You burst in like the first green grass and the meadowlarks singing. All were announcing they were back. The prairie was no longer locked in winter. She started for the door, and Mrs. Swenson grabbed her arm.

"It's bad luck to see the groom on your wedding day before the ceremony, a'course."

"All right, if you insist, but can I send him a message?"

The two women in the room with her looked at each other and shrugged.

Cordellia, eyes shining, announced, "I'll go tell him."

"Tell him. . ." Belle closed her eyes. "Tell him all is well."

"That all?"

"Yes, that is all." She'd signed the letter almost that way, only "All will be well." And he'd answered. Letters had been her lifeline in the months since that day after Christmas when he'd ridden north to his new job.

She returned in a minute. "You shoulda seen his face—like the sun lit it."

Belle felt peace settle over her. She looked over to the corner where one of her friends had picked up the baby. At five months, Angel charmed everyone.

A knock at the door, and Reverend Swenson asked, "You ready?"

"Yes." Belle picked up her bouquet of pink prairie roses, one of her favorite spring and summer flowers, and Cordellia, carrying Angel, walked out first. Belle followed her and paused at the door. Abel stepped in beside her and grinned up at her.

"He's up front." His whisper could have carried clear to Fargo.

Belle nodded.

The man to the right of the reverend turned with a smile that encompassed his entire face.

At the reverend's slight nod, a woman started to sing. "Holy, holy, holy, Lord God Almighty."

Belle repeated her vows to love, honor, and obey with a firm voice, looking into eyes that searched clear to her soul.

Angel chortled from the front row. Abel snickered, and a titter ran through those present. This was too special an occasion not to smile and rejoice.

"You may kiss your bride." Belle floated into Jeremiah's arms and heard Angel again. Angels singing? How appropriate. With her cowboy at her side, Belle took the first step in the journey to her new life. And all would be well, for the God who had brought them together and guided them to this point would never leave. When Reverend Swenson gave the blessing, everyone said, "Amen." And Angel, who had stolen the cowboy's heart at their first meeting, chortled again.

A Badlands Christmas

Marcia Gruver

Dedication

To Noela Nancarrow, my Australian angel and new best mate. Thank you for the blessing of your friendship and for the gracious loan of your delightful name. This book belongs to you.

Acknowledgments

First and foremost to Noela, Allen, and Nathan, the Nancarrow family. Without you, I couldn't have written my Aussie characters. Any mistakes made in this endeavor are entirely my own and due to no lack of enthusiasm on your part. Your help was invaluable. You've given me enough information and research material to write a series set in Australia. Maybe one day.

To my husband, Lee: You faithfully whisk me away to the most amazing book settings. Medora, North Dakota, will remain one of my favorites.

My thanks to the town of Medora, North Dakota (www.medora.com), gatekeepers of the rich history of an incredible land. And to the Theodore Roosevelt National Park (www.nps.gov/thro), a region of indescribable beauty. Thank you for guarding the memory of one of our country's great statesmen. He loved Medora, too.

And Jesus said unto him, Foxes have holes, and birds of the air have nests; but the Son of man hath not where to lay his head.
LUKE 9:58

Chapter 1

New York City
October 1885

Fifth Avenue bustled with grand carriages pulled by splendid teams, their manes neatly braided, the equine bodies brushed to a sheen. Twin muzzles proudly tossed, though not as high as the well-bred noses of the passengers the horses conveyed. The pompous, high-stepping mares appeared to tiptoe through puddles along the sodden street, and the drivers, sitting tall in their seats, pretended no splatter of mud dotted their top hats and coats.

Noela touched her mouth to hide a smile.

Glancing at the midday sun, she stepped up her pace. Father had rolled the pastry for beef steak and kidney pie before she left. Considering his fondness for meat pies, he wouldn't appreciate holding lunch.

The autumn breeze chilled her back, and the scent of burning leaves wafted on the air. She tucked her hands inside her wrap and wished she'd aired out Mum's warm coat. She adored the fitted sable garment lined in black velvet. The auburn fur looked nice against her fair complexion and set off her russet hair.

That morning she'd run her fingers over the luxurious collar then left it on a hook in the closet.

"New York society considers furs and gaudy ornamentation unfit attire for unmarried ladies," Mrs. Baumann's strident voice rang in her head. "And one must always adhere to the dictates of New York society."

Noela smirked. Even if one happened to be a true-blue Australian girl from the shores of Coolangatta?

"I say, young Miss Nancarrow. . .what folly amuses you today?"

She glanced up, and her heart lurched. Butterflies took flight in the pit of her stomach, and the glee she fought to suppress twitched at her lips.

Julian Van der Berg strolled her way, looking smart in a knee-length topcoat and fleece collar. Tilting his carefully groomed head to the side, he slapped his gloves playfully against the palm of his slender hand. "Oh yes, my dear, I saw. You can't hide a smile as bright as sunrise."

He tucked his handsome, dimpled chin. "Care to share? I could use an occasion for mirth. Pleasurable diversions are few in this dreary city of ours."

"G'day, Mr. Van der Berg, and kindly mind your tongue. New York is ace in my book."

Without invitation, he took her arm and walked alongside, gazing at her with bold admiration. "I do believe you mean it. I detect a sparkle in those pretty green eyes."

Folding down the brim of her hat, she turned away from the biting north wind and stared toward the East River Bridge. "I'm ever so chuffed you got the color right. I'm told you miss on occasion."

He feigned shock. "Would you suggest I'm a philanderer?"

She met his saucy pout with a grin. "No worries, sir. I believe only the best of you."

Amusement flickered in his eyes. "And I of you, my trusting lamb." He drew her arm closer and held it snug against the warmth of his body. "Now then, where have you been this morning? Are you up to any mischief?"

"I was summoned to Mrs. Baumann's house." Her chest swelled with joy at the unexpected honor. "She appointed me to the planning committee for the Christmas ball."

"Of course." He sniffed as though he'd caught a whiff of something foul. "The annual soirée of black tie and beaded gown waltzing beneath the crystalline glow of Edith Baumann's chandelier, the watchful eyes of her cherished Degas—resplendent in gilded frame—overseeing the terpsichorean display."

Julian prided himself on the liberal use of multisyllabic words, blithely slipping them into the conversation each time an opportunity presented itself.

Without an inkling of what he'd just said, Noela frowned. "I sense a lack of enthusiasm."

Julian reclined his head and closed his eyes. "My dear, I can hardly wait for one more boring social affair."

His weary gaze shifted down to her. "Then again"—he raised one tapered brow—"you, my dear, hold the power to make the night seem somewhat bearable. Have I mentioned how utterly charmed I am by your accent?"

She affected a flirtatious simper. "You should book passage to Queensland without delay. You'd stay well charmed there, because everyone sounds the same as I do."

"No one could compare with the magic of your lilting tone." He studied her lips as if contemplating a kiss. "I can't imagine anything more desirable than your voice in my ear all evening."

She tensed, anticipation crowding her throat. An invitation to accompany him to the ball would surely follow. As for the kiss, he wouldn't dare be so bold in the middle of Fifth Avenue in broad daylight.

She swallowed hard, her legs weak beneath her. Or would he?

His undeniably feminine lashes swept up and down in a languid blink. "Promise to save a dance for me?"

Her stomach fell, but she fought to recover. "Of—of course I will." It wouldn't do to let him sense her disappointment.

"Delightful!" He tipped his chin at something behind her. "And here you are, delivered safely to your door."

And so she was. His presence had engaged her so fully, he could've marched her off the Hudson River pier. She might've noticed once the water closed over her head.

She beamed her brightest. "Thank you for seeing me home, Julian."

"My pleasure."

Reluctant to see him go, she gripped the banister of the two-story brownstone. "Won't you please join us for lunch? There's always plenty, and we'd love to have you."

A cocky glint returned to his eyes. "Your father won't share your enthusiasm."

"Rubbish. If he were standing here now, he'd extend the invitation himself."

Julian backed away, bowing slightly. "Let's not test your theory, my dear." He winked and shot her a rakish grin. "Farewell, little lamb. Another time perhaps?"

Struggling to return his smile, she fingered the threads of her crocheted waistband and nodded. "Very well then. Another time."

Noela stared after him until he reached the end of the block. An invitation to share one dance wasn't exactly what she'd hoped for, but it would do for now. She'd find a way to persuade him.

She opened the door to eerie silence. Her steps clattered in the entry hall and bounced off the great room's high ceiling.

Curious, she ducked to peer up the deserted staircase. One might assume the quiet house was abandoned, yet nothing could be further from the truth.

Somewhere inside the ornate walls dwelled a high-spirited father and an exasperating young sister. She loved Beatrice, but since the dawn of the girl's fourteenth birthday, she'd made every effort to try Noela's patience.

Like a siren's song, the little sitting room to the left of the fireplace beckoned. Crossing to it, she stood on the threshold, her fists knotted at her stomach, before entering the room with quiet, measured steps.

Poignant mementos of her mother's life rushed from every corner.

Distant strains of "Wild Colonial Boy" echoed in Noela's heart as she passed the piano. She could almost see her smiling mum bobbing on the bench, her dancing fingers pounding on the keys.

Picking up the snow globe, Mum's most treasured bauble, Noela gave it a shake. Staring into the miniature storm that mirrored the tempest in her soul, she slid into a nearby chair.

Rosewater scent lifted from the upholstered arms, along with a fine misting of dust. Noela's chest ached, and tears sprang to her eyes. Two years hadn't erased Mum's fragrance any more effectively than easing the pain of her loss.

Leaving Queensland was meant to heal their grief. Parting with their home in Coolangatta and all they held dear felt dreadful then and no less wrenching now.

Father promised it would help. He said nowhere in the homeland could they escape the reality of Mum's lingering illness and painful death. He hadn't realized the memories lived in their hearts and would follow them to America.

Noela lifted her face to the heavens and released a shuddering sigh. "We're stuck, God, the three of us. We can't return to the past because death stands in the way. Yet we can't go forward into the future for the same reason."

Looking around, she bit back a sob. If Father wanted to forget, why had he shipped her mum's things to America and fashioned this room into a shrine?

Pushing out of the chair, she left the study and made her way down the hall. Composing her face, she entered the dining room and slipped into her place. As she hoped, Father remained buried in the *New York Times*.

Beatrice scrunched up her nose, the sprinkle of tiny freckles across the bridge disappearing in the folds. "You're late. We've already said grace."

Noela's eyes flashed a warning.

"Well, you are late. I saw you from the window. Talking to that silly Julian Van der Berg. How can you cling to the arm of that strutting peacock?"

Noela longed to reach across and yank her blond curls. "Oh be quiet."

"And the way he talks. Admit it—you don't understand half of what he says."

"The way *he* talks? We're the ones fresh off the boat."

"Yes, but we don't spout Webster's dictionary with every breath."

Noela shrugged and looked away. "Big words come naturally to Julian. He's an educated man."

"He's a rogue, and you know it. Every girl in Washington Square has found him out. You can do better than that pompous lothario."

"Beatrice, where do you pick up such vulgar words?"

Her brow furrowed. "I've asked you to call me Bea."

Noela shook out her napkin and placed it in her lap. "Well, I won't. You have a perfectly nice name. Bea is too common."

"Like your lothario?"

"No." Noela glared. "Like your vocabulary."

"Girls," Father growled from behind the paper—a sufficient deterrent to further discussion.

Noela tucked her chin and took a demure bite of her meat pie.

Beatrice followed suit, signaling a temporary truce while they finished their plates.

"Pass me the biscuits, please," Noela said, lifting the kettle and pouring a steaming cup of tea.

Beatrice rolled her eyes and lifted the silver platter. "Cookies, Noela. They call them *cookies* in America. Why must you be so dense?"

Noela bit a chunk from the crisp round confection. "Call it what you will, it's delicious."

Without warning, the forbidding newspaper lowered, revealing their father's resolute face. "I've made my decision."

Noela tensed. Those particular words, spoken in that tone, had never boded well.

He tossed the folded paper aside and slapped his hands down on the table. "Daughters, we're going away." The last time he'd made the same announcement, they'd journeyed to America.

Noela blinked across the kettle at her sister.

Beatrice seemed to take the news with a little more cheer. "Where, Daddy?"

He took off his reading glasses. "To Medora. In the western Dakota Territory."

He might have said the moon.

"Medora?" Traitor Beatrice beamed. "What an odd-sounding place."

"It's a new settlement. A rather small town in the heart of the wilderness."

Noela's heart raced. "This is all very sudden, isn't it?" She swallowed hard and tried to think. After all, we're finally beginning to adjust to New York."

Beatrice made a sassy face. "You're not. You still call a cookie a biscuit."

"You hush," Noela warned then sought her father's eyes. "Why now? And why into a barren wilderness?"

"For the adventure!" he said, pounding the table. "For the thrill of the quest."

Beatrice clasped her hands. "Hurrah! We're going on holiday."

"*Vacation*," Noela corrected. "Why must you be so dense?"

Her sister stuck out her tongue.

Gathering her wits, Noela tried again. "This is hardly the best time for a trip, is it, Father?"

"Rubbish. It's the perfect time." By the set of his jaw, he'd made up his mind.

Noela's jumbled thoughts leaped in circles. "Very well. We should go soon, if we're going, so we can be home in time for Christmas."

His eyes shifted to the side. "We won't be in New York for the holidays."

Noela rose with a whoosh of her skirts. Bracing her arms on the table, she leaned to stare at him. "That's impossible. I'm on Mrs. Baumann's planning committee."

Cutting a deliberate bite from his pie, he shook his head. "They'll have to do without you, Noela. You'll see no Christmas ball, I'm afraid."

A vision of swirling across the ballroom floor in Julian's arms turned to mist and wafted to the rafters. "How can you just decree this? You're forgetting that we have a life here at last. We have friends and plans and. . .well, prospects."

He put down his fork, his brows lofty peaks. "Julian Van der Berg? You'll find I side with Beatrice on the matter of that prospect."

"You haven't given Julian a chance."

"Forget him, Noela. He was never a proper match for you."

Her eyes narrowed to slits. "Where has all this come from?"

He cocked his head. "I've never warmed to that boy, and you know it."

"I'm referring to this sudden trip of yours. Who's been filling your ears with adventuresome tales this time?"

Averting his eyes, he tugged at the offending earlobe. "I did have a bit of a chin-wag with Theodore Roosevelt."

Beatrice frowned up at him. "Who, Daddy?"

"Your sister remembers him. He's that young politician Edith Baumann invited to her masquerade ball. She paraded him around the room, serving him to her guests like sweets on a platter."

Noela cast him a dubious frown. "I remember him. Go on."

"He said the Dakota Territory is a wild and free land, wide open to stouthearted men." He hooked his thumb at his chest. "Men like me, for instance."

"You? But you're—" Halting, she bit her lip. Her brawny, handsome father had always been the daring sort. He sported a head full of hair and the build of a younger man, but he'd aged since Mum's death in subtle, troubling ways.

She sighed. "I suppose I should be grateful he wasn't quoting lines from *Robinson Crusoe*, or else we'd be castaways battling savage cannibals for our entrails."

Her father released a weary breath. "Spare me, Noela, and kindly sit."

She kept to her feet, quaking inside at her boldness. "We're not going on holiday, are we? This is another scheme you've cooked up to line your pockets."

He ducked his head. "I reckon I do have a bit of business there."

Her shoulders slumped. "Oh Father. . ."

Cornered, he tried out his boyish grin. "You'll like Medora, love. I'm certain of it. Mr. Roosevelt spends most of his time there." His smile lit up the room. "Tamin' the Badlands."

Agitation building in her chest, Noela tapped her toe beneath the table. *I pray he works fast. If there's any taming to do once we get there, you won't be around long enough to contribute.*

Father's grin eased into a sober stare. "The man lost his wife last year, you know. His mum as well. On the same day, if you can imagine the luck."

Pain throbbed in Noela's chest, and she shivered. "How dreadful. How could he bear it?"

Alarm widened Father's eyes. He'd stumbled too close to their own heartbreak.

Pushing his plate aside, he stood. "Decide what you'd have the servants to pack, and give them instructions. We'll be leaving right soon."

Slumping into her chair, Noela pleaded with her eyes. "Don't do this, Father."

His expression hardened. "I fear it's done." Pulling his gaze from her brimming eyes, he crossed to the door. "Bring plenty of clothes, girls. We'll be gone a fair spell."

Chapter 2

Western Dakota Territory
November 1885

T hat's the last one, boys," Hiram McGregor shouted, kicking the gate closed with the toe of his boot. Staring after the bobbing heads of the longhorn steers, he drew in deep of the crisp, clean air and whispered a grateful prayer.

A line rider's life was hard work in any terrain. Wintertime in the Dakota Badlands meant bitter conditions for man and beast. The weather had proved mild for November in Medora, but a deep chill was on the way.

The cattle would spend the night in a holding pen on the Maltese Cross Ranch. At dawn they'd drive them to the prairie east of the Little Missouri River. From there the ranchmen would set up camps along the line to keep the herd in check.

Roy, the wide-eyed greenhorn Bill Sewall had saddled Hiram with, rode up fast and spun in beside him. Hiram cut his gaze to the boy's beaming face. "Don't look so relieved. That was the easy part."

"You think we'll lose any? Mr. Sewall claims the cows and heifers fare better than the bulls. Why's that?"

Hiram flipped up his collar and ducked lower into the warmth of his woolen coat. "They're more likely to eat through the snow and gnaw frozen stumps or the roots of prairie grass. The bulls tend to crawl off and die. I can't say why."

He scowled, gazing toward the vast gorge behind them. "But I don't intend to lose a single head, and you'd best entertain the same notion. Mr. Roosevelt is counting on us."

The little politician from New York had a big stake in the thousand-plus head of cattle he'd purchased to raise on his two ranches, the Maltese Cross and the Elkhorn. Since the livestock fared so well last year, he figured to start up cattle ranching in earnest.

To Hiram's way of thinking, the man's instincts were good, and the Little Missouri River Valley was an ideal location. With no shortage of clean water or rich grass and with ample gullies and coulees for shelter, the land took care of the animals for a rancher. Until the first blizzard. With the howl of the wind and the relentless cold, the land became a frightening enemy.

Hiram and his pa had survived many a Dakota winter. Unlike Texas, where he was born, the Dakota Territory had four distinct seasons. They reminded him of passing grub at the table. If you didn't like what was on the platter, sit back and wait for the next round. It was bound to be different.

Hiram slid off his horse and squatted at the edge of the bluff, staring across the canyon at the banded clay buttes. Jagged peaks in assorted shades of purple, brown, and red stretched across the rocky ground clear to the horizon. "It's like the Almighty ladled out the rock in layers."

Roy tethered his horse and joined him, easing to the ground and dangling his feet off the cliff. "It's as pretty a sight as I've ever seen."

They sat together in silence, gazing at the soaring flats and weathered ravines.

Hiram nudged Roy with his elbow. "In a few weeks, those scarlet crests will disappear under a clean white blanket of snow. Makes a man feel like all that's wrong in the world is erased to give him another chance."

Roy hooted and slapped his leg. "Listen at you. I'm riding the range with a poet." He chuckled under his breath. "Partner, you've got stars in your eyes."

Firing a warning glare, Hiram stood. "No more time to waste. We've got to meet the supply train."

Swinging his legs around, Roy struggled to his feet and caught Hiram by the sleeve. "Hold up there. I didn't mean to poke fun." He offered a shy smile. "You really love this place, don't you?"

A reluctant smile tugged at Hiram's lips. "The way a man loves a faithful wife."

Laughing, they saddled up and ambled toward town.

The overland into Little Missouri, or Little Misery as the townsfolk called the faded outpost, generally met with an enthusiastic welcoming committee, and today was no different. The big engine pulled in loaded with much needed supplies and a smattering of travelers, the majority of them bound for somewhere else.

Careworn men stood along the tracks, their shoulders stooped by hard work, their gaunt faces lined by harsh sunlight and ruthless wind. For the most part, they were farmers and settlers awaiting shipments of grain or catalog orders for their wives. Hiram and Roy worked their way to the door of the boxcar and took their place in line while rail men unloaded stacks of crates and burlap bags.

Roy whistled, two soft, measured tones. "Will you look at her?"

Hiram followed his spellbound gaze to the passenger car. A lovely young woman stood next to the conductor, one hand on the rail, the other extended to a big fellow on the ground.

The color of her hair was like a tin of coffee beans, with warm reds, browns, and near blacks in the mix. The unruly waves shone in the distance as if she'd doused them in shellac. He couldn't see her eyes from where he stood, but he'd bet his last dollar they were green.

Followed off the train by a young girl with blond curly hair, she stepped down beside the man Hiram assumed was their father. Her face the color of wood ash, she spun in a slow circle, taking in the squalid scatter of dingy shops and ramshackle hotels. Turning a fierce glare on the burly man beside her, she muttered in an irate tone.

In response, his voice raised a notch, but he shrank from her wrath.

The little blond girl added fat to the fire with waving arms and shrill cries.

Hiram had never found the private affairs of strangers the least bit enticing, but he couldn't pull his gaze from the lovely high-strung lady. He handed off a box of goods to Roy. "Handle the rest of the load. I think they may need help."

Roy glanced past Hiram's shoulder with a twinkle in his eye. "Sure thing, partner."

Striding toward the squabbling group, Hiram nearly changed his mind. Someone had sure put a bramble in the berry patch.

"This is Theodore Roosevelt's promised land?" the scowling girl demanded. "There's not even a proper platform. They've cast us out alongside the tracks."

"Now, love. . ." The man reached out a shaky hand, but she withdrew.

Utterly charmed by her peculiar manner of speech, Hiram took off his hat and cleared his throat. "Excuse me? Is there something I can do for you folks?"

The big man spun with an impatient frown. "What's that?"

From a distance, while shrinking under the gaze of an angry woman, he had appeared less threatening.

Hiram gulped and fingered his hat, briefly meeting the lady's flashing eyes—bright green, as he'd suspected, and swimming with tears. "My apologies. The name's Hiram McGregor, and I live around here. I noticed you just rode in, and I wondered if I could assist you."

The stranger's smile eased the angry lines on his face and melted the tightness in Hiram's chest. "Jonathan Nancarrow here. You might point the way to Medora's livery. I reckon we have need of a wagon."

Hiram shifted his feet. "Well sir, I would. But this isn't Medora."

Mr. Nancarrow's brows crowded together. "But the conductor said—"

Hiram motioned him aside a few paces and pointed across the banks of the Little Missouri. "Medora's the new settlement right across the river. I can take you there, if you'd like."

The man smiled over his shoulder at his daughters. "Our curse has lifted, girls. The Lord sent Moses to deliver us."

Chapter 3

The obliging ranch hand offered to take them wherever they needed to go. He left his friend with instructions to hire a wagon for the goods they'd loaded off the train, and then Noela, Beatrice, and their father climbed aboard his chariot for a trip across the Red Sea.

More accurately, they crowded into his buckboard for a ride across the Little Missouri River. Despite the scenic backdrop, the rustic, squalid town of Little Missouri gave Noela a chill that had little to do with the climate. The difference, once they'd crossed the river, was encouraging. On the eastern bank beneath a wide bluff stood proud structures fashioned with new lumber and an atmosphere of hope.

They rumbled past a scattering of houses, and the young man beamed with pride. "This here's Medora. It was founded by a Frenchman, the Marquis de Mores."

He smiled over his shoulder at Noela. "He named the town after his wife. In fact, he built a house for her not far from here. The Chateau de Mores we call it. It has twenty-six rooms in two stories with twenty servants to run it."

A French nobleman? A chateau manned by servants? Noela's heart greatly eased. With the primitive railroad town behind her and the promise of a genteel society close by, her father's trip began to make more sense.

Noela longed to ask questions, but she'd forgotten the name their "Moses" gave when he introduced himself. Gazing at his profile while he continued talking to Father, she realized for the first time how handsome he was.

Was his hair really so black, or did the shadow of his hat create the striking illusion? He wore facial hair, an overgrown brush on his chin bleeding into a light moustache, over full, expressive lips. Overall, his eyes were his best feature. Lively and kind, they were deep set and a warm shade of brown. And at the moment, staring right at her.

She blinked. "I'm sorry?"

Tiny wrinkles formed between his brows, and he offered a shy smile. "I was wondering what you think."

Her face on fire, she glanced away. She couldn't exactly tell him what she'd been thinking.

Her father peered over his shoulder. "Noela? Mr. McGregor's asking how you like Medora."

Beatrice giggled.

Noela gave her skinny leg a swift bump with a knee. "Forgive me, Mr. McGregor. I didn't mean to ignore you."

"Call me Hiram. We don't stand on ceremony out here." He lifted questioning eyes to Father. "If your pa doesn't mind, that is."

Father shook his head. "Not at all, mate. You may call me Jonathan."

He twisted around. "Noela, the man's still waiting for your opinion of Medora." He shot her a hopeful smile. "I wouldn't mind hearing it myself."

She pretended interest in her surroundings. "I find this part of town quite nice."

Hiram's eyes crinkled at the corners. "I'm glad. It's the only part we've got."

Beatrice leaned her arms on the back of his seat and flashed her perfect teeth. "I like it, Hiram."

"Well that's fine, Beatrice." His winsome grin stirred Noela's heart. She could imagine the effect it had on her sister at such close range. Beatrice romanticized the smallest gestures.

Ignoring Noela's warning pinch, the impish girl raised her dainty chin and batted her lashes. "Please, call me Bea."

Hiram's chuckle rang out in the cold, thin air. "All right, Bea."

Noela jerked her sister's arm, pulling her back to her proper place.

Hiram grinned and glanced at their father. "Where am I taking you folks?"

Father pulled a folded paper from his breast pocket and opened it on his knee. "It says here we're to go to a place called Vine House."

Noela smiled to herself. It was the first he'd mentioned of their prospective quarters. Vine House brought to mind a quaint cottage with moss-covered roof and trailing plants on the walls.

Hiram frowned and tilted his head at the typewritten page. "Are you certain you have that right?"

Father peered closer at the document and tapped it with a forefinger. "That's what it says." He shot Hiram an anxious look. "Why, son? Is it far?"

"No sir. Just a few miles out of town."

"Can you take us there?"

Hiram cleared his throat. "Well sure. If you say so." Had the man grown slightly pale?

They passed a few more houses before the road curved away from Medora. Sick with curiosity and dread, Noela perched at the edge of her seat. Too nervous to relax and too embarrassed to ask the questions her father should be asking, she rode in frustrated silence.

At last, Hiram broke the stillness. "Jonathan, forgive me if you find this impolite, but may I ask why we're headed to Vine House?"

Father folded the curious paper he'd been studying and returned it to his pocket. "I don't mind your question. The girls and I will be lodging there for a spell."

Hiram's head whipped around. "Are you jesting?"

"I'm entirely serious."

"Sir, you can't stay there."

Father's jaw twitched. "Why not?"

"It's not a proper house."

Beads of sweat dotted Father's brow. "By what definition?"

"It's a soddie, Mr. Nancarrow. A sorry excuse for one at that."

Escaping Noela's grasp, Beatrice wriggled forward. "What's a soddie, Hiram?"

Father seemed to age before their eyes. His throat worked furiously, and when he spoke, his voice cracked. "Yes, son. . . What the devil is a soddie?"

Hiram propped his boot on the rail and nudged back his hat. "Trees are scarce out here in the plains. The settlers had to find other ways to build shelter. They came up with sod houses, homes built out of bricks cut from the earth."

"Dirt houses?" Beatrice said, her eyes aglow.

He nodded. "Dirt and grass. It's a fine idea really. Cheap to build. The home is cool in the summer and traps heat in the winter."

Father scratched along his jaw. "What holds them up?"

"The roots grow together and bind the blocks. They become fairly strong in most cases. Not so for Vine House."

Narrowing his eyes, Father appeared to chew on the question before he spat it out. "Why not?"

"Shoddy workmanship maybe, or the roots failed to knit. The house is drafty, shaky, and subject to collapse. Your family won't survive a Dakota winter there."

"Can't we go someplace else?" Beatrice asked.

Father shook his head. "There's nowhere else to go."

He sat in silence for so long, worry niggled at Noela's mind. She sat forward and touched his arm. "Are you all right?"

"I haven't told you girls the truth," he muttered. "We haven't come to Medora for a holiday. We're here to stay."

Her hand slid away from him. "What?"

He spun on the seat with terrible fear in his eyes. "Forgive me, Noela. I couldn't tell you before. You wouldn't have come."

Her stomach heaved. She'd been kicked in the chest by a mule. Trampled by a runaway team. She fought the urge to bolt from the buckboard and run clear back to the station.

"We live here, now?" Beatrice cried. "In this pretty place?"

Hiram reined in his horse and pulled to a stop. Shifting on the seat, he studied their father with a troubled gaze. "I don't know what's going on here, Jonathan, but you can't live out there. Not at Vine House."

Dismal silence descended. Father drummed his fingers on his knee. Beatrice watched, her mouth parted in anticipation of what he'd say next. Hiram cast worried glances at Noela.

Ignoring him, she lurched forward and gripped the seat. "It's not a catastrophe, you know. We'll just go back to the city."

Father's raised a stricken face. "Noela—"

"We don't have to stay another day. We'll go home to New York on the next train out."

Tears tipped over her father's bottom lashes, cascading down his ruddy cheeks. "There is no home in New York, Noela. I lost the house."

"What are you saying?" she whispered. "I don't understand."

"I'm saying I trusted a dishonest bloke with an investment." His head drooped to his chest. "We're flat busted and homeless because of me. If we can't make a go of it here, we're doomed."

Hope drained from Noela and pooled at her feet. Fury warred in her chest with heartbreaking pity. She stood in the wagon, her clenched hands itching to pummel him, her heart longing to comfort.

She squeezed past Beatrice and gathered him in consoling arms. "No worries, now. We're Nancarrows, aren't we? We'll be all right in the end."

Admiration shone from Hiram's eyes.

Noela flashed him a weak smile. "After all, God sent us our own Moses. He can surely help us find a way out of this wilderness, can't He?"

"Noela's right, Daddy," Beatrice sobbed behind them. "You'll see."

He spun on the seat, one arm tight around Noela, the other groping for Beatrice. "I don't deserve my girls."

When the tumult settled to sniffs and sighs, Hiram cleared his throat. "If you'd like, Jonathan, I can help you find another house."

Shaking his head, Father patted the pocket where he'd slid the folded document. "I'm contracted to Vine House through the government's Homestead Act. I'm committed to live there and farm the land for the next five years."

"Five years?" Noela's voice quavered along with her courage.

"Yes, and then it will be ours, all 160 acres."

Father sniffed and raised his chin. "I'm sorry to involve you in our shameful business, young man. If you decide to unload us here and not look back, I won't fault you."

Despite the chilly air, Hiram took off his hat and swiped his brow with his sleeve. "Not a chance, sir. My offer to help still stands."

Father placed a trembling hand on his shoulder. "Then we'd best complete our journey. I reckon we Nancarrows need to take a gander at our new home."

Chapter 4

Gloom crouched over the buckboard for the remainder of the ride.

Beatrice ceased her chatter, watching the countryside pass with buttoned lips and folded hands. Grateful for her sister's silence, Noela spent the time trying to picture a house made of sod, but she couldn't conceive of it.

"Is it much farther, young Hiram?" her father asked.

"Just ahead, sir."

Father shaded his eyes and peered toward the horizon. "She's out in back of nowhere, ain't she?"

They crossed a barren plain, the long brown grass rippling in the wind. Hiram pointed toward a gentle rise and steered the wagon toward it. "Vine House is right over there, tucked in the bottom of a coulee." He grimaced. "A good thing in this case, or the wind would bring it down."

Beatrice swiveled on the seat. "Coulee? That's a curious word. What's it mean?"

"A French term, I believe. I don't know the exact translation. Around here, it refers to the low spots carved out by glaciers. An area too small to be a valley, too wide and shallow to be a ravine."

Father considered him carefully. "Your cowhand veneer is deceptive, Hiram. You're an educated man—am I right?"

Hiram's cheeks flamed beneath his tan. "Just an only child reared by an intelligent woman. Ma passed on her love of reading to me."

He circled behind the sloping hill and stopped. "Here we are, folks. Welcome to Vine House."

Noela's mouth parted, but no sound escaped her lips. The atrocity Father referred to as home leered at her from across the yard, its crooked windows staring like glazed, hopeless eyes.

Short, squatty walls. A roof that dipped and leaned as if a large thumb descended out of heaven to squash it. A narrow structure so small it would fit three times on Mrs. Baumann's ballroom floor.

Noela's fanciful musing had been of a moss-covered roof, not moldy straw. Of trailing plants on the walls, not ugly, exposed roots. Hysteria rose like bile in her throat.

Beside her, Beatrice whimpered. Little sister's indomitable spirit had met its match. "We live *here*?" Her chin quivered and her eyes brimmed with tears. "Why, this isn't pretty at all!"

Pale as a ghoul, Father absently patted her hand. "Now, now. Let's have a look around first." Casting a grim look at Hiram, he hauled himself over the side with a grunt.

Noela's legs had turned to mush. She kept to her seat and tracked her father's grave, studied walk about the grounds.

He started with the barn, part wood and part sod. The latter construction hadn't fared as well as the first. A large portion of the back half of the barn, roof and all, lay on the ground.

Crossing to another building, this one comprised all of wood, he gave it a shake to test for soundness. Whatever its purpose, the small edifice held.

"It's the privy," Father called.

Beatrice giggled through her tears.

Noela blushed to her toes.

His gait slowed as he turned and approached the shoddy dwelling. One hand at his hip, the other cupping his chin, he watched as if waiting for the house to speak.

He was wasting his time. If the dilapidated ruin had the capacity of speech, it wouldn't have one good thing to say.

Hiram climbed out and strolled to Father's side. Noela forced herself down from the rig and fell in behind him. Beatrice followed, grasping her hand.

"Why isn't it built on high ground?" Father asked. "Why hidden behind these mounds?"

"In the plains there are few windbreaks, so the gusts are fierce. In the winter, it cuts you to the marrow. We find whatever we can to shield us."

Nodding, Father took a few halting steps closer. Leaning over the threshold, he gazed at the ceiling. "What's holding it up?"

Hiram joined him, stepping carefully into the room. "Very little, I'm afraid. A few tangled roots." He pointed. "I see the problem now. Notice how small those sod bricks are and how the light filters between them? They're supposed to be three foot squares at least four inches thick, with layers to form walls two or three bricks deep."

"Then it's a poor job of building like you said. A poor job indeed."

Hiram grunted. "I suppose that's why the last man left, most likely at the first freeze."

Father puffed his cheeks then exhaled. "And the first freeze is upon us. What will it take to begin repairs?"

Hiram glanced at Noela and Beatrice. "To start, it needs bracing before you can go inside. It's not safe in this condition."

Father flexed his jaw. "Then I'd better start making her safe. We have nowhere else to sleep tonight."

❧

Hiram ached for the spirited man. "That's where you're wrong, Jonathan. My pa would disown me if I didn't bring you folks home." He smiled. "He's getting on in years a bit, but he's still a lively dinner companion. You might not feel the warmth of hospitality we offered when Ma was alive, but we get by."

Noela's chin came up. Grief flickered in her eyes, and she gave him a sympathetic smile. Her reaction explained why no Mrs. Nancarrow traveled with the family.

He returned her smile and patted her father's back. "Let's get you settled at my place so the ladies can rest and have a bite to eat. I have an early cattle drive tomorrow, but very soon we'll ride out here and shore this place up."

"You'd do that, son?"

"My pleasure. I'll even round up a few men in town. With extra hands, it won't be long before you'll have a suitable place to live."

Beaming, Jonathan spun on the ball of his foot. "We've been thrown a lifeline, girls. What do you think?"

Noela's dark lashes swept her cheeks. Standing meekly, she gave the impression of calm, but her chest rose and fell too fast, and a pulse raced in her delicate throat. "I appreciate the wonderful gesture"—she lifted her eyes and gave her father a pointed look—"but we don't want to impose, do we? I believe I saw a hotel back in town."

Blushing, Hiram tucked his chin. "You saw the Metropolitan. It's a brand-new hotel and clean as a fresh dollar bill. Of course you'll be more comfortable there."

"Noela!" Jonathan's stern tone made both his daughters jump. "You've offended our new friend. We'll accept his hospitality and be grateful."

Hiram read a clear message in Jonathan's harsh reaction. The man couldn't afford a hotel.

"Well, that's fine, sir," he said. "When you taste your meal tonight, you'll realize you made a wise decision. The overpriced fare at the Metropolitan can't compete with our cook's beef stew." With a tight smile, he herded them to the buckboard for a somber ride home.

Hiram turned off the main road onto his lane and scattered a parading flock of prairie chickens. Several male birds, puffed and strutting, had declared the grassy field a breeding ground. Long, dark feathers stuck out behind their heads, and yellow sacs inflated on each side of their necks as they pranced and sparred for the females' attention.

"Look at the funny chooks," Beatrice called. "Whose are they?"

Father chuckled. "Those aren't barnyard chickens, darlin'. They're wild creatures."

"Why are they fighting?"

He shot Hiram an amused wink. "They're waltzing for the ladies, love. The old boys are showing out a little, that's all."

Grinning, Hiram watched the silly birds as they passed. "A legend among the Apsáalooke—the Crow Indians—says that Old Man Coyote made the prairie chicken to teach the other animals how to dance."

"Is Old Man Coyote their name for God?" Noela asked.

"No." He craned his neck to see her better. "I believe it's something they came up with in their search for God."

She slumped against the seat and stared into the distance. "How sad."

Hiram nodded. "How sad, indeed."

He followed the rutted lane until it curved in front of his modest cabin. As predicted, Pa seemed delighted to have company.

Leaning on his knobby cane, his face lit by a broad smile, he hobbled onto the porch to greet them. "I was just complaining to the Almighty about the solitude, and look—He's answered my prayer." His dim gaze swept the inhabitants of the rig. "Who's this you've brought me, boy?"

Hiram slid off the seat. "Pa, I'd like you to meet the Nancarrows. Jonathan, Noela, and Bea," he said, pointing to each one. "I've invited them to stay with us for a few days."

Pa grinned up at him. "You don't say? Well, that's mighty fine news."

He leaned across the buckboard and extended his hand to Jonathan. "God exacts a stiff penalty of loneliness in exchange for living in this beautiful land. It's a rare treat when He blesses us with company. I'm glad to meet you, sir."

"Likewise," Jonathan said, pumping his hand. "We're grateful for the offer."

Pa drew back in surprise. "I know that accent. You folks came from Australia."

Noela's shoulders relaxed. "You're familiar with our country, Mr. McGregor?"

"Quite familiar, pretty lady." He took her hand and helped her down from the wagon. "I journeyed there in my impetuous youth. Liked it so much, I lingered for a spell."

Hiram reached for Beatrice's hand and guided her to the ground. "I'm sure they're travel-weary, Pa. Let's take them inside and get them settled."

Chapter 5

Hiram McGregor and his father lived simply. There were no ballrooms inside the modest log cabin, no spacious drawing rooms or libraries like those in the brownstones back East. But each night, Noela washed in a clean porcelain bowl and slept in a downy, soft bed.

For several days, while her father, Hiram, and his men worked at making Vine House habitable, she'd enjoyed Mr. McGregor's generous hospitality, relished the tales of his travels, and laughed at his jokes.

In the evenings, while sharing food and conversation around the dining table, she'd grown to respect and admire Hiram—a moral man and dutiful son, not to mention witty, intelligent, and of striking good looks. In a very short time, they'd become friends.

Every night after tea, the two of them retired to the corner where Hiram taught her to play chess. She had a real knack for the game, improving at a rapid pace under his gifted tutelage.

Squirming, she jerked her thoughts to Julian Van der Berg, heretofore the brightest and handsomest man she'd ever known. Hadn't fate destined them to marry? Ordained her to a life of status and ease as the mistress of Van der Berg Manor?

Instead, her father tricked her and brought her to Medora, never to see Julian again. As if that dismal prospect was not dreadful enough, tomorrow she would move into a house made entirely of mud.

Groaning, she sat up in bed, wondering at the time. Dusky light framed the curtains, and a rooster crowed in the yard.

Her bedmate grumbled disagreeably and flipped to face the wall. Noela smiled and tucked the cover around her sister's shoulder. "All right, sleepy girl. Take a few more minutes."

A rumble deep in her stomach inspired her to hurry and dress for the day. The aroma of frying pork wafting beneath the door drew her into the hallway, eager to trace the source.

She entered the kitchen still pinning her hair, expecting to see the McGregors' German cook. Instead, Hiram stood at the stove, a comical sight in Ursula's cotton apron.

He peered over his shoulder and smiled. "Good morning. I hope you're hungry. Where's Bea?"

Noela pointed behind her. "She can't find the floor this morning. The poor girl is knackered, but I reckon she'll be along soon."

Nibbling hard on her lip to hide a grin, she took the pitcher of milk he held out and placed it on the table. "More to the point, where's the cook?"

He jerked his thumb at his chest. "You're looking at him. When Ma died, I realized Pa couldn't heat a kettle, so I took on the kitchen duties. We found Ursula so Pa wouldn't starve after I hired on at the Maltese Cross."

He jerked his hand away from a sizzling spatter of grease. "Looks like I'm a bit out of practice. Ursula's feeling poorly today, so I'm manning the stove."

"I'm glad."

Hiram frowned and tilted his head.

"Not glad the poor thing is ill," she amended. "But for the chance to spend time with you." She would never speak so boldly to Julian. With Hiram, she felt comfortable being herself.

His cheeks glowing a little brighter, he nodded at the table. "Sit down and help yourself. I'll have this bacon ready in a jiffy."

By the time Noela had buttered a steaming slice of fragrant bread and ladled a spoonful of scrambled eggs onto her plate, Hiram had served two slices of bacon alongside them and pulled out a chair to join her. Under the spell of his charm, she took a moment to realize they were eating alone.

"Where's my father? And yours for that matter?"

Hiram shot her a playful wink. "Not everyone can sleep all day."

He explained while pouring them each a mug of coffee. "I fed them early, and they left. Your father was eager to get started, and Pa rode along to judge our progress. He won't rest if the house isn't comfortable for you and Bea."

Noela scowled and placed a napkin in her lap. "Is such a thing possible?"

Hiram sobered and slid his chair closer. "May I ask you something? If it's none of my business, you don't have to answer."

Intrigued, she watched him over the rim of her cup. "I've come to know a little something about your character. A man like you would never ask an inappropriate question of a lady."

He pretended to leer. "Maybe there's a side to me you don't know."

"Oh stop!" Her laughter echoed in the high ceiling. "The last thing you are is a rogue."

He's a rogue, and you know it. Her sister's estimation of Julian Van der Berg rang in her head. She'd never once considered Julian in a bad light, but she had to admit he didn't compare well to the man seated across the table.

Noela pushed her disloyal thoughts aside. Tucking both fists under her chin, she propped her arms on the table. "Go ahead. Ask your question."

"Do any of you know the first thing about farming?" His finger shot up. "More to the point, do you know about farming a harsh, unforgiving land where one careless mistake may be your last?"

He leaned in. "Do you understand that the wind will freeze your teardrops, the mist of your breath?" His stern gaze roamed her face. "This brand of cold freezes sweat on a man's brow, drool on a baby's cheek. Is your father prepared for the challenge he's undertaken?"

Choking fear crowded out her playful mood. "That's more than one question, and the answer is no to them all."

She pressed her eyes with the heel of her hands, trying to block the dismal picture he'd painted. "What am I to do, Hiram? How can I convince him to abandon this dreadful plan?"

He pulled her hands from her face and held them, his gentle fingers cool on her flesh. "It's more than a plan to him now. In his mind, Vine House is the last hope. You should see him out there, Noela, his hands blistered and bleeding, his back bent over the task. I've never seen a man so driven by courage and determination."

Noela's throat swelled with pride. "He's a Nancarrow, and he's acting like one."

Hiram smiled. "You Nancarrows are proving to be a hearty breed, all right." He shrugged. "By himself, I'd bet on Jonathan to make it, but. . ."

She stilled. "With me and Beatrice, he won't?"

"He's running himself aground to make it work for you girls. At the pace he's going, he'll be too spent to make the winter."

Fighting tears, Noela lifted her chin. "He'll make it just fine. Beatrice and I will help him."

Hiram's smile threatened her resolve. If she succumbed to his comforting warmth, her courage would puddle at his feet.

He pursed his lips and shrugged. "Then I'll help, too."

She searched his face across their uneaten breakfast. "I can't allow it."

He cocked one brow. "It's not up to you."

"But why? You've done too much already."

"For the chance to spend time with you," he said softly, repeating her earlier words. "And because your father is going to need another man on the place."

The depth of her gratitude brimmed in her eyes.

Bracing his elbow on the table, Hiram stroked her chin and swiped the moisture from her cheek with his finger. "Here now, we can't have tears with our eggs. Too salty."

Breaking the heady spell, he leaned to peer down the hall. "We may need to wake Bea. I have orders to bring you two to Vine House this morning."

Nodding, Noela folded her napkin next to her plate. "Your men were called back to the ranch last night, weren't they? Which means Father is rather shorthanded this morning." She sighed. "If we're going to rally 'round him, I reckon it's time we start to pitch in."

She pushed back her chair. "I'll go rouse the lazy girl."

Hiram stood and pulled her to her feet. "Noela, I put off telling you as long as I could." Grim lines creased his brow. "Your father said to bring your things."

Her heart plunged. "We're not scheduled to move until tomorrow."

With a tight smile, he shook his head. "Schedules are another thing you've left behind for good."

She slumped against the table, massaging her temple. "I stayed awake last night plotting my next move on the chessboard. I had hoped to finish our game after the evening meal."

He curled his finger and lifted her chin. Compassion and regret shone in his eyes. "Best save your fancy move for later. I don't expect we'll be playing chess tonight."

Chapter 6

Withered grass crunched beneath the wheels as Hiram drove the buggy into the yard at Vine House. A blast of air lifted the back of his coat, raising goose flesh along his arms. Shading his eyes against the late morning sun, he scowled across the field.

A rogue scatter of pronghorn antelope grazed across the distant plains. Confused by the mild weather, they'd missed the October migration, but they wouldn't stay around for long.

Noela touched his arm. "What's the matter?"

"The wind has shifted. It's coming out of the north. The snow will be right behind it. I can already smell it."

Bea crowded up between them. "Smell snow? What a silly notion."

Hiram raised his face to the sky and drew in deeply through his nose. "Close your eyes and take a whiff. You'll see."

She lifted her head and sniffed. Her expression of total concentration paired with a twitching nose was too much for Hiram. Laughter rattled from his chest.

Bea smacked his arm. "You're teasing, aren't you?"

He chuckled. "No ma'am, I'm not. The ability to smell snow is a proven fact."

"Well, I don't smell a thing," Bea said. "Besides, I like snow. In New York, we fall back and make snow angels. Like this. . ." She held out her arms and waved them up and down. "Then we bring snowballs inside and pour honey over them. It's delicious."

He tapped her chin. "You'll have to be the only angel in Medora, I'm afraid. You won't be making the other kind very often. It gets too cold to play outside."

Muted voices near the house drew their attention. Hiram's pa leaned on his cane, watching Jonathan, perched halfway up a ladder. Flushed and straining, the poor man struggled to lay in a fresh-cut square of earth.

Hiram set the brake and hit the ground running.

The girls were fast on his heels.

"Hold up there!" he called. "Let me help."

Placing one foot on a rung of the ladder and the other against the house, he raised himself level with Jonathan and heaved the crumbling block of dirt into place.

Back on the ground, Jonathan brushed off his shirtsleeves and offered a shaky smile. "Much obliged, mate. It's easier with an extra pair of hands."

He glanced at the roof. "I had it up there once. It didn't stay."

"Might've done, if you'd heeded my advice," Pa grumbled. "Hiram, I told him to stretch tarp paper over the opening first, but he wouldn't listen. So a whole blessed square of sod wound up in the kitchen sink."

Jonathan scowled. "How did I know you'd be right for once? Nothing you've said so far has been."

Despite the short time they'd known each other, the two men squabbled like old friends.

Noela leaned on the house and peered through the smudges on the window. "There's a block of dirt inside?"

Pa patted her back. "We shoveled most of it out. It needs to be swept, but I couldn't find a broom."

He wound his arm through hers. "Your pa's worked mighty hard to make the place nice for you girls. Would you care to see?"

With a forlorn set to her shoulders, she nodded.

Hiram folded his arms to keep from pulling her close and smoothing her hair. The urge to comfort a female in distress was an untried impulse until Noela, but it felt right somehow.

Jonathan led the way, ducking beneath the low entrance, then standing aside while the others filed in.

The last to enter, Noela gripped the door frame and stepped over the threshold. Her stoic face revealed nothing. Her anguished eyes were another matter. The struggle to put on a brave front sapped all the color from her cheeks.

The interior of the soddie looked better than Hiram had expected. Aside from the remaining dirt Pa had mentioned, the room gave an impression of tidiness. Unlike most sod houses, this one had a raised wooden floor instead of cold, wet dirt.

A quick assessment of the furnishings revealed that Pa had generously contributed to the project. Striped paper on the kitchen wall came from the leftover rolls stored in the barn at home. The new window and wooden frame had once rested in a corner of the shed, along with the tarp paper tacked to the remaining walls and ceiling. Two blankets, hanging from the rafters for modesty's sake, Hiram last saw in his linen closet.

Noela stood with folded arms, surveying the room. Deep creases marred the smooth skin of her forehead. Hiram narrowed his eyes and tried to see the place from a woman's point of view.

The planks beneath their feet were rough and buckled. Without a good sanding, a barefooted walk across the floor would be risky. The tarp paper would keep out some of the mice, but not all. Meanwhile, the unseemly evidence of their presence dotted the crude tabletop and the corners of the built-in shelves.

A gust from outside blasted the north-facing wall. The girls' hems and sleeves ballooned and tendrils of their hair lifted. The dirt that fell from the ceiling rose like a giddy specter, becoming a small, swirling tornado in the kitchen floor.

Beatrice stared with bulging eyes. "Father?" Her plaintive cry sounded frightened.

Noela clutched her sister's shoulders and drew her away from the uninvited twister.

Jonathan sprang into action. Kicking the roll of tarp against the wall, he jerked up a long sheet and held it in place. "No worries, lamb. We missed a few spots, is all."

With the draft blocked, the swirl lost its legs and fell, salting the entire room with soil.

Jonathan cast a desperate glance over his shoulder. "Pass me the hammer, will you? It's there on the window sill."

Hiram grabbed the mallet and a handful of tacks while his pa limped to help Jonathan hold the tarp. Between them, they got the opening secured.

Laughter bubbled in Hiram's throat, but the girls' stricken faces choked it down. "There you are, ladies. All fixed."

Pa chuckled. "It's a good thing we found it before the weather turned, or you'd wake up one morning with a snowdrift instead of a whirligig."

Jonathan shuffled over and touched Noela's arm. His sagging shoulders added years to his appearance. "I'm sorry, love. It's not the standard you girls are accustomed to."

Her pale lips faintly trembled. "It needs a woman's touch, to be sure." She raised her chin defiantly. "But we'll get along all right." She tightened her arm around her sister. "Won't we, Beatrice?"

Staring up at Noela, the doubt in Bea's eyes began to fade. "Y–yes. We'll be just fine."

"There's my girls!" Jonathan shouted, clutching them in a crushing hold, his booming laughter echoing off the walls.

Noela's brave words opposed the despair shining beneath her lowered lashes. With her proud pa so close to tears, she let him believe what he needed to.

Relief flooded Jonathan's face. "You girls are just what this house needs. In no time, you'll have the place as cozy as our parlor in the brownstone."

Frowning, Noela peered up at him. "And what of the brownstone, Father? I know you sold it along with the furnishings, but where are our things? The personal items we left behind?"

His excitement sputtered and died. Shifting his stance, he rested his hands on his hips. "Blast it. I never know when to can it."

Chapter 7

Father's shoulders tensed and his guilty gaze flickered up. "I left your things behind, Noela."

Her breath caught. "Left them where?"

"In the house. I let the new owner dispose of them. I had no heart for the task."

She stared. Struggled to comprehend. "Everything? The photo album, our hope chests"—she swallowed against the painful lump in her throat—"the family Bible?"

"What choice did I have? I didn't want you to realize we weren't coming back."

Deathly cold flushed Noela's veins. Her body swayed as the blood rushed from her head. "Not Mum's sitting room. You left the piano? Her chair?"

He stood quietly, pain brewing in the eyes she knew so well.

Bile rose in her throat. "Tell me you didn't do this."

He lowered his lashes, turned his face aside.

Noela struggled for breath. Rage choked her. Fire roared from her heated glare, spilling onto flaming cheeks.

"How could you?" Censure oozed from every bitter word.

His outstretched arms took in the surroundings. "We couldn't bring them here, could we? Besides, Mummy's things upset you girls. You said so, remember?"

Sordid emotion welled in Noela's chest. An angry spew of pent-up accusations leaped to the tip of her tongue. She bit them back until she tasted blood.

Father reached for her, but she jerked away, gripping the edge of the table to steady herself. "I need some fresh air. Please don't follow." Spinning away, she stumbled out the door with Beatrice's anxious voice an echo behind her.

Frigid gusts assailed Noela from behind, driving her across the yard. She staggered mindlessly, unaware of where she headed until she reached the barn door. Her legs quaking, she leaned against the threshold for support, but it sagged beneath her weight.

Large black shapes arose and flapped in the overhead loft. Gasping, she drew back then clutched her heart in relief as her eyes adjusted to the dimness. Only more unsightly tarp paper rustling in the wind that blew past the missing wall.

Groping her way to a protected corner, she sank to her knees on a thatch of moldy hay and buried her face in her hands. *Why have you forsaken me, God? First Mum. Now this?*

Tears flowed from a wellspring inside. Noela curled into a tight ball and wept like an abandoned child, her body wracked with shuddering sobs.

Strong hands lifted her. Gentle arms gathered her from behind, drawing her close. "There now, honey. Come here."

"Oh Hiram," she whispered. Cradled against his strong, steady heartbeat, she clung to his shirt and vented her grief.

His tender touch moved over her face—cupping her chin with his palm, sweeping away tears with a nimble thumb, smoothing her hair with his fingers—soothing her soul. She hadn't felt small or vulnerable in a very long time. In that moment, she felt like a babe in its mother's arms.

The thought brought reminiscences of her mum along with a fresh wave of tears. Hiram held her until the last sigh and hiccup.

Noela pressed close to him, the heat of his body shielding her from the cold. Hidden away in the dim, cozy corner, a blanket of hay beneath and the wind whistling overhead, they seemed tucked away in a secret den.

Hiram lowered his face and brushed her cheek with his. "So smooth," he whispered. His heartbeat raced beneath her hands.

Unsure if he drew her or she rose to meet him, Noela's free arm snaked up and wound around his neck, her fingertips teasing his hair. She'd never drawn so deeply from another's soul. Never felt their warmth, inhaled their breath.

A fleeting thought of impropriety crept in, but her befuddled mind cast it away. He was bringing comfort. That was all.

Hiram sat up, easing her arm from around him. Settling her against the wall, he pushed a curl from her eyes and plucked a straw from her hair. "Feeling better?"

He seemed to be avoiding her eyes.

Cheeks blazing, she lowered her gaze to her hands. "Yes, thanks to you."

"I wasn't sure I should barge in on you, so I waited." He jerked his thumb toward the door. "Then I heard you crying and figured you needed a. . .friend."

A smile tugged at her lips. She understood his pause. The last few moments hadn't felt like friendly communion.

Noela glanced at him, and his dark lashes swept up, revealing pain in a determined stare. "Forgive me if I got out of line. I didn't mean to—that is, I'd never. . ."

"I know you wouldn't."

His shoulders eased, and he returned her smile. "I'm glad."

She sniffed and swiped her nose with the back of her hand. "I must look a fright."

He shook his head. "You're beautiful."

"You're being a gentleman. I've seen myself after a good cry. My lips swell and my nostrils flare."

He chuckled and tweaked her nose. "Maybe a little."

She laughed. "I have my mum to blame. I inherited her fair complexion." Father's terrible betrayal crushed her again, and she glanced away, pain throbbing in her chest.

Hiram lifted his brows. "Would you like to talk about it?"

She clenched her fists. "I'm so frightfully angry, Hiram. I did say my mum's belongings upset me. I said it over and over again." A lingering sob brought a catch to her throat. "But to hear him use it to excuse what he did—"

He shook his head. "I'm sorry, Noela."

"Now that her things are gone, I realize how much I needed them." She leaned her head against the wall and let the tears flow unchecked. "They were all I had left."

Hiram gripped her hand and squeezed. "We kept a few of Ma's things. Her reading glasses. Her hairbrush. It helps to take them out sometimes and look at them, remember her using them."

Noela nodded. "I slipped into her sitting room several times each day to touch her scarves or sit in her chair. It helped me feel close to her."

Confusion furrowed his brow. "I'm a little baffled by this room you speak of. I thought your ma passed away in Australia."

The question caught Noela off guard. "W–well yes, she did. Father brought over her favorite things, you see, and set them up in our new home. A tribute of sorts." She'd never realized before how peculiar it sounded.

He gave a firm shake of his head. "That wouldn't do for Pa and me. Too hurtful."

Crossing her arms, Noela peered over his head in deep thought. "To be perfectly honest, it was a mistake for us as well. The space became more of a shrine than a tribute."

"I'm thinking it would make letting go a hard thing to do."

She bit the corner of her lip. "You must be right. I haven't managed it yet."

Past the opening in the barn door, snowflakes danced like the little storm in Mum's snow globe—the one Noela would never see again. Perhaps it was a good thing.

She sat up and pointed. "Your sensitive nose was spot on. Look, it's started to snow."

As if he hadn't heard, Hiram sat with a distant haze in his eyes. "This Christmas will mark three years since Ma died."

The familiar ache resurfaced, and she touched his hand. "On Christmas? How dreadful."

"She was a frail woman but stubborn as a post. Tending Pa and me was all she lived for, and in the end, it took her life. She wound up with pneumonia brought on by exhaustion."

"I'm so sorry. She sounds wonderful."

His eyes glinted with unshed tears. "Ma wasn't afraid to die"—his voice quavered—"but the thought of leaving us alone scared her senseless."

Noela released a breath. "Three years, and you're still grieving. I thought it got easier."

"I suppose we'll always grieve. When I start to miss her, I remind myself what the Bible says about the death of a saint."

"Share it with me, please."

He glanced up, blotches of color rising in his cheeks. "You know, the part that reads, 'O death, where is thy sting? O grave, where is thy victory?' " He shrugged. "I can't quote the rest exactly, but it says our labor in the Lord is not in vain. As hard as Ma worked, it's a comfort to think she traded a bent back and calloused hands for robes of righteousness and eternal rest. So I try not to be selfish and wish her back." He smiled. "Most days I succeed—until I burn the biscuits or Pa tries his hand at the skillet." The wounded look returned, his attempt at humor failing him. "Or until I wake up hearing her footsteps in the hall and realize it was just a dream. Or I catch Pa staring at the hearth with tears shining in his eyes."

Noela's heart swelled to bursting. "Oh Hiram. . ."

She scooted closer, and they clasped hands. The distance between them felt like miles instead of inches. She longed to slip back in his arms and press her cheek against his chest, to hear his heartbeat, to smooth his face as he'd done hers and try to ease his pain.

Their eyes locked, and bittersweet emotion churned in her chest. She swayed to meet him, and—

"Noela!"

They sprang apart. "Beatrice Nancarrow, you frightened the life out of us."

Her sister peered into the gloom, her head and shoulders dotted with snow. "Pa's in a terrible state. Please come inside and forgive him."

Minutes ago, the request would've stung Noela to the quick. Now, thanks to Hiram, her heart yawned as wide as the Dakota skies.

"Go tell him I'm coming."

Beatrice darted away, and Hiram helped Noela to her feet. "Why the sudden change?"

She smiled up at him. "Our discussion helped me realize something important. We must cherish the parent we still have, wouldn't you say?"

His grin lit up the shadowed barn. "Yes indeed."

"And Hiram, the scripture is a lovely tribute to your mum. I plan to memorize it for myself. Thank you for telling me."

He widened the door for her to pass through. "No worries, mate. After all, what are. . .friends for?"

Chapter 8

Y ou're up early, Son."

The flapjack Hiram flipped in the air landed half in the skillet and half in the fire, the drips of batter dotting the stovetop and sizzling into tiny round cakes. Hoisting the pan, he juggled the hotcake with the spatula until he had it wrangled into place.

He scowled over his shoulder. "It's too early to be sneaking up on a man."

Pa chuckled. "I haven't been able to slip up on you since I got this cane. What's got your mind so busy your ears can't hear?" He crowded in beside Hiram to pour coffee in his battered tin mug. "Or should I say *who*?"

Hiram pretended to glare. "You're not so smart, old man."

Pa nudged him with an elbow. "I may be crippled, but I'm not blind."

"I like listening to her, that's all." Hiram grinned. "She sounds funny."

"Funny, eh? And that's the extent of her charms?" He snorted. "I don't suppose she's ever heard the likes of you before either. We brought a big load of Texas to Medora when we came."

He watched Hiram over the rim of his cup, amusement dancing on his face. "Be sure and give my regards to the Nancarrows this morning."

"What makes you think I'm going out there?"

Laughing, Pa hobbled to the table and sat down. "It's not hard to figure since you spent all your time there before you left on your stint at the ranch. And considering you haven't seen her in two weeks, well. . ."

Hiram made a wry face. "Show off."

He stretched across the table and plopped a thick slice of fried ham on Pa's plate. "It's not just about Noela. Jonathan needs my help." Worry gnawed his insides. "Pa, I've never seen a man less suited for wilderness living. His clumsy efforts were funny at first, but now it's downright concerning. I fear they won't make it in Medora."

Pa grunted. "With the state of Jonathan's affairs, that could be bad."

Hiram stared out the window at the jagged row of icicles. "The girls are not doing well either. Especially Noela. The deeper the snow gets, the lower her spirits dive."

He pulled out his chair and sat down. "She's working too hard. It's draining the life out of her."

Pa's troubled gaze mirrored Hiram's dire thoughts of his ma. Forking a slice of ham, he shook his head. "Jonathan can't let that happen."

"I can't let that happen."

Pa put down his fork, the bite of food uneaten. "You've decided that's your responsibility?"

Hiram squirmed under his direct stare. "It feels that way."

Reaching across the table, Pa gripped his hand. "Because you're a good man. You're a credit to me, Son."

The words spread pleasant warmth through Hiram. "You'd do the same if you were able. I just need to see them through the winter. Whatever they decide come spring will be up to them."

Pa shook his head. "Up to God, whichever way it goes."

He patted Hiram's wrist and went back to the business of eating. "I won't stand in your way, Son. Just don't neglect your chores. And don't shirk your duties on Mr. Roosevelt's ranch. He's counting on you men to keep his herd alive until spring."

Releasing a determined breath, Hiram nodded. "I won't let him down. And you can count on me, too."

Pa stuffed his mouth with buttered pancake. "I always could. By the way, how is that new ranch hand working out?"

Hiram flashed a wry grin. "Roy? That tenderfoot headed south at the first snowfall."

Pa chuckled. "I'm not surprised. Not many Texans can handle this harsh climate."

The dishes washed and dripping on the rack, Hiram saddled a horse and turned up the lane for the ride to Vine House.

His saddlebag held a sack of tenpenny nails he'd picked up for Jonathan and the spool of blue thread Beatrice asked for. He had a surprise for Noela tucked away in the bottom. He hoped the rock candy, sweet brown crystals dotting a length of string like a beaded necklace, might cheer her up.

The sky held the promise of a good day. Despite a foot of snow on the ground, the sun shone brightly, and the breeze at his back had lost its chill.

Two hundred yards from the Nancarrow house, piercing screams gripped his gut. Burying his heel in the horse's flank, he thundered toward the frenzied shrieks. Spinning around the windbreak, he leaped out of the saddle before his mount fully stopped, hitting the ground in a run.

The incredible sight in the yard dragged him to a stop.

Noela, in nightdress and slippers, danced in circles in the melting snow, beating the top of her head with both hands.

Beatrice kept time on the side, one hand over her laughing mouth, the other reaching for her sister each time she swept past. "Noela, be still!" she cried, giggling so hard she could barely speak. "How can I get him out with you bouncing like that?"

Hiram reached them in two strides. Gripping Noela's arm with one hand, he latched onto the mouse with the other and pulled him from the tangle of matted hair.

The small gray creature cowered in the folds of his glove, his sides heaving, his beady eyes wild with fright. "Look, he's harmless. You've frightened him nearly to death."

Hugging herself, Noela took one look and wheeled away. "Get that horrid thing away from me. I can't abide sharing a home with snakes, insects, and rodents. If it's not mice in my hair, it's muddy rainwater dripping into my skillet."

Biting back a smile, Hiram stepped aside and knelt to the ground. The mouse sailed off his hand and scurried for the barn.

"There he goes!" Beatrice called. "He's gone, Noela. You can open your eyes."

She peeked then gasped. "You let it go? For pity's sake, Hiram. He'll be back in the larder before nightfall." She punctuated her words with a violent shudder.

"Hold still," Hiram said. "The little fellow left you a gift." Reaching into the untidy mane draped over her shoulder, he pinched a tiny black pellet between his fingers and flung it away.

"Ew!" she shrieked. The war dance recommenced while she furiously shook out her hair.

Beatrice howled with glee. "You should've been here, Hiram. The poor little mouse fell out of the ceiling while Noela was washing dishes. I haven't seen her trip so lightly since dancing the Virginia reel with horrid old Julian Van der Berg."

Noela whirled. "You leave him out of this."

The fury in her eyes and the glint of sudden tears seared a hole in Hiram's stomach. Could this man be a beau from back home? He clamped his mouth shut to keep from asking the question burning in his chest.

A sound akin to a horse's whinny, ending in a shrill bray, came from behind the windbreak. Jonathan rode into sight sitting astride a big red mule. "G'day, Hiram. You're a welcome sight."

Hiram took off his hat. "Morning, sir. I came to see how you folks were getting on."

Jonathan's gaze slid to his daughters. "I heard those two yowling from a mile away."

Hiram grinned. "They gave me quite a turn. I guess you're relieved to see they're all right."

"Never doubted it, mate. When you share a roof with two high-strung gals, you grow accustomed to yowling."

A startled glance at Noela and his amusement turned to outrage. "Go find your clothes, young lady. What in blazes are you thinkin'?"

Her eyes rounded. She held her flowing nightdress out to the sides and stared in disbelief. Spinning on her heels, she dashed for the door, slamming it behind her.

Beatrice threw back her head and brayed like Jonathan's mule.

Her pa swung down off his mount and tied the reins. "Restrain yourself, Daughter. That isn't how a lady behaves."

With a gasp like the last breath of a drowning man, her laughter shifted to a higher gear. She whirled for the house with a loud snort and bounded inside.

Jonathan stared after her for several seconds, a deep furrow growing between his brows. "Did you ever see the like?"

Dangerously close to braying himself, Hiram shook his head. "Can't say that I have."

The humor of the situation struck Jonathan at last. A grin spread over his face and his generous belly shook. "I sure need their mum. I've done a poor job thus far. One parades half clothed in the blessed light of day. The other cackles like a chook and grunts like a pig in the mud."

Hiram couldn't contain his laughter. "You've got your hands full, sir. That you do." Wiping his eyes, he ran his hand along the mule's muzzle. "You've got yourself a fine animal here."

Beaming with pride, Jonathan patted her back. "She's a fat, cheeky girl, all right. A fine little hinny. I've dubbed her Mollie."

"You got her from Mr. Evart in town, didn't you? He bred his stallion with a little jenny last year."

Jonathan nodded. "He's promised us a milk cow, too. The bloke struck a fair bargain. He's letting us work off the debt."

"Work it off?"

"That's right. I'll help him tend his cattle, and the girls will keep his house."

A dull ache struck the pit of Hiram's stomach. "Are you sure that's a wise decision?"

Jonathan glanced up. "It's a fine arrangement. Mr. Evart is aging and all alone. We're able-bodied and in need of a plow animal. We made a gentleman's agreement and shook on it."

Hiram struggled to contain his frustration. "I don't know, Jonathan. . . ."

"I can't see what you're getting so worked up about."

"I'm wondering if you can do what you've agreed to, that's all. Even a small herd like Evart's is a full-time job."

"I'll have you know, I spent ten years droving cattle through the bush country."

Frowning, Hiram shifted his weight. "That was a few years back, and you didn't have a struggling farm to think of. Forgive me, but I don't think you can do it."

Mottled splotches rose on Jonathan's cheeks, and a white line rimmed his mouth. "I don't mean to rub you the wrong way, mate. I reckon I'm grateful for all you've done. But in matters concerning this farm, you'd best leave me to do the thinkin'."

Tense silence settled between them. Hiram gnawed his bottom lip while Jonathan fiddled with the mule's harness. Their eyes met across the top of Mollie's back.

"I apologize, sir," he said to Jonathan. "I stepped out of line."

A bit of sparkle returned to the man's eyes. "Apology accepted."

"But as your friend, I have to tell you I still have concerns. May I speak frankly?"

Jonathan raised one brow. "You haven't already?"

"To be honest, I'm worried about your daughter."

Jonathan's bottom lip jutted. "Noela? She's bushed, but she'll be all right."

"I disagree," Hiram said. "Haven't you noticed the state of her? This time of the morning, and she's still not dressed. Her skin is pale, and her eyes are tired. Doesn't that tell you anything?"

Nibbling on his thumbnail, Jonathan stared across the plain. "Now that you mention it, I've never seen her hair in such a mess. My girls have always minded their appearance." He nodded. "She can do better. Don't worry, I'll speak to her."

Hiram's hand shot up. "That's the worst you could do. Noela's doing her best, but the burden of running the farm is draining her. Do you really think pressing her to spruce up or sending her to clean Mr. Evart's house is the answer? You'll be the death of her."

Jonathan regarded Hiram as if he'd sprouted extra ears. "Rubbish. The Nancarrows are hearty stock."

Hiram sighed. "So I've heard. But you have young daughters, sir. Not sons."

Jonathan waved a dismissive hand. "No worries, young Hiram. In the end, you'll see what my girl's made of. Now stop all your blather and go inside. I'll be along once I tend to Mollie."

Whistling a carefree tune, he strolled toward the barn with the mule in tow.

Hiram massaged his throbbing temples. If ever a parent had lost touch with his offspring, Jonathan Nancarrow was that man. He seemed more aware of his mule's needs than those of his own daughter.

Chapter 9

Noela swung her feet to the floor then jerked them up and felt for her slippers. Shivering, she pushed aside the makeshift curtain surrounding her bed and winced at the rush of cold air. Half asleep, she squinted at the hearth. Only embers glowed in the ashes.

It was Father's job to tend the fire at night. Noela and Beatrice kept it during the daylight hours. Casting a resentful glance as she passed his sleeping mat, she rushed to add logs and kindling to the coals, holding her breath until they ignited into welcome flames.

The unseasonal warmth on what Hiram teasingly called "the day of the mouse" changed the next day to an ice storm. The rest of November and into December had brought sleet and heavy snow.

Despite her father's promise to improve on the meager life he'd provided, their plight had only worsened. Noela feared she'd reached the end of her endurance.

He muttered fitfully in his sleep and rolled toward the warmth of the hearth. Deep shadows lined his face, darkening the bags under his eyes to hollows. His body sagged heavily on the bed as if he'd lost the fight with gravity.

White-hot shame pricked her conscience. How could she be angry with him? He worked in the early morning darkness until long past sundown, trying to make a go of the farm—a mulish, unappreciative farm buried beneath a blanket of ice.

He moaned as if in pain, and she turned away. The sight of him so frail was unbearable. She longed to pull the cover up over his shoulders but didn't dare wake him. Placing another log on the fire, she inched closer and held out her hands to the heat.

The calendar hanging over the mantelpiece caught her eye. Idly, she studied the marked-off days until a startling realization hit.

One week until Christmas? Impossible!

"Isn't it exciting?" Beatrice slid up beside her, pulling her nightdress tight against her body to warm her behind.

Nodding at their sleeping father, Noela held a finger to her lips. "You shouldn't creep up on people," she whispered

"I saw you looking at the calendar," Beatrice whispered back. "Only one more week. I can hardly wait."

New York's bright lights, cheery carols, and joyful greetings swam in Noela's head. Fifth Avenue would overflow with holiday shoppers, their arms loaded down with bundles of presents or children wrapped in muffs and gloves, clutching candy canes and holly. Laughing couples arm-in-arm would make their way down busy streets on their way to festive parties.

She compared the picture in her head with the dismal soddie, and hot tears stung her eyes. "There's very little to look forward to stuck way out here."

Confusion etched her sister's brow. "Christmas is Christmas wherever you are. We'll just get busy and make it nice. We have a whole week to weave garlands, make presents, and plan the meal."

"What shall we weave into garlands, my balmy girl?" Noela said, not bothering to lower her voice. "Dead grass? Go on, make Christmas pies out of dried beans and carve gifts from icicles. I plan to skip Christmas this year."

Father growled and pulled a pillow over his head. "Kindly stop yammerin' like a couple of scrub jays. It's not yet daylight."

"Sorry, Daddy," Beatrice called.

Noela's cheeks flamed hotter than the hearth. He must have heard her harsh tirade. "It's time to be up and about anyway. I need to light the lanterns and start breakfast."

Father rolled up with a mournful sigh. He scrubbed his face with both hands then shook his head like a cattle dog, his cheeks flapping. Squinting up at her, he blinked to focus. "Hiram came home from the ranch yesterday. I reckon he'll be out this morning."

A flicker of joy surged in her chest. The day might be bearable after all.

Father peered from under bushy brows. "What say we put on our clothes before he arrives? No need in showing off another nightgown."

Beatrice ducked her head and giggled.

Noela bristled, crossing her arms self-consciously. "I don't need to be told to dress for company."

A warning flashed in his eyes. "If memory serves, you do." He gestured at her hair. "While you're at it, run a comb through your rat's nest and pin it up."

"Not rat's nest, Father." Beatrice teased. "It's a mouse nest."

Clenching her fists, Noela stalked across the room to heat the stove.

She prepared the morning meal—making more noise than usual with her pots and pans—while Father and Beatrice washed and dressed. Before sitting down to the table, she slipped on her clothes and tidied her hair.

Hiram arrived, bringing laughter and warmth to the dismal house. He stood on the threshold, stamping snow from his boots and peeling a scarf from around his neck. Noela's heart lifted at the sight of him.

She reached to relieve him of his coat, and their fingers tangled beneath the bundle of cloth. Hiram held on, and her breath caught.

He smiled, and his soulful brown eyes conveyed more than a simple greeting. "You were gone longer this time," she told him.

"Couldn't be helped, I assure you."

"How are things at the Elkhorn?" Father blurted, oblivious to the tender reunion. Or pretending to be.

Releasing her hand, Hiram plucked off his hat and dropped it on a hook by the door. "The usual struggle to keep the cattle alive." He laughed. "And their owner. Last week, Mr. Roosevelt rode a storm home from a hunting trip in the Badlands. Things are always lively when he's around."

"The man does like to hunt."

Hiram nodded. "He claims to have killed every kind of plains game there is, and he has most of the trophies to prove it."

"Sit down and tell me while we eat a bite."

"Thank you, but I had breakfast with Pa this morning."

Father waved at the coffeepot on the stove. "Have a cuppa at least to warm your bones. Pour him a mug full, Noela."

After a pleasant time around the table, Father stood up, patting his belly. "There are a couple of things in the barn I could use a hand with."

"Sure thing, sir," Hiram said. Draining the last of his coffee, he followed him to the door.

Noela cleared her throat. "Can you stay for tea?"

His brow creased. "I'm not much for tea, but I wouldn't mind another cup of coffee later on."

She laughed. "Tea is what we call the evening meal."

He screwed up his face. "So. . .you eat your tea?"

Covering her mouth to suppress a giggle, she nodded.

Smiling, he dropped his hat on his head and winked. "In that case, count me in."

Watching him go, Noela seethed with disappointment. Hiram had just arrived. Why had Father pulled him away so soon? She set about her chores but spent an unreasonable amount of time checking the front window for sight of them.

Morning stretched into late afternoon. Noela prepared the meal, more anxious than ever to have them return.

After setting the table, she sliced a fresh hot loaf of bread. She had just turned out a pan of potatoes still in their jackets when the clatter of boots on the porch gave her a start. Smoothing her hair, she hurried to the stove to start a fresh pot of coffee for Hiram.

He ducked inside after Father, caught sight of her, and smiled. "It smells good in here."

Flushing with pleasure, she placed a tray of roast venison on the table. "The water's fresh in the pitcher. You can wash up."

Beatrice sat cross-legged by the fire brushing Rowland's Macassar Oil into her hair. Nimble as a cricket, she sprang up and rushed to the washbowl. "Me first."

An angry red flush dotted Father's cheeks. "Show some manners, girl, and back out of Hiram's way."

"But Father, I don't want to use a man's dirty water." She shuddered. "You two have been clutching udders."

The color of Father's face heightened with the strain of stifled laughter. He turned aside, but his shaking shoulders gave him away.

Chuckling, Hiram lifted her shiny blond curls. "Hold still and let me see."

"See what?" Beaming, she bunched her shoulders. "Stop, that tickles."

"I'm searching for pointed ears," Hiram said. "You're an elf, aren't you?"

"I am not!" Her delicate complexion clouded pink, and she yanked her hair from his grasp. "You're being silly."

An unfamiliar sensation tugged at Noela, but she shoved it away. Heaven forbid she be jealous of her own sister.

Furious with herself, she scowled. "Beatrice, do as you're told and move away from the washstand."

Hiram turned with a grin. "Let her go ahead of me. I don't mind. How dirty could one little pixie be?"

Beatrice clasped her hands under her chin and awaited Father's answer. He nodded at the washstand. "Go on then."

Beatrice curtsied for Hiram, her lively curls bouncing. "You have my utmost appreciation, kind sir." Noela smelled the delightful fragrance of the Macassar Oil from where she stood.

Hiram bowed. "Anything for you, milady."

Spinning, Noela busied herself at the sink. She smelled of raw meat and potato peels and couldn't remember the last time she'd laughed so freely or felt lighthearted.

She pulled a lock of dry, stringy hair over her shoulder to examine it. How long since she'd cared how it looked?

Her gaze slid to the hand clutching the wispy strands of hair. The red, chafed fingers with brittle nails couldn't possibly be hers.

She swiped her lips with her tongue. Cracked and crusted skin met its touch.

Beatrice looked like the whimsical creature Hiram had called her, a delicate, fresh-faced sprite. Noela resembled a troll.

Blast Medora's dry wind and weather! Dash the work and worry of Vine House!

As if he'd read her mind, Hiram brought up the subject of their home while finishing the last few bites of his meal. "There's an upside to living in a soddie. Like I told you once before, they stay cool in the summer, warm in the winter. In case of a prairie fire, you can bring your livestock and anything else of value inside with you and keep it safe."

"Fire?" Beatrice's mind appeared to be whirling.

He patted her hand. "Don't fret, honey. We don't see them often."

Her shoulders relaxed, and she smiled up at him. "Is it always so dreadfully cold here?"

"Patience, little elf," Hiram said. "Medora thaws out and comes to life in the springtime. These cliffs and gullies teem with wildlife. Prairie grass comes up in a dozen shades of green as far as the eye can see."

He pointed at the low ceiling. "Including the patch over your head. Some folks sow flower seeds on the roof. The colorful blooms really perk up the place."

A dreamy daze settled over Beatrice. She propped her chin and stared in the distance. "Like an enchanted cottage. May we plant flowers on the roof, Father?"

Forking a chunk of potato, he grinned. "If it makes you happy, love."

Noela refilled their coffee mugs. "What sort of wildlife, Hiram?"

"Well, let's see. . . . There are bobcats, coyotes, elk, prairie dogs, and badgers." He paused, staring as if he saw them in his mind. "Mustangs and bison roam in herds across the plain, and eagles soar over skies so blue they bring a man to tears."

He drew a shaky breath and shook his head. "There's no place on earth like Medora in the spring."

Noela marveled at his glowing eyes and quavering voice. How could the harsh, frozen ground outside her door ever inspire such devotion in a man? She'd have to see Medora the way he described with her own eyes before she'd believe it.

Moonstruck, Beatrice gazed at him. "You make it sound so nice. Back home we just have roos and wallabies. And eucalyptus trees."

He cut his eyes to Noela and winked. "Just kangaroos? Imagine that."

Father cleared his throat. "Girls, let the poor bloke eat in peace. You've about talked his ear off."

Hiram nudged his plate aside. "I couldn't hold another bite, sir. Mighty fine meal though."

Noela smiled. She'd discovered a hidden talent in cooking. It pleased her that he noticed.

Pushing away from the table, Hiram stretched out his long legs and crossed his ankles. "If you don't mind, Noela, there's a matter we need to discuss."

She settled back in her chair twisting her napkin. "All right."

"There's a dinner party on Christmas Eve at the Chateau de Mores. I'm acquainted with the marquis and his wife through Mr. Roosevelt, so they've asked me to come." His eyes flickered toward her father. "With your pa's permission, I'd like you to go with me."

Noela pulled her chafed hands off the table and tucked them in the folds of her skirt. "Oh Hiram. I don't know. . ."

Father's bulging cheeks lifted in a smile. "You should go," he mumbled around a mouthful of venison.

She fingered her brittle hair. "I couldn't possibly."

Beatrice shot straight up in her chair. "I'll go."

"There's little chance of that," Father said. "Besides, Noela is going. A night out will do her good."

"I think so, too," Hiram said softly.

Noela shook her head. "I don't have a proper dress to wear."

Certain she could influence a swift return to New York, she'd defiantly gone against Father's edict to pack plenty of clothing. She'd left most of her best things, along with the lovely gown she commissioned to wear to Mrs. Baumann's Christmas gala, hanging in her dressing chamber in the brownstone. How she wished she had it now.

Father raised an expectant brow. "Can't you make something?"

How like a man. If she *could* sew that fast, she didn't own a machine.

Beatrice pouted her mouth. "I did so want to meet the marquis's wife."

"Madame de Mores?" Hiram's features softened. "She's a wonderful lady. You'd like her, Bea. She was Medora von Hoffman when the marquis met her. The daughter of a wealthy American banker, though you'd never know. She's as comfortable on a game hunt as any man. The marquis claims she's a better shot than he is."

Her sulk fading like a puff of smoke, Beatrice leaned in. "She sounds wonderful. Tell me more."

Hiram pressed his knuckles to his lips "Let me see, what else? Ah yes, she speaks seven languages."

"All at once?"

The corners of his mouth twitched. "No, one at a time. She's also an accomplished pianist and a fine artist. She paints in watercolor."

"Is she pretty?"

Rubbing his chin, Hiram considered the question then nodded. "She cleans up nice."

Father's hand shot up to block the next question. "Give us a turn, girl. Hiram, will Mr. Roosevelt be at this do?"

"Yes sir. He and the marquis quarreled awhile back. A misunderstanding over a cattle deal followed by some ugly business that nearly led to a duel. Both men are eager to prove they've mended fences."

Beatrice wrinkled her nose. "Who cares about quarrels and duels? Tell us about the chateau."

"That's actually a name given by the locals in jest." He grinned. "The marquis calls it a hunting cabin."

Noela gasped. "A twenty-seven-room hunting cabin?"

He chuckled. "With ten bedrooms."

She stared wistfully out the window. "I would dearly love to see it."

Hiram perked up. "So you'll go?"

A vision of the only nice dress she still owned flashed in her mind. A beige off-the-shoulder with an empire waistline. She could reposition the bow and add a few well-placed tucks in the bodice. Madame de Mores would recognize it as last year's fashion, and Noela would burn with shame, but. . .

"I'd love to go, Hiram. I couldn't bear to miss it."

Beatrice cheered, and Father gave a satisfied nod.

Hiram's smile alone made her hasty decision worthwhile.

Chapter 10

Noela's first glimpse of the Chateau de Mores would stay with her for the rest of her life. The lone structure, backed by rocky crags and a soaring flat plateau, took her breath. The claret-red roof, matching shutters, and pale gray coat of paint stood out on the surrounding ocean of snow like piping on a cake.

There might be grander homes back East, but after weeks of staring at dirt walls, none could be more welcome to Noela's eager eyes. "She's a beaut, isn't she?"

Seated next to her in the wagon, Hiram watched her with a tender smile. "That she is."

Her brows rose to peaks. "I'm referring to the chateau."

His smile deepened. "The chateau's nice, but I'd rather look at you."

Speechless, Noela squeezed his hand. She'd felt like a maiden aunt for so long, Hiram's attentive stares felt wonderful.

Judging by her reflection in the mirror at home, his reaction held the slightest merit. Since the invitation, she'd worked to repair the consequences of neglect. Beatrice helped, along with her bottle of Rowlands' Macassar Oil. Now Noela's hands and shoulders were supple, her hair silky soft and glowing.

Hiram stopped in front of the house and set the brake. Hurrying around, he helped her down, a proud, eager smile on his face. Taking her arm, he escorted her onto the porch. A servant opened the door at their knock and held it wide for them to enter.

A fair-skinned, doe-eyed woman stood behind him smiling a welcome. Her light brown hair, artfully pinned and laced with ribbons, had a reddish cast. The marquise did, in fact, clean up nice.

"Come inside, you two. Out of the dreadful cold."

She leaned to kiss Hiram on the cheek. "Dear boy, where has Theodore kept you hidden?"

Hiram laughed and took her hand. "You're one of the few in town he allows the liberty of that name. To the rest of us, he's *Mr.* Roosevelt."

He winked at Noela. "Madame de Mores, may I present Miss Noela

Nancarrow of New York City? By way of Queensland, Australia, of course."

Noela was gripped with a sudden fear that he would mention Vine House. Then a sinking realization hit. The people of Medora were certain to know of her plight.

Madame de Mores took her hand. "Noela. A beautiful name for a lovely young woman."

"Thank you, madame. I'm honored to meet you."

Another servant appeared and collected their wraps. Noela breathed a sigh of relief that she'd packed Mother's sable. The lovely coat was the only proof left of the life she'd once lived.

The marquise led them down the hall. On the way, Noela stole a peek inside several rooms. Unlike dismal Vine House, where the days passed in dreary sameness, the Christmas season was evident in the festive decorations. Her heart ached with sudden longing for her brownstone in the city.

Madame had an affinity for jewel tones. Royal blue dominated the sitting room on the left, from the upholstered couch to the fringed scarf over the mantelpiece. She'd chosen red as her accent color—no surprise considering the red roof and shutters of the house.

In a corner of the formal living room stood a box grand piano, the top adorned with family photographs and sheet music. Hiram had mentioned that the lady played.

Noela's heart leaped painfully at the reminder. She'd never see her mum's piano again.

Their hostess glanced over her shoulder as she walked. "The silly men in the parlor are determined to ruin our evening with talk of a blizzard, but pay them no mind. It wouldn't dare snow on our party."

"I'm going to agree with them this time," Hiram said. "The signs are clear. Bad weather is on the way."

"Don't you turn traitor on me, Hiram McGregor. I won't have it."

She laughed and waved for them to cross the next threshold. "Go through to the dining room then, and let's get you fed in a timely fashion." She winked. "Just in case you're right."

Sensing Noela's hesitation, she patted her arm. "Sit where you like, dear. Wherever you feel most comfortable. We don't stand on formalities in Medora."

Before Hiram could escort her inside, a tall, slender man strolled toward them at a leisurely pace. "*Mais non.* We happily left ceremony behind us in France. A refreshing change, *n'est-ce pas?*"

Madame de Mores swung around to greet him. "Perfect timing. You've saved me a trip to collect you." She placed a hand on his shoulder and introduced him to Noela as her husband, the Marquis de More.

Haunting eyes in an angular yet handsome face appraised her carefully. His full mouth seemed to pout beneath a thin, waxed moustache. "I am pleased to meet you, *mademoiselle.*" He bowed slightly. "Welcome to our home."

Several men approached from behind the marquis, one vaguely familiar. In his mid- to late twenties perhaps, the dapper gentleman sported a slim build and full moustache. Intelligent eyes peered from behind large round spectacles.

Curiosity dancing in his eyes, he reached for Noela's hand. "I beg your pardon. Have we met?"

His strong, commanding voice jarred her memory. "We have indeed, Mr. Roosevelt. At the home of Edith Baumann of New York. I'm Noela, the daughter of Jonathan Nancarrow."

"Of course. The masquerade ball. You were standing beneath an Impressionist painting mounted over the fireplace. A Degas, I believe." He winked at Hiram. "As I recall, I couldn't decide which work of art to study."

The marquis reared back his head and laughed. "Pay him no mind, my dear. He's harmless."

A servant appeared at the head of the table, his manner aloof, his face expressionless.

The marquis smiled. "I believe the staff is ready to serve. Shall we be seated, *s'il vous plaît?*"

The lavish meal, served in endless courses by black-tied waiters and sober kitchen servants, consisted of fish prepared three ways, a savory roast, wild game, several salads, roasted vegetables, and a fruit platter, followed by a delectable French dessert. The proprietress of Medora's largest hunting cabin seemed overjoyed to pamper her guests.

For those few minutes, seated at a grand table, surrounded by well-dressed people engaged in lively discussion, Noela felt as if she'd returned to New York City. Better yet, gone home to Coolangatta.

The marquis smiled from his place at the head of the table. "Noela, how fitting you should grace our table on *la veille de Noël*—Christmas Eve in *français*. In France we call Christmas *Noël*. The word comes from the phrase '*les bonnes nouvelles.*' It means 'the good news' and is referring to the Gospel."

"How lovely. I didn't know." A touch of shame pierced her heart. Lately she'd been anything but good news.

Madame blotted pastry cream from her mouth with a lace napkin. "What sort of celebration have you planned for tomorrow, my dear? A nice dinner perhaps?"

Noela nearly choked on her bite of pastry, the flaky crust turning to dust in her mouth. How could she admit to this woman, who heaped bountiful food and gracious good cheer on a stranger, that she had no plans at all for her loved ones?

Floundering for words, she panted and stared like the frightened little mouse Hiram had plucked from her hair.

He sat forward and cleared his throat. "Her family will dine with us, madame. I'm preparing the Christmas meal this year."

Noela flashed him a grateful smile.

The marquise nodded. "How good of you, Hiram. This time of year, it's nice to gather with family and friends." She leaned across the table and widened her eyes. "A man who can cook, Noela. A rare specimen, don't you think?"

The waiters removed the last empty dessert plate, and the marquis pushed back his chair. "Gentlemen? I don't want any of you caught in a blizzard, so I won't be offended if you must take your leave. For those who would partake, please join me in the parlor for a cordial and a cigar."

After-dinner drinks and pleasant conversation while Father braves the cold alone to do the evening chores.

Standing, the marquis bowed to his wife and kissed the tips of his fingers. "A wonderful meal, *ma chère*."

Noela cringed. A wonderful meal indeed while her sister dined on leftovers.

Guilt sickened her. When had she become shortsighted and self-focused? Her family circumstances were a tragedy that affected them all. Not just her.

"Hiram?"

He paused half out of his chair. "Are you all right? You're pale as a sheet."

"I'd like to leave now, if you don't mind."

Madame de Mores clucked her tongue. "You men have frightened her with your dire predictions." She hurried around the table to help Noela stand. "Someone fetch her wrap."

Mr. Roosevelt pushed away from the table. "I'll go have their wagon brought around."

Hiram reached her side and took her elbow. She tried to blink away her tears, but his strained expression meant she'd failed. "Come on, honey. Let's get you home."

Chapter 11

An ominous haze met Noela outside, so dense it blotted out the horizon. Silent lightning laced the sky, and storm clouds dragged their bloated bellies over the prairie. Hiram took one look, gripped her elbow, and rushed her down the steps to the wagon.

Neither of them spoke as they pulled away from the chateau. Noela feared she'd burst into tears if she opened her mouth. Hiram chewed his lip and cast anxious glances her way.

A few miles out, the wind picked up, and a heavy snow began to fall. After a few false starts, Hiram cleared his throat and blurted the question he must have been building the courage to ask. "What happened back there?"

She shrugged and pulled her coat tighter.

"I know it had nothing to do with the weather."

She longed to explain, but he was the last person she dared to confide in. Confessing her faults would make him think the worst of her. More than anything, she hoped he didn't already see her in a bad light.

The weather worsened with every turn of the wheels. Driving snow wiped out the road, and Noela wondered how Hiram kept the horse on track. Pulling her scarf over her face, she gripped his arm. "This is dreadful. Shouldn't we turn back?"

Hiram sat rigid and tense, his worried gaze fixed straight ahead. "It's too late. We're halfway to Vine House."

She moaned. "We should never have left."

He glanced back, guilt shining in his eyes. "I'm sorry, honey. All I could think of was getting you home."

"No, Hiram. It's not your fault. I'm the one who—"

The horse stumbled, and the wagon dipped. Noela screamed and slid forward on the seat, grasping for a hold on Hiram's sleeve.

"Hang on!" he cried, clinging to the reins.

The mare fought to regain her footing. With painstaking strides, she hauled forward, pulling them up out of a deep coulee and back onto the road.

On level ground, Hiram pulled back on the reins and set the brake. Gripping Noela's arms, his frantic gaze swept over her. "Are you all right?"

"Yes, I think so."

"You're sure?"

She swallowed hard and nodded.

"Wait here. I'll go see about the horse."

Noela sat alone within the terrifying gale, wishing Hiram would hurry back to her. When he climbed up beside her at last, she trembled with relief.

"The mare can't go any farther. She's come up lame."

Stunned, Noela groped for words. "That can't be. We're miles from home."

Wrapping his arm around her shoulder, he bundled her close. "Don't worry. I think we passed the Rowley farm less than a quarter mile back."

Fear swirled in her belly. "It might as well be ten miles in this blizzard."

A strong gust caught the wagon in its teeth and shook it. Driving snow pelted Noela's head, stinging through her hat and scarf. Once the shrill whistle of the wind subsided, she tugged on Hiram's sleeve. "There are blankets under the seat. We could wrap up tight and wait it out right here. The storm will die down before long."

He raised his face to the overhead sky. "This squall is just getting started. We have to find shelter."

Her stomach tightened. "Suppose we get lost? I've heard stories of poor souls wandering blindly in their own yards, freezing to death ten feet from the door. What if we—"

Hiram spun her around to face him, his eyes dark hollows in the waning light. "We have to try, Noela. Otherwise, they'll find us right here in the morning."

Her feverish mind filled in the rest. She gulped, her throat raw from the frigid air, and nodded. "Of course. I'm sorry."

Hiram wrapped the lap blanket around her shoulders and jumped to the ground. "Wait there," he shouted over the howling wind. "I want to free the horse."

Noela leaned over the rail. "Why? You said she's lame."

"Her leg's too weak to bear a load, but I think she can walk. Her senses are keener than ours. She'll guide us to John Rowley's place."

"Why would she go there?"

"She won't. She'll head straight home. But Rowley's is in her path."

He returned leading the skittish mare. Her nostrils flared, and she jerked against her restraints, clearly eager to be away.

Noela felt her angst.

Hiram offered his arm, and she clambered off the rig.

Wheeling, the horse picked her way through the drift at the side of the road and baled in the direction Hiram predicted.

Hiram clung to the reins with one hand. The other held Noela's wrist so tightly her flesh stung.

She kept up the best she could, tripping and stumbling behind him. "Can't you slow her down?"

"I'm trying," he shouted back. "If I lose you, stay put. I'll pull her around and find you again."

Noela shuddered and picked up the pace. She couldn't imagine anything coaxing the single-minded animal to turn. She seemed well set on a destination.

The mare faltered repeatedly, and Noela prayed she wouldn't go down—for the animal's sake as well as theirs. If she fell, they'd have to leave her to her fate. Then what would become of them?

An eternity passed in a frigid blur, the horse's labored breaths the only sound. Staggering forward at Hiram's insistent bidding, Noela tried to call out, but the wind took her breath.

Her body had gone numb beneath her, burning lungs and the pinch of Hiram's determined grip the only sensations left.

A drowsy fog descended on her mind, and she longed to lie down. She imagined breaking free of Hiram's grip and falling away, sinking into the mounded snow and giving way to blissful sleep.

"Whoa! Whoa there!" Hiram's frantic shout roused her from her daze. The horse had bolted, pulling ahead. Hiram held on until the last inch of the reins slid out of his hand, dragging him to the ground.

Noela cried out and made her way to him. "Are you all right?"

"I'm fine," he said, pushing to his knees in the snow. "But I'm afraid we're on our own."

She helped him to his feet. "Did something spook her?"

"Maybe."

"Will she be all right?"

"If she can keep to her feet, she'll find her way to our barn. Otherwise—"

He stilled and shaded his eyes against the snow. "Did you see that?"

Noela stared in the direction he pointed. A relentless wall of white blinded her. "How can you see anything in this?"

He held her fast. "Keep watching."

In a faint lull between the punishing gusts, the barest flicker appeared in the distance. Her heart surged. "Is it far?"

"I don't think so. Let's go."

He drew her close, and she trudged on beneath the shelter of his arm. Hope chased away the urge to sleep, and all she could think of was warming her hands by a fire. Each time Hiram lost his sense of direction, he'd stop and wait for a glimpse of the light. They stumbled onto the weathered barn sooner than Noela expected, and she shed thankful tears.

Hiram found the side door and pushed his way in, pulling her in behind him. Instantly, miraculously, they exchanged brutal cold for warmth, a blinding white tempest for yellow straw and a lantern's soft glow.

On the other side of a corral, a large animal stirred and gave a low moan. Two men kneeling beside it stood up and stared dumbly over the rail.

"John? It's Hiram McGregor. I have a friend with me."

The older man scratched the side of his face. "Hiram? What are you folks doing out on a night like this?"

"Our horse came up lame."

"You walked from the road, boy?"

Hiram nodded. "Across your field."

"You're lucky you made it."

Hiram glanced at Noela. "Yes, and we're grateful." He placed a protective hand on her shoulder. "Gentlemen, this is Miss Nancarrow. Her pa is Jonathan, the fellow homesteading Vine House."

John nodded. "I've seen them around town."

"Noela, meet John Rowley and his son, Jake."

They tipped their hats. "Glad to know you, ma'am," young Jake said.

"Likewise," she managed through chattering teeth. Somewhere along the way, probably when Hiram fell to the ground, Noela had lost the lap blanket from around her shoulders.

Hiram tightened the scarf around her neck. "John, the lady's freezing. Do you mind if we wait out the storm with you?"

John pointed to the hulking black cow at his feet. "We're not going anywhere for a while. Old Trudy here is trying to birth a calf. Not having an easy time of it, I fear."

The cow sprawled on the hay-strewn floor, her abdomen swollen and her sides heaving from exertion. A birthing pain seized her, and she raised her head and bawled in protest.

Hiram studied the poor creature. "Reckon it's turned?"

Jake shook his head. "Doesn't feel like it. It's her first calf, is all." He gave a shy smile. "Nothing time won't cure."

John pointed to a corner of the barn. "Hiram, dig out a hollow in that pile of straw for Miss Nancarrow. Try to keep her warm until we can do better by her."

Hiram led her to the spot and dug out a cozy burrow just big enough for her. He helped her lie down and then covered her with handfuls of hay. Her mind leaped to the mice, snakes, and insects she'd kept company with of late and wondered how many of their relatives might be sharing her nest.

Hiram fussed over her like a protective parent. "Are you all right? Warm enough?"

She struggled to control her chattering teeth and nodded.

He took off his heavy coat and prepared to place it over her, but she held up her hand. "It's still too cold in here for that. Put it on again, please. I'm starting to warm up."

He hesitated but only briefly. Already he'd started to shiver. "All right, but promise to call me if you need it."

"I promise."

With a wink, he scurried back to the Rowley men and their birthing cow.

Noela snuggled down and tried to relax. Her thoughts drifted to the party at the chateau, and her cheeks flamed. What must they think of her?

And now her frantic behavior and rude departure had been for naught. Her desperation to return home had failed to get her there.

Father would be so worried. She pictured him walking the splintered floor of the soddie, watching at the windows and running his hands through his hair.

Suppose he saddled Mollie and set out in the blizzard to search for her? *Please God. . .don't let that happen.*

With sudden insight, she realized her father spent most of his evenings brooding and pacing the floor. She'd failed to notice because she'd been blind to anyone's suffering but her own.

One bad decision, perhaps driven by greed, had lost them everything and landed them in this harsh land. But he'd paid for his mistake with hard work and grief from the moment they came to Medora.

In a rush of tenderness, Noela forgave him. Choking on bitter tears, she vowed never again to hold it against him. She only hoped he and Beatrice could forgive her for wallowing in self-pity.

She groaned inside. And for cheating them out of Christmas.

"I'm so sorry, God," she whispered past the flickers of light on the ceiling. "Give me the chance to make it up to them."

At her confession, blessed peace swept over her soul. The urgency to rush home melted into drowsy contentment. She yawned and closed her eyes, basking in a strong sense of assurance.

Startled awake by the men's excited voices, Noela turned her head and peered toward the dusky light at the window. Sometime in the night, the snow had stopped.

"We've got a young bull!" Mr. Rowley cried.

Past the slats of the corral, the mother cow rose to her feet and began licking her baby to clean him. In the faint glow of the lantern, the little newborn fought to gain his feet.

The three men stood over the animals, their bodies casting tall shadows on the wall. They reminded Noela of the wise men and another hushed birth in a distant manger. Another baby born in a faraway place and time.

Jesus came to earth in humble circumstances and lived a modest life. He once said of himself, "Foxes have holes, and the birds of the air have nests; but the Son of man has nowhere to lay his head." In comparison, Vine House seemed like the Chateau de Mores, and Noela couldn't wait to get home.

"Hiram?"

Smiling, he left the corral and came to kneel at her side. "You're awake. How are you feeling?"

"Wonderful. It's Christmas morning."

He grinned. "Yes it is. Merry Christmas."

"I need you to take me home right away. I have a celebration meal to prepare, worthy of Bea's expectations and Father's sacrifice."

"Is that so?" He seemed bursting with pride.

"I've wasted enough time, don't you think?"

Joy transformed his weary face. "Do you realize you called her Bea?"

Noela grinned. "Yes, but you must never tell her."

His hearty laugh echoed in the rafters. "If you're serious about that meal, I know a couple of fellows who wouldn't turn down an invitation." He raised his brow and sweetened the deal. "I'll throw in a pair of fat prairie chickens."

She propped up on her elbows. "I just remembered. You told the marquise you were cooking for me today."

He shot her a sheepish grin. "I'll keep my word, too, if you'll settle for bacon and flapjacks. It's all I know how to cook."

They laughed until Noela's stomach ached; then she sat up and reached for his hand. "Oh Hiram, I want more than anything to see Vine House succeed."

He turned her arm over. Sliding her glove halfway down, he dropped soft kisses on her wrist. "There's only one way to assure your father's success," he murmured.

With an effort, she pulled her attention from the delicious warmth of his lips. "What is it? I'll do anything."

He glanced up, a smile stealing over his face. "Do you mean it? Because what he needs is an able-bodied son-in-law who knows how to farm this land."

At her sharp intake of breath, Hiram lifted his head and carefully searched her eyes. "I love you, little Australian girl. I want you for my bride."

Noela slid into his arms, caressing his face with her fingertips the way she'd longed to do. "I won't need to open any more presents. God has granted me the best gift of my life."

His eyes glowed as he hugged her close. "I'll take that as a yes."

This time, when she rose to meet him, he didn't push her away. His searching mouth found hers, their eager press a vow of his heartfelt commitment.

Bea's voice echoed in her head. *Christmas is Christmas wherever you are.* From this day forward, it would be where Hiram was as well.

He held her at arms' length. "I do have one question, honey. Who is Julian Van der Berg?"

Laugher bubbled up in her chest. "No one important, love. Absolutely no one at all."

Buckskin Bride

Vickie McDonough

Chapter 1

Oklahoma Territory
December 1889

Mattie Carson stared at the thin dirt trail that wound through the trees and veered out of sight. Three weeks had passed since her father left on that same path, and he'd never been gone this long before. Where was he?

Birds overhead sang a cheerful tune that did little to lift her sagging spirits. She sensed something awful had happened to her papa. Was she strong enough—wise enough—to keep her two sisters safe if he never returned?

"Watching that path won't bring Papa home any sooner."

Mattie spun around and glared at her twin sister, Milly. "At least I haven't given up hope that he *will* return."

Milly's expression softened. "I haven't lost hope, but maybe I'm being more realistic than you. In the nine years since Mama died, he's never been gone longer than a week. Not once." She glanced over to where their younger sister, Jess, sat, cracking pecans between two rocks. Milly leaned in closer, lowering her voice. "I fear something dreadful has happened to Papa."

Mattie nodded. "Me, too." And that meant she was now in charge, even though Milly was the oldest by five minutes.

"What will we do?" Milly grabbed hold of one of her long braids and held the end of it to her lips, as she always did when she worried.

"We'll stay here as long as we can. If Papa is still alive, this is where he will come." *Please come.* Though her father had told her she was born a leader in spite of her birth order, she didn't want the responsibility. But there was no one else. Milly didn't have the gumption needed to protect them, and hunting turned her stomach. If they wanted to eat, it was up to Mattie to find game.

Milly nodded. "That sounds like a good idea. I best get to work on our supper." She walked a few steps then turned back. "When will you skin the deer you shot this morning?"

"Soon, but I want to check on the horses first."

"The skin will make a nice pair of pants for Jess."

Milly headed toward their tipi, and Mattie swung around to check on their horses. After a short walk down the trail, she stepped through the trees into a small clearing and found both bays grazing. To her right, a creek burbled along a rocky bed, creating a peaceful setting. She wished they could set up the tipi closer to the water, but her father had always instructed them to place it somewhere that it was hidden by the trees and not out in the open. That wasn't always an easy task, especially on the prairie they'd been traveling through. This land was called the Oklahoma Territory. Her papa had told her *Oklahoma* was a Choctaw Indian word that meant "red people," and that was a fitting name since this area was where many of the country's Indians had been relegated to live after they were moved off their homelands.

A twig snapped in the trees to her left, and Mattie froze. She scanned the area but saw no one. A horse whinnied, and she darted back into the trees. She ran, careful not to make a noise, like her father had taught her. She paused, peering through the trees, and saw a man on a horse. What could he want?

She backed toward camp, trying to watch the man. He turned in her direction, and she froze. Had he heard her? Seen her?

He sat atop his horse, looking around. She hoped he didn't ride in the other direction—he would discover their horses.

Mattie had to warn her sisters. She crept through the brush until she caught a glimpse of their camp. Then she whistled the *hey, sweetie* sound of a chickadee's call.

Milly spun around and stared into the trees for a brief moment then grabbed Jess's hand, hauling her to her feet. She helped the nine-year-old shinny up the tree she'd been leaning against and then followed her up.

With her sisters safe, Mattie crept back to where she could watch the intruder. She hid behind the trunk of a downed tree surrounded by tall prairie grass. The man wove his horse through the trees, looking at the ground for a time, and then he stopped and scanned the area again.

What was he looking for? Mattie's heart pounded. Although she had hunted all types of wildlife, she'd never had to pull her gun or knife on another human. But she would. She had to protect her sisters.

The man looked a few years older than her nineteen years. Rather than wear a western hat like many men in these parts preferred, he wore a round cap with a bill, and his coat was a style she wasn't familiar with. He lifted his cap and forked his fingers through his black hair, which glistened in the morning sunlight like a raven's wing. He dropped the cap back on his head and reined his horse in the direction she was hiding.

Mattie held her breath as he rode within four feet of her. She didn't fear that he'd see her, since her buckskin clothing blended well with the natural surroundings, but she was concerned he'd spot the tipi. He sat a moment, his gaze scanning the area. Did he sense someone was near? If he spotted one of them, would he harm them?

She struggled to keep her breathing quiet when worry and concern made it come out ragged. The man clucked to his horse, and it moved forward—right down the path she'd taken to the creek. But he was riding away from the creek, straight toward their tipi.

❧

Conall Donegan guided his horse slowly up the trail that led through the wooded area. Something wasn't quite right. The birds and insects he normally heard while hunting were silent, as if warning him of someone else's presence. But other than an odd pattern of footprints, he hadn't seen anything to make him think an intruder was on his property. He reined the bay gelding through the trees, and his heart nearly jumped from his chest at the sight he encountered. A tan tipi stood tall, well-hidden among the birch, cottonwood, and pine trees that grew thick in this area. He rode closer and searched the area but saw no signs of life. He started to dismount to peek inside the tipi, but then he noticed the same odd footprints he'd seen earlier, going in all directions—two different sizes of them. And near a tree sat a pile of pecans—half-cracked. People had been here quite recently.

But where were they now? Were they hiding among the shrubs, watching him? He swallowed the lump in his throat and backed up his horse. He'd heard plenty of Indian tales, both good and bad, since settling in the Oklahoma Territory after the land rush, but Indians were not supposed to be in this area that had been called the Unassigned Lands. No Indians had settled in this part of the territory.

He clucked to his horse and ducked as the gelding rode under a low tree limb. He needed to tell Brian about the squatters—if they were still around. He knew enough about Indians to know that those who lived in tipis were generally nomads—and nomads always took their tipis with them whenever they left an area. That meant either the Indians were still around or something had happened to them.

❧

Mattie waited a good while after the man rode off before she stood. A brilliant cardinal landed on the end of the log she sat beside. His drab-colored mate lighted on a nearby shrub; then, as if he'd signaled to her, they flew off in unison. The male's red feathers stood out well against the browns of winter.

Hunkering down, lest the man still be watching, she dodged from tree to tree. As she approached their camp, she finally straightened, convinced he was gone—and now they needed to pack up and leave.

She whistled the call for "all clear" and gazed up in the oak tree, one of the few that was still clothed in a gown of russet leaves. Milly deftly climbed down and dropped to the ground. "Who do you think he was?"

Shrugging, Mattie watched as Jessamine made her way down, at a slower pace than Milly, but almost as skillfully. The girl had been hiding in trees longer than she could walk.

Jess swung onto the lower limb. Mattie turned toward the tipi, but Jess cried out. She spun back around, watching helplessly as her little sister fell sideways. Jess stuck out one leg, landed with a sickening crack, and then fell to the ground.

Jess gasped and emitted a high-pitched squeal, just like an animal sometimes did when shot with an arrow. Mattie and Milly rushed to her side as Jess writhed on the ground.

"Where does it hurt?" Milly ran her hands down Jess's pant leg.

"The other one. Oh. . .my ankle." Jess reached for her leg, but Mattie pulled her hand back.

Milly untied Jess's moccasin, tossed it aside, then slid up her pant leg. "It's swelling already." She glanced at Mattie, shook her head, and mouthed, "Broken."

Standing, Milly turned to Mattie. "Let's get her down to the creek. The cool water will help with the swelling and pain. Then I'll mix up some chamomile tea while you sit with her."

Milly helped Mattie to lift Jess, and Mattie held her close, supporting the injured leg and hating that her little sister was in so much pain. The gun that was tied around Mattie's neck and hid beneath her buckskin shirt, pressed hard against her chest.

"It hurts." Jess rested her head on Mattie's shoulder. The girl rarely fussed, so the tears streaming down her face and her soft moans proved her discomfort.

"I know, chickadee. I'm sorry."

"I want Papa," Jess whimpered.

Me, too. Mattie didn't mind watching over her sisters for a short while when their father went hunting, but she didn't know if she was capable of doing it forever. Jess's injury and her own confusion about what to do for her sister were perfect examples of her shortcomings.

Jess needed a doctor. Though Milly tended their cuts, scrapes, and other minor wounds, she'd never set a broken bone. Mattie shifted Jess higher. How could she carry the nine-year-old all the way to the creek? Maybe she should get one of the horses. She heard a sound in the woods behind her and turned around.

Milly hurried from the tipi, holding her medical basket, teakettle, and tin of tea. "What are you waiting on? We need to soak Jess's foot."

"Shh. . .listen. I hear voices."

The sound of something crashing through the brush behind Mattie made her turn. Her heart jolted. Though he hadn't yet reached them, the man had returned—and he wasn't alone.

Chapter 2

I promise it's not blarney. I saw a tipi—and footprints." Conall glanced at his brother Brian, but he could tell he didn't believe him.

"Then why did you not see any Indians?"

"Like I said, they either were hiding, gone, or something happened to them."

"Ah now, I think you're pulling my leg, as they say in these parts." Brian grinned.

A screech tore through the peaceful woods, and both brothers spun toward the eerie cry. "Sounds like they're on the warpath." Brian reached for the pistol in the holster on his hip.

"Ah. . .so you believe me now, do you?"

Conall nudged his horse to a trot. That cry had sounded more like someone in pain than an attack, and since he still hadn't seen any Indians, he suspected his hunch was right. They rode down the path, and he saw the top of the tipi up ahead. He pulled his gun from his waistband, just in case. They broke through the trees, and he saw an Indian dressed in buckskin clothing holding a child in his arms.

He reined his horse to a quick stop, as did Brian. The Indian wearing pants was a woman—a woman with long blond braids, blue eyes, and skin tanner than he'd ever seen on a white woman.

He glanced at Brian. His brother twisted his mouth and shrugged.

Squaws rarely traveled alone—he knew that much about Indians—so where were their men? Were these women captives who'd been stolen from their families at a young age?

The squaw holding a basket and other items suddenly dropped them and shinnied up the nearest oak tree, faster than any cat he'd ever seen. He stared up into the branches, wondering what had inspired her to do such a thing. His sister wouldn't be caught dead up a tree. Conall shook his head and dragged his gaze back to the other woman. His heart lurched. She no longer held the child but rather a gun—and it was aimed at him.

"Conall." Brian's soft warning came too late.

He lowered his weapon but kept it handy on his lap. "We don't mean you any harm."

Brian leaned over. "Maybe they don't speak English."

The child moaned and grabbed her leg. Conall gazed at her swollen ankle. If he wasn't mistaken, it was broken. He refocused on the woman who seemed to be in charge. "We'd like to help the girl. We have a cottage a short ways from here, and my sister is quite good at doctoring."

"And one of our closest neighbors is an old army doc," Brian said. "He could help, too."

The tree rustled as the other woman climbed down and then dropped to the ground. Conall looked from one female to the other. Both were lovely, and there was no doubt these two were twins. They looked younger than Brian. In fact, he doubted they'd even reached twenty yet. What were they doing here?

"The child is in pain." Conall softened his voice, hoping they wouldn't see him as a threat. "And we have laudanum."

The twin from the tree walked over to her sister and whispered in her ear. The woman with the gun scowled and shook her head.

Conall glanced around, hoping to find some sign they had a man with them, but if not for the tipi, the items the woman dropped, and the pile of half-cracked pecans, he wouldn't have known anyone had been living here. They must have kept the area clean for that purpose. "Do you have a man to take care of you?"

The twin with the gun yanked her gaze back to his. Sharp blue-jay colored eyes assessed him. He smiled, but it didn't ease her somber expression. She flicked the gun in the air, indicating for him to leave.

He hated abandoning them when he knew they could help the child, but what more could he do if they didn't want his help?

"What if we go and get Glynna? Could be they'd be more willing to accept a woman's assistance," Brian said.

"I don't even know as they understood a word we said."

"Then we should go. It's obvious they don't trust us."

Conall blew out a sigh and nodded. He stuck his gun back into his waistband and looked at the woman again. "We have a cottage just a short ways from here. Follow this path, and it will take you there. Please come if you'd like us to help you."

Brian reined his horse back toward home. Conall sat there a moment longer, feeling like he was in a standoff. What were they so afraid of that they were willing to let the girl suffer?

He turned his horse toward home. Maybe they wouldn't accept his aid, but at least he could pray for them.

❧

Mattie kept an eye on the last man as Milly tugged on her sleeve. "Why didn't you accept their offer?"

Mattie snapped her gaze to her sister's. Looking into Milly's face was kindred to gazing into a mirror. "You know what Papa always told us—avoid men at all cost."

"But those two sounded kind—and they were quite handsome." A rosy glow tinged Milly's cheeks. "Don't you think?"

Blowing out a loud breath, Mattie ignored her sister's pointless question. "Let's get Jess to the creek."

"But if they know of a doctor. . ." Milly nibbled her lower lip. "I don't know how to set a bone."

Mattie gave her sister a hug. "It might have all been a lie, just to get us to go along with them. Let's get Jess to the creek, then I'll follow the trail and see if it leads to a cabin."

"All right."

A short while later, Mattie stood at the edge of the tree line starring at a cabin. Behind it sat a barn, and all around were fallow fields. She followed the tree line around to the east side of the house. A privy sat between her and the cabin. If only she could get there without being seen. She lifted the twine that held the gun over her neck. Then with a final look around, she darted across the field. Her feet sunk in the soft earth, slowing her steps, but she made it to the back of the privy without anyone crying alarm.

A door banged, and Mattie jumped. She peered around the side of the wooden structure, holding her breath. Even though it was December and cool out, the privy still reeked. The man she'd seen twice now stepped off the side of the porch.

"And why did you not bring them here?" A woman followed the boss man into view.

He walked along the side of the cabin, eating up the ground with his long-legged gait. The woman rushed to keep up.

"Conall. Stop."

He spun around. "I already told you. Either they didn't want our assistance, or they couldn't understand what I was saying."

"So you just left them there, and with a hurting child?"

"What more could I do, Glynna? Throw them on my horse and force them to come?"

The woman's irritation blew away like leaves in a strong gust. "Sure now, I'm sorry. It just pains me to know a child is hurting, and we could help. Maybe I should go to them?"

"No! Not unless I take you."

Mattie bristled. Did he think she'd hurt the woman? Certainly not, unless she had a good reason to.

She wished her father was here. He always dealt with any men who came to their camp while they all hid. Papa would know what to do.

Jess's whimpering still taunted her. Her little sister was brave and hadn't cried, but she was suffering. If these people had laudanum, that alone could ease her pain. And if her sister's ankle wasn't set properly, would she be able to walk once it healed? The thought of her lively sister being forced to sit all day and never run or climb trees again twisted in her stomach like a knife.

She leaned against the building. What should she do? Papa taught her the first rule was always to keep her sisters safe. If she allowed these people to help them, would she be compromising their safety?

The man called Brian strode out of the barn, leading a different horse than he'd previously ridden. "I'm going over to Doc Scott's place and see what he thinks."

"Try to bring him back." The woman hurried over to the man's side and rested her hand on his shoulder. "Maybe he can talk those women into letting him help the girl. He was a doctor in the army."

"We know that, Glynna," the man with the horse said. "That's why I'm going."

Milly thought they should trust the men, and she was usually a good judge of character. Heaving a sigh, Mattie hid her gun beneath her shirt and stepped out into the open.

Three sets of eyes swiveled in her direction. The man who seemed the leader walked toward her, making no move toward the weapon resting in his waistband. He smiled, and she realized Milly was right. He was a handsome man, with that thick, curly dark hair and blue eyes. She wanted to trust him, but she'd never relied on a man other than her father or uncle before. She swallowed hard.

"Good day to you." The man tipped his cap. "I don't believe I properly introduced myself earlier. I'm Conall Donegan; this here's my sister, Glynna; and Brian, my wee brother." Brian frowned, which made Mattie want to smile, but she fought to maintain a sober expression.

"Have you come to ask our help with the child?"

Mattie nodded. "Yes. She is my sister Jess."

Conall's brows lifted. "So you do speak English?"

Mattie scowled. Wasn't that obvious since she'd just spoken to him?

Brian strode forward. "I'm riding over to the doc's right now. Bring your sister to the house, and we'll meet you here. Glynna can care for her until we return."

Mattie searched the eyes of each Donegan, looking for signs of trickery or falsehood, but all three held the same open, friendly gaze. She felt certain she could trust this family. "We will stay at our camp. Bring the man to us."

She ducked back into the trees before they could object. It would be much easier on Jess not to have to ride all this way, and Mattie felt safer in woodlands.

She could only hope she hadn't made a terrible mistake.

Chapter 3

Mattie stared up at the dreary pewter sky. The air held the scent of rain. She needed to check on the horses—to move them to a new spot of winter grass, but her wooden legs refused to budge. Jess had cried out several times from inside the tipi where the doctor was tending her, but all had been quiet for some time now.

Mattie bent down and yanked free a stem of dried yellow grass and plucked seed after seed off. How long would it take that doctor to finish setting Jess's ankle?

Staring at the tipi, she wished she had stood her ground and stayed inside instead of abiding by the doctor's request that only Milly assist him. Mattie forced her tense body to relax. Of course it should be Milly. Her sister knew far more about tending ailing folks.

"Your sister will be fine."

Spinning around, she was surprised Conall Donegan had sneaked up on her. She rarely got so lost in thought that she was caught unaware, and that only increased her anxiety. What if he'd meant to harm her? Her father had warned her so many times to beware of men and to avoid them.

He smiled, relieving her concerns, and his blue eyes lit up in an intriguing manner. He was much calmer than the other men she'd met, and worries rolled off him like rain on the oiled canvas of their tipi. "I've been prayin' for your sister, and I believe the good Lord means to heal her leg."

"How do you know?" Her mother had been a praying woman and believed in God, but not her father. Mattie had tried talking to God on different occasions, but He never answered her requests, so she had quit asking for His help.

Conall gazed at the sky. He wasn't a stocky man but had wide shoulders that looked accustomed to hard work. He cleared his throat. "The Bible says to 'ask and ye shall receive.'" He looked down again, his blue eyes capturing hers, and then he smiled, revealing his straight white teeth. "And I believe God's Word."

Mattie's heart flip-flopped. Conall Donegan was a handsome man and talked to her so freely. She'd rarely conversed with the men who visited their camp. Her father always dealt with them. Milly would serve them food and drink, while Mattie generally hid out in the trees with her Hawken rifle, keeping watch in case the men attempted to overpower her pa.

"We are all God's children, Miss Carson. And like any good father, He cares for His children."

"Your faith is strong."

He cocked a brow, as if asking, "And yours isn't?"

The tipi's opening flapped back, and the doctor crawled out. He rose and pushed his fist in the small of his back. The man Conall had called Edward Scott ambled toward them. Wrinkles creased his leathery skin and bags rested beneath kind brown eyes. "Your sister's ankle is broken, but I fully expect her to recover and be able to use it again, providing she stays off it for the next month or so. No walking."

Thoughts stampeded across her mind faster than an elk fleeing a hungry wolf. That meant no tree climbing. No hiding from strangers. And keeping their active sister off her feet would be no easy task.

"You understand?" Dr. Scott raised his voice.

Mattie nodded.

"Good. I set and wrapped your little sister's foot and ankle. Don't remove the binding, even if she complains about it. I'll come back and check on it in a week. I left your sister Millicent some laudanum to give Jessamine for the pain."

"Thank you." Mattie ducked her head. She hadn't gotten used to being in one man's presence, much less two. If only her father were here. What would he do if he were? She suddenly realized she owed the doctor for his services. "I have no money, but I do have a deer I killed this morning. Will you take that as payment?"

He nodded, and Mattie relaxed, even though losing the deer meant they had no meat for today and no hide for Jess's pants.

Milly exited the tipi. "If you can wait around for a little while, Doctor, I'll prepare some coffee for you and a bite to eat."

He glanced up at the sky. "Thank you, but I should be getting home. Looks like we're in for a toad strangler tonight."

A heavy rain would only make hunting and tending Jess more difficult, but there was little Mattie could do about that. "If you'll follow me, Doctor, I'll take you to the deer. It should be bled out by now." Mattie waited for his nod then started up the path to where she'd hung the deer. Like her father had taught her, she never hung a carcass near their camp in case a wolf or bear caught the scent and came hunting for it.

"Conall," she heard the doctor say, "be seeing you around." Hoofbeats soon followed her, and ten minutes later, she reached the spot where the deer hung. She climbed the tree, untied the rope, and then lowered down the carcass. The deer would have fed them for several days—longer if they'd been able to make jerky, but now she'd need to go hunting again. Unless she found something before the rains came, supper tonight would be slim fare.

"I don't hardly feel right taking the whole deer." The doctor dismounted and rubbed his whiskers.

"You said you have to return. You will earn it."

He studied her for a moment then nodded. He secured the carcass behind his saddle then remounted. After a tip of his hat, he reined his horse back up the path and soon disappeared through the trees.

Mattie blew out a sigh then walked down to the clearing to check on the horses. She untied the hobbles on each one and led them to the creek to drink and then to a new patch of winter grass. With Jess injured, she and her sisters would have to stay here longer than they'd planned. She needed to build some kind of enclosure rather than keeping her horses hobbled, but Conall Donegan had said this was his land. How would he feel about them living on it for a month? But what choice did they have?

If he wanted them off his land, she could build a travois for Jess to ride on, since sitting on the back of a horse would probably cause her ankle to hurt with all the flopping around it would do.

She rechecked the hobbles, making sure her horses were secure, then walked back to camp. Conall was gone, but his sister and brother had arrived—and a delicious aroma made her stomach complain of its emptiness.

Milly smiled and rushed to her side. "Glynna Donegan has brought us some stew." She wrinkled her forehead. "She called it Bubble and Squeak, such an odd name for the cabbage and potato mixture, but it does smell tasty."

Mattie stared at Glynna's backside as the woman stirred the pot cooking on a new campfire someone had built. She wondered how Glynna managed to keep from catching her wide skirt on fire. Mattie frowned, glad she didn't have to mess with all that fabric. Climbing a tree would be nearly impossible, as would sneaking through the woods or riding astride.

First, Brian Donegan had fetched Dr. Scott, and now his sister was cooking for them. Mattie didn't like being beholden to the Donegan family. What would they require in exchange for the niceties they were doing?

Milly shook her shoulder. "Did you hear me?"

"Yes. How's Jess?"

"Better. Resting." Milly turned and watched Glynna then moved closer to Mattie. She picked up one of her braids and rolled it around her finger. "I wonder how my hair would look done up like Glynna's. And don't you love her dress? It's the exact same color as a bluebird, and it's so, so feminine."

"*Humph.* Looks dangerous to me."

"You're impossible. You'll never catch the eye of a man with that attitude." Milly sighed. "I think we should take the Donegans up on their offer to stay with them. Jess would be warmer and much more comfortable in a soft bed than lying on furs on the ground."

Mattie turned and caught her sister's eye. They hadn't known the Donegans a full day, and Milly was ready to take up their way of living. "We're staying here unless they tell us we must leave their land. I'll not be any more beholden to those people than we already are."

"Then we should take Jess to a town and get a room in a boardinghouse."

"No!"

"But—"

Mattie gave a quick shake of her head, cutting off her sister. "Pa left me in charge. We're staying put."

Spinning around, Mattie stomped off, in spite of how her stomach grumbled at leaving behind such enticing food. She'd find some dried berries or maybe catch a fish for dinner, but she wouldn't touch the Donegans' food.

Down at the creek, she sat on the bank holding a cane rod over the water. The wind had picked up, chilling her to the bone, and a few sprinkles dampened her hair. She had never felt so overwhelmed. The cheerless iron-colored sky mirrored her emotions, but Conall's gentle encouragement that God cared what happened to them gave her a measure of hope. "God, are You really up there? Do You care about us like Ma used to say?"

Tears burned her eyes, even though she never cried, not even when she sliced her palm with her knife the first time she tried to skin a rabbit. "Show me what to do."

Some time later, Mattie shivered and awoke to rain splattering her face. She wiped her eyes and realized she must have dropped the fishing pole after falling asleep. She would have to look for it tomorrow after the sun came out, since that pole held her last hook. Hurrying up the slippery path, she was thankful for her buckskins and how they shed water.

Just before she reached the tipi, the skies opened up. She dove under the flap covering the opening then set several stones along the bottom lip to secure it back into place. The warmth of the fire heated her back, stealing away the cold chill. Mattie squeezed what water she could from her braid then looked across the small fire at her sisters. All she could make out of Jess was the top of her head as she huddled under a heavy bearskin. Milly lay between Jess and the fire to protect their little sister, who tended to roll around in her sleep.

Rain pelted the outside of the tipi. The canvas walls lit up from lightning then went dark again. Mattie added several pieces of wood they'd collected earlier to the fire, warming her chilled flesh. Droplets of water fell down from the opening overhead and hissed as they hit the fire. Thankfully the rain came at an angle and not straight down, or they would have a lot more water to deal with. Mattie removed her muddy moccasins and crawled under an elk hide. She couldn't help being a little envious of the Donegans and their cabin. Was she wrong to make her sisters stay here?

She yawned, exhausted from the stress of the day. Tomorrow she would have to endure the mud and go hunting again. Maybe tomorrow her father would return.

❧

Conall rode into the Carsons' camp and waved at one of the twins, who tossed an animal hide over a shrub. He hadn't yet figured out how to tell them apart. The woman smiled. "Ah, Milly, right?"

"How did you know?"

He slid to the ground and tied his horse to a sapling. "You tend to smile, while your sister frowns at me."

"Don't think the worst of Mattie. She has a lot of responsibility with our father gone and now with Jess hurt."

He picked up a wet hide from the pile on the ground and threw it over another skeleton of a shrub. "I see that last night's rain got inside your tipi. I wondered about that, since you have a hole in the top."

Milly nodded and brushed her hands together, glancing past Conall down the trail. "Is Brian coming to visit?"

Conall shook his head. "He's mending some shakes that the wind blew off the roof during the storm. Wild, wasn't it?"

Milly shrugged and smiled. "I slept through—at least until the rain started gushing through the hole and put out our fire."

"How's your sister?"

"Which one?"

Conall wanted to ask about Mattie, considering it was odd that he hadn't seen her yet. "Is Jess faring well?"

Milly wrapped her arms around herself. "I'm worried about her. We got so much rain last night that it seeped under the tipi, and Jess's hair was wet, as were her buckskins. She has a fever now, and I can't get a fire going in the tipi because things are so damp."

"You should bring her to our cabin. It's warm and dry. Your sister can have my bed."

Milly shook her head. "Mattie doesn't want to leave here, in case our father returns."

Conall considered what to say to sway the woman. The girl needed to be somewhere warm. "Do you always do what Mattie says?"

Shrugging, Milly stared off toward the trees. "Father put her in charge. I'm good at cooking, sewing—domestic things, but. . ." She picked up one braid and brushed the end of it across her lips. "Mattie is smart. That's why Pa put her in charge, and it was the right choice. She can hunt, fish, track, and she doesn't get flustered like I do."

She was right. Mattie's self-control was what attracted him to her—that and those intense blue eyes that seemed to stare right through a man's soul and find him lacking. He wanted to prove to her that he could be trusted. "Try to talk her into bringing Jess to our place. We're happy to have you. Brian and I can move to the barn—or maybe the dugout we lived in before building the cabin—so you won't have to worry about us. Glynna would enjoy the company of other women. She gets lonely."

He knew by Milly's reaction that the words had hit home, and he also knew that she was more sympathetic of others' feelings—yet another reason Mattie should be in charge. She wasn't swayed by emotions.

He cleared his throat. "Where is Mattie?"

Cocking her head, Milly stared at him a moment, and then a knowing smile pulled at her lips. "She was out late, probably hunting since she gave our deer to the doctor, so she's still resting. She came in sometime after I went to sleep."

Conall didn't like the idea of Mattie out after dark all alone. What if she encountered a pack of wolves? Or one of the groups of cowboys or other men who often traveled through central Oklahoma Territory as they journeyed from Texas to Kansas?

His mother had drilled into them that a man cares for a woman, no matter what. But how was a man supposed to do that when the woman refused his help? Brain had asked that once, Conall remembered. "Shower her with kindness," had been his mam's response. Conall smiled. "Is there anything I can do to help you?"

"Thank you for your assistance with the furs. They're heavy when they're wet." Milly nibbled her lip and looked around. Her eyes brightened. "Would you have any dry wood we could use? Ours is almost used up, and what's out here is soakin' wet. I'd like to keep Jess warm."

"I do have some—quite a lot, actually. I'll return home and fetch it, and maybe by then Glynna will have some food ready to send."

The flap on the tipi flew up and stuck to the wet side. Mattie climbed out, her hair mussed and in bare feet. She splashed over to him. "I can take care of my family."

Conall wondered why Mattie found accepting their help so difficult. It's what people out here on the prairie did. They survived by neighbor helping neighbor.

Mild-mannered Milly surprised him and took a step toward her sister, her expression hardening. "No, you listen, Matilda Carson. Jess woke up cryin', wet with a fever. She needs to be some place dry. You don't want her to get worse and d–die, do you?"

Mattie's tanned skin turned pale, and her eyes widened. She stared at her sister for a moment then glanced at him. Conall smiled, hoping to dispel her fears. "She can have my bed, and my brother and I can stay—"

"I heard." Mattie lifted her chin. "Why do you want to help us?"

Conall considered what to say that wouldn't push her away. "Because we're Christians, and it's what people out here do. We have to help one another, or none of us would be able to make it."

Mattie crossed her arms. "And what do you want in exchange?"

He blinked, trying to make sense of her question. He held out his hands. "Nothing. It gives us pleasure to know that we helped someone in need. My family wants to help yours, and we don't expect a thing a'tall in return." Conall winced at how his Irish accent was more prominent when he was flustered. How was it this stubborn snippet of a woman could agitate him when he was trying to do them a favor?

Mattie held his gaze. She twisted her lips up on one side, and a number of expressions crossed her pretty face. "Fine. We will stay with you, but we're taking all of our belongings with us."

Chapter 4

Where did she get those horses?" Brian nudged his chin toward the two large bays that pulled the Carsons' belongings toward their cabin.

"From a leprechaun, if you ask me." Conall leaned back against the barn and grinned. "It's fascinating how they pack up that tipi and use the poles to make a travois."

Brian nodded. "It's good they brought the little girl to our cabin, although I don't look forward to sleeping in the barn. I'll miss my bed."

"Maybe we should ask to borrow one of the Carsons' bear hides to sleep on. Better that than getting poked by hay."

"Be my guest. Can you just imagine what those must smell like? I'll settle for a wool blanket or two."

Conall pushed away from the barn, remembering the pungent odor of the hide he'd thrown over a bush earlier, and walked toward the Carson women. He'd offered to help pack up the tipi, but Mattie had insisted she and her sister could do it—and she'd been correct.

"How's Jess?" one of the twins asked.

"Sleeping, last time Glynna looked in on her."

He stared at the twins as they stood side by side. Their similarity was uncanny. The twin on the right—the one with a tiny mole under her left eye—blushed under his perusal, while the other scowled, and then he knew which was which. If Mattie ever smiled at him, he'd think she was Milly, but there was as much chance of that as there was that he'd find a pot of gold at the end of an Oklahoma rainbow.

"Do you want to set up the tipi again?"

Mattie eyed the sky. "It will be dark soon. We will lay out the lodge poles and spread the canvas across them for tonight."

"Can we be of assistance?" Conall asked.

Mattie stared at him for a long moment, and he struggled to hold her gaze. He'd never met a woman like her. Strong, tenacious, beautiful. Finally, she nodded and turned back to her horse and began untying the long poles that held up the tipi. They clattered to the ground, and the horse that had pulled them didn't flinch a muscle. How many times had the bay borne that load and had the poles dropped to the ground near his hooves?

Mattie lifted the end of one pole then glanced at him. "Where should we put it?"

He scanned the yard then pointed to the right of the house. A large open area close to one of the turned-under fields would work. "There."

Mattie and Milly both dragged a ten-foot-long rod over to the place he'd indicated, dropped it, then returned for another. Conall grabbed three poles and placed them next to theirs. In just a few minutes, they had the posts all aligned and the tipi laid out across them.

Conall dusted his palms, rubbing them together. "See, an extra set of hands helps finish a task quicker."

"Thank you for helping us." Milly smiled. "I'm going to look in on Jess."

"I'll go, too," Mattie muttered. She followed her sister then paused, looking back at him, and gave a brief nod.

He repeated the action, and much to his surprise, a tiny smile quirked at the corner of her lips. The difference was startling, and it stirred something deep in his gut. He stood taller as he watched her walk toward the cabin. How was it he was attracted to one twin and not the other when they so closely resembled one another?

He had wanted to marry for a long time, but until he had land and a home, he had little to offer a woman. Now he had both but found himself attracted to a woman dressed in buckskin britches whose home traveled on tree limbs behind a horse. He shook his head and walked back to the barn. The only reason Mattie had stepped inside his home was because her sister was injured and ill. He doubted she'd ever consent to living in a cabin, and he was foolish to allow his heart to stray in her direction.

&

Conall sat at the table, staring into his half-emptied cup of coffee. Mattie had shoveled down her breakfast and hurried out the door to who knew where. The woman drove him crazy. How was he supposed to protect her when she gallivanted alone all over the prairie?

He blew out a sigh. She didn't want his protection, and he knew it, but was a man supposed to change his nature to suit one puny female? He had offered to go hunting with her, but she was used to being alone.

"I love lookin' at your books," Jess said, her voice carrying from his and Brian's bedroom. "We only have one book—*Swiss Family Robinson*, but I love to have my sisters read it over and over."

Where Mattie was stoic and silent, her youngest sister was cordial and chatty. Milly fell somewhere in between the two in personality.

"Is that why you climb trees?" Glynna asked.

Milly walked out of the room carrying Jess's breakfast plate and set it on the table. She smiled. Conall stood. "How long do you think Mattie will be gone?"

"Don't worry about her. She's been wandering off, hunting and fishing, since she was younger than Jess. I used to fuss about it, but our pa said let her be. She can take care of herself."

He nodded but wondered how she could so easily watch her sister leave all the time. What if something happened? How would Mattie get back? What would Milly do if—God forbid—Mattie never returned one day? He cleared his throat and decided to ask a question that had been on his mind since he first met the Carson women. "What happened to your father?"

Milly shrugged and dropped down into the chair across the table, so Conall sat, too. "We don't know. He went hunting one day and never came back. He's never left us this long before."

"You're worried something happened to him?"

She nodded. "But I don't dare tell Mattie that. She firmly believes he'll return. It's why she's so adamant about not leaving the area—and why I'm so ever grateful that you and your kind siblings have taken us in." She looked in the direction of the cabin's front window. "If Pa hasn't returned by the time Jess is well, I doubt he ever will."

The despondency in her voice created an ache in Conall's chest. He knew what it was like to lose a parent—both parents, actually. "May I ask what happened to your mother?"

"She died shortly after Jessamine was born. Back then, we lived in a cozy house in Michigan. Pa was a trapper and gone for weeks on end. Ma taught school to Mattie and me, as well as to four neighbor children to earn some extra money."

"How did you end up living in a tipi?"

"After our mother died, Pa didn't want to leave us alone. He found an Indian woman to wet-nurse Jess and then packed us all up and took off for the hills."

Conall took a sip of his lukewarm coffee as he pondered how hard things must have been in the early days that the Carsons lived on the trail. "How did your father learn how to live off the land?"

Milly stacked up the dirty plates. "You may have heard of Kit Carson. He's a famous frontiersman, and he's my father's kin. He taught him much about nature and living in the wild. Mattie took to it like a duckling to water, but it was much more difficult for me. I was always closer to Ma than she was, and I missed her so much." Her eyes glistened. She popped up and carried the dishes over to the dry sink.

No wonder Mattie was so independent. "Oh, Brian asked me to tell you that he's out in the barn and would like to talk with you."

Milly spun around, all trace of tears gone. "He did? Well then, I should go see what he wants." She untied the apron Glynna had loaned her, patted her hair, then scurried out the door. Conall smelled a romance brewing between his brother and Mattie's sister, but he wasn't sure how he felt about it. Milly seemed much more willing to adopt to their style of living than her sister. If things became serious between his brother and Milly, what would happen to Mattie and Jess? It would be nearly impossible for Mattie to hunt *and* care for a nine-year-old all by herself—but he was certain she'd find a way to do so.

Glynna glided into the room. "Where is Milly off to?"

"I told her Brian wanted to talk with her, and you'd've thought someone had lit her skirts afire the way she scurried outside." He chuckled.

Eyes twinkling, Glynna waggled her eyebrows. "Wouldn't it be lovely if romance was blossoming?"

Conall sobered, causing Glynna to do the same. "I don't see how it would all work out." Time to change the subject. "Something's bothering me."

"What's that?"

"With the poor harvest we had this fall, I don't know how long our food will last now that we've twice as many folks to feed. We could have managed with just the three of us, but now. . ."

"Don't you be worrying, Conall. The good Lord will provide."

"Then He'd best get to work." Conall knew that his tone bordered on irreverence, but he was worried about their dwindling food supplies—and there was precious little money to buy more. With the heat of the long summer and lack of rain, their crops hadn't yielded what he'd hoped they would. How would he feed six people with the little stored in their dugout?

The door opened, and Mattie strode in as if she'd lived there all her life. He doubted it ever occurred to her to knock and wait for someone to answer. But from what he'd observed so far, that was Mattie. She plowed her way through and did what had to be done.

She aimed straight for the kitchen and flipped a bag off her shoulder onto the table with a loud thump. She pulled a fat, plucked turkey out of the bag then turned and walked outside again.

Conall glanced at Glynna and found her eyes sparkling, a smirk on her face. "As I said so shortly ago, the Lord provides, brother. He does indeed."

⁓

Mattie finished the last line of the chapter and peeked over the top of the book at Jess. Her sister's eyes were closed, the heavy breath of sleep upon her. Love for Jess warmed Mattie's heart, but keeping her sister still was getting increasingly difficult. If not for the books the Donegans had loaned them, it would have been nigh impossible.

She quietly closed the book and set it on the side table, grimacing when the bed creaked as she stood. Tiptoeing from the room, she was thankful for Jess's improved health. As much as she didn't want to admit it, bringing her to the Donegans' warm cabin had helped her sister, but the walls were closing in on Mattie. She shut the bedroom door and glanced around the combined parlor/kitchen for Milly or Glynna.

Outside, Mattie looked for the women but again saw neither. She ducked inside the tipi and retrieved the two arrowheads, a pair of shafts she'd whittled from tree limbs, and a couple of leather strips, and then she sat on a deerskin she'd dragged outside. She'd seen several flocks of geese fly overhead and hoped to take one down for tomorrow's meals. Taking a bird down with an arrow was more difficult then with a bullet, but it meant the meat didn't carry the scent of gunpowder.

The sound of voices pulled her gaze from the sky. Mattie's jaw tightened as Milly and Brian strolled out of the barn, walking far too close to one another for casual conversation. She scowled at her sister's attire—a dark blue calico that Glynna had traded to Milly for two coon hides that would have brought them some good money for supplies. What did Milly need with a fabric dress? She certainly couldn't climb a tree in it or traipse around the woods in search of berries or wild onions. Milly giggled and swished her hips like some flirting ladies she'd once seen in Kansas City.

She needed to have a talk with her twin. It wouldn't do her sister any good to get attached to the Donegans and their way of living when they would be leaving next month. Milly and Brian walked along the far side of the house and out of view, but that didn't ease Mattie's concern. It only made things worse.

The dried grass crunched as Conall ambled out of the woods toward her in his constant relaxed state, which never failed to intrigue her. He was the obvious head of his family, and though he worked hard, he never seemed to worry or feel burdened providing for them. Was that just his manner, or was it simply because he was a man? In some ways, Conall reminded her of her pa.

"What are you doing there?" He squatted down and picked up an arrowhead. "Did you find those around here?"

Mattie tensed. Did he think she was stealing from him? "No, I've seen few signs of Indians in these parts. I found those up in the Dakota Territory."

He whistled through his teeth. "That's a ways from here. Oh, and the Dakotas were split up and made into two states last month."

Jerking her gaze toward his, Mattie saw no deception in his beguiling blue eyes. He was just relaying news—news that she hadn't heard—and not trying to best her with his knowledge like some men would do. Mattie slit one end of the shaft and stuck the narrow, flattened end of the arrowhead in it, then picked up a thin strip of leather and began wrapping it around the shaft to secure the two pieces.

"I've never seen anyone make an arrow before. Mind if I try it?"

Mattie did but shrugged one shoulder.

Conall picked up her knife, slit the top of the second shaft, and stuck the last arrowhead in it. He reached for a length of leather, and the arrowhead plopped onto the ground. He frowned, picked it up, and stretched for the leather again, but this time he wobbled and lost his balance, falling onto his side with an *oomph*.

Mattie tried not to laugh, but a giggle slipped out. Instead of getting angry, Conall lithely hopped up and bowed in her direction, as if he'd planned the feat just to entertain her. This time he grabbed the leather and sat down beside her, watching closely as she wove the leather around, through a loop, and pulled it tight and then repeated the process. He leaned closer, his arm touching hers, making her insides fidget. He was no threat—she knew that now—yet he still made her nervous.

As he watched her work, she sidled a glance at his profile. He didn't look as rugged as many of the men they crossed paths with, but he was still manly. His nose was straight and rounded on the end, his lashes long and dark, and his almost ebony hair flopped over across his forehead in a boyish manner. His gaze swiveled sideways, latching on to hers. Mattie felt certain her heart had just dislodged itself and dropped into her belly. His breath warmed her cheeks, and a light kindled deep in his eyes. His gaze dropped down to her lips, stealing away Mattie's breath. Suddenly, Conall blinked, as if surprised to catch himself staring, and turned away.

Mattie swallowed. What just happened? And why did she react as she did? Her insides swirled like dirt caught up in a dust devil. She liked Conall more than she cared to admit. He was kind and gentle, and he made her smile at times. Even though she rejected his offer to help most times, the fact that he offered made her feel good. No man other than her father had treated her like Conall did. She was attracted to the handsome man. Was it possible he felt the same about her?

The thought was so far-fetched—created such a riot of confusion in her— that she tossed aside the arrow she was working on and shot to her feet. She needed to get away and all but ran to the barn to check on her horses. Quick footsteps followed her, and she wished more than anything that the Donegans hadn't cleared this part of their land and that there was a bushy tree she could climb.

Chapter 5

Mattie. Wait!" Conall hadn't meant to offend her, and judging by the way she stormed off, he certainly had. He hadn't meant to stare, either, but she was so pretty—so intriguing. He wanted to know everything about the courageous, closed-mouth woman, but getting her to talk was about as easy as trying to pluck a live turkey. Her steps slowed. He pulled even with her and lightly took hold of her arm to keep her from fleeing again. "Did I say or do something that upset you?"

She shrugged and wouldn't look at him.

Conall lifted up his cap and ran his hands through his hair. He had little experience with women and had no idea what to say to make Mattie more at ease around him. When he'd turned and looked her straight in the face, he hadn't expected the lightning bolt that sent charges of delicious attraction zigzagging through his body. And when his gaze landed on her lips—by Paddy's pig, he'd wanted to kiss her, then and there, where anyone could have seen them. But Mattie probably would have scalped him. How could he expect her to be comfortable around him when being around her made him jittery?

But truth be told, she had stared back, and with longing, if he wasn't mistaken.

"What are you grinning at?" Mattie shoved her hands to her hips.

Conall sobered. He didn't realize his delight at discovering Mattie might feel a little something for him had been reflected in his expression. In Gaelic, he crooned, "Ah now, what's not to be happy about?"

"Huh? Speak English?"

Conall chuckled and decided to impress her with his Irish accent. "And what would be the pleasure in that, me lady? Such a fine mornin' 'tis. And well it deserves the lyrical tongue of one such as I, born in the fine land of Erin."

A tiny smile danced in one corner of Mattie's pretty mouth; then she shook her head and mumbled, "Numskull." She strode back to her tipi, gathered up the arrow supplies, and then ducked inside. Milly had shown it to him and Brian yesterday. He could see the practicality of living in such a home, especially if one moved from place to place, but he still preferred the security of a wood cabin.

As he waited for Mattie to come back, he studied the thin canvas flap. While it might work well as a door for privacy, it was a poor barrier. If a wolf—or man—wanted in, little would keep him out—except Mattie's rifle. A shiver snaked down Conall's back. It was one thing for two women to live out in the wild with their father, but it was something else for them to try to manage on their own. If they only had wildlife to be concerned about, they'd probably be safe, but many lonely men had moved to this area—and some of them would do just about anything to have a pretty, resourceful woman like Mattie or Milly by their side. His gut tightened.

Mattie stooped as she crawled out, carrying her bow and a quiver of arrows. She cast a quick glance in his direction. As if dismissing him, she started for the woods, and again, he trailed after her. If she meant to put herself in harm's way, he intended to be there to rescue her, if by chance she needed him.

A few feet into the woods, she suddenly stopped and whirled around, the fringe on her buckskin top slapping the leather. "Why are you still here?"

He could hardly explain that he wanted to protect her, especially since he wasn't carrying his rifle, but neither would he lie to her. "I. . .uh. . .would like to learn how to hunt better. I go out for a full day but don't come back with as much game as you catch in an hour."

"That's because you stomp around the woods like a moose in mating season, scaring away all the game." Her cheeks suddenly reddened.

Conall's mouth gaped open for a moment before he slammed it shut, as he struggled to respond to her scathing accusation. Then he chuckled. This colleen certainly had a blunt way of saying things, and that only made him like her more. So many women he'd met batted their lashes, as if that would help them catch a man, and then they'd prattle about useless drivel like fashion, in which he had no interest. He continued walking, but his foot snagged on a tree root. He stumbled several steps until he grabbed hold of a sapling just off the trail and righted himself. Birds screeched and fled the nearby bushes.

Mattie slowly turned, her eyes narrowed. "You see what I mean? You're frightening away all of the game. If you want meat for your supper, I suggest you go back and let me hunt."

Conall ducked his head, embarrassed that he'd proven her right. It wouldn't do any good to tell her he'd stumbled because he'd been thinking about her—comparing her to other women. He ought to go back home. Plenty of work awaited him, but he didn't want to leave her alone in the woods. Still, he stayed where he was and allowed her to go on without him. He'd wait a few minutes then follow. While assuring himself she was safe, he might also learn a thing or two about hunting. Farming, building things from wood, and laying tracks for the railroad was about all he was proficient in. He'd had precious little time to go hunting since his family moved to the 160 acres he'd won in the April 22 land rush.

Five minutes later, Conall tiptoed down the dirt trail, making sure not to step on twigs or crunchy dried leaves that could alert Mattie to his presence. But as he rounded corner after corner, there was no sign of the vixen. He'd lost her.

❧

Mattie was glad to have shed her shadow. She didn't understand why Conall made her nervous, especially whenever he touched her or was so close she could feel his breath on her cheek. Just the thought of it made her breath catch in her throat and her heart thump. Maybe it happened because he was a man. Her father had warned her about men, but now her family was at the mercy of two of them. She didn't know what to do.

She feared she was losing Milly, and if her middle sister decided to stay with the Donegans, Jess would probably want to also. Both sisters were enamored with the soft beds and felt safer inside the wooden house. Mattie couldn't stand the thought of walking off and leaving them behind. It would be like abandoning them. But neither could she settle here.

There was no easy answer.

Mattie trudged through the dried bushes, halfway wishing she'd let Conall join her. She hated the conflicting feelings raging through her and didn't want to admit that she enjoyed his company. Stooping down, she checked one of her rabbit snares. She clenched her fist. The trap had been sprung, but there was no rabbit. The same was true at the next one, but the dirt was scratched around the snare and small bits of fur clung to the yellowed grass. She gritted her teeth and blew a loud breath from her nose. Someone had stolen her rabbits.

If only a single snare had been sprung, she'd have thought it an accident, but not three. After resetting the trap, she stood and listened. Birds sang in the branches overhead, and two yellow and black goldfinches chased one another from bush to bush. In the distance, Mattie heard a loud crack. She jerked her head in that direction then set off to find the rabbit thief. People who stole from traps might have no qualms about going into a home and helping themselves. If there were vandals on the Donegans' land, Conall and Brian needed to know.

Five minutes later, she crept toward two men in a small clearing. One man was skinning her rabbits, while the other was breaking dead branches for a campfire. Mattie clenched her jaw. That was her family's food and skins, which could be traded for things they needed. But she had to be sensible, and even though she had her bow and arrow, she was no match against two grown men. She took a step backward and rammed into something hard—something that hadn't been there a few moments ago.

"Well, well, lookie what we have here, gents."

❧

Conall followed Mattie's moccasin prints for several minutes, but they suddenly stopped right in the middle of the path. Straightening, he looked around. Mattie couldn't have just up and disappeared, but why did her footprints end? His cap caught on a low-hanging branch, so he reached up and tugged it free. He glanced at the branch for a moment then looked down. The limb stuck out over the path, and it was low enough that Mattie could have jumped up and caught a hold of it. Had she seen or heard something that scared her, causing her to climb to safety?

And if she had, where was she now?

He twisted his mouth to one side as the truth settled on him like a cold fog. She'd deliberately tried to lose him. He crossed his arms and heaved a loud sigh.

"Fine then. If ye do not want my company, ye shall not have it." He spun around and headed back home, irritated that he let Mattie get to him. A man had his pride, after all, and he had work that needed doing. He didn't have time to chase after a stubborn loner who didn't want him around.

After several long strides, his steps slowed. Though his manhood had felt challenged by the intriguing, resourceful woman, he felt a tug—no something stronger—a compelling urgency to find her. He turned back. Had something happened to Mattie?

Walking back down the path, he lifted his gaze upward. "Is that You, Lord? Are You tellin' me that Mattie is in need of my help?"

A fire lit in his gut, and he knew he had to find her. Back at the tree, he studied the branches. Mattie could have climbed through the limbs and dropped down on the other side. He worked his way through the tall, dried grasses and shrubs, walking in widening circles until he found what he was looking for. There. Mattie had dropped down, making heavier impressions in the dirt than when walking. The footprints were hard to follow in the grass, but there was a broken limb on a shrub and another footprint in a bare area, and then she picked up the trail again about a hundred yards from where she'd left it. He walked a short ways and passed several rabbit snares. Mattie's flat footprints surrounded each trap. No wonder she caught so many rabbits. He studied the snare and knew that he could make one of his own; then he continued on. Mattie had veered off to the left for some reason and smashed down the short grass, leaving an easy trail to follow.

Laughter echoed across the hills. Male raucous laughter. Conall froze, listening, trying to determine which direction the noise had come from. Goose bumps charged up his arms. If Mattie had stumbled across a group of men, she'd be defenseless. Hunkering down, he searched for several walnut-sized stones and shoved them in his coat pocket. He crept toward the voices.

His gut clenched when he finally found her. A man held Mattie captive, but she thrashed and struggled, fighting him. The man yanked on one of her braids, and she cried out. She jerked her head back, colliding with his face. He yelled but didn't lose his grip on her. Conall wanted to rush in and rescue her, but that could cause them both to be captured—or worse.

He forced himself to study the scene. Best he could tell, there were three men, but one of them lay on the ground, not moving. Conall didn't know how he could sleep through all the noise. The third man sat across the campfire, skinning rabbits, evidently content to watch the wrestling match between Mattie and his cohort.

Conall wished he'd brought his rifle, but he wasn't totally unarmed. He tugged his slingshot out of his pocket, loaded a stone in it, then jumped up. He made several quick swings, and just as he released the first stone, the man by the fire noticed him. Before he could react, the stone hit its mark. His eyes rolled up in his head, and he fell back.

Chapter 6

Mattie's mind raced, searching for a way of escape, as she struggled with the man who held her. These men were the kind her father had warned her about. Men who took what they wanted and had no respect for women. Men who didn't care who they hurt. Her head ached where she'd rammed the man's face, and she was sure her ribs were close to breaking from his tight grip around her chest.

Three horses tied to nearby trees pranced and snorted, disturbed by the ruckus. Mattie kicked her captor's shin and struggled to break free. He yelped out a curse.

Mattie knew if she didn't get away soon, she'd run out of strength. She closed her eyes. *Help! God, if You're up there, help me.*

The man kissed the back of her neck. Chills marched down her arms, and she jerked her head forward. Her gaze landed on the man's hand. Something her father taught her charged across her mind. One of her arms had broken free, and she reached down and yanked her captor's little finger backward. He roared in pain, dropping her. The moment she hit the ground, she scrambled away and searched for the other men. The one she'd punched in the throat when he'd approached her still lay on the ground unconscious, but where had the other man gone?

She dove toward the man on the ground and tugged his pistol out of the holster. Spinning around, she pointed it at the scoundrel who'd kissed her. Off to her right—glory be!—Conall stood, swinging one arm in a circle. The man who'd held her captive pulled out his own weapon but turned toward Conall. Mattie's heart lurched. Something whizzed through the air and collided with the man's forehead. He grimaced, his eyes rolled up in his head, and then he fell sideways. Jumping to her feet, she frantically searched for the third man. But like her captor, he too lay sprawled on the ground.

Mattie lowered the pistol, every bone and muscle in her body shaking. She dropped to her knees. God had answered her cry for help. She was safe.

Conall rushed to her side and pulled her up. His worried gaze roved her face, down the length of her body and back up. "Are you hurt?"

His concern was her undoing. Tears blurred her view of the handsome man, and she fell against him. If he hadn't come when he had. . . She couldn't bear the thought. He hugged her close, brushing one hand over her mussed hair and murmuring soft comforting words. "You're all right now. They can't hurt you."

Shamelessly, she clung to him, so grateful to have someone else to lean on for a change. Her siblings meant more to her than anything, but being in charge, being the one who had to find food, shelter, and keep them safe, was exhausting. And now this frightening encounter.

When she thought she could stand on her own, she turned loose of Conall, but instantly, she wished he'd pull her back into his arms. Never could she remember being so shaken, not even the day her mother died.

"We must tie up these scalawags before they revive."

Mattie nodded. He was right. Forcing her feet into motion, she searched for a rope. She discovered one still tied to a saddle and tossed it to Conall. He dragged one man over to a tree and tied him up then did the same to a second one. The only other thing she could find to bind the third man were the reins from the horses' bridles. She carried them over to Conall; then she poured some water from a canteen onto her hands and washed her face. She'd need a dip in the stream or the Donegans' washtub to feel clean again.

After all three men had been bound to different trees, Conall walked up to her and ran one hand down the side of her right arm. "Brian and I can return to collect these varmints and take them into Guthrie. Are you ready to head home?"

She licked her lips. Home. If only she had one. A place to call home, not a tipi that could be hauled around from mountains to plains and back. The thought surprised her. Sleeping behind the locked doors of the Donegans' cabin sounded so much safer than spending another night in her family's tipi.

"Mattie? Are you all right?"

Glancing up at Conall, she pursed her lips and forced herself to nod. Then she ducked her head, not wanting him to know she hadn't been totally truthful. Making a wide path around the rousing men, she collected her bow and quiver, and her rabbits, then hurried back to Conall's side. The encounter with the scoundrels had shaken her more than she could ever have imagined. She looked around at the gray barren trees interspersed with a few dark green pines. Would she ever feel safe alone in the woods again?

❧

Mattie sat in a chair next to Jess's bed and watched her sister stitch together two squares cut from rabbit pelts. "You're doing a nice job."

Jess glanced up and smiled. "You think Glynna will like the pillow?"

Mattie brushed her hand down one side of her little sister's head. "She will love it, and it will mean all the more because you made it yourself."

Eyes gleaming, Jess nibbled her lower lip and took another cautious stitch.

Finding tasks to keep her busy was becoming increasingly difficult now that her leg wasn't paining her as much.

Mattie stared at the cabin wall, longing to go hunting but afraid to do so. Since those men had attacked her a week ago, she hadn't wandered any farther than the Donegans' barn to collect her horses and tie them to trees near some winter grass. Even then, when she was close to the tree line, her heart raced and hands shook. One time when she heard a crack in the woods, she nearly ran all the way back to the cabin.

She clenched her fist. She hated feeling vulnerable. Hated how she was afraid to walk in the woods that had always been her refuge. How was she to overcome her fear? When Jess could walk again, they would leave the Donegans, even though Glynna had invited them to stay the winter.

If she didn't get Milly away soon, she never would. Mattie shifted on the hard wooden chair. She found sitting on soft furs on the ground much more comfortable. And though the cabin's bedroom was less drafty, it was chillier than sitting in the cozy tipi with a fire going, except on rainy nights. The heat from the stove didn't reach into this room unless the door remained open.

The soft padding of Milly's moccasins drew her gaze to the door. Her sister smiled as she sashayed toward them in the dark green calico Glynna had given her, the ruffles of her petticoats peeking out every now and then. Her hair, no longer braided, was done up in a knot on the back of her head. Mattie sighed. If not for the moccasins, Milly's transformation to farm woman would be complete.

Dropping down on the end of Jess's bed, Milly smiled, her eyes dreamy. "That Brian Donegan is the nicest man I've ever met. And his eyes are such a lovely shade of blue, although at times, I'd declare they must be gray."

Brian was a handsome man, Mattie would allow, but Conall was much better looking. Both brothers had the same shade of black hair with a hint of curl, but Conall's eyes were a much more vibrant shade of blue than his brother's. And he was at least an inch taller. Mattie scowled. Why was she comparing the two?

Milly reached out and laid her hand on Mattie's arm. "Brian has gone out of his way to let me know that we're welcome to stay the winter. He said Glynna gets lonely and would enjoy the company."

To her thinking, it was Brian who wanted Milly's company. Mattie twisted her lips to one side and shook her head. "When Jess is better, we'll move on. I don't want to abuse the Donegans' hospitality."

Milly shot up and shoved her hands to her hips. "Don't I have a say in the matter? I am the oldest, after all."

Standing, Mattie glanced through the open door to the kitchen, thankful no one was there to overhear them. "Pa put me in charge."

"That doesn't mean you get to make *all* of the decisions."

"I pretty much have since he's been gone."

Milly stamped her foot in a rare display of temper. "Well, I don't want to leave. I'm tired of living in a tipi and wearing buckskins and smelling like an animal. I'm sick of moving all the time and having to lug that heavy tipi and those putrid hides—and—and cooking over a smoky fire." Tears filled her eyes, and she rushed from the room.

Mattie glanced down at Jess, who stared at the doorway, wide-eyed, her sewing forgotten. She licked her lips. "I kind of like it here, too, but I'm tired of being stuck in this bed. Glynna is a good cook, and she bakes treats sometimes."

Eyes stinging from the disagreement with Milly and both sisters' desertion, Mattie forced a smile. "Don't worry about the future, chickadee. Things will work out."

Jess studied her for a moment then shrugged and went back to work on her pillow. Needing time alone, Mattie fled the cabin and hurried to the tipi. Inside, she dropped down the flap and curled up on a bear skin, unable to stem her tears. Everything was falling apart, and she didn't know what to do. A rank odor assaulted her nose. Milly was right about the furs smelling, but she hadn't noticed it until she'd slept several weeks on Glynna's sun-kissed sheets.

Mattie sighed. Surely, Milly understood that they couldn't stay with the Donegans forever. And when they did leave, she'd have to face the woods again. She would need to go hunting, and she'd probably never see Conall or his siblings again. Mattie swallowed hard. Why did things have to become so complicated?

"Um. . .knock, knock."

Recognizing Glynna's voice, Mattie bolted upright, swiping the tears off her face. "Come on in."

Sunlight stretched its warm fingers inside the open flap, and Glynna crawled in. She glanced around the tipi then crept over to sit next to Mattie. Her friendly smile soothed Mattie. "It's rather cozy in here. I can see why you like it."

She tried to look at the place through her friend's eyes. The furs did smell, but they were comfortable—if you didn't mind the fact there were no chairs. And the tipi reeked of smoke from the fires lit on cold nights. Even her buckskins carried a strong, unladylike aroma.

Glynna cleared her throat. "I'm sorry, but I was in my bedroom and overheard some of what Milly said. She's talked to me several times about her desires."

Mattie stiffened. If Glynna came to try to talk her into staying, she was wasting her time. The sooner she and her sisters left, the sooner things would get back to normal.

"I know things have been hard for you since your father has been gone so long." Her eyes dimmed, and she frowned. "It was like that for me when I lost Ben, the man I'd planned to marry."

Mattie sucked in a breath. This was the first she'd heard of Glynna losing her intended, but it made sense that she would have had one, since she was older than her brothers. "I'm sorry."

"Thank you. It was several years ago, although I still miss Ben. But that's not what I wanted to talk about." She smoothed out the wrinkles of her dress and stared up at the hole in the top for a moment. "I never would have made it through those dark days if not for the Lord's help. He was my comfort and strength. My hope for the future."

The moment when Mattie had cried out to God when those men held her captive rushed across her mind. She'd almost forgotten how God had so quickly answered her prayer.

"God loves you and your sisters, Mattie. He will help you understand what to do if you'll seek Him."

Fiddling with a piece of buckskin fringe, Mattie glanced at Glynna. "I asked for His help when those men. . ." She swallowed hard. "He sent Conall to help me."

Glynna's smile warmed Mattie's insides. "I'm so glad to hear that you called upon Him. He longs to help you all the time, like He did then. Just talk to Him as you do me or your sisters. The Bible says that if we believe on the name of God's Son, Jesus, we shall be saved, and we become children of God. I hope you'll consider that. God loves you even more than your own father does." She glanced down, picked a piece of lint off her dark blue dress, and flicked it aside. "Would you like me to pray for you?"

Mattie tensed. "You mean here? Now?"

Glynna nodded, and Mattie did, too. If God would send her a rescuer when she desperately needed one, maybe He would also help her in her day-to-day decisions. Maybe He could help her to not be afraid.

Reaching out to clutch Mattie's hand, Glynna closed her eyes and bowed her head. "Heavenly Father, I beseech You to reveal Yourself to Mattie. Give her the assurance that You love her and care about her future. Help her to know what to do concerning staying the winter with us or moving on. And, Lord, we ask that if it's possible, You bring her father back to her."

That night, as Mattie shared a bed with Milly, she thought about all that Glynna had said. She was so tired of battling her sisters, of making the decisions and carrying the weight of everything on her shoulders. She stared into the darkness of the room but no longer felt alone as she had before Glynna prayed for her. *God, will You help me? Would You accept me as Your child? Show me what to do.*

Chapter 7

This is where we lived when we first claimed this land." Conall lifted the lantern, illuminating Mattie's face. "Someone hewed this dugout from the side of the hill long before we came. What do you think of the place?"

She shrugged. "It would keep the wind out, but I imagine it gets chilly since you can't have a fire in here."

"To be honest, the temperature pretty much stays the same, summer or winter." As he set the lamp down on the battered old table, memories of his first days on this land marched through his mind. They were hardscrabble but rewarding days. He pointed to several shelves along one wall. "As you can see, this is where we store our extra produce and the things Glynna cans."

"Saves you from havin' to dig a root cellar." She smiled, and his insides turned to mush. "Still, I prefer the tipi."

"Do you not like the cabin?"

Mattie walked across the small room and ran her hand along the shelf holding the canned vegetables. "It's a very nice cabin, but it's yours, not mine, so what I think shouldn't matter."

Her opinion did matter, but he wasn't quite ready to tell her that. He needed to analyze his attraction to her and pray before voicing it. "Do you think you could ever be happy living in one?"

She cast him a curious glance; then one side of her pretty mouth cocked up. "Milly sure loves it."

He wasn't interested in what her sister thought, although the news would make Brian happy. His brother had fallen hard for Milly. If the women left at some point, Brian would have a rough time of it. For that matter, he would, too. He liked Mattie far more than he was sure she did him. Everything about her intrigued him—except the thought of her one day riding out of his life.

A strong gust of humid wind blew in the open door like an unwanted visitor. He stepped to the doorway and looked out. The sky had darkened. Ugly grayish-green clouds overhead caused his heart to lurch. He'd only seen those twice before, and the first time had resulted in a cyclone. He grabbed the lantern and clutched Mattie's hand, tugging her outside. "Come on. We need to get to the cabin."

The warm, clammy wind pummeled them, threatening to yank Mattie's hand from his. Her concerned gaze shot upward, and he knew she understood the need to hurry. "Look how fast those clouds are moving. They're the kind you see before a tornado hits. We saw one once in Kansas."

Conall wished they could run, but he didn't want to risk breaking the lantern. Still, he quickened his pace. "From what I've heard from neighbors who have some Indian friends, this warm weather is not common for December." As they neared the barn, he handed the lantern to Mattie. "I'll get the horses inside and lock up."

"No! They'll have a better chance if they're outside."

"I don't have time to argue. They're protected inside."

Mattie shook her head. "Put yours in but leave mine out. They'll find their way to safety."

Conall scowled. "Fine. It will save me time."

As he ran toward the pasture, he argued with himself. Maybe he should just put her horses in the barn, too. Mattie had been in charge so long that she always had to have a say in things. Even his horses had the sense to get inside because they waited at the gate, but Mattie's two bays were nowhere to be seen. He threw open the gate, grabbed the halters of his horse and their big draft horse and all but let them pull him to the barn. He locked them in their stalls, closed the barn windows, and then the double doors.

His gaze lifted toward the heavens. From the looks of things, they didn't have much time.

⁓

Mattie burst through the cabin's door, drawing Milly's and Glynna's surprised gazes. She set the lantern on the table.

"Where's the fire?" Glynna grinned and set down a silver bowl she'd been polishing.

"No fire. A tornado!"

Both women gasped and glanced toward the front door.

"I'll secure the shutters. Get Jess and bring her in here."

"No!" Milly and Mattie shouted in unison.

Mattie glanced at her sister and nudged her chin toward the bedroom. "We need to get outside. Tornadoes destroy buildings."

Glynna clutched her bodice. "We can't go out there. We could get swept up in the storm or hit by debris."

"The dugout is safer." Mattie didn't have time to argue—didn't have time to tell Glynna about the memories she had of seeing much of the town of Irving, Kansas, destroyed after a tornado hit it ten years ago. She had to get her sisters to safety.

Milly had spread a quilt on the floor and set Jess in the middle. Mattie grabbed two corners and then walked her hands up the sides and got a good hold on it. Milly did the same then looked at Mattie. She nodded, and they both lifted the quilt and their sister.

"I'm scared." Jess hugged her doll, eyes wide. Her lower lip trembled.

"We'll be fine, but we must hurry." Shuffling their feet, they hauled her into the great room.

Glynna rushed out of her room, looking frightened. "Where's Conall? Oh, I do hope Brian will have the sense to stay in town until the storm passes."

"It may not even go toward Guthrie. Don't think the worst. Grab the lantern, and come with us."

"No, I can't go." Glynna shook her head and clutched the door frame.

Conall charged in the front door. His brows shot up to his hairline when he looked at Mattie. "Where are you going?"

"The dugout. Buildings are unsafe during a tornado."

He shut the door. "You can't go out there. This cabin is solid. Safe."

Mattie glared at him. "Move out of the way. I thank you for your hospitality, but you can't order us around just because we're in your debt."

He crossed his arms across his chest, as if saying, "Make me."

"Conall. Let them go." Glynna's soft entreaty surprised Mattie after her vehement refusal to leave the house.

Conall pleaded with his eyes for her to stay, but Mattie couldn't let him sway her. She—not him—was responsible for her sisters.

She padded toward him, carrying Jess. "I'm sorry. Please move, Conall."

His eyes blinked several times, but he stepped aside and pulled the door open.

Mattie hated going against his wishes, but she couldn't explain that everything within her was telling her to get out of that cabin. "Come with us. Please."

He shook his head, a sad look in his eyes.

They stepped outside, and Mattie felt sure she had just broken whatever it was that had been growing between them. Already grieving his loss, she glanced up at the clouds then over to Milly.

"Hurry!"

❧

The door to the dugout rattled on its wooden frame. Only the facade of the dirt house was made of wood, and she prayed that it held up under the fierce winds. Debris thumped and thudded against the front of the house, like a bully flinging rocks—a bully angered because it couldn't reach them. Mattie pressed her back against the cool dirt walls, thankful for the protection of the earthen cave. How were Conall and Glynna faring? Should she have listened and stayed with them?

"That wind sounds like the train that passed us in Nebraska, remember?" Jess said, her voice sounding only a little nervous.

"It does." Milly bumped Mattie's shoulder as she hugged Jess, who sat between them. "That train was so big and loud—like a ferocious beast."

"And it was smelly."

Mattie chuckled at Jess's comment, glad for some humor in a tense situation. "It liked to have scared the horses to death."

"And Pa had to chase one down." Milly cleared her throat.

After a long moment when no one talked, Jess said, "What do you think happened to Pa?"

Something whacked hard against the dugout's facade, and they all jumped. The log wall creaked and groaned. If it caved in, they'd be facing the storm with no protection. Mattie closed her eyes in spite of the darkness. *Please, God. Keep the Donegans and us safe.*

"It's almost Christmas," Jess whispered. She sniffled. "I miss Pa."

Mattie groped in the dark for her sister's hand. "We all do, chickadee. Pa will come back to us—if he can."

Jess leaned her head against Mattie's arm. "Do you think he's dead?"

"I don't know." Mattie thought of her hearty father. He'd taught her all she knew about living off the land, and she found it difficult to believe he was dead.

Milly sniffled, and Jess did, too.

"Don't fall apart on me now. Listen, I believe the wind is dying down."

Milly coughed. "So you think the cyclone has passed us?"

The angry black twister Mattie had seen on the horizon as they raced for the dugout had been unlike anything she'd ever encountered. A fat, swirling black beast bent on devouring them. But it hadn't—and it was gone. Mattie sucked in a strengthening breath and stood. She lifted off the wooden brace that had been the only thing keeping the storm out, set it down, then pushed open the door. Sunlight poured in, and only a remnant of clouds remained. Limbs ripped from trees hundreds of feet away, wooden shakes, clothing, and debris of all kinds littered the land. A pitchfork had lodged itself in the dugout's facade, its handle sticking straight out into the air. Something white—one of Glynna's shirt waists—hung from the end of the handle, like a flag of surrender. Only she wasn't sure if it was the pitchfork or the storm that had surrendered. Just past the dugout, she recognized two of the long poles from her tipi lying on the ground. She swallowed hard, thankful they hadn't taken shelter there.

Pulling her gaze away, she looked across the field for the cabin—but it wasn't there. Mattie gasped. A knifelike pain pierced her heart, and she started walking then broke into a run.

"Mattie, what's wrong?" Milly shouted behind her.

Only one thought etched her mind—had Conall and Glynna survived?

Chapter 8

Conall coughed. The darkness faded, and he lifted an arm over his eyes as a brilliant shaft of sunlight bore through the cloud of dust that had enveloped him. Where was he? Why were his clothes wet? Why was Glynna shouting at him?

As his head and vision cleared, he remembered. The storm! He leaned up on one elbow, gazing around. The roof of his house was gone, and the walls had collapsed. A pain stabbed his head, matching the one in his leg. He blinked several times as his vision blurred. He finally focused on the roof's crossbeam, which had broken in half with one section lying across his thighs. Pushing hard, he was unable to move it. He lay back, praying the swirling fog would leave.

"Conall."

"Glynna!" He attempted to sit, instantly sorry for the sudden movement, but his legs were held immobile by the log lying across them. They were sore, but he could tell nothing was broken. Brushing at a tickle on his forehead, he searched for his sister. When he pulled back his hand, it was covered in blood and dirt.

"Here. Under the table."

Slowly, he turned his head, searching the rubble that had been his family's home—a home they'd only lived in for six months. Nothing looked the same except for the black iron stove that stood up from the rubble, looking proud and untouched. The table had collapsed, but one corner was propped up on a chair, and his sister's skirt stuck out from under it. She moved her leg, but he couldn't see the top half of her body. A jumble of chairs and a large tree branch blocked his view. "Are you hurt?"

"Only a little, I think. But I'm stuck."

Conall tried tugging his legs free, but the beam refused to move. "I am, too. We'll have to wait for help. Try to keep still." He lay back, looking at the amazingly blue sky, which was so different than the angry gray one he'd seen only minutes before. He shivered, probably more from his wet clothing than the temperature. Sure, it had dropped after the storm, but it still remained warmer than the first weeks of early December. That was something he could be thankful for. If the weather was frigid, he and Glynna might freeze before help came. "Help us, Lord. Keep Brian safe. And Mattie."

Mattie! He pushed up again and looked toward the dugout, but his view was blocked by the mound of logs that had been the walls of the cabin. *Please, God, let Mattie and her sisters be safe.* Lying back again, he wondered if he shouldn't have listened to her. She'd been so insistent that the cabin wasn't safe—and she had been correct.

"Conall!"

Mattie's cry brought a flood of joy, warming his chest, and in that moment, he knew he loved her. He'd never dreamed he'd fall for a woman so quickly, but he had, and the splash of her feet brought her closer each second. "Mattie, be careful of nails—broken glass. They can pierce your moccasins."

The footsteps stopped, but then Mattie's face appeared to the side of the heap of logs. "Where are you? Where's Glynna?"

He pushed up onto his elbows and welcomed the relief in her gaze when she saw him. He smiled, hoping to alleviate some of her concern. "As luck would have it, I'm pinned down, and so is Glynna."

"How bad are you hurt? There's blood on your face."

"Not bad." He shook his head, and though it pained him, the ache was less severe. "Can you get to Glynna? She's by the table."

Mattie rose up on her tiptoes, he surmised, and gazed around the rubble. "I think I could get to you easier. Let me fetch one of the horses to haul away some of this rubble."

"How did your sisters fare?"

"They're fine. Still in the dugout."

Her gaze caught his and held. There was no I-told-you-so. Only genuine concern and—dare he hope—something more. Then she was gone.

As he lay listening to the uncommon silence, he gazed upward again. *Why did this have to happen? What lesson would You have me learn from this, Lord?*

☙

Mattie rushed to the barn, tossed open the doors, then found the harness for Conall's stock horse, thankful that the structure had withstood the rigors of the storm. Patches of sky shone overhead where the shakes had been blow off and in several cracks in the walls, but the structure was still standing and in good condition. As she harnessed the large horse, she thought again of the relief that flooded her when she saw Conall in the collapsed cabin. The blood on his face scared her, but he was alive. She didn't have time to analyze her feelings for the man, but she would need to face them soon. Thoughts of him being crushed and dead had scared the wits out of her as she ran toward the house.

Milly rushed into the barn, obviously distraught. "The house is gone. Are Glynna and Conall—"

"They're alive, but they need our help. Where's Jess?" Mattie backed the horse out of his stall.

"I moved her over to the doorway of the dugout so she could look out. She was worried about the Donegans."

"Grab those ropes on the wall and c'mon." Mattie jogged back to the cabin's remains, glad to have her sister's help. She handed the horse's reins to Milly then carefully crawled through the debris, watching for nails and sharp objects.

" 'Twas kind of you to return with such haste, *lachóigín*. I'd stand, considering I'm a gentleman, but as you can see, my legs are encumbered."

Mattie smiled at Conall's exaggerated accent, even though she had no idea what *lack-o-geen* meant. She was so thankful he wasn't seriously hurt, but on second thought. . . "Sounds like that bump on the head knocked you silly."

He chuckled, his eyes twinkling, and Mattie found breathing difficult. She sucked some oxygen back into her lungs and surveyed the scene. A large log, which had split in half, lay across Conall's thighs, but thankfully the overturned settee had broken its fall. She swallowed hard, not wanting to think of what would have happened to Conall's legs if not for the settee. But how could she free him without hurting him?

"I've been studying the situation, and I think if you could wedge something else under the end of the log where the couch is, and if we can lift this other side, I could slide free."

Mattie studied the scene, not wanting to be rushed yet knowing she needed to free both siblings quickly. She crawled farther into the debris and found the trunk she was looking for, only inches from where it had been before the storm. Kicking and tossing things out of her way, she dragged it over to the log and wedged it underneath. Then she worked her way the few more feet to Conall's side and stooped down. He lifted his dirty hand and clasped hers, gazing into her eyes, sending an unspoken message straight to her heart. He cared for her—and she did him. She didn't know what could become of their attraction, but she knew that something had changed between them. She leaned across the beam, taking care not to put her weight on it, and brushed his hair back so she could look at his wound.

" 'Tis not all that bad, so stop your worryin'. Just get me out of here."

Mattie shot him a glance that said she'd worry if she wanted to then turned to Milly. "Toss one end of the rope to me, then tie the two ropes together—good and tight."

She stepped past Conall, kicking away pieces of her life and the Donegans'—a tattered shirt she recognized as Brian's, a tin cup someone had used for coffee just that morning, and a man's shoe she didn't remember seeing before. The pillow Jess had made for Glynna lay a foot away. Mattie picked it up and brushed it off, no worse for wear in spite of the storm.

"Let me have that—and Brian's shirt."

She handed the items to Conall, and he shoved them under the beam and against his side. He held out his hand, and Mattie passed the rope, watching as he secured it around the beam.

"Is there a board or something strong you can give me to use as a lever and something I can wedge under the log when you lift it?"

Mattie unearthed a muddy bucket and a four-foot-long tree branch, casting a glance in Glynna's direction. She'd not heard a word from her and prayed that she was not badly hurt. With the items in place, she moved to the side of the house and lifted the rope over the mound of logs. She could only pray they held long enough to free Conall. Mattie checked that Milly had secured the other end of the rope to the horse's harness and prayed that it, too, held. *Please, God, help us get them out of here.*

She motioned for Milly to back up the horse and hurried to Conall's side. The rope creaked, the logs groaned, and the beam across Conall's legs slowly lifted. "A little more," she shouted to her sister. The beam rose, and Mattie shoved the bucket under it as Conall slid backward.

"I'm free!"

Tension released and the rope relaxed with the log resting on top of the bucket.

Mattie squatted next to Conall and watched him rub his legs. His gaze, filled with gratitude, lifted to hers. "Thank you, lachóigín."

She smiled and caressed his dirty cheek. "What does that mean?"

"Pretty girl."

Heat warmed her face. No one other than her pa had called her pretty. Embarrassed down to her damp toes, she chose to ignore it. "Can you stand?"

"I think so." He pushed up and wobbled a bit, and then he grasped Mattie's shoulder and tugged her closer. "I'm sorry I didn't listen to you."

Mattie smiled against his wet shirt. "You were right about the barn though. It's still standing."

"Is it now?" His finger lifted her chin, and she gazed into those brilliant blue eyes she adored. Conall leaned down, his breath warm on her face, and kissed her—sweet and chaste. Mattie didn't have time to consider how her insides were spinning faster than that tornado before he stepped back.

"W–we need to help Glynna." Mattie blinked, trying to regain her sense of equilibrium.

A scuffling drew their attention across the room to where Glynna sat. "I'm almost free. Just my skirt is caught."

"Stay here." Conall squeezed Mattie's hand and winked.

She watched him carefully make his way through the debris, casting aside part of a broken chair, a tree branch, and other small items. He freed Glynna's skirt, helped her up, and hugged her. Mattie couldn't help being amazed how God had brought them all safely through the awful storm and destruction.

Chapter 9

Mattie stretched as the early sunlight brightened the eastern side of the tipi. The scarred structure had seen better days, but with it mended, at least they had shelter. She gazed around the dying fire, thankful that no lives had been lost in the terrible storm. Glynna lay beside Milly, softly snoring. Though she had some cuts and bruises, she was not seriously hurt. Doc had placed several stitches in Conall's head and said he hoped he'd had some sense knocked into him.

Mattie smiled. The longer she stayed with the Donegans, the more she felt at home. She blew out a breath. But it wasn't their home. Leaving would be difficult, but they would soon have to. The Donegans no longer had a home, only the barn, where the men slept, and the dugout, where the supplies that had been salvaged from the cabin remains were stored. Their being here created more of a hardship for Conall's family. But getting Milly to leave would be no easy task. She'd practically flown into Brian's arms when he raced his horse to the cabin the day of the storm, worried about his family. And the way he kissed her sister—it reminded her of Conall's kiss. She touched her lips, knowing it was the only time she could allow that to happen. If he kissed her again, she feared she'd never leave.

A horse's whinny and the sound of voices drew her to the tipi's opening. Brian walked beside a wagon, talking to the two men sitting on the bench. Behind them, wagon after wagon followed, most driven by a man with a woman sitting next to him, and more men riding alongside on their horses. What was going on?

Conall didn't know when he'd ever been so tired. The whack on the head had taken more out of him than he'd expected. Doc Scott had harped at him all day long that he should be resting instead of working, but a man couldn't lie abed when a town full of kindhearted folks had come to rebuild his home. And rebuild it, they did.

Conall stared at the clapboard walls, already completed. Even the door stood attached to the frame. Only the glass for the windows, which had to be ordered from Kansas City, and the roof, which he and Brian would finish, remained. By Christmas, just eight days away, they should be back in their home. Granted, it was smaller than the first cabin, with just one bedroom, but they'd make do and could add on come spring.

Mattie walked up to him carrying a bucket and smiling. "Would you like some water?"

He nodded, although all he really needed was another look at the woman he loved. Still, he took the ladle she handed him and downed the cool liquid.

"It was kind of all these folks to come and help. We have so much leftover food that we probably won't need to hunt or cook much for days." She shook her head. "I can't get over how these people—some you don't even know—rallied today to rebuild your cabin."

The wonder in her voice made him question whether she'd ever known what it was like to live in a community. Yes, most of these families lived somewhat isolated on their own land, at least a mile away from the nearest neighbor, but they were all neighbors, and they banded together when someone needed help. "I imagine things wouldn't have come together so fast if there had been others who lost their homes."

Mattie nodded. "That's true. I'm glad no one else did."

"Me, too."

"I was surprised how most of the folks here today didn't even frown at my buckskins, and they were all nice to us." Mattie waved at several departing wagons and watched as they drove down the trail. "I never knew that strangers would do such a turn of kindness for others. Pa never let us stay in a town."

Conall took the bucket from her arm and set it down. "Your father is a wise man."

Mattie's brow creased. "Why do you say that? If we'd have lived in a town, we would have learned how to live among others and would not always have had to live alone."

He brushed back a lock that had come loose from Mattie's braid and tucked it over her ear. "If I had three daughters half as pretty as you and your sisters, I'd keep them hidden, too."

She stared up at him with those amazing, penetrating eyes as if she thought he was joking.

"I'm serious. I'm sure he did that to protect you from men like the ones who attacked you."

She pursed her lips and ducked her head. "You may be right, but if he'd stayed around instead of leaving us alone so often, he would have been there to protect us."

Conall cupped her arms then realized they were out in the open where anyone could see. He tugged her behind the new walls of the cabin and around to the side with no window openings. "Your father did what he thought best, and you had to trust him. He was a man alone with three daughters to raise, and that can't have been easy. Forgive him if he made the wrong choices sometimes."

Mattie shrugged and blew out a sigh. "I do, but I suppose I just realized today what we've been missing."

"But you no longer have to miss such things."

"What do you mean?"

"I mean. . ." Conall took a deep breath and prayed that Mattie felt the way he did. "I don't want you to leave. Stay here. With me."

Mattie's eyebrows dipped down. "In your cabin?"

"Yes. No. Well, maybe for a time until we can build our own cabin."

Her mouth opened and eyes widened.

Conall rubbed the back of his neck. "That didn't come out right. I love you, Mattie. I want you to be my wife."

Her mouth and eyes widened even more. Then her lips snapped together for a long moment. "I know nothing about being a wife. I don't even own a dress."

Conall tugged her close. "Then be my bride in buckskin. I don't care if you never wear a dress, except maybe on our wedding day."

Mattie smiled, and tears glistened in her eyes. "Are you sure? Taking me as your wife wouldn't be easy, and it means you'd be saddled with my two sisters."

He brushed his finger down her cheek, and her eyes drifted shut. Leaning closer, he whispered, "I don't think we have to worry about Milly. If he hasn't yet, Brian will soon be staking a claim."

"You truly wouldn't mind being married to someone like me? You know, I can barely cook a thing—and I can't sew."

He tapped her nose. "Maybe not, but you can learn. And who else will have a wife who can hunt and skin a rabbit in two minutes flat?"

Mattie grinned. "Not many, I reckon."

"So, will you marry me, lachóigín?"

Mattie's throat tightened. She'd never been a crying woman, but tears stung her eyes. This wonderful, handsome man wanted her—a half-wild woman—to be his wife. He deserved much better than her, but when he looked at her with such love in his eyes, all she could do was nod.

He grinned then pulled her close, all but crushing her to his chest. His lips touched hers, gentle at first, but then increasing in pressure and intensity. Yet there was no fear like there had been when she was attacked. Only happiness—and delightful sensations she'd never encountered before. When Conall finally stepped back, she knew that a future with this amazing man was all she wanted.

Christmas Day

Mattie followed Conall as he carried Jess into the house from the tipi where she'd been resting. The table was crowded with all manner of food, some they'd prepared themselves and other items that kind neighbors had contributed. Brian, carrying a large platter of meat cut fresh from the pig that was roasting, met them at the door with Milly close on his heels.

"That smells good." Jess held out a hand. "Can I have a bite?"

"Not until we're at the table, missy." Milly wagged her finger, though the grin on her face belied her scolding.

Glynna smiled when they'd all made their way inside. "Any sign of Doc yet?"

Conall shook his head. "If he doesn't arrive soon, I say we eat without him. He may have been called out to care for someone."

Pursing her lips as if undecided, Glynna finally nodded. "I suppose that's a possibility. Why don't you go ahead and take your places?"

Conall set Jess down then pulled out the chair beside her for Mattie. She smiled and leaned close to his ear. "Why thank you, kind sir."

He ran a finger down her cheek. "My pleasure."

A loud knock pulled everyone's gaze to the door, but Mattie jumped. She hadn't seen a soul when they were outside only a minute ago. Doc must have come from a different direction than normal, because she'd scanned the road looking for him.

Conall opened the door, and there Doc stood, but behind him was another man. Doc strode in, grinning like a possum, then stepped aside. Mattie's heart lurched, and she took a step away from the table. The man's tired gaze collided with hers, and he smiled.

"Papa?"

"It's me, my darlin'."

Mattie rushed toward the door at the same time as Milly. Their father wrapped an arm around each of them and chuckled, that deep-throated laugh she adored. He'd lost weight and smelled clean instead of like a wild man, and he was here—alive—in time for Christmas dinner.

A pounding on the table drew her attention.

"Papa! What about me?" Jess held her arms out to him.

Mattie and Milly stepped aside, and their father strode farther into the room and lifted his youngest daughter in his arms. After a long hug that brought tears to Mattie's eyes, he leaned back and lifted up Jess's leg. "And what's this? I'm gone for a little while and you go and get hurt."

Jess pursed her lips and frowned at him. "You were gone for a *long* time, Pa."

He blew out a loud sigh. "That I was, darlin', that I was. I took sick on my way back to you all, but a kind doctor in Guthrie had mercy on me, took me in, and nursed me back to health. Soon we all will be back on the trail. I've a hankerin' to see California."

California. Mattie's heart took another jolt. She couldn't bear to see him go off again—and what about Jess? Would he take her away?

Milly pushed past her, dragging Brian along with her. "Pa, we're not going anywhere."

He looked up, surprise wrinkling his leathery skin. "What's that you say?"

Milly stamped her foot and shook her head. "This is Brian Donegan—the man I mean to marry."

Pa stood there blinking for a moment then grinned. "He can come, too."

Milly's mouth dropped open, clearly unprepared for such a response.

Mattie walked through the crowded room and stopped in front of Pa. "I'm not leaving either, Pa." She waved to Conall, and he stepped to her side. "Milly and I are getting married."

He frowned and scratched behind his ear. "You and Milly?"

Mattie chuckled, her cheeks warming. "No, of course not. Milly is marrying Brian, and I'm marrying Conall Donegan. They're brothers." She looped one arm around Conall's then motioned at Glynna. "And this is their sister, Glynna."

Her father stared at Mattie as if searching for the truth in her gaze. She'd never disappointed him before, and if she did this time, her heart would break, but she knew what her future held. God had made that clear to her the day the tornado hit. "It's true, Pa. The Donegans are good people. They took us in when Jess got hurt and even fetched Dr. Scott to see to her." She hugged Conall's arm, a bit uncomfortable voicing her feelings aloud where all could hear, but she felt she must. "I love Conall, and Milly loves Brian."

Pa snorted and shifted his feet like an angry buffalo then turned to Conall. "Do you love my daughter, young man?"

Conall straightened, but Mattie could feel the tremble that coursed through him. "Yes sir. I do. I. . .uh. . .mean I love Mattie—Matilda."

"She must like you a heap if'n she told you her given name." He winked at her and Conall then looked at Brian. "And what about you?"

Brian glanced at Milly and cleared his throat. "Aye, sir. . .um. . .I also love your daughter. . .uh. . .this one." He wrapped his arm around Milly's shoulders. "If you take her away, I'll just follow."

Pa stroked his beard, looking contemplative. He glanced at Jess. "And what about you?"

Jess crossed her arms. "I just wish everyone would sit down so we can eat."

A smile broke out on Pa's weathered face. "Knowin' that you twins have found men who love you and that you love is the best news I've heard since Dr. Peters said I was going to live."

An audible sigh filled the room, and Mattie grinned up at Conall. Her father had given his blessing.

Glynna clapped her hands. "If you would all please find a seat, we'll eat. Brian, please get the rocker off the porch so Mr. Carson has a seat. I'll get another place setting.

Later that evening, Mattie and Milly talked with their father. He explained how his time at the doctor helped him to see that sometimes they needed the help of others. He couldn't stay forever but would for a time, and Jess could stay with her sisters if that's what she wanted. Mattie snuggled down beneath her bearskin, happier than she could ever remember. This Christmas was the best she'd had since her mother's passing, and the way things looked, there would be many more wonderful Christmases in the future. She closed her eyes, fully prepared to dream of her handsome husband-to-be.

The Gold Rush Christmas

Michelle Ule

Dedication

For the adventurers who sailed to Alaska with me:
Robert, Christopher, Jonathan, Nicholas, and Devin;
and for the one still awaiting adventure:
Michael

*I sent messengers unto them, saying, I am doing a great work,
so that I cannot come down: why should the work cease,
whilst I leave it, and come down to you?*
NEHEMIAH 6:3

Chapter 1

Port Orchard, Washington
August 1897

Here's the last quilt." Samantha Harris brushed tears from her eyes and tossed her heavy gold braid over her shoulder.

Mrs. Parker sighed as she folded the wedding ring quilt into the final crate. "I remember your dear mother stitching the quilts on the veranda. She tucked a prayer for your future husband and Peter's future wife into each stitch. I'm sorry she'll never learn who they are."

Peter grinned. "I'm sure Samantha can find a husband in Alaska territory."

"I'm hunting for Pa, not a husband."

"Maybe you'll find both." Peter set her indigo carpet bag with the luggage. "Alaska's a land of golden opportunities. We're throwing off civilization's shackles and sailing to a territory of unlimited prospects. I'm ready to go."

Mrs. Parker frowned. "You're like your father—never satisfied. You've always wanted to be somewhere else. How your mother fretted over your rash schemes."

Samantha glanced at her twin as she set her father's carved candlesticks on the quilt. She stuffed in the last two feather pillows, sprinkled dried lavender on top, and spread a clean sheet over them. Peter nailed on the lid. The Parkers would store their few remaining possessions.

"Look how your sister taught at the Port Orchard School the last three years. She never complained about taking care of your mother while your father. . ." Mrs. Parker hesitated.

"Shared the Gospel with the Indians?" Samantha grabbed the heavy crate, which also contained her mother's cherished china, and carried it to the door with Peter's help. She heard the Parkers' horse clopping up the road with a cart.

"I don't know what she saw in your father. An itinerant preacher who itched to preach to ruffians even after Port Orchard became civilized. He got his travels, but your mother paid a pretty penny for them. She wouldn't approve of your taking Samantha off to the wilderness. You should be ashamed of yourself, Peter Harris."

"I'll return next year to attend the University of Washington." Samantha hoped her brother's promises and her mother's dream would come true. "But we need to find Pa first."

Reverend Parker entered carrying four Bibles under his arm and gripping a letter in his hand. He scowled at Peter. "Muscular Christianity sounds like your idea."

"Sir?"

"You challenged Miles, didn't you? You told him to abandon his books for action. Are these not your words?"

Peter stood at attention. Samantha froze.

"According to this, my son left seminary just short of his ordination exams." Reverend Parker shook the letter. "He wants to explore his faith in practical ways and take his chances in the Klondike goldfields. He's headed to Alaska, and we are not to discourage him, only pray." Reverend Parker offered the Bibles. "If so, he'll need these extra Bibles."

Mrs. Parker gasped.

Samantha advanced on her brother. "Did you invite him to come with us?"

"Miles wants to be a preacher. Miners have spiritual needs. I told him Alaska could prove his calling to ministry." Peter set the Bibles with their luggage.

"You talked Miles into going to Alaska? He's. . ." She chose her word carefully. "He's clumsy!"

Reverend Parker read aloud. "Don't try to stop me. I prayed and believe this is God's direction for my life right now. I love you. Tell Peter and Samantha I will see them in the north."

"Where would he obtain the money?" Mrs. Parker clutched her throat.

Reverend Parker examined the letter. "He borrowed funds from a friend. Miles purchased his provisions in Seattle and mailed this letter from the docks before he sailed."

"Sailed?" his mother cried. "Who would have loaned him so much money?"

Samantha squelched the urge to strike Peter. "You didn't!"

Samantha watched two men lift her mother's prized pump organ onto the cart. She gulped a sob as she recalled Mama singing and playing hymns, particularly on nights when they missed Pa.

Peter cleared his throat. "That's done. Let's say good-bye to Mother." They walked up the dirt road to the cemetery.

"What were you thinking inviting Miles?"

"How could we go on an adventure and not take our third musketeer? We need him."

Samantha sighed. "You know what he's been like the last couple years. He'll propose again."

Peter snorted. "He loves you. You just don't appreciate him."

Samantha swatted at Queen Anne's lace. "His head is so full of God—not that there's anything wrong with loving the Lord—he misses obvious things.

Alaska could kill him." When they were growing up, pudgy, bespectacled Miles was always falling out of trees, getting stung by bees, or tripping over his own feet.

Peter stopped. "He's shorter than you. That's the real reason you turned him down."

She stomped her foot. "That's not true."

"You're six feet tall, Sam. Your chances of finding a guy tall enough to suit you are slim."

"I'm five-eleven and a half."

He laughed. "You're still taller than most men. But maybe giants like us live in Alaska."

Samantha shut her eyes and counted to ten, like Mama always advised. She lowered her voice to soften her anger. "You told me we sold our household goods to pay our way on the steamship and for our supplies. I signed over my bank account to cover unexpected travel incidentals. Are my savings funding Miles's trip?"

Her high-spirited brother turned his blue eyes away. The cheekbones above his beard turned pink.

She smelled the damp Washington soil and the decaying rot of soggy plants as the summer day dwindled to dusk. "Please tell me the truth."

"I promised to find Pa," Peter said. "Once we find him, you can stay with him through the winter and Miles and I will go to the Klondike. I'll reimburse you. You'll only lose one year. I've waited my whole life for an adventure beyond this little town. If I had to sit at that desk in the lumber mill one more day I'd go crazy."

"We couldn't have survived without your hard work." She patted his arm. "But why does Miles have to come?"

Peter unlatched the squeaky cemetery gate. "I can't prospect alone, and I trust him. Besides, the Klondikers will hear the Gospel if he's with me. I'll work and he'll preach. Pa will like that. Don't worry. We've always saved Miles before. We'll do it again. We need him. I promise he'll be safe with me."

They pushed past the overgrown phlox to their mother's fresh grave. Thin grass blades poked through the ruddy earth around the beloved azalea Samantha had transplanted from their garden.

Could so much have changed in only a month?

Peter's shoulders shook. "She'd be proud of us—you'll see. Mother wanted us to spend more time with Pa. It's our job to tell him about her passing. We'll find him."

Samantha let the tears flow. How often had Mama warned Samantha to use her head and curb Peter's fancies? How many times had Mama told her to watch out for bookish Miles?

"I'll do my best to trust you, Peter," she sniffed. "I'll try to be thankful Miles is with us, because it means the Parkers will be on their knees. We'll need their prayers."

Peter brushed leaves off the grave. "Mother would like that."

Samantha pressed her lips together and stared at the headstone. She wasn't so sure.

Would Mama have approved of anything about this scheme?

Chapter 2

Seattle docks

Miles Parker shoved the bowler hat down over his forehead, only to have it pop up again. He should cut off the fair curls his mother liked so much. They got unruly and made him look like a tall child instead of the man he wanted to be.

Miles corrected his thinking. He was a twenty-one-year-old man voyaging to uncharted lands. Alaska's adventures would prove he was a man that women, particularly Samantha, could admire.

Miles was counting on it.

He peered over the hordes swarming Seattle's docks, searching for the towering Harris twins. When Peter sent the money and the packing list last week, he'd ordered Miles to supervise the purchase and loading of their provisions onto the steamship *Alki*.

Miles spent the first dime at the Seattle Hardware Company on *Facts for Klondikers*. He knew the booklet would more than repay them with gained insight. In addition, the outfitters Coopers and Levy had suggested several items. Figuring it better to be safe than sorry, Miles added snow glasses and cozy knitted hats.

Miles checked his coat pockets. His extra pair of spectacles remained secure. His small New Testament rode, as always, in his breast pocket close to his heart.

"Excuse me, sirs." Miles lifted his hat to the scowling faces of gold-fevered men.

When they didn't budge, Miles gently pushed through the crowd with his broad shoulders. Two men resisted, so he put on his charming smile.

"What's your rush?" one growled.

"I have a ticket." He'd learned that speaking slowly in a cordial tone worked better for him than belligerence.

The crowd parted.

Miles watched stevedores hauling cargo onto the *Alki*. The ship creaked against the quay as travelers crossed the gangplank to board. He could hear the frantic barking dogs, bleating sheep, and neighing horses that would spend the six-day journey in the ship's hold.

A whiff of coal-fired smoke mixed with the tangy sea air and press of humanity. He straightened and his heart skipped a beat when he saw Samantha.

Miles waved his bowler and whistled their childhood signal. Samantha turned in his direction. Peter grasped her elbow and pulled a cart behind them loaded with baggage. Samantha didn't need help, but it always pleased Miles when Peter recognized his sister was a young woman and not merely a shorter version of himself.

"Everything on board?" Peter demanded.

Miles ignored him. "Hello, Samantha. I bet you're surprised to see me."

"That doesn't half express my thoughts," Samantha murmured. "Peter said you purchased our equipment?"

"Yes. I bought everything on Peter's list. My research suggested beefing up on antiscurvy items, so I purchased four bottles of lime juice. They loaded our provisions on the ship this morning."

"What research?" Peter stepped closer.

Miles held up *Facts for Klondikers*.

"I figured I'd ask men who've been to Alaska before," Peter said.

"Sourdoughs? An excellent idea. I suspect, however, most of the voyagers on the *Alki* will be Argonauts; that's another name for folks headed to the goldfields."

"I've heard that." Samantha elbowed the man behind her. "This crowd is rough."

Miles tapped his chin, the old sign for the musketeers to bow close. "I haven't seen many gentlewomen boarding. I'm concerned about the people Samantha will encounter."

"What do you mean?" Peter asked.

Samantha frowned. "I can take care of myself."

"Certainly." Her lilac scent reminded him of home. "You're strong and resourceful, but desperate times may require desperate measures."

Samantha's sigh dismissed him, but Miles continued. "Where's Samantha supposed to sleep? I've seen few women except"—he leaned toward Peter—"the wrong type."

Peter had always been the most cunning of the three. Miles watched him consider his sister, taller than most of the other passengers, and the surly men around them. He met Miles's eyes. "Should we disguise her?"

"You can't be serious." Samantha stepped back. "We're adults, not kids playing *Twelfth Night*. You want me to masquerade as a man?"

Peter nodded. "We need to decide now, before we embark."

"It's for your own good," Miles explained. "You can sleep between us on deck if they think you're a boy. We can protect you."

Samantha looked down her nose at him, but Miles didn't flinch. He was used to it.

"We need to cut her hair, and she can wear my clothes. I've got a change in my carpetbag." Peter ignored her protests. "It's only until we get to Alaska. Then you can put your corset on again."

Samantha reached for her blond knot. "Pa called my hair a crown of golden glory. How can I cut it off?"

Miles winced at the threat to Samantha's splendid hair, but he steeled himself. "There's not much time."

"Let's go. I'll use my knife. Watch our luggage." Peter seized his sister's arm and dragged her toward a nearby building.

Smoke belched from the forward smokestack, and the throng grew more restless. The twins returned with Peter's expression stiff and Samantha's eyes red. Her hair stuck out in pitiful tufts, and Peter's clothes hung on her.

Loss pricked Miles. When he had suggested Peter leave Samantha behind, his oldest friend refused. "We've always said all for one—we can't leave her behind. Sam's yearned for Pa since the day he left. Besides, the trip will keep her mind off losing Mother."

What did Miles know about missing a parent? His parents had fussed over him his entire life. He'd agreed to go with Peter just to keep an eye on Samantha.

Miles removed his bowler. "Wear this, Samantha."

"It's Sam," Peter said.

In Peter's tightly belted pants with the hems rolled up four inches, her angular frame resembled that of an adolescent boy. Sam grabbed the hat. If no one looked too closely, she would pass.

"Give me your necklace," Peter commanded.

Sam clutched the carved cross around her neck. "Pa made this. I never take it off."

"Do you see any other men wearing necklaces?"

Sam turned away to remove the chain. Miles patted her arm. "Time to board."

Peter led the way, hauling their personal baggage. Miles slung his blanket roll across his shoulders and toted a rust-colored carpetbag crammed with saltine crackers, ginger root, and other soothing food in case seasickness struck. Growing up, the trio had sailed a small boat in Sinclair Inlet with Mr. Harris. Miles never had a problem, but Samantha's stomach was another story.

The *Alki* had large open deck areas front and back with passenger cabins two stories high in the center. Travelers bustled about arranging their gear into a space to call home for the voyage. The Port Orchard trio found a spot on top behind the smokestack near the lifeboats. Peter pointed at Miles. "Pray for clear weather or we'll get wet."

"We grew up in the Pacific Northwest. I think we can handle rain." He put cheer in his voice to encourage them.

Sam stared west toward home and the summer snow-topped Olympic Mountains. She fidgeted with something in her pocket. Miles tapped the bowler. "What're you thinking, Sam?"

She pulled out the bulky golden braid Peter loved to tug but Miles feared to touch. She smoothed it between her hands. "I just want to find my father."

Chapter 3

Inland Passage

Miles fussed about arranging things and defending their spot against interloping Argonauts. When Peter invited her to watch the ship cast off, Samantha shook her head. She felt hollow and assaulted, too drained by recent events to budge.

A horn blasted for departure. Hoarse voices shouted, "Alaska, Alaska!" but Samantha covered her ears and face to forget the milling crowds, rumbling engines, and squalling sea birds. Her grieving heart longed for a home now lost and a cherished mother whose voice she'd never hear again.

Mama would be horrified at their recent actions. They'd sold their possessions, abandoned Port Orchard, bought steamship tickets, chopped off Samantha's hair, and now she wore Peter's clothes. But what choices did she have? Mama was dead. Pa was missing. Peter had spent her savings. Until he earned more money, she had neither home nor future.

All Samantha had was hope she'd see her father again. Two years was a long time not to hear Pa's warm voice reading the Bible. She yearned for his calm reminders that Jesus loved her and God had a good plan for her life.

But where was Pa? He'd sent the last letter in June from somewhere near Skagway, explaining he missed them but had important work to finish by Christmas. He'd come home then. Mama had read the letter aloud. "Remember how God sent Nehemiah to help his people? Pa is doing the same thing."

Mama had folded the pages carefully, coughed into her handkerchief, and found solace in her Bible, as always. Peter had paced and run his hands through his hair, his frustration barely contained.

Samantha craved Pa's strong arms. With her mother dead, she needed his comfort. Surely he would understand the trip, her shorn hair, and Peter's ambitious plans.

She took a deep breath and told herself to appreciate the freedom of not wearing a pinching corset. Her disguise depended on her ability to behave like her brother. She willed herself to act manlike. Perhaps she should spit or scratch.

Or order someone to do something he didn't want to do.

Peter returned. "You shouldn't be mooning up here. This is a turning point in your life. Everything will be different from now on."

"What if I didn't want my life to change?"

"You don't have a choice, Sam. The past is gone. This is your new life. Are you going to embrace it or sulk?"

Peter's eyes danced with excitement, and he brimmed with confidence.

Miles tripped up, his hair curling above his ears like a toddler. His round cheeks already looked sunburned above his scraggly beard. "Just like when we were kids, Sam, and played three musketeers. One for all, all for one."

She really looked at him for the first time. "When did you start growing whiskers?"

"As soon as I heard about the trip." He hooked his scholar's tweed jacket over his shoulder and played his jovial role. "We should eat in shifts, one of us guarding our spot. You two go first."

Samantha wasn't hungry, but she stepped over the neighbor sprawling beside their gear and followed Peter down the steep stairway. They skirted the outside cabins to a line at the dining hall on the back end of the ship. "Best get the eats while they're hot," mumbled the Sourdough in front of them.

They waited an hour before space opened at a long table. Distracted white-coated stewards passed metal plates and flung cutlery before sliding large bowls of grub—the obvious description of the food—before them.

Her nose prickled at the sour smell of boiled cabbage and a slab of unrecognizable meat, but she ate it. Peter handed her a chunk of bread, she drank a mug of water, and then the stewards evicted them to make room for other diners.

"I'll relieve Miles. Do you want to explore?" Peter asked.

"Yes." Samantha squeezed past Klondikers clogging the interior hallway between the staterooms. Belongings spilled out narrow doorways.

"I paid for a double berth," a dandy bristled. "Who are all these other people?"

The harried steward consulted a paper. "We've got too many people on board. Two hundred travelers need beds."

"Six men are in here. I want my money back."

The steward eyed him. "We could sell your berthing space ten times over. Are you sure?"

The man swore and shoved in.

Three doors down a woman in a low-cut emerald dress leaned against the wall. "Hiya, honey, are you going to Alaska?"

Sam jumped. "Me?"

"Sure thing." The woman drew a scarlet fingernail along Sam's cheek. "You're kind of young to be traveling alone. You looking for a place to stay?"

"No. I want the toilet."

The woman shook her silky black hair. "They call it the 'head' on a ship, honey. Though why a boy would need our head I don't know." She peered closer.

"Or do I? It's the last door on the left. If you need privacy to change, come here. There's no room for modesty on a ship like this."

After using the cramped and nose-wrinkling head, Sam returned to the top deck. Miles, full of details and holding a booklet, was lecturing to the men camped around them.

"The *Alki* is 215 feet long and can make up to ten knots an hour. She's a powerful beauty." Miles patted the white lifeboat beside him. No one asked any questions.

Sam pushed a carpetbag out of the way when Miles joined her beside their luggage. "The food's awful, but you should eat."

"Soon enough. I haven't had a chance to tell you how sorry I am about your mother."

Miles had missed the funeral. He'd been so busy at seminary, she hadn't seen him since Christmas. "Thanks."

He ducked his head. "Mrs. Harris was always kind. She wrote every week like clockwork."

"Really?"

"She sent encouraging notes, telling me to stay true to the calling God had placed on my heart and assuring me of her prayers."

Sam rocked back. "I had no idea."

"Your pa left her behind because she was too delicate and refined for the frontier, but she had a missionary spirit." Miles raised his chin. "I hope to have a wife like her someday, a woman who will support me no matter how hard a life God sends."

Sam shuddered and put up her hands. "Don't ask."

"This is not a proposal, Sam." He emphasized her nickname. "I'm just saying your mother understood personal sacrifice for the spread of the Gospel. I admired her."

"Thank you. How do you know so much about the ship?"

He jabbed her forearm like she was a boy. "I always do my research."

Samantha sighed. "Do you know what you're getting into?"

"Yes. How about you?"

Peter wouldn't lead the musketeers into danger, would he?

"I'm not sure."

That's what scared her the most.

Chapter 4

At sea along the Inland Passage

Other than crossing Puget Sound on his way to the Seattle seminary, Miles had never been outside of Port Orchard. He leaned on the ship's railing, entranced by the views. They journeyed among small islands covered in evergreens, ocean birds whirling in the skies, and a variety of logging or fishing boats.

He relished the sharp ocean air. When the ship sailed close enough to land, he could smell cedar and rotting kelp on the beach. When they hit a wave, he tasted salty spray. So far the weather had been dry and sunny, just as he'd prayed.

As the *Alki* steamed north, they passed Indian families digging clams and fishing. Too bad the ship's cook didn't do the same. The fare plopped onto the crowded tables often made the passengers gag. Miles ate it only to keep hunger at bay.

Beside him, a miserable Sam hung over the railing. She paid no attention to the scenery as she heaved over the side. Miles coaxed her to sip water and nibble soda crackers, but nothing stayed down. Even the ginger root didn't help.

Peter joined them. "Seen any killer whales?"

Sam groaned.

Miles shaded his eyes with *Facts for Klondikers*. "Scientists call them orcas."

Peter lifted an eyebrow. "Do you know everything, Miles?"

"I read up on the flora and fauna. I wanted to know what I would see."

Peter leaned on the railing. "What else do you know?"

Miles consulted his pamphlet. "As soon as we reach the end of Vancouver Island, we'll be out of sheltered water. The seas can be fierce in Queen Charlotte's Sound."

Sam moaned.

Miles dared to pat her back. "Come below. Maybe they'll serve broth today."

Normally Sam shied away, but this time she slumped against him. "I need the head."

Leaving Peter behind, Miles helped her downstairs, conscious they didn't look very manly. At the bottom, they met Faye, a saucy brunette who licked her lips into a lascivious smile. "How's our *boy* doing?"

Sam ducked her head and held her stomach.

"You men ready for some real entertainment yet?"

"Join us tonight," Miles said. "I'm preaching from the book of John."

"Not likely. But if either one of you needs a soft bed, we could find room in our berth. Especially for this one whose voice hasn't dropped."

"No thanks," Miles muttered.

Faye laughed after them.

❧

Miles watched Sam choke down the bean swill. The warm broth revived her, and she raised her head to study the jam-packed dining area. "I've never seen women dressed like that before." She nodded in Faye's direction. "Is she wearing face paint?"

Miles adjusted his glasses. "Possibly."

"She's very friendly."

He concentrated on his food. "But in need of the Gospel."

Sam peered at him. "Your whiskers are growing. It becomes you."

He smoothed the stubble on his chin and didn't try to hide his smile.

Two dozen Argonauts lounged against their bags smoking pungent cigars and playing cards when he opened his study Bible that evening. Miles recited John 1:10–12 from his heart.

"He was in the world, and the world was made by him, and the world knew him not. He came unto his own, and his own received him not. But as many as received him, to them gave he power to become the sons of God, even to them that believe on his name."

"Preach it, brother," hiccupped a man brandishing a brown bottle.

Two women sat on a lifeboat swinging their legs. A half-dozen Klondikers huddled nearby, trying to make conversation. Few people seemed to be paying attention. Miles continued. The word of God did not return void, even if they pretended otherwise.

No one asked questions when he finished his sermon, so he returned to their section of the deck. Sam slept wrapped in a blanket with her carpetbag as pillow.

Peter held up his thumb. "Good job. Your father would be pleased."

"Yours, too, I hope. He must preach to people like this." Miles gestured to the groups of motley men.

"Probably. He's always liked savages and rough characters. Pa said they recognized their need for a savior better than civilized folks. He knows how to talk in ways they can understand. That's why he went to Alaska."

Miles was always confused when Peter spoke about his father. Miles knew his friend loved and missed Donald Harris, but underlying bitterness always tainted his words. "Do you think he meant to be gone so long?"

Peter shrugged. "He was doing a good work and could not come back. That's what Mother always said. Maybe he lost track of time. Maybe he forgot his son would like to see the world, too. He always said he'd send for me when the time was right. He needs me now and I'm coming, even if he doesn't know it."

"Any more thoughts on the plan? What'll we do first?"

Peter stared at the stars prickling the twilight. "I've been talking with the Sourdoughs."

Miles nodded.

"There's good money to be made hauling other people's cargo over the pass. I think we should do that. We can ask around for Pa while we're working so I can repay Sam faster."

"Do you think it'll take long to find your pa?" Miles asked.

"Who knows? He could be anywhere."

Miles spoke slowly. "If we found him right off, Sam could see him and then sail home. But where would she live?"

"She'll want to stay with Pa for a while. If she decided to return, I figure your folks would take her in until classes start at the university. Sam wanted out of Port Orchard, too." Peter snickered. "Her idea about college made Mother happy and gave her a respectable way to leave. Me, I'd rather not spend my life indoors. Sam's more like you, wanting to teach and help people."

A window of hope opened in his heart. "I appreciate your advice. I need to spend time in the world before I can minister to it. If I only know people like me, how will I understand how to help those not like me?"

Peter squeezed Miles's shoulder. "You're a good man. Thanks for coming. This adventure wouldn't feel right without you and Sam. I'm going to walk around the ship before bedtime."

"All for one," Miles murmured as the boldest person he knew hopped lightly over the men sleeping on deck.

But then Peter's words penetrated.

"What do you mean 'repay' Sam?"

Peter had disappeared.

Chapter 5

At sea

When the *Alki* entered the Queen Charlotte Straits, Samantha thought she would lose her mind as well as her stomach over the roiling, rocking, rolling waves.

On day five, however, she opened her eyes to a bright morning and felt weak but no longer nauseous. "I think I'm going to live."

Miles closed his Bible. "You've finally got your sea legs. You'll be fine the rest of the trip."

"Promise?"

He cocked his head as if listening to something. "Yes. I brought you a cup of tea. It may still be warm."

Samantha held the thick mug to her nose and inhaled the thin spicy scent. Before she sipped, she frowned. "What's on your face?"

Miles's fingers went to his left cheekbone. "Nothing."

"Did one of those women *kiss* you?"

He rubbed the red mark into his flushed skin. "I don't want to talk about it. Peter will be back soon. Let's eat."

Samantha swallowed the tasteless, lumpy porridge in the congested dining area and felt almost alert for the first time. Faye noticed the difference when they met her in the companionway.

"You're looking better, honey. Maybe a kiss will do you good, too."

As Miles recoiled, Sam shook her head. "No thanks."

Faye's enveloping perfume improved the moldy hallway. "Lover boy there may be too innocent to know," the woman murmured, "but you're not fooling us. Your face is too smooth and your voice and movements aren't masculine. Be careful. Men on this ship need to be tamed or manipulated."

Sam stuttered. "I don't know what you mean."

Faye's lips twitched and her drop earrings danced. "A real man would've slugged me. Let me help." She kissed Sam's cheek. "Leave it there and the Klondikers will be envious, not suspicious."

Laughter followed Sam and Miles's hasty exit.

Upon return to their encampment, Samantha took in the scenery. The air smelled of ocean brine and promise. Icy blue and white glaciers glowed pink in the morning sun. Miles joined her at the railing where Sam pointed to a log sculpture on a nearby beach. "What's that?"

"A totem pole. The Indians use them to tell stories and remember their myths." He shuddered. "Savages."

"But those are the type of people my father serves," Sam said.

Miles blinked. "You're right. But don't you wonder if he might have served God better by staying with his family?"

Sam said nothing. Mama never allowed traitorous thoughts.

Miles tossed his head the way he always did when anxious. "I've seen several on shore. Pretty impressive carving."

"Maybe Pa went to the Indians." Sam reached for her missing necklace. "He likes to carve. Have I missed anything else?"

"Natives paddling long canoes and golden eagles soaring to the sun. Enormous trees and spectacular mountains. If I never pick up a nugget of gold, I'll still feel I've gotten rich from this trip." Miles removed his steel-framed glasses and rubbed the lenses clean.

He looked taller, somehow, in his torn and rumpled clothing. Sam fingered a tear in the sleeve of his denim shirt. "What happened here?"

"I ripped it on a nail."

"Any other mishaps?"

He looked sideways. "Be careful around our neighbors. Most don't like me." He squinted at the sun. "I don't have your father's way with rough men."

Samantha should have expected problems. "What happened?"

"They're tired of being on board. I've knocked things over, spilled drinks, kicked luggage, the usual."

She nodded, fluffed her dusty wool blanket, and stretched it over their bags to air. "There hasn't been any rain. Peter must be pleased with your prayers. Where is he?"

Miles put on his glasses. "I research in books. Peter picks up information from people. He's been learning about Alaska from Sourdoughs. We'll be in Skagway tomorrow."

"Wouldn't you love to see Pa standing on the dock?"

Miles stared at her. "Yeah."

She didn't remember him being so focused; Miles had always been the bumbling musketeer. Confused by his intensity, she gestured at the area. "Look at this disorder. I need a broom."

The Klondiker next door scowled when she pushed the carpetbags aside. "Watch what you're doing, kid."

"I'm sorry."

"I mean it," he bellowed.

She suppressed a chuckle. He sounded like one of her eight-year-old students. "I apologize. I'd like to straighten up."

The man clamored to his feet. "Watch yourself,. We don't need you sweeping anything onto our luggage. You can't stand the stink, go home to your mama."

Sam trembled and dropped her chin toward the deck. If she didn't look at him, maybe he'd leave her alone.

"Hey! I'm talking to you."

She stood tall and clenched her fists. He was half a foot shorter. "I'm trying to be a good neighbor."

"I don't like your lip."

Miles spoke in a slow, reasonable voice. "Leave her alone."

A crowd moved in their direction.

"Yeah, *her*. That's a good one A regular pansy, this kid."

Samantha turned her cheek.

"Will you look at that?" He sneered. "The little boy got himself a kiss." He grabbed Sam's arm. "Look at me when I'm talking to you."

Butterflies stormed her gut while she located her classroom voice. "I beg your pardon, sir. I assumed you were speaking to another."

His foul breath forced her backward. "Speaking to another? He talks like a schoolmarm. You need some toughening up before you hit the north. Spending time with the sporting women is a good start, but don't bring their marks up here to torment us. You need a lesson."

His fist struck Sam's jaw with a sharp pain that snapped her head and sent her reeling against the luggage.

Miles lunged, but others beat him to the man. Shoving, kicking, yelling, and the smack of fists turned the top deck into a brawl. Three men tripped over Sam. Wooden boxes scattered, along with luggage, blankets, and the dirty flotsam from a week on a crowded ship.

Sam crunched herself into a cowering ball. Peter yanked her away.

Two sailors blew shrill whistles and broke up the fight. Miles's glasses were askew, his lip bled, and he panted with rage. His shirt had lost a sleeve.

"Miles got into a fight?" Peter snickered.

"A Klondiker hit me." Sam rubbed her throbbing jaw.

"Which one?"

She shook her head. "It doesn't matter. We're supposed to turn the other cheek."

"Not on the frontier. Turning the other cheek is a good way to get killed."

"What do you mean?"

Peter's eyebrows drew together. "Alaska's far rougher than I imagined. You better stay a man as long as possible."

"What will Pa think?"

"He'd want you safe."

Sam touched the remains of Faye's kiss. The task might be harder than her brother thought.

Chapter 6

Skagway, Alaska Territory

Miles's body ached from the fistfight, but the physical pain wasn't as bad as his disappointment when he first saw Skagway's scraggly tents and half-finished buildings.

Ragged mountains marched to the sea at the head of the Lynn Canal and towered above the narrow Skagway River delta. The canal continued northwest through another channel between imposing peaks and ended at Dyea, where travelers could climb the arduous Chilkoot Pass to the Yukon's Klondike River goldfields.

Miles looked from his information pamphlet to the scenery when the *Alki* anchored well offshore. "No dock?"

"No." Peter pointed to log rafts headed their way. "We'll unload onto those shallow barges and transfer ashore."

"I'm glad I'm wearing trousers," Sam said. "It'll be easier to climb a rope ladder without worrying about a skirt."

"Be thankful you're not livestock. They have to swim ashore." Peter strapped the blanket roll onto his carpetbag. "Let's go."

They met Faye, teasing and rosy, at the ladder. "I've got my pretty knickers on, boys, so enjoy the sight." She tossed her bag to a stevedore and winked at Sam. "Go before me, honey. I figure I can trust you."

Sam dropped her baggage onto the barge, grabbed the ladder, and climbed over the side. Faye's full silk skirts slapped Sam's face as Faye maneuvered down. Miles followed, careful to avoid squashing the sporting woman's feathered hat.

The ship's stevedores and anxious Argonauts manhandled crates onto the barge, rocking it with every load. Overhead slings swung out from the deck and dropped screaming horses into the cold water with a thunderous splash. One Argonaut jumped in with them, climbed onto a frantic steed, and urged the herd toward land.

Sam steadied herself on the bouncing deck. "Oh no! The poor horses. What kind of a place is this? Why is Pa here?"

Miles faced the cluster of tents and shacks nestled along the shoreline. Behind them, a black-green spruce forest separated the hamlet from rugged mountains. Miles swallowed. This adventure might be more dangerous than he had pictured at his seminary desk. *Facts for Klondikers* hadn't mentioned Skagway's brooding and forlorn setting.

"Isn't this great?" Peter and two stevedores pushed off from the steamship and poled the barge toward land.

They ran aground in the stinking mudflats ten feet offshore. Argonauts shoved crates toward the rocky beach. Miles slipped into heart-stabbing icy water up to his hips. The shoals lapped to Peter's thighs as he cheerfully hauled their goods to land.

A soaked Sam sloshed up to them. "I couldn't decide what to do, and that Faye pushed me in."

Miles's face felt hot as soon as he saw her, and he peeled off his jacket. "You better wear this."

She glanced down, gasped, and thrust her arms into the heavy sleeves. *Facts for Klondikers* fell from the coat pocket and floated away before Miles could grab it.

"The sporting woman needs help," Miles muttered. Faye waved from the nearly empty barge.

Peter snorted. "Do you want to carry her ashore or shall I? Sam, grab those barrels. I bet they're hers."

Miles and Sam wrestled the barrels ashore, panting from the effort. Peter arrived with a flutter of Faye's skirts and giggles. He retreated before she could bestow another florid kiss.

"Welcome to Skagway. You gents want to store your goods?" A small man wearing a friendly smile and a preacher's collar stuck out his hand.

"Thanks." Miles reached to shake.

"We'll be fine." Peter stepped between them. "Sam, you guard our gear while we scout a tent site."

"Try east." The preacher pointed toward the edge of town.

"Thanks." Peter picked up two carpetbags and jerked his head north. Miles followed.

Men milled around a row of tents surrounded by stacks of wooden crates. Pounding hammers and scratching saws made a deafening noise. The air smelled of cedar. "Is it wise to leave Sam alone with the gear?"

"Wiser than leaving you," Peter said. "She's suspicious by nature and you're not."

"He was being helpful." Miles shifted a wet canvas bag from one arm to the next. "It's important to be polite when entering a new community."

"Did you notice the goons behind him?"

Miles spun around. The "preacher" stalked the waterfront greeting Argonauts, shadowed by ruffians wearing heavy revolvers. Sam scowled and paced around their boxes, arms folded tight across her chest. Faye, he noticed, had found men to carry her luggage as she sashayed toward the business district.

"We can't leave her alone. I'll wait with Samantha and not speak to a soul."

"Fine. I'll mark a spot at the end of this street." Peter indicated an area near the forest. "We'll haul everything ourselves."

"Deal." Miles spied a wooden shack beyond the tents. "Hey, we can send a telegram home to let them know we arrived." He gulped. "Five dollars is a lot of money, but it will ease my mother's worry."

"Telegraph? Here?" Peter peered at the building and frowned. "Do you see any telegraph wires?"

"No." Miles's jaw dropped "That's dishonest."

"Assume everyone wants to steal our money," Peter said. "Sourdoughs say there are two types of people in Skagway: the skinned and the skinners. We've landed in a lawless town on the edge of nowhere."

Miles trudged toward the beach. How could Peter discern people's motives so much better than he could?

Barges continued moving toward shore. The *Alki* steamed a plume of smoke as she rode at anchor, an insignificant piece of civilization against the dramatic Alaskan backdrop. Dozens of horses shook themselves dry on the rocky beach as Argonauts organized their soaked possessions. The thin sunshine provided little warmth, and a chill blew from the high mountains. Miles shivered in his wet clothes, but Sam needed his jacket more.

At the water's edge, Sam ignored the fast-talking men who addressed her. With her lanky frame and Miles's bowler pulled low over her ears, it took sharp eyes to see her feminine features. Indeed, as she kicked at boxes and spat, she reminded Miles of Peter.

Certainly she'd behaved more manly than Miles.

Miles reached for a barrel when he joined her. "Peter says we shouldn't trust anybody."

"He's right," Sam said. "See him waving? He must have found a spot."

They shuffled their goods a quarter mile down the muddy path. When they finally got everything moved, Peter pried opened a crate and pulled out a heavy canvas tent.

Miles read the directions while Sam and Peter erected it.

Peter pulled out another tent.

"Why two?"

He felt his face grow hot. "We're not kids anymore. I thought Samantha needed privacy."

Peter turned to his sister. "Will you be comfortable in a tent by yourself?"

Sam stopped pounding stakes to push the hat off her face. "As long as you two are next to me, yes. If we find Pa, I may not be here long anyway. When can we start looking?"

Peter shuffled his feet. "I'll make inquiries tomorrow when I look for work."

"Work?" Sam frowned.

"I figure to kill two birds with one stone: hunt for Pa and earn money. The people who got rich during the California gold rush were the folks who sold to the forty-niners. We'll ask around for Pa, but if we carry freight over the White Pass at the same time, we can earn hard cash."

"I came to find Pa. He's the only reason I'm here."

Peter picked up the white canvas and motioned for Miles to stretch his end over the tent poles. "We'll start tomorrow."

Miles had trouble falling asleep after a week rocking on the *Alki*. Peter snoozed soundly beside him, but Miles eventually got up and pushed out the tent flap. A full moon rose over the mountains, and muffled voices rumbled from nearby tents. A bonfire lit the beach, and music called from Broadway, a mere block away. An owl hooted, and Miles looked up, amazed at the splendid stars filling the sky.

"The heavens declare the glory of God," he whispered.

"And the firmament declares his handiwork." Samantha stepped from her tent. "You're not sleeping."

He could see her clearly in the moonlight, her chopped hair sticking up in all directions. The left side of her face was swollen, and Miles's muscles tensed remembering the fight. At least she looked more feminine in a white nightgown.

Nightgown.

"Why are you dressed like that? What if someone sees you?"

She scratched at the remains of her hair. "It felt so good to get out of Peter's dirty clothes after a week, I didn't think. I'll go in the tent."

"It's more prudent." Miles hated to see her go.

"You're right." Samantha sighed. "Thank you. I appreciate how you watched out for me on the ship."

"I'll always defend you."

Samantha touched the cut on his cheek. "Good night."

Miles smiled. He could sleep now.

Except he tripped on the stake peg and toppled Samantha's tent.

"Oh Miles!" Samantha groaned. "Forget what I said."

They re-erected her tent in silence and returned to bed.

But Miles lay awake most of the night. Why had he thought Samantha would treat him any differently in Alaska?

Chapter 7

Skagway
September 1897

"You want me to do what?" Sam dropped the frying pan.

"Packing freight is the fastest way to prosperity," Peter said. "We'll split the jobs three ways in a rotation. One of us will stay in town to rest and hunt for Pa. The other two will haul goods to the pass for the Klondikers."

"I can't manage horses or mules. Why don't we look for Pa first? Once we find him, you can go on your way," Sam said.

"Even if we found him, there's no money to return you to Washington." Peter uncharacteristically twisted his hat in his hands.

Sam gaped at Miles. "You spent all my money?"

"Peter told me to spend it all to outfit us. I'd have been more careful if I'd known it was your savings." He picked up the frying pan.

Peter patted the money belt he wore under his shirt. "All we have left is here. Thirty dollars. It might pay your way if we begged the steamship captain, but then what? What would you live on?"

The betrayal stabbed all the way to her spine. Three years of teaching hooligans in a small Port Orchard classroom had been transformed into the crated goods stacked around them. Tents, clothing, food, and equipment were the physical remains of her college dream. She didn't care if she was supposed to be a young man, she let them see her eyes pool with tears. What would Mama have said?

"The packers driving horse teams make twenty-five dollars a day. With all three of us working, we can earn a lot of money in no time. Then when we find Pa, you can decide what you want to do." Peter's voice rang with his traditional confidence.

Sam snatched the frying pan and slammed it against a crate. Peter could not keep making life-changing decisions for her. "I came to find Pa, nothing else."

"We'll ask around for him. The sooner we get jobs, though, the sooner you'll have your money. Deal?"

"No. I came to find Pa. We need to look for him."

"We'll ask around today. Somebody must know something about him, since he sent a letter from here," Peter said. "But we've got to act quickly if we're going to work. People want to get over the pass before winter. Now's the time to haul goods."

"You can't just keep making decisions without discussing them with us. All for one and one for all means we discuss what we're going to do before one of us just decides. Isn't that right, Miles?"

He put up his hands. "I'm here to support both of you. But we do need to look for your father."

"We're going to look for him," Peter said. "But we're going to look for work, too. Sam needs her money back."

Did she have a choice? It burned that she had to agree, but his argument made sense yet again. "Miles, you need to pray we find Pa soon. I don't trust Peter. He's probably made some other bargain with God."

"Maybe we should eat," Miles said.

Miles read the directions for constructing the camp stove and then dropped most of the pieces in the mud trying to set it up. Peter got the metal contraption burning hot within minutes. Samantha mixed flour, soda, and water to make flapjacks. They drank boiling coffee with condensed milk as sweetener, secured their possessions, and then explored Skagway.

The town crackled with activity. Argonauts organized their possessions and argued among themselves. Whiskered Klondikers with determined faces packed heavy loads to Broadway, turned north, and headed up the Skagway River to White Pass. Grim men plodded the rutted muddy road, leading sickly nags overburdened with goods.

The sawmill at the water's edge shrieked out planks in a cloud of pungent cedar sawdust. Barking dogs and the jingling reins of pack animals livened the chilly morning. Samantha watched three young women enter a two-story building with a steep-pitched roof. Lace curtains hung in the upper windows. Faye leaned out to shout hello.

"Don't look at her," Miles said. "We don't want people to think we're acquainted with her type of woman."

Peter squinted in the sunlight. "They say Doc Runnalls handles the mail. Let's see if he knows anything about Pa."

They picked their way along the mucky street lined with new buildings to a hovel marked Mail Office. "He's the closest thing we got to a postmaster," a grizzled Sourdough explained. "He meets the steamers when they come into port and hands off the mail. Twenty-five cents a letter—expensive."

"Harris?" The bespectacled doctor shook his head. "Don't know the name."

"He's a missionary, a big man like my brother," Sam said. "Pa sent a letter in June saying he was headed this way to finish a job."

"Haven't seen many missionaries in Skagway. It's too crude and lawless with people mostly passing through. A fellow they call Peg Leg lives down the canal with some Tlingits, but I never heard his real name or if he's a missionary."

"That wouldn't be him," Peter said. "Pa's a strong man. He's been traveling well-nigh two years. He's got both his legs."

Runnalls shrugged. "Soapy Smith might know him. He'll be at his saloon."

When they reached the saloon, which reeked of cheap liquor even on the boardwalk, Samantha noticed the shorefront minister entering ahead of them. Peter set his jaw. "Take Miles's wallet and stay outside, Sam."

She stuck the wallet and her hand into the trousers' front pocket and leaned against the building in a casual manlike way. Four women flounced by wearing colorful dresses and heavily fringed silk shawls. She stared after their saucy confidence.

"No luck," Miles said when the two men rejoined her. "They offered to hire us to haul freight, but we turned them down. We'll check with more reputable packers."

"This Soapy Smith controls the town." Peter put on his hat. "Stay away from him and his con men."

When Sam described the fancy women, Peter drew his eyebrows together. "This is a dangerous place. Keep to yourself."

"How will I find Pa without talking to people?"

"Do you think Pa would know sporting women and con men?"

Samantha had not seen her father in two years. She had no idea.

❧

Peter and Miles left before dawn the next morning. They would lead a string of pack mules six miles to Liarsville at the base of White Pass and return to Skagway late in the afternoon. "I'll try to get back early." Miles wore worry lines across his forehead. "I'll go with you to ask around for your pa then. Don't go near anyone who looks threatening."

Sam shook her head. "Folks see me as a boy. I'll be safe. Help Peter find his fortune."

"It's not like that," he began, but Sam turned away.

She asked at the lumber mill if they'd heard of Donald Harris or seen a very tall man with fair hair starting to thin. No one had.

Sam rubbed her hands as she tramped toward the business district. Would Pa still have hair? Two years in a cold climate might have changed him.

She stopped in the shops lining Broadway: a real estate investment office, a hardware store, and a mercantile. Mr. Brown at the mercantile looked through a ledger he kept behind the counter. "No Harris listed. If he's been in the store, he must have paid cash. Sorry, sonny."

She steered clear of the pool hall and passed four men throwing dice against the jail.

The door burst open at a saloon, and a black-goateed man tossed out a native. "Don't come back."

The mahogany-skinned man rolled in the dirt and moaned. Sam stepped toward him. "Do you need help?"

He groaned in a tongue she didn't understand, shook her off, and crept away on hands and knees. Giggles sounded from a neighboring window. "You can help me, honey," shouted a fleshy woman dressed in a loose wrapper.

Sam cringed and headed north.

By the time she'd reached the end of the street, Sam had no leads on her father and a disgust with the town. Was no one honorable?

"Hey there, boy, do you want a job?"

A petite woman wearing a flour sack tied around her waist beckoned from a rough log hut. A placard reading, RESTAURANT, hung over the entry. "I need someone to wash dishes. I'll pay two bits."

The woman ushered Sam into a crowded room where a pot of water boiled on the stove. "Start there. I've got an hour before customers return. I'm Mollie."

A plank table with crude benches ran the width of the restaurant. Mollie pushed stray hairs off her face with her forearm and returned to chopping onions, chattering the entire time.

"You a *cheechako*? I'm a newcomer, too. I got here last week, and Reverend Dickey found me this job working for Mr. Brown who owns the mercantile. You headed to the Klondike?" Her blade never stopped moving. "Once you finish, I'll pay you to peel potatoes."

Sam kept her head down, not trusting her voice.

"How old are you?" Mollie asked. "Fifteen, sixteen?"

"Yeah."

Mollie showed Sam how to keep track of the bread baking in the tiny ten-inch-square oven. "Do you know how to cook flapjacks? We'll need filling when the stew runs out."

"Yes ma'am."

Men trooped in when the friendly bread aroma seeped from the cabin. Sam fried flapjacks while Mollie served food, collected money, joshed with the Argonauts, and made everyone feel at home. By the time they scraped the last of the stew from the pot, they'd fed three dozen men.

Mollie jingled the coins in her pocket, pushed the hair out of her eyes, and bustled to the stove. "You got yourself a job if you'll come back tomorrow at dawn."

"Yes ma'am. I will."

Mollie laughed. "What's your real name, sweetie? Since we'll be working together, I'd like to make sure you're a girl."

"Samantha Harris." Sam felt her face flush.

"It's hard to be a single woman in this town," Mollie said. "Maybe I should dress as a man. Do you think I can fool anyone?"

With her curly hair, sparkling eyes, trim shape, and small hands, Mollie was all female. It took a tall, spare figure like Sam's hiding in men's clothing to stride through the town without concern.

Sam grinned. "No one would mistake your fair sex."

Mollie held out her hand. "Your secret is safe with me."

They shook on it.

Sam whistled as she walked to her tent after work, hands in her pockets. She could make her own plans. Peter didn't dictate her life. She'd find Pa without him.

Chapter 8

White Pass and Skagway
October 1897

Miles hated freighting work.

Everything about the job disgusted him.

The vulgar, arrogant men desperate for riches. The abused horses forced to carry overweight loads. The glacial Skagway River he sloshed into several times a day. The fear he might stumble off the narrow trail into canyons spiked with boulders. The interminable hours of waiting when the foul path backed up because something far ahead had broken or fallen and blocked traffic.

The change in Peter over the last six weeks bothered him even more.

Always craving adventure and excitement, Peter now had a bad case of gold fever. He strapped on his snow glasses and went to work every morning with determination. While Miles appreciated Peter's resolve to repay Samantha, his single-minded fervor for every cent was troubling.

"Everyone has a price, and these Argonauts need to pay for what they're getting," Peter explained during one of their waits. The hard labor, long hours, and frigid wind had pared down their features, giving Peter a golden wolfish look. Miles had taken in his belt two notches, and his shirts felt tight across the shoulders.

"Why does it always have to be about money? Is it necessary to charge for every service?" Miles preferred to include minor assists in his daily fee, but Peter debited everything and expected a tip as well.

"Yes. It's a brutal world, and traveling to the Yukon to prospect for gold in the Klondike River isn't going to be easy on them."

"What about us?" Miles asked. "How will we manage?"

Peter raised his jacket lapels and tugged the knit cap over his ears. The mule beside him shifted, and Peter adjusted its load. The line of Klondikers ahead grumbled and kicked at rocks.

"Don't you feel stronger? You climb this pass without wheezing now. You needed to get into shape before our hard work begins."

Miles removed his glasses and fished out his red calico kerchief to polish the lenses. "This has been training for me?"

Peter poked him. "Your fat's gone and your endurance is much improved. We've got money in our pockets and information. We'll be ready to hike over the pass for ourselves soon."

Miles replaced his glasses and pulled out his pocket New Testament. If they got too delayed, he liked to walk along the pack line offering to read encouraging scripture. He held out the book to Peter. "Do you want to read today?"

"I'll manage the animals so you can." Peter rubbed his mule's nose. "The way packers treat these poor animals is the worst part of this job. I'm glad Sam isn't here. She couldn't handle the violence."

Miles agreed. The restaurant job kept her safe and warm, though he wondered at the wisdom of two women serving food to strange men. Of course, no one knew Sam was a woman. He shook his head. He couldn't imagine how men could be so blind. Every time he looked at her, his heart raced.

He opened his New Testament and reread the note she'd slipped him that morning: "I thank my God, making mention of thee always in my prayers."

Miles kissed the note. He'd cherish Philemon 1:4 forever.

Miles and Peter usually only hauled freight to Liarsville, where they cached the goods for Klondikers to pick up later. They often managed two trips a day. That day, however, they were going higher, and Miles worried about leaving Sam alone in the unguarded tent overnight. "Do you think she'll be okay?"

"For the ninth time, yes. I left her the gun, and she's a better shot than you anyway. If she gets scared, she can stay with Mollie."

"Not if she's a boy." Miles brushed a snowflake off his nose.

Peter shrugged. "With the new preacher setting up a church, I think she'll transform into respectable Samantha soon."

"Which will make Skagway even more dangerous for her. Why won't you help her look for your father? She's visited every tent and shack in town. It's not safe. She's talking about hiking outside of town to look, and that's plain foolish."

"I ask everyone I see. The weather's turning bad, and he hasn't come into town. I don't know where he is. Runnalls hasn't gotten any mail."

"What about that Peg Leg living with the Tlingits? Why don't you check him out?"

Peter snorted. "My father would have said something in his letter if he'd been injured. Besides, Runnalls says it's a four-hour hike in good weather if you can find someone to guide you. There's no reason to risk our lives and lose two days of hauling fees without anything more to go on."

"So you have made inquiries?"

"I'm trying to be pragmatic. If I don't get my hopes up, I can better cope if we never find him." Peter slapped at the thickening snowflakes.

Miles's heart sank. He'd been afraid of the same thing. But what about Sam's feelings? How could he protect her from the inevitable? "Have I earned enough money yet? I'd like to stay in town."

"Sam can take care of herself. You don't need to protect her." Peter tugged the mule forward.

Miles shook his head. "No. Skagway's dangerous. I'll ask for a job at the mercantile for the winter. I'd like to help build the new church anyway."

"Suit yourself. You won't make as much money."

The snowflakes gusted. Miles tucked his scarf over his beard and thought of Sam's desperate searching. "Money isn't everything."

≈

"I'm glad you're working in town," Sam said as she picked up supplies for the restaurant.

Miles nodded. He ate every meal at the restaurant and stayed into the evening with the two women. "The job is better, and I get to see you more."

She hesitated before leaning over the mercantile counter to whisper. "It makes me feel safer knowing you're nearby."

Before Miles could respond, Sam spun around and exited. He watched her try to walk like a man on the boardwalk and chuckled. She couldn't fool him, no matter what she wore.

Miles battled guilt every morning he sat on a stool beside a crackling stove while Peter hauled the trail alone. Snow covered the ground now, and dark clouds often loomed over the narrow Skagway valley. He watched the sky every afternoon, wondering what would happen to those on the trail in a blizzard.

Peter insisted he'd charge more.

Miles prayed more.

Whenever a Sourdough entered to make a purchase, Miles asked if he knew Donald Harris. No one recognized the name. One or two had heard rumors, but most thought missionaries lived further down the west side of Lynn Canal in Haines. One Tlingit tribe southeast of Skagway hosted a *skokum*, but no one knew his real name.

"Old man," explained a Tlingit in broken English who had come in to buy cornmeal. "No hair, bad leg, round belly." His description didn't match the robust *skokum*—man—Miles knew from childhood.

From his seat in the warm mercantile, Miles daily witnessed Alaska's heartbreak. If he hadn't lost *Facts for Klondikers*, he would have burned it in disgust. No words could have prepared him for Skagway. He saw Argonauts scrambling to land their possessions on shore. He watched Soapy Smith's gang fleece newcomers and the mostly futile attempts by responsible citizens to intervene. Packs of abandoned dogs roamed town fighting over food scraps.

The most troubling residents were the sporting women.

Flocks arrived on every steamship, fancy women wearing elaborate hairstyles and paint on their pretty faces. They pranced up slushy Broadway to the two-story houses across the street. He seldom saw them leave, and indignation fired his soul. Why would a woman choose a life of degradation?

In the doorway, Mr. Brown sniffed as the women strolled past swinging their

422

hips. "We're trying to build a civilized town, and those women are bad elements. As a minister, you should steer clear of them."

"I'm not ordained yet," Miles reminded him. He tried not to think of the women and what they did in the house across the street.

"You're close enough for this town." Mr. Brown left for the waterfront to claim supplies sent on the most recent steamship.

Miles stepped to the shelves to rearrange the stock. The door opened and Faye entered wearing a sweet-scented silk shawl over a blazing blue dress. "I've wanted to stop in and say hello, honey, but old sourpuss wouldn't let me through the door."

"How may I help you?" Miles looked past her, hoping no one would peer in the window.

"I've come for Pear's Soap. This climate affects my complexion."

She sounded stiff, and he glanced out the corner of his eyes. Dimples of irritation appeared on either side of her pursed ruby lips. "Are you too proud to take my cash?"

"I'll check our supply."

"You're looking good, preacher man. I'm surprised working in this store could cause such a change in your physique."

He found a bar of Pear's Soap and laid it on the counter, still not looking at her.

"Where's young Sam these days? She's not bulked up like you, is she?"

Startled, Miles finally met her eye. "No. She's working up the street with Mollie."

Faye's eyes shocked wide open and her voice shrilled. "What do you mean up the street? I thought you were a God-fearing man. Which crib? I should slap you." Her face flushed with rage.

Horror dawned. "She's not working—" Miles couldn't say the words. "She and Mollie run a restaurant." He pushed the soap across the counter. "Ten cents."

Faye lifted her chin. "Is she still dressing as a boy?"

He nodded.

"Keep her that way. The men in this town can't be trusted." She dropped a coin from her crimson velvet bag and picked up the soap. Faye swept to the door and paused. "You, preacher man, should pay more attention to how Jesus treated sinners and Pharisees."

The door shut behind her with a soft click.

Chapter 9

November brought snowdrifts and ice to the Skagway waterfront, while the pass became nearly impossible to traverse. Sam watched men trudge by the restaurant each day. Were they all as determined as Peter with his chapped red skin and thick beard? How long could they go on?

"Until they close the pass," Peter said. "Then they'll shift to the Chilkoot."

"Will you hunt for Pa then?" Sam stirred the oatmeal on the restaurant stove. She prepared him a hot breakfast every morning to guard against the arctic conditions.

"I've been asking. No news."

Sam splatted oatmeal into a bowl and thrust it at her brother. "What about the outlying areas? We're practically snowed in here—when will you visit the natives?"

"It's not that easy, Sam." Peter stared at his breakfast.

"Only because you haven't looked." Fury vied with despair. To give her hands something to do, she passed the coffeepot to Miles.

He shook his head. "No word at the mercantile either."

"Christmas is coming." She tried to steady her voice. Peter never responded well to anger. "He said he had a project to finish up here and then he'd come home. Where is he?"

"Is Christmas significant?" Mollie returned the coffeepot to the hot stove.

Sam slumped at the table, chin in hand. "Pa loves Christmas. He thinks Jesus' birth is the best way to explain God coming to earth and being accessible to all."

"True." Miles picked up his spoon.

"I don't think we're going to hear from him by Christmas." Peter stretched his arm across the table to take her hand. "You need to face facts, Sam. I don't think he's coming back."

All the air disappeared from her chest, and the frozen chill of fear that had haunted her stabbed Sam's soul. "Is that why you haven't looked for him? You think he's dead?"

"Everyone knows we're looking for him. You torment Runnalls about the mail every other day. You buttonhole every native you see. I don't have to go to the outlying areas. Everyone in Alaska knows Mollie's assistant Sam is looking for his father." He pushed back from the table and reached for his knit cap.

"What are we going to do?" Sam crossed her arms tight against her body and tried not to whimper.

"I'm going to haul over the pass. Another couple weeks of this and I'll have enough to send you back to Washington. You can go to school in the spring." He stuffed a loaf of bread into his pack and banged out the door, taking her hopes and unanswered questions with him.

Miles cleared away the remains of breakfast. Sam stared at nothing, trying to slow her breathing and absorb Peter's words. Mollie took her knife to the onions and began to chop. They worked in silence for a time before Miles slid in beside her and took her hands.

"Peter doesn't know everything. He's just as scared as you are. All he can do is take care of you as best he can."

Sam nodded. She knew that.

"You've got to have faith," Mollie said. "Maybe your father's working so hard he hasn't needed to come to town. Maybe he'll hear of the church being built and want to come see it even if he can't get home. It'll be finished by Christmas."

"We can't give up hope," Miles agreed. "Anything can happen."

"I just want to see Pa again." Sam put her head on the table. "I'm not giving up before Christmas."

֍

Mollie had sailed to Skagway on the same ship as the Reverend R. M. Dickey, and they were fast friends. Caught up by the reverend's enthusiastic vision, the civilized townspeople had banded together to construct a church building. Funds had come from all walks of life: Sourdoughs, businessmen, packers, even Soapy Smith. Mollie kept a jar at the restaurant and encouraged customers to donate tips for the lumber and nails.

Mollie, Samantha, and Miles volunteered to help the effort. The women made coffee and served sandwiches, but after Miles split a board, hammered his thumb, and nearly fell off the roof, Pastor Dickey asked him to teach a small Bible study. Samantha agreed with the preacher's carefully chosen words: "Let's build the congregation while we construct God's house. God can better use Miles's Bible skills in a less physical way."

Mollie offered the restaurant as a meeting place with Mr. Brown's approval. "Sam and I can listen to the lessons while we clean up."

Sam loved the lectures. Miles had learned a lot at the seminary. His teaching blew a glow of pride into her heart.

Miles began every meeting with prayer for Donald Harris. He asked each student if he'd heard the name. No one ever had, but the fact others knew to look for him eased Sam's worry. She announced a prize to the men who bundled into the restaurant: "If you find my father, I'll praise God and make you an apple pie."

On the evenings they finished kitchen duties early, Sam and Mollie helped the students locate and read passages from Miles's extra Bibles. Sam assisted men writing letters home. Miles shared information about the Klondike goldfields he had gleaned while doing research and from working at the mercantile.

"You must be pleased folks want to learn about the Bible," Mollie said one night after the students left.

"You're the reason the men come, Mollie." Miles adjusted his glasses. "How many marriage proposals did you get today?"

"Two serious, three fake. What do you suppose will happen when Sam reveals her true identity?"

"The class will double." Miles held out her coat. Sam slipped her arms into the sleeves.

"How much longer can you get away with your disguise?" Miles murmured.

Mollie laughed. "Good question."

"When the church is finished, I will worship God as a lady." Sam put on Miles's old bowler hat.

"Then the real trouble will begin." He buttoned up his parka.

Mollie saw them out.

The cold night air hit their faces like a chisel. Sam took Miles's arm, and they huddled together on their walk home.

"Do you like Mollie?" Sam asked.

Miles nodded. "She's the finest person I've met here."

During their months in Skagway, the town had taken on a more established look. Buildings now stood on either side of Mollie's restaurant, and while the rutted frozen streets were dark, the snow reflected enough light that they could see. "Mollie's talking about opening her own restaurant at the top of the pass," Samantha said.

"Do you want to go with her?" Miles stepped carefully; he'd tripped the night before and sprawled face down into a drift.

"No. Listening and helping you makes me miss teaching. If anything, I'd like to start a school. There's enough children in town." She squeezed his arm. "Your work on the trail gave you practical applications for your lessons. Some men may come to admire Mollie, but you're telling stories about God they want to hear. You're a good teacher."

Miles clutched the Bibles to his chest. "Thank you," he whispered. "Your words mean a great deal."

She leaned closer. Miles no longer acted like the bungling boy she'd grown up with. "The beard makes you look distinguished."

He smiled. "Will I look proper enough to escort you to church soon?"

Sam laughed. "Only if you wear your bowler."

As they turned off the boardwalk, a shadow scurried from behind a two-story house. "Are you one of the preachers?"

"He is." Sam dropped her hand. She'd forgotten about her disguise in the dark street.

"Please, sir, I need help." The woman's voice wavered. "I want out, and they're after me. Can you take me somewhere safe?"

Miles stiffened. "Who's after you?"

"Please," she coughed. "They'll beat me. I have nowhere to go."

Two figures loomed. Sam plucked off her hat and pushed it on the frail woman's head. She took the woman's arm and dragged her in the direction of their tents two rows away. The neighboring tents glowed from the lanterns inside, leaving a cool whiteness gleaming on the snowbank. "What's your name? How can we help you?"

"Lucy." She shivered. "They're coming for me. I know they are.

Sam opened the tent flap. The woman trembled. "I can't go in there."

Miles stopped. "She's right, Sam, your reputation will suffer."

Two brutes ran up. "You've got something that belongs to us." The taller one reached for Lucy.

"Pretty strange doings," the shorter man said. "You fancy yourself a preacher, and here you're taking a sporting girl to your tent."

"You can't take her if she doesn't want to go!" Sam put her hand on Lucy's arm.

"You don't think so?" The big man shoved her. Sam fell against Miles, and the two stumbled against the tent. The men dragged a screaming Lucy down the street.

The bowler hat rolled to a stop beside Sam, who struggled to catch her breath.

"I'm so sorry. Did they hurt you?" Miles held her close. "We'll find Lucy and help her. I'm here, and I won't leave you. I'll keep you safe."

As she nestled against him, Samantha knew she didn't want to be manly anymore.

Chapter 10

December

The respectable citizens of Skagway completed Union Church a week before Christmas. True to her word, Samantha put away her nickname, returned Peter's borrowed clothes, cinched up her corset, and swept into church wearing a woolen skirt. Mollie had trimmed her ragged hair straight across. She held her chin high, and male heads turned as she and Peter took seats in the third row.

Mollie hugged her. "You're beautiful. We'll have even longer lines outside the restaurant today."

Miles figured she was right.

Samantha seemed oblivious to the stares as she focused on Reverend Dickey's words. She sang the hymns and Christmas carols with her pleasing soprano. Men clustered about her after the service, and Samantha brushed them off with a lighthearted, "Time for work."

When she caught Miles's eye, Samantha winked.

As they exited the church, Peter pulled Miles aside. "The pass will close after the next snowstorm. Hauling is finished here until spring."

Miles nodded. "We need to find better quarters for the winter. Will you hunt for your father now?"

"There's plenty of packing work on the Chilkoot Trail," Peter said through cracked lips. "I figure two more weeks and I'll have enough money for Sam's college in the spring. It won't be everything I owe her, but enough to start. I'm going to head over there."

"She wants to find your father. Why don't you help her?" Miles couldn't keep the annoyance out of his voice.

"He was coming to the Skagway River area. Here we are. No one's heard of him. Your parents haven't forwarded a letter. He probably wandered off and couldn't be bothered to write, if he's even alive."

"You can't break Sam's heart." Miles sighed.

"Her heart's going to be broken when he doesn't turn up by Christmas. I'll talk to her tonight."

"How can you abandon her?" Miles demanded. "Especially if your father is dead. When are you coming back?"

Peter's hand came down on his shoulder. "You'll be here. I figure she can bunk with Mollie. Can you winter in your store until we've got enough money to head to the Klondike?"

Miles had already gotten permission. "I'll give you my earnings. Skip the Chilkoot and do a thorough search for your father."

Peter shook his head. "I'm counting on your pay to see us through the next year."

Miles should have thought of that.

Mollie had invited the men to spend the day in the relatively warm restaurant. When they arrived, they found Mollie in tears and Samantha indignant.

"We have to do something about this town. Mollie saw a woman she knew from home working as a sporting woman. It was Lucy. When we tried to talk to her, Soapy Smith's gang threatened us."

"Did they recognize you?" Miles had feared this.

"What does it matter? Lucy's the one in trouble." Samantha paced the cramped room.

Miles removed his gloves. "Do you know which house she's in?"

"No. She wants to escape, and they've snagged her twice now." Samantha tripped on her long skirt. "She's ill."

Mollie reached for a knife. "I'll chop onions while we think of something to do."

Peter shook his head. Miles had no ideas. Samantha kneaded the bread dough with vengeance and stuffed it into pans for the oven.

Night fell around four o'clock. Just before the dinner rush, Faye entered. "Is this where Mollie lives?"

"What do you want?" Miles stood up.

"I'm looking for Mollie. Lucy over at the house is sick and needs help."

The sporting woman who had sailed from Seattle didn't look confident or saucy anymore. Her dull hair slumped. Her face paint no longer precisely outlined her lips. Powder to cover the circles under Faye's eyes accentuated her weariness. Miles felt a tug of pity, which he quickly covered with bravado.

"Why don't you take care of her?"

Long, blackened lashes blinked twice. "She wants Mollie."

"Mollie's busy," Peter said.

Faye pressed her lips together and glared at Miles. "What if Lucy's dying and wants a preacher man? Will you come?"

He frowned.

"How can you not go?" Samantha whispered.

"I'm not ordained," he muttered.

"Go."

Mollie grabbed her coat. "Peter, will you stay and help Samantha feed the men? Miles can fill in until Reverend Dickey can come. Let's go."

Miles carried his Bible and tried to estimate the damage to his reputation as he followed Mollie and Faye past Soapy Smith's pool hall and the mercantile. He shuddered as they entered the two-story establishment reeking of cheap perfume and filled spittoons. Faye led them down a gloomy hallway into a tiny room. Lucy lay coughing on an iron cot.

Mollie knelt at the bedside and ran her hand across Lucy's perspiring forehead. "We're here, little one," she crooned. "Miles will read you the stories."

How could he not?

By the light of a small wax candle, he read the Gospel of John, assuring Lucy of God's love for her and willingness to forgive her sins. The woman coughed and panted, but her eyes focused on Miles.

Mollie straightened the bedclothes, wiped Lucy's brow with a damp cloth, and tried to coax liquid into her. Faye stopped in periodically with broth for the woman, but it soon became apparent Lucy wouldn't survive long. When Reverend Dickey arrived, Miles had reached a contentment about sitting with her he could not explain.

Lucy's face softened, relaxed, and slid into peace as Reverend Dickey pronounced absolution over her soul. Miles stood in a corner to watch. And so he remained when the young woman passed into eternity, taking a surprisingly sympathetic piece of his heart with her.

Two days later, Reverend Dickey hosted Lucy's funeral at Union Church over the objections of many in his fledgling congregation. Disgruntled townspeople stayed away.

With no flowers available in snowy Skagway, Samantha used Miles's buck knife to cut evergreen boughs and bunches of red berries. He helped carry them to the church and followed her decorating directions, hanging the boughs along the wall.

When they finished, the new church smelled of pine and winterberries.

Miles centered a Bible on the plain wooden altar.

"Christmas is coming." Samantha squeezed her eyes shut. "Dare I ask to see my father for Christmas?"

He couldn't help himself. Miles stretched his arms to her, and Samantha went into them, trembling. "I'm starting to lose hope we'll find him, and then I don't know what I'll do. What good was it to come here?"

Miles rubbed circles on her back and kissed her hair. "You've made this church and this town a better place by your presence. Don't you know that?"

She nodded against his chest, and he continued. "Your hard work enables Peter to climb the pass every day with pockets full of food. Your voice cheers discouraged men. Your contributions have put together a church in a lawless place. You've made a difference here. I thank God for your presence."

"We couldn't have managed without you." Samantha rested her cheek on his shoulder. "You've been patient with Peter, helped build this church, and you've protected me. I don't know what I'd do if I lost you, too."

He closed his eyes to let her words sink in. Maybe coming to Alaska was proving his calling in more than one way.

"There's more to be done." Samantha broke away. "I need to help."

At ten o'clock, Miles, Peter, and two Sourdoughs carried in Lucy's plain cedar casket. Reverend Dickey waited near the altar at the foot of an elaborately carved cross three Tlingit natives had delivered to the church that morning.

Almost every sporting woman in Skagway, close to fifty in number, filled the pews. Samantha, Miles, Peter, and Mollie sat in the front row, singing the funeral hymns in full voice. Miles leaned forward in professional respect when Reverend Dickey challenged the mourners.

"Dear Sisters," he said, "listen to this invitation from Jesus. 'Come unto me all ye that are weary.' You are weary of the life you have been living. Leave it. It holds nothing for you but sorrow, suffering, and shame. Jesus received Mary Magdalene. He said to another who had been led into sin, 'Neither do I condemn you—go and sin no more.'"

The women wailed so loudly the hair on Miles's arms stood up.

After Reverend Dickey pronounced the benediction, Miles set his old bowler on his head and slipped outside. His soul churned, and he needed to calm down. Was it possible sporting women could repent after just one sermon?

He walked along the shore, his boots crunching on sand and rocks mixed with ice, where he saw Captain O'Brien, a steamship captain, conversing with a Sourdough named Jim.

"What's the news, Mr. Parker?"

Miles described Lucy's funeral, still astonished at Reverend Dickey's invitation for the women to give up the sporting life.

The captain spoke slowly. "Do you think any of them will do it?"

"How could they? They have no place to go," Miles said.

"Go to the church and tell them I have plenty of room on my ship tomorrow. I'll take anyone who wants to return to Seattle for free. It won't cost them a cent."

Miles's mouth dropped open. Here, he thought, was true Christianity—seeing a need and responding to it. Hope flared, but he shook his head. "What good will that do? They've no money. They'll have to return to the same way of life in Seattle."

"No they won't," Jim said. "I already found my bonanza. I'll give Captain O'Brien money to cover all their needs."

The men shook hands. Miles retraced his steps, his soul reeling.

Two doors from the church, a gang of Soapy Smith's men leaned against a building and glared at him. Three held clubs.

He straightened his shoulders and took a deep breath. Would he be able to help the sporting women escape Skagway's thugs?

Chapter 11

Samantha and Mollie brewed tea and served biscuits to the sorrowful women. A dozen wept while others touched dainty handkerchiefs to their damp eyes and sniffed.

Miles burst through the door waving his arms. Samantha set down the teapot and hurried to him. His ruddy face and flashing eyes made him look confident and in charge, taller.

Mollie joined them as he described Captain O'Brien's offer to Reverend Dickey. Mollie clapped her hands. "God is using you! Thanks be to God!"

Samantha felt a stab of jealousy. Why didn't she say that?

Reverend Dickey climbed onto a pew. "For those women interested in a fresh start, Captain O'Brien will take you to Seattle tomorrow for free. Anyone who wants to take him up on the offer, come tell me."

Thirty women gathered around Reverend Dickey, burbling with excitement. Samantha and Mollie hugged each other. "Lucy will not have died in vain if these women escape," Mollie exclaimed.

Miles joined them. "A little problem. They want their possessions and are afraid to retrieve them." He rubbed his full-bearded chin. "Soapy Smith's gang won't like this."

Samantha surveyed the room. "What can we do?"

"Where's Peter?"

"He went to the tent."

Miles blew out his breath. "Reverend Dickey is making a list of what each woman wants from her room. I'll get the lists and then go for the marshal and Peter. We can't do this without their help."

"I'm coming with you." Samantha put on her cloak when Miles had the list and followed him out.

"It's not safe. You've already been assaulted by these men. You saw with Lucy what they've done to the sporting women. Stay here at church." Miles marched down the street.

"One for all, Miles. I want to help you." Happiness bubbled inside her, and she took his arm. "We'll do this together."

Six of Soapy's men loitered outside a pool hall. The scowls on their hairy faces made her stomach curl. Samantha shivered.

Miles slowed his steps and patted her hand. "Let's not make them suspicious."

"Okay." She kissed his cheek.

"Samantha!"

"A good distraction, right? Keep walking."

Snowflakes swirled and dreary clouds threatened more as they entered the hovel that housed official Skagway justice. The marshal sprawled in a chair leaned against the wall, a potbellied stove emitting toasty heat.

When Miles described the situation, the marshal's chair thudded forward. "Are you out of your mind? Don't you know Soapy's income depends on these women turning over their earnings to him? He and his men won't give them up without a fight. I can't do this."

"How can you not?" Miles asked.

Samantha's heart soared with Miles's confidence. But she also remembered how her body ached from the skirmish over Lucy. How could they thwart the thugs outside?

"What kind of preacher man are you?" the marshal grumbled. "This is going to cause me no end of trouble, but I'll do it if the church folks will back me."

"We'll need God's help to be successful. Let's pray. Then I'll send Samantha for her giant brother. Round up some men, and we'll meet you at Mollie's restaurant."

"Our boy has grown up." Peter laughed when Samantha told him of Miles's plan.

"Why do you say things like that?" Samantha demanded. "You belittle him. He's taken a principled stand and is facing real danger for the good of these women. You have no reason to make fun of him."

Peter's eyebrows went up, and he crossed his arms over his chest. "Are you finally recognizing Miles's value?"

"One for all and all for one," Samantha retorted. "I'm changing my clothes."

"Why?"

"I'm going with you."

Peter blocked her exit. "No you're not. This isn't safe. The sporting women houses are no place for my sister."

She narrowed her eyes. "I'm not going as your sister. I'm going as Sam, your brother. Besides, you know I'm a better shot than Miles."

They met the marshal and half a dozen deputies at Mollie's restaurant. Miles sighed when he saw Sam dressed in her brother's clothes. "I suppose you had to come along, but you'll stay with Peter and me."

The marshal divided them into three squads, gave each group a list, and directed them to the church when done. "Soapy's gang knows something's up, but let's keep them confused as long as possible. As soon as we've got everything, we'll escort the women to the ship. They'll be safe there."

Miles led Peter and Sam to the house on Broadway across from the mercantile. They stepped into a wallpapered parlor stuffy with horsehair furniture and Victorian furbelows. The cloying scent made Sam wrinkle her nose.

A squat man with a plug moustache tromped down the stairs. "The girls are out. Only Faye's here. You'll have to take your turn."

"May we see Faye?" Sam asked. Miles displayed the list.

"I can't let you go through their things," the man sputtered. "Does Soapy know about this?"

"I'll handle them, Billy." Faye glided downstairs. Red eyes sagged in her gaunt face.

"Soapy's not going to like it," Billy growled.

"Follow me, Sam. The other two should stay below." Faye led Sam to the first door at the top of the stairs. "We have to work fast. Let me see the list."

Faye stripped the dingy pillowcase off the bed and rummaged through the plain bureau to find what the woman wanted. Sam examined the cramped, windowless room: dresses and a worn silk wrapper hung on nails. Face paint littered the bureau top, and a small round mirror hung above. A wooden chair draped with clothing and a pair of overturned boots on the floor gave the room color and texture. The rumpled bed linens needed to be washed.

Sam turned away. The whole room reeked of a cheap sadness that suggested endless tears.

Seven women's names were on the list. Faye went through their possessions while Sam carried the pillowcases and tried not to react to the grim living situations. Most of the women in this house would travel to Seattle. Sam stopped at the last door where a window faced the street. "Is this your room? What are you bringing?"

Faye's shoulders slumped. "I'm not coming."

"Why not? This is your chance. They'll help you start over. You don't have to live like this."

Faye closed her eyes a moment and then straightened. Her voice turned sassy, and she stretched her lips into a confident smile. "I came north for the Klondike. Skagway is a stopping off point before I cross the pass and make my fortune come spring. I'll turn civilized when I've got a big enough poke to buy me a big house in Seattle with a water view. You got to stay focused, Sam, to get what you want."

"No," Sam shook her head. "This isn't what you want."

Faye's eyes narrowed. "It's what I want today, missy, and it's my business. You need to decide what's important to you. That preacher man loves you. Ask yourself what you want, and then choose how you'll live. Time for you to go."

Was Faye right? Could Samantha choose how she wanted to live her life? Had her presence in Skagway really helped others as Miles said? If she never found Pa, would this trip still have been worthwhile?

Sam followed Faye's swaying hips and clicking high heels back down the hall. At the stairs, Faye pointed. "Go. Tell my girls good-bye. Don't come back."

Samantha considered Faye one long moment and then hurried downstairs. She handed the pillowcases to Peter and Miles. Billy gnawed the end of a moldy cigar.

"Remember," Miles told him. "You don't need to stay in this life either."

"Get out of here." The man stood back from the open doorway. "I ain't seen nothing."

Across the street, a bearded man wearing a suit with a bolo tie pushed a black Stetson off his forehead. He ambled over to greet them in the middle of Broadway.

"Good afternoon, Mr. Smith," Miles said.

Samantha turned wide eyes to Peter. He silenced her with a look and braced his shoulders. Sam followed suit, scrunching her face into a snarl.

"What have we got here, preacher man?" Soapy Smith drawled around a pungent cigar. "Ransacking the home of honest citizens?"

A low mutter rose from the boardwalk where four brutes glared.

Miles pushed his glasses higher on his nose. "No sir, just picking up some items for friends. You'll excuse me, but we're wanted at the church."

"I don't think so. Step into my parlor, I'd like to have a word with you. Your boys are welcome to join us if they leave their weapons at the bar." Smith removed the cigar from his mouth and breathed smoke.

Sam prayed for wisdom.

Miles waited long enough for Soapy's men to grow restless. His blond curls stuck out from under his bowler hat. "I'm sorry, sir, but I'm doing a good work, and I can't go into your parlor. We're needed at the church."

Soapy Smith dropped his cigar into the slush. "I helped build that church. They can wait for you."

"We appreciate your monetary contribution, but we must be gone. Good day, sir." Miles turned to walk away.

"Soapy! Come quick," shouted a man running down Broadway. "They're stealing our girls."

Smith and his men took off, and the three musketeers hastened to Union Church. They handed the pillowcases to their owners and sat down. The frazzled marshal and his deputies burst through the doors an hour later, their arms full of women's finery and bags. A dozen townspeople followed.

The marshal rubbed his lined forehead. "I may need to get on that ship myself. Soapy's mighty riled. You should consider leaving town for a while, preacher man. He pulled a gun on me."

"How did you get away?" Reverend Dickey asked.

The marshal nodded toward the townspeople. "They came up and took our side. Someone shot into the air, and Soapy's men scattered.

Miles smiled. "God protects those doing his work."

Mr. Brown from the mercantile joined them. "Soapy's outside with his men, but they don't like the numbers. More folks are headed this way. I knew if enough people went to church, those thugs would back down. We licked 'em today."

Once the women obtained their possessions, Reverend Dickey offered a prayer. As the afternoon waned toward sunset and flurries filled the air, dozens of church members escorted the women to the shore. They cheered as the majority of Skagway's sporting women climbed aboard a barge.

"That Soapy's nothing but a bully," screamed a woman as they cast off. "Good-bye and good riddance!"

"Without the Lord's help we never could have accomplished this," Miles said.

Sam hugged him. "The Lord's help and you being in the right place at the right time. I'm so proud of you."

His eyes shone. "I'll take another one of those."

Peter intervened. "No you won't. It's time for me to shake your hand. I'm proud of you, too."

The enormous mountains loomed to the west across the gray canal, aloof and frozen in surprise. Three women fluttered handkerchiefs when they reached the steamship. Samantha's soul soared. Even if they never found Pa, something good had come of their time in Skagway, and Miles had instigated it.

Doc Runnalls crunched across the snowy shoreline carrying the canvas mailbag.

Miles reached into his coat pocket. "With all the excitement this morning, I forgot to give you my letter." He handed it to the mailman with two bits for postage.

Runnalls examined the envelope. "What's this town? Port Orchard, Washington?"

"Yes. We're from there."

"How very curious. I've got another letter for Port Orchard, brought in this morning." Runnalls noticed Samantha. "What's your name again, sonny?"

"I'm Samantha Harris from Port Orchard."

"Samantha? You don't look like a Samantha to me." Runnalls dug through the mail bag and extracted a discolored envelope. "This is for a Mrs. Mary Harris of Port Orchard, Washington."

"My mother. She's dead. That's why we're here."

"Dead?" He held out the cheap envelope. "If she's dead, I believe I can pass this on to her next of kin."

Samantha gasped at the slashing scrawl. "Where did this letter come from?"

"The Tlingits brought it with the cross for the church this morning. Peg Leg sent it. I hope it's the news you've wanted." Runnalls cleared his throat. "I need to get the mailbag to the steamship."

Samantha ripped open the envelope. "Pa's alive!"

Chapter 12

South of Skagway

Miles and Peter huddled around Samantha as she read the letter aloud.

> *My darling, what I feared has come to pass. I must ask you to send my son. I need Peter to help me. Only his young strength and manhood can bring me home to you.*
>
> *Dr. Harry Runnalls of Skagway, Alaska Territory, has a letter giving directions on how to find me. If Peter will come, Dr. Runnalls will help him. If you do not have the funds, go to the good John Parker. I know my brother in Christ will lend Peter the money he needs.*
>
> *Bestow a kiss on Samantha's crown of golden glory. The good work is finished. I pray I will see you all soon. I will not be there in time this year, but Merry Christmas.*
>
> *Your loving husband,*
> *Donald Harris*

Samantha's eyes shone as she clutched the letter to her chest. Miles watched Peter blink rapidly and swallow.

When he got control of himself, Peter whooped and spun his sister around. "I knew it. Pa needed us."

Samantha laughed when he put her down. She stroked her still golden, but not much of a crown, hair. "I knew he'd be disappointed Peter chopped off my hair."

"You cut it for good reason," Miles said. "He won't care."

Dr. Runnalls returned. "I take it you have good news."

"The best," Samantha said.

Peter indicated the letter. "It says you've got directions for how to find Pa."

Dr. Runnalls shouldered his bag. "Come up to the office."

A blizzard blew in during the night and shut down White Pass for the rest of the winter. While Miles sought time off from the mercantile, Peter scoured the waterfront looking for someone to guide them down the southeast side of the canal. Samantha could scarcely wait to find the village Donald Harris indicated in the letter left with Runnalls, but Tlingits rarely visited Skagway.

December twenty-fourth dawned clear and cold. A Tlingit Indian hiked into town that morning on a beach trail. After picking up mail and several items from the mercantile, he agreed to escort them to his village and Peg Leg.

The trio stowed clothes, bedrolls, and foodstuffs into packs and followed him.

The small dark man in a thick bearskin coat walked briskly along the rocky shoreline. A bone-chilling wind blew off the water, and sea spray soaked them more than once. They scrambled over driftwood and boulders, grateful for low tide.

Miles was thankful for the days spent on the trail; he had no trouble keeping up.

"Why Peg Leg?" Samantha asked as she dodged a sudden wave.

Peter and Miles didn't know. Their guide spoke only broken English.

When she struggled in her long skirts over large boulders and nearly slipped, Miles held out his hand. She took it and did not let go, even when the path smoothed. Peter raised an eyebrow but said nothing.

Miles's heart thumped with optimism. "Are you looking forward to returning to Washington?"

Samantha tripped on a piece of driftwood. "I don't know."

He hated to say it, but he needed to know her plans. "You probably can begin in the second semester, only one term late."

She bit her lip. "But I don't feel like I'm done in Skagway. How can I leave now, when there's talk of a school?"

Miles stopped. "You would stay to teach school? I thought you didn't like this town."

"Things have changed since Lucy's funeral. People are different. Did you notice the children at church? I can be useful in Skagway. I can't stay by myself, but with Mama gone, maybe Pa won't want to go back to Port Orchard."

Miles tucked her hand under his elbow. His blood pounded in his ears all the way down the coast as he contemplated how to tell her of his own change in heart.

Two hours later, the winter night and rising tide were nearly upon them when they reached a river mouth. Three native lodges sprawled three hundred yards from the shore. Canoes were beached high above the surf line. A pack of barking mongrels rushed to greet them.

Their guide led them to the first house—a long cedar-planked building with a peaked roof covered in bark. They pushed through a door into a great room smelling of smoke and close living. Four decorated corner posts held up the roof, and the floor was dug down in the middle, providing earthen seating around a central fire. Wooden partitions to divide the area into sleeping compartments lined the walls. The fire in the center and two kerosene lanterns provided dim light.

Twenty people startled at their entry, and the deerskin-clad women recoiled in surprise, calling their children to them. An elderly man stepped forward and addressed them in the sliding guttural Tlingit language.

When Miles, Peter, and Samantha removed their wraps, the chief laughed. "I think you speak English. *Tillicum*"—he motioned to a seated man smoothing a totem pole in the far corner.

"Papa," Samantha cried, starting forward. Her brother followed.

"Peter? Samantha?" Donald Harris's deep voice cracked. "But I just sent the letter. How are you here so soon?"

"We've been in Skagway looking for you." Samantha fell at his feet.

Miles blinked back tears.

Donald sat on a skin-covered box with one leg stretched before him, a carved crutch at his feet. His big hands shook as he embraced the twins. His bare head, now shaved bald, shone in the firelight, and his coarse beard was white. The hearty man who had led the trio on hikes and taught them about the outdoors years before looked diminished in the longhouse.

The natives around Miles gabbled in a language he could not understand. Possessions filled the room, fishing gear hung on the walls, and the families obviously were preparing a meal. Their trail guide slipped away, leaving Miles towering over the Tlingit families. Peter looked like a giant.

Donald ruffled his hands along Samantha's head with a chuckle. "Your crowning glory is shorn these days. Did you think to find riches in your golden hair?"

"Peter and Miles thought I would be safer if I blended in with the Klondikers. I've been wearing trousers and pretending to be a man."

"Your mother agreed to a disguise?" Donald laughed.

The twins shared a glance.

"That's why we're here, Pa." Peter took his father's hands. "Mother died in June. We've been in Skagway since August looking for you."

Donald's joy crumbled. "Mary's dead?"

His distress caught the ear of the natives. The elder who had greeted them stepped closer, and a nearby woman moaned. Miles scanned the room; all the Tlingits watched Donald, waiting. For what?

The man buried his face in his hands. "Tell me."

Samantha recounted her mother's illness, the hours spent reading the Bible, the moments of her death. Peter described the decision to close up the house and head north. "We needed to find you."

Donald's shoulders shook, and Samantha hugged him. Peter completed the circle, and the three cried together.

At their tears, the Tlingits murmured a low sympathy. Miles went to his friends. Peter pulled him, too, into the wide embrace.

There in a native house on the edge of nowhere, the civilized, cultured, devout Mary Harris's death was fully mourned by those who loved her best.

❧

Donald opened his watch and gazed at a photograph of his wife while the native women served them dried salmon and tea. Miles chewed on the salted smoked fish. Sips of spruce tea cleared his sinuses.

"This is not what I expected," Donald finally said. "She never wrote of illness. Mary's refinement had no place in Alaska, which is why she stayed behind. She argued she would get in the way of God's work and slow me down. She always sent me without her."

"But you wanted to return to Port Orchard." Peter leaned forward. "That's what you said in the letter."

Donald gestured to his leg. "I broke it right after I wrote in June. I can't walk without a crutch. I finished my task—the totem—and I wanted to see my family. But now Mary's gone."

"You have us, Pa," Samantha said. "And Miles."

Donald scrutinized him. "Ah, Miles. How did you escape your mother?"

Miles set his jaw. "I sent my parents a letter and said I was leaving. Here I am."

The Tlingit chief joined them around the fire. Behind them, the families prepared their meals, settled their children to sleep, and murmured among themselves. A log shifted on the fire, and the light danced. With his stomach full and his body finally warm, Miles should have relaxed, but Donald's steady gaze held a challenge. He smoothed his beard and moustache.

Samantha rubbed Miles's arm. "He's done very well, Pa."

Donald noted her movement. "Were you ordained?"

"No sir. I finished my coursework but missed ordination. The missions board members laid hands on me before I left and charged me to preach the gospel."

His questioner's right eyebrow went up just like Peter's. "Have you done so?"

"He has." Samantha declared. "He preached to the Sourdoughs and sporting women on the ship. He read his Bible to packers on White Pass. He nearly killed himself building the church, and then he started teaching Bible study in the restaurant."

She gazed at him with shining eyes. Miles's heart hammered. "He's the one who instigated the sporting women leaving Skagway, and then he took on Soapy Smith when we collected their belongings. The town has seen God in action ever since Miles arrived."

Peter slapped Miles on the back. "Miles bought our provisions. He's watched out for Sam. We never could have made this trip without him. 'All for one,' we always said, but it's really been all Miles for us."

Donald smiled "The Tlingits like nothing better than a good story. My three musketeers have all grown up. I'd like to hear about your adventures."

They told their story long into the night.

Chapter 13

Tlingit Village
Christmas

Samantha woke the next morning fully clothed but wrapped in a blanket beside the banked fire.

Peter and her father snored softly while the Tlingits moved quietly about their chores. Miles's bedroll lay folded in a neat pile. Samantha stretched, pulled on her boots and coat, and headed outside.

Dawn took a long time coming in the December north, and at the shoreline she saw a broad-shouldered man wearing a misshapen bowler hat watching the waves. He stepped backward as a roller slipped far up the beach and bumped into a driftwood log.

She sighed, but he stepped nimbly over it and laughed.

Pa was right. Miles had changed.

So had Samantha's opinion of him. She went to her childhood friend with a shyness she'd never felt before.

"Merry Christmas." He put his arm around her shoulders to protect her when a gust of frigid air threatened to knock them over.

"The same to you."

"I wonder if mistletoe grows here."

Samantha tilted her head. "Why?"

"After what you said to your father last night, I'd like to kiss you." The cold wind blew ruddiness into his face.

Satisfaction swelled from deep within. "We don't need mistletoe. I'd be honored to kiss you."

His brow wrinkled. "Do you mean it?"

"I do."

He considered her. The water crashed; a shorebird scooted past. The village dogs barked, and a curl of cedar smoke reminded her breakfast would be ready soon.

She held her breath.

"What happens next, Sam?" Miles asked in a husky voice.

"Pa will tell the Christmas story."

"Will you stay in Alaska?"

She gazed toward the jagged white mountains across the canal. "Mollie is taking her restaurant to the top of the pass in the spring. You and Peter are headed to the Klondike."

"I'm not going to the Klondike." Miles pushed at the driftwood with his heavy boot. "I feel like your Pa. He stayed because of the work he believed God called him to do. Reverend Dickey heads over the Chilkoot soon. He means to start a church in Dawson."

"Will you take his place?"

"Only if I don't have to minister alone. I'm not as strong as your father and mother."

Her lips parted. She moved within a breath of a kiss but stopped when she heard rocks shift on the beach.

Peter jogged up. "Happy Christmas. You need to come inside. Pa's going to explain his totem pole. Hey. What's happening here?"

Miles gazed a rueful moment longer and then tapped Samantha's chin. "Everything."

They made their way back to the longhouse, shucked off their wraps, then joined the clan seated around the central fire hearth. Babies cuddled on their mothers' laps, small children played at their feet, and the men stood behind. Donald leaned on his carved crutch beside a blond totem, the scent of freshly cut wood still in the air. The trio found spots beside the fire.

"I came to you a year ago," Donald said. "You asked me to tell more about the good news other missionaries brought. It has been an honor to read the scriptures and to teach some of you to read. But not all can read the words, and so for this Christmas, I did what missionaries asked me to do when I came: I've carved a totem so you can remember God and how he came to earth to live with his people."

Samantha's father spoke in simple English with a young interpreter by his side, but the way he communicated with the native people filled her with pride. They wanted to hear the story of the Creator who sent His Son to teach them about love and how to know Him better. The contrast between the "savages" in a wooden longhouse hungering for the Christmas story and the thugs controlling Skagway couldn't have been plainer.

Her father pointed to the top figure on the totem. "Raven is the emissary of the great Chief of Heavens who holds the Christmas star."

"Raven is a sort of an angel here, but he often is a joker," Miles whispered.

Peter nudged her. "Trust Miles to have done his homework, even on native tribes."

In the past, she would have laughed with her brother at Miles's need for research, but that day Samantha thought about how thorough Miles had been in his preparations. He not only learned about the Alaskan country before he left his books at the seminary, but he investigated the beliefs of people he expected to meet.

She smiled to herself, however, realizing how he had miscalculated on the sporting women.

"Joseph is the wood carver who led Mary on a journey to Bethlehem. Here I've represented him by a man holding a canoe paddle." Donald pointed midway up the totem at a mother and child. "Many people came to the potlatch where the powerful chief wanted to display his wealth. Mary gave birth to the baby Jesus at the gathering."

Samantha took Miles's hand. He had provisioned their trip and made sure they had what they needed. He worked the pass with her brother, but he came back to Skagway to watch over her. Because he loved her.

Just like that, she knew what she wanted.

"The bear lives in a cave, or a manger," Donald explained, "and the keepers of the fish trap, the men who tended animals, proclaimed the good news. The chief beneath them is one of the three wise men who brought gifts to the newborn king."

Miles brought his talents to worship his God in Skagway, Samantha thought. He tried to build the church but then got correctly diverted to teach instead. She shook herself—she needed to pay attention to her father's story, not think about Miles.

The bottom two characters were the frog, symbolizing the angel who appeared to Joseph in his dream, and the upside-down chief, symbolizing evil King Herod who was outwitted by the angel.

Samantha told Miles, "You were the angel who outwitted Soapy Smith."

Peter and Miles both laughed.

Donald blessed his congregation and hummed the opening bars of "Joy to the World." Men in leggings, women in deerskin, children, and the Americans from Port Orchard put their hands into the air and sang.

Worshipping God, Samantha thought, could be done anywhere with anyone who believed.

Salmon, seafood, dried berries, and more spruce tea made up the natives' Christmas potlatch. Her father brightened when Samantha pulled dried apple turnovers from her backpack, along with sourdough to make flapjacks.

The women crowded to watch as Samantha greased the skillet with salt pork and poured in the batter. "I've learned a lot at the restaurant."

"She has," Peter agreed. "Her cooking is almost edible now."

When she made a fist in his direction, her brother put up his hands. "You're not Sam anymore. You're a real woman. Act like one."

Miles and her father shrugged together.

The four sat by the fire after the Tlingits had their fill of flapjacks, and they ate their meal on tin plates. They drank coffee from metal mugs and reminisced about Christmases past eaten on china plates.

"What happens to you now?" Donald asked when they finished their meal.

"We'll take you back with us tomorrow." Peter stretched his feet toward the fire. "You're crippled, and you're a long way from civilization. Samantha will travel home with you from Skagway."

They watched the fire crackle in a companionable silence.

"I've been thinking and praying since last night," Donald finally said. "I've not lived in a town or a house for two years. It won't hurt me to stay with these people now that Mary's gone."

Peter shook his head. "With these simple natives?"

Donald looked around the longhouse and smiled. "They're the most honest people I've met in Alaska. I can continue teaching them to read and to understand the Scriptures, and I can help them deal with the white men. It's a good work for someone like me."

Samantha kissed him. "I think Pa should stay here."

"Without us?" Peter shook his head.

"With people who care about him and whom he loves," Samantha said. "He's needed here. We have our own lives now."

Peter pulled a small canvas bag out of his money belt. "Fine. Here's most of the money I owe you. Now you can return to Washington and go to college."

Samantha touched the rough, dirty pouch. "Where is my home? Washington or Skagway?"

Miles moved closer.

"You can't live in Skagway by yourself. It's not safe. Take the money." Peter held out the bag.

Miles took her hand. "She doesn't have to be alone. I'm not going over the pass with you, Peter. I'm staying in Skagway. The two of you dragged me into a ministry I never dreamed of at seminary. Samantha made me confront evil with good because she saw the need in the sporting women's hearts. Now the town has built a church and needs men to preach the gospel. That's a harvest richer than Klondike gold and one I mean to pursue."

"You're not going with me to the Klondike?"

"No."

"Surely you've met others you can travel with," Samantha said.

"Yes." Peter looked troubled. "But I don't trust anyone like I do Miles. I thought I'd do the heavy work while he could minister to the miners, just like we did on the trail. I'm not a preacher. I can't do that."

"Here we have it." Donald clasped his son by both shoulders. "I've prayed you would embrace the man God created you to be. You don't have to be a missionary to serve God. Your desire to go to the Klondike could be for gold. But maybe it's really an adventure for a young man who stayed with his mother and sister far longer than he wanted so his father could do a good work. This is your time, Peter. Go into the world and follow where God is leading you. You have my blessing."

"Do you want to come with me, Sam?" her twin asked.

Samantha stood. "I love you, Peter, but it's time we went our own ways.

I don't want to go to the Klondike. I've found what I want here."

The Tlingits hummed. Her father stirred the fire. Miles stood beside her and tilted her chin toward him. "We're both doing a good work in Skagway. Will you marry me so we can serve the town together?"

Samantha gazed into his eyes a long moment. "Wait a minute." She looked him up and down. "Have you grown, Miles? How tall are you?"

"Six feet. Why?"

Peter burst into laughter.

"I would love to marry you," Samantha said. "Pa can do the honors."

"What does my height have to do with it?"

Samantha hugged him. "Absolutely nothing."

Donald stood to pronounce a benediction. "Mary was proud of all three of you, but today your plans complete her dreams and prayers."

He faced his son. "I know how thankful she was you stayed in Port Orchard. You go to the Klondike with her blessing and mine."

Donald smiled at Samantha. "She would have rejoiced that you finally learned you don't have to live in Peter's shadow. She wanted you to choose what is important for your own life."

He shook Miles's hand. "Mary prayed long for your calling, Miles, and would have been even more grateful you stood by your friends and gave them the opportunity to find themselves." He caressed Samantha's cheek. "I think you've got the best end of this deal."

Donald gathered the three into another hug. "Mary, I am sure, is rejoicing with the angels right now. Peter will have his adventure, and today we'll have a wedding. Anything else?"

Miles smiled at Samantha. "May I kiss my bride?"

Samantha looked up at him. "Yes."

Historical Notes

While Miles and the Harris family are fictional characters, the story of the sporting women's exodus from Skagway after hearing Rev. R. W. Dickey's funeral sermon is true. Steamship captain O'Brien met Dickey on the beach after the service and volunteered to take the sporting women back to Seattle at no cost. Sourdough Jim contributed one thousand dollars to cover their costs. Mollie Walsh knew "Lucy," and Mollie set up a restaurant at the top of White Pass in the spring of 1898.

The Christmas totem pole described in *The Gold Rush Christmas* was carved by Rev. David Fison of Alaska in 1987. I used the concept with his permission and my thanks. You can see a photo of it at my website: www.michelleule.com.